PARA HANDY
AND OTHER TALES

BY THE SAME AUTHOR.

THE LOST PIBROCH.
JOHN SPLENDID.
FANCY FARM.
JAUNTY JOCK.
GILIAN THE DREAMER.
THE NEW ROAD.
DOOM CASTLE.
CHILDREN OF TEMPEST.
THE DAFT DAYS.
SHOES OF FORTUNE.
AYRSHIRE IDYLLS.

PARA HANDY
AND OTHER TALES

BY

HUGH FOULIS
(NEIL MUNRO)

William Blackwood and Sons Ltd.
Edinburgh and London
1937

First Impression . . . . . . November 1931
Second Impression . . . . . . January 1933
Third Impression . . . . . . August 1937

. . . .

FOREWORD

THIRTY years ago the readers of the "Evening News"
of Glasgow discovered in the columns of that journal
the first of a series of light sketches which, in their shrewd
humour and fresh presentation of native comedy, revealed
the arrival of a humorist whose certainty of touch could not
be denied.

No daily paper in Scotland had produced anything in
the same vein so unfailingly good or so wide in its Scottish
appeal ; but Neil Munro, the author of these tales, chose
to have his work appear anonymously, so that for many
years the majority of the readers of the "Evening News,"
though keenly appreciative of their excellence, were uncertain of their origin.

But from those who studied the pages of the "News" more
discerningly, who were aware of the author of the famous
"Views and Reviews" column and recognised his brilliant
journalism in the weekly "Looker-On" causerie, the hand
of Munro could not be hid, for "the Munro touch" per-
meated these gaily chronicled histories of Erchie, Para Handy,
and Jimmy Swan. The manner of them betrayed the man.
To those critics the gently ironic philosophy of Para Handy
could obviously have been recorded by no other pen.

Yet Neil Munro was never more than mildly interested
in the popularity of his humorous tales. They were written
for the hour, mere by-products from the literary workshop
in which he fashioned his serious novels—"The New Road,"
"Gilian the Dreamer," "John Splendid," and the others.
And it was only after considerable persuasion from newspaper
colleagues and friends that he permitted these sketches to
appear in book form. Even so, they were published cheaply,

and under the pseudonym of Hugh Foulis. " Erchie " proved
an astonishingly popular volume, and Hugh Foulis became
a local " best seller " in Glasgow and the West of Scotland.
Other and equally successful collections of his humorous
sketches followed, but from the beginning Munro had made
it clear to his publishers that, having satisfied a local demand,
he had no desire to encourage any wider circulation of the
books.

But " Para Handy "—Peter, son of Sandy—survives, for his
racy humour is more enduring than the flimsy " wisecrack "
comedy of the cinema, more penetrating than the colourless
" humour " mechanically evolved by trick writing. He has
been discovered absorbing the interest of Cambridge Uni-
versity Dons, who set themselves examination papers on
his voyages and vernacular. He is cherished by numerous
Scottish exiles in the Colonies. And one traveller has confessed to carrying leather-bound copies of the first two Para
Handy volumes on all his tours abroad—one in his bag, the
other in his pocket !

In this " omnibus " book the Erchie, Para Handy, and
Jimmy Swan tales are to be found together for the first
time. It is published in response to the very numerous
and appreciative references made to Neil Munro's humorous
writings after his death last December.

October 1931.

CONTENTS

IN HIGHLAND HARBOURS
WITH PARA HANDY

HURRICANE JACK OF THE *VITAL SPARK*

ERCHIE, MY DROLL FRIEND

CONTENTS

JIMMY SWAN, THE JOY TRAVELLER

THE *VITAL SPARK*

THE *VITAL SPARK*

I

PARA HANDY, MASTER MARINER

A SHORT, thick-set man, with a red beard, a hard round felt hat, ridiculously out of harmony with a blue pilot jacket and trousers and a seaman's jersey, his hands immersed deeply in those pockets our fathers (and the heroes of Rabelais) used to wear behind a front flap, he would have attracted my notice even if he had not, unaware of my presence so close behind him, been humming to himself the chorus of a song that used to be very popular on gabbarts, but is now gone out of date, like "The Captain with the Whiskers took a Sly Glance at Me." You may have heard it thirty years ago, before the steam puffer came in to sweep the sailing smack from all the seas that lie between Bowling and Stornoway. It runs—

> "Young Munro he took a notion
> For to sail across the sea,
> And he left his true love weeping,
> All alone on Greenock Quay,"

and by that sign, and by his red beard, and by a curious gesture he had, as if he were now and then going to scratch his ear and only determined not to do it when his hand was up, I knew he was one of the Macfarlanes. There were ten Macfarlanes, all men, except one, and he was a valet, but the family did their best to conceal the fact, and said he was away on the yachts, and making that much money he had not time to write a scrape home.

3

"I think I ought to know you," I said to the vocalist with the hard hat. "You are a Macfarlane: either the Beekan, or Kail, or the Nipper, or Keep Dark, or Para Handy——"

"As sure as daith," said he, "I'm chust Para Handy, and I ken your name fine, but I cannot chust mind your face." He had turned round on the pawl he sat on, without taking his hands from his pockets, and looked up at me where I stood beside him, watching a river steamer being warped into the pier.

"My goodness!" he said about ten minutes later, when he had wormed my whole history out of me; "and you'll be writing things for the papers? Cot bless me! and do you tell me you can be makin' a living off that? I'm not asking you, mind, hoo mich you'll be makin', don't tell me; not a cheep! not a cheep! But I'll wudger it's more than Mac-lean the munister. But och! I'm not saying: it iss not my business. The munister has two hundred in the year and a coo's gress; he iss aye the big man up yonder, but it iss me would like to show him he wass not so big a man as yourself. Eh? But not a cheep! not a cheep! A Mac-farlane would never put his nose into another man's oar."

"And where have you been this long while?" I asked, having let it sink into his mind that there was no chance to-day of his learning my exact income, expenditure, and how much I had in the bank.

"Me!" said he; "I am going up and down like yon fellow in the Scruptures—what wass his name? Sampson —seeking what I may devour. I am out of a chob. Chust that: out of a chob. You'll not be hearin' of anybody in your line that iss in want of a skipper?"

Skippers, I said, were in rare demand in my line of business. We hadn't used a skipper for years.

"Chust that! chust that! I only mentioned it in case. You are making things for newspapers, my Cot! what will they not do now for the penny? Well, that is it; I am out of a chob ; chust putting bye the time. I'm not vexed for myself, so mich as for poor Dougie. Dougie wass mate, and I wass skipper. I don't know if you kent the *Fital Spark* ? "

The *Vital Spark*, I confessed, was well known to me as the most uncertain puffer that ever kept the Old New-Year in Upper Lochfyne.

" That wass her ! " said Macfarlane, almost weeping. " There was never the bate of her, and I have sailed in her four years over twenty with my hert in my mooth for fear of her boiler. If you never saw the *Fital Spark*, she is aal hold, with the boiler behind, four men and a derrick, and a watter-butt and a pan loaf in the fo'c'sle. Oh man ! she wass the beauty ! She was chust sublime ! She should be carryin' nothing but gentry for passengers, or nice genteel luggage for the shooting-lodges, but there they would be spoilin' her and rubbin' all the pent off her with their coals, and sand, and whunstone, and oak bark, and timber, and trash like that."

" I understood she had one weakness at least, that her boiler was apt to prime."

" It's a —— lie," cried Macfarlane, quite furious ; " her boiler never primed more than wance a month, and that wass not with fair play. If Dougie wass here he would tell you.

" I wass ass prood of that boat ass the Duke of Argyll, ay, or Lord Breadalbane. If you would see me waalkin' aboot on her dake when we wass lyin' at the quay ! There wasna the like of it in the West Hielan's. I wass chust sublime ! She had a gold bead aboot her ; it's no lie I am tellin' you, and I would be pentin' her oot of my own pocket every time we went to Arran for gravel. She drawed four feet forrit and nine aft, and she could go like the duvvle."

" I have heard it put at five knots," I said maliciously.

Macfarlane bounded from his seat. " Five knots ! " he cried. " Show me the man that says five knots, and I will make him swallow the hatchet. Six knots, ass sure ass my

name iss Macfarlane ; many a time between the Skate and
Otter. If Dougie wass here he would tell you. But I am
not braggin' aboot her sailin' ; it wass her looks. Man,
she was smert, smert ! Every time she wass new pented I
would be puttin' on my Sunday clothes. There wass a time
yonder they would be callin' me Two-flag Peter in Loch
Fyne. It wass wance the Queen had a jubilee, and we had
but the wan flag, but a Macfarlane never wass bate, and I
put up the wan flag and a regatta shirt, and I'm telling you
she looked chust sublime ! "

" I forget who it was once told me she was very wet," I
cooed blandly ; " that with a head wind the *Vital Spark*
nearly went out altogether. Of course, people will say nasty
things about these hookers. They say she was very ill to
trim, too."

Macfarlane jumped up again, grinding his teeth, and his
face purple. He could hardly speak with indignation.
" Trum ! " he shouted. " Did you say ' trum ' ? You could
trum her with the wan hand behind your back and you
lookin' the other way. To the duvvle with your trum !
And they would be sayin' she wass wet ! If Dougie wass
here he would tell you. She would not take in wan cup
of watter unless it wass for synin' oot the dishes. She wass
that dry she would not wet a postage stamp unless we
slung it over the side in a pail. She wass sublime, chust
sublime !

" I am telling you there iss not many men following the
sea that could sail the *Fital Spark* the way I could. There
iss not a rock, no, nor a chuckie stone inside the Cumbrie
Heid that I do not have a name for. I would ken them
fine in the dark by the smell, and that iss not easy, I'm
telling you. And I am not wan of your dry-land sailors.
I wass wance at Londonderry with her. We went at night,
and did Dougie no' go away and forget oil, so that we had
no lamps, and chust had to sail in the dark with our ears
wide open. If Dougie wass here he would tell you. Now

and then Dougie would be striking a match for fear of a collusion."

" Where did he show it ? " I asked innocently. " Forward or aft ? "

" Aft," said the mariner suspiciously. " What for would it be aft ? Do you mean to say there could be a collusion aft ? I am telling you she could do her six knots before she cracked her shaft. It wass in the bow, of course ; Dougie had the matches. She wass chust sublime. A gold bead oot of my own pocket, four men and a derrick, and a watter-butt and a pan loaf in the fo'c'sle. My bonnie wee *Fital Spark* ! "

He began to show symptoms of tears, and I hate to see an ancient mariner's tears, so I hurriedly asked him how he had lost the command.

" I will tell you that," said he. " It was Dougie's fault. We had yonder a cargo of coals for Tarbert, and we got doon the length of Greenock, going fine, fine. It wass the day after the New Year, and I wass in fine trum, and Dougie said, ' Wull we stand in here for orders ? ' and so we went into Greenock for some marmalade, and did we no' stay three days ? Dougie and me wass going about Greenock looking for signboards with Hielan' names on them, and every signboard we could see with Campbell, or Macintyre, on it, or Morrison, Dougie would go in and ask if the man came from Kilmartin or anyway roond aboot there, and if the man said no, Dougie would say, ' It's a great peety, for I have cousins of the same name, but maybe you'll have time to come oot for a dram ? ' Dougie was chust sublime !

" Every day we would be getting sixpenny telegrams from the man the coals was for at Tarbert, but och ! we did not think he wass in such an aawful hurry, and then he came himself to Greenock with the *Grenadier*, and the only wans that wass not in the polis-office wass myself and the derrick. He bailed the laads oot of the polis-office, and ' Now,' he said, ' you will chust sail her up as fast as you can, like smert laads, for my customers iss waiting for their coals, and I will go over and see my good-sister at Helensburgh, and go back to Tarbert the day efter to-morrow.' ' Hoo can we be going and us with no money ? ' said Dougie—man, he wass sublime ! So the man gave me a paper pound of money, and went away to Helensburgh, and Dougie wass coilin' up a hawser forrit ready to start from the quay. When he wass away, Dougie said we would maybe chust be as weel to wait another tide, and I said I didna know, but what did he think, and he said, ' Ach, of course ! ' and we went aal back into Greenock. ' Let me see that pound ! ' said Dougie, and did I not give it to him ? and then he rang the bell of the public-hoose we were in, and asked for four tacks and a wee hammer. When he got the four tacks and the wee hammer he nailed the pound note on the door, and said to the man, ' Chust come in with a dram every time we ring the bell till that's done ! ' If Dougie wass here he would tell you. Two days efter that the owner of the *Fital Spark* came doon from Gleska and five men with him, and they went away with her to Tarbert."

" And so you lost the old command," I said, preparing to go off. " Well, I hope something will turn up soon."

" There wass some talk aboot a dram," said the mariner. " I thought you said something aboot a dram, but och ! there's no occasion ! "

A week later, I am glad to say, the Captain and his old crew were reinstated on the *Vital Spark*.

II

THE PRIZE CANARY

" CANARIES ! " said Para Handy contemptuously, " I have a canary yonder at home that would give you a sore heid to hear him singing. He's chust sublime. Have I no', Dougie ? "

It was the first time the mate had ever heard of the Captain as a bird-fancier, but he was a loyal friend, and at Para Handy's wink he said promptly, " You have that, Peter. Wan of the finest ever stepped. Many a sore heid I had wi't."

" What kind of a canary is it ? " asked the Brodick man jealously. " Is it a Norwich ? "

Para Handy put up his hand as usual to scratch his ear, and checked the act half-way. " No, nor a Sandwich ; it's chust a plain yellow wan," he said coolly. " I'll wudger ye a pound it could sing the best you have blin'. It whustles even-on, night and day, till I have to put it under a bowl o' watter if I'm wantin' my night's sleep."

The competitive passions of the Brodick man were roused. He considered that among his dozen prize canaries he had at least one that could beat anything likely to be in the possession of the Captain of the *Vital Spark*, which was lying at Brodick when this conversation took place. He produced it—an emaciated, sickle-shaped, small-headed, bead-eyed, business-looking bird, which he called the Wee Free. He was prepared to put up the pound for a singing contest anywhere in Arran, date hereafter to be arranged.

" That's all right," said Para Handy, " I'll take you on. We'll be doon this way for a cargo of grevel in a week, and if the money's wi' the man in the shippin'-box at the quay, my canary 'll lift it."

" But what aboot your pound ? " asked the Brodick man. " You must wudger a pound too."

" Is that the way o't ? " said the Captain. " I wass never up to the gemblin', but I'll risk the pound," and so the contest was arranged.

" But you havena a canary at aal, have you ? " said Dougie, later in the day, as the *Vital Spark* was puffing on her deliberate way to Glasgow.

" Me ? " said Para Handy, " I would as soon think of keepin' a hoolet. But och, there's plenty in Gleska if you

A*

have the money. From the needle to the anchor. Forbye,
I ken a gentleman that breeds canaries ; he's a riveter, and
if I wass gettin' him in good trum he would maybe give me
a lend o' wan. If no', we'll take a dander up to the Bird
Market, and pick up a smert wan that'll put the hems on
Sandy Kerr's Wee Free. No man wi' any releegion aboot
him would caal his canary a Wee Free."

The captain and the mate of the *Vital Spark* left their
noble ship at the wharf that evening—it was a Saturday
—and went in quest of the gentleman who bred canaries.
He was discovered in the midst of an altercation with his
wife which involved the total destruction of all the dishes
on the kitchen-dresser, and, with a shrewdness and consideration that were never absent in the Captain, he apologised for the untimely intrusion and prepared to go away.
" I see you're busy," he said, looking in on a floor covered
with the debris of the delf which this ardent lover of bird
life was smashing in order to impress his wife with the fact
that he was really annoyed about something—" I see you're
busy. Fine, man, fine ! A wife need never weary in this
hoose—it's that cheery. Dougie and me wass chust wantin'
a wee lend of a canary for a day or two, but och, it doesna
matter, seein' ye're so throng ; we'll chust try the shops."

It was indicative of the fine kindly humanity of the riveter
who loved canaries that this one unhesitatingly stopped his
labours, having disposed of the last plate, and said, " I
couldna dae't, chaps ; I wadna trust a canary oot o' the
hoose ; there's nae sayin' the ill-usage it micht get. It
would break my he'rt to ha'e onything gang wrang wi'
ony o' my birds."

" Chust that, Wull, chust that ! " said Para Handy
agreeably. " Your feelings does you credit. I would be
awful vexed if you broke your he'rt ; it'll soon be the only
hale thing left in the hoose. If I wass you, and had such a
spite at the delf, I would use dunnymite," and Dougie and
he departed.

" That's the sort of thing that keeps me from gettin'
merrit," the Captain, with a sigh, confided to his mate,
when they got down the stair. " Look at the money it
costs for dishes every Setturday night."

" Them riveters iss awfu' chaps for sport," said Dougie
irrelevantly.

" There's nothing for't now but the Bird Market," said
the Captain, leading the way east along Argyle Street. They
had no clear idea where that institution was, but at the
corner of Jamaica Street consulted several Celtic compatriots,
who put them on the right track. Having reached the
Bird Market, the Captain explained his wants to a party
who had " Guaranteed A1 Songsters " to sell at two shillings.
This person was particularly enthusiastic about one bird
which in the meantime was as silent as " the harp that
once through Tara's halls." He gave them his solemn
assurance it was a genuine prize roller canary ; that when
it started whistling, as it generally did at breakfast time,
it sang till the gas was lit, with not even a pause for refreshment. For that reason it was an economical canary to
keep ; it practically cost nothing for seed for this canary.
If it was a songster suitable for use on a ship that was
wanted, he went on, with a rapid assumption that his
customers were of a maritime profession, this bird was
peculiarly adapted for the post. It was a genuine imported
bird, and had already made a sea voyage. To sell a bird
of such exquisite parts for two shillings was sheer commercial suicide ; he admitted it, but he was anxious that
it should have a good home.

" I wish I could hear it whustlin'," said the Captain,
peering through the spars at the very dejected bird, which
was a moulting hen.

" It never sings efter the gas is lighted," said the vendor
regretfully, " that's the only thing that's wrang wi't. If
that bird wad sing at nicht when the gas was lit, it wad
solve the problem o' perpetual motion."

Para Handy, considerably impressed by this high warrandice, bought the canary, which was removed from the cage and placed in a brown paper sugar-bag, ventilated by holes which the bird-seller made in it with the stub of a lead pencil.

" Will you no' need a cage ? " asked Dougie.

" Not at aal, not at aal ! " the Captain protested ; " wance we get him doon to Brodick we'll get plenty o' cages," and away they went with their purchase, Para Handy elate at the imminent prospect of his prize canary winning an easy pound.   Dougie carefully carried the bag containing the bird.

Some days after, the *Vital Spark* arrived at Brodick, but the Captain—who had not yet staked his pound with the man in the shipping-box as agreed on, curiously enough showed no disposition to bring off the challenge meeting between the birds.   It was by accident he met the Brodick man one day on the quay.

" Talking about birds," said Para Handy, with some diffidence, " Dougie and me had a canary yonder——"

" That's aal off," said the Brodick man hurriedly, getting very red in the face, showing so much embarrassment, indeed, that the Captain of the *Vital Spark* smelt a rat.

" What way off ? " he asked.   " It sticks in my mind that there wass a kind of a wudger, and that there's a pound note in the shupping-box for the best canary."

" Did you bring your canary ? " asked the Brodick man anxiously.

" It's doon there in the vessel singin' like to take the rivets oot o' her," said Para Handy.   " It's chust sublime to listen to."

" Weel, the fact iss, I'm not goin' to challenge," said the Brodick man.   " I have a wife yonder, and she's sore against bettin' and wudgerin' and gemblin', and she'll no let me take my champion bird Wee Free over the door."

" Chust that ! " said Para Handy.   " That's a peety. Weel, weel, the pund'll come in handy.   I'll chust go away down to the shupping-box and lift it. Seeing I won, I'll stand you a drink."

The Brodick man maintained with warmth that as Para Handy had not yet lodged his stake of a pound the match was off ; an excited discussion followed, and the upshot was a compromise. The Brodick man, having failed to produce his bird, was to forfeit ten shillings, and treat the crew of the *Vital Spark*.

They were being treated, and the ten shillings were in Para Handy's possession, when the Brodick sportsman rose to make some disconcerting remark.

"You think you are very smert, Macfarlane," he said, addressing the Captain. "You are thinkin' you did a good stroke to get the ten shullin's, but if you wass smerter it iss not the ten shullin's you would have at aal, but the pound. I had you fine, Macfarlane. My wife never said a word aboot the wudger, but my bird is in the pook, and couldna sing a note this week. That's the way I backed oot."

Para Handy displayed neither resentment nor surprise. He took a deep draught of beer out of a quart pot, and then smiled with mingled tolerance and pity on the Brodick man.

"Ay, ay!" he said, "and you think you have done a smert thing. You have mich caause to be ashamed of yourself. You are nothing better than a common swundler. But och, it doesna matter ; the fact iss, oor bird's deid."

"Deid!" cried the Brodick man. "What do you mean by deid?"

"Chust that it's no' livin'," said Para Handy coolly. "Dougie and me bought wan in the Bird Market, and Dougie was carryin' it doon to the vessel in a sugar-poke when he met some fellows he kent in Chamaica Street, and went for a dram, or maybe two. Efter a while he didna mind what he had in the poke, and he put it in his troosers pockets, thinkin' it wass something extra for the Sunday's dinner. When he brought the poor wee bird oot of his pocket in the mornin', it wass chust a' remains."

III

THE MALINGERER

THE crew of the *Vital Spark* were all willing workers, except The Tar, who was usually as tired when he rose in the morning as when he went to bed. He said himself it was his health, and that he had never got his strength right back since he had the whooping-cough twice when he was a boy. The Captain was generally sympathetic, and was inclined to believe The Tar was destined to have a short life unless he got married and had a wife to look after him. "A wife's the very thing for you," he would urge; "it's no' canny, a man as delicate as you to be having nobody to depend on."

"I couldna afford a wife," The Tar always maintained. "They're all too grand for the like of me."

"Och ay! but you might look aboot you and find a wee, no' aawfu' bonny wan," said Para Handy.

"If she was blin', or the like of that, you would have a better chance of gettin' her," chimed in Dougie, who always scoffed at The Tar's periodical illnesses, and cruelly ascribed his lack of energy to sheer laziness.

The unfortunate Tar's weaknesses always seemed to come on him when there was most to do. It generally took the form of sleepiness, so that sometimes when he was supposed to be preparing the dinner he would be found sound asleep on the head of a bucket, with a half-peeled potato in his hand. He once crept out of the fo'c'sle rubbing his eyes after a twelve-hours' sleep, saying, "Tell me this and tell me no more, am I going to my bed or comin' from it?"

But there was something unusual and alarming about the illness which overtook The Tar on their way up Lock Fyne to lift a cargo of timber. First he had shivers all down his back; then he got so stiff that he could not bend to lift a bucket, but had to kick it along the deck in front of him, which made Dougie admiringly say, "Man! you are an aawful handy man with your feet, Colin"; his appetite, he declared, totally disappeared immediately after an un- usually hearty breakfast composed of six herrings and two eggs ; and finally he expressed his belief that there was nothing for it but his bed.

"I'll maybe no trouble you long, boys," he moaned lugu- briously. "My heid's birling roond that fast that I canna even mind my own name two meenutes."

"You should write it on a wee bit paper," said Dougie unfeelingly, "and keep it inside your bonnet, so that you could look it up at any time you were needin'."

Para Handy had kinder feelings, and told The Tar to go and lie down for an hour or two and take a wee drop of something.

"Maybe a drop of brandy would help me," said The Tar, promptly preparing to avail himself of the Captain's advice.

"No, nor brandy ; a drop of good Brutish spurits will suit you better, Colin," said the Captain, and went below to dispense the prescription himself.

The gusto with which The Tar swallowed the prescribed dram of British spirits and took a chew of tobacco after it to enhance the effect, made Para Handy somewhat suspicious, and he said so to Dougie when he got on deck, leaving The Tar already in a gentle slumber.

"The rascal's chust scheming," said Dougie emphatically. "There iss nothing in the world wrong with him but the laziness. If you'll notice, he aalways gets no weel when we're going to lift timber, because it iss harder on him at the winch.

The Captain was indignant, and was for going down there and then with a rope's-end to rouse the patient, but Dougie confided to him a method of punishing the malingerer and at the same time getting some innocent amusement for them- selves.

Dinner-time came round. The Tar instinctively wakened and lay wondering what they would take down to him to eat.

The *Vital Spark* was puff-puffing her deliberate way up the loch, and there was an unusual stillness on deck. It seemed to The Tar that the Captain and Dougie were moving about on tiptoe and speaking in whispers. The uncomfortable feeling this created in his mind was increased when his two shipmates came down with slippers on instead of their ordinary sea-boots, creeping down the companion with great caution, carrying a bowl of gruel.

"What's that for?" asked The Tar sharply. "Are you going to paste up any bills?"

"Wheest, Colin," said Para Handy, in a sick-room whisper. "You must not excite yourself, but take this gruel. It'll do you no herm. Poor fellow, you're looking aawful bad." They hung over his bunk with an attitude of chastened grief, and Dougie made to help him to the gruel with a spoon as if he were unable to feed himself.

"Have you no beef?" asked The Tar, looking at the gruel with disgust. "I'll need to keep up my strength with something more than gruel."

"You daurna for your life take anything but gruel," said the Captain sorrowfully. "It would be the daith of you at wance to take beef, though there's plenty in the pot. Chust take this, like a good laad, and don't speak. My Chove! you are looking far through."

"You're nose is as sherp as a preen," said Dougie in an awed whisper, and with a piece of engine-room waste wiped the brow of The Tar, who was beginning to perspire with alarm.

"I don't think I'm so bad ass aal that," said the patient. "It wass chust a turn; a day in my bed 'll put me aal right —or maybe two."

They shook their heads sorrowfully, and the Captain turned away as if to hide a tear. Dougie blew his nose with much ostentation and stifled a sob.

"What's the metter wi' you?" asked the Tar, looking at them in amazement and fear.

" Nothing, nothing, Colin," said the Captain. " Don't say a word. Iss there anything we could get for you ? "

" My heid's bad yet," the patient replied. " Perhaps a drop of spurits——"

" There's no' another drop in the ship," said the Captain.

The patient moaned. " And I don't suppose there's any beer either ? " he said hopelessly.

He was told there was no beer, and instructed to cry if he was requiring any one to come to his assistance, after which the two nurses crept quietly on deck again, leaving him in a very uneasy frame of mind.

They got into the quay late in the afternoon, and the captain and mate came down again quietly, with their caps in their hands, to discover The Tar surreptitiously smoking in his bunk to dull the pangs of hunger that now beset him, for they had given him nothing since the gruel.

" It's not for you, it's not for you at aal, smokin' ! " cried Para Handy in horror, taking the pipe out of his hand. " With the trouble you have, smoking drives it in to the hert and kills you at wance."

" What trouble do you think it iss ? " asked the patient seriously.

" Dougie says it's—it's—what did you say it wass, Dougie ? "

" It's convolvulus in the inside," said Dougie solemnly ; " I had two aunties that died of it in their unfancy."

" I'm going to get up at wance ! " said The Tar, making to rise, but they thrust him back in his blankets, saying the convolvulus would burst at the first effort of the kind he made.

He began to weep. " Fancy a trouble like that coming on me, and me quite young ! " he said, pitying himself seriously. " There wass never wan in oor femily had it."

" It's sleep brings it on," said Dougie, with the air of a specialist who would ordinarily charge a fee of ten guineas— " sleep and sitting doon. There iss nothing to keep off convolvulus but exercise and rising early in the morning. Poor fellow! But you'll maybe get better; when there's hope there's life. The Captain and me wass wondering if there wass anything we could buy ashore for you—some grapes, maybe, or a shullin' bottle of sherry wine."

"Mercy on me! am I ass far through ass that?" said The Tar.

"Or maybe you would like Macphail, the enchineer, to come doon and read the Scruptures a while to you," said Para Handy.

"Macphail!" cried the poor Tar; "I wudna let a man like that read a song-book to me."

They clapped him affectionately on the shoulders; Dougie made as if to shake his hand, and checked himself; then the captain and mate went softly on deck again, and the patient was left with his fears. He felt utterly incapable of getting up.

Para Handy and his mate went up the town and had a dram with the local joiner, who was also undertaker. With this functionary in their company they were moving towards the quay when Dougie saw in a grocer's shop-door a pictorial card bearing the well-known monkey portrait advertising a certain soap that won't wash clothes. He went chuckling into the shop, made some small purchase, and came out the possessor of the picture. Half an hour later, when it was dark, and The Tar was lying in an agony of hunger which he took to be the pains of internal convolvulus, Para Handy, Dougie, and the joiner came quietly down to the fo'c'sle, where he lay. They had no lamp, but they struck matches and looked at him in his bunk with countenances full of pity.

"A nose as sherp as a preen," said Dougie; "it must be the galloping kind of convolvulus."

"Here's Macintyre the joiner would like to see you, Colin," said Para Handy, and in the light of a match the patient saw the joiner cast a rapid professional eye over his proportions.

" What's the joiner wantin' here ? " said The Tar, with a frightful suspicion.

"Nothing Colin, nothing—six by two—I wass chust passing —six by two—chust passing, and the Captain asked me in to see you. It's—six by two, six by two—it's no' very healthy weather we're havin'. Chust that ! "

The fo'c'sle was in darkness, and The Tar felt already as if he was dead and buried. " Am I lookin' very bad ? " he ventured to ask Dougie.

" Bad's no' the name for it," said Dougie. " Chust look at yourself in the enchineer's looking-gless." He produced from under his arm the engineer's little mirror, on the face of which he had gummed the portrait of the monkey cut out from the soap advertisement, which fitted neatly into the frame. The Captain struck a match, and in its brief and insufficient light The Tar looked at himself, as he thought, reflected in the glass.

" Man, I'm no' that awful changed either ; if I had a shave and my face washed. I don't believe it's convolvulus at aal," said he, quite hopefully, and jumped from his bunk.

For the rest of the week he put in the work of two men.

IV

WEE TEENY

THE last passenger steamer to sail that day from Ardrishaig was a trip from Rothesay. It was Glasgow Fair Saturday, and Ardrishaig Quay was black with people. There was a marvellously stimulating odour of dulse, herring, and shell-fish, for everybody carried away in a handkerchief a few samples of these marine products that are now the only sea-side souvenirs not made in Germany. The *Vital Spark*, in ballast, Clydeward bound, lay inside the passenger steamer, ready to start when the latter had got under weigh, and Para Handy and his mate meanwhile sat on the fo'c'sle-head of

" the smertest boat in the tred " watching the frantic efforts of lady excursionists to get their husbands on the steamer before it was too late, and the deliberate efforts of the said husbands to slink away up the village again just for one more drink. Wildly the steamer hooted from her siren, fiercely clanged her bell, vociferously the Captain roared upon his bridge, people aboard yelled eagerly to friends ashore to hurry up, and the people ashore as eagerly demanded to know what all the hurry was about, and where the bleezes was Wull. Women loudly defied the purser to let the ship go away without their John, for he had paid his money for his ticket, and though he was only a working man his money was as good as anybody else's ; and John, on the quay, with his hat thrust back on his head, his thumbs in the arm-holes of his waistcoat and a red handkerchief full of dulse at his feet, gave a display of step-dancing that was responsible for a great deal of the congestion of traffic at the shore end of the gangway.

Among the crowd who had got on board was a woman with eleven children. She was standing on the paddle-box counting them to make sure—five attached to the basket that had contained their food for the day, other four clinging to her gown, and one in her arms. " Yin, twa, three, fower, and fower's eight, and twa's ten, and then there's Wee Teeny wi' her faither doon the caibin." She was quite serene. If she could have seen that the father—at that moment in the fore-saloon singing

> " In the guid auld summer time,
> In the guid auld summer time,
> She'll be your tootsy-wootsy
> In the guid auld summer time."

had no Wee Teeny with him, she would have been distracted. As it was, however, the steamer was miles on her way when a frantic woman with ten crying children all in a row behind her, and a husband miraculously sobered, made a vain appeal to the Captain to go back to Ardrishaig for her lost child.

The child was discovered on the quay by the local police ten minutes after the excursion steamer had started, and just when Para Handy was about to cast off the pawls. She was somewhere about three years old, and the only fact that could be extracted from her was that her name was Teeny. There had probably not been a more contented and self-possessed person on Ardrishaig Quay that day : she sucked her thumb with an air of positive relish, smiled on the slightest provocation, and showed the utmost willingness to go anywhere with anybody.

" The poor wee cratur ! " said Para Handy sympathetically. " She minds me fearfully of my brother Cherlie's twuns. I wudna wonder but she's a twuns too ; that would be the way the mistake would be made in leavin' her ; it's such a terrible thing drink. I'm no' goin' to ask you, Dougie, to do anything you wudna like, but what would you be sayin' to us takin' the wean wi' us and puttin' her ashore at Rothesay ? Mind you, chust if you like yoursel'."

" It's your own vessel, you're the skipper of her, and I'm sure and I have no objections, at aal at aal," said Dougie quite heartily, and it was speedily arranged with the police that a telegram should be sent to wait the captain of the excursion steamer at Rothesay, telling him the lost child was following in the steam-lighter *Vital Spark.*

Macphail the engineer, and The Tar, kept the child in amusement with pocket-knives, oil-cans, cotton-waste, and other maritime toys, while the Captain and Dougie went hurriedly up the village for stores for the unexpected passenger.

" You'll not need that mich," was Dougie's opinion ; " she'll fall asleep as soon as it's dark, and no' wake till we put her ashore at Rothesay."

" Ah, but you canna be sure o' them at that age," said the Captain. " My brother Cherlie wass merrit on a low-country woman, and the twuns used to sit up at night and greet in the two languages, Gaalic and Gleska, till he had to put plugs in them."

" God bless me ! plugs ? " said Dougie astonished.

" Ay, chust plugs," said the Captain emphatically. " You'll see them often. They're made of kahouchy, with a bone ring on them for screwing them on and off. It's the only thing for stopping them greetin'."

The adventures of Wee Teeny from this stage may be better told as Para Handy told it to me some time afterwards.

" To let you ken," he said, " I wass feared the wean would sterve. Nothing in the ship but sea biscuits and salt beef. I went into wan shop and got a quart of milk on draught, half a pound of boiled ham the same as they have at funerals, and a tin tinny For a Good Girl. Dougie wasna slack either ; he went into another shop and got thruppence worth of sweeties and a jumpin'-jeck. It wass as nice a thing ass ever you saw to see the wee cratur sittin' on the hatches eatin' away and drinkin' wi' the wan hand, and laughing like anything at the jumpin'-jeck wi' the other. I never saw the ship cheerier ; it wass chust sublime. If Dougie wass here himsel' he would tell you. Everything wass going first-rate, and I wass doon below washing my face and puttin' on my other jecket and my watch-chain oot o' respect for the passenger, when Dougie came doon in a hurry wi' a long face on him, and says—

" ' She's wantin' ta-ta.'

" ' Mercy on us, she canna be more ta-ta than she iss unless we throw her over the side,' I says to Dougie. But I went up on dake and told her she would be ta-ta in no time becaase the ship was loggin' six knots and the wind wi' us.

" ' Ta-ta,' says she, tuggin' my whuskers the same as if I wass merrit on her—ah, man ! she wass a nice wee thing. And that good-natured ! The best I could do wass to make The Tar show her the tattoo marks on his legs, and Dougie play the trump (Jew's harp), and when she wass tired o' that I carried her up and doon the dake singin' ' Auld Lang Syne ' till she was doverin' over.

" ' She's goin' to sleep noo,' I says to Dougie, and we put her in my bunk wi' her clothes on. She wanted her clothes off, but I said, ' Och ! never mind puttin' them off, Teeny ; it's only a habit.' Dougie said, if he minded right, they always put up a kind of a prayer at that age. ' Give her a start,' I says to Dougie, and he said the 23rd Psalm in Gaalic, but she didn't understand wan word of it, and went to sleep wi' a poke o' sweeties in her hand.

" We were off Ardlamont, and Macphail wass keepin' the boat bangin' at it to get to Rothesay before the mother went oot of her wuts, when I heard a noise doon below where Teeny wass. I ran doon and found her sittin' up chokin' wi' a sweetie that wass a size too lerge for her. She wass black in the face.

" ' Hut her on the back, Peter ! ' said Dougie.

" ' Hut her yoursel' ; I wudna hurt her for the world,' I says, and Dougie said he wudna do it either, but he ran up for The Tar, that hasna mich feelin's, and The Tar saved her life. I'm tellin' you it wass a start ! We couldna trust her below, herself, efter that, so we took her on dake again. In ten meenutes she fell down among Macphail's engines, and nearly spoiled them. She wasna hurt a bit, but Macphail's feelin's wass, for she wass wantin' the engines to her bed wi' her. She thought they were a kind of a toy. We aye keep that up on him yet.

" ' My Chove ! this wean's no' canny,' said Dougie, and we took her up on dake again, and put up the sail to get as mich speed oot of the vessel as we could for Rothesay. Dougie played the trump even-on to her, and The Tar walked on his hands till she was sore laughing at him. Efter a bit we took oor eyes off her for maybe two meenutes, and when we turned roond again Teeny wass fallin' doon into the fo'c'sle.

" ' This iss the worst cargo ever we had,' I says, takin'

her up again no' a bit the worse. ' If we don't watch her like a hawk aal the time she'll do something desperate before we reach Rothesay. She'll jump over the side or crawl doon the funnel, and we'll be black affronted.'

" ' I wudna say but you're right,' said Dougie. We put her sittin' on the hatch wi' the jumpin'-jeck, and the tin tinny For a Good Girl, and my watch and chain, Dougie's trump, the photygraph of The Tar's lass, and Macphail's new carpet sluppers to play wi', and the three of us sat roond her watchin' she didna swallow the watch and chain.

" When I handed her over to her mother and father on Rothesay Quay, I says to them, ' I'm gled I'm no' a mother ; I would a hunder times sooner be a sailor.'

" But it's a nice thing a wean, too ; for a week efter that we missed her awful," concluded the Captain pensively.

v

THE MATE'S WIFE

THAT the Captain of the *Vital Spark* should so persistently remain a bachelor surprised many people. He was just the sort of man, in many respects, who would fall an easy prey to the first woman on the look-out for a good home. He had rather a gallant way with the sex, generally said "mem" to them all, regardless of class ; liked their society when he had his Sunday clothes on, and never contradicted them. If he had pursued any other calling than that of mariner I think he would have been captured long ago ; his escape doubtless lay in the fact that sailing about from place to place, only briefly touching at West-Coast quays, and then being usually grimed with coal-dust, he had never properly roused their interest and natural sporting instincts. They never knew what a grand opportunity they were losing.

" I'm astonished you never got married, Captain," I said to him recently.

" Ach, I couldn't be bothered," he replied, like a man who had given the matter his consideration before now. " I'm that busy wi' the ship I havena time. There's an aawful lot of bother aboot a wife. Forbye, my hert's in the *Fital Spark*—there's no' a smerter boat in the tred. Wait you till I get her pented ! "

" But a ship's not a wife, Captain," I protested.

" No," said he, " but it's a responsibulity. You can get a wife any time that'll stick to you the same as if she wass riveted as long's you draw your pay, but it takes a man with aal his senses aboot him to get a ship and keep her. And chust think on the expense ! Oh, I'm not sayin', mind you, that I'll not try wan some day, but there's no hurry, no, not a bit."

" But perhaps you'll put it off too long," I said, " and when you're in the humour to have them they won't have you."

He laughed at the very idea.

" Man ! " he said, " it's easy seen you have not studied them. I ken them like the Kyles of Bute. The captain of a steamer iss the most popular man in the wide world —popularer than the munisters themselves, and the munisters iss that popular the weemen put bird-lime in front of the Manses to catch them, the same ass if they were green-linties. It's worse with sea-captains—they're that dashing, and they're not aalways hinging aboot the hoose wi' their sluppers on."

" There's another thing," he added, after a little pause, " I couldna put up with a woman comin' aboot the vessel every pay-day. No, no, I'm for none o' that. Dougie's wife's plenty."

" But surely she does not invade you weekly ? " I said, surprised.

" If the *Fital Spark's* anywhere inside Ardlamont on a Setturday," said Para Handy, " she's doon wi' the first steamer from Gleska, and her door-key in her hand, the same ass if it wass a pistol to put to his heid. If Dougie was here himsel' he would tell you. She's a low-country woman, wi' no' a word o' Gaalic, so that she canna understand Dougie at his best. When it comes to bein' angry in English, she can easy bate him. Oh, a cluvver woman: she made Dougie a Rechabite, and he's aalways wan when he's at home, and at keepin' him trum and tidy in his clothes she's chust sublime. But she's no' canny aboot a ship. The first week efter she merried him we were lyin' at Innellan, and doon she came on the Setturday wi' her door-key at full cock. When Dougie saw her comin' doon the quay he got white, and turned to me, sayin', 'Peter, here's the Mustress; I wish I hadna touched that dram, she'll can tell it on me, and I'm no' feared for her, but it would hurt her feelings.'

"'Man!' I said, 'you're an aawful tumid man for a sailor; but haste you doon the fo'c'sle and you'll get a poke of pepper-mint sweeties in my other pocket I had for the church to-morrow. Chust you go like the duvvle, and I'll keep her in conversation till you get your breath shifted.'

"Dougie bolted doon below, and wass up in a shot. 'I got the sweeties, Peter,' he said, 'but, oh! she's as cunning as a jyler, and she'll chalouse something if she smells the pepper-mints. What would you say to the whole of us takin' wan or two sweeties so that we would be aal the same, and she wouldna suspect me?' 'Very weel,' I said, 'anything to obleege a mate,' and when the good leddy reached the side of the vessel the enchineer and The Tar and me and Dougie wass standin' in a row eating peppermints till you would think it wass the front sate of the Tobermory Free Church.

"'It's a fine day and an awfu' smell o' losengers,' was the first words she said when she put her two feet on the deck. And she looked very keen at her man.

"'It is that, mem,' I said. 'It's the cargo.'

"'What cargo?' said she, looking at Dougie harder than ever. 'I'll cargo him!'

"'I mean the cargo of the boat, mem,' I said quite smert.

' It's a cheneral cargo, and there's six ton of peppermint sweeties for the Tarbert fishermen.'

" ' What in the wide world dae the Tarbert fishermen dae wi' sae mony sweeties ? ' said she.

" ' Och, it's chust to keep them from frightening away the herrin' when they're oot at the fishin',' I said. Man ! I'm tellin' you I had aal my wuts aboot me that day ! It wass lucky for us the hatches wass doon, so that she couldna see the cargo we had in the hold. There wasna wan sweetie in it.

" I couldna but be nice to the woman, for she wasna my wife, so I turned a bucket upside doon and gave her a sate, and let on that Dougie was chust ass mich a man of conse-quence on the *Fital Spark* as myself. It does not do to let a wife see wi' her own eyes that her man iss under you in your chob, for when she'll get him at home she'll egg him on to work harder and get your place, and where are you then, eh ! where are you then, I'm asking ? She wass a cluvver woman, but she had no sense. ' Weel,' said she, ' I don't think muckle o' yer boat. I thocht it was a great big boat, wi' a cabin in it. Instead o' that, it's jist a wee coal yin.'

" Man ! do you know that vexed me ; I say she wasna the kind of woman Dougie should have married at aal, at aal. Dougie's a chentleman like mysel' ; he would never hurt your feelings unless he wass tryin'.

" ' There's nothing wrong with the *Fital Spark*, mem,' I said to her. ' She's the most namely ship in the tred ; they'll be writing things aboot her in the papers, and men often come to take photographs of her.'

" She chust sniffed her nose at that, the way merrit women have, and said, ' Jist fancy that ! '

" ' Yes ; chust fancy it ! ' I said to her. ' Six knots in a gale of wind if Macphail the enchineer is in good trum, and maybe seven if it's Setturday, and him in a hurry to get home. She has the finest lines of any steamboat of her size coming oot of Clyde ; if her lum wass pented yellow and she had a bottom strake or two of green, you would take her for a

yat. Perhaps you would be thinkin' we should have a
German band on board of her, with the heid fuddler goin'
aboot gaitherin' pennies in a shell, and the others keekin'
over the ends of their flutes and cornucopias for fear he'll
pocket some. What ? H'm ! Chust that ! '

" Efter a bit she said she would like to see what sort of
place her man and the rest of us slept in, so there was
nothing for it but to take her doon to the fo'c'sle, though it
wass mich against my will. When she saw the fo'c'sle she
wass nestier than ever. She said, ' Surely this iss not a place
for Christian men ' ; and I said, ' No, mem, but we're chust
sailors.'

" ' There's nae richt furniture in't,' she said.

" ' Not at present, mem,' I said. ' Perhaps you were
expectin' a piano,' but, och ! she wass chust wan of them
Gleska women, she didna know life. She went away up the
toon there and then, and came back wi' a bit of waxcloth, a
tin of black soap, a grocer's calendar, and a wee lookin'-gless,
hung her bonnet and the door-key on a cleat, and started
scrubbin' oot the fo'c'sle. Man, it wass chust peetiful !
There wass a damp smell in the fo'c'sle I could feel for months
efter, and I had a cold in my heid for a fortnight. When she
had the floor of the fo'c'sle scrubbed, she laid the bit of waxcloth, got two nails from The Tar, and looked for a place to
hang up the calendar and the wee lookin'-gless, though there
wass not mich room for ornaments of the kind. ' That's
a little mair tidy-like,' she said when she was feenished, and
she came up lookin' for something else to wash. The Tar
saw the danger and went ashore in a hurry.

" ' Are ye merrit ? ' she asked me before she left the vessel
wi' Dougie's pay.

" ' No, mem,' I said, ' I'm not merrit yet.'

" ' I could easy see that,' she said, sniffin' her nose again,
the same ass if I wass not a captain at aal, but chust before the mast. ' I could easy see that. It's time you were
hurryin' up. I ken the very wife wad suit **you** ; she's a

kizzen o' my ain, a weedow wumman no' a bit the worse o'
the wear.'

" ' Chust that ! ' said I, ' but I'm engaged.'

" ' Wha to ? ' she asked quite sherp, no' very sure o' me.

" ' To wan of the Maids of Bute, mem,' I told her, meanin'
yon two pented stones you see from the steamer in the
Kyles of Bute ; and her bein' a Gleska woman, and not
traivelled mich, she thocht I wass in earnest.

" ' I don't ken the faimily,' she said, ' but it's my opeenion
you wad be better wi' a sensible weedow.'

" ' Not at aal, mem,' I said, ' a sailor couldna have a
better wife nor wan of the Maids of Bute ; he'll maybe no'
get mich tocher with her, but she'll no' come huntin' the
quays for him or his wages on the Setturday.' "

VI

PARA HANDY—POACHER

THE *Vital Spark* was lying at Greenock with a cargo of
scrap-iron, on the top of which was stowed loosely an extraordinary variety of domestic furniture, from bird cages to
cottage pianos. Para Handy had just had the hatches off
when I came to the quay-side, and he was contemplating
the contents of his hold with no very pleasant aspect.

" Rather a mixed cargo ! " I ventured to say.

" Muxed's no' the word for't," he said bitterly. " It puts
me in mind of an explosion. It's a flittin' from Dunoon.
There would be no flittin's in the *Fital Spark* if she wass
my boat. But I'm only the captain, och aye ! I'm only
the captain, thirty-five shullin's a-week and liberty to put
on a pea-jecket. To be puttin' scrap-iron and flittin's in
a fine smert boat like this iss carryin' coals aboot in a
coach and twice. It would make any man use Abyssinian
language."

" Abyssinian language ? " I repeated, wondering.

"Chust that, Abyssinian language—swearing, and the like of that, you ken fine, yoursel', withoot me tellin' you. Fancy puttin' a flittin' in the *Fital Spark*! You would think she wass a coal-laary, and her with two new coats of pent out of my own pocket since the New Year."

"Have you been fishing?" I asked, desirous to change the subject, which was, plainly, a sore one with the Captain. And I indicated a small fishing-net which was lying in the bows.

"Chust the least wee bit touch," he said, with a very profound wink. "I have a bit of a net there no' the size of a pocket-naipkin, that I use noo and then at the river-mooths. I chust put it doon—me and Dougie—and whiles a salmon or a sea-troot meets wi' an accident and gets into't. Chust a small bit of a net, no' worth speakin' aboot, no' mich bigger nor a pocket-naipkin. They'll be calling it a splash-net, you ken yoursel' withoot me tellin' you." And he winked knowingly again.

"Ah, Captain!" I said, "that's bad! Poaching with a splash-net! I didn't think you would have done it."

"It's no' me; it's Dougie," he retorted promptly. "A fair duvvle for high jeenks, you canna keep him from it. I told him many a time that it wasna right, becaause we might be found oot and get the jyle for't, but he says they do it on aal the smertest yats. Yes, that iss what he said to me—'They do it on aal the first-cless yats; you'll be bragging the *Fital Spark* iss chust ass good ass any yat, and what for would you grudge a splash-net?'"

"Still it's theft, Captain," I insisted. "And it's very, very bad for the rivers."

"Chust that!" he said complacently. "You'll likely be wan of them fellows that goes to the hotels for the fushing in the rivers. There's more sport aboot a splash-net; if Dougie wass here he would tell you."

"I don't see where the sport comes in," I remarked, and he laughed contemptuously.

" Sport ! " he exclaimed. " The best going. There wass wan time yonder we were up Loch Fyne on a Fast Day, and no' a shop open in the place to buy onything for the next mornin's breakfast. Dougie says to me, ' What do you think yoursel' aboot takin' the punt and the small bit of net no' worth mentionin', and going doon to the river mooth when it's dark and seeing if we'll no' get a fush ? '

" ' It's a peety to be poaching on the Fast Day,' I said to him.

" ' But it's no' the Fast Day in oor parish,' he said. ' We'll chust give it a trial, and if there's no fush at the start we'll come away back again.' Oh ! a consuderate fellow, Dougie ; he saw my poseetion at wance, and that I wasna awfu' keen to be fushin' wi' a splash-net on the Fast Day. The end and the short of it wass that when it wass dark we took the net and the punt and rowed doon to the river and began to splash. We had got a fine haul at wance of six great big salmon, and every salmon Dougie would be takin' oot of the net he would be feeling it all over in a droll way, till I said to him, ' What are you feel-feelin' for, Dougie, the same ass if they had pockets on them ? I'm sure they're all right.'

" ' Oh, yes,' he says, ' right enough, but I wass frightened they might be the laird's salmon, and I wass lookin' for the luggage label on them. There's none. It's all right ; they're chust wild salmon that nobody planted.'

" Weel, we had got chust ass many salmon ass we had any need for when somebody birled a whustle, and the river watchers put off in a small boat from a point outside of us to catch us. There wass no gettin' oot of the river mooth, so we left the boat and the net and the fush and ran ashore, and by-and-by we got up to the quay and on board the *Fital Spark*, and paaused and consudered things.

" ' They'll ken it's oor boat,' said Dougie, and his clothes wass up to the eyes in salmon scales.

" ' There's no doo't aboot that,' I says. ' If it wassna the Fast Day I wouldna be so vexed ; it'll be an awful disgrace to be found oot workin' a splash-net on the Fast Day. And it's a peety aboot the boat, it wass a good boat, I wish we could get her back.'

" ' Ay, it's a peety we lost her,' said Dougie ; ' I wonder in the wide world who could have stole her when we were doon the fo'c'sle at oor supper ? ' Oh, a smert fellow, Dougie ! when he said that I saw at wance what he meant.

" ' I'll go up this meenute and report it to the polis office,' I said quite firm, and Dougie said he would go with me too, but that we would need to change oor clothes, for they were covered with fush-scales. We changed oor clothes and went up to the sercheant of polis, and reported that some-body had stolen oor boat. He wass sittin' readin' his Bible, it bein' the Fast Day, wi' specs on, and he keeked up at us, and said, ' You are very spruce, boys, with your good clothes on at this time of the night.'

" ' We aalways put on oor good clothes on the *Fital Spark* on a Fast Day,' I says to him ; ' it's as little as we can do, though we don't belong to the parish.'

" Next day there wass a great commotion in the place aboot some blackguards doon at the river mooth poachin' with a splash-net. The Factor wass busy, and the heid gamekeeper wass busy, and the polis wass busy. We could see them from the dake of the *Fital Spark* goin' aboot buzzin' like bum-bees.

" ' Stop you ! ' said Dougie to me aal of a sudden. ' They'll be doon here in a chiffy, and findin' us with them scales on oor clothes—we'll have to put on the Sunday wans again.'

" ' But they'll smell something if they see us in oor Sunday clothes,' I said. ' It's no' the Fast Day the day.'

" ' Maybe no' here,' said Dougie, ' but what's to hinder it bein' the Fast Day in oor own parish ? '

" We put on oor Sunday clothes again, and looked the Almanac to see if there wass any word in it of a Fast Day any place that day, but there wass nothing in the Almanac but tides, and the Battle of Waterloo, and the weather for next winter. That's the worst of Almanacs ; there's nothing in them you want. We were fair bate for a Fast Day any place, when The Tar came up and asked me if he could get to the funeral of a cousin of his in the place at two o'clock.

" ' A funeral ! ' said Dougie. ' The very thing. The Captain and me'll go to the funeral too. That's the way we have on oor Sunday clothes.' Oh, a smert, smert fellow, Dougie !

" We had chust made up oor mind it wass the funeral we were dressed for, and no' a Fast Day any place, when the polisman and the heid gamekeeper came doon very suspeecious, and said they had oor boat. ' And what's more,' said the gamekeeper, ' there's a splash-net and five stone of salmon in it. It hass been used, your boat, for poaching.'

" ' Iss that a fact ? ' I says. ' I hope you'll find the blackguards,' and the gamekeeper gave a grunt, and said somebody would suffer for it, and went away busier than ever. But the polis sercheant stopped behind. ' You're still in your Sunday clothes, boys,' said he ; ' what iss the occasion to-day ? '

" ' We're going to the funeral,' I said.

" ' Chust that ! I did not know you were untimate with the diseased,' said the sercheant.

" ' Neither we were,' I said, ' but we are going oot of respect for Colin.' And we went to the funeral, and nobody suspected nothin', but we never got back the boat, for the gamekeeper wass chust needin' wan for a brother o' his own. Och, ay ! there's wonderful sport in a splash-net."

VII

THE SEA COOK

THE TAR'S duties included cooking for the ship's company. He was not exactly a chef who would bring credit to a first-class club or restaurant, but for some time after he joined the *Vital Spark* there was no occasion to complain of him. Quite often he would wash the breakfast-cups to have them clean for tea in the evening, and it was only when in a great hurry he dried plates with the ship's towel. But as time passed, and he found his shipmates not very particular about what they ate, he grew a little careless. For instance, Para Handy was one day very much annoyed to see The Tar carry forward the potatoes for dinner in his cap.

"That's a droll way to carry potatoes, Colin," he said mildly.

"Och! they'll do no herm; it's only an old kep anyway," said The Tar. "Catch me usin' my other kep for potatoes!"

"It wass not exactly your kep I wass put aboot for," said the Captain. "It wass chust running in my mind that maybe some sort of a dish would be nater and genteeler. I'm no' compleenin', mind you, I'm chust mentioning it."

"Holy smoke!" said The Tar. "You're getting to be aawful polite wi' your plates for potatoes, and them no peeled!"

But the want of variety in The Tar's cooking grew worse and worse each voyage, and finally created a feeling of great annoyance to the crew. It was always essence of coffee, and herring—fresh, salt, kippered, or red—for breakfast, sausages or stewed steak and potatoes for dinner, and a special treat in the shape of ham and eggs for Sundays. One unlucky day for the others of the crew, however, he discovered the convenience of tinned corned beef, and would

feed them on that for dinner three or four days a week.
Of course they commented on this prevalence of tinned
food, which the engineer with some humour always called
"malleable mule," but The Tar had any number of reasons
ready for its presence on the midday board.

"Sorry, boys," he would say affably, "but this is the
duvvle of a place ; no' a bit of butcher meat to be got in't
till Wednesday, when it comes wi' the boat from Gleska."
Or "The fire went oot on me, chaps, chust when I wass
making a fine thing. Wait you till Setturday, and we'll
have something rare ! "

"Ay, ay ; live, old horse, and you'll get corn," the Captain
would say under these circumstances, as he artistically
carved the wedge of American meat. "It's a mercy to get
anything ; back in your plate, Dougie."

It became at last unbearable, and while The Tar was ashore
one day in Tarbert, buying bottled coffee and tinned meat
in bulk, a conference between the captain, the engineer, and
the mate took place.

"I'm no' going to put up wi't any longer," said the engineer
emphatically. "It's all very well for them that has no thinking to do wi' their heids to eat tinned mule even on, but an
engineer that's thinking aboot his engines all the time, and
sweatin' doon in a temperature o' 120, needs to keep his
strength up."

"What sort o' heid-work are you talking aboot ? " said
the Captain. "Iss it readin' your penny novelles ? Hoo's
Lady Fitzgerald's man gettin' on ? " This last allusion was
to Macphail's passion for penny fiction, and particularly to
a novelette story over which the engineer had once been
foolish enough some years before to show great emotion.

"I move," said Dougie, breaking in on what promised to
be an unprofitable altercation,—"I move that The Tar be
concurred."

"Concurred ! " said the engineer, with a contemptuous
snort. "I suppose you mean censured ? "

" It's the same thing, only spelled different," said the mate.

" What's censured ? " asked the Captain.

" It's giving a fellow a duvvle of a clourin'," answered Dougie promptly.

" No, no, I wouldna care to do that to The Tar. Maybe he's doin' the best he can, poor chap. The Tar never saw mich high life before he came on my boat, and we'll have to make an allowance for that."

" Herrin' for breakfast seven days a week ! it's a fair scandal," said the engineer. " If you were maister in your own boat, Macfarlane, you would have a very different kind of man makin' your meat for you."

" There's not mich that iss wholesomer than a good herrin'," said Para Handy. " It's a fush that's chust sublime. But I'll not deny it would be good to have a change noo and then, if it wass only a finnen haddie."

" I have a cookery book o' the wife's yonder at home I'll bring wi' me the next time we're in Gleska, and it'll maybe give him a tip or two," said the engineer, and this was, in the meantime, considered the most expedient thing to do.

Next trip, on the way to Brodick on a Saturday with a cargo of bricks, The Tar was delicately approached by the Captain, who had the cookery book in his hand. " That wass a nice tender bit of tinned beef we had the day, Colin," he said graciously. " Capital, aaltogether ! I could live myself on tinned beef from wan end of the year to the other, but Dougie and the enchineer there's compleenin' that you're givin' it to them too often. You would think they were lords ! But perhaps I shouldna blame them, for the doctor told the enchineer he should take something tasty every day, and Dougie's aye frightened for tinned meat since ever he heard that the enchineer wance killed a man in the Australian bush. What do you say yoursel' to tryin' something fancy in the cookery line ? "

" There's some people hard to please," said The Tar ;

" I'm sure I'm doin' the best I can to satisfy you aal. Look at them red herrin's I made this mornin' ! "

" They were chust sublime ! " said the Captain, clapping him on the back. " But chust try a change to keep their mooths shut. It'll only need to be for a little, for they'll soon tire o' fancy things. I have a kind of a cookery book here you might get some tips in. It's no' mine, mind you, it's Macphail's."

The Tar took the cookery book and turned over some pages with contemptuous and horny fingers.

" A lot o' nonsense ! " he said. " Listen to this : ' Take the remains of any cold chicken, mix with the potatoes, put in a pie-dish, and brown with a salamander.' Where are you to get the cold chucken ? and where are you to take it ? Fancy callin' it a remains ; it would be enough to keep you from eatin' chucken. And what's a salamander ? There's no' wan on this vessel, at any rate."

" It's chust another name for cinnamon, but you could leave it oot," said the Captain.

" Holy smoke ! listen to this," proceeded The Tar : " ' How to make clear stock. Take six or seven pounds of knuckle of beef or veal, half a pound of ham or bacon, a quarter of a pound of butter, two onions, one carrot, one turnip, half a head of salary, and two gallons of water.' You couldna sup that in a week."

" Smaal quantities, smaal quantities, Colin," explained the Captain. " I'm sorry to put you to bother, but there's no other way of pleasin' them other fellows."

" There's no' a thing in this book I would eat except a fowl that's described here," said The Tar, after a further glance through the volume.

" The very thing ! " cried the Captain, delighted. " Try a fowl for Sunday," and The Tar said he would do his best.

" I soon showed him who wass skipper on this boat," said the Captain going aft to Dougie and the engineer. " It's to be fowls on Sunday."

There was an old-fashioned cutter yacht at anchor in Brodick Bay with a leg of mutton and two plucked fowls hanging openly under the overhang of her stern, which is sometimes even yet the only pantry a yacht of that type has, though the result is not very decorative.

"Look at that!" said the engineer to The Tar as the *Vital Spark* puffed past the yacht. "There's sensible meat for sailors; no malleable mule. I'll bate you them fellows has a cook wi' aal his wuts aboot him."

"It's aal right, Macphail," said The Tar; "chust you wait till to-morrow and I'll give you fancy cookin'."

And sure enough on Sunday he had two boiled fowls for dinner. It was such an excellent dinner that even the engineer was delighted.

"I'll bate you that you made them hens ready oot o' the wife's cookery book," he said. "There's no' a better cookery book on the South-side of Gleska; the genuine Aunt Kate's. People come far and near for the lend o' that when they're havin' anything extra."

"Where did you buy the hens?" inquired the Captain, nibbling contentedly at the last bone left after the repast.

"I didna buy them at aal," said the Tar. "I couldna be expected to buy chuckens on the money you alloo me. Forbye, it doesna say anything aboot buying in Macphail's cookery book. It says, 'Take two chickens and boil slowly.' So I chust had to take them."

"What do you mean by that?" asked Para Handy, with great apprehension.

"I chust went oot in a wee boat late last night and took them from the stern o' yon wee yacht," said The Tar coolly; and a great silence fell upon the crew of the *Vital Spark*.

"To-morrow," said the Captain emphatically at last— "to-morrow you'll have tinned meat; do you know that, Colin? And you'll never have chucken on the boat again, not if Macphail was breakin' his he'rt for it."

VIII

LODGERS ON A HOUSE-BOAT

A MAN and his wife came down Crarae Quay from the village. The man carried a spotted yellow tin box in one hand and a bottle of milk in the other. He looked annoyed at something. His wife had one child in her arms, and another walked weeping behind her, occasionally stopping the weeping to suck a stalk of The Original Crarae Rock. There was a chilly air of separation about the little procession that made it plain there had been an awful row. At the quay the *Vital Spark* lay with her hold half covered by the hatches, after discharging a cargo. Her gallant commander, with Dougie, stood beside the winch and watched the family coming down the quay.

" Take my word for it, Dougie," said Para Handy, " that man's no' in very good trum ; you can see by the way he's banging the box against his legs and speaking to himsel'. It's no' a hymn he's going over, I'll bate you. And hersel's no' mich better, or she wouldna be lettin' the poor fellow carry the box."

The man came forward to the edge of the quay, looked at the newly-painted red funnel of the *Vital Spark*, and seemed, from his countenance, to have been seized by some bright idea.

" Hey ! you with the skipped kep," he cried down eagerly to Dougie, " when does this steamer start ? "

Para Handy looked at his mate with a pride there was no concealing. " My Chove ! Dougie," he said in a low tone to him. " My Chove ! he thinks we're opposeetion to the *Lord of the Isles* or the *King Edward*. I'm aye tellin' you this boat iss built on smert lines ; if you and me had brass buttons we could make money carryin' passengers."

" Are ye deaf ? " cried the man on the quay impatiently, putting down the tin box, and rubbing the sweat from his brow. " When does this boat start ? "

" This iss not a boat that starts at aal," said the Captain. " It's a—it's a kind of a yat."

" Dalmighty ! " exclaimed the man, greatly crestfallen, " that settles it. I thocht we could get back to Gleska wi' ye. We canna get ludgin's in this place, and whit the bleezes are we to dae when we canna get ludgin's ? "

" That's a peety," said the Captain. " It's no' a very nice thing to happen on a Setturday, and there's no way you can get oot of Crarae till Monday unless you have wan of them motor cars."

" We havena oors wi' us," said the wife, taking up a position beside her husband and the tin box. " I'm vexed the only thing o' the kind I ha'e 's a cuddy, and if it wasna for him we would ha'e stayed at Rothesay, whaur you can aye get ludgin's o' some kind. Do ye no' think ye could gie us twa nicht's ludgin's on your boat ? I'm shair there's plenty o' room."

" Bless my sowl, where's the plenty o' room ? " asked the Captain. " This boat cairries three men and an enchineer, and we're crooded enough in the fo'c'sle."

" Where's that ? " she asked, taking all the negotiations out of the hands of her husband, who sat down on the spotted tin box and began to cut tobacco.

" Yonder it is," said Para Handy, indicating the place with a lazy, inelegant, but eloquent gesture of his leg.

" Weel, there's plenty o' room," persisted the woman,— " ye can surely see for yersel' there's plenty o' room ; you and your men could sleep at the—at the—the stroup o' the boat there, and ye could mak' us ony kind o' a shake-down doon the stair there "—and she pointed at the hold.

" My coodness ! the stroup o' the boat ! " exclaimed Para Handy ; " you would think it wass a teapot you were taalkin' aboot. And that's no' a doon-stairs at aal, it's the howld. We're no' in the habit of takin' in ludgers in the coastin' tred ; I never had wan in the *Fital Spark* in aal my life except the time I cairried Wee Teeny. We havena right accommodation for ludgers ; we have no napery, nor enough knives and forks——"

" Onything wad dae for a shove-bye," said the woman. " I'm shair ye wouldna see a dacent man and his wife and twa wee hameless lambs sleepin' in the quarry as lang as ye could gie them a corner to sit doon in on that nice clean boat o' yours."

She was a shrewd woman ; her compliment to the *Vital Spark* found the soft side of its captain's nature, and, to the disgust of Macphail the engineer and the annoyance of The Tar—though with the hearty consent of the mate— Jack Flood and his family, with the tin box and the bottle of milk, were ten minutes later installed in the fo'c'sle of the *Vital Spark* as paying guests. The terms arranged were two shillings a night. " You couldna get ludgin's in a good hotel for mich less," said the Captain, and Mrs Flood agreed that that was reasonable.

The crew slept somewhat uncomfortably in the hold, and in the middle watches of the night the Captain wakened at the sound of an infant crying. He sat up, nudged Dougie awake, and moralised.

" Chust listen to that, Dougie," he said, " the wee cratur's greetin' ass naitural ass anything, the same ass if it wass a rale ludgin's or on board wan of them ships that carries passengers to America. It's me that likes to hear it ; it's ass homely a thing ass ever happened on this vessel. I wouldna say but maybe it 'll be good luck. I'm tellin' you what, Dougie, we'll no' cherge them a d—— ha'penny ; what do you think, mate ? "

" Whatever you say yoursel'," said Dougie.

The wail of the infant continued ; they heard Jack Flood get up at the request of his wife and sing. He sang " Rocked in the Cradle of the Deep "—at least he sang two lines of it over and over again, taking liberties with the air that would have much annoyed the original composer if he could have heard him.

B*

"It's chust sublime!" said Para Handy, stretched on a rolled-up sail. "You're a lucky man, Dougie, that iss mairried and has a hoose of your own. Oor two ludgers iss maybe pretty cross when it comes to the quarrelling, but they have no spite at the weans. You would not think that man Flood had the sense to rise up in the muddle of the night and sing ' Rocked in the Cradle of the Deep ' at his child. It chust shows you us workin'-men have good he'rts."

" Jeck may have a cood enough he'rt," said Dougie, " but, man! he has a poor, poor ear for music! I wish he would stop it and no' be frightenin' the wean. I'm sure it never did him any herm."

By and by the crying and the music ceased, and the only sound to be heard was the snore of The Tar and the lapping of the tide against the run of the vessel.

Sunday was calm and bright, but there was no sign of the lodgers coming on deck till late in the forenoon, much to the surprise of the Captain. At last he heard a loud peremptory whistle from the fo'c'sle, and went forward to see what was wanted. Flood threw up four pairs of boots at him. " Gie them a bit polish," he said airily. " Ye needna be awfu' parteecular," he added, " but they're a' glaur, and we like to be dacent on Sunday."

The Captain, in a daze, lifted the boots and told The Tar to oil them, saying emphatically at the same time to Dougie, " Efter aal, we'll no' let them off with the two shillin's. They're too dirty parteecular."

There was another whistle ten minutes later, and Dougie went to see what was wanted.

" I say, my lad," remarked Mr Flood calmly, " look slippy with the breakfast ; we canna sterve here ony langer."

" Are you no' comin' up for't ? " asked Dougie in amazement. " It's a fine dry day."

" Dry my auntie ! " said Mr Flood. " The wife aye gets her breakfast in her bed on Sundays whether it's wet or dry.

Ye'll get the kippered herrin' and the loaf she brung last nicht beside the lum.''

The Tar cooked the lodgers' breakfast under protest, saying he was not paid wages for being a saloon steward, and he passed it down to the fo'c'sle.

" Two shillin's a night ! " said the Captain. " If I had known what it wass to keep ludgers, it wouldna be two shillin's a night I would be cherging them.''

He was even more emphatic on this point when a third whistle came from the fo'c'sle, and The Tar, on going to see what was wanted now, was informed by Mrs Flood that the cooking was not what she was accustomed to. " I never saw a steamer like this in my life," she said, " first cless, as ye micht say, and no' a table to tak' yer meat aff, and only shelfs to sleep on, and sea-sick nearly the hale nicht to the bargain ! Send us doon a pail o' water to clean oor faces.''

Para Handy could stand no more. He washed himself carefully, put on his Sunday clothes and his watch chain, which always gave him great confidence and courage, and went to the fo'c'sle-head. He addressed the lodgers from above.

" Leezy," he said ingratiatingly (for so he had heard Mr Flood designate his wife), " Leezy, you're missing aal the fun doon there ; you should come up and see the folk goin' to the church ; you never saw such style among the women in aal your days.''

" I'll be up in a meenute," she replied quickly ; " Jeck, hurry up and hook this.''

On the whole, the lodgers and the crew of the *Vital Spark* spent a fairly pleasant Sunday. When the Flood family was not ashore walking in the neighbourhood, it was lying about the deck eating dulse and picking whelks culled from the shore by Jack. The mother kindly supplied the infant with as much dulse and shell-fish as it wanted, and it had for these a most insatiable appetite.

" You shouldna eat any wulks or things of that sort when

there's no ' r's ' in the month," Para Handy advised her.
" They're no' very wholesome then."

" Fiddlesticks ! " said Mrs Flood.   " I've ett wulks every
Fair since I was a wee lassie, and look at me noo ! Besides,
there's an ' r ' in Fair, that puts it a' richt."

That night the infant wailed from the moment they went
to bed till it was time to rise in the morning ; Jack Flood
sang " Rocked in the Cradle of the Deep " till he was hoarse,
and the crew in the hold got up next morning very sorry for
themselves.

" You'll be takin' the early steamer ? " said Para Handy
at the first opportunity.

" Och ! we're gettin' on fine," said Jack cheerfully ;
" Leezy and me thinks we'll just put in the week wi' ye,"
and the wife indicated her hearty concurrence.

" You canna stay here," said the Captain firmly.

" Weel, we're no' goin' to leave, onywye," said Mr Flood,
lighting his clay pipe. " We took the ludgin's, and though
they're no' as nice as we would like, we're wullin' to put up
with them, and ye canna put us oot withoot a week's warnin'."

" My Chove ! do you say that ? " said Para Handy in
amazement. " You're the first and last ludger I'll have
on this vessel ! "

" A week's notice ; it's the law o' the land," said the
admirable Mr Flood, " isn't that so, Leezy ? "

" Everybody that has sense kens that that's richt," said
Mrs Flood. And the Flood family retired en masse to the
fo'c'sle.

Ten minutes later the Vital Spark was getting up steam,
and soon there were signs of her immediate departure from
the quay.

" Whaur are ye gaun ? " cried Jack, coming hurriedly on
deck.

" Outward bound," said Para Handy with indifference.
" That's a sailor's life for you, here the day and away
yesterday."

" To Gleska ? " said Mr Flood hopefully.

" Gleska ! " said Para Handy. " We'll no' see it for ten months ; we're bound for the Rio Grande."

" Whaur's that in a' the warld ? " asked Mrs Flood, who had joined her husband on deck.

" Oh ! chust in foreign perts," said Para Handy. " Away past the Bay of Biscay, and the first place on your left-hand side after you pass New Zealand. It's where the beasts for the Zoo comes from."

In four minutes the Flood family were off the ship, and struggling up the quay with the spotted tin trunk, and the *Vital Spark* was starting for Bowling.

" I'm a stupid man," said Para Handy in a few minutes after leaving the quay. " Here we're away and forgot aal aboot the money for the ludgin's."

IX

A LOST MAN

It was a dirty evening, coming on to dusk, and the *Vital Spark* went walloping drunkenly down Loch Fyne with a cargo of oak bark, badly trimmed. She staggered to every shock of the sea ; the waves came combing over her quarter, and Dougie the mate began to wish they had never sailed that day from Kilcatrine. They had struggled round the point of Pennymore, the prospect looking every moment blacker, and he turned a dozen projects over in his mind for inducing Para Handy to anchor somewhere till the morning. At last he remembered Para's partiality for anything in the way of long-shore gaiety, and the lights of the village of Furnace gave him an idea.

" Ach ! man, Peter," said he, " did we no' go away and forget this wass the night of the baal at Furnace ? What do you say to going in and joining the spree ? "

" You're feared, Dougie," said the Captain ; " you're

scaared to daith for your life, in case you'll have to die and leave your money. You're thinkin' you'll be drooned, and that's the way you want to put her into Furnace. Man! but you're tumid, tumid! Chust look at me—no' the least put aboot. That's becaause I'm a Macfarlane, and a Macfarlane never was bate yet, never in this world! I'm no' goin' to stop the night for any baal—we must be in Clyde on Friday; besides, we havena the clothes wi' us for a baal. Forbye, who'll buy the tickets? Eh? Tell me that! Who'll buy the tickets?"

"Ach! you don't need tickets for a Furnace baal," said Dougie, flicking the spray from his ear, and looking longingly at the village they were nearing. "You don't need tickets for a Furnace baal as long as you ken the man at the door and taalk the Gaalic at him. And your clothes 'll do fine if you oil your boots and put on a kind of a collar. What's the hurry for Clyde? It'll no' run dry. In weather like this, too! It's chust a temptin' of Providence. I had a dream yonder last night that wasna canny. Chust a temptin' of Providence."

"I wudna say but it is," agreed the Captain weakly, putting the vessel a little to starboard; "it's many a day since I was at a spree in Furnace. Are you sure the baal's the night?"

"Of course I am," said Dougie emphatically; "it only started yesterday."

"Weel, if you're that keen on't, we'll maybe be chust as weel to put her in till the mornin'," said Para Handy, steering hard for Furnace Bay; and in a little he knocked down to the engines with the usual, "Stop her, Macphail, when you're ready."

All the crew of the *Vital Spark* went to the ball, but they did not dance much, though it was the boast of Para Handy that he was "a fine strong dancer." The last to come down to the vessel in the morning when the ball stopped, because the paraffin-oil was done, was the Captain, walking on his heels, with his pea-jacket tightly buttoned on his chest, and his round, go-ashore pot hat, as he used to say himself, "on three hairs." It was a sign that he felt intensely satisfied with everything.

"I'm feeling chust sublime," he said to Dougie, smacking his lips and thumping himself on the chest as he took his place at the wheel, and the *Vital Spark* resumed her voyage down the loch. "I am chust like the eagle that knew the youth in the Scruptures. It's a fine, fine thing a spree, though I wass not in the trum for dancing. I met sixteen cousins yonder, and them all in the committee. They were the proud men last night to be having a captain for a cousin, and them only quarry-men. It's the educaation, Dougie; educaation gives you the nerve, and if you have the nerve you can go round the world."

"You werena very far roond the world, whatever o't," unkindly interjected the engineer, who stuck up his head at the moment.

The Captain made a push at him angrily with his foot. "Go down, Macphail," he said, "and do not be making a display of your ignorance on this ship. Stop you till I get you at Bowling! Not round the world! Man, I wass twice at Ullapool, and took the *Fital Spark* to Ireland wance, without a light on her. There iss not a port I am not acquent with from the Tail of the Bank to Cairndow, where they keep the two New Years. And Campbeltown, ay, or Barra, or Tobermory. I'm telling you when I am in them places it's Captain Peter Macfarlane iss the mich-respected man. If you were a rale encheneer and not chust a fireman, I would be asking you to my ludgings to let you see the things I brought from my voyages."

The engineer drew in his head and resumed the perusal of a penny novelette.

"He thinks I'm frightened for him," said the Captain, winking darkly to his mate. "It iss because I am too cuvil to him : if he angers me, I'll show him. It is chust spoiling the boat having a man like that in cherge of her enchines, and her such a fine smert boat, with me, and a man like me, in command of her."

"And there's mysel', too, the mate," said Dougie ; "I'm no' bad mysel'."

Below Minard rocks the weather grew worse again : the same old seas smashed over the *Vital Spark*. "She's pitching aboot chust like a washin'-boyne," said Dougie apprehensively. "That's the worst of them oak-bark cargoes."

"Like a washin'-boyne !" cried Para Handy indignantly ; "she's chust doing sublime. I wass in boats in my time where you would need to be baling the watter out of your top-boots every here and there. The smertest boat in the tred ; stop you till I have a pound of my own, and I will paint her till you'll take her for a yat if it wasna for the lum. You and your washin'-boyne ! A washin'-boyne wudna do you any herm, my laad, and that's telling you."

They were passing Lochgair ; the steamer *Cygnet* overtook and passed them as if they had been standing, somebody shouting to them from her deck.

Para Handy refrained from looking. It always annoyed him to be passed this way by other craft ; and in summer time, when the turbine *King Edward* or the *Lord of the Isles* went past him like a streak of lightning, he always retired below to hide his feelings. He did not look at the *Cygnet*. "Ay, ay," he said to Dougie, "if I was telling Mr Macbrayne the umpudence of them fellows, he would put a stop to it in a meenute, but I will not lose them their chobs ; poor sowls ! maybe they have wifes and femilies. That'll be Chonny Mactavish takin' his fun of me ; you would think he wass a wean. Chust like them brats of boys that come to the riverside when we'll be going up the Clyde at Yoker and cry, 'Columbia, ahoy !' at us—the duvvle's own !"

As the *Cygnet* disappeared in the distance, with a figure

waving at her stern, a huge sea struck the *Vital Spark* and swept her from stem to stern, almost washing the mate, who was hanging on to a stay, overboard.

" Tar ! Tar ! " cried the Captain. " Go and get a ha'ad o' that bucket or it'll be over the side."

There was no response. The Tar was not visible, and a wild dread took possession of Para Handy.

" Let us pause and consider," said he to himself ; " was The Tar on board when we left Furnace ? "

They searched the vessel high and low for the missing member of the crew, who was sometimes given to fall asleep in the fo'c'sle at the time he was most needed. But there was no sign of him. " I ken fine he wass on board when we started," said the Captain, distracted, " for I heard him sputtin'. Look again, Dougie, like a good laad." Dougie looked again, for he, too, was sure The Tar had returned from the ball with them. " I saw him with my own eyes," he said, " two of him, the same as if he was a twins ; that iss the curse of drink in a place like Furnace." But the search was in vain, even though the engineer said he had seen The Tar an hour ago.

" Weel, there's a good man gone ! " said Para Handy. " Och ! poor Tar ! It was yon last smasher of a sea. He's over the side. Poor laad ! poor laad ! Cot bless me, dyin' without a word of Gaalic in his mooth ! It's a chudgment on us for the way we were carryin' on, chust a chudgment ; not another drop of drink will I drink, except maybe beer. Or at a New Year time. I'm blaming you, Dougie, for making us stop at Furnace for a baal I wudna give a snuff for. You are chust a disgrace to the vessel, with your smokin' and your drinkin', and your ignorance. It iss time you were livin' a better life for the sake of your wife and femily. If it wass not for you makin' me go into Furnace last night, The Tar would be to the fore yet, and I would not need to be sending a telegram to his folk from Ardrishaig. If I wass not steering the boat, I would break

my he'rt greetin' for the poor laad that never did anybody
any herm.   Get oot the flag from below my bunk, give it a
syne in the pail, and put it at half-mast, and we'll go into
Ardrishaig and send a telegram—it'll be a sixpence.   It'll
be a telegram with a sore he'rt, I'll assure you.   I do not
know what I will say in it, Dougie.   It will not do to break
it too much to them ; maybe we will send the two telegrams
—that'll be a shilling.   We'll say in the first wan—' Your
son, Colin, left the boat to-day ' : and in the next wan we
will say—' He iss not coming back, he is drooned.'   Och !
och ! poor Tar, amn't I sorry for him ?   I was chust going
to put up his wages a shillin' on Setturday."

The *Vital Spark* went in close to Ardrishaig pier just as
the *Cygnet* was leaving after taking in a cargo of herring-
boxes.   Para Handy and Dougie went ashore in the punt,
the Captain with his hands washed and his watch-chain on
as a tribute of respect for the deceased.   Before they could
send off the telegram it was necessary that they should
brace themselves for the melancholy occasion.   "No drinking, chust wan gless of beer," said Para Handy, and they
entered a discreet contiguous public-house for this purpose.

The Tar himself was standing at the counter having a
refreshment, with one eye wrapped up in a handkerchief.

"Dalmighty ! " cried the Captain, staggered at the sight,
and turning pale.   "What are you doing here with your eye
in a sling ? "

"What's your business ? " retorted The Tar coolly.   "I'm
no' in your employ anyway."

"What way that ? " asked Para Handy sharply.

"Did you no' give me this black eye and the sack last
night at the baal, and tell me I wass never to set foot on
the *Vital Spark* again ?   It was gey mean o' you to go away
withoot lettin' me get my dunnage oot, and that's the way
I came here with the *Cygnet* to meet you.   Did you no' hear
me roarin' on you when we passed ? "

"Weel done ! weel done ! " said Para Handy soothingly,

with a wink at his mate. " But ach ! I wass only in fun,
Colin ; it wass a jeenk ; it wass chust a baur aalthegither.
Come away back to the boat like a smert laad. I have a
shilling here I wass going to spend anyway. Colin, what'll
you take ? We thought you were over the side and drooned,
and you are here, quite dry as usual."

X

HURRICANE JACK

I very often hear my friend the Captain speak of Hurricane
Jack in terms of admiration and devotion, which would
suggest that Jack is a sort of demigod. The Captain always
refers to Hurricane Jack as the most experienced seaman of
modern times, as the most fearless soul that ever wore oilskins, the handsomest man in Britain, so free with his money
he would fling it at the birds, so generally accomplished
that it would be a treat to be left a month on a desert island
alone with him.

" Why is he called Hurricane Jack ? " I asked the Captain
once.

" What the duvvle else would you caal him ? " asked
Para Handy. " Nobody ever caals him anything else than
Hurricane Jeck."

" Quite so, but why ? " I persisted.

Para Handy scratched the back of his neck, made the
usual gesture as if he were going to scratch his ear, and then
checked himself in the usual way to survey his hand as if
it were a beautiful example of Greek sculpture. His hand,
I may say, is almost as large as a Belfast ham.

" What way wass he called Hurricane Jeck ? " said he.
" Well, I'll soon tell you that. He wass not always known
by that name ; that wass a name he got for the time he stole
the sheep."

" Stole the sheep ! " I said, a little bewildered, for I failed to see how an incident of that kind would give rise to such a name.

" Yes ; what you might call stole," said Para Handy hastily ; " but, och ! it wass only wan smaal wee sheep he lifted on a man that never went to the church, and chust let him take it ! Hurricane Jeck would not steal a fly— no, nor two flies, from a Chrustian ; he's the perfect chentleman in that."

" Tell me all about it," I said.

" I'll soon do that," said he, putting out his hand to admire it again, and in doing so upsetting his glass. " Tut, tut ! " he said. " Look what I have done—knocked doon my gless ; it wass a good thing there wass nothing in it.

" Hurricane Jeck," said the Captain, when I had taken the hint and put something in it, " iss a man that can sail anything and go anywhere, and aalways be the perfect chentleman. A millionaire's yat or a washing-boyne—it's aal the same to Jeck ; he would sail the wan chust as smert as the other, and land on the quay as spruce ass if he wass newly come from a baal. Oh, man ! the cut of his jeckets ! And never anything else but 'lastic-sided boots, even in the coorsest weather ! If you would see him, you would see a man that's chust sublime, and that careful about his 'lastic-sided boots he would never stand at the wheel unless there wass a bass below his feet. He'll aye be oil-oiling at his hair, and buying hard hats for going ashore with : I never saw a man wi' a finer heid for the hat, and in some of the vessels he wass in he would have the full of a bunker of hats. Hurricane Jeck wass brought up in the China clupper tred, only he wassna called Hurricane Jeck then, for he hadna stole the sheep till efter that. He wass captain of the *Dora Young*, wan of them cluppers ; he's a hand on a gaabert the now, but aalways the perfect chentleman."

" It seems a sad downcome for a man to be a gabbart hand after having commanded a China clipper," I ventured to remark. " What was the reason of his change ? "

" Bad luck," said Para Handy. " Chust bad luck. The fellow never got fair-play. He would aye be somewhere takin' a gless of something wi' somebody, for he's a fine big cheery chap. I mind splendid when he wass captain on the clupper, he had a fine hoose of three rooms and a big decanter, wi' hot and cold watter, oot at Pollokshaws. When you went oot to the hoose to see Hurricane Jeck in them days, time slupped bye. But he wassna known as Hurricane Jeck then, for it wass before he stole the sheep."

" You were just going to tell me something about that," I said.

" Jeck iss wan man in a hundred, and ass good ass two if there wass anything in the way of trouble, for, man ! he's strong, strong ! He has a back on him like a shipping-box, and when he will come down Tarbert quay on a Friday night after a good fishing, and the trawlers are arguing, it's two yerds to the step with him and a bash in the side of his hat for fair defiance. But he never hit a man twice, for he's aye the perfect chentleman iss Hurricane Jeck. Of course, you must understand, he wass not known as Hurricane Jeck till the time I'm going to tell you of, when he stole the sheep.

" I have not trevelled far mysel' yet, except Ullapool and the time I wass at Ireland ; but Hurricane Jeck in his time has been at every place on the map, and some that's no'. Chust wan of Brutain's hardy sons—that's what he iss. As weel kent in Calcutta as if he wass in the Coocaddens, and he could taalk a dozen of their foreign kinds of languages if he cared to take the bother. When he would be leaving a port, there wassna a leddy in the place but what would be doon on the quay wi' her Sunday clothes on and a bunch o' floo'ers for his cabin. And when he would be sayin' good-bye to them from the brudge, he would chust take off his hat and give it a shoogle, and put it on again ; his manners wass complete. The first thing he would do when he reached any place wass to go ashore and get his boots brushed, and then sing ' Rule

Britannia' roond aboot the docks. It wass a sure way to get freend or foe aboot you, he said, and he wass aye as ready for the wan as for the other. Brutain's hardy son!

"He made the fastest passages in his time that wass ever made in the tea trade, and still and on he would meet you like a common working-man. There wass no pride or nonsense of that sort aboot Hurricane Jeck; but, mind you, though I'm callin' him Hurricane Jeck, he wasna Hurricane Jeck till the time he stole the sheep."

"I don't like to press you, Captain, but I'm anxious to hear about that sheep," I said patiently.

"I'm comin' to't," said Para Handy. "Jeck had the duvvle's own bad luck; he couldna take a gless by-ordinar' but the ship went wrong on him, and he lost wan job efter the other, but he wass never anything else but the perfect chentleman. When he had not a penny in his pocket, he would borrow a shilling from you, and buy you a stick pipe for yourself chust for good nature——"

"A stick pipe?" I repeated interrogatively.

"Chust a stick pipe—or a wudden pipe, or whatever you like to call it. He had three medals and a clock that wouldna go for saving life at sea, but that wass before he wass Hurricane Jeck, mind you; for at that time he hadna stole the sheep."

"I'm dying to hear about that sheep," I said.

"I'll soon tell you about the sheep," said Para Handy. "It wass a thing that happened when him and me wass sailing on the *Elizabeth Ann*, a boat that belonged to Girvan, and a smert wan too, if she wass in any kind of trum at aal. We would be going here and there aboot the West Coast with wan thing and another, and not costing the owners mich for coals if coals wass our cargo. It wass wan Sunday we were passing Caticol in Arran, and in a place yonder where there wass not a hoose in sight we saw a herd of sheep eating gress near the shore. As luck would have it, there wass not a bit of butcher-meat on board the *Elizabeth Ann* for the Sunday dinner, and Jeck cocked his eye at the sheep and says to me, ' Yonder's some sheep lost, poor things ; what do you say to taking the punt and going ashore to see if there's anybody's address on them ? '

" ' Whatever you say yoursel',' I said to Jeck, and we stopped the vessel and went ashore, the two of us, and looked the sheep high and low, but there wass no address on them. ' They're lost, sure enough,' said Jeck, pulling some heather and putting it in his pocket—he wassna Hurricane Jeck then—' they're lost, sure enough, Peter. Here's a nice wee wan nobody would ever miss, that's chust the very thing for a coal vessel,' and before you could say ' knife ' he had it killed and carried to the punt. Oh, he iss a smert, smert fellow with his hands ; he could do anything.

" We rowed ass caalm ass we could oot to the vessel, and we had chust got the deid sheep on board when we heard a roarin' and whustling.

" ' Taalk about Arran being releegious ! ' said Jeck. ' Who's that whustling on the Lord's day ? '

" The man that wass whustling wass away up on the hill, and we could see him coming running doon the hill the same ass if he would break every leg he had on him.

" ' I'll bate you he'll say it's his sheep,' said Jeck. ' Weel, we'll chust anchor the vessel here till we hear what he hass to say, for if we go away and never mind the cratur he'll find oot somewhere else it's the *Elizabeth Ann.*'

" When the fermer and two shepherds came oot to the *Elizabeth Ann* in a boat, she wass lying at anchor, and we were all on deck, every man wi' a piece of heather in his jecket.

" ' I saw you stealing my sheep,' said the fermer, coming on deck, furious. ' I'll have every man of you jiled for this.'

" ' Iss the man oot of his wuts ? ' said Jeck. ' Drink—chust drink ! Nothing else but drink ! If you were a sober Christian man, you would be in the church at this 'oor in

Arran, and not oot on the hill recovering from last night's carry-on in Loch Ranza, and imagining you are seeing things that's not there at aal, at aal.'

" ' I saw you with my own eyes steal the sheep and take it on board,' said the fermer, nearly choking with rage.

" ' What you saw was my freend and me gathering a puckle heather for oor jeckets,' said Jeck, ' and if ye don't believe me you can search the ship from stem to stern.'

" ' I'll soon do that,' said the fermer, and him and his shepherds went over every bit of the *Elizabeth Ann*. They never missed a corner you could hide a moose in, but there wass no sheep nor sign of sheep anywhere.

" ' Look at that, Macalpine,' said Jeck. ' I have a good mind to have you up for inflammation of character. But what could you expect from a man that would be whustling on the hill like a peesweep on a Sabbath when he should be in the church. It iss a good thing for you, Macalpine, it iss a Sabbath, and I can keep my temper.'

" ' I could swear I saw you lift the sheep,' said the fermer, quite vexed.

" ' Saw your auntie !   Drink ; nothing but the cursed drink ! ' said Jeck, and the fermer and his shepherds went away with their tails behind their legs.

" We lay at anchor till it was getting dark, and then we lifted the anchor and took off the sheep that wass tied to it when we put it oot.   ' It's a good thing salt mutton,' said Hurricane Jeck as we sailed away from Caticol, and efter that the name he always got wass Hurricane Jeck."

" But why ' Hurricane Jeck ' ? " I asked, more bewildered than ever.

" Holy smoke ! am I no' tellin' ye ? " said Para Handy. " It wass because he stole the sheep."

But I don't understand it yet.

XI

PARA HANDY'S APPRENTICE

THE owner of the *Vital Spark* one day sent for her Captain, who oiled his hair, washed himself with hot water and a scrubbing-brush, got The Tar to put three coats of blacking on his boots, attired himself in his good clothes, and went up to the office in a state of some anxiety. " It's either a rise in pay," he said to himself, " or he's heard aboot the night we had in Campbeltown. That's the worst of high jeenks ; they're aye stottin' back and hittin' you on the nose ; if it's no' a sore heid, you've lost a pound-note, and if it's nothing you lost, it's somebody clypin' on you." But when he got to the office and was shown into the owner's room, he was agreeably enough surprised to find that though there was at first no talk about a rise of pay, there was, on the other hand, no complaint.

" What I wanted to see you about, Peter," said the owner, " is my oldest boy Alick. He's tired of school and wants to go to sea."

" Does he, does he ? Poor fellow ! " said Para Handy. " Och, he's but young yet, he'll maybe get better. Hoo's the mustress keepin' ? "

" She's very well, thank you, Peter," said the owner. " But I'm anxious about that boy of mine. I feel sure that he'll run away some day on a ship ; he's just the very sort to do it and I want you to help me. I'm going to send him one trip with you, and I want you to see that he's put off the notion of being a sailor—you understand ? I don't care what you do to him so long as you don't break a leg on him, or let him fall over the side. Give him it stiff."

" Chust that ! " said the Captain. " Iss he a boy that reads novelles ? "

" Fair daft for them ! " said the owner. " That's the cause of the whole thing."

" Then I think I can cure him in wan trip, and it'll no' hurt him either."

" I'll send him down to the *Vital Spark* on Wednesday, just before you start," said the owner. " And, by the way, if you manage to sicken him of the idea, I wouldn't say but there might be a small increase in your wages."

" Och, there's no occasion for that," said Para Handy.

On the Wednesday a boy about twelve years of age, with an Eton suit and a Saturday-to-Monday hand-bag, came down to the wharf in a cab alone, opened the door of the cab hurriedly, and almost fell into the arms of Para Handy, who was on shore to meet him.

" Are you the apprentice for the *Fital Spark* ? " asked the Captain affably. " Your name 'll be Alick ? "

" Yes," said the boy. " Are you the Captain ? "

" That's me," said the Captain. " Gie me a haad o' your portmanta," and taking it out of Alick's hand, he led the way to the side of the wharf, where the *Vital Spark* was lying, with a cargo of coals that left her very little freeboard, and all her crew on deck awaiting developments. " I'm sorry," he said, " we havena any gangway, but I'll hand you doon to Dougie, and you'll be aal right if your gallowses 'll no' give way."

" What ! is THAT the boat I'm to go on ? " cried the boy astounded.

" Yes," said the Captain, with a little natural irritation. " And what's wrong with her ? The smertest boat in the tred. Stop you till you see her goin' roond Ardlamont ! "

" But she's only a coal boat ; she's very wee," said Alick. " I never thought my father would apprentice me on a boat like that."

" But it's aye a beginnin'," explained the Captain, with remarkable patience. " You must aye start sailorin' some way, and there's many a man on the brudge of Atlantic liners the day that began on boats no bigger than the *Fital Spark*. If you don't believe me, Dougie 'll tell you himsel'.

Here, Dougie, catch a haad o' oor new apprentice, and watch you don't dirty his clean collar wi' your hands." So saying, he slung Alick down to the mate, and ten minutes later the *Vital Spark*, with her new apprentice on board, was coughing her asthmatic way down the river outward bound for Tarbert. The boy watched the receding wharf with mixed feelings.

" What do you say to something to eat ? " asked the Captain, as soon as his command was under way. " I'll tell The Tar to boil you an egg, and you'll have a cup of tea. You're a fine high-spurited boy, and a growin' boy needs aal the meat he can get. Watch that rope ; see and no' dirty your collar ; it would never do to see an apprentice wi' a dirty collar."

Alick took the tea and the boiled egg, and thought regretfully that life at sea, so far, was proving very different from what he had expected.

" Where are we bound for ? " he asked.

" Oh ! a good long trup," said the Captain. " As far as Tarbert and back again. You'll be an A.B. by the time you come back."

" And will I get wearing brass buttons ? " inquired Alick.

" Brass buttons ! " exclaimed Para Handy. " Man, they're oot o' date at sea aalthegither ; it's nothing but hooks and eyes, and far less trouble to keep them clean."

" Can I start learning to climb the mast now ? " asked Alick, who was naturally impatient to acquire the elements of his new profession.

" Climb the mast ! " cried Para Handy horrified. " There wass never an apprentice did that on my vessel, and never will ; it would dirty aal your hands ! I see a shoo'er o' rain comin' ; there's nothing worse for the young sailor than gettin' damp ; away doon below like a good boy, and rest you, and I'll give you a roar when the rain's past."

Alick went below bewildered. In all the books he had read there had been nothing to prepare him for such coddling on a first trip to sea; so far, there was less romance about the business than he could have found at home in Athole Gardens. It rained all afternoon, and he was not permitted on deck; jelly " pieces" were sent down to him at intervals. The Tar was continually boiling him eggs; he vaguely felt some dreadful indignity in eating them, but his appetite compelled him, and the climax of the most hum-drum day he had ever spent came at night when the Captain insisted on his taking gruel to keep off the cold, and on his fastening his stocking round his neck.

Alick was wakened next morning by The Tar standing at the side of his bunk with tea on a tray.

" Apprentices aye get their breakfast in their bed," said The Tar, who had been carefully coached by the Captain what he was to do. " Sit up and take this, and then have a nice sleep to yoursel', for it's like to be rainin' aal day, and you canna get on deck."

" Surely I can't melt," said the boy, exasperated. " I'll not learn much seamanship lying here."

" You would maybe get your daith o' cold," said The Tar, " and a nice-like job we would have nursin' you." He turned to go on deck when an idea that Para Handy had not given him came into his head, and with great solemnity he said to the boy, " Perhaps you would like to see a newspaper; we could put ashore and buy wan for you to keep you from wearyin'."

" I wouldn't object to ' Comic Cuts,' " said Alick, finding the whole illusion of life on the deep slipping from him.

But " Comic Cuts" did not come down. Instead, there came the Captain with a frightful and familiar thing—the strapful of school-books to escape from which Alick had first proposed a sailor's life. Para Handy had sent to Athole Gardens for them the previous day.

" Shipmate ahoy!" he cried, cheerily stumping down to the fo'c'sle. " You'll be frightened you left your books behind, but I sent The Tar for them, and here they are."

and, unbuckling the strap, he poured the unwelcome volumes on the apprentice's lap.

" Who ever heard of an apprentice sailor taking his school books to sea with him ? " said Alick, greatly disgusted.

" Who ever heard o' anything else ? " retorted the Captain. " Do you think a sailor doesna need any educaation ? Every apprentice has to keep going at his Latin and Greek, and Bills of Parcels, and the height of Ben Nevis, and Grammar, and aal the rest of it. That's what they call navigation, and if you havena the navigation, where are you ? Chust that, where are you ? "

" Do you mean to tell me that when you were an apprentice you learned Latin and Greek, and all the rest of that rot ? " asked Alick, amazed.

" Of course I did," said the Captain unblushingly. " Every day till my heid wass sore ! "

" Nature Knowledge, too ? " asked Alick.

" Nature Knowledge ! " cried Para Handy. " At Nature Knowledge I wass chust sublime ! I could do it with my eyes shut. Chust you take your books, Alick, like a sailor, and wire into your navigation, and it'll be the brudge for you aal the sooner."

There were several days of this unromantic life for the boy, who had confidently expected to find the career of a sea apprentice something very different. He had to wash and dress himself every morning as scrupulously as ever he did at home for Kelvinside Academy ; Para Handy said that was a thing that was always expected from apprentices, and he even went further and sent Alick back to the water-bucket on the ground that his neck and ears required a little more attention. A certain number of hours each day, at least, were ostensibly devoted to the study of " Navigation," which, the boy was disgusted to find, was only another name for the lessons he had had at the Academy. He was not allowed on deck when it was wet without an umbrella, which the Captain had unearthed from somewhere ; it was in vain he rebelled against breakfast in bed, gruel, and jelly " pieces."

" If this is being a sailor, I would sooner be in a Sunday School," said Alick finally.

" Och! you're doin' splendid," said Para Handy. " A fine high-spurited laad! We'll make a sailor of you by the time we're back at Bowling if you keep your health. It's pretty cold the night; away doon to your bunk like a smert laad, and The Tar 'll take doon a hot-watter bottle for your feet in a meenute or two."

When the *Vital Spark* got back to the Clyde, she was not three minutes at the wharf when her apprentice deserted her.

Para Handy went up to the owner's office in the afternoon with the boy's school-books and the Saturday-to-Monday bag.

" I don't know how you managed it," said Alick's father, quite pleased; " but he's back yonder this morning saying a sailor's life's a fraud, and that he wouldn't be a sailor for any money. And by the fatness of him, I should say you fed him pretty well."

" Chust that!" said Para Handy. " The Tar would be aye boilin' an egg for him noo and then. Advice to a boy iss not much use; the only thing for it iss kindness, chust kindness. If I wass wantin' to keep that boy at the sailin', I would have taken the rope's-end to him, and he would be a sailor chust to spite me. There wass some taalk aboot a small rise in the pay, but och——"

" That's all right, Peter; I've told the cashier," said the owner, and the Captain of the *Vi'al Spark* went down the stair beaming.

XII

QUEER CARGOES

" The worst cargo ever I sailed wi'," said Macphail the engineer, " was a wheen o' thae Mahommedan pilgrims: it wasna Eau de Colong they had on their hankies."

" Mahommedans ! " said Para Handy, with his usual suspicions of the engineer's foreign experience—" Mahommedans ! Where were they bound for ? Was't Kirkintilloch ? "

" Kirkintilloch's no' in Mahommeda," said Macphail nastily. " I'm talkin' aboot rale sailin', no' wyding in dubs, the way some folk does a' their days."

" Chust that ! chust that ! " retorted the Captain sniffing. " I thought it wass maybe on the Port-Dundas Canal ye had them."

" There was ten or eleeven o' them died every nicht," proceeded Macphail, contemptuous of these interruptions. " We just gied them the heave over the side, and then full speed aheid to make up for the seven meenutes."

" Like enough you would ripe their pockets first," chimed in Dougie. " The worst cargo ever I sailed with wass leemonade bottles ; you could hear them clinking aal night, and not wan drop of stumulents on board ! It wass duvilish vexing."

" The worst cargo ever I set eyes on," ventured The Tar timidly, in presence of these hardened mariners, " wass sawdust for stuffing dolls."

" Sawdust would suit you fine, Colin," said the Captain. " I'll warrant you got plenty of sleep that trup.

" You're there and you're taalking about cargoes," proceeded Para Handy, " but there's not wan of you had the experience I had, and that wass with a cargo of shows for Tarbert Fair. They were to go with a luggage-steamer, but the luggage-steamer met with a kind of an accident, and wass late of getting to the Broomielaw : she twisted wan of her port-holes or something like that, and we got the chob. It's me that wassna wantin' it, for it wass no credit to a smert boat like the *Fital Spark*, but you ken yoursel' what owners iss ; they would carry coal tar made up in delf crates if they get the freight for it."

" I wouldna say but what you're right," remarked Dougie agreeably.

" A stevedore would go wrong in the mind if he saw the hold of the vessel efter them showmen got their stuff on board. You would think it wass a pawn-shop struck wi' a sheet o' lightning. There wass everything ever you saw at a show except the cocoanuts and the comic polisman. We started at three o'clock in the mornin', and a lot of the show people made a bargain to come wi' us to look efter their stuff. There wass the Fattest Woman in the World, No-Boned Billy or the Boy Serpent, the Mesmerising Man, another man very namely among the Crowned Heads for walkin' on stilts, and the heid man o' the shows, a chap they called Mr Archer. At the last meenute they put on a wee piebald pony that could pick oot any card you asked from a pack. If you don't believe me, Macphail, there's Dougie ; you can ask him yoursel'."

" You're quite right, Peter," said Dougie emphatically. " I'll never forget it. What are you goin' to tell them aboot the Fair ? " he added suspiciously.

" It's a terrible life them show folk has ! " resumed the Captain, without heeding the question. " Only English people would put up with it ; poor craturs, I wass sorry for them ! Fancy them goin' aboot from place to place aal the year roond, wi' no homes ! I would a hundred times sooner be a sailor the way I am. But they were nice enough to us, and we got on fine, and before you could say ' knife ' Dougie wass flirtin' wi' the Fattest Woman in the World."

" Don't believe him, boys," said the mate, greatly embarrassed. " I never even kent her Chrustian name."

" When we got the shows discherged at Tarbert, Mr Archer came and presented us aal with a free pass for everything except the stilts. ' You'll no' need to put on your dress clothes,' says he. He wass a cheery wee chap, though he wass chust an Englishman. Dougie and me went ashore and had a royal night of it. I don't know if ever you wass at a Tarbert Fair, Macphail—you were aye that busy learnin' the names of the foreign places you say you traivelled to, that you wouldn't have the time ; but I'll warrant you it's worth while seein'. There's things to be seen there you couldna see the like of in London. Dougie made for the tent of the mesmeriser and the Fattest Woman in the World whenever we got there : he thought she would maybe be dancin' or something of that sort, but aal she did was to sit on a chair and look fat. There wass a crood roond her nippin' her to make sure she wasna padded, and when we got in she cried, ' Here's my intended man, Mr Dugald ; stand aside and let him to the front to see his bonny wee rosebud. Dugald, darling, you see I'm true to you and wearin' your ring yet,' and she showed the crood a brass ring you could tie boats to.''

" She wass a caaution ! '' said Dougie. " But what's the use of rakin' up them old stories ? ''

" Then we went to the place where No-Boned Billy or the Boy Serpent wass tying himself in knots and jumpin' through girrs. It was truly sublime ! It bates me to know hoo they do it, but I suppose it's chust educaation.''

" It's nothing else,'' said the mate. " Educaation 'll do anything for you if you take it when you're young, and have the money as weel.''

" Every noo and then we would be takin' a gless of yon red lemonade they sell at aal the Fairs, till Dougie got dizzy and had to go to a public-house for beer.''

" Don't say a word aboot yon,'' interrupted the mate anxiously.

" It's aal right, Dougie, we're among oorsel's. Weel, as I wass sayin', when he got the beer, Dougie, right or wrong, wass for goin' to see the fortune-teller. She wass an Italian-lookin' body that did the spaein', and for a sixpence she gave Dougie the finest fortune ever you heard of. He wass to be left a lot of money when he wass fifty-two, and mairry the dochter of a landed chentleman. But he wass to watch a man wi' curly hair that would cross his path, and he wass to mind and never go a voyage abroad in the month o'

c

September. Dougie came out of the Italian spaewife's in fine trum wi' himsel', and nothing would do him but another vusit to the Fattest Woman in the World."

"Noo, chust you be canny what you're at next!" again broke in the mate. "You said you would never tell anybody."

"Who's tellin' anybody?" asked Para Handy impatiently. "I'm only mentionin' it to Macphail and Colin here. The mesmeriser wass readin' bumps when we got into the tent, and Dougie wass that full o' the fine fortune the Italian promised him that he must be up to have his bumps read. The mesmeriser felt aal the bumps on Dougie's heid, no' forgettin' the wan he got on the old New Year at Cairndow, and he said it wass wan of the sublimest heids he ever passed under his hands. 'You are a sailor,' he said to Dougie, 'but accordin' to your bumps you should have been a munister. You had a fine, fine heid for waggin'. There's great strength of will behind the ears, and the back of the foreheid's packed wi' animosity.'

"When the readin' of the bumps wass done, and Dougie wass nearly greetin' because his mother didna send him to the College in time, the mesmeriser said he would put him in a trance, and then he would see fine fun."

"Stop it, Peter," protested the mate. "If you tell them, I'll never speak to you again."

Para Handy paid no attention, but went on with his narrative. "He got Dougie to stare him in the eye the time he wass working his hands like anything, and Dougie was in a trance in five meenutes. Then the man made him think he wass a railway train, and Dougie went on his hands and knees up and doon the pletform whustlin' for tunnels. Efter that he made him think he wass a singer—and a plank of wud—and a soger—and a hen. I wass black affronted to see the mate of the *Fital Spark* a hen. But the best of the baur was when he took the Fattest Woman in the World up on the pletform and mairried her to Dougie in front of the whole of Tarbert."

" You gave me your word you would never mention it," interrupted the mate, perspiring with annoyance.

" Then the mesmeriser made Dougie promise he would come back at twelve o'clock the next day and take his new wife on the honeymoon. When Dougie wass wakened oot of the trance, he didn't mind onything aboot it."

" Neither I did," said the mate.

" Next day, at ten meenutes to twelve, when we were makin' ready to start for the Clyde, my mate here took a kind of a tirrivee, and wass for the shows again. I saw the dregs of the mesmerisin' wass on the poor laad, so I took him and gave him a gill of whisky with sulphur in it, and whipped him on board the boat and off to the Clyde before the trance came on at its worst. It never came back."

" Iss that true ? " asked The Tar.

" If Dougie wass here—— Of course it iss true," said the Captain.

" All I can mind aboot it is the whisky and sulphur," said Dougie. " That's true enough."

XIII

IN SEARCH OF A WIFE

THE TAR had only got his first week's wages after they were raised a shilling, when the sense of boundless wealth took possession of him, and went to his head like glory. He wondered how on earth he could spend a pound a week. Nineteen shillings were only some loose coins in your pocket, that always fell through as if they were red-hot : a pound-note was different, the pleasure of not changing it till maybe to-morrow was like a wage in itself. He kept the pound-note untouched for three days, and then dreamed one night that he lost it through a hole in his pocket. There were really holes in his pockets, a fact that had never troubled him before ; so the idea of getting a wife to mend them flashed on him.

He was alarmed at the notion at first—it was so much out of his daily routine of getting up and putting on the fire, and cooking for the crew, and working the winch, and eating and sleeping—so he put it out of his head; but it always came back when he thought of the responsibility of a pound a week, so at last he went up to Para Handy and said to him sheepishly, " I wass thinking to mysel' yonder that maybe it wouldna be a bad plan for me to be takin' a kind of a wife."

" Captial! First-rate! Good for you, Colin!" said the Captain. " A wife's chust the very thing you're needing, Your guernsays iss no credit to the *Fital Spark*—indeed they'll be giving the boat a bad name; and I aalways like to see everything in nice trum aboot her. I would maybe try wan mysel', but I'm that busy on the boat with wan thing and another, me being Captain of her, I havena mich time for keeping a hoose. But och! there's no hurry for me; I am chust nine and two-twenties of years old, no' countin' the year I wass workin' in the sawmull. What wass the gyurl you were thinkin' on? "

" Och, I didna get that length," said The Tar, getting very red in the face at having the business rushed like that.

" Weel, you would need to look slippy," said Para Handy. " There's fellows on shore with white collars on aal the time going aboot picking up the smert wans."

" I wass chust thinkin' maybe you would hear of somebody aboot Loch Fyne that would be suitable: you ken the place better nor me."

" I ken every bit of it," said Para Handy, throwing out his chest. " I wass born aal along this loch-side, and brocht up wi' an auntie. What kind of a wan would you be wantin'? "

" Och, I would chust leave that to yoursel'," said The Tar. " Maybe if she had a puckle money it wouldna be any herm."

" Money!" cried the Captain. " You canna be expectin'

money wi' the first.   But we'll consider, Colin.   We'll paause and consider."

Two days later the *Vital Spark* was going up to Inveraray for a cargo of timber, Para Handy steering, and singing softly to himself—

> " As I gaed up yon Hieland hill,
>   I met a bonny lassie ;
> She looked at me and I at her,
>   And oh, but she was saucy.
>   With my rolling eye,
>   Fal tee diddle dye,
>   Rolling eye dum derry,
>   With my rolling eye."

The Tar stood by him peeling potatoes, and the charming domestic sentiment of the song could not fail to suggest the subject of his recent thoughts.   " Did you have time to consider yon ? " he asked the Captain, looking up at him with comical coyness.

" Am I no' considering it as hard as I'm able ? " said Para Handy.   " Chust you swept aal them peelin's over the side and no' be spoiling the boat, my good laad."

" I wass mindin', mysel', of a femily of gyurls called Macphail up in Easdale, or maybe it wass Luing," said The Tar.

" Macphails ! " cried Para Handy.   " I never hear the name of Macphail but I need to scratch mysel'.   I wouldna alloo any man on the *Fital Spark* to mairry a Macphail, even if she wass the Prunce of Wales.   Look at that man of oors that caals himsel' an enchineer ; he's a Macphail, that's the way he canna help it."

" Och, I wass chust in fun," The Tar hastened to say soothingly.   " I don't think I would care for any of them Macphail gyurls whatever.   Maybe you'll mind of something suitable before long."

Para Handy slapped himself on the knee.   " My Chove ! " said he, " I have the very article that would fit you."

" What's—what's her name ? " asked The Tar alarmed at the way destiny seemed to be rushing him into matrimony.

" Man, I don't know," said the Captain, " but she's the laandry-maid up here in the Shurriff's—chust a regular beauty. I'll take you up and show her you to-morrow."

" Will we no' be awfu' busy to-morrow ? " said The Tar hastily. " Maybe it would be better to wait till we come back again. There's no' an awfu' hurry."

" No hurry ! " cried the Captain. " It's the poor heid for business you have, Colin ; a gyurl the same as I'm thinkin' on for you will be snapped up whenever she gets her Mertinmas wages."

" I'm afraid she'll be too cluver for me, her being a laandry-maid," said The Tar. " They're aawfu' high-steppers, laandry-maids, and aawfu' stiff."

" That's wi' working among starch," explained Para Handy. " It'll aal come oot in the washin'. Not another word, Colin ; leave it to me. And maybe Dougie, och ay, Dougie and me 'll see you right."

So keenly did the Captain and Dougie enter into the matrimonial projects of The Tar that they did not even wait till the morrow, but set out to interview the young lady that evening. " I'll no' put on my pea-jecket or my watch-chain in case she might take a fancy to mysel'," the Captain said to his mate. " A man in a good poseetion like me canna be too caautious." The Tar, at the critical moment, showed the utmost reluctance to join the expedition. He hummed and hawed, protested he " didna like," and would prefer that they settled the business without him ; but this was not according to Para Handy's ideas of business, and ultimately the three set out together with an arrangement that The Tar was to wait out in the Sheriff's garden while his ambassadors laid his suit in a preliminary form before a lady he had never set eyes on and who had never seen him.

There was a shower of rain, and the Captain and his mate

had scarcely been ushered into the kitchen on a plea of "important business" by the Captain, than The Tar took shelter in a large wooden larder at the back of the house.

Para Handy and Dougie took a seat in the kitchen at the invitation of its single occupant, a stout cook with a humorous eye.

"It was the laandry-maid we were wantin' to see, mem," said the Captain, ducking his head forward several times and grinning widely to inspire confidence and create a genial atmosphere without any loss of time. "We were chust passing the door, and we thought we would give her a roar in the by-going."

"You mean Kate?" asked the cook.

"Ay! chust that, chust that—Kate," said the Captain, beaming warmly till his whiskers curled. "Hoo's the Shurriff keeping himsel'?" he added as an afterthought. "Iss he in good trum them days?" And he winked expansively at the cook.

"Kate's not in," said the domestic. "She'll be back in a while if you wait."

The Captain's face fell for a moment. "Och perhaps you'll do fine yoursel'," said he cordially, at last. "We have a fellow yonder on my boat that's come into some money, and what iss he determined on but to get mairried? He's aawfu' backward, for he never saw much Life except the Tarbert Fair, and he asked us to come up here and put in a word for him."

"Is that the way you do your courtin' on the coalgabbarts?" said the cook, greatly amused.

"Coal-gaabert!" cried Para Handy, indignant. "There iss no coal-gaabert in the business; I am the Captain of the *Fital Spark*, the smertest steamboat in the coastin' tred——"

"And I'm no' slack, mysel'; I'm the mate," said Dougie, wishing he had brought his trump.

"He must be a soft creature not to speak for himself," said the cook.

"Never mind that," said the Captain; "are you game to take him?"

The cook laughed. "What about yoursel'?" she asked chaffingly, and the Captain blenched.

"Me!" he cried. "I peety the wumman that would mairry me. If I wass not here, Dougie would tell you— would you no', Dougie?—I'm a fair duvvle for high jeenks. Forbye, I'm sometimes frightened for my health."

"And what is he like, this awfu' blate chap?" asked the cook.

"As smert a laad as ever stepped," protested Para Handy. "Us sailors iss sometimes pretty wild; it's wi' followin' the sea and fightin' hurricanes, here the day and away yesterday; but Colin iss ass dacent a laad ass ever came oot of Knapdale if he wass chust letting himself go. Dougie himsel' will tell you."

"There's nothing wrong wi' the fellow," said Dougie. "A fine riser in the mornin'."

"And for cookin', there's no' his equal," added the Captain.

"It seems to me it's my mistress you should have asked for," said the cook; "she's advertising for a scullery-maid." But this sarcasm passed over the heads of the eager ambassadors.

"Stop you!" said the Captain, "and I'll take him in himsel'; he's oot in the garden waiting on us." And he and the mate went outside.

"Colin!" cried Para Handy, "come away and be engaged, like a smert laad." But there was no answer, and it was after considerable searching they discovered the ardent suitor sound asleep in the larder.

"It's no' the laandry-maid; but it's a far bigger wan," explained the Captain. "She's chust sublime. Aal you have to do now is to come in and taalk nice to her."

The Tar protested he couldn't talk to her unless he had some conversation lozenges. Besides, it was the laundry-maid he had arranged for, not the cook.

"She'll do fine for a start ; a fine gyurl," the Captain assured him, and with some difficulty they induced The Tar to go with them to the back-door, only to find it emphatically shut in their faces.

"Let us paause and consuder, what day iss this ? " asked the Captain, when the emphasis of the rebuff had got time to sink into his understanding.

"Friday," said Dougie.

"Tuts ! wass I not sure of it ? It's no' a lucky day for this kind of business. Never mind, Colin, we'll come to-morrow when the laandry-maid's in, and you'll bring a poke of conversation lozenges. You mustna be so stupid, man ; you were awfu' tumid ! "

"I wasna a bit tumid, but I wasna in trum," said The Tar, who was walking down to the quay with a curious and unusual straddle.

"And what for would you not come at wance when I cried you in ? " asked the Captain.

"Because," said The Tar pathetically, "I had a kind of an accident yonder in the larder : I sat doon on a basket of country eggs."

XIV

PARA HANDY'S PIPER

If you haven't been at your favourite coast resort except at the time of summer holidays, you don't know much about it. At other seasons of the year it looks different, smells different, and sounds different—that is, when there's any sound at all in it. In those dozing, dreamy days before you come down with your yellow tin trunk or your kit-bag, there's only one sound in the morning in the coast resort— the sizzling of frying herring. If it is an extra lively day, you may also hear the baker's van-driver telling a dead secret to the deaf bellman at the other end of the village, and the cry of sea-gulls. Peace broods on that place then

c*

like a benediction, and (by the odour) some one is having
a sheep's head singed at the smithy.

I was standing one day on Brodick Quay with Para Handy
when the place looked so vacant, and was so quiet we
unconsciously talked in whispers for fear of wakening somebody. The *Vital Spark* shared the peace of that benign
hour : she nodded idly at the quay, her engineer half asleep
with a penny novelette in his hands ; The Tar, sound asleep
and snoring, unashamed, with his back against the winch ;
Dougie, the mate, smoking in silent solemnity, and occasionally scratching his nose, otherwise you would have taken
him for an ingenious automatic smoking-machine, set agoing
by putting a penny in the slot. If anybody had dropped
a postage-stamp in Brodick that day, it would have sounded
like a dynamite explosion. It was the breakfast hour.

Suddenly a thing happened that seemed to rend the very
heavens : it was the unexpected outburst of a tinker piper,
who came into sight round the corner of a house, with his
instrument in the preliminary stages of the attack.

" My Chove ! " said Para Handy, " isn't that fine ?
Splendid aalthegether ! "

" What's your favourite instrument ? " I asked.

" When Dougie's in trum it's the trump," said he in a
low voice, lest the mate (who was certainly very vain of
his skill on the trump—that is to say, the Jew's harp) should
hear him ; " but, man ! for gaiety, the pipes. They're
truly sublime ! A trump's fine for small occasions, but
for style you need the pipes. And good pipers iss difficult
nooadays to get ; there's not many in it. You'll maybe
can get a kind of a plain piper going aboot the streets of
Gleska noo and then, but they're like the herrin', and the
turnips, and rhubarb, and things like that—you don't get
them fresh in Gleska ; if you want them at their best, you
have to go up to the right Hielands and pull them off the
tree. You ken what I mean yoursel'."

And the Captain of the *Vital Spark* widely opened his

mouth and inhaled the sound of the bagpipe with an air of great refreshment.

"That's ' The Barren Rocks of Aden ' he iss on now," he informed me by and by. "I can tell by the sound of it. Oh, music ! music ! it's me that's fond of it. It makes me feel that droll I could bound over the mountains, if you understand. Do you know that I wance had a piper of my own ? "

" A piper of your own ! "

"Ay, chust that, a piper of my own, the same ass if I wass the Marquis of Bute. You'll be thinkin' I couldna afford it," Para Handy went on smiling slyly, "but a Macfarlane never wass bate. Aal the fine gentry hass their piper that plays to them in the mornin' to put them up, and goes playin' roond the table at dinner-time when there's any English vusitors there, and let them chust take it ! It serves them right ; they should stay in their own country. My piper wass a Macdonald."

" You mean one of the tinker pipers ? " I said mischievously, for I knew a tribe of tinker pipers of that name.

Para Handy was a little annoyed. "Well," he said, "I wouldna deny but he wass a kind of a tinker, but he wass in the Militia when he wass workin', and looked quite smert when he wass sober."

" How long did you keep the piper ? " I asked, really curious about this unexpected incident in the Captain's career.

" Nearly a whole day," he answered. "Whiles I kept him and whiles he wass going ashore for a dram.

" To let you understand, it wass the time of the fine fushin's in Loch Fyne, and I had a cousin yonder that wass gettin' mairried at Kilfinan. The weddin' wass to be on a Friday, and I wass passin' up the loch with a cargo of salt, when my cousin hailed me from the shore, and came oot in a small boat to speak to me.

" ' Peter,' he said to me, quite bashful, ' they're sayin'

I'm goin' to get mairried on Friday, and I'm lookin' for you to be at the thing.'

" ' You can depend on me bein' there, Dougald,' I assured him. ' It would be a poor thing if the Macfarlanes would not stick by wan another at a time of trial.'

" ' Chust that ! ' said my cousin ; ' there's to be sixteen hens on the table and plenty of refreshment. What's botherin' me iss that there's not a piper in Kilfinan. I wass thinkin' that maybe between this and Friday you would meet wan on your trevels, and take him back with you on your shup.'

" ' Mercy on us ! You would think it wass a parrot from foreign perts I wass to get for you,' I said. ' But I'll do my best,' and off we went. I watched the hillsides aal the way up the loch to see if I could see a piper ; but it wass the time of the year when there's lots of work at the hay, and the pipers wass keepin' oot of sight, till I came to Cairndow. Dougie and me wass ashore at Cairndow in the mornin', when we saw this Macdonald I'm telling you aboot standin' in front of the Inns with pipes under his oxter. He wass not playin' them at the time. I said to him, ' There's a weddin' yonder at Kilfinan to-morrow, that they're wantin' a piper for. What would you take to come away doon on my vessel and play for them ? '

" ' Ten shillin's and my drink,' he said, as quick as anything.

" ' Say five and it's a bargain,' I said ; and he engaged himself on the spot. He wass a great big fellow with a tartan trooser and a cocketty bonnet, and oh, my goodness ! but his hair wass rud ! I couldna but offer him a dram before we left Cairndow, for we were startin' there and then, but he wouldna set foot in the Inns, and we went on board the *Vital Spark* withoot anything at all, and started doon the loch. I thought it wass a droll kind of a piper I had that would lose a chance.

" When we would be a mile or two on the passage, I said

to him, ' Macdonald, tune up your pipes and give us the Macfarlanes' Merch.'

" He said he didna know the Macfarlanes had a Merch, but would do the best he could by the ear, and he began to screw the bits of his pipes together. It took him aboot an hour, and by that time we were off Strachur.

" ' Stop you the boat,' he said, ' I'll need to get ashore a meenute to get something to soften the bag of this pipes ; it's ass hard ass a bit of stick.'

" ' You can get oil from the enchineer,' I said to him.

" ' Oil ! ' said he ; ' do you think it's a clock I'm mendin' ? No, no ; there's nothing will put a pipe bag in trum but some treacle poured in by the stock.'

" Well, we went ashore and up to the Inns, and he asked if they could give him treacle for his bagpipes. They said they had none. ' Weel,' said he, ' next to that the best thing for it iss whusky—give me a gill of the best, and the Captain here will pay for it ; I'm his piper.' He got the gill, and what did he do but pour a small sensation of it into the inside of his pipes and drink the rest ? ' It comes to the same thing in the long-run,' said he, and we got aboard again, and away we started.

" ' There's another tune I am very fond of,' I said to him, watchin' him workin' away puttin' his drones in order. ' It's " The 93rd's Farewell to Gibraltar." '

" ' I ken it fine,' he said, ' but I don't ken the tune. Stop you, and I'll give you a trate if I could get this cursed pipe in order. What aboot the dinner ? '

" The dinner wass nearly ready, so he put the pipes past till he wass done eatin', and then he had a smoke, and by the time that wass done we were off Lochgair. ' That puts me in mind,' said he ; ' I wonder if I could get a chanter reed from Maclachlan the innkeeper ? He plays the pipes himself. The chanter reed I have iss bad, and I would like to do the best I could at your cousin's weddin'.'

" We stopped, and Dougie went ashore in the smaal boat

with him, and when they came back in half-an-hour the piper said it wass a peety, but the innkeeper wasna a piper efter aal, and didna have a reed, but maybe we would get wan in Ardrishaig.

" ' We're no' goin' to Ardrishaig, we're goin' to Kilfinan,' I told him, and he said he couldna help it, but we must make for Ardrishaig, right or wrong, for he couldna play the pipes right withoot a new reed. ' When you hear me playing,' he said, ' you will be glad you took the trouble. There iss not my equal in the three parishes,' and, man, but his hair wass rud, rud !

" We wouldna be half-an-oor oot from Lochgair when he asked if the tea would soon be ready. He wass that busy puttin' his pipes in order, he said, he was quite fatigued. Pipers iss like canaries, you have to keep them going weel with meat and drink if you want music from them. We gave him his tea, and by the time it wass finished we were off Ardrishaig, and he made me put her in there to see if he could get a reed for his chanter. Him and Dougie went ashore in the smaal boat. Dougie came back in an oor wi' his hair awfu' tousy and nobody wi' him.

" ' Where's my piper ? ' I said to him.

" ' Man, it's terrible ! ' said Dougie ; ' the man's no' a piper at aal, and he's away on the road to Kilmertin. When he wass standin' at Cairndow Inns yonder, he was chust holdin' the pipes for a man that wass inside for his mornin', and you and me 'll maybe get into trouble for helpin' him to steal a pair o' pipes.'

" That wass the time I kept a piper of my own," said Para Handy, in conclusion. " And Dougie had to play the trump to the dancin' at my cousin's weddin'."

XV

THE SAILORS AND THE SALE

PARA HANDY's great delight was to attend farm sales. " A sale's a sublime thing," he said, " for if you don't like a thing you don't need to buy it. It's at the sales a good many of the other vessels in the tred get their sailors." This passion for sales was so strong in him that if there was one anywhere within twelve miles of any port the *Vital Spark* was lying at, he would lose a tide or risk demurrage rather than miss it. By working most part of a night he got a cargo of coals discharged at Lochgoilhead one day in time to permit of his attending a displenishing sale ten miles away. He and the mate, Dougie, started in a brake that was conveying people to the sale ; they were scarcely half-way there when the Captain sniffed.

" Hold on a meenute and listen, Dougie," said he. " Do you no' smell anything ? "

Dougie sniffed too, and his face was lit up by a beautiful smile as of one who recognises a friend. " It's not lemon kali at any rate," he said knowingly, and chuckled in his beard.

" Boys ! " said the Captain, turning round to address the other passengers in the brake, who were mainly cattle dealers and farmers—" Boys ! this iss going to be a majestic sale ; we're five miles from the place and I can smell the whisky already."

At that moment the driver of the brake bent to look under his seat, and looked up again with great vexation written on his countenance. " Isn't it not chust duvvelish ? " he said. " Have I not gone away and put my left foot through a bottle of good spurits I wass bringing up wi' me in case anybody would take ill through the night."

" Through the night ! " exclaimed one of the farmers, who was plainly not long at the business. " What night are you taalking aboot ? "

"This night," replied the driver promptly.

"But surely we'll be back at Lochgoilhead before night?" said the farmer, and all the others in the coach looked at him with mingled pity and surprise.

"It's a ferm sale we're going to, and not a rent collection," said the driver. "And there's thirty-six gallons of ale ordered for it, no' to speak of refreshments. If we're home in time for breakfast from this sale it's me that'll be the bonny surprised man, I'm telling you."

At these farm sales old custom demands that food and drink should be supplied " ad lib." by the outgoing tenant. It costs money, but it is a courtesy that pays in the long-run, for if the bidding hangs fire a brisk circulation of the refreshments stimulates competition among the buyers, and adds twenty per cent. to the price of stots. It would be an injustice to Para Handy and Dougie to say they attended sales from any consideration of this sort; they went because of the high jeenks. At the close of the day sometimes they found that they had purchased a variety of things not likely to be of much use on board a steam-lighter, as on the occasion when Dougie bought the rotary churn.

"Keep away from the hoosehold furniture aaltogither!" said the Captain, this day. "We have too mich money in oor pockets between us, and it'll be safer no' to be in sight of the unctioneer till the beasts iss on, for we'll no' be tempted to buy beasts."

"I would buy an elephant for the fun of the thing, let alone a coo or two," said Dougie.

"That's put me in mind," said the Captain, "there's a cousin of my own yonder in Kilfinan wantin' a milk coo for the last twelvemonth; if I saw a bargain maybe I would take it. But we'll do nothing rash, Dougie, nothing rash; maybe we're chust sailors, but we're no' daft aalthegither."

By this time they were standing on the outside of a crowd of prospective purchasers interested in a collection of farm utensils and household sundries, the disposal of which pre-

ceded the rouping of the beasts. The forenoon was chilly;
the chill appeared to affect the mood of the crowd, who
looked coldly on the chain harrows, turnip-cutters, and
other articles offered to them at prices which the auctioneer
said it broke his heart to mention, and it was to instil a
little warmth into the proceedings that a handy man with
red whiskers went round with refreshments on a tray.

"Streetch your hand and take a gless," he said to the
Captain. "It'll do you no herm."

"Man, I'm not mich caring for it," drawled the Captain.
"I had wan yesterday. What do you think, Dougie?
Would it do any herm chust to take wan gless to show
we're freendly to the sale of impliments and things?"

"Whatever you say yoursel'," replied Dougie diffidently,
but at the same time grasping the glass nearest him with
no uncertain hand.

"Weel, here's good prices!" said the Captain, fixing to
another glass, and after that the sun seemed to come out
with a genial glow.

The lamentable fact must be recorded that before the
beasts came up to the hammer the mate of the *Vital Spark*
had become possessor of a pair of curling-stones—one of
them badly chipped—a Dutch hoe, and a baking-board.

"What in the world are you going to do with that trash?"
asked the Captain, returning from a visit to the outhouse where
the ale was, to find his mate with the purchases at his feet.

"Och! it's aal right," said Dougie, cocking his eye at
him. "I wassna giving a docken for the things mysel',
but I saw the unctioneer aye look-looking at me, and I didna
like no' to take nothing. It's chust, as you might say, for
the good of the hoose. Stop you and you'll see some fun."

"But it's a rideeculous thing buying curling-stones at this
time of the year, and you no' a curler. What?"

Dougie scratched his neck and looked at his purchases.
"They didn't cost mich," he said; "and they're aye handy
to have aboot you."

When the cattle came under the hammer it was discovered that prices were going to be very low. All the likely buyers seemed to be concentrated round the beer-barrel in the barn, with the result that stots, queys, cows, and calves were going at prices that brought the tears to the auctioneer's eyes. He hung so long on the sale of one particular cow for which he could only squeeze out offers up to five pounds that Para Handy took pity on him, and could not resist giving a nod that put ten shillings on to its price and secured the animal.

" Name, please ? " said the auctioneer, cheering up wonderfully.

" Captain Macfarlane," said Para Handy, and, very much distressed at his own impetuosity, took his mate aside. " There you are, I bought your coo for you," he said to Dougie.

" For me ! " exclaimed his mate. " What in the world would I be doing with a coo ? "

" You said yoursel' you would take a coo or two for the fun o' the thing," said Para Handy.

" When I'm buying coos I'm buying them by my own word o' mooth ; you can chust keep it for your cousin in Kilfinan. If I wass buyin' a coo it wouldna be wan you could hang your hat on in fifty places. No, no, Peter, I'm Hielan', but I'm no' so Hielan' ass aal that."

" My goodness ! " said Para Handy, " this iss the scrape ! I will have to be taking her to Lochgoilhead, and hoisting her on the vessel, and milking her, and keeping her goodness knows what time till I'll have a cargo the length of Kilfinan. Forbye, my cousin and me's no' speakin' since Whitsunday last."

" Go up to the unctioneer and tell him you didna buy it at aal, that you were only noddin' because you had a tight collar," suggested the mate, and the Captain acted on the suggestion ; but the auctioneer was not to be taken in by any such story, and Para Handy and his mate were accordingly seen on the road to Lochgoil late that night with a cow, the possession of which took all the pleasure out of their day's outing. Dougie's curling-stones, hoe, and bake-board were to follow in a cart.

It was a long time after this before the *Vital Spark* had any occasion to go to Lochgoilhead. Macphail the engineer had only to mention the name of the place and allude casually to the price of beef or winter feeding, and the Captain would show the most extraordinary ill-temper. The fact was he had left his purchase at a farmer's at Lochgoil to keep for him till called for, and he never liked to think upon the day of reckoning. But the *Vital Spark* had to go to Lochgoilhead sooner or later, and the first time she did so the Captain went somewhat mournfully up to the farm where his cow was being kept for him.

" It's a fine day ; hoo's the mustress ? " he said to the farmer, who showed some irritation at never having heard from the owner of the cow for months.

" Fine, but what aboot your coo, Peter ? "

" My Chove ! iss she living yet ? " said the Captain. " I'll be due you a penny or two."

" Five pounds, to be exact ; and it'll be five pounds ten at the end of next month."

" Chust the money I paid for her," said Para Handy. " Chust you keep her for me till the end of next month, and then pay yoursel' with her when my account iss up to the five pound ten," a bargain which was agreed on ; and so ended Para Handy's most expensive high jeenk.

XVI

A NIGHT ALARM

THE wheel of the *Vital Spark* was so close to the engines that the Captain could have given his orders in a whisper, but he was so proud of the boat that he liked to sail her with all the honours, so he always used the knocker. He would catch the brass knob and give one, two, or three knocks as the circumstances demanded, and then put his mouth to the speaking-tube and cry coaxingly down to the engineer, " Stop her, Dan, when you're ready." That would be when she was a few lengths off the quay. Dan, the engineer, never let on he heard the bell ; he was very fond of reading penny novelettes, and it was only when he was spoken to soothingly down the tube that he would put aside " Lady Winifred's Legacy," give a sigh, and stop his engine. Then he would stand upright—which brought his head over the level of the deck, and beside the Captain's top-boots—wiping his brow with a piece of waste the way real engineers do on the steamers that go to America. His great aim in taking a quay was to suggest to anybody hanging about it that it was frightfully hot in the engine-room—just like the Red Sea—while the fact was that most of the time there was a draught in the engine-room of the *Vital Spark* that would keep a cold store going without ice.

When he stuck up his head he always said to the Captain, " You're aye wantin' something or other ; fancy goin' awa' and spoilin' me in the middle o' a fine baur."

" I'm sorry, Dan," Para Handy would say to him in an agony of remorse, for he was afraid of the engineer because that functionary had once been on a ship that made a voyage to Australia, and used to say he had killed a man in the Bush. When he was not sober it was two men, and he would weep. " I'm sorry, Dan, but I did not know you would be busy." Then he would knock formally to reverse the engine, and cry down the tube, " Back her, Dan, when you're ready ; there's no hurry," though the engineer was, as I have said, so close that he could have put his hand on his head.

Dan drew in his head, did a bit of juggling with the machinery, and resumed his novelette at the place where Lady Winifred lost her jewels at the ball. There was some-thing breezy in the way he pulled in his head and moved in the engine-room that disturbed the Captain. " Dan's no' in good trum the day," he would say, in a hoarse whisper to the mate Dougie under these circumstances. " You daurna say wan word to him but he flies in a tiravee."

" It's them cursed novelles," was always Dougie's explanation ; " they would put any man wrong in the heid, let alone an enchineer. If it wass me wass skipper of this boat, I wadna be so soft with him, I'll assure you."

" Ach, you couldna be hard on the chap and him a Macphail," said the Captain. " There wass never any holdin' o' them in. He's an aawful fellow for high jeenks ; he killed a man in the Bush."

One afternoon the *Vital Spark* came into Tarbert with a cargo of coals that could not be discharged till the morning, for Sandy Sinclair's horse and cart were engaged at a country funeral. The Captain hinted at repainting a strake or two of the vessel, but his crew said they couldn't be bothered, forbye Dougie had three shillings ; so they washed their faces after tea and went up the town. Peace brooded on the *Vital Spark*, though by some overlook Macphail had left her with almost a full head of steam. Sergeant Macleod, of the constabulary, came down when she lay deserted. " By Cheorge ! " said he to himself, " them fellows iss coing to get into trouble this night, I'm tellin' you," for he knew the *Vital Spark* of old. He drew his tippit more firmly about him, breathed hard, and went up the town to survey the front of all the public-houses. Peace brooded on the *Vital Spark* —a benign and beautiful calm.

It was ten o'clock at night when her crew returned. They came down the quay in a condition which the most rigid moralist could only have described as jovial, and went to their bunks in the fo'c'sle. A drizzling rain was falling. That day the Captain had mounted a new cord on the steam whistle, so that he could blow it by a jerk from his position at the wheel. It was drawn back taut, and the free end of it was fastened to a stanchion. As the night passed and the rain continued falling, the cord contracted till at last it acted on the whistle, which opened with a loud and croupy hoot that rang through the harbour and over the town. Otherwise peace still brooded on the *Vital Spark*. It took fifteen minutes to waken the Captain, and he started up in wild alarm. His crew were snoring in the light of a small globe lamp, and the engineer had a "Family Herald Supplement" on his chest.

"That's either some duvvlement of somebody's or a warnin'," said Para Handy, half irritated, half in superstitious alarm. "Dougie, are you sleepin'?"

"What would I be here for if I wass not sleepin'?" said Dougie.

"Go up like a smert laad and see who's meddlin' my whustle."

"I canna," said Dougie; "I havena but the wan o' my boots on. Send up The Tar." The Tar was so plainly asleep from his snoring that it seemed no use to tackle him. The Captain looked at him. "Man!" he said, "he hass a nose that minds me o' a winter day, it's so short and dirty. He would be no use any way. It's the enchineer's chob, but I daurna waken him, he's such a man for high jeenks." And still the whistle waked the echoes of Tarbert.

"If I wass skipper of this boat I would show him," said Dougie, turning in his bunk, but showing no sign of any willingness to turn out. "Give him a roar, Peter, or throw the heel of yon pan loaf at him."

"I would do it in a meenute if he wasna a Macphail," said the Captain, distracted. "He wance killed a man in the Bush. But he's the enchineer; the whustle's in his depairtment. Maybe if I spoke nice to him he would see aboot it. Dan!" he cried softly across the fo'c'sle to the man with the "Family Herald Supplement" on his chest—"Dan, show a leg, like a good laad, and go up and stop that cursed whustle."

"Are you speakin' to me?" said the engineer, who was awake all the time.

"I was chust makin' a remark," explained the Captain hurriedly. "It's not of any great importance, but there's a whustle there, and it's wakin' the whole toon of Tarbert. If you werena awfu' throng sleepin', you might take a bit turn on dake and see what is't. Chust when you're ready, Dan, chust when you're ready."

Dan ostentatiously turned on his side and loudly went to sleep again. And the whistle roared louder than ever.

The Captain began to lose his temper. "Stop you till I get back to Bowling," he said, "and I'll give every man of you the whole jeeng-bang, and get rale men for the *Fital Spark*. Not a wan of you iss worth a spittle in the hour of dancher and trial. Look at Macphail there tryin' to snore like an enchineer with a certeeficate, and him only a fireman! I am not a bit frightened for him; I do not believe he ever killed a man in the Bush at aal—he hass not the game for it; I'll bate you he never wass near Australia—and what wass his mother but wan of the Macleans of Kenmore? Chust that; wan of the Macleans of Kenmore! Him and his pride! If I had my Sunday clothes on I would give him my opeenion. And there you are, Dougie! I thocht you were a man and not a mice. You are lying there in your ignorance, and never wass the length of Ullapool. Look at me—on the vessels three over twenty years, and twice wrecked in the North at places that's not on the maps."

The two worthies thus addressed paid no attention and snored with suspicious steadiness, and the Captain turned his attention to The Tar.

"Colin!" he said more quietly, "show a leg, like a cluvver fellow, and go up and put on the fire for the breakfast." But The Tar made no response, and in the depth of the fo'c'sle Para Handy's angry voice rose up again, as he got out of his bunk and prepared to pull on some clothes and go up on deck himself.

"Tar by by-name and Tar by nature!" said he. "You will stick to your bed that hard they could not take you off without half-a-pound of saalt butter. My goodness!

have I not a bonny crew? You are chust a wheen of
crofters. When the owners of vessels wass wantin' men
like you, they go to the Kilmichael cattle-market and drag
you down with a rope to the seaside. You will not do the
wan word I tell you. I'll wudger I'll not hammer down
to you again, Dan, or use the speakin'-tube, the same ass
if you were a rale enchineer; I'll chust touch you with
the toe of my boot when I want you to back her, mind
that! There iss not a finer nor a faster vessel than the
Fital Spark in the tred; she iss chust sublime, and you
go and make a fool of her with your drinking and your laziness and your ignorance."

He got up on deck in a passion, to find a great many
Tarbert people running down the quay to see what was
wrong, and Sergeant Macleod at the head of them.

"Come! come! Peter, what iss this whustlin' for on a
wet night like this at two o'clock in the mornin'?" asked
the sergeant, with a foot on the bulwark. "What are you
blow-blow-blowin' at your whustle like that for?"

"Chust for fun," said the Captain. "I'm a terrible
fellow for high jeenks. I have three fine stots from the
Kilmichael market down below here, and they canna sleep
unless they hear a whustle."

"The man's in the horrors!" said the sergeant in a
whisper to some townsmen beside him on the quay. "I
must take him to the lock-up and make a case of him, and
it's no' a very nice chob, for he's as strong ass a horse.
Wass I not sure there would be trouble when I saw the
Fital Spark the day? It must be the lock-up for him,
and maybe Lochgilphead, but it iss a case for deleeberation
and caaution—great caaution.

"Captain Macfarlane," he said in a bland voice to the
Captain, who stood defiant on the deck, making no attempt
to stop the whistling. "Mr Campbell the banker wass wantin'
to see you for a meenute up the toon. Chust a meenute!
He asked me to come doon and tell you."

" What will the banker be wantin' wi' me ? " said the Captain, cooling down and suspecting nothing. " It's a droll time o' night to be sendin' for onybody."

" So it is, Captain Macfarlane," admitted the constable mildly. " I do not know exactly what he wants, but it iss in a great hurry. He said he would not keep you wan meenute. I think it will be to taalk about your cousin Cherlie's money."

" I'll go wi' you whenever I get on my bonnet," said the Captain, preparing to go below.

" Never mind your bonnet ; it iss chust a step or two, and you'll be back in five meenutes," said the sergeant ; and, thus cajoled, the Captain of the *Vital Spark*, having cut the cord and stopped the whistle, went lamb-like to the police office.

Peace fell again upon the *Vital Spark*.

XVII

A DESPERATE CHARACTER

THOUGH Para Handy went, like a lamb, with Sergeant Macleod, he had not to suffer the ignominy of the police office, for the sergeant found out on the way that the Captain belonged to the Wee Free, and that made a great deal of difference. Instead of putting the mariner into a cell, he took him into his own house, made a summary investigation into the cause of the whistling of the *Vital Spark*, found the whole thing was an accident, dismissed the accused without a stain on his character, gave him a dram, and promised to take him down a pair of white hares for a present before the vessel left Tarbert.

" I am glad to see you belong to the right Church, Peter," he said. " Did I not think you were chust wan of them unfuduls that carries the rud-edged hime-books and sits at the prayer, and here you are chust a dacent Christian like mysel'. My goodness! It shows you a man cannot be too caautious. Last year there wass but a small remnant of us Christians to the fore here—myself and Macdougall the merchant, and myself and the Campbells up in Clonary Farm, and myself and the steamboat aagent, and myself and my cousins at Dunmore; but it'll be changed days when we get a ha'ad o' the church. They'll be sayin' there's no hell; we'll show them, I'll assure you! We are few, but firm— firm; there's no bowin' of the knee with us, and many a pair of white hares I'll be gettin' from the Campbells up in Clonary. I have chust got to say the word that wan of the rale old Frees iss in a vessel at the quay, and there will be a pair of white hares doon for you to-morrow."

"I'm a staunch Free," said Para Handy, upsetting his glass, which by this time had hardly a drop left in it. "Tut! tut!" he exclaimed apologetically, "it's a good thing I never broke the gless. Stop! stop! stop in a meenute; I'm sure I'm no needin' any more. But it's a cold wet nicht, whatever. I'm a staunch Free. I never had a hime-book on board my boat; if Dougie wass here he would tell you."

"You'll no' get very often to the church, wi' you goin' about from place to place followin' the sea?" said the sergeant.

"That's the worst of it," said Para Handy, heaving a tremendous sigh. "There's no mich fun on a coal vessel; if it wasna the *Fital Spark* wass the smertest in the tred, and me the skipper of her, I would mairry a fine strong wife and start a business. There wass wan time yonder, when I wass younger, I wass very keen to be a polisman."

"The last chob!" cried the sergeant. "The very last chob on earth! You would be better to be trapping rabbits. It iss not an occupation for any man that has a kind he'rt, and I have a he'rt mysel' that's no slack in that direction, I'm tellin' you. Many a time I'll have to take a poor laad in and cherge him, and he'll be fined, and it's mysel' that's the first to get the money for his fine."

" Do you tell me you pay the fine oot of your own pocket ? "
asked Para Handy astonished.

" Not a bit of it ; I have aal my faculties about me. I go
roond and raise a subscruption," explained the sergeant. " I
chust go roond and say the poor laad didna mean any herm,
and his mother wass a weedow, and it iss aal right, och aye !
it iss aal right at wance wi' the folk in Tarbert. Kind, kind
he'rts in Tarbert—if there's any fushing. But the polis iss
no chob for a man like me. Still and on it's a good pay, and
the uniform, and a fine pair of boots, and an honour, so I'm
no' complaining. Not a bit ! "

Para Handy put up his hand with his customary gesture
to scratch his ear, but as usual thought better of it, and
sheered off. " Do you ken oor Dougie ? " he asked.

" Iss it your mate ? " replied the constable. " They're
telling me aboot him, but I never had him in my hands."

" It's easy seen you're no' long in Tarbert," said the Captain. " He wass wan time namely here for makin' trouble ;
but that wass before he wass a kind of a Rechabite. Did
you hear aboot him up in Castlebay in Barra ? "

" No," said the sergeant.

" Dougie will be aye bouncin' he wass wan time on the
yats, and wearing a red night-kep aal the time, and whiten-
ing on his boots, the same ass if he wass a doorstep, but,
man ! he's tumid, tumid ! If there's a touch of a gale he
starts at his prayers, and says he'll throw his trump over
the side. He can play the trump sublime—reels and things
you never heard the like of ; and if he wass here, and him in
trum, it's himself would show you. But when the weather's
scoury, and the *Fital Spark* not at the quay, he'll make up
his mind to live a better life, and the first thing that he's
going to stop 's the trump. ' Hold you on, Dougie,' I'll be
sayin' to him ; ' don't do anything desperate till we see if the
weather 'll no lift on the other side of Minard.' It's a long
way from Oban out to Barra ; many a man that hass gold
braid on his kep in the Clyde never went so far, but it's

nothing at aal to the *Fital Spark*. But Dougie does not like
that trup at aal, at aal. Give him Bowling to Blairmore in
the month of Aagust, and there's no' a finer sailor ever put on
oilskins."

"Och, the poor fellow!" said the sergeant, with true
sympathy.

"Stop you!" proceeded Para Handy. "When we would
be crossing the Munch, Dougie would be going to sacrifice
his trump, and start releegion every noo and then ; but when
we had the vessel tied to the quay at Castlebay, the merchants had to shut their shops and make a holiday."

"My Chove! do you tell me?" cried the sergeant.

"If Dougie was here himsel' he would tell you," said the
Captain. "It needed but the wan or two drams, and Dougie
would start walkin' on his heels to put an end to Castlebay.
There iss not many shops in the place aaltogether, and the
shopkeepers are aal MacNeils, and cousins to wan another ;
so when Dougie was waalkin' on his heels and in trum for
high jeenks, they had a taalk together, and agreed it would
be better chust to put on the shutters."

"Isn't he the desperate character!" said the constable.
"Could they no' have got the polis?"

"There's no a polisman in the island of Barra," said Para
Handy. "If there wass any need for polismen they would
have to send to Lochmaddy, and it would be two or three
days before they could put Dougie on his trial. Forbye,
they kent Dougie fine ; they hadna any ill-wull to the laad,
and maybe it wass a time there wasna very mich business
doin' anyway. When Dougie would find the shops shut he
would be as vexed as anything, and make for the school.
He would go into the school and give the children a lecture
on music and the curse of drink, with illustrations on the
trump. At last they used to shut the school, too, and give
the weans a holiday, whenever the *Fital Spark* was seen off
Castle Kismul. He wass awfu' popular, Dougie, wi' the weans
in Castlebay."

" A man like that should not be at lerge," said the constable emphatically.

" Och ! he wass only in fun ; there wass no more herm in Dougie than a fly. Chust fond of high jeenks and recreation ; many a place in the Highlands would be gled to get the lend of him to keep them cheery in the winter-time. There's no herm in Dougie, not at aal, chust a love of sport and recreation. If he wass here himsel' he would tell you."

" It iss a good thing for him he does not come to Tarbert for his recreation," said the constable sternly ; " we're no' so Hielan' in Tarbert ass to shut the shops when a man iss makin' himsel' a nuisance. By Cheorge ! if he starts any of his high jeenks in Tarbert he'll suffer the Laaw."

" There iss no fear of Tarbert nowadays," said the Captain, " for Dougie iss a changed man. He mairried a kind of a wife yonder at Greenock, and she made him a Good Templar, or a Rechabite, or something of the sort where you get ten shillin's a week if your leg's broken fallin' doon the stair, and nobody saw you. Dougie's noo a staunch teetotaller except aboot the time of the old New Year, or when he'll maybe be takin' a dram for medicine. It iss a good thing for his wife, but it leaves an awfu' want in Barra and them other places where they kent him in his best trum."

XVIII

THE TAR'S WEDDING

It was months after The Tar's consultation with Para Handy about a wife : The Tar seemed to have given up the idea of indulgence in any such extravagance, and Para Handy had ceased to recommend various " smert, muddle-aged ones wi' a puckle money " to the consideration of the young man, when the latter one day sheepishly approached him, spat awkwardly through the clefts of his teeth at a patch in the funnel of the *Vital Spark*, and remarked, " I wass thinkin' to mysel' yonder, Captain, that if there wass nothing parteecular doing next Setturday, I would maybe get mairried."

"Holy smoke!" said the Captain; "you canna expect me to get a wife suitable for you in that time. It's no reasonable. Man, you're gettin' droll—chust droll!"

"Och, I needn't be puttin' you to any trouble," said The Tar, rubbing the back of his neck with a hand as rough as a rasp. "I wass lookin' aboot mysel', and there's wan yonder in Campbeltown 'll have me. In fact, it's settled. I thocht that when we were in Campbeltown next Setturday, we could do the chob and be dune wi't. We were roared last Sunday——"

"Roared!" said the Captain. "Iss it cried, you mean?"

"Yes, chust cried," said The Tar, "but the gyurl's kind of dull in the hearing, and it would likely need to be a roar. You'll maybe ken her—she's wan of the MacCallums."

"A fine gyurl," said the Captain, who had not the faintest idea of her identity, and had never set eyes on her, but could always be depended on for politeness. "A fine gyurl! Truly sublime! I'm not askin' if there's any money; eh? —not a word! It's none of my business, but, tuts! what's the money anyway, when there's love?"

"Shut up aboot that!" said the scandalised Tar, getting very red. "If you're goin' to speak aboot love, be dacent and speak aboot it in the Gaalic. But we're no' taalkin' aboot love; we're taalkin' aboot my merrage. Is it aal right for Setturday?"

"You're a cunning man to keep it dark till this," said the Captain, "but I'll put nothing in the way, seein' it's your first caper of the kind. We'll have high jeenks at Campbeltown."

The marriage took place in the bride's mother's house, up a stair that was greatly impeded by festoons of fishing-nets, old oars, and net-bows on the walls, and the presence of six stalwart Tarbert trawlers, cousins of The Tar's, who were asked to the wedding, but were so large and had so many guernseys on, they would of themselves have filled the room in which the ceremony took place ; so they had agreed, while the minister was there at all events, to take turn about of going in to countenance the proceedings. What space there was within was monopolised by the relatives of the bride, by Para Handy and Dougie, The Tar in a new slop-shop serge suit, apparently cut out by means of a hatchet, the bride—a good deal prettier than a Goth like The Tar deserved—and the minister. The wedding-supper was laid out in a neighbour's house on the same stair-landing.

A solemn hush marked the early part of the proceedings, marred only by the sound of something frying in the other house and the shouts of children crying for bowl-money in the street. The minister was a teetotaller, an unfortunate circumstance which the Captain had discovered very early, and he was very pleased with the decorum of the company. The MacCallums were not church-goers in any satisfactory sense, but they and their company seemed to understand what was due to a Saturday night marriage and the presence of " the cloth." The clergyman had hardly finished the ceremony when the Captain began manœuvering for his removal. He had possessed himself of a bottle of ginger cordial and a plate of cake.

" You must drink the young couple's health, Mr Grant," he said. " We ken it's you that's the busy man on the Setturday night, and indeed it's a night for the whole of us goin' home early. I have a ship yonder, the *Fital Spark*, that I left in cherge of an enchineer by the name of Macphail, no' to be trusted with such a responsibility."

The minister drank the cheerful potion, nibbled the corner of a piece of cake, and squeezed his way downstairs between the Tarbert trawlers.

" We're chust goin' away oorsel's in ten meenutes," said the Captain after him.

" Noo that's aal right," said Para Handy, who in virtue of his office had constituted himself master of ceremonies. " He's a nice man, Mr Grant, but he's not strong, and it would be a peety to be keeping him late out of his bed on a Setturday night. I like, mysel', yon old-fashioned munisters that had nothing wrong wi' them, and took a Chrustian dram. Pass oot that bottle of chinger cordial to the laads from Tarbert and you'll see fine fun."

He was the life and soul of the evening after that. It was he who pulled the corks, who cut the cold ham, who kissed the bride first, who sang the first song, and danced with the new mother-in-law. " You're an aawful man, Captain Macfarlane," she said in fits of laughter at his fun.

" Not me ! " said he, lumberingly dragging her round in a polka to the strains of Dougie's trump. " I'm a quate fellow, but when I'm in trum I like a high jeenk noo and then. Excuse my feet. It's no' every day we're merryin' The Tar. A fine, smert, handy fellow, Mrs MacCallum ; you didn't make a bad bargain of it with your son-in-law. Excuse my feet. A sailor every inch of him, once you get him wakened. A pound a-week of wages an' no incumbrance. My feet again, excuse them ! "

" It's little enough for two," said Mrs MacCallum ; " but a man's aye a man," and she looked the Captain in the eye with disconcerting admiration.

" My Chove ! she's a weedow wuman," thought the Captain ; " I'll have to ca' canny, or I'll be in for an engagement."

" I aye liked sailors," said Mrs MacCallum ; " John—that's the depairted, I'm his relic—was wan."

" A poor life, though," said the Captain, " especially on the steamers, like us. But your man, maybe, was sailin' foreign, an' made money ? It's always a consuderation for a weedow."

" Not a penny," said the indiscreet Mrs MacCallum, as Para Handy wheeled her into a chair.

At eleven o'clock The Tar was missing. He had last been

seen pulling off his new boots, which were too small for him, on the stair-head; and it was only after considerable searching the Captain and one of the Tarbert cousins found him sound asleep on the top of a chest in the neighbour's house.

"Colin," said the Captain, shaking him awake, "sit up and try and take something. See at the rest of us, as jovial as anything, and no' a man hit yet. Sit up and be smert for the credit of the *Fital Spark*."

"Are you angry wi' me, Captain?" asked The Tar.

"Not a bit of it, Colin! But you have the corkscrew in your pocket. I'm no' caring myself, but the Tarbert gentlemen will take it amiss. Forbye, there's your wife; you'll maybe have mind of her—wan Lucy MacCallum? She's in yonder, fine and cheery, wi' two of your Tarbert cousins holding her hand."

"Stop you! I'll hand them!" cried the exasperated bridegroom, and bounded into the presence of the marriage-party in the house opposite, with a demonstration that finally led to the breaking-up of the party.

Next day took place The Tar's curious kirking. The MacCallums, as has been said, were not very regular church-goers; in fact, they had overlooked the ordinances since the departed John died, and forgot that the church bell rang for the Sabbath-school an hour before it rang for the ordinary forenoon service.

Campbeltown itself witnessed the bewildering spectacle of The Tar and his bride, followed by the mother and Para Handy, marching deliberately up the street and into the church among the children. Five minutes later they emerged, looking very red and ashamed of themselves.

"If I knew there wass so mich bother to mind things, I would never have got merried at all," said the bridegroom.

D

XIX

A STROKE OF LUCK

IT was a night of harmony on the good ship *Vital Spark*. She was fast in the mud at Colintraive quay, and, in the den of her, Para Handy was giving his song, " The Dancing Master "—

" Set to Jeanie Mertin, tee-teedalum, tee-tadulam,
    Up the back and doon the muddle, tee-tadalum, tee-tadulam.
    Ye're wrong, Jeck, I'm certain ; tee-tadalum, tee-tadulam,"

while the mate played an accompaniment on the trump— that is to say, the Jew's harp, a favourite instrument on steam-lighters where the melodeon has not intruded. The Captain knew only two verses, but he sang them over several times. " You're getting better and better at it every time," The Tar assured him, for The Tar had got the promise of a rise that day of a shilling a week on his pay. " If I had chust on my other boots," said the Captain, delighted at this appreciation. " This ones iss too light for singin' with——" and he stamped harder than ever as he went on with the song, for it was his idea that the singing of a song was a very ineffective and uninteresting performance unless you beat time with your foot on the floor.

The reason for the harmony on the vessel was that Dougie the mate had had a stroke of luck that evening. He had picked up at the quay side a large and very coarse fish called a stenlock, or coal-fish, and had succeeded, by sheer effrontery, in passing it off as a cod worth two shillings on a guileless Glasgow woman who had come for the week to one of the Colintraive cottages.

" I'm only vexed I didna say it wass a salmon," said Dougie, when he came back to the vessel with his ill-got florin. " I could have got twice ass much for't."

" She would ken fine it wasna a salmon when it wasna in a tin," said the Captain.

" There's many a salmon that iss not in a canister," said the mate.

" Och ay, but she's from Gleska ; they're awfu' Hielan' in Gleska aboot fush and things like that," said the Captain. " But it's maybe a peety you didn't say it wass a salmon, for two shullin's iss not mich among four of us."

" Among four of us ! " repeated Dougie emphatically. " It's little enough among wan, let alone four ; I'm going to keep her to mysel'."

" If that iss your opeenion, Dougie, you are maakin' a great mistake, and it'll maybe be better for you to shift your mind," the Captain said meaningly. " It iss the jyle you could be getting for swundling a poor cratur from Gleska that thinks a stenlock iss a cod. Forbye, it iss a tremendous risk, for you might be found oot, and it would be a disgrace to the *Fital Spark*."

Dougie was impressed by the possibility of trouble with the law as a result of his fish transaction, which, to do him justice, he had gone about more as a practical joke than anything else. " I'm vexed I did it, Peter," he said, turning the two shillings over in his hand. " I have a good mind to go up and tell the woman it wass chust a baur."

" Not at aal ! not at aal ! " cried Para Handy. " It wass a fine cod right enough ; we'll chust send The Tar up to the Inns with the two shullin's and the jar, and we'll drink the Gleska woman's health that does not ken wan fush from another. It will be a lesson to her to be careful ; chust that, to be careful."

So The Tar had gone to the Inn for the ale, and thus it was that harmony prevailed in the fo'c'sle of the *Vital Spark*.

" Iss that a song of your own doing ? " asked Dougie, when the Captain was done.

" No," said Para Handy, " it iss a low-country song I heard wance in the Broomielaw. Yon iss the place for seeing life. I'm telling you it iss Gleska for gaiety if you have the money. There is more life in wan day in the

Broomielaw of Gleska than there iss in a fortnight on Loch Fyne."

"I daarsay there iss," said Dougie; "no' coontin' the herring."

"Och! life, life!" said the Captain, with a pensive air of ancient memory; "Gleska's the place for it. And the fellows iss there that iss not frightened, I'm telling you."

"I learned my tred there," mentioned the engineer, who had no accomplishments, and had not contributed anything to the evening's entertainment, and felt that it was time he was shining somehow.

"Iss that a fact, Macphail? I thocht it wass in a coal-ree in the country," said Para Handy. "I wass chust sayin', when Macphail put in his oar, that yon's the place for life. If I had my way of it, the *Fital Spark* would be going up every day to the Chamaica Brudge the same as the *Columba*, and I would be stepping ashore quite spruce with my Sunday clothes on, and no' lying here in a place like Colintraive, where there's no' even a polisman, with people that swundle a Gleska woman oot of only two shullin's. It wass not hardly worth your while, Dougie." The ale was now finished.

The mate contributed a reel and strathspey on the trump to the evening's programme, during which The Tar fell fast asleep, from which he wakened to suggest that he should give them a guess.

"Weel done, Colin!" said the Captain, who had never before seen such enterprise on the part of The Tar. "Tell us the guess if you can mind it."

"It begins something like this," said The Tar nervously: "'Whether would you raither——' That's the start of it."

"Fine, Colin, fine!" said the Captain encouragingly. "Take your breath and start again."

"'Whether would you raither,'" proceeded The Tar— "'whether would you raither or walk there?'"

"Say 't again, slow," said Dougie, and The Tar repeated his extraordinary conundrum.

" If I had a piece of keelivine (lead pencil) and a lump of paper I could soon answer that guess," said the engineer, and the Captain laughed.

" Man Colin," he said, " you're missing half of the guess oot. There's no sense at aal in ' Whether would you raither or walk there ? ' "

" That's the way I heard it, anyway," said The Tar, sorry he had volunteered. " ' Whether would you raither or walk there ? ' I mind fine it wass that."

" Weel, we give it up anyway ; what's the answer ? " said the Captain.

" Man, I don't mind whether there wass an answer or no'," confessed The Tar, scratching his head ; and the Captain irritably hit him with a cap on the ear, after which the entertainment terminated, and the crew of the *Vital Spark* went to bed.

Next forenoon a very irate-looking Glasgow woman was to be observed coming down the quay, and Dougie promptly retired into the hold of the *Vital Spark*, leaving the lady's reception to the Captain.

" Where's that man away to ? " she asked Para Handy. " I want to speak to him."

" He's engaged, mem," said the Captain.

" I don't care if he's married," said the Glasgow woman ; " I'm no' wantin' him. I jist wanted to say yon was a bonny like cod he sell't me yesterday. I biled it three oors this mornin', and it was like leather when a' was done."

" That's droll," said the Captain. " It wass a fine fush, I'll assure you ; if Dougie was here himsel' he would tell you. Maybe you didna boil it right. Cods iss curious that way. What did you use ? "

" Watter ! " snapped the Glasgow woman ; " did you think I would use sand ? "

" Chust that ! chust that ! Watter ? Weel, you couldna use anything better for boilin' with than chust watter. What kind of coals did you use ? "

" Jist plain black yins," said the woman. " I bocht them frae Cameron along the road there," referring to a coal agent who was a trade rival to the local charterer of the *Vital Spark.*

" Cameron ! " cried Para Handy. " Wass I not sure there wass something or other wrong ? Cameron's coals wouldna boil a wulk, let alone a fine cod. If Dougie wass here he would tell you that himsel'."

XX

DOUGIE'S FAMILY

THE size of Dougie the mate's family might be considered a matter which was of importance to himself alone, but it was astonishing how much interest his shipmates took in it. When there was nothing else funny to talk about on the *Vital Spark*, they would turn their attention to the father of ten, and cunningly extract information from him about the frightful cost of boys' boots and the small measure of milk to be got for sixpence at Dwight's dairy in Plantation.

They would listen sympathetically, and later on roast him unmercifully with comments upon the domestic facts he had innocently revealed to them.

It might happen that the vessel would be lying at a West Highland quay, and the Captain sitting on deck reading a week-old newspaper, when he would wink at Macphail and The Tar, and say, " Cot bless me ! boys, here's the price of boots goin' up ; peety the poor faithers of big femilies." Or, " I see there's to be a new school started in Partick, Dougie ; did you flit again ? "

" You think you're smert, Peter," the mate would retort lugubriously. " Fun's fun, but I'll no' stand fun aboot my femily."

" Och ! no offence, Dougald, no offence," Para Handy would say soothingly. " Hoo's the mustruss keepin' ? "

and then ask a fill of tobacco to show his feelings were quite friendly.

In an ill-advised moment the parental pride and joy of the mate brought on board one day a cabinet photograph of himself and his wife and the ten children.

" What do you think of that ? " he said to Para Handy, who took the extreme tip of one corner of the card between the finger and thumb of a hand black with coal-grime, glanced at the group, and said—

" Whatna Sunday School trup's this ? "

" It's no' a trup at aal," said Dougie with annoyance.

" Beg pardon, beg pardon," said the Captain, " I see noo I wass wrong ; it's Quarrier's Homes. Who's the chap wi' the whuskers in the muddle, that's greetin' ? "

" Where's your eyes ? " said Dougie. " It's no' a Homes at aal ; that's me, and I'm no' greetin'. What would I greet for ? "

" Faith, I believe you're right," said the Captain. " It's yoursel' plain enough, when I shut wan eye to look at it ; but the collar and a clean face make a terrible dufference. Well, well, allooin' that it's you, and you're no greetin', it's rideeculous for you to be goin' to a dancin'-school."

" It's no' a dancin'-school, it's the femily," said the mate, losing his temper. " Fun's fun, but if you think I'll stand——"

" Keep caalm, keep caalm ! " interrupted the Captain hurriedly, realising that he had carried the joke far enough. " I might have kent fine it wass the family ; they're aal ass like you both ass anything, and that 'll be Susan the eldest."

" That ! " said Dougie, quite mollified—" that's the mustress hersel'."

" Well, I'm jeegered," said the Captain, with well-acted amazement. " She's younger looking than ever ; that's a woman that's chust sublime."

The mate was so pleased he made him a present of the photograph.

But it always had been, and always would be, a distressing task to Dougie to have to intimate to the crew (as he had to do once a year) that there was a new addition to the family, for it was on these occasions that the chaff of his shipmates was most ingenious and galling. Only once, by a trick, had he got the better of them and evaded his annual roastings. On that occasion he came to the *Vital Spark* with a black muffler on, and a sad countenance.

" I've lost my best freend," said he, rubbing his eyes to make them red.

" Holy smoke ! " said Para Handy, " is Macmillan the pawnbroker deid ? "

" It's no' him," said Dougie, manfully restraining a sob, and he went on to tell them that it was his favourite uncle, Jamie. He put so much pathos into his description of Uncle Jamie's last hours, that when he wound up by mentioning, in an off-hand way, that his worries were complicated by the arrival of another daughter that morning, the crew had, naturally, not the heart to say anything about it.

Some weeks afterwards they discovered by accident that he never had an Uncle Jamie.

" Man ! he's cunning ! " said Para Handy, when this black evidence of Dougie's astuteness came out. " Stop you till the next time, and we'll make him pay for it."

The suitable occasion for making the mate smart doubly for his deceit came in due course. Macphail the engineer lived in the next tenement to Dougie's family in Plantation, and he came down to the quay one morning before the mate, with the important intelligence for the Captain that the portrait group was now incomplete.

" Poor Dugald ! " said the Captain sympathetically. " Iss it a child or a lassie ? "

" I don't ken," said the engineer. " I just got a rumour frae the night polisman, and he said the wife was fine."

" Stop you and you'll see some fun with Dougie," said the Captain. " I'm mich mistaken if he'll swundle us this twict."

Para Handy had gone ashore for something, and was back before his mate appeared on board the *Vital Spark*, which was just starting for Campbeltown with a cargo of bricks. The mate took the wheel, smoked ceaselessly at a short cutty pipe, and said nothing ; and nobody said anything to him.

"He's plannin' some other way oot of the scrape," whispered the Captain once to the engineer ; "but he'll not get off so easy this time. Hold you on ! "

It was dinner-time, and the captain, mate, and engineer were round the pot on deck aft, with The Tar at the wheel, within comfortable hearing distance, when Para Handy slyly broached the topic.

"Man, Dougie," he said, "what wass I doin' yonder last night but dreamin' in the Gaalic aboot you ? I wass dreamin' you took a charter of the *Fital Spark* doon to Ardkinglas with a picnic, and there wass not a park in the place would hold the company."

Dougie simply grunted.

"It wass a droll dream," continued the Captain, diving for another potato. "I wass chust wonderin' hoo you found them aal at home. Hoo's the mustress keepin' ? "

The mate got very red. "I wass chust goin' to tell you aboot her," he said with considerable embarrassment.

"A curious dream it wass," said Para Handy, postponing his pleasure, like the shrewd man he is, that he might enjoy it all the more when it came. "I saw you ass plain ass anything, and the *Fital Spark* crooded high and low with the picnic, and you in the muddle playing your trump. The mustress wass there, too, quite spruce, and— But you were goin' to say something aboot the mustress, Dougie. I hope she's in her usual ? "

"That's chust it," said Dougie, more and more embarrassed as he saw his news had to be given now, if ever. "You would be thinkin' to yourself I wass late this mornin', but the fact iss we were in an aawful habble in oor hoose——"

"Bless me ! I hope the lum didn't take fire nor nothing

D*

like that ? " said Para Handy anxiously ; and The Tar, at the wheel behind, was almost in a fit with suppressed laughter.

" Not at aal ! worse nor that ! " said Dougie in melancholy tones. " There's—there's—dash it ! there's more boots than ever needed yonder ! "

" Man, you're gettin' quite droll," said Para Handy. " Do you no' mind you told me aboot that wan chust three or four months ago ? "

" You're a liar ! " said Dougie, exasperated ; " it's a twelvemonth since I told you aboot the last."

" Not at aal ! not at aal ! your mind's failin'," protested the Captain. " Five months ago at the most ; you told me aboot it at the time. Surely there's some mistake ? "

" No mistake at aal aboot it," said the mate, shaking his head so sadly that the Captain's heart was melted.

" Never mind, Dougald," he said, taking a little parcel out of his pocket. " I'm only in fun. I heard aboot it this mornin' from Macphail, and here's a wee bit peeny and a pair o' sluppers that I bought for't."

" To the muschief ! It's no' an ' it,' " said Dougie ; " it's —it's—it's a twuns ! "

" Holy smoke ! " exclaimed Para Handy. " Iss that no chust desperate ? " And the mate was so much moved that he left half his dinner and went forward towards the bow.

Para Handy went forward to him in a little and said, " Cheer up, Dougie ; hoo wass I to ken it wass a twuns ? If I had kent, it wouldna be the wan peeny and the wan sluppers ; but I have two or three shillin's here, and I'll buy something else in Campbeltown."

" I can only—I can only say thankye the noo, Peter ; it wass very good of you," said the mate, deeply touched, and attempting to shake the Captain's hand.

" Away ! away ! " said Para Handy, getting very red himself ; " none of your chat ! I'll buy peenies and sluppers if I like."

XXI

THE BAKER'S LITTLE WIDOW

ON the night after New Year's Day the Captain did a high-spirited thing he had done on the corresponding day for the previous six years ; he had his hair cut and his beard trimmed by Dougie the mate, made a specially careful toilet—taking all the tar out of his hands by copious applications of salt butter—wound up his watch (which was never honoured in this way more than once or twice a twelvemonth), and went up the quay to propose to Mrs Crawford. It was one of the rare occasions upon which he wore a topcoat, and envied Macphail his Cairngorm scarfpin. There was little otherwise to suggest the ardent wooer, for ardent wooers do not look as solemn as Para Handy looked. The truth is, he was becoming afraid that his persistency might wear down a heart of granite, and that this time the lady might accept him.

The crew of the *Vital Spark*, whom he thought quite ignorant of his tender passion for the baker's widow, took a secret but intense interest in this annual enterprise. He was supposed to be going to take tea with a cousin (as if captains took the tar off their hands to visit their own cousins !), and in order to make the deception more complete and allay any suspicions on the part, especially, of Macphail, who, as a great student of penny novelettes, was up to all the intrigues of love, the Captain casually mentioned that if it wasn't that it would vex his cousin he would sooner stay on the vessel and play Catch the Ten with them.

" I hate them tea-pairties," he said ; " chust a way of wasting the New Year. But stay you here, boys, and I'll come back ass soon ass ever I can."

" Bring back some buns, or cookies, or buscuits wi' you," cried Dougie, as the Captain stepped on to the quay.

" What do you mean ? " said Para Handy sharply, afraid he was discovered.

" Nothing, Peter, nothing at aal," the mate assured him, nudging The Tar in the dark. " Only it's likely you'll have more of them than you can eat at your cousin's tea-pairty."

Reassured thus that his secret was still safe, Para Handy went slowly up the quay. As he went he stopped a moment to exchange a genial word with everybody he met, as if time was of no importance, and he was only ashore for a daunder. This was because, dressed as he was, if he walked quickly and was not particulary civil to everybody, the whole of Campbeltown (which is a very observant place) would suspect he was up to something and watch him.

The widow's shop was at a conveniently quiet corner. He tacked back and forward off it in the darkness several times till a customer, who was being served, as he could see through the glass door, had come out, and a number of boys playing at " guesses " at the window had passed on, and then he cleared his throat, unbuttoned his topcoat and jacket to show his watch-chain, and slid as gently as he could in at the glass door.

" Dear me, fancy seeing you, Captain Macfarlane ! " said the widow Crawford, coming from the room at the back of the shop. " Is it really yourself ? "

" A good New Year to you," said the Captain, hurried and confused. " I wass chust goin' up the toon, and I thought I would give you a roar in the by-going. Are you keeping tip-top, Mery ? "

His heart beat wildly ; he looked at her sideways with a timid eye, for, hang it ! she was more irresistible than ever. She was little, plump, smiling, rosy-cheeked, neat in dress, and just the exact age to make the Captain think he was young again.

" Will you not come ben and warm yourself ? It's a nasty, damp night," said Mrs Crawford, pushing the back door, so that he got the most tempting vision of an interior with firelight dancing in it, a genial lamp, and a tea-table set

" I'll chust sit doon and draw my breath for a meenute or two. You'll be busy ? " said the Captain, rolling into the back room with an elephantine attempt (which she skilfully evaded) at playfully putting his arm round the widow's waist as he did so.

" You're as daft as ever, I see, Captain," said the lady. " I was just making myself a cup of tea ; will you take one ? "

" Och, it's puttin' you to bother," said the Captain.

" Not a bit of it," said the widow, and she whipped out a cup, which was suspiciously handy in a cupboard, and told the Captain to take off his coat and he would get the good of it when he went out.

People talk about young girls as entrancing. To men of experience like the Captain girls are insipid. The prime of life in the other sex is something under fifty ; and the widow, briskly making tea, smiling on him, shaking her head at him, pushing him on the shoulder when he was impudent, chaffing him, surrounding him with an intoxicating atmosphere of homeliness, comfort, and cuddleability, seemed to Para Handy there and then the most angelic creature on earth. The rain could be heard falling heavily outside, no customers were coming in, and the back room of the baker's shop was, under the circumstances, as fine an earthly makeshift for Paradise as man could ask for.

Para Handy dived his hand into his coat pocket. " That minds me," said he ; " I have a kind of a bottle of scent here a friend o' mine, by the name of Hurricane Jeck, took home for me from America last week. It's the rale Florida Water ; no' the like o't to be got here, and if you put the least sensation on your hanky you'll feel the smell of it a mile away. It's chust sublime."

" Oh ! it's so kind of you ! " said the widow, beaming on him with the merriest, brownest, deepest, meltingest of eyes, and letting her plump little fingers linger a moment on his as she took the perfume bottle. The Captain felt as if golden harps were singing in the air, and fairies were tickling him down the back with peacocks' feathers.

" Mery," he said in a little, " this iss splendid tea.   Capital, aalthegether ! "

" Tuts ! Captain," said she, " is it only my tea you come to pay compliments to once a year ?   Good tea's common enough if you're willing to pay for it.   What do you think of myself ? "

The Captain neatly edged his chair round the corner of the table to get it close beside hers, and she just as neatly edged her chair round the other corner, leaving their relative positions exactly as they had been.

" No, no, Captain," said she, twinkling ; " hands off the widow.   I'm a done old woman, and it's very good of you to come and have tea with me ; but I always thought sailors, with a sweetheart, as they say, in every port, could say nice things to cheer up a lonely female heart.   What we women need, Captain—the real necessity of our lives—is some one to love us.   Even if he's at the other end of the world, and unlikely ever to be any nearer, it makes the work of the day cheery.   But what am I haverin' about ? " she added, with a delicious, cosy, melting, musical sigh that bewitchingly heaved her blouse.   " Nobody cares for me, I'm too old."

" Too old ! " exclaimed the Captain, amused at the very idea.   " You're not a day over fifty.   You're chust sublime."

" Forty-nine past, to be particular," said the widow, " and feel like twenty.   Oh ! Captain, Captain ! you men ! "

" Mery," entreated Para Handy, putting his head to one side, " caal me Peter, and gie me a ha'ad o' your hand." This time he edged his chair round quicker than she did hers, and captured her fingers.   Now that he had them he didn't know very well what to do with them, but he decided after a little that a cute thing to do was to pull them one by one and try to make them crack.   He did so, and got slapped on the ear for his pains.

"What do you mean by that?" said she.

"Och, it was chust a baur, Mery," said Para Handy. "Man, you're strong, strong! You would make a sublime wife for any sober, decent, good-looking, capable man. You would make a fine wife for a sailor, and I'm naming no names, mind ye; but "—here he winked in a manner that seemed to obliterate one complete side of his face—" they caal him Peter. Eh? What?"

"Nobody would have me," said the widow, quite cheerfully, enjoying herself immensely. "I'm old—well, kind of old, and plain, and I have no money."

"Money!" said Para Handy contemptuously; "the man I'm thinking of does not give wan docken for money. And you're no more old than I am mysel', and as for bein' plain, chust look at the lovely polka you have on and the rudness of your face. If Dougie was here he would tell— no, no, don't mention a cheep to Dougie—not a cheep; he would maybe jalouse something."

"This is the sixth time of asking, Captain," said the widow. "You must have your mind dreadful firm made up. But it's only at the New Year I see you; I'm afraid you're like all sailors—when you're away you forget all about me. Stretch your hand and have another London bun."

"London buns iss no cure for my case," said the Captain, taking one, however. "I hope you'll say yes this time."

"I'll—I'll think about it," said the widow, still smiling; "and if you're passing this way next New Year and call in, I'll let you know."

The crew of the *Vital Spark* waited on deck for the return of the skipper. Long before he came in sight they heard him clamping down the quay singing cheerfully to himself—

> "Rolling home to bonnie Scotland,
>   Rolling home, dear land, to thee;
> Rolling home to bonnie Scotland,
>   Rolling home across the sea."

"Iss your cousin's tea-pairty over already?" said Dougie innocently. "Wass there many at it?"

"Seven or eight," said Para Handy promptly. "I chust came away. And I'm feeling chust sublime. Wan of Brutain's hardy sons."

He went down below, and hung up his topcoat and his watch and took off his collar, which uncomfortably rasped his neck. "Mery's the right sort," said he to himself; "she's no' going ram-stam into the business. She's caautious like mysel'. Maybe next New Year she'll make her mind up."

And the widow, putting up her shutters that night, hummed cheerfully to herself, and looked quite happy. "I wish I HAD called him Peter," she thought; "next year I ll not be so blate."

XXII

THREE DRY DAYS

On the first day of February the Captain of the *Vital Spark* made an amazing resolution. Life in the leisure hours of himself and his crew had been rather strenuous during the whole of January, for Dougie had broken the Rechabites. When Dougie was not a Rechabite, he always carried about with him an infectious atmosphere of gaiety and a half-crown, and the whole ship's company took its tone from him. This is a great moral lesson. It shows how powerful for good or evil is the influence and example of One Strong Man. If Dougie had been more at home that month, instead of trading up the West Coast, his wife would have easily dispelled his spirit of gaiety by making him nurse the twins, and she would have taken him herself to be reinstalled in the Rechabites, for she was " a fine, smert, managin' woman," as he admitted himself; but when sailors are so often and so far away from the benign influences of home, with nobody

to search their pockets, it is little wonder they should sometimes be foolish.

So the Captain rose on the first day of the month with
a frightful headache, and emphatically refused to adopt
the customary method of curing it. " No," he said to his
astonished mates, " I'm no' goin' up to the Ferry Hoose
nor anywhere else ; I'm teetotal."

" Teetotal ! " exclaimed Dougie, much shocked. " You
shouldna make a joke aboot things like that, and you no'
feelin' very weel ; come on up and take your mornin'."

" Not a drop ! " said Para Handy firmly.

" Tut, tut, Peter ; chust wan beer," persisted the mate
patiently.

" Not even if it wass jampaigne," said the Captain, drying
his head, which he had been treating to a cold douche. " My
mind's made up. Drink's a curse, and I'm done wi't, for
I canna stand it."

" There's nobody askin' you to stand it," explained the
mate. " I have a half-croon o' my own here."

" It's no odds," said the Captain. " I'm on the teetotal
tack. Not another drop will I taste——"

" Stop, stop!" interrupted Dougie, more shocked than ever.
" Don't do anything rash. You might be struck doon deid,
and then you would be sorry for what you said. Do you mean
to tell us that you're goin' to be teetotal aalthegether ? "

" No," said the Captain, " I'm no' that desperate. I
wouldna care chust to go aal that length, but I'm goin' to
be teetotal for the month o' February."

" Man, I think you're daft, Peter," said the mate.
" February, of aal months ! In February the New Year's
no' right bye, and the Gleska Fair's chust comin' on ; could
you no' put it off for a more sensible time ? "

" No," said the Captain firmly, " February's the month
for me ; there's two or three days less in't than any other
month in the year."

So the crew filed ashore almost speechless with astonishment—annoyed and depressed to some extent by this inflexible virtue on the part of Para Handy.

" He's gettin' quite droll in his old age," was Dougie's explanation.

" Fancy him goin' away and spoilin' the fun like that ! " said The Tar incredulously.

" I aye said he hadna the game in him," was the comment of Macphail the engineer.

Para Handy watched them going up to the Ferry House, and wished it was the month of March.

The first day of his abstinence would have passed without much more inclination on his part to repent his new resolution were it not for the fact that half a score of circumstances conspired to make it a day of unusual trial. He met friends that day he had not met for months, all with plenty of time on their hands ; Hurricane Jack, the irresistible, came alongside in another vessel, and was immediately for celebrating this coincidence by having half a day off, a proposal the Captain evaded for a while only by pretending to be seriously ill and under medical treatment ; the coal merchant, whose cargo they had just discharged, presented the crew with a bottle of whisky ; there was a ball at the George Hotel ; there was a travelling piper on the streets, with most inspiring melodies ; the headache was away by noon—only a giant will-power could resist so many circumstances conducive to gaiety. But Para Handy never swerved in his resolution. He compromised with the friends who had plenty of time and the inclination for merriment by taking fills of tobacco from them ; confiscated the bottle of whisky as Captain, and locked it past with the assurance to his crew that it would be very much the more matured if kept till March ; and the second time Hurricane Jack came along the quay to see if the Captain of the *Vital Spark* was not better yet, he accompanied him to the Ferry House, and startled him by saying he would have " Wan small half of lime-juice on draught."

" What's that, Peter ? " said Hurricane Jack. " Did I hear you say something aboot lime-juice, or does my ears deceive me ? "

" It's chust for a bate, Jeck—no offence," explained the Captain hurriedly. " I have a bate on wi' a chap that I'll no' drink anything stronger this month ; but och ! next month, if we're spared, wait you and you'll see some fine fun."

Hurricane Jack looked at him with great disapproval. " Macfarlane," he said solemnly, " you're goin' far, far wrong, and mind you I'm watchin' you. A gembler iss an abomination, and gemblin' at the expense of your inside iss worse than gemblin' on horses. Us workin' men have nothing but oor strength to go on, and if we do not keep up oor strength noo and then, where are we ? You will chust have a smaal gill, and the man that made the bate wi' you 'll never be any the wiser."

" No, Jeck, thank you aal the same," said the Captain, " but I'll chust take the lime-juice. Where 'll you be on the first o' Merch ? "

Hurricane Jack grudgingly ordered the lime-juice, and asked the landlady to give the Captain a sweetie with it to put away the taste, then looked on with an aspect of mingled incredulity and disgust as Para Handy hurriedly gulped the unaccustomed beverage and chased it down with a drink of water.

" It's a fine thing a drap watter," said Para Handy, gasping.

" No' a worse thing you could drink," said Hurricane Jack. " It rots your boots ; what 'll it no' do on your inside ? Watter's fine for sailin' on—there's nothing better —but it's no' drink for sailors."

On the second day of the great reform Para Handy spent his leisure hours fishing for saithe from the side of the vessel, and was, to all appearance, firmer than ever. He was threatened for a while by a good deal of interference from his crew, who resented the confiscation of the presentation bottle, but he turned the tables on them by coming out in the *rôle* of temperance lecturer. When they approached him, he sniffed suspiciously, and stared at their faces in a way that was simply galling—to Dougie particularly, who was naturally of a rubicund countenance. Then he sighed deeply, shook his head solemnly, and put on a fresh bait.

"Are you no' better yet?" Dougie asked. "You're looking ass dull ass if the shup wass tied up to a heid-stone in the Necropolis o' Gleska. None o' your didoes, Peter; give us oot the spurits we got the present o'. It's Candlemas."

Para Handy stared at his fishing-line, and said gently, as if he were speaking to himself, "Poor sowls! poor sowls! Nothing in their heids but drink. It wass a happy day for me the day I gave it up, or I might be like the rest o' them. There's poor Dougald lettin' it get a terrible grup o' him; and The Tar chust driftin', driftin' to the poor's-hoose, and Macphail iss sure to be in the horrors before Setturday, for he hasna the heid for drink, him no' bein' right Hielan'."

"Don't be rash; don't do anything you would be vexed for, but come on away up the toon and have a pant," said Dougie coaxingly. "Man, you have only to make up your mind and shake it off, and you'll be ass cheery ass ever you were."

"He's chust takin' a rise oot o' us; are you no', Captain?" said The Tar, anxious to leave his commander an honourable way of retreat from his preposterous position.

Para Handy went on fishing as if they were not present.

"Married men, too, with wifes and femilies," he said musingly. "If they chust knew what it wass, like me, to be risin' in the mornin' wi' a clear heid, and a good conscience, they would never touch it again. I never knew what happiness wass till I joined the teetotal, and it'll be money in my pocket forbye."

" You'll go on, and you'll go on with them expuriments too far till you'll be a vegetarian next," said Dougie, turning away. " Chust a vegetarian, tryin' to live on turnips and gress, the same ass a coo. If I was a Macfarlane I wouldna care to be a coo."

Then they left him with an aspect more of sorrow than of anger, and he went on fishing.

The third day of the month was Saturday ; there was nothing to do on the *Vital Spark*, which was waiting on a cargo of timber, so all the crew except the Captain spent the time ashore. Him they left severely alone, and the joys of fishing saithe and reading a week-old newspaper palled.

" The worst of bein' good iss that it leaves you duvelish lonely," said the Captain to himself.

An hour later, he discovered that he had a touch of tooth-ache, and, strongly inclined for a temporary suspension of the new rules for February, he went to the locker for the presentation bottle.

It was gone !

XXIII

THE VALENTINE THAT MISSED FIRE

A FORTNIGHT of strict teetotalism on the part of the Captain was too much of a joke for his crew. " It's just bounce," said the mate ; " he's showin' off. I'm a Rechabite for six years, every time I'm in Gleska ; but I never let it put between me and a gless of good Brutish spurits wi' a ship-mate in any port, Loch Fyne or foreign."

" It's most annoyin'," said The Tar. " He asked me yesterday if my health wassna breakin' doon wi' drink, the same ass it would break doon wi' aal I take."

" Chust what I told you ; nothing but bounce ! " said Dougie gloomily. " Stop you ! Next time he's in trum, I'll no' be so handy at pullin' corks for him. If I wass losin' my temper wi' him, I would give him a bit o' my mind."

The engineer, wiping his brow with a wad of oily waste, put down the penny novelette he was reading and gave a contemptuous snort. " I wonder to hear the two o' ye talkin'," said he. " Ye're baith feared for him. I could soon fix him."

" Could you, Macphail ? " said Dougie. " You're aawful game : what would you do ? "

" I would send him a valentine that would vex him," replied the engineer promptly ; " a fizzer o' a valentine that would mak' his hair curl for him."

The mate impulsively smacked his thigh. " My Chove ! Macphail," said he, " it's the very ticket ! What do you say to a valentine for the Captain, Colin ? "

" Whatever you think yersel'," said The Tar.

That night Dougie and The Tar went ashore at Tarbert for a valentine. There was one shop-window up the town with a gorgeous display of penny " mocks," designed and composed to give the recipient in every instance a dull, sickening thud on the bump of his self-esteem. The two mariners saw no valentine, however, that quite met the Captain's case.

" There 'll be plenty o' other wans inside on the coonter," said Dougie diplomatically. " Away you in, Colin, and pick wan suitable, and I'll stand here and watch."

" Watch what ? " inquired The Tar suspiciously. " It would be more like the thing if you went in and bought it yoursel' ; I'll maybe no' get wan that 'll please you."

" Aal you need to ask for iss a mock valentine, lerge size, and pretty broad, for a skipper wi' big feet. I would go in mysel' in a meenute if it wassna that—if it wassna that it would look droll, and me a muddle-aged man wi' whuskers."

The Tar went into the shop reluctantly, and was horrified to find a rather pretty girl behind the counter. He couldn't for his life suggest mock valentines to her, and he could not with decency back out without explanation.

"Have you any—have you any nice unvelopes?" he inquired bashfully, as she stood waiting his order.

"What size?" she asked.

"Lerge size, and pretty broad, for a skipper wi' big feet," said The Tar in his confusion. Then he corrected himself, adding, "Any size, muss, suitable for holdin' letters."

"There's a great run on that kind of envelope this winter," the lady remarked, being a humorist. "How many?"

"A ha'pennyworth," said The Tar. "I'll chust take them wi' me."

When The Tar came out of the shop the mate was invisible, and it was only after some search he found him in a neighbouring public-house.

"I chust came in here to put by the time," said Dougie; "but seein' you're here, what am I for?"

The Tar, realising that there must be an unpleasant revelation immediately, produced the essential threepence and paid for beer.

"I hope you got yon?" said the mate anxiously.

"Ass sure ass daith, Dougie, I didna like to ask for it," explained the young man pathetically. "There's a gasalier and two paraffin lamps bleezin' in the shop, and it would gie me a rud face to ask for a mock valentine in such an illumination. Iss there no other wee dark shop in the toon we could get what we want in?"

The mate surveyed him with a disgusted countenance. "Man, you're a coward, Colin," he said. "The best in the land goes in and buys mock valentines, and it's no disgrace to nobody so long ass he has the money in his hand. If I had another gless o' beer I would go in mysel'."

"You'll get that!" said The Tar gladly, and produced another threepence, after which they returned to the shop-window, where Dougie's courage apparently failed him, in spite of the extra glass of beer. "It's no' that I give a docken for anybody," he explained, "but you see I'm that weel kent in Tarbert. What sort o' body keeps the shop ? "

" Och, it's chust an old done man wi' a sore hand and wan eye no' neebours," replied The Tar strategically. " Ye needna be frightened for him ; he'll no' say a cheep. To bleezes wi' him ! "

Dougie was greatly relieved at this intelligence. " Toots ! " he said. " Iss that aal ? Watch me ! " and he went banging in at the door in three strides.

The lady of the shop was in a room behind. To call her attention Dougie cried, " Shop ! " and kicked the front of the counter, with his eyes already on a pile of valentines ready for a rush of business in that elegant form of billet-doux. When the pretty girl came skipping out of the back room, he was even more astounded and alarmed than The Tar had been.

" A fine night," he remarked affably ; " iss your faither at the back ? "

" I think you must have made a mistake in the shop," said the lady. " Who do you want ? "

" Him with the sore hand and the wan eye no' right neebours," said the mate, not for a moment suspecting that The Tar had misled him. " It's parteecular business ; I'll no' keep him wan meenute."

" There's nobody here but myself," the girl informed him, and then he saw he had been deceived by his shipmate.

" Stop you till I get that Tar ! " he exclaimed with natural exasperation, and was on the point of leaving when the pile of valentines met his eye again, and he decided to brazen it out.

" Maybe you'll do yoursel'," said he, with an insinuating leer at the shopkeeper. " There iss a shipmate o' mine standin' oot there took a kind o notion o' a mock valentine and doesna like to ask for't. He wass in a meenute or two ago—you would know him by the warts on his hand— but he hadna the nerve to ask for it."

"There you are, all kinds," said the lady, indicating the pile on the counter, with a smile of comprehension. "A penny each."

Dougie wet his thumb and clumsily turned over the valentines, seeking for one appropriate to a sea captain silly enough to be teetotal. "It's chust for a baur, mind you," he explained to the lady. "No herm at aal, at aal; chust a bit of a high jeenk. Forbye, it's no' for me: it's for the other fellow, and his name's Colin Turner, but he's blate, blate." He raised his voice so that The Tar, standing outside the window, could hear him quite plainly; with the result that The Tar was so ashamed, he pulled down his cap on his face and hurriedly walked off to the quay.

"There's an awful lot o' them valentines for governesses and tylers and polismen," said Dougie; "the merchant service doesna get mich of a chance. Have you nothing smert and nippy that'll fit a sea captain, and him teetotal?"

The shopkeeper hurriedly went over her stock, and discovered that teetotalism was the one eccentricity valentines never dealt with; on the contrary, they were all for people with red noses and bibulous propensities.

"There's none for teetotal captains," said she; "but here's one for a captain that's not teetotal," and she shoved a valentine with a most unpleasant-looking seaman, in a state of intoxication, walking arm-in-arm with a respectable-looking young woman.

"Man, that's the very tup!" said Dougie, delighted. "It's ass clever a thing ass ever I seen. I wonder the way they can put them valentines thegather. Read what it says below, I havena my specs."

The shopkeeper read the verse on the valentine:

"The girl that would marry a man like you
    Would have all the rest of her life to rue;
A sailor soaked in salt water and rum
    Could never provide a happy home."

"Capital!" exclaimed the mate, highly delighted. "Ass smert ass anything in the works of Burns. That wan 'll do splendid."

"I thought it was for a teetotal captain you wanted one," said the lady, as she folded up the valentine.

"He's only teetotal to spite us," said Dougie. "And that valentine fits him fine, for he's coortin' a baker's weedow, and he thinks we don't know. Mind you, it's no' me that's goin' to send the valentine, it's Colin Turner; but there's no herm, chust a bit of a baur. You ken yoursel'."

Then an embarrassing idea occurred to him—Who was to address the envelope?

"Do you keep mournin' unvelopes?" he asked.

"Black-edged envelopes—yes," said the shopkeeper.

"Wan," said Dougie; and when he got it he put the valentine inside and ventured to propose to the lady that, seeing she had pen and ink handy, she might address the envelope for him, otherwise the recipient would recognise Colin Turner's hand-of-write.

The lady obliged, and addressed the document to

CAPTAIN PETER MACFARLANE,

SS. VITAL SPARK,

TARBERT.

Dougie thanked her effusively on behalf of The Tar, paid for his purchases and a penny stamp, and went out. As he found his shipmate gone, he sealed the envelope and posted it.

When the letter-carrier came down Tarbert quay next morning, all the crew of the *Vital Spark* were on deck—the Captain in blissful unconsciousness of what was in store for him, the others anxious not to lose the expression of his countenance when he should open his valentine.

It was a busy day on the *Vital Spark*; all hands had to help to get in a cargo of wood.

"A mournin' letter for you, Captain," said the letter-carrier, handing down the missive.

Para Handy looked startled, and walked aft to open it. He took one short but sufficient glimpse at the valentine, with a suspicious glance at the crew, who were apparently engrossed in admiration of the scenery round Tarbert. Then he went down the fo'c'sle, to come up a quarter of an hour later with his good clothes on, his hat, and a black tie.

" What the duvvle game iss he up to noo ? " said Dougie, greatly astonished.

" I hope it didna turn his brain," said The Tar. " A fright sometimes does it. Wass it a very wild valentine, Dougie ? "

Para Handy moved aft with a sad, resigned aspect, the mourning envelope in his hand. " I'm sorry I'll have to go away till the efternoon, boys," he said softly. " See and get in that wud nice and smert before I come back."

" What's wrong ? " asked Dougie mystified.

The Captain ostentatiously blew his nose, and explained that they might have noticed he had just got a mourning letter.

" Was't a mournin' wan ? I never noticed," said Dougie.

" Neither did I," added The Tar hurriedly.

" Yes," said the Captain sadly, showing them the envelope ; " my poor cousin Cherlie over in Dunmore iss no more ; he just slipped away yesterday, and I'm goin' to take the day off and make arrangements."

" Well, I'm jiggered ! " exclaimed Dougie, as they watched Para Handy walking off on what they realised was to be a nice holiday at their expense, for they would now have his share of the day's work to do as well as their own.

" Did ye ever see such a nate liar ? " said The Tar, lost in admiration at the cunning of the Captain.

And then they fell upon the engineer, and abused him for suggesting the valentine.

THE DISAPPOINTMENT OF ERCHIE'S NIECE

PARA HANDY never had been at a Glasgow ball till he went to the Knapdale Natives', and he went there simply to please Hurricane Jack. That gallant and dashing mariner came to him one day at Bowling, treated him to three substantial refreshments in an incredibly short space of time, and then delivered a brilliant lecture on the duty of being patriotic to one's native place, " backing up the boys," and buying a ticket for the assembly in question.

" But I'm not a native of Knapdale," said the Captain. " Forbye, I'm kind of oot o' the dancin' ; except La Va and Petronella I don't mind wan step."

" That's aal right, Peter," said Hurricane Jack encouragingly ; " there's nobody 'll make you dance at a Knapdale ball if you're no' in trum for dancin'. I can get you on the committee, and aal you'll have to do will be to stand at the door of the committee room and keep the crood back from the beer-bottles. I'm no' there mysel' for amusement : do you ken Jean Mactaggart ? "

" Not me," said Para Handy. " What Mactaggarts iss she off, Jeck ? "

" Carradale," said Hurricane Jack modestly. " A perfect beauty ! We're engaged."

The Captain shook hands mournfully with his friend and cheerlessly congratulated him. " It's a responsibulity, Jeck, he said, " there's no doot it's a responsibulity, but you ken yoursel' best."

" She's a nice enough gyurl so far ass I know," said Hurricane Jack. " Her brother 's in the Western Ocean tred What I'm wantin' you on the committee for iss to keep me back from the committee room, so that I'll not take a drop too much and affront the lassie. If you see me desperate keen on takin' more than would be dacent, take a dozen strong smert fellows in wi' you at my expense and barricade the door. I'll maybe taalk aboot tearin' the hoose doon, but och, that 'll only be my nonsense."

The Captain accepted the office, not without reluctance, and went to the ball, but Hurricane Jack failed to put in any appearance all night, and Para Handy considered himself the victim of a very stupid practical joke on the part of his friend.

Early next forenoon Hurricane Jack presented himself on board the *Vital Spark* and made an explanation. " I'm black affronted, Peter," he said, " but I couldna help it. I had a bit of an accident. You see it wass this way, Peter. Miss Mactaggart wass comin' special up from Carradale and stayin' with her uncle, old Macpherson. She wass to put her clothes on there, and I wass to caal for her in wan of them cabs at seven o'clock. I wass ready at five, all spruce from clew to earing, and my heid wass that sore wi' wearin a hat for baals that I got hold of a couple of men I knew in the China tred and went for chust wan small wee gless. What happened efter that for an oor or two's a mystery, but I think I wass drugged. When I got my senses I wass in a cab, and the driver roarin' doon the hatch to me askin' the address.

" ' What street iss it you're for ? ' said he.

" ' What streets have you ? ' I asked.

" ' Aal you told me wass Macfarlane's shup,' he said ; ' do you think we're anyway near it ? '

" When he said that I put my heid oot by the gless and took an observation.

" ' Iss this Carrick Street or Monday mornin' ? ' says I to him, and then he put me oot of his cab. The poor sowl had no fear in him ; he must have been Irish. It wass not much of a cab ; here's the door handles, a piece of the wud, and the man's brass number ; I chust took them with me for identification, and went home to my bed. When I wakened

this mornin' and thought of Jean sittin' up aal night waitin'
on me, I wass clean demented."

"It's a kind of a peety, too, the way it happened," said
Para Handy sympathetically. "It would put herself a bit
aboot sittin' aal night wi' her sluppers on."

"And a full set o' new sails," said Hurricane Jack pathetically. "She was sparin' no expense. This 'll be a lesson to
me. It 'll do me good ; I wish it hadna happened. What I
called for wass to see if you'll be kind enough, seein' you were
on the committee, to go up to 191 Barr Street, where she's
stayin' wi' Macpherson, and put the thing ass nicely for me
ass you can."

Para Handy was naturally shy of the proposal. "I never
saw the lassie," said he. "Would it no' look droll for me
to go instead of yoursel'."

"It would look droll if you didna," said Hurricane Jack
emphatically. "What are you on the committee for, and
in cherge of aal the beer, unless you're to explain things ?
I'll show you the close, and you'll go up and ask for two
meenutes' private conversation with Miss Mactaggart, and
you'll tell her that I'm far from weel. Say I wass on my way
up last night in fine time and the cab collided with a tramway
car. Break it nice, and no' frighten the poor gyurl oot of
her senses. Say I was oot of my conscience for seven 'oors,
but that I'm gettin' the turn, and I'm no' a bit disfigured."

Para Handy was still irresolute. "She'll maybe want to
nurse you, the way they do in Macphail's novelles," said he,
"and what 'll I tell her then ? "

This was a staggerer for Hurricane Jack. He recognised
the danger of arousing the womanly sympathies of Miss
Mactaggart. But he was equal to all difficulties of this
kind. "Tell her," said he, "there's nobody to get speakin'
to me for forty-eight 'oors, but that I'll likely be oot on
Monday."

The Captain agreed to undertake this delicate mission, but
only on condition that Dougie the mate should accompany

him to back him up in case his own resourcefulness as a liar should fail him at the critical moment.

"Very well," said Hurricane Jack, "take Dougie wi' you, but watch her uncle; I'm told he's cunning, cunning, though I never met him—a man Macpherson, by the name of Erchie. Whatever you tell her, if he's there at the time, tell it to her in the Gaalic."

Para Handy and his mate that evening left Hurricane Jack at a discreet public bar called the "Hot Blast," and went up to the house of Erchie Macpherson. It was himself who came to answer their knock at his door, for he was alone in the house.

"We're no' for ony strings o' onions, or parrots, or ony-thing o' that sort," he said, keeping one foot against the door and peering at them in the dim light of the rat-tail burner on the stair-landing. "And if it's the stair windows ye want to clean, they were done yesterday."

"You should buy specs," said the Captain promptly— "they're no' that dear. Iss Miss Mactaggart in?"

Erchie opened the door widely, and gave his visitors admission to the kitchen.

"She's no' in the noo," said he. "Which o' ye happens to be the sailor chap that was to tak' her to the ball last nicht?"

"It wasna any o' us," said Para Handy. "It wass another gentleman aalthegather."

"I micht hae kent that," said Erchie. "Whit lock-up is he in? If it's his bail ye're here for, ye needna bother. I aye tell't my guid-sister's dochter she wasna ill to please when she took up wi' a sailor. I had a son that was yince a sailor himself, but thank the Lord he's better, and he's in the Corporation noo. Were ye wantin' to see Jean?"

"Chust for a meenute," said Para Handy, quietly taking a seat on the jawbox. "Will she be long?"

"Five feet three," said Erchie, "and broad in proportion. She hasna come doon sae much as ye wad think at her disappointment.''

" That's nice," said Para Handy. " A thing o' the kind would tell terribly on some weemen. You're no' in the shuppin' tred yoursel', I suppose? I ken a lot o' Macphersons in the coast line. But I'm no' askin,' mind ye; it's chust for conversation. There wass a femily of Macphersons came from the same place ass mysel' on Lochfyne side; fine smert fellows they were, but I daresay no relation. Most respectable. Perhaps you ken the Gaalic? ''

" Not me! '' said Erchie frankly—" jist plain Gleska. If I'm Hielan' I canna help it; my faither took the boat to the Broomielaw as soon as he got his senses.''

The conversation would have languished here if Dougie had not come to the rescue. " What's your tred? '' he asked bluntly.

" Whiles I beadle and whiles I wait," replied Erchie, who was not the man to be ashamed of his calling. " At ither times I jist mind my ain affairs; ye should gie 't a trial —it'll no hurt ye.''

The seamen laughed at this sally: it was always a virtue of both of them, that they could appreciate a joke at their own expense.

" No offence, no offence, Mr Macpherson," said Para Handy. " I wish your niece would look slippy. You'll be sorry to hear aboot what happened to poor Jeck.''

Erchie turned quite serious. " What's the maitter wi' him? '' he said.

" The cab broke doon last night," said the Captain solemnly, " and he got a duvvle of a smash.''

" Puir sowl! '' said Erchie, honestly distressed. " This'll be a sair blow for Jeanie.''

" He lost his conscience for 'oors, but there's no disfeegurement, and he'll be speechless till Monday mornin'. It's a great peety. Such a splendid voice ass he had, too; it wass truly sublime. He's lyin' yonder wi' his heid in a sling and not wan word in him. He tell't me I was to say to——"

Here Dougie, seeing an inconsistency in the report, slyly nudged his captain, who stopped short and made a very good effort at a sigh of deep regret.

" I thocht ye said he couldna speak," said Erchie suspiciously.

" My mistake, my mistake," said the Captain. " What I meant wass that he could only speak in the Gaalic ; the man's fair off his usual.   Dougie 'll tell you himsel'."

Dougie shook his head lugubriously. " Ay," said he, " he's yonder wi' fifteen doctors roond him waitin' for the turn."

" What time did it happen ? " inquired Erchie. " Was it efter he was here ? "

" He wass on his way here," said Para Handy. " It was exactly half-past seven, for his watch stopped in the smash."

At this Erchie sat back in his chair and gave a disconcerting laugh. " Man," he said, " ye're no' bad at a baur, but ye've baith put yer feet in't this time. Will ye tak' a refreshment ?   There's a drop speerits in the hoose and a bottle or two o' porter."

" I'm teetotal mysel' at present," said Para Handy, " but I have a nesty cold.   I'll chust take the spurits while you're pullin' the porter.   We'll drink a quick recovery to Jeck."

" Wi' a' my he'rt," said Erchie agreeably.   " I hope he'll be oot again afore Monday. Do ye no' ken he came here last nicht wi' the cab a' richt, but was that dazed Jeanie wadna gang wi' him.   But she got to the ball a' the same, for she went wi' Mackay the polisman."

" My Chove ! " said the Captain, quite dumbfoundered. " He doesna mind, himsel', a thing aboot it."

" I daresay no'," said Erchie, " that's the warst o' trevellin' in cabs ; he should hae come in a motor-caur."

When the Captain and Dougie came down Macpherson's stair, they considered the situation in the close.

" I think mysel'," said the Captain, " it wouldna be salubrious for neither o' the two of us to go to the ' Hot Blast ' and break the news to Jeck the night."

" Whatever ye think yoursel'," said Dougie, and they headed straight for home.

XXV

PARA HANDY'S WEDDING

IT is possible that Para Handy might still have been a bachelor if Calum Cameron had not been jilted. Three days before Calum was to have been married, the girl exercised a girl's privilege and changed her mind. She explained her sad inconstancy by saying she had never cared for him, and only said " yes " to get him off her face. It was an awkward business, because it left the baker's widow, Mrs Crawford, with a large bride's-cake on her hands. It is true the bride's-cake had been paid for, but in the painful circumstances neither of the parties to the broken contract would have anything to do with it, and it continued to lie in the baker's window, a pathetic evidence of woman's perfidy. All Campbeltown talked about it ; people came five and six miles in from the country to look at it. When they saw what a handsome example of the confectioner's art it was, they shook their heads and said the lassie could have no heart, let alone good taste.

Mrs Crawford, being a smart business woman, put a bill in the window with the legend—

EXCELLENT BRIDE'S-CAKE
SECOND-HAND
17/6

But there were no offers, and she was on the point of disposing of it on the Art Union principle, when, by one of those providential accidents that are very hard on the sufferer but lead by a myriad consequent circumstances to the most beneficent ends, a man in Carrick Street, Glasgow, broke his leg. The man never heard of Para Handy in all his life, nor of the *Vital Spark* ; he had never been in Campbeltown, and if he had not kept a pet tortoise he would never have figured in this book, and Para Handy might not have been married, even though Calum Cameron's girl had been a jilt.

The Carrick Street man's tortoise had wandered out into the close in the evening ; the owner, rushing out hurriedly at three minutes to ten to do some shopping, tripped over it, and was not prevented by the agony of his injured limb from seizing the offending animal and throwing it into the street, where it fell at the feet of Para Handy, who was passing at the time.

"A tortoise ! " said the Captain, picking it up. " The first time ever I kent they flew. I'll take it to Macphail —he's keen on birds anyway," and down he took it to the engineer of the *Vital Spark*.

But Macphail refused to interest himself in a pet which commended itself neither by beauty of plumage nor sweetness of song, and for several days the unhappy tortoise took a deck passage on the *Vital Spark*, its constitution apparently little impaired by the fact that at times The Tar used it as a coal-hammer.

" I'll no' see the poor tortoise abused this way," said Para Handy, when they got to Campbeltown one day ; " I'll take it up and give it to a friend o' mine," and, putting it into his pocket in the evening, he went up to the baker's shop.

The widow was at the moment fixing a card on the bride's-cake intimating that tickets for the raffle of it would cost sixpence each, and that the drawing would take place on the following Saturday. Her plump form was revealed in the small shop-window ; the flush of exertion charmingly irradiated her countenance as she bent among her penny buns and bottles of fancy biscuits ; Para Handy, gazing at her from the outside, thought he had never seen her look more attractive. She blushed more deeply when she saw him looking in at her, and retired from the window with some embarrassment as he entered the shop.

"Fine night, Mery," said the Captain. "You're pushin' business desperate, surely, when you're raffling bride's-cakes."

"Will you not buy a ticket ? " said the lady smiling. "You might be the lucky man to get the prize."

"And what in the world would I do wi' a bride's-cake ? " asked the Captain, his manly sailor's heart in a gentle palpitation. "Where would I get a bride to—to—to fit it ? "

"I'm sure and I don't know," said the widow hurriedly, and she went on to explain the circumstances that had left it on her hands. The Captain listened attentively, eyed the elegant proportions of the cake in the window, and was seized by a desperate resolve.

"I never saw a finer bride's-cake," he said ; "it's chust sublime ! Do you think it would keep till the Gleska Fair ? "

"It would keep a year for that part o't," said the widow. "What are you askin' that for ? "

"If it'll keep to the Fair, and the Fair suits yoursel'," said Para Handy boldly, "we'll have it between us. What do you say to that, Mery ? " and he leaned amorously over the counter.

"Mercy on me ! this is no' the New Year time," exclaimed the widow ; "I thought you never had any mind of me except at the New Year. Is this a proposal, Captain ? "

"Don't caal me Captain, caal me Peter, and gie me a haad o' your hand," entreated Para Handy languishingly.

"Well, then—Peter," murmured the widow, and the Captain went back to the *Vital Spark* that night an engaged man : the bride's-cake was withdrawn from the window, and the tortoise took up its quarters in the back shop.

.   .   .   .

Of all the ordeals Para Handy had to pass through before his marriage, there was none that troubled him more than his introduction to her relatives, and the worst of them was Uncle Alick, who was very old, very deaf, and very averse to his niece marrying again. The Captain and his " fiancée " visited him as in duty bound, and found him in a decidedly unfavourable temper.

" This is Peter," said the widow by way of introduction ; and the Captain stood awkwardly by her side, with his pea-jacket tightly buttoned to give him an appearance of slim, sprightly, and dashing youthfulness.

" What Peter ? " asked the uncle, not taking his pipe out of his mouth, and looking with a cold, indifferent eye upon his prospective relative.

" You know fine," said the lady, flushing. " It's my lad."

" What did you say ? " inquired Uncle Alick, with a hand behind his ear.

" My lad," she cried. " Peter Macfarlane—him that's Captain on the *Vital Spark*."

" Catched him in a park," said Uncle Alick. " I'll wudger you didna need to run fast to catch him. Whatna park was it ? "

" The *Fital Spark*," roared the Captain, coming to Mary's assistance. " I'm captain on her."

" Are you, are you ? " said Uncle Alick querulously. " Weel, you needna roar at me like that ; I'm no' that deaf. You'll be wan o' the Macfarlanes from Achnatra ; they were aal kind of droll in the mind, but hermless."

The Captain explained that he was a member of a different family altogether, but Uncle Alick displayed no interest in the explanation. " It's none of my business," said he.

" Mery thinks it is," rejoined the Captain. " That's the reason we're here."

" Beer ! " said Uncle Alick. " No, no, I have no beer for you. I never keep drink of any sort in the hoose."

" I never said beer," exclaimed Para Handy.

"I'll be telling a lie then," said Uncle Alick. "The same ass if I didn't hear you with my own ears. You'll be the man that Mery's goin' to merry. I canna understand her; I'm sure she had plenty of trouble wi' Donald Crawford before he went and died on her. But it's none o' my business: I'm only an old done man, no' long for this world, and I'm not goin' to interfere wi' her if she wass to merry a bleck. She never consulted me, though I'm the only uncle she has. You shouldna put yoursel's to bother tellin' me anything aboot it; I'm sure I would have heard aboot it from some o' the neebours. The neebours iss very good to me. They're sayin' it's a droll-like thing Mery merryin' again, and her wi' a nice wee shop o' her own. What I says to them iss, 'It's her own business: perhaps she sees something takin' in the man that nobody else does. Maybe,' I says to them, 'he'll give up his vessel and help her in the shop.'"

"Och, you're chust an old haiver!" remarked the Captain *sotto voce*, and of course the deaf man heard him.

"A haiver!" said he. "A nice-like thing to say aboot the only uncle Mery has, and him over eighty-six. But you're no' young yoursel'. Maybe it wass time for you to be givin' up the boats."

"I'm no' thinkin' o' givin' them up, Uncle," said Para Handy cheerfully. "The *Vital Spark*'s the smertest boat in the tred. A bonny-like hand I would be in a shop. No, no, herself here—Mery, can keep the shop or leave it, chust ass it pleases hersel', it's aal wan to me; I'm quite joco. I hope you'll turn up at the weddin' on the fufteenth, for aal langsyne."

"What's your wull?" inquired Uncle Alick.

"I hope you'll turn up at the weddin' and give us support," bellowed the Captain.

"Give you sport," said the old man indignantly. "You'll surely get plenty of sport withoot takin' it off a poor old man like me."

"Och! to the muschief!" exclaimed the Captain somewhat impatiently. " Here's a half pound o' tobacco me and Mery brought you, and surely that 'll put you in better trum."

" What wey did you no' say that at first ? " said Uncle Alick. " Hoo wass I to know you werena wantin' the lend o' money for the weddin' ? Stop you and I'll see if there's any spurits handy."

.   .   .   .   .   .

I was not at the wedding, but the Captain told me all about it some days afterwards. " It would be worth a bit in the papers," he said with considerable elation. " I'll wudger there wasna another weddin' like it in Kintyre for chenerations. The herrin' trawlers iss not back at their work yet, and herrin's up ten shullin's a box in Gleska. Dougie and The Tar and their wifes wass there, quite nate and tidy, and every noo and then Macphail would be comin' doon to the boat and blowin' her whustle. Och, he's not a bad chap Macphail, either, but chust stupid with readin' them novelles.

" I never saw Mery lookin' more majestic ; she wass chust sublime ! Some of them said I wassna lookin' slack mysel', and I daarsay no', for I wass in splendid trum. When the knot was tied, and we sat doon to a bite, I found it wass a different bride's-cake aalthegither from the wan that julted Cameron.

" ' What's the meanin' of that ? ' I whuspered to the mustress. ' That's no' the bride's-cake you had in the window.'

" ' No,' says she, ' but it's a far better one, isn't it ? '

" ' It's a better-lookin' wan,' I says, ' but the other wan might have done the business.'

" ' Maybe it would,' she said, ' but I have all my wuts aboot me, and I wasna goin' to have the neighbours say that both the bride and bride's-cake were second-hand.' Oh ! I'm tellin' you she's a smert wan the mustress ! "

" Well, I wish you and your good lady long life and happiness, Captain," I said.

" Thanky, thanky," said he. " I'll tell the mustress.

Could you no put a bit in the papers sayin', ' The rale an
only belle o' Captain Macfarlane's weddin' wass the young
lady first in the grand merch, dressed in broon silk.' "

"Who was the young lady dressed in brown?" I asked.

"What need you ask for?" he replied. "Who would it
be but the mustress?"

IN HIGHLAND
HARBOURS WITH
PARA HANDY
S.S. *VITAL SPARK*

IN HIGHLAND
HARBOURS WITH
PARA HANDY

A NEW COOK

THE s.s. *Texa* made a triumphal entry to the harbour by steaming in between two square-rigged schooners, the *Volant* and *Jehu*, of Wick, and slid silently, with the exactitude of long experience, against the piles of Rothesay quay, where Para Handy sat on a log of wood. The throb of her engine, the wash of her propeller, gave place to the strains of a melodeon, which was playing "Stop yer ticklin', Jock," and Para Handy felt some sense of gaiety suffuse him, but business was business, and it was only for a moment he permitted himself to be carried away on the divine wings of music.

"Have you anything for me, M'Kay?" he hailed the *Texa's* clerk.

The purser cast a rapid glance over the deck, encumbered with planks, crates, casks of paraffin oil, and herring-boxes, and seeing nothing there that looked like a consignment for the questioner, leaned across the rail, and made a rapid survey of the open hold. It held nothing maritime—only hay-bales, flour-bags, soap-boxes, shrouded mutton carcases, rolls of plumbers' lead, two head-stones for Ardrishaig, and the dismantled slates, cushions, and legs of a billiard-table for Strachur.

"Naething the day for you, Peter," said the clerk; "unless it's yin o' the heid-stanes," and he ran his eye down the manifest which he held in his hand.

" Ye're aawful smert, M'Kay," said Para Handy.   " If ye wass a rale purser wi' brass buttons and a yellow-and-black strippit tie on your neck, there would be no haadin' ye in ! It's no' luggage I'm lookin' for ; it's a kind o' a man I'm expectin'.   Maybe he's no' in your depairtment ; he'll be traivellin' saloon.   Look behind wan o' them herring-boxes, Lachie, and see if ye canna see a sailor."

His intuition was right ; the *Texa's* only passenger that afternoon was discovered sitting behind the herring-boxes playing a melodeon, and smiling beatifically to himself, with blissful unconsciousness that he had arrived at his destination.   He came to himself with a start when the purser asked him if he was going off here ; terminated the melody of his instrument in a melancholy squawk, picked up a carelessly-tied canvas bag that lay at his feet, and hurried over the plank to the quay, shedding from the bag as he went a trail of socks, shoes, collars, penny ballads, and seaman's biscuits, whose exposure in this awkward fashion seemed to cause him no distress of mind, for he only laughed when Para Handy called them to his attention, and left to one of the *Texa's* hands the trouble of collecting them, though he obligingly held the mouth of the sack open himself while the other restored the dunnage.   He was a round, short, red-faced, clean-shaven fellow of five-and-twenty, with a thin serge suit, well polished at all the bulgy parts, and a laugh that sprang from a merry heart.

" Are you The Tar's kizzen ?   Are you Davie Green ? " asked Para Handy.

" Right-oh !   The very chap," said the stranger.   " And you'll be Peter ?   Haud my melodeon, will ye, till I draw my breath.   Right-oh ! "

" Are ye sure there's no mistake ? " asked Para Handy as they moved along to the other end of the quay where the *Vital Spark* was lying.   " You're the new hand I wass expectin', and your name's Davie ? "

" My name's Davie, richt enough," said the stranger, " but

I seldom got it ; when I was on the Cluthas they always ca'd me Sunny Jim."

"Sunny Jum!" said the Captain. "Man! I've often heard aboot ye ; you were namely for chumpin' fences ? "

"Not me !" said Davie. "Catch me jumpin' onything if there was a hole to get through. Is that your vessel ? She's a tipper ! You and me 'll get on A1. Wait you till ye see the fun I'll gie ye ! That was the worst o' the Cluthas— awfu' short trips, and every noo and then a quay ; ye hadn't a meenute to yerself for a baur at all. Whit sort o' chaps hae ye for a crew ? "

"The very pick !" said Para Handy, as they came along-side the *Vital Spark*, whose crew, as a matter of fact, were all on deck to see the new hand. "That's Macphail, the chief enchineer, wan of Brutain's hardy sons, wi' the wan gallows ; and the other chap's Dougie, the first mate, a Cowal laad ; you'll see him plainer efter his face iss washed for the tea. Then there's me, mysel', the Captain. Laads, this iss Colin's kizzen, Sunny Jum."

Sunny Jim stood on the edge of the quay, and smiled like a sunset on his future shipmates. "Hoo are yez, chaps ? " he cried genially, waving his hand.

"We canna compleen," said Dougie solemnly. "Are ye in good trum yersel' ? See's a grup o' your hold-aal, and excuse the gangway."

Sunny Jim jumped on board, throwing his dunnage-bag before him, and his feet had no sooner touched the deck than he indulged in a step or two of the sailor's hornpipe with that proficiency which only years of practice in a close-mouth in Crown Street, S.S., could confer. The Captain looked a little embarrassed ; such conduct was hardly business-like, but it was a relief to find that The Tar's nominee and successor was a cheery chap at any rate. Dougie looked on with no disapproval, but Macphail grunted and turned his gaze to sea, disgusted at such free-and-easy informality.

" I hope ye can cook as weel's ye can dance," he remarked coldly.

Sunny Jim stopped immediately. " Am I supposed to cook ? " he asked, concealing his surprise as he best could.

" Ye are that ! " said Macphail. " Did ye think ye were to be the German band on board, and go roon' liftin' pennies ? Cookin's the main thing wi' the second mate o' the *Vital Spark*, and I can tell ye we're gey particular ; are we no', Dougie ? "

" Aawful ! " said Dougie sadly. " Macphail here hass been cookin' since The Tar left ; he'll gie ye his receipt for haddies made wi' enchine-oil."

The *Vital Spark* cast off from Rothesay Quay on her way for Bowling, and Sunny Jim was introduced to several pounds of sausages to be fried for dinner, a bag of potatoes, and a jar of salt, with which he was left to juggle as he could, while the others, with expectant appetites, performed their respective duties. Life on the open sea, he found, was likely to be as humdrum as it used to be on the Cluthas, and he determined to initiate a little harmless gaiety. With some difficulty he extracted all the meat from the uncooked sausages, and substituted salt. Then he put them on the frying-pan. They had no sooner heated than they began to dance in the pan with curious little crackling explosions. He started playing his melodeon, and cried on the crew, who hurried to see this unusual phenomenon.

" Well, I'm jeegered," said the Captain ; " what in aal the world iss the matter wi' them ? "

" It's a waarnin'," said Dougie lugubriously, with wide-staring eyes.

" Warnin', my auntie ! " said Sunny Jim, playing a jig-tune. " They started jumpin' like that whenever I begood to play my bonnie wee melodeon."

" I daarsay that," said Para Handy ; " for you're a fine, fine player, Jum, but—but it wassna any invitation to a baal I gave them when I paid for them in Ro'sa'."

"I aye said sausages werena meat for sailors," remarked the engineer, with bitterness, for he was very hungry. "Ye'll notice it's an Irish jig they're dancin' to," he added with dark significance.

"I don't see mysel'," said the Captain, "that it matters whether it iss an Irish jeeg or the Gourock Waltz and Circassian Circle."

"Does it no'?" retorted Macphail. "I suppose ye'll never hae heard o' Irish terrier dugs? I've ett my last sausage onywye! Sling us ower that pan-loaf," and seizing the bread for himself he proceeded to make a spartan meal.

Sunny Jim laughed till the tears ran down his jovial countenance. "Chaps," he exclaimed, with firm conviction, "this is the cheeriest ship ever I was on; I'm awful gled I brung my music."

Dougie took a fork and gingerly investigated. "As hard ass whun-stanes!" he proclaimed; "they'll no' be ready by the time we're at the Tail o' the Bank. Did you ever in your mortal life see the like of it?" and he jabbed ferociously with the fork at the bewitched sausages.

"That's richt!" said Macphail. "Put them oot o' pain."

"Stop you!" said Para Handy. "Let us pause and consuder. It iss the first time ever I saw sassages with such a desperate fine ear for music. If they'll no' fry, they'll maybe boil. Put them in a pot, Jum."

"Right-oh!" said Sunny Jim, delighted at the prospect of a second scene to his farce, and the terpsichorean sausages were consigned to the pot of water which had boiled the potatoes. The crew sat round, staving off the acuter pangs of hunger with potatoes and bread.

"You never told us what for they called you Sunny Jum, Davie," remarked the Captain. "Do you think it would be for your complexion?"

"I couldna say," replied the new hand, "but I think mysel' it was because I was aye such a cheery wee chap.

The favourite Clutha on the Clyde, when the Cluthas was rinnin', was the yin I was on ; hunners o' trips used to come wi' her on the Setturdays on the aff-chance that I wad maybe gie them a baur. Mony a pant we had ! I could hae got a job at the Finnieston Ferry richt enough, chaps, but they wouldna alloo the melodeon, and I wad sooner want my wages."

" A fine, fine unstrument ! " said Para Handy agreeably. " Wi' it and Dougie's trump we'll no' be slack in passin' the time."

" Be happy !—that's my motto," said Sunny Jim beaming upon his auditors like one who brings a new and glorious evangel. " Whatever happens, be happy, and then ye can defy onything. It's a' in the wye ye look at things. See ? "

" That's what I aalways say mysel' to the wife," said Dougie in heart-broken tones, and his eye on the pot, which was beginning to boil briskly.

" As shair as daith, chaps, I canna stand the Jock o' Hazeldean kind o' thing at a'—folk gaun aboot lettin' the tear doon-fa a' the time. Gie me a hearty laugh and it's right-oh ! BE HAPPY !—that's the Golden Text for the day, as we used to say in the Sunday School."

" I could be happy easy enough if it wassna that I wass so desperate hungry," said Dougie in melancholy accents, lifting the lid to look into the pot. He could see no sign of sausages, and with new forebodings he began to feel for them with a stick. They had disappeared ! " I said from the very first it wass a waarnin' ! " he exclaimed, resigning the stick to the incredulous engineer.

" This boat's haunted," said Macphail, who also failed to find anything in the pot. " I saw ye puttin' them in wi' my ain eyes, and noo they're no' there."

Para Handy grabbed the spirtle, and feverishly explored on his own account, with the same extraordinary results.

" My Chove ! " he exclaimed, " did you ever see the like of that, and I havena tasted wan drop of stimulants since

last Monday.   Laads !   I don't know what you think aboot
it, but it's the church twice for me to-morrow ! "

Sunny Jim quite justified his nickname by giving a pleasant
surprise to his shipmates in the shape of a meat-tea later in
the afternoon.

PENSION FARMS

THE *Vital Spark* was making for Lochgoilhead, Dougie at
the wheel, and the Captain straddled on a water-breaker,
humming Gaelic songs, because he felt magnificent after his
weekly shave.   The chug-chug-chug of the engines was the
only other sound that broke the silence of the afternoon,
and Sunny Jim deplored the fact that in the hurry of em-
barking early in the morning he had quite forgotten his
melodeon—those peaceful days at sea hung heavy on his
urban spirit.

" That's Ardgoil," remarked Macphail, pointing with the
stroup of an oil-can at the Glasgow promontory, and Para
Handy gazed at the land with affected interest.

" So it iss, Macphail," he said ironically.   " That wass it
the last time we were here, and the time before, and the
time before that again.   You would think it would be shifted.
It's wan of them guides for towerists you should be, Macphail,
you're such a splendid hand for information.   What way do
you spell it ? "

" Oh, shut up ! " said the engineer with petulance ; " ye
think ye're awfu' clever.   I mind when that wee hoose at
the p'int was a hen farm, and there's no' a road to't.   Ye
could only get near the place wi' a boat."

" If that wass the way of it," said Dougie, " ducks would
suit them better ; they could swim.   It's a fine thing a
duck."

" But a goose is more extraordinar'," said Macphail with

meaning. " Anyway it was hens, and mony a time I wished
I had a ferm for hens."

" You're better where you are," said the Captain, " oilin'
engines like a chentleman. A hen ferm iss an aawful speculation, and you need your wuts aboot you if you start wan.
All your relations expect their eggs for nothing, and the
very time o' the year when eggs iss dearest, hens takes a
tirrievee and stop the layin'. Am I no' tellin' the truth,
Dougie ? "

" You are that ! " said the mate agreeably ; " I have
noticed it mysel'."

" If ye didna get eggs ye could live aff the chickens,"
suggested Sunny Jim. " I think a hen ferm would be top,
richt enough ! "

" It's not the kind o' ferm I would have mysel' whatever
o't," said Para Handy; " there's far more chance o' a dacent
livin' oot o' rearin' pensioners."

" Rearin' pensioners ? " remarked Macphail ; " ye would
lie oot o' your money a lang while rearin' pensioners ; ye
micht as weel start growin' trees."

" Not at aal ! not at aal ! " said Para Handy ; " there's
quick returns in pensioners if you put your mind to the thing
and use a little caation. Up in the Islands, now, the folks
iss givin' up their crofts and makin' a kind o' ferm o' their
aged relations. I have a cousin yonder oot in Gigha wi' a
stock o' five fine healthy uncles—no' a man o' them under
seventy. There's another frien' o' my own in Mull wi'
thirteen heid o' chenuine old Macleans. He gaithered them
aboot the islands wi' a boat whenever the rumours o' the pensions started. Their frien's had no idea what he wanted wi'
them, and were glad to get them off their hands. ' It's
chust a notion that I took,' he said, ' for company ; they're
great amusement on a winter night,' and he got his pick o'
the best o' them. It wassna every wan he would take ;
they must be aal Macleans, for the Mull Macleans never
die till they're centurions, and he wouldna take a man that

wass over five and seventy. They're yonder, noo, in Loch Scridain, kept like fightin' cocks ; he puts them oot on the hill each day for exercise, and if wan o' them takes a cough they dry his clothes and give him something from a bottle."

" Holy smoke ! " said Dougie ; " where's the profits comin' from ? "

" From the Government," said Para Handy. " Nothing simpler ! He gets five shillings a heid in the week for them, and that's £169 in the year for the whole thirteen—enough to feed a regiment ! Wan pensioner maybe wadna pay you, but if you have a herd like my frien' in Mull, there's money in it. He buys their meal in bulk from Oban, and they'll grow their own potatoes ; the only thing he's vexed for iss that they havena wool, and he canna clip them. If he keeps his health himsel', and doesna lose his heid for a year or twa, he'll have the lergest pension ferm in Scotland, and be able to keep a gig. I'm no' a bit feared for Donald, though ; he's a man o' business chust ass good ass you'll get on the streets o' Gleska."

" Thirteen auld chaps like that aboot a hoose wad be an awfu' handful," suggested Sunny Jim.

" Not if it's at Loch Scridain," answered Para Handy ; " half the time they're on the gress, and there's any amount o' fanks. They're quite delighted swappin' baurs wi' wan another aboot the way they could throw the hammer fifty years ago, and they feel they're more important noo than ever they were in a' their lives afore. When my frien' collected them, they hadna what you would caal an object for to live for except it wass their own funerals ; noo they're daft for almanacs, and makin' plans for living to a hundred, when the fermer tells them that he'll gie them each a medal and a uniform. Oh ! a smert, smert laad, Donal'. Wan o' Brutain's hardy sons ! Nobody could be kinder ! "

" It's a fine way o' makin' a livin'," said Macphail. " I hope they'll no' go wrang wi' him."

" Fine enough," said Para Handy, " but the chob iss not

withoot responsibilities. Yonder's my cousin in Gigha wi'
his stock o' five, and a nice bit ground for them, and you
wouldna believe what it needs in management. He got two
of them pretty cheap in Salen, wan o' them over ninety, and
the other eighty-six ; you wouldna believe it, but they're
worse to manage than the other three that's ten years
younger. The wan over ninety's very cocky of his age, and
thinks the other wans iss chust a lot o' boys. He says it's a
scandal givin' them a pension ; pensions should be kept for
men that's up in years, and then it should be something
sensible—something like a pound. The wan that iss eighty-
six iss desperate dour, and if my cousin doesna please him,
stays in his bed and says he'll die for spite.''

" That's gey mean, richt enough ! " said Sunny Jim ;
" efter your kizzen takin' a' that trouble ! "

" But the worst o' the lot's an uncle that he got in Eigg ;
he's seventy-six, and talkin' aboot a wife ! "

" Holy smoke ! " said Dougie ; " isn't that chust desperate ! "

" Ay ; he hass a terrible conceity notion o' his five shillin's
a-week ; you would think he wass a millionaire. ' I could
keep a wife on it if she wass young and strong,' he tells my
cousin, and it takes my cousin and the mustress aal their
time to keep him oot o' the way o' likely girls. They don't
ken the day they'll lose him.''

" Could they no' put a brand on him ? " asked Dougie.

" Ye daurna brand them,'' said the Captain, " nor keel
them either. The law 'll not allo' it. So you see yersel's
there's aye a risk, and it needs a little capital. My cousin
had a bit of a shop, and he gave it up to start the pension
ferm ; he'll be sayin' sometimes it wass a happier man
he wass when he wass a merchant, but he's awfu' prood
that noo he hass a chob, as you might say, wi' the Brutish
Government.''

PARA HANDY'S PUP

ONE night when the *Vital Spark* lay at Port Ellen quay, and all the crew were up the village at a shinty concert, some one got on board the vessel and stole her best chronometer. It was the property of Macphail, had cost exactly 1s. 11½d., and kept approximate time for hours on end if laid upon its side. Macphail at frequent intervals repaired it with pieces of lemonade wire, the selvedges of postage stamps, and a tube of seccotine.

"Holy smoke!" said the Captain, when the loss was discovered; "we'll be sleepin' in in the efternoons as sure as anything. Isn't this the depredation!"

"The champion wee nock!" said Macphail, on the verge of tears. "Set it to the time fornenst yon nock o' Singerses at Kilbowie, and it would tick as nate as onything to the Cloch."

"Right enough!" said Sunny Jim impressively; "I've biled eggs wi't. There's the very nail it hung on!"

"It's the first time I ever knew that nock to go without Macphail doin' something to it wi' the stroup o' an oil-can," said Dougie.

It was decided that no more risks of quay-head burglary were to be run, and that when evening entertainments called the rest of the crew ashore, the charge of the ship should depend on Sunny Jim.

"I couldna tak' it in haund, chaps!" he protested feelingly. "Ye've nae idea hoo silly I am at nicht when I'm my lane; I cod mysel' I'm seein' ghosts till every hair on my heid's on end."

"I'm like that mysel'!" confessed Para Handy. "I can gie mysel' a duvvle o' a fright, but it's only nonsense, chust fair nonsense! there's no' a ghost this side o' the Sound o' Sleat; nothing but imagination."

"Ye shouldna be tumid!" counselled Dougie, who never

could stay in the fo'c'sle alone at night himself for fear of spirits.

" Ye'll can play your melodian," said Macphail; " if there's onything to scare the life oot o' ghosts it's that."

But Sunny Jim was not to be induced to run the risk, and the Captain wasn't the sort of man to compel a body to do a thing he didn't like to do, against his will. Evening entertainments at the ports of call were on the point of being regretfully foresworn, when Sunny Jim proposed the purchase of a watch-dog. " A watch-dug's the very ticket," he exclaimed. " It's an awfu' cheery thing on a boat. We can gie't the rin o' the deck when we're ashore at nicht, and naebody 'll come near't. I ken the very dug—it belangs to a chap in Fairfield, a rale Pompanion, and he ca's it Biler. It has a pedigree and a brass-mounted collar, and a' its P's and Q's."

" Faith ! there's worse things than a good dog ; there's some o' them chust sublime ! " said Para Handy, quite enamoured of the notion. " Iss it well trained, your frien's Pompanion ? "

" Top ! " Sunny Jim assured him. " If ye jist seen it ! It would face a regiment o' sodgers, and has a bark ye could hear from here to Campbeltown. It's no awfu' fancy-lookin', mind ; it's no' the kind ye'll see the women carryin' doon Buchanan Street in their oxters ; but if ye want sagaciosity——! " and Sunny Jim held up his hands in speechless admiration of the animal's intelligence. " It belangs to a rivetter ca'd Willie Stevenson, and it's jist a pup. There's only the wan fau't wi't, or Willie could live aff the prizes it wad lift at shows—it's deaf."

" That's the very sort o' dug we wad need for a boat like this," said Macphail, with his usual cynicism. " Could ye no' get yin that was blin' too ? " But nobody paid any attention to him ; there were moments when silent contempt was the obvious attitude to the engineer.

" The worst about a fine, fine dog like that," said Para

Handy reflectively, " iss that it would cost a lot o' money, and aal we want iss a dog to watch the boat and bark daily or hourly ass required."

" Cost ! " retorted Sunny Jim ; " it wad cost naething ! I wad ask Willie Stevenson for the len' o't, and then say we lost it ower the side. It has far mair sense than Willie himsel'. It goes aboot Govan wi' him on pay Setturdays, and sleeps between his feet when he's sittin' in the public-hooses backin' up the Celts. Sometimes Willie forgets it's wi' him, and gangs awa' without waukenin' 't, but when Biler waukens up and sees its maister's no there, it stands on its hind legs and looks at the gless that Willie was drinkin' frae. If there's ony drink left in't it kens he'll be back, and it waits for him."

" Capital ! " said Para Handy. " There's dogs like that. It's born in them. It's chust a gift ! "

The dog Biler was duly borrowed by Sunny Jim on the next run to Glasgow, and formally installed as watch of the *Vital Spark*. It was distinctly not the sort of dog to make a lady's pet ; its lines were generously large, but crude and erratic ; its coat was hopelessly unkempt and ragged, its head incredibly massive, and its face undeniably villain-ous. Even Sunny Jim was apologetic when he produced it on a chain. " Mind, I never said he was onything awfu' fancy," he pleaded. " But he's a dug that grows on ye."

" He's no' like what I thocht he would be like at aal, at aal," admitted the Captain, somewhat disappointed. " Iss he a rale Pompanion ? "

" Pure bred ! " said Sunny Jim ; " never lets go the grip. Examine his jaw."

" Look you at his jaw, Dougie, and see if he's the rale Pompanion," said the Captain ; but Dougie declined. " I'll wait till we're better acquent," he said. " Man ! doesn't he look desperate dour ? "

" Oor new nock's a' richt wi' a dug like that to watch it," said Macphail ; " he's as guid as a guardship."

Biler surveyed them curiously, not very favourably impressed, and deaf, of course, to all blandishments. For a day or two the slightest hasty movement on the part of any of his new companions made him growl ferociously and display an appalling arsenal of teeth. As a watch-dog he was perfect ; nobody dared come down a quay within a hundred yards of the *Vital Spark* without his loud, alarming bay. Biler spoiled the quay-head angling all along Loch Fyne.

In a week or two Para Handy got to love him, and bragged incessantly of his remarkable intelligence. " Chust a pup ! " he would say, " but as long in the heid as a weedow woman. If he had aal his faculties he would not be canny, and indeed he doesna seem to want his hearin' much ; he's ass sharp in the eye ass a polisman. A dog like that should have a Board of Tred certuficate."

Dougie, however, was always dubious of the pet. " Take my word, Peter," he would say solemnly, " there's muschief in him ; he's no a dog you can take to your he'rt at aal, at aal, and he barks himsel' black in the face wi' animosity at Macphail."

" Didn't I tell you ? " would the Captain cry, exultant. " Ass deaf ass a door, and still he can take the measure o' Macphail ! I hope, Jum, your frien' in Fairfield's no' in a hurry to get him back."

" Not him," said Sunny Jim. " He's no expectin' him back at a'. I tell't him Biler was drooned at Colintraive, and a' he said was ' ye micht hae tried to save his collar.' "

And Dougie's doubts were fully justified in course of time. The *Vital Spark* was up with coals at Skipness, at a pier a mile away from the village, and Para Handy had an invitation to a party. He dressed himself in his Sunday clothes, and, redolent of scented soap, was confessed the lion of the evening, though Biler unaccountably refused to accompany him. At midnight he came back along the shore, to the ship, walking airily on his heels, with his hat at a dashing angle. The crew of the *Vital Spark* were all asleep, but the faithful Biler held the deck, and the Captain heard his bark.

"Pure Pompanion bred!" he said to himself. "As wise as a weedow woman! For the rale sagacity give me a dog!"

He made to step from the quay to the vessel's gunnel, but a rush and a growl from the dog restrained him; Biler's celebrated grip was almost on his leg.

"Tuts, man," said the Captain, "I'm sure you can see it's me; it's Peter. Good old Biler; stop you and I'll give you a buscuit!"

He ventured a foot on the gunnel again, and this time Biler sampled the tweed of his trousers. Nothing else was stirring in the *Vital Spark*. The Captain hailed his shipmates for assistance; if they heard, they never heeded, and the situation was sufficiently unpleasant to annoy a man of better temper even than Para Handy. No matter how he tried to get on board, the trusty watch-dog kept him back. In one attempt his hat fell off, and Biler tore it into the most impressive fragments.

"My Cot," said the Captain, "issn't this the happy evenin'? Stop you till I'll be pickin' a dog again, and it'll be wan wi' aal his faculties."

He had to walk back to the village and take shelter ashore for the night; in the morning Biler received him with the friendliest overtures, and was apparently astonished at the way they were received.

"Jum," said the Captain firmly, "you'll take back that dog to your frien' in Fairfield, and tell him there's no' a bit o' the rale Pompanion in him. He's chust a common Gleska dog, and he doesna know a skipper when he sees him, if he's in his Sunday clothes."

TREASURE TROVE

SUNNY JIM proved a most valuable acquisition to the *Vital Spark*. He was a person of humour and resource, and though they were sometimes the victims of his practical jokes, the others of the crew forgave him readily because of the fun he made.   It is true that when they were getting the greatest entertainment from him they were, without thinking it, generally doing his work for him—for indeed he was no sailor, only a Clutha mariner—but at least he was better value for his wages than The Tar, who could neither take his fair share of the work nor tell a baur.   Sunny Jim's finest gift was imagination ; the most wonderful things in the world had happened to him when he was on the Cluthas—all intensely interesting, if incredible : and Para Handy, looking at him with admiration and even envy, after a narrative more extraordinary than usual, would remark, " Man ! it's a peety listenin' to such d——d lies iss a sin, for there iss no doobt it iss a most pleeasant amuusement ! "

Macphail the engineer, the misanthrope, could not stand the new hand. " He's no' a sailor at a' ! " he protested ; " he's a clown ; I've see'd better men jumpin' through girrs at a penny show."

" Weel, he's maybe no' aawful steady at the wheel, but he hass a kyind, kyind he'rt ! " Dougie said.

" He's chust sublime ! " said Para Handy.   " If he wass managed right there would be money in him ! "

Para Handy's conviction that there was money to be made out of Sunny Jim was confirmed by an episode at Tobermory, of which the memory will be redolent in Mull for years to come.

The *Vital Spark*, having discharged a cargo of coal at Oban, went up the Sound to load with timber, and on Calve Island, which forms a natural breakwater for Tobermory harbour, Dougie spied a stranded whale.   He was not very much of a

whale as whales go in Greenland, being merely a tiny fellow
of about five-and-twenty tons, but as dead whales here are
as rarely to be seen as dead donkeys, the *Vital Spunh* was
steered close in to afford a better view, and even stopped
for a while that Para Handy and his mate might land
with the punt on the islet and examine the unfortunate
cetacean.

" My Chove ! he's a whupper ! " was Dougie's comment,
as he reached up and clapped the huge mountain of sea-flesh
on its ponderous side. " It wass right enough, I can see,
Peter, aboot yon fellow Jonah ; chust look at the accommodation ! "

" Chust waste, pure waste," said the skipper ; " you can
make a meal off a herrin', but whales iss only lumber, goin'
aboot ass big as a land o' hooses, blowin' aal the time, and
puttin' the fear o' daith on aal the other fushes. I never had
mich respect for them."

" If they had a whale like that aground on Clyde,"
said Dougie, as they returned to the vessel, " they would
stick bills on't ; it's chust thrown away on the Tobermory
folk."

Sunny Jim was enchanted when he heard the whale's
dimensions. " Chaps," he said with enthusiasm ; " there's
a fortune in't ; right-oh ! I've see'd them chargin' tuppence
to get into a tent at Vinegar Hill, whaur they had naethin'
fancier nor a sea-lion or a seal."

" But they wouldna be deid," said Para Handy ; " and
there's no' mich fun aboot a whale's remains. Even if there
was, we couldna tow him up to Gleska, and if we could, he
wouldna keep."

" Jim'll be goin' to embalm him, rig up a mast on him, and
sail him up the river ; are ye no', Jim ? " said Macphail with
irony.

" I've a faur better idea than that," said Sunny Jim.
" Whit's to hinder us clappin' them tarpaulins roon' the
whale whaur it's lyin', and showin' 't at a sixpence a heid to

the Tobermory folk? Man! ye'll see them rowin' across in hunners, for I'll bate ye there's no' much fun in Tobermory in the summer time unless it's a Band o' Hope soiree. Give it a fancy name—the 'Tobermory Treasure'; send the bellman roond the toon, sayin' it's on view to-morrow from ten till five, and then goin' on to Oban; Dougie'll lift the money, and the skipper and me'll tell the audience a' aboot the customs o' the whale when he's in life. Macphail can stand by the ship at Tobermory quay."

"Jist what I said a' alang," remarked Macphail darkly. "Jumpin' through girrs! Ye'll need a big drum and a naphtha lamp."

"Let us first paause and consider," remarked Para Handy, with his usual caution; "iss the whale oors?"

"Wha's else wad it be?" retorted Sunny Jim. "It was us that fun' it, and naebody seen it afore us, for it's no' mony oors ashore."

"Everything cast up on the shore belangs to the Crown; it's the King's whale," said Macphail.

"Weel, let him come for't," said Sunny Jim; "by the time he's here we'll be done wi't."

The presumption that Tobermory could be interested in a dead whale proved quite right; it was the Glasgow Fair week, and the local boat-hirers did good business taking parties over to the island where an improvised enclosure of oars, spars, and tarpaulin and dry sails concealed the "Tobermory Treasure" from all but those who were prepared to pay for admission. Para Handy, with his hands in his pockets and a studied air of indifference, as if the enterprise was none of his, chimed in at intervals with facts in the natural history of the whale, which Sunny Jim might overlook in the course of his introductory lecture.

"The biggest whale by three feet that's ever been seen in Scotland," Sunny Jim announced. "Lots o' folk thinks a whale's a fish, but it's naething o' the kind; it's a hot-blooded mammoth, and couldna live in the watter mair nor a wee while at a time withoot comin' up to draw its breath. This is no' yin o' thae common whales that chases herrin', and goes pechin' up and doon Kilbrannan Sound ; it's the kind that's catched wi' the harpoons and lives on naething but roary borealises and icebergs."

" They used to make umbrella-rubs wi' this parteecular kind," chimed in the skipper diffidently, " forbye, they're full o' blubber. It's an aawful useful thing a whale, chentlemen." He had apparently changed his mind about the animal, for which the previous day he had said he had no respect.

" Be shair and tell a' your friends when ye get ashore that it's maybe gaun on to Oban to-morrow," requested Sunny Jim. " We'll hae it up on the Esplanade there and chairge a shillin' a heid ; if we get it the length o' Gleska, the price 'll be up to hauf-a-croon."

" Is it a ' right ' whale ? " asked one of the audience in the interests of exact science.

" Right enough, as shair's onything ; isn't it, Captain ? " said Sunny Jim.

" What else would it be ? " said Para Handy indignantly. " Does the chentleman think there iss onything wrong with it ? Perhaps he would like to take a look through it ; eh, Jum ? Or maybe he would want a doctor's certeeficate that's it's no a dromedary."

The exhibition of the " Tobermory Treasure " proved so popular that its discoverers determined to run their entertainment for about a week. On the third day passengers coming into Tobermory with the steamer *Claymore* sniffed with appreciation, and talked about the beneficial influence of ozone ; the English tourists debated whether it was due to peat or heather. In the afternoon several yachts in the bay hurriedly got up their anchors and went up Loch Sunart, where the air seemed fresher. On the fourth day the residents of Tobermory overwhelmed the local chemist with demands for camphor, carbolic powder, permanganate

of potass, and other deodorants and disinfectants ; and
several plumbers were telegraphed for to Oban. The public
patronage of the exhibition on Calve Island fell off.

" If there's ony mair o' them wantin' to see this whale,"
said Sunny Jim, " they'll hae to look slippy."

" It's no' that bad to windward," said Para Handy.
" What would you say to coverin' it up wi' more tarpaulins ? "

" You might as weel cover't up wi' crape or muslin," was
Dougie's verdict. " What you would need iss armour-plate,
the same ass they have roond the cannons in the man-o'-
wars. If this wind doesn't change to the west, half the
folk in Tobermory 'll be goin' to live in the cellar o' the
Mishnish Hotel."

Suspicion fell on the " Tobermory Treasure " on the
following day, and an influential deputation waited on the
police sergeant, while the crew of the *Vital Spark*, with
much discretion, abandoned their whale, and kept to their
vessel's fo'c'sle. The sergeant informed the deputation that
he had a valuable clue to the source of these extraordinary
odours, but that unfortunately he could take no steps without a warrant from the Sheriff, and the Sheriff was in Oban.
The deputation pointed out that the circumstances were
too serious to permit of any protracted legal forms and ceremonies ; the whale must be removed from Calve Island
by its owners immediately, otherwise there would be a
plague. With regret the police sergeant repeated that he
could do nothing without authority, but he added casually
that if the deputation visited the owners of the whale and
scared the life out of them, he would be the last man to
interfere.

" Hullo, chaps ! pull the hatch efter yez, and keep oot
the cold air ! " said Sunny Jim, as the spokesman of the
deputation came seeking for the crew in the fo'c'sle. " Ye'd
be the better o' some odecolong on your hankies."

" We thought you were going to remove your whale to
Oban before this," said the deputation sadly.

"I'm afraid," said Para Handy, "that whale hass seen its best days, and wouldna be at aal popular in Oban."

"Well, you'll have to take it out of here immediately anyway," said the deputation. "It appears to be your property."

"Not at aal, not at aal!" Para Handy assured him; "it belongs by right to His Majesty, and we were chust takin' care of it for him till he would turn up, chairgin' a trifle for the use o' the tarpaulins and the management. It iss too great a responsibility now, and we've given up the job; aren't we, Jum?"

"Right-oh!" said Sunny Jim, reaching for his melodeon; "and it's time you Tobermory folk were shiftin' that whale."

"It's impossible," said the deputation, "a carcase weighing nearly thirty tons—and in such a condition!"

"Indeed it is pretty bad," said Para Handy; "perhaps it would be easier to shift the toon o' Tobermory."

But that was, luckily, not necessary, as a high tide restored the "Tobermory Treasure" to its natural element that very afternoon.

LUCK

PARA HANDY, gossiping with his crew, and speaking generally of "luck" and the rewards of industry and intelligence, always counted luck the strongest agent in the destiny of man. "Since ever I wass a skipper," he said, "I had nobody in my crew that was not lucky; I would sooner have lucky chaps on board wi' me than tip-top sailors that had a great experience o' wrecks. If the *Fital Spark* hass the reputation o' bein' the smertest vessel in the coastin' tred, it's no' aalthegither wi' navigation; it's chust because I had luck mysel', and aalways had a lot o' lucky laads aboot me. Dougie himsel' 'll tell you that."

"We have plenty o' luck," admitted Dougie, nursing a

wounded head he had got that day by carelessly using it as
a fender to keep the side of the ship from the piles of Tarbert
quay. " We have plenty of luck, but there must be a lot o'
cluver people never mindin' mich aboot their luck, and gettin'
aal the money."

" Money ! " said the Captain with contempt; " there's
other things to think aboot than money. If I had as mich
money ass I needed, I wouldna ask for a penny more. There's
nothing bates contentment and a pleesant way o' speakin'
to the owners. You needna empty aal the jar o' jam, Macphail; give him a rap on the knuckles, Jum, and tak' it
from him."

Macphail relinquished the jam-jar readily, because he had
finished all that was in it. " If ye had mair luck and less
jaw aboot it," said he snappishly, " ye wadna hae to wait
so lang on the money ye're expectin' frae your cousin Cherlie
in Dunmore. Is he no deid yet ? "

" No," said Para Handy dolefully; " he's still hangin'
on; I never heard o' a man o' ninety-three so desperate
deleeberate aboot dyin', and it the winter-time. Last
Friday week wass the fifth time they sent to Tarbert for the
munister, and he wasna needed."

" That was your cousin Cherlie's luck," said the engineer,
who was not without logic.

" I don't caal that luck at aal," retorted Para Handy;
" I call it just manœuvrin'. Forbye, it wasna very lucky for
the munister."

Cousin Cherlie's deliberation terminated a week later, when
the *Vital Spark* was in Loch Fyne, and the Captain borrowed
a hat and went to the funeral. " My own roond hat iss
a good enough hat and quite respectable," he said, " but
someway it doesna fit for funerals since I canna wear it on
my heid except it's cocked a little to the side. You see, I
have been at so many Tarbert Fairs with it, and high jeenks
chenerally."

The crew helped to make his toilet. Macphail, with a

piece of oily engine-room waste, imparted a resplendent polish to the borrowed hat, which belonged to a Tarbert citizen, and had lost a good deal of its original lustre. Dougie contributed a waistcoat, and Sunny Jim cheerfully sacrificed his thumb-nails in fastening the essential, but unaccustomed, collar on his Captain's neck. "There ye are, skipper," he said; "ye look A1 if ye only had a clean hanky."

"I'm no feelin' in very good trum, though," said the Captain, who seemed to be almost throttled by the collar; "there's no' mich fun for us sailor chaps in bein' chentlemen. But of course it's no' every day we're buryin' Cherlie, and I'm his only cousin, no' coontin' them MacNeills."

"Hoo much did ye say he had?" asked Macphail. "Was it a hunder pounds and a free hoose? or a hunder free hooses and a pound?"

"Do you know, laads," said the Captain, "his money wasna in my mind!"

"That's wi' the ticht collar," said the engineer unfeelingly; "lowse yer collar and mak' up yer mind whit yer gaun to dae wi' the hunder pounds. That's to say, if the MacNeills don't get it."

The Captain's heart, at the very thought of such disaster, came to his throat, and burst the fastenings of his collar, which had to be rigged up anew by Sunny Jim.

"The MacNeills," he said, "'ll no' touch a penny. Cherlie couldna stand them, and I wass aye his favourite, me bein' a captain. Money would be wasted on the MacNeills; they wouldna know what to do wi't."

"I ken whit I wad dae wi' a hunder pound if I had it," said Macphail emphatically.

"You would likely gie up the sea and retire to the free hoose wi' a ton or two o' your penny novelles," suggested the Captain.

"I wad trevel," said the engineer, heedless of the unpleasant innuendo. "There's naething like trevel for widenin' the mind. When I was sailin' foreign I saw a lot

F

o' life, but I didna see near sae much as I wad hae seen if I had the money."

"Fancy a sailor traivellin'!" remarked Sunny Jim. "There's no much fun in that."

"I don't mean traivellin' in boats," explained Macphail. "Ye never see onything trevellin' in boats; I mean trains. The only places abroad worth seein' 's no' to be seen at the heid o' a quay; ye must tak' a train to them. Rome, and Paris, and the Eytalian Lakes—that sort o' thing. Ye live in hotels and any amount o' men's ready to carry yer bag. Wi' a hunder pound a man could trevel the world."

"Never heed him, Peter," said Dougie; "trevellin's an anxious business; you're aye losin' your tickets, and the tips you have to give folk 's a fair ruination. If I had a hunder pound and a free hoose, I would let the hoose and tak' a ferm."

"A ferm's no' bad," admitted Para Handy, "but there's a desperate lot o' work aboot a ferm."

"There's a desperate lot o' work aboot anything ye can put your hand to, except enchineerin'," said Dougie sadly, "but you can do wonders if you have a good horse and a fine strong wife. You wouldna need to be a rale fermer, but chust wan o' them chentleman fermers that wears knickerbockers and yellow leggin's."

"There's a good dale in what you say, Dougie," admitted the Captain, who saw a pleasing vision of himself in yellow leggings. "It's no' a bad tred, chentleman fermin'."

"Tred!" said Dougie; "it's no a tred—it's a recreation, like sailin' a yat. Plooin'-matches and 'ool-markets every other day; your own eggs and all the mutton and milk you need for nothing. Buy you a ferm, Peter, I'm tellin' you!"

"Chust that!" said the Captain cunningly. "And then maybe you would be skipper of the *Fital Spark*, Dougie."

"I wasna thinkin' aboot that at aal!" protested the mate.

"I wasna sayin' you were," said the Captain, "but the mustress would give you the notion."

"If I was you I wad tak' a shop in Gleska," said Sunny Jim. "No' an awfu' big shop, but a handy wee wan ye could shut when there was any sport on withoot mony people noticin'."

Para Handy buttoned his coat, and prepared to set out for the funeral. "Whether it wass trevellin', or a ferm, or a shop, I would get on sublime, for I'm a lucky, lucky man, laads ; but I'm no lettin' my mind dwell on Cherlie's money, oot o' respect for my relative. I'll see you aal when I come back, and maybe it might be an Occasion."

Dougie cried after him when he was a little up the quay, "Captain, your hat's chust a little to the side."

Para Handy was back from the funeral much sooner than was expected, his collar in his pocket, and the borrowed hat in his hand. He went below to resume his ordinary habiliments without a word to the crew, who concluded that he was discreetly concealing the legacy. When he came up, they asked no questions, from a sense of proper decorum, but the Captain seemed surcharged with great emotion.

"Dougie," he said to the mate, "what would be the cost o' a pair o' yellow leggin's ? "

"Aboot a pound," said the mate, with some exultation. "Have you made up your mind for fermin' ? "

"No," said the Captain bitterly; "I might afford the leggin's off my cousin Cherlie's legacy, but it wouldna go the length o' knickerbockers."

SALVAGE FOR THE *VITAL SPARK*

THE vessel was rounding Ardlamont in a sou'-wester that set her all awash like an empty herring-box. Over her snub nose combed appalling sprays ; green seas swept her fore and aft ; she was glucking with internal waters, and her squat red funnel whooped dolorously with wind. "Holy smoke ! " gasped Para Handy, "isn't this the hammerin' ! "

" A sailor's life ! " said Dougie bitterly, drawing a soaking sleeve across his nose ; " I would sooner be a linen-draper."

In flaws of the wind they could hear Macphail break coals in the engine-room, and the wheezy tones of Sunny Jim's melodeon as he lay on his bunk in the fo'c'sle quelling his apprehensions to the air of " The Good Old Summer-Time." Together at the wheel the Captain and his mate were dismal objects, drenched to the hide, even below their oil-skins, which gave them the glistening look of walruses or seals. They had rigged a piece of jib up for a dodger ; it poorly served its purpose, and seemed as inefficient as a handkerchief as they raised their blinking eyes above it and longingly looked for the sheltering arms of the Kyles.

" I wish to the Lord it wass Bowlin' quay and me sound sleepin'," said the mate. " Yonder's the mustress in Plantation snug and cosy on't, and I'll wager she's no' a bit putaboot for her man on the heavin' bullow. It makes me quite angry to think of it. Eggs for her tea and all her orders, and me with not a bite since breakfast-time but biscuits."

" Holy smoke ! you surely wouldna like her to be wi' you here," said Para Handy, shocked.

" No," said Dougie, " but I wish she could see me noo, and I wish I could get her and her high tea at the fireside oot o' my heid ; it's bad enough to be standing here like a flag-pole thinkin' every meenute 'll be my next."

" Toot ! man, Dougie, you're tumid, tumid," said the Captain. " Draw your braith as deep's you can, throw oot your chest, and be a hero. Look at me ! my name's Macfarlane and I'm wan of Brutain's hardy sons ! "

The *Vital Spark* got round the Point, and met a wave that smashed across her counter and struck full in the face the mariners at the wheel. Dougie, with his mouth inelegantly open, swallowed a pint or two, and spluttered. Para Handy shook the water from his beard like a spaniel, and looking more anxiously than before through smarting eyes, saw a gabbart labouring awkwardly close on the shore of Ettrick Bay.

"Dougie," said he, "stop giggling a bit, and throw your eye to starboard—is yon no' the *Katherine-Anne* ?"

"It wassna giggling I wass," said Dougie irritably, coughing brine, "but I nearly spoiled the Kyles o' Bute. It's the *Katherine-Anne* right enough, and they've lost command o' her; stop you a meenute and you'll hear an awfu' dunt."

"She'll be ashore in a juffy," said the Captain tragically. "Man ! iss it no' chust desperate ! I'm no' makin' a proposeetion, mind, but what would you say to givin' a slant across and throwin' a bit o' a rope to her ?"

Dougie looked wistfully at Tighnabruaich ahead of them, and now to be reached in comfort, and another at the welter of waves between them and the struggling gabbart. "Whatever you say yoursel', Peter," he replied, and for twenty minutes more they risked disaster. At one wild moment Para Handy made his way to the fo'c'sle hatch and bellowed down to Sunny Jim, "You there wi' your melodeon—it would fit you better if you tried to mind your Psalms."

When they reached the *Katherine-Anne*, and found she had been abandoned, Para Handy cursed at first his own soft heart that had been moved to the distress of a crew who were comfortably on their way to Rothesay. He was for leaving the gabbart to her fate, but Macphail, the engineer, and Sunny Jim remarked that a quite good gabbart lacking any obvious owners wasn't to be picked up every day. If they towed her up to Tighnabruaich they would have a very pretty claim for salvage.

"Fifty pounds at least for ship and cargo," said Macphail ; "my share 'll pay for my flittin' at the term, jist nate."

"Fifty pounds !" said Para Handy. "It's a tidy sum, and there might be more than fifty in't when it came to the bit, for fifty pounds iss not an aawful lot when the owner gets his wheck of it. What do you think yoursel', Dougie ?"

" I wass chust thinkin'," said Dougie, " that fifty pounds would be a terrible lot for poor MacCallum, him that owns the *Katherine-Anne* ; he hasna been very lucky wi' her."

" If we're no' gaun to get the fifty pound then, we can just tow her up to Tignabruaich for a baur," said Sunny Jim. " It doesna dae to be stickin'. If there's naething else in't, we'll get a' oor names in the papers for a darin' deed at sea. Come on, chaps, be game ! "

" I wish to peace the *Katherine-Anne* belonged to any other man than John MacCallum," said the skipper. " You're an aawful cluver laad, Macphail ; what iss the law aboot salvage ? "

" Under the Merchant Shippin' Act," said Macphail glibly, " ye're bound to get your salvage ; if ye divna claim't, it goes to the King the same as whales or onything that's cast up by the sea."

" Ach ! it disna maitter a docken aboot the salvage," said Sunny Jim. " Look at the fun we'll hae comin' into Tighnabruaich wi' a boat we fun' the same as it was a kitlin. See's a rope, and I'll go on board and mak' her fast."

When they had towed the *Katherine-Anne* to Tighnabruaich, Dougie was sent ashore with a telegram for the owner of the *Vital Spark*, suggesting his immediate appearance on the scene. Later in the afternoon the crew of the *Katherine-Anne* came by steamer to Tignabruaich, to which port she and they belonged, and the captain and owner ruefully surveyed the vessel he had abandoned, now lying safe and sound at his native quay. He sat on a barrel of paraffin-oil and looked at Para Handy in possession.

" Where did you pick her up ? " said MacCallum sadly.

" Oh, chust doon the road a bit," said Para Handy. " It's clearin' up a nice day."

" It's a terrible business this," said MacCallum, nervously wiping his forehead with his handkerchief.

" Bless me ! what is't ? " exclaimed Para Handy. " I havena seen the paper this week yet."

" I mean about havin' to leave the *Katie-Anne* almost at our own door, and you finding her."

" Chust that ; it wass Providence," remarked Para Handy piously, " chust Providence."

" I'll hae to gie you something for your bother," said MacCallum.

" I wouldna say but you would," replied the skipper. " It's a mercy your lifes wass saved. Hoo are they keepin', aal, in Ro'sa' ? "

" Are ye no' comin' ashore for a dram ? " remarked MacCallum, and Para cocked at him a cunning eye.

" No, John," he said ; " I'm no' carin' mich aboot a dram the day ; I had wan yesterday."

But he succumbed to the genial impulse an hour later, and leaving his mate in possession of the *Katherine-Anne*, went up the village with the owner of that unhappy craft. MacCallum took him to his home, where Para Handy found himself in the uncomfortable presence of a wife and three daughters dressmaking. The four women sewed so assiduously, and were so moist about the eyes with weeping, that he was sorry he came.

" This is the gentleman that found the *Katie-Anne*," remarked MacCallum by way of introduction, and the eldest daughter sobbed.

" Ye're aal busy ! " said Para Handy, with a desperate air of cheerfulness.

" Indeed, aye ! we're busy enough," said the mother bitterly. " We're workin' oor fingers to the bane, but we're no' makin' much o't ; it's come wi' the wind and gang wi' the water," and the second daughter sobbed in unison with her sister as they furiously plied their needles.

" By Chove ! " thought Para Handy, " a man would need to have the he'rt o' a hoose-factor on a chob like this ; it puts me aal oot o' trum," and he drank his glass uncomfortably.

" I think ye mentioned aboot fifty pounds ? " said Mac-Callum mournfully, and at these words all the four women laid their sewing on their knees and wept without restraint. " Fi-fi-fifty p-p-pounds ! " exclaimed the mother, " where in the wide world is John MacCallum to get fifty pounds ? "

Para Handy came hurriedly down the quay and called Dougie ashore from the *Katherine-Anne*.

" Somebody must stay on board of her, or we'll have trouble wi' the salvage," said the mate.

" Come ashore this meenute," commanded the Captain, " for I'm needin' some refreshment. There's four women yonder greetin' their eyes oot at the loss o' fifty pounds."

" Chust that ! " said Dougie sympathetically. " Poor things ! "

" I would see the salvage to the duvvle," said the Captain warmly, " if we hadna sent that telegram to oor owner. Four o' them sew-sew-sewing yonder, and dreepin', like the fountain oot in Kelvingrove ! "

" Man, it wass lucky, too, aboot the telegram," said Dougie, " for I didna like to send it and it's no' away."

Para Handy slapped him on the shoulder. "Man ! " he said, " that's capital ! To the muschief with their fifty pounds ! Believe you me, I'm feelin' quite sublime ! "

PARA HANDY HAS AN EYE TO BUSINESS

IT was a lovely day, and the *Vital Spark*, without a cargo, lay at the pier of Ormidale, her newly-painted under-strakes reflected in a loch like a mirror, making a crimson blotch in a scene that was otherwise winter-brown. For a day and a half more there was nothing to be done. " It's the life of a Perfect Chentleman," said Dougie. The engineer, with a novelette he had bought in Glasgow, was lost in the love affairs of a girl called Gladys, who was excessively poor, but looked, at Chapter Five, like marrying a Colonel of Hussars who seemed to have no suspicion of the fate in store for him ; and Sunny Jim, with the back of his head showing at the fo'c'sle scuttle, was making with his melodeon what sounded like a dastardly attack on " The Merry Widow."

" I wass thinkin', seein' we're here and nothing else doin', we might be givin' her the least wee bit touch o' the tar-brush," remarked Para Handy, who never cared to lose a chance of beautifying his vessel.

" There it is again ! " exclaimed Macphail, laying down his novelette in exasperation. " A chap canna get sittin' doon five meenutes in this boat for a read to himsel' withoot some-body breakin' their legs to find him a job. Ye micht as weel be in a man-o'-war." Even Dougie looked reproachfully at the Captain ; he had just been about to pull his cap down over his eyes and have a little sleep before his tea.

" It wass only a proposeetion," said the Captain soothingly. " No offence ! Maybe it'll do fine when we get to Tarbert. It's an awfu' peety they're no' buildin' boats o' this size wi' a kind of a study in them for the use o' the enchineers," and he turned for sympathy to the mate, who was usually in the mood to rag Macphail. But this time Dougie was on Macphail's side.

" There's some o' your jokes like the Carradale funerals—there's no' much fun in them," he remarked. " Ye think it's great sport to be tar-tar-tarring away at the ship ; ye never consult either oor healths or oor inclinations. Am I right, Macphail ? "

" Slave-drivin' ! that's whit I ca't," said Macphail emphati-cally. " If Lloyd George kent aboot it, he would bring it before the Board o' Tred."

The Captain withdrew, moodily, from his crew, and ostentatiously scraped old varnish off the mast. This business engaged him only for a little ; the weather was so plainly made for idleness that he speedily put the scraper aside and entered into discourse with Sunny Jim.

" Whatever you do, don't you be a Captain, Jum," he advised him.

" I wisht I got the chance ! " said Sunny Jim.

F*

" There's nothing in't but the honour o' the thing, and a shilling or two extra ; no' enough to pay the drinks to keep up the poseetion.   Here am I, and I'm anxious to be frien'ly wi' the chaps, trate them the same's I wass their equal, and aalways ready to come-and-go a bit, and they go and give me the name o' a slave-driver !   Iss it no' chust desperate ? "

" If I was a Captain," said Sunny Jim philosophically, " I wad dae the comin' and mak' the ither chaps dae the goin', and d—— smert aboot it."

" That's aal right for a Gleska man, but it's no' the way we're brocht up on Loch Long ; us Arrochar folk, when we're Captains, believe in a bit o' compromise wi' the crews.   If they don't do a thing when we ask them cuvilly, we do't oorsel's, and that's the way to vex them."

" Did ye never think ye wad like to change your job and try something ashore ? " asked Sunny Jim.

" Many   a   time ! "   confessed   the   Captain.   " There's yonder jobs that would suit me fine.   I wass nearly, once, an innkeeper.   It wass at a place called Cladich ; the man came into a puckle money wi' his wife, and advertised the good-wull at a great reduction.   I left the boat for a day and walked across to see him.   He wass a man they caalled MacDiarmid, and he wass yonder wi' his sleeves up puttin' corks in bottles wi' a wonderful machine.   Did you ever see them corkin' bottles, Jum ? "

" I never noticed if I did," said Sunny Jim ; " but I've seen them takin' them oot."

" Chust that !   This innkeeper wass corkin' away like hey-my-nanny.

" ' You're sellin' the business ? ' says I.

" ' I am,' says he ; and him throng corkin' away at the bottles.

" ' What's your price ? ' says I.

" ' A hundred and fifty pounds for the good-wull and the stock the way it stands,' says he.

" ' What aboot the fixtures ? ' then says I.

"'Oh, they're aal right!' said the innkeeper, cork-cork-corkin' away at the bottles; 'the fixtures goes along with the good-wull.'

"'What fixtures iss there?' says I.

"'There's three sheep fermers, the shoemaker doon the road, and Macintyre the mail-driver, and that's no' coontin' a lot o' my Sunday customers,' said the innkeeper."

"You didna tak' the business, then?" said Sunny Jim.

"Not me!" said Para Handy. "To be corkin' away at bottles aal my lone yonder would put me crazy. Forbye, I hadna the half o' the hunder-and-fifty. There wass another time I went kind o' into a business buyin' eggs——"

"Eggs!" exclaimed Sunny Jim with some astonishment —"whit kin' o' eggs?"

"Och! chust egg eggs," said the Captain. "It wass a man in Arran said there wass a heap o' money in them if you had the talent and a wee bit powney to go roond the countryside. To let you ken: it wass before the *Fital Spark* changed owncrs; the chentleman that had her then wass a wee bit foolish; nothing at aal against his moral and releegious reputaation, mind, but apt to go over the score with it, and forget whereaboots the vessel would be lying. This time we were for a week or more doin' nothin' in Loch Ranza, and waitin' for his orders. He couldna mind for the life o' him where he sent us, and wass telegraphin' aal the harbour-masters aboot the coast to see if they kent the whereaboots o' the *Fital Spark*, but it never came into his heid that we might be near Loch Ranza, and there we were wi' the best o' times doin' nothing."

"Could ye no' hae sent him a telegraph tellin' him where ye wiz?" asked Sunny Jim.

"That's what he said himsel', but we're no' that daft, us folk from Arrochar; I can tell you we have aal oor faculties. Dougie did better than that; he put a bit o' paper in a bottle efter writin' on't a message from the sea—'s.s *Fital Spark* stranded for a fortnight in a fit o' absent-mind ; aal hands quite joco, but the owner lost.'

" We might have been lyin' in Loch Ranza yet if it wassna that I tried Peter Carmichael's business. 'When you're doin' nothing better here,' he said to me, 'you micht be makin' your fortune buyin' and sellin' eggs, for Arran's fair hotchin' wi' them.'

" ' What way do you do it ? ' says I.

" ' You need a wee cairt and a powney,' said Peter Carmichael, 'and I've the very cairt and powney that would suit you. You go roond the island gatherin' eggs from aal the hooses, and pay them sixpence a dozen—champion eggs ass fresh ass the mornin' breeze. Then you pack them in boxes and send them to Gleska and sell them at a profit.'

" ' What profit do you chenerally allow yoursel' ? ' I asked Peter.

" ' Oh ! chust nate wan per cent,' said Peter ; 'you chairge a shillin' in Gleska for the eggs ; rale Arran eggs, no' foreign rubbadge. Folk 'll tell you to put your money in stone and lime ; believe me, nothing bates the Arran egg for quick returns. If the people in Gleska have a guarantee that any parteecular egg wass made in Arran, they'll pay any money for it ; it's ass good ass a day at the coast for them, poor craturs ! '

" Seein' there wass no prospeck o' the owner findin' where we were unless he sent a bloodhound oot to look for us, I asked Carmichael hoo long it would take to learn the business, and he said I could pick it up in a week. I agreed to buy the cairt and powney and the good-wull o' the business if the chob at the end o' the week wass like to bring in a pleasin' wage, and Dougie himsel' looked efter the shup. You never went roond the country buyin' eggs ? It's a chob you need a lot o' skill for. Yonder wass Peter Carmichael and me goin' roond by Pirnmill, Machrie, and Blackwaterfoot, Sliddery, and Shiskine——"

"Ach! ye're coddin'!" exclaimed Sunny Jim; "there's no such places."

"It's easy seen you were a' your days on the Clutha steamers," said the Captain patiently; "I'll assure you that there's Slidderys and Shiskines oot in Arran. Full o' eggs! The hens oot yonder's no' puttin' bye their time!

"Three days runnin' Peter and me and the powney scoured the country and gaithered so many eggs that I begun to get rud in the face whenever I passed the least wee hen. We couldna get boxes enough to hold them in Loch Ranza, so we got some bales o' hay and packed them in the hold of the *Fital Spark*, and then consudered. 'There's nothing to do noo but to take them to the Broomielaw and sell them quick at a shillin',' said Carmichael. 'The great thing iss to keep them on the move, and off your hands before they change their minds and start for to be chuckens. Up steam, smert, and off wi' ye! And here's the cairt and powney—fifteen pounds.'

"'Not at aal, Carmichael!' I said to him; 'I'll wait till I'll see if you wass right aboot the wan per cent of profits. Stop you here till I'll come back.'

"I telegraphed that day to the owner o' the vessel, sayin' I was comin' into the Clyde wi' a cargo, and when we got to Gleska he wass standin' on the quay, and not in the best o' trum.

"'Where in a' the world were you?' says he; 'and me lookin' high and low for you! What's your cargo?'

"'Eggs from Arran, Mr Smuth,' says I, 'and a bonny job I had gettin' them at sixpence the dozen.'

"'Who are they from?' he asked, glowerin' under the hatches.

"'Chust the cheneral population, Mr Smuth,' says I.

"'Who are they consigned to?' he asked then—and man he wassna in trum at aal, at aal!

"'Anybody that'll buy them, sir,' said I; 'it's a bit of a speculation.'

"He scratched his heid and looked at me. 'I mind o' orderin' eggs,' says he, 'but I never dreamt I wass daft enough to send for a boatload o' them. But noo they're here I suppose we'll have to make the best o' them.' So he sold the eggs, and kept the wan per cent for freight and responsibeelity, and I made nothin' off it except that I shifted my mind aboot takin' a chob ashore, and didn't buy Carmichael's cairt and powney.''

A VEGETARIAN EXPERIMENT

THE *Vital Spark* had been lying for some time in the Clyde getting in a new boiler, and her crew, who had been dispersed about the city in their respective homes, returned to the wharf on a Monday morning to make ready for a trip to Tobermory.

"She's a better boat than ever she was," said Macphail with satisfaction, having made a casual survey. "Built like a lever watch ! We'll can get the speed oot o' her noo. There's boats gaun up and doon the river wi' red funnels, saloon caibins, and German bands in them, that havena finer engines. When I get that crank and crossheid tightened, thae glands packed and nuts slacked, she'll be the gem o' the sea."

"She's chust sublime !" said Para Handy, patting the tarred old hull as if he were caressing a kitten ; "it's no' coals and timber she should be carryin' at aal, but towrist passengers. Man ! if we chust had the accommodation !"

"Ye should hae seen the engines we had on the Cluthas !" remarked Sunny Jim, who had no illusions about the *Vital Spark* in that respect. "They were that shiney I could see my face in them."

"Could ye, 'faith ?" said Macphail ; "a sicht like that must have put ye aff yer work. We're no' that fond o' polish in the coastin' tred that we mak' oor engines shine like an Eyetalian ice-cream shop ; it's only vanity. Wi' us it's speed——"

" Eight knots," murmured Sunny Jim, who was in a nasty Monday-morning humour. " Eight knots, and the chance o' nine wi' wind and tide."

" You're a liar ! " said the Captain irritably, " and that's my advice to you. Ten knots many a time between the Cloch and the Holy Isle," and an argument ensued which it took Dougie all his tact to put an end to short of bloodshed.

" It's me that's gled to be back on board of her anyway," remarked Para Handy later ; " I suppose you'll soon be gettin' the dinner ready, Jum ? See and have something nice, for I'm tired o' sago puddin'."

" Capital stuff for pastin' up bills," said Dougie ; " I've seen it often in the cookin'-depots. Wass the wife plyin' ye wi' sago ? "

" Sago, and apples, potatoes, cabbage, cheese, and a new kind o' patent coffee that agrees wi' the indigestion ; I havena put my two eyes on a bit of Christian beef since I went ashore ; the wife's in wan of her tirravees, and she's turned to be a vegetarian."

" My Chove ! " said Dougie incredulously ; " are you sure, Peter ? "

" Sure enough ! I told her this mornin' when I left I would bring her home a bale of hay from Mull, and it would keep her goin' for a month or two. Women's a curious article ! "

" You should get the munister to speak to her," said Dougie sympathetically. " When a wife goes wrong like that, there's nothing bates the munister. She'll no' be goin' to the church ; it's aalways the way wi' them fancy new releegions. Put you her at wance in the hands o' a dacent munister."

" I canna be harsh wi' her, or she'll greet," said Para Handy sadly.

" It's no' harshness that's wanted," counselled the mate,

speaking from years of personal experience ; " what you need iss to be firm. What way did this ●alamity come on her ? Don't be standin' there, Jum, like a soda-water bottle, but hurry and make a bit of steak for the Captain ; man ! I noticed you werena in trum whenever I saw you come on board. I saw at wance you hadn't the agility. What way did the trouble come on her ? "

" She took it off a neighbour woman," explained the Captain. " She wass aal right on the Sunday, and on the Monday mornin' she couldna bear to look at ham and eggs. It might happen to anybody. The thing was at its heid when I got home, and the only thing on the table wass a plate of maccaroni."

" Eyetalian ! " chimed in the engineer. " I've seen them makin' it in Genoa and hingin' it up to bleach on the washin'-greens. It's no' meat for men ; it's only for passin' the time o' organ-grinders and ship-riggers."

" ' Mery,' I said to her, ' I never saw nicer decorations, but hurry up like a darlin' wi' the meat.' ' There'll be no more meat in this hoose, Peter,' she said, aal trumblin' ; ' if you saw them busy in a slaughter-hoose you wadna eat a chop. Forbye, there's uric acid in butcher meat, and there's more nourishment in half a pound o' beans than there iss in half a bullock.' ' That's three beans for a sailor's dinner ; it's no' for nourishment a man eats always ; half the time it's only for amusement, Mery,' said I to her, but it wass not the time for argyment. ' You'll be a better man in every way if you're a vegetarian,' she said to me. ' If it iss a better man you are wantin',' I says to her, wonderful caalm in my temper, ' you are on the right tack, sure enough ; you have only to go on with them expuriments wi' my meat and you'll soon be a weedow woman.'

" But she wouldna listen to reason, Mery, and for a fortnight back I have been feedin' like the Scribes and Sadducees in the Scruptures."

" Man ! iss it no chust desperate ? " said Dougie compassionately, and he admiringly watched his Captain a little later make the first hearty meal for a fortnight. " You're lookin' a dufferent man already," he told him ; " what's for the tea, Jum ? "

" I kent a vegetarian yince," said Sunny Jim, " and he lived maist o' the time on chuckie soup."

" Chucken soup ? " repeated Dougie interrogatively.

" No ; chuckie soup. There was nae meat o' ony kind in't. A' ye needed was some vegetables, a pot o' hot water, and a parteecular kind o' chuckie-stane. It was fine and strengthenin'."

" You would need good teeth for't, I'm thinkin'," remarked the Captain dubiously.

" Of course ye didna eat the chuckie-stane," Sunny Jim explained ; " it made the stock ; it was instead o' a bane, and it did ower and ower again."

" It would be a great savin'," said Dougie, fascinated with the idea. " Where do you get them parteecular kinds of chuckies ? "

" Onywhere under high water," replied Sunny Jim, who saw prospects of a little innocent entertainment.

" We'll get them the first time we're ashore, then," said the mate, " and if they're ass good ass what you say, the Captain could take home a lot of them for his vegetarian mustress."

At the first opportunity, when he got ashore, Sunny Jim perambulated the beach and selected a couple of substantial pieces of quartz, and elsewhere bought a pound of margarine which he put in his pocket. " Here yez are, chaps—the very chuckie ! I'll soon show ye soup," he said, coming aboard with the stones, in which the crew showed no little interest. " A' ye have to do is to scrub them weel, and put them in wi' the vegetables when the pot's boilin'."

They watched his culinary preparations closely. He prepared the water and vegetables, cleaned the stones, and solemnly popped them in the pot when the water boiled. At a moment when their eyes were off him he dexterously added the unsuspected pound of margarine. By-and-by the soup was ready, and when dished, had all the aspect of the ordinary article. Sunny Jim himself was the first to taste it *pour encourager les autres*.

" Fair champion ! " he exclaimed.

The engineer could not be prevailed to try the soup on any consideration, but the Captain and the mate had a plate apiece, and voted it extraordinary.

" It's a genius you are, Jum ! " said the delighted Captain ; " if the folk in Gleska knew that soup like this was to be made from chuckie-stanes they wouldna waste their time at the Fair wi' gaitherin' cockles."

And the next time Para Handy reached the Clyde he had on board in all good faith a basket-load of stones culled from the beach at Tobermory for his vegetarian mistress.

THE COMPLETE GENTLEMAN

" THE finest chentleman I ever knew was Hurricane Jeck," said Para Handy. " His manners wass complete. Dougie himsel' will tell you."

" A nice laad," said the mate agreeably ; " he had a great, great faculty."

" Whaur did he mak' his money ? " asked Sunny Jim, and they looked at him with compassion.

" There iss men that iss chentlemen, and there iss men that hass a puckle money," said the Captain impressively ; " Hurricane Jeck wass seldom very rife with money, but he came from Kinlochaline, and that iss ass good ass a Board of Tred certuficate. Stop you till you're long enough on the *Fital Spark*, and you'll get your educaation. Hurricane Jeck was a chentleman. What money he had he would spend like the wave of the sea."

" It didna maitter wha's money it was, either," chimed in Macphail unsympathetically. " I kent him ! Fine ! "

" Like the wave of the sea," repeated the Captain, meeting the engineer's qualification with the silence of contempt. "Men like Jeck should never be oot of money, they distribute it with such a taste."

" I've seen chaps like that," remarked Sunny Jim, who was sympathetic to that kind of character. " When I was on the Cluthas——"

" When you was on the Cluthas, Jum, you were handlin' nothing but ha'pennies ; Hurricane Jeck wass a chentleman in pound notes, and that's the dufference."

"My Jove!" said Sunny Jim, "he must hae been weel aff!"

" There wass wan time yonder," proceeded the Captain, " when Jeck came into a lot o' money from a relative that died—fifty pounds if it wass a penny, and he spent it in a manner that was chust sublime. The very day he got it, he came down to the *Fital Spark* at Bowlin' for a consultation. ' You'll no' guess what's the trouble, Peter,' said he ; ' I'm a chentleman of fortune,' and he spread the fifty notes fornent him, with a bit of stone on each of them to keep them doon, the same as it wass a bleachin'-green. ' Fifty pounds and a fortnight to spend it in, before we sail for China. Put bye your boat, put on your Sunday clothes, and you and me'll have a little recreaation.'

" ' I canna, Jeck,' says I—and Dougie himsel' 'll tell you —' I canna, Jeck ; the cargo's in, and we're sailin' in the mornin'.'

" ' That's the worst o' money,' said Hurricane Jeck ; ' there's never enough o't. If Uncle Willy had left me plenty I would buy your boat and no' let a cargo o' coals interfere wi' oor diversion.'

" ' Put it in the bank,' I said to him.

" ' I'm no that daft,' he said. ' There's no' a worst place in the world for money than the banks ; you never get the good o't.'

" ' Oh, there's plenty of other ways of gettin' rid of it,' I told him.

" ' Not of fifty pounds,' said Jeck. ' It's easy spendin' a pound or two, but you canna get rid o' a legacy withoot assistance.' Wassn't that the very words of him, Dougie ? "

" Chust his own words ! " said the mate ; " your memory iss capital."

" ' There's a lot o' fun I used to think I would indulge in if I had the money,' said Hurricane Jeck, ' and now I have the opportunity if I only had a friend like yoursel' to see me doin' it. I'm goin' to spend it aal in trevellin'.' "

" And him a sailor ! " commented the astonished Sunny Jim.

" He wass meanin' trevellin' on shore," said Para Handy. " Trains, and tramway cars, and things like that, and he had a brulliant notion. It wass aye a grief to Jeck that there wass so many things ashore you darena do withoot a prosecution. ' The land o' the Free ! ' he would say, ' and ye canna take a tack on a train the length o' Paisley withoot a bit of a pasteboard ticket ! ' He put in the rest of that day that I speak of trevellin' the Underground till he wass dizzy, and every other hour he had an altercaation wi' the railway folk aboot his ticket. ' Take it oot o' that,' he would tell them, handin' them a pound or two, and he quite upset the traffic. On the next day he got a Gladstone bag, filled it with empty bottles, and took the train to Greenock. ' Don't throw bottles oot at the windows,' it says in the railway cairrages ; Jeck opened the windows and slipped oot a bottle or two at every quarter mile, till the Caledonian system looked like the mornin' efter a Good Templars' trip. They catched him doin' it at Pollokshields.

" ' What's the damage ? ' he asked them, hangin' his arm on the inside strap o' a first-cless cairrage and smokin' a fine cigar. You never saw a fellow that could be more genteel.

" ' It might be a pound a bottle,' said the railway people ; ' we have the law for it.'

" ' Any reduction on takin' a quantity ? ' said Jeck ; ' I'm havin' the time o' my life ; it's most refreshin'.'

" That day he took the train to Edinburgh—didn't he, Dougie ? "

" He did that ! " said Dougie. " You have the story exactly."

" He took the train to Edinburgh. It was an express, and every noo and then he would pull the chain communication wi' the guard. The train would stop, and the guard would come and talk with Jeck. The first time he came along Jeck shook him by the hand, and said he only wanted to congratulate him.

" ' What aboot ? ' said the guard, no' lookin' very well pleased.

" ' On your cheneral agility,' said Hurricane Jeck. ' Your cairrages iss first-rate ; your speed iss astonishin' quick ; your telegraph communication iss workin' A1 ; and you stopped her in two lengths. I thocht I would chust like you to take my compliments to the owners.'

" ' It's five pounds o' a fine for pullin' the cord,' said the guard.

" ' That's only for the wan cord ; I pulled the two o' them,' said Jeck, quite nice to him ; ' first the port and then the starboard. You canna be too parteecular. There's the money and a shillin' extra for a dram.'

" The guard refused the money, and said he would see aboot it at Edinburgh, and the train went on. Jeck pulled the cords till he had them all in the cairrage wi' him, but the train never stopped till it came to Edinburgh, and then a score o' the offeecials came to the cairrage.

" ' What are you doin' with them cords ? ' they asked him.

" ' Here they are, all coiled up and flemished-down,' said Jeck, lightin' another cigar. ' When does this train go back ? ' and he hands them over a bunch o' notes, and told them never to mind the change."

" Man ! he was the comic ! " exclaimed Sunny Jim. " Fair champion ! "

" In Edinburgh," proceeded Para Handy, " he waalked

aboot till he came on a fire alarm where it said it would cost a heavy fine to work it unless there wass a fire. Jeck rung the bell, and waited whustlin' till the Fire Brigade came clatterin' up the street.

" ' Two meenutes and fifty seconds,' he says to them, holdin' his watch ; ' they couldna do better in Gleska. I like your helmets. Noo that we're aal here, what iss it goin' to be, boys ? '

" ' Are you drunk, or daft ? ' said the Captain o' the Fire Brigade, grippin' him by the collar.

" ' Not a drop since yesterday ! ' said Jeck. ' And I'm no' daft, but chust an honest Brutish sailor, puttin' bye the time and spreadin' aboot my money. There's me and there's Mr Carnegie. His hobby is libraries ; on the other hand I'm for Liberty. The Land of the Free and the Brave ; it says on the fire alarm that I mustna break it, and I proved I could. Take your money oot o' that,'—and he hands the Captain the bundle of notes. ' If there iss any change left when you pay yoursel's for your bother, send home the enchines and we'll aal adjourn to a place.' "

" Capital ! " exclaimed Dougie.

" It took three days for Jeck to get rid of his fortune in cheneral amusement of that kind, and then he came to see me before he joined his shup for China.

" ' I had a fine time, Peter,' he said ; ' couldna have better. You would wonder the way the week slipped by. But it's the Land of the Free, right enough ; there's no' half enough o' laws a chentleman can break for his diversion ; I hadna very mich of a selection.' "

AN OCEAN TRAGEDY

It was a lovely afternoon at the end of May, and the *Vital Spark* was puffing down Kilbrannan Sound with a farmer's flitting. Macphail, the engineer, sat " with his feet among

the enchines and his heid in the clouds," as Dougie put it—
in other words, on the ladder of his engine-room, with his
perspiring brow catching the cool breeze made by the vessel's
progress, and his emotions rioting through the adventures of
a governess in the " Family Herald Supplement." Peace
breathed like an exhalation from the starboard hills ; the
sea was like a mirror, broken only by the wheel of a stray
porpoise, and Sunny Jim indulged the Captain and the mate
with a medley on his melodeon.

" You're a capital player, Jum," said the Captain in a
pause of the entertainment. " Oh, yes, there's no doot you
are cluver on it ; it's a gift, but you havena the selection ;
no, you havena the selection, and if you havena the selection
where are you ? "

" He's doin' his best," said Dougie sympathetically, and
then, in one of those flashes of philosophy that come to the
most thoughtless of us at times—" A man can do no more."

" Whit selections was ye wantin' ? " asked the musician,
with a little irritation ; " if it's Gaelic sangs ye're meanin'
I wad need a drum and the nicht aff."

" No, I wassna thinkin' aboot Gaelic sangs," explained
Para Handy ; " when we're consuderin' them we're consuderin' music ; I wass taalkin' of the bits of things you
put on the melodeon ; did you ever hear ' Napoleon ' ? " and
clearing his throat he warbled—

" Wa-a-n night sad and dree-ary
    Ass I lay on my bed,
And my head scarce reclined on the pillow ;
A vision surprisin' came into my head,
And I dreamt I wass crossin' the billow.
And ass my proud vessel she dashed o'er the deep——"

" It wasna the *Vital Spark*, onywye," remarked Macphail
cynically ; " afore I got her biler sorted she couldna dash
doon a waterfall——"

" I beheld a rude rock, it was craggy and steep,"

(proceeded the vocalist, paying no attention),

" " 'Twas the rock where the willow iss now seen to weep,
    O'er the grave of the once-famed Napo-o-o-ole-on ! ' "

" I never heard better, Peter," said the mate approvingly.
" Take your breath and give us another touch of it.   There's
nothing bates the old songs."

" Let me see, noo, what wass the second verse ? " asked
the Captain, with his vanity as an artist fully roused ; " it
was something like this—

" And ass my proud vessel she near-ed the land,
    I beheld her clad in green, his bold figure ;
    The trumpet of fame clasped firm in his hand,
    On his brow there wass valour and vigour."

" Balloons ! balloons ! " cried Macphail, imitating some
Glasgow street barrow vendor.   " Fine balloons for rags and
banes."

" Fair do ! gie the Captain a chance," expostulated Sunny
Jim.   " Ye're daein' fine, Captain ; Macphail's jist chawed
because he canna get readin'."

" ' Oh, stranger,' he cried, ' dost thou come unto me,
    From the land of thy fathers who boast they are free ;
    Then, if so, a true story I'll tell unto thee
    Concerning myself—I'm Napo-o-o-ole-on,' "

proceeded the Captain, no way discouraged, and he had no
sooner concluded the final doleful note than a raucous voice
from the uncovered hold cried " Co-co-coals ! "

Even Dougie sniggered ; Macphail fell into convulsions of
laughter, and Sunny Jim showed symptoms of choking.

" I can stand Macphail's umpudence, but I'll no' stand
that nonsense from a hoolit on my own shup," exclaimed the
outraged vocalist, and, stretching over the coamings, he
grabbed from the top of a chest of drawers in the hold a cage
with a cockatoo.   " Come oot like a man," said he, " and
say't again."

" Toots ! Peter, it's only a stupid animal ; I wouldna
put myself a bit aboot," remarked Dougie soothingly.   " It's

weel enough known them cockatoos have no ear for music.
Forbye, he wassna meanin' anything when he cried ' Coals ! '
he was chust in fun."

"Fun or no," said Macphail, "a bird wi' sense like that's
no' canny. Try him wi' another verse, Captain, and see if
he cries on the polis."

"If he says another word I'll throw him over the side,"
said Para Handy. "It's nothing else but mutiny," and with
a wary eye on the unsuspecting cockatoo he sang another
verse—

" ' You remember that year so immortal,' he cried,
' When I crossed the rude Alps famed in story,
With the legions of France, for her sons were my pride,
And I led them to honour and glory——' "

"Oh, crickey ! Chase me, girls ! " exclaimed the cockatoo,
and the next moment was swinging over the side of the *Vital
Spark* to a watery grave.

The fury of the outraged Captain lasted but a moment ;
he had the vessel stopped and the punt out instantly for
a rescue ; but the unhappy bird was irrecoverably gone,
and the tea-hour on the *Vital Spark* that afternoon was
very melancholy. Macphail, particularly, was inexpressibly
galling in the way he over and over again brought up the
painful topic.

"I canna get it oot o' my heid," he said ; "the look it
gied when ye were gaun to swing it roon' your heid and
gie't the heave ! I'll cairry that cockatoo's last look to my
grave."

"Whit kin' o' look was it ? " asked Sunny Jim, eager for
details ; "I missed it."

"It was a look that showed ye the puir bird kent his last
oor was come," explained the engineer. "It wasna anger,
and it wasna exactly fricht ; it was—man ! I canna picture it to ye, but efter this ye needna tell me beasts have nae
sowls ; it's a' my aunty. Yon bird——"

"I wish I hadna put a finger on him," said the Captain, sore stricken with remorse. "Change the subject."

"The puir bird didna mean ony hairm," remarked Sunny Jim, winking at the engineer. "'Coals!' or 'Chase me, girls!' is jist a thing onybody would say if they heard a chap singin' a sang like yon; it's oot o' date. Fair do! ye shouldna hae murdered the beast; the man it belangs to 'll no' be awfu' weel pleased."

"Murdered the beast!" repeated the conscience-stricken Captain; "it's no' a human body you're talkin' aboot," and the engineer snorted his amazement.

"Michty! Captain, is that a' ye ken?" he exclaimed. "If it's no' murder, it's manslaughter; monkeys, cockatoos, and parrots a' come under the Act o' Parliament. A cockatoo's no' like a canary; it's able to speak the language and give an opeenion, and the man that wad kill a cockatoo wad kill a wean."

"That's right enough, Peter," said Dougie pathetically; "everybody kens it's manslaughter. I never saw a nicer cockatoo either; no' a better behaved bird; it's an awful peety. Perhaps the polis at Carradale will let the affair blow bye."

"I wassna meanin' to herm the bird," pleaded Para Handy. "It aggravated me. Here wass I standin' here singin' 'Napoleon,' and the cockatoo wass yonder, and he hurt my feelin's twice; you would be angry yoursel' if it wass you. My nerves got the better o' me."

"If the polis cross-examine me," said the engineer emphatically, "I'll conceal naething. I'll no' turn King's evidence or onything like that, mind, but if I'm asked I'll tell the truth, for I don't want to be mixed up wi' a case o' manslaughter and risk my neck."

Thus were the feelings of the penitent Para Handy lacerated afresh every hour of the day, till he would have given everything he possessed in the world to restore the cockatoo to life. The owner's anger at the destruction of his bird

was a trifle to be anticipated calmly ; the thought that made
Para Handy's heart like lead was that cockatoos DID speak,
that this one even seemed to have the gift of irony, and that
he had drowned a fellow-being ; it was, in fact, he admitted
to himself, a kind of manslaughter. His shipmates found a
hundred ways of presenting his terrible deed to him in fresh
aspects.

" Cockatoos iss mentioned in the Scruptures," said Dougie ;
" I don't exactly mind the place, but I've seen it."

" They live mair nor a hundred years if they're weel
trated," was Sunny Jim's contribution to the natural history
of the bird.

" Naebody ever saw a deid cockatoo," added the engineer.

" I wish you would talk aboot something else," said the
Captain piteously ; " I'm troubled enough in mind withoot
you bringin' that accursed bird up over and over again,"
and they apologised, but always came back to the topic
again.

" I wid plead guilty and throw mysel' on the mercy o' the
coort," was Macphail's suggestion. " At the maist it'll no'
be mair nor a sentence for life."

" Ye could say ye did it in self-defence," recommended
Sunny Jim. " Thae cockatoos bites like onything."

" A great calamity ! " moaned Dougie, shaking his head.

When the cargo of furniture was discharged and delivered,
the farmer discovered the absence of his cockatoo, and came
down to make inquiries.

" He fell over the side," was the Captain's explanation.
" We had his cage hanging on the shrouds, and a gale struck
us and blew it off. His last words wass, ' There's nobody
to blame but mysel'.' "

" There was no gale aboot here," said the farmer, suspecting nothing. " I'm gey sorry to lose that cage. It was a
kind o' a pity, too, the cockatoo bein' drooned."

" Say nothing aboot that," pleaded the Captain. " I
have been mournin' about that cockatoo all week ; you

wouldna believe the worry it haas been for me, and when all iss said and done I consider the cockatoo had the best of it."

THE RETURN OF THE TAR

A YACHTSMAN with " R.Y.S. Dolphin " blazoned on his guernsey came down Campbeltown quay and sentimentally regarded the *Vital Spark*, which had just completed the discharge of a cargo of coals under circumstances pleasing to her crew, since there had been a scarcity of carts, two days of idleness, and two days' demurrage. Para Handy saw him looking—" The smertest shup in the tred," he remarked to Sunny Jim ; " you see the way she catches their eye ! It's her lines, and cheneral appearance ; stop you till I give her a touch of paint next month ! "

" He'll ken us again when he sees us," said Sunny Jim, unpleasantly conscious of his own grimy aspect, due to eight hours of coal dust. " Hey, you wi' the sign-board, is't a job you're wantin' ? " he cried to the yachtsman ; and started to souse himself in a bucket of water.

The stranger pensively gazed at the Captain, and said, " Does your eyes deceive me or am I no' Colin ? "

" Beg pardon ! " replied the Captain cautiously.

" Colin," repeated the stranger. " Surely you must mind The Tar ? "

" Holy smoke ! " exclaimed Para Handy, " you're no' my old shupmate, surely ; if you are, there's a desperate change on you. Pass me up my spy-gless, Dougie."

The yachtsman jumped on board, and barely escaped crashing into the tea-dishes with which Sunny Jim proposed to deal when his toilet was completed. " And there's Dougie himsel'," he genially remarked ; " —— and Macphail, too ; it's chust like comin' home. Are ye aal in good condeetion ? "

" We canna complain," said Dougie, shaking the proffered

hand with some dubiety. "If you were The Tar we used to have you wouldna miss them plates so handy wi' your feet." They stood around and eyed him shrewdly; he certainly looked a little like The Tar if The Tar could be imagined wideawake, trim, clean-shaven, and devoid of diffidence. The engineer, with a fancy nourished on twenty years' study of novelettes, where fraudulent claimants to fortunes and estates were continually turning up, concluded at once that this was really not The Tar at all, but a clever impersonator, and wondered what the game was. The Captain took up a position more non-committal; he believed he could easily test the bona-fides of the stranger.

"And how's your brother Charles?" he inquired innocently.

"Cherles," said the yachtsman, puzzled. "I never had a brother Cherles."

"Neither you had, when I mind, now; my mistake!" said the Captain; "I wass thinkin' on another hand we used to have that joined the yats. Wass I not at your mairrage over in Colintraive?"

"I wasna mairried in Colintraive at all!" exclaimed the puzzled visitor. "Man, Captain! but your memory's failin'."

"Neither you were," agreed the Captain, thinking for a moment. "It wass such a cheery weddin', I forgot."

"If you're the oreeginal Tar," broke in the engineer, "you'll maybe gie me back my knife: ye mind I gied ye a len' o't the day ye left, and I didna get it back frae ye," but this was an accusation the visitor emphatically denied.

"You'll maybe no' hae an anchor tatooed aboot you anywhere?" asked the mate. "It runs in my mind there wass an anchor."

"Two of them," said the visitor, promptly baring an arm, and revealing these interesting decorations.

"That's anchors right enough," said the Captain, closely

examining them, and almost convinced. " I canna say mysel' I mind o' them, but there they are, Dougie."

" It's easy tatooin' anchors," said the engineer ; " whaur's your strawberry mark ? "

" What's a strawberry mark ? " asked the baffled stranger.

" There ! " exclaimed Macphail triumphantly. " Everybody kens ye need to hae a strawberry mark. Hoo are we to ken ye're the man ye say ye are if ye canna produce a strawberry mark ? " And again the confidence of the Captain was obviously shaken.

" Pass me along that pail," said the mate suddenly to the stranger, who, with his hands in his pockets, slid the pail along the deck to the petitioner with a lazy thrust of his foot that was unmistakably familiar.

The Captain slapped him on the shoulder. " It's you yoursel', Colin ! " he exclaimed. " There wass never another man at sea had the same agility wi' his feet ; it's me that's gled to see you. Many a day we missed you. It's chust them fancy togs that makes the difference. That and your hair cut, and your face washed so parteecular."

" A chentleman's life," said The Tar, later, sitting on a hatch with his bona-fides now established to the satisfaction of all but the engineer, who couldn't so readily forget the teachings of romance. " A chentleman's life. That's oor yat oot there ; she comes from Cowes, and I'm doin' fine on her. I knew the tarry old hooker here ass soon ass I saw her at the quay."

" You're maybe doin' fine on the yats," said the Captain coldly, " but it doesna improve the mainners. She wassna a tarry old hooker when you were earnin' your pound a-week on her."

" No offence ! " said The Tar remorsefully. " I wass only in fun. I've seen a wheen o' vessels since I left her, but none that had her style nor nicer shupmates."

" That's the truth ! " agreed the Captain, mollified immediately. " Come doon and I'll show you the same old bunk

'ou did a lot o' sleepin' in," and The Tar agreeably followed
him with this sentimental purpose. They were below ten
minutes, during which time the engineer summed up the
whole evidence for and against the identity of the claimant,
and proclaimed his belief to Dougie that the visitor had come
to the *Vital Spark* after no good. He was so righteously
indignant at what he considered a deception that he even
refused to join the party when it adjourned into the town to
celebrate the occasion fittingly at the Captain's invitation.

The Tar retired to his yacht in due course ; Para Handy,
Dougie, and Sunny Jim returned, on their part, to the
Vital Spark, exhilarated to the value of half-a-crown handsomely disbursed by the Captain, who had never before been
seen with a shilling of his own so far on in the week. They
were met on board by Macphail in a singularly sarcastic
frame of mind, mingled with a certain degree of restrained
indignation.

" I hope your frien' trated ye well," he said.

" Fine ! " said the Captain. " Colin was aye the chentleman. He's doin' capital on the yats."

" He'll be daein' time oot o' the yats afore he's done," said
the engineer. " I kent he was efter nae guid comin' here,
and when ye had him doon below showin' him whaur The
Tar bunked, he picked my Sunday pocket o' hauf-a-croon.
The man's a fraud, ye're blin' no' to see't ; he hadna even a
strawberry mark."

" Whatever you say yoursel'," replied the Captain, with an
expansive wink at the mate and Sunny Jim. " If he's not
The Tar, and took your money, it wass lucky you saw through
him."

THE FORTUNE-TELLER

TARBERT Fair was in full swing ; the crew of the *Vital
Spark* had exhausted the delirious delights of the hobby-
horses, the shooting-gallery, Aunt Sally, Archer's Lilliputian

Circus, and the booth where, after ten, they got pink fizzin
drinks that had " a fine, fine appearance, but not mich fu:
in them," as Para Handy put it, and Dougie stumbled upo:
a gipsy's cart on the outskirts of the Fair, where a woma:
was telling fortunes. Looking around to assure himse!
that he was unobserved by the others, he went behind th:
cart tilt and consulted the oracle, a proceeding which too!
ten minutes, at the end of which time he rejoined the Captain
betraying a curious mood of alternate elation and depression

"Them high-art fizzy drinks iss not agreeing with you
Dougie," said the Captain sympathetically ; " you're losin:
all your joviality, and it not near the mornin'. Could yo:
not get your eye on Macphail ? I'll wudger he'll have some
thing sensible in a bottle ! "

" Macphail ! " exclaimed the mate emphatically ; " :
wouldna go for a drink to him if I wass dyin' ; I wouldna b:
in his reverence."

" Holy smoke ! but you're gettin' desperate independent,'
said the Captain ; " you had more than wan refreshmen:
with him the day already," and the mate, admitting it remorsefully, relapsed into gloomy silence as they loitered
about the Fair-ground.

" Peter," he said in a little, " did you ever try your fortune ? "

" I never tried anything else," said the Captain ; " but
it's like the herrin' in Loch Fyne the noo—it's no' in't."

" That's no what I mean," said Dougie ; " there's a
cluver woman roond in a cairt yonder, workin' wi' cairds
and tea-leaves and studyin' the palm o' the hand, and she'll
tell you everything that happened past and future. I gave
her a caal mysel' the noo, and she told me things that wass
most astonishin'."

" What did it cost you ? " asked Para Handy, with his
interest immediately aroused.

" Ninepence."

" Holy smoke ! she would need to be most extraordinar'

astonishin' for ninepence ; look at the chap in Archer's circus tying himself in knots for front sates threepence ! Forbye, I don't believe in them spae-wifes ; half the time they're only tellin' lies."

" This wan's right enough, I'll warrant you," said the mate ; " she told me at once I wass a sailor and came through a lot of trouble."

"What did she predict ?—that's the point, Dougie ; they're no' mich use unless they can predict ; I could tell myself by the look o' you that you had a lot o' trouble, the thing's quite common."

" No, no," said the mate cautiously ; " pay ninepence for yoursel' if you want her to predict. She told me some eye-openers."

The Captain, with a passion for eye-openers, demanded to be led to the fortune-teller, and submitted himself to nine-pence worth of divination, while Dougie waited outside on him. He, too, came forth, half-elated, half-depressed.

" What did she say to you ? " asked the mate.

" She said I wass a sailor and seen a lot o' trouble," replied the Captain.

" Yes, but what did she predict ? "

" Whatever it wass it cost me ninepence," said the Captain, " and I'm no' givin' away any birthday presents any more than yoursel' ; it's time we were back noo on the vessel."

Getting on board the *Vital Spark* at the quay they found that Para Handy's guess at the engineer's possession of something sensible in a bottle was correct. He hospitably passed it round, and was astonished to find the Captain and mate, for the first time in his experience, refuse a drink. They not only refused but were nasty about it.

" A' richt," he said ; " there'll be a' the mair in the morn for me an' Jim. I daursay ye ken best yersel's when ye've gane ower faur wi't. I aye believe, mysel', in moderation."

The manner of Para Handy and his mate for a week after this was so peculiar as to be the subject of unending

G

speculation on the part of the engineer and Sunny Jim.   The
most obvious feature of it was that they both regarded the
engineer with suspicion and animosity.

"I'm shair I never did them ony hairm," he protested to
Sunny Jim, almost in tears; "I never get a ceevil word frae
either o' them. Dougie's that doon on me, he wad raither
gang withoot a smoke than ask a match aff me."

"It's cruel, that's whit it is!" said Sunny Jim, who had a
feeling heart; "but they're aff the dot ever since the nicht
we were at Tarbert. Neither o' them 'll eat fish, nor gang
ashore efter it's dark. They baith took to their beds on
Monday and wouldna steer oot o' their bunks a' day, pre-
tendin' to be ill, but wonderfu' sherp in the appetite."

"I'll give them wan chance, and if they refuse it I'll wash
my hands o' them," said Macphail decisively, and that evening after tea he produced a half-crown and extended a general
invitation to the nearest tavern.

"Much obleeged, but I'm not in the need of anything,"
said the Captain. "Maybe Dougie——"

"No thanky," said the mate with equal emphasis; "I
had a dram this week already"—a remark so ridiculous that
it left the engineer speechless. He tapped his head significantly with a look at Sunny Jim, and the two of them went
ashore to dispose of the half-crown without the desired
assistance.

Next day there was an auction sale in the village, and
Para Handy and his mate, without consulting each other,
found themselves among the bidders.

"Were you fancyin' anything parteecular?" asked the
Captain, who plainly had an interest in a battered old eight-
day clock.

"No, nothing to mention," said the mate, with an eye
likewise on the clock. "There's capital bargains here,
see, in crockery."

But the Captain seemed to have no need for crockery;
he hung about an hour or two till the clock was put to the

hammer, and offered fifteen shillings, thus completely discouraging a few of the natives who had concealed the hands and weights of the clock, and hoped to secure the article at the reasonable figure of about a crown. To the Captain's surprise and annoyance, he found his mate his only competitor, and between them they raised the price to thirty shillings, at which figure it was knocked down to the Captain, who had it promptly placed on a barrow and wheeled down to the quay.

" Were you desperate needin' a nock ? " asked the mate, coming after him.

" I wass on the look-out for a nock like that for years," said the Captain, apparently charmed with his possession.

" I'll give you five and thirty shillings for't," said the mate, but Para Handy wasn't selling. He had the clock on board, and spent at least an hour investigating its interior, with results that from his aspect seemed thoroughly disappointing. He approached Dougie and informed him that he had changed his mind, and was willing to hand over the clock for five-and-thirty shillings. The bargain was eagerly seized by Dougie, who paid the money and submitted his purchase to an examination even more exhaustive than the Captain.

Half an hour later the engineer and Sunny Jim had to separate the Captain and the mate, who were at each other's throats, the latter frantically demanding back his money or a share of whatever the former had found inside the clock.

" The man's daft," protested Para Handy ; " the only thing that was in the nock wass the works and an empty bottle."

" The Tarbert spae-wife said I would find a fortune in a nock like that," spluttered Dougie.

" Holy smoke ! She said the same to me," confessed the Captain. " And did she say that eatin' fish wass dangerous ? "

" She did that," said the mate. " Did she tell you to keep your bed on the first o' the month in case of accidents."

"Her very words!" said the Captain. "Did she tell you to beware o' a man wi' black whiskers that came from Australia?" and he looked at the engineer.

"She told me he was my bitterest enemy," said the mate.

"And that's the way ye had the pick at me!" exclaimed the engineer. "Ye're a couple o' Hielan' cuddies; man, never wass nearer Australia than the River Plate."

On the following day a clock went cheap at the head o' the quay for fifteen shillings, and the loss was amicably shared by Para Handy and his mate, but any allusion to Tarbert Fair and fortune-telling has ever since been bitterly resented by them both.

THE HAIR LOTION

DOUGIE, the mate, had so long referred to his family album as a proof of the real existence of old friends regarding whom he had marvellous stories to tell, that the crew finally demanded its production. He protested that it would be difficult to get it out of the house, as his wife had it fair in the middle of the parlour table, on top of the Family Bible.

"Ye can ask her for the len' o't, surely," said the Captain. "There's nobody goin' to pawn it on her. Tell her it's to show your shupmates what a tipper she wass hersel' when she wass in her prime."

"She's in her prime yet," said the mate, with some annoyance.

"Chust that!" said Para Handy. "A handsome gyurl, I'm sure of it; but every woman thinks she wass at her best before her husband mairried her. Let you on that you were bouncin' aboot her beauty, and tell her the enchineer wass dubious——"

"Don't drag me into't," said the engineer. "You micht hae married Lily Langtry for a' I care; put the blame on the Captain; he's what they ca' a connysure among the girls," a statement on which the Captain darkly brooded for several days after.

The mate ultimately rose to the occasion, and taking advantage of a visit by his wife to her good-sister, came on board one day with the album wrapped in his oilskin trousers. It created the greatest interest on the *Vital Spark*, and an admiration only marred by the discovery that the owner was attempting to pass off a lithograph portrait of the late John Bright as that of his Uncle Sandy.

" My mistake ! " he said politely, when the engineer corrected him ; " I thocht it wass Uncle Sandy by the whuskers ; when I look again I see he hasna the breadth across the shouthers."

" Wha's this chap like a body-snatcher ? " asked the engineer, turning over another page of the album. " If I had a face like that I wad try and no' keep mind o't."

" You're a body snatcher-yoursel'," said the mate warmly, " and that's my advice to you. Buy specs, Macphail ; you're spoilin' your eyes wi' readin' them novelles."

" Holy smoke ! " cried the Captain ; " it's a picture o' yoursel', Dougie. Man ! what a heid o' hair ! "

" I had a fair quantity," said the mate, passing his hand sadly over a skull which was now as bare as a bollard. " I'm sure I don't ken what way I lost it."

" Short bunks for sleepin' in," suggested the Captain kindly ; " that's the worst o' bein' a sailor."

" I tried everything, from paraffin oil to pumice-stone, but nothing did a bit of good ; it came oot in handfuls."

" I wad hae left her," said the engineer. " When a wife tak's her hands to ye the law says ye can leave her and tak' the weans wi' ye."

" I see ye hae been consultin' the lawyers," retorted the mate readily ; " what way's your ear keepin' efter your last argument wi' the flet-iron ? " and Macphail retired in dudgeon to his engines.

Sunny Jim regarded Dougie's portrait thoughtfully.

" Man ! " he said, " if the Petroloid Lotion had been invented in them days ye could hae had your hair yet. That's the stuff ! Fair champion ! Rub it on the doorstep and ye didna need to keep a bass. The hair mak's a difference richt enough ; your face is jist the same's it used to be but the hair in the photo mak's ye twenty years younger It's as nice a photo as ever I seed ; there's money in't."

" None o' your dydoes noo ! " said the mate, remembering how Sunny Jim had found money in the exploitation of the Tobermory whale. " If you think I would make an exhibeetion o' my photygraph——"

" Exhibeetion my aunty ! " exclaimed Sunny Jim. " Ye're no' an Edna May. But I'll tell ye whit we could dae. Thae Petroloid Lotion folks is keen on testimonials. A' ye hae to dae is to get Macphail to write a line for ye saying ye lost yer hair in a biler explosion, and tried Petroloid, and it broch it back in a couple o' weeks. Get a photograph o' yersel the way ye are the noo and send it, and this yin wi' the testimonial, lettin' on the new yin's the way ye looked immediately efter the explosion, and this yin's the way ye look since ye took to usin' the lotion."

" Capital ! " cried the Captain, slapping his knees. " For ingenuity you're chust sublime, Jum."

" Sublime enough," said Dougie cautiously, " but I thocht you said there wass money in it."

" So there is," said Sunny Jim. " The Petroloid Lotion folk 'll gie ye a pound or twa for the testimonial ; I kent a chap that made his livin' oot o' curin' himsel' o' diseases he never had, wi' pills he never saw except in pictures. He was a fair don at describin' a buzzin' in the ear, a dizzy heid, or a pain alang the spine o' his back, and was dragged back frae the brink o' the grave a thoosand times, by his way o't, under a different name every time. Macphail couldna touch him at a testimonial for anything internal, but there's naething to hinder Macphail puttin' a bit thegither aboot the loss and restoration o' Dougie's hair. Are ye game, Dougie ? "

The mate consented dubiously, and the engineer was called upon to indite the requisite document, which took him a couple of evenings, on one of which the mate was taken ashore at Rothesay and photographed in the Captain's best blue pilot pea-jacket. The portraits and the testimonial were duly sent to the address which was found in the advertisement of Petroloid's Lotion for the Hair, a gentle hint being included that some " recognition " would be looked for, the phrase being Sunny Jim's. Then the crew of the *Vital Spark* resigned themselves to a patient wait of several days for an acknowledgment.

Three weeks passed, and Sunny Jim's scheme was sadly confessed a failure, for nothing happened, and the cost of the Rothesay photograph, which had been jointly borne by the crew on the understanding that they were to share alike in the products of it, was a subject of frequent and unfeeling remarks from the engineer, who suggested that the mate had got a remittance and said nothing about it. But one afternoon the Captain picked up a newspaper, and turning, as was his wont, to the pictorial part of it, gave an exclamation on beholding the two portraits of his mate side by side in the midst of a Petroloid advertisement.

" Holy smoke ! Dougie," he cried, " here you are ass large ass life like a futbaal player or a man on his trial for manslaughter."

" Michty ! iss that me ? " said the mate incredulously. " I had no notion they would put me in the papers. If I kent that I would never have gone in for the ploy."

" Ye look guilty," said the engineer, scrutinising the blurred lineaments of his shipmate in the newspaper. " Which is the explosion yin ? The testimonial's a' richt onyway ; it's fine," and he read his own composition with complete approval—

I unfortunately lost all my hair in a boiler explosion, and tried all the doctors, but none of them could bring it back. Then I heard of your wonderful Petroloid Lotion, and got a small bottle, which I rubbed in night and morning as described. In a week there was a distinct improvement. In a fortnight I had to have my head shorn twice, and now it is as thick as ever it was. I will recommend your Lotion to all my friends, and you are at liberty to make any use of this you like.—(Signed) Dougald Campbell, Captain, *Vital Spark*.

" What's that ? " cried Para Handy, jumping up. " Captain ! who said he was captain ? "

" The advertisement," said the engineer guiltily. " I never wrote ' captain ' ; they've gone and shifted a lot o' things I wrote, and spiled the grammar and spellin'. Fancy the way they spell distinck ! "

. . . .

A few days later a box was delivered on the *Vital Spark* which at first was fondly supposed to be a case of whisky lost by somebody's mistake, but was found on examination to be directed to the mate. It was opened eagerly, and revealed a couple of dozen of the Petroloid specific, with a letter containing the grateful acknowledgments of the manufacturers, and expressing a generous hope that as the lotion had done so much to restore their correspondent's hair, he would distribute the accompanying consignments among all his bald-headed friends.

" Jum," said the Captain sadly, "when you're in the trum for makin' money efter this, I'll advise you to tak' the thing in hand yoursel' and leave us oot of it."

PARA HANDY AND THE NAVY

MACPHAIL the engineer sat on an upturned bucket reading the weekly paper, and full of patriotic alarm at the state of the British Navy.

" What are you groanin' and sniffin' at ? " asked the

Captain querulously. "I should think mysel' that by this time you would be tired o' Mrs Atherton. Whatna prank iss she up to this time ? "

"It's no' Mrs Atherton," said the reader ; "it's something mair important ; it's the Germans."

"Holy smoke ! " said Para Handy, "are they findin' them oot, noo ? Wass I not convinced there wass something far, far wrong wi' them ? Break the full parteeculars to me chently, Mac, and you, Jim, go and get the dinner ready ; you're far too young to hear the truth aboot the Chermans. Which o' the Chermans iss it, Mac ? Some wan in a good poseetion, I'll be bound ! It's a mercy that we're sailors ; you'll no' find mich aboot the wickedness o' sailors in the papers."

"The British Navy's a' to bleezes ! " said Macphail emphatically. "Here's Germany buildin' Dreadnought men-o'-war as hard's she can, and us palaverin' awa' oor time."

Para Handy looked a little disappointed. "It's politics you're on," said he ; "and I wass thinkin' it wass maybe another aawful scandal in Society. That's the worst o' the newspapers—you never know where you are wi' them ; a week ago it wass nothing but the high jeenks of the beauteous Mrs Atherton. Do you tell me the Brutish Navy's railly done ? "

"Complete ! " said the engineer.

"Weel, that's a peety ! " said Para Handy sympathetically ; "it'll put a lot o' smert young fellows oot o' jobs ; I know a Tarbert man called Colin Kerr that had a good poseetion on the *Formidable*. I'm aawful sorry aboot Colin."

The engineer resumed his paper, and the *Vital Spark* chug-chugged her sluggish way between the Gantocks and the Cloch, with Dougie at the wheel, his nether garments hung precariously on the half of a pair of braces. "There's nothing but dull tred everywhere," said he. "They're stoppin' a lot o' the railway steamers, too."

G*

" The state o' the British Navy's mair important than the stoppage o' a wheen passenger steamers," explained the engineer. " If you chaps read the papers ye would see this country's in a bad poseetion. We used to rule the sea——"

" We did that ! " said the Captain heartily ; " I've seen us doin' it ! Brutain's hardy sons ! "

" And noo the Germans is gettin' the upper hand o' us ; they'll soon hae faur mair Dreadnoughts than we hae. We're only buildin' four. Fancy that ! Four Dreadnoughts at a time like this, wi' nae work on the Clyde, and us wi' that few Territorials we hae to go to the fitba' matches and haul them oot to jine by the hair o' the heid. We've lost the two-Power standard."

" Man, it's chust desperate ! " said the Captain. " We'll likely advertise for't. What's the—what's the specialty aboot the Dreadnoughts ? "

" It's the only cless o' man-o'-war that's coonted noo," said the engineer ; " a tip-top battle-winner. If ye havena Dreadnoughts ye micht as weel hae dredgers."

" Holy smoke ! what a lot o' lumber aal the other men-o'-war must be ! " remarked the Captain. " That'll be the way they're givin' them up and payin' off the hands."

" Wha said they were givin' them up ? " asked the engineer snappishly.

" Beg pardon ! beg pardon ! I thocht I heard you mention it yon time I remarked on Colin Kerr. I thocht that maybe aal the other boats wass absolute, and we would see them next week lyin' in the Kyles o' Bute wi' washin's hung oot on them."

" There's gaun to be nae obsolete boats in the British Navy efter this," said the engineer ; " we're needin' every man-o'-war that'll haud thegither. The Germans has their eye on us."

" Dougie," said the Captain firmly, with a glance at the deshabille of his mate, " go doon this instant and put on your jecket ! The way you are, you're not a credit to the boat."

A terrific bang broke upon the silence of the Firth ; the crew of the *Vital Spark* turned their gaze with one accord towards the neighbourhood of Kilcreggan, whence the report seemed to have proceeded, and were frightfully alarmed a second or two afterwards when a shell burst on the surface of the sea a few hundred yards or so from them, throwing an enormous column of water into the air.

" What did I tell ye ! " cried Macphail, as he dived below to his engine-room.

" Holy smoke ! " exclaimed Para Handy ; " did ye notice anything, Dougie ? "

" I think I did ! " said the mate, considerably perturbed ; ' there must be some wan blastin'."

" Yon wassna a blast," said the Captain ; " they're firin' cannons at us from Portkill."

" There's a pant for ye ! " exclaimed Sunny Jim, dodging behind the funnel.

" What for would they be firin' cannons at us ? " asked the mate, with a ludicrous feeling that even the jacket advised a minute or two ago by the Captain would now be a most desirable protection.

Another explosion from the fort at Portkill postponed the Captain's answer, and this time the bursting shell seemed a little closer.

" Jim," said the mate appealingly, " would ye mind takin' ha'd o' this wheel till I go down below and get my jacket ? If I'm to be shot, I'll be shot like a Hielan' chentleman and no' in my shirt sleeves."

" You'll stay where you are ! " exclaimed the Captain, greatly excited ; " you'll stay where you are, and die at your post like a Brutish sailor. This iss WAR. Port her heid in for Macinroy's Point, Dougald, and you, Macphail, put on to her every pound of steam she'll cairry. I wish to Providence I had chust the wan wee Union Jeck."

"Whit would ye dae wi' a Union Jeck?" asked the engineer, putting up his head and ducking nervously as another shot boomed over the Firth.

"I would nail it to the mast!" said Para Handy, buttoning his coat. "It would show them Cherman chentlemen we're the reg'lar he'rts of oak."

"Ye don't think it's Germans that's firin', dae ye?" asked the engineer, cautiously putting out his head again. "It's the Garrison Arteelery that's firin' frae Portkill."

"Whit are the silly duvvles firin' at us for, then?" asked Para Handy; "I'm sure we never did them any herm."

"I ken whit for they're firin'," said the engineer maliciously; "they're takin' the *Vital Spark* for yin o' them German Dreadnoughts. Ye have nae idea o' the fear o' daith that's on the country since it lost the two-Power standard."

This notion greatly charmed the Captain, being distinctly complimentary to his vessel; but his vanity was soon dispelled, for Sunny Jim pointed out that the last shot had fallen far behind them, in proximity to a floating target now for the first time seen. "They're jist at big-gun practice," he remarked with some relief, "and we're oot o' the line o' fire."

"Of course we are!" said Para Handy. "I kent that aal along. Man, Macphail, but you were tumid, tumid! You're losin' aal your nerve wi' readin' aboot the Chermans."

PIRACY IN THE KYLES

"I'M goin' doon below to put on my sluppers," said the Captain, as the vessel puffed her leisured way round Buttock Point; "keep your eye on the *Collingwood*, an' no' run into her; it would terribly vex the Admirality."

The mate, with a spoke of the wheel in the small of his back, and his hands in his trousers pockets, looked along the Kyles towards Colintraive, and remarked that he wasn't altogether blind.

"I didna say you were," said the Captain ; "I wass chust advisin' caaution. You canna be too caautious, and if anything would happen it's mysel' would be the man responsible. Keep her heid a point away, an' no' be fallin' asleep till I get my sluppers on ; you'll mind you were up last night pretty late in Tarbert."

Macphail, the engineer, projected a perspiring head from his engine-room, and wiped his brow with a wad of oily waste. "Whit's the argyment ? " he asked. "Is this a coal-boat or a Convention o' Royal Burghs ? I'm in the middle o' a fine story in the ' People's Frien',' and I canna hear mysel' readin' for you chaps barkin' at each other. I wish ye would talk wee."

Para Handy looked at him with a contemptuous eye, turned his back on him, and confined his address to Dougie. "I'll never feel safe in the Kyles of Bute," he said, "till them men-o'-war iss oot o' here. I'm feared for a collusion."

"There's no' much chance of a collusion wi' a boat like that," said the mate, with a glance at the great sheer hulk of the discarded man-o'-war.

"You would wonder ! " said Para Handy. "I haf seen a smert enough sailor before now come into a collusion wi' the whole o' Cowal. And he wassna tryin't either ! Keep her off yet, Dougald."

With his slippers substituted for his sea-boots, the Captain returned on deck, when the *Collingwood* was safely left astern ; and, looking back, watched a couple of fishermen pulling mussels off the lower plates of the obsolete ship of war. "They're a different cless of men aboot the Kyles from what there used to be," said he, "or it wouldn't be only bait they would be liftin' off a boat like that. If she wass there when Hurricane Jeck wass in his prime, he would have the very cannons off her, sellin' them for junk in Greenock. There's no' that hardy Brutish spirit in the boys

that wass in't when Hurricane Jeck and me wass on the
Aggie."

" Tell us the baur," pleaded Sunny Jim, seated on an
upturned bucket, peeling the day's potatoes.

" It's not the only baur I could tell you about the same
chentleman," said the Captain, " but it's wan that shows
you his remarkable agility. Gie me a haud o' that wheel
Dougie ; I may ass well be restin' my back ass you, and me
the skipper. To let you ken, Jum, Hurricane Jeck wass a
perfect chentleman, six feet two, ass broad in the back as
a shippin'-box, and the very duvvle for contrivance. He
wass a man that wass namely in the clipper tred to China, and
the Board o' Tred had never a hand on him ; his navigation wass complete. You know that, Dougie, don't you ? "

" Whatever you say yoursel'," replied the mate agreeably
cutting himself a generous plug of navy-blue tobacco. "
have nothing to say against the chap—except that he cam
from Campbeltown."

" He sailed wi' me for three or four years on the *Aggie*,"
said the Captain, " and a nicer man on a boat you wouldn
meet, if you didna contradict him. There wass nothin
at aal against his moral character, except that he alway
shaved himsel' on Sunday, whether he wass needin' it o
no'. And a duvvle for recreation ! Six feet three, if h
wass an inch, and a back like a shippin'-box ! "

" Where does the British spirit come in ? " inquired th
engineer, who was forced to relinquish his story and joi
his mates.

" Hold you on, and I'll tell you that," said Para Handy
" We were lyin' wan winter night at Tighnabruaich wi'
cargo o' stones for a place they call Glen Caladh, that was
buildin' at the time, and we wanted a bit o' rope for some
thing in parteecular—I think it wass a bit of a net. Ther
wass lyin' at Tighnabruaich at the time a nice wee steame
yat belonging to a chentleman in Gleska that was busy
at his business, and nobody wass near her. " We'll borrow

a rope for the night from that nice wee yat,' said Hurricane
Jeck, as smert as anything, and when it wass dark he took
the punt and went off and came back wi' a rope that did the
business. 'They havena much sense o' ropes that moored
that boat in the Kyles,' said he ; 'they had it flemished
down and nate for liftin'. They must be naval architects.'
The very next night did Jeck no' take the punt again and
go oot to the wee steam-yat, and come back wi' a couple o'
india-rubber basses and a weather-gless ? "

"Holy smoke !" said Dougie. "Wasn't that chust
desperate ? "

"We were back at Tighnabruaich a week efter that,"
continued Para Handy, "and Jeck made some inquiries.
Nobody had been near the wee steam-yat, though the name
o' her in the Gaelic was the *Eagle*, and Jeck made oot it wass
a special dispensation. 'The man that owned her must
be deid,' said he, ' or he hasna his wuts aboot him ; I'll
take a turn aboard the night wi' a screw-driver, and see
that aal's in order.' He came back that night wi' a bag
o' cleats, a binnacle, half a dozen handy blocks, two dozen
o' empty bottles, and a quite good water-breaker.

"'They may call her the *Eagle* if they like,' says he,
' but I call her the *Silver Mine*. I wish they would put lights
on her ; I nearly broke my neck on the cabin stairs.'

"'Mind you, Jeck,' I says to him, ' I don't ken anything
aboot it. If you're no' comin' by aal them things honest,
it'll give the *Aggie* a bad name.'

"'It's aal right, Peter,' says he, quite kind. 'Flotsam
and jetsam ; if you left them there, you don't ken who
might lift them !' Oh, a smert, smert sailor, Jeck ! Six
feet four in his stockin's soles, and a back like a couple o'
shippin'-boxes."

"He's gettin' on !" remarked the engineer sarcastically.
"I'm gled I wasna his tailor."

"The Glen Caladh job kept us comin' and goin' aal winter,"
pursued the Captain, paying no attention. "Next week

we were back again, and Jeck had a talk with the polisman
at Tighnabruaich aboot the lower clesses. Jeck said the
lower clesses up in Gleska were the worst you ever saw ;
they would rob the wheels off a railway train. The polisman
said he could weel believe it, judgin' from the papers, but,
thank the Lord ! there wass only honest folk in the Kyles
of Bute. ' It's aal right yet,' said Jeck to me that night ;
' the man that owns the *Silver Mine* 's in the Necropolis,
and never said a word aboot the wee yat in his will.' In
the mornin' I saw a clock, a couple o' North Sea charts, a
trysail, a galley-stove, two kettles, and a nice decanter lyin'
in the hold.

" ' Jeck,' I says, ' is this a flittin' ? '

" ' I'll not deceive you, Peter,'' he says, quite honest,
' it's a gift' ; and he sold the lot on Setturday in Greenock.''

" A man like that deserves the jyle,'' said the engineer
indignantly.

" I wouldna caal it aalthegither fair horny,'' admitted the
Captain, " parteecularly as the rest of us never got more
than a schooner o' beer or the like o't oot of it ; but, man !
you must admit the chap's agility ! He cairried the business
oot single-handed, and there wass few wass better able ; he
wass six feet six, and had a back on him like a Broomielaw
shed. The next time we were in the Kyles, and he went off
wi' the punt at night, he came back from the *Silver Mine*
wi' her bowsprit, twenty faddom o' chain, two doors, and
half a dozen port-holes.''

" Oh, to bleezes ! '' exclaimed Sunny Jim incredulously,
" noo you're coddin' ! What wye could he steal her port-
holes ? ''

" Quite easy ! '' said Para Handy. " I didna say he took
the holes themsel's, but he twisted off the windows and
the brass aboot them. You must mind the chap's agility !
And that wassna the end of it, for next time the *Aggie* left
the Kyles she had on board a beautiful vernished dinghy, a
couple o' masts, no' bad, and a fine brass steam-yat funnel.''

" Holy smoke ! " said Dougie ; " it's a wonder he didna trip the lead off her."

" He had it in his mind," exclaimed the Captain ; " but, mind, he never consulted me aboot anything, and I only kent, as you might say, by accident, when he would be standin' me another schooner. It wass aalways a grief to Jeck that he didna take the boat the way she wass, and sail her where he would be properly appreciated. 'My mistake, chaps ! ' he would say ; 'I might have kent they would miss the masts and funnel ! ' "

AMONG THE YACHTS

MACPHAIL was stoking carefully and often, like a mother feeding her first baby ; keeping his steam at the highest pressure short of blowing off the safety valve, on which he had tied a pig-iron bar ; and driving the *Vital Spark* for all he was worth past Cowal. The lighter's bluff bows were high out of water, for she was empty, and she left a wake astern of her like a liner.

" She hass a capital turn of speed when you put her to it," said the Captain, quite delighted ; " it's easy seen it's Setturday, and you're in a hurry to be home, Macphail. You're passin' roond that oil-can there the same ass if it wass a tea-pairty you were at, and nobody there but women. It's easy seen it wass a cargo of coals we had the last trip, and there's more in your bunkers than the owner paid for. But it's none o' my business ; please yoursel' ! "

" We'll easy be at Bowlin' before ten," said Dougie, consulting his watch. " You needna be so desperate anxious."

The engineer mopped himself fretfully with a fistful of oily waste and shrugged his shoulders. " If you chaps like to palaver awa' your time," said he, " it's all the same to me, but I was wantin' to see the end o' the racin'."

"Whatna racin'?" asked the Captain.

"Yat-racin'," said the engineer, with irony. "Ye'l' maybe hae heard o't. If ye havena, ye should read tho papers. There's a club they ca' the Royal Clyde at Hunter's Quay, and a couple o' boats they ca' the *Shamrock* and the *White Heather* are sailin' among a wheen o' ithers for a cup I wouldna care if I saw the feenish; you chaps needna bother just pull doon the skips o' your keps on your e'en when ye pass them, and ye'll no' see onything."

"I don't see much in aal their yat-racin'," said Para Handy.

"If I was you, then, I would try the Eye Infirmary," retorted the engineer, "or wan o' them double-breisted spy-glesses. Yonder the boats; we're in lots o' time——" and he dived again among his engines, and they heard the hurried clatter of his shovel.

"Anything wi' Macphail for sport!" remarked the Captain sadly. "You would think at his time o' life, and the morn Sunday, that his meditaations would be different. . . Give her a point to starboard, Dougie, and we'll see them better. Yonder's the *Ma'oona*; if the duvvle wass wise he would put aboot at wance or he'll hit that patch o' calm."

"There's an aawful money in them yats!" said the mate, who was at the wheel.

"I never could see the sense o't," remarked the Captain . . . "There's the *Hera* tacking; man, she's smert! smert! Wan o' them Coats's boats; I wish she would win; I ken a chap that plays the pipes on her."

Dougie steered as close as he could on the racing cutters with a sportsman's scrupulous regard for wind and water. "What wan's that?" he asked, as they passed a thirty-rater which had struck the calm.

"That's the *Pallas*," said the Captain, who had a curiously copious knowledge of the craft he couldn't see the sense of. "Another wan o' the Coats's; every other wan you see

belongs to Paisley. They buy them by the gross, the same
ass they were pirns, and distribute them every noo and then
among the faimely. If you're a Coats you lose a lot o' time
makin' up your mind what boat you'll sail to-morrow; the
whole o' the Clyde below the Tail o' the Bank is chock-a-
block wi' steamboat-yats and cutters the Coats's canna hail
a boat ashore from to get a sail, for they canna mind their
names. Still-and-on, there's nothing wrong wi' them—tip-
top sportin' chentlemen!"

"I sometimes wish, mysel', I had taken to the yats,"
said Dougie; "it's a suit or two o' clothes in the year,
and a pleasant occupaation. Most o' the time in canvas
sluppers."

"You're better the way you are," said Para Handy;
"there's nothing bates the mercantile marine for makin'
sailors. Brutain's hardy sons! We could do withoot yats,
but where would we be withoot oor coal-boats? Look at
them chaps sprauchlin' on the deck; if they saw themsel's
they would see they want another fut on that main-sheet.
I wass a season or two in the yats mysel'—the good old
Marjory. No' a bad job at aal, but aawful hurried. Holy
smoke! the way they kept you jumpin' here and there the
time she would be racin'! I would chust as soon be in a
lawyer's office. If you stopped to draw your breath a
minute you got yon across the ear from a swingin' boom.
It's a special breed o' sailor-men you need for racin'-yats,
and the worst you'll get iss off the Islands."

"It's a cleaner job at any rate than carryin' coals," remarked the mate, with an envious eye on the spotless decks
of a heeling twenty-tonner.

"Clean enough, I'll alloo, and that's the worst of it," said
Para Handy. "You might ass weel be a chamber-maid—
up in the mornin' scourin' brass and scrubbin' floors, and
goin' ashore wi' a fancy can for sixpenceworth o' milk and
a dozen o' syphon soda. Not much navigation there, my
lad! . . . If I wass that fellow I would gybe her there and

set my spinnaker to starboard ; what do you think yoursel',
Macphail ? "

" I thocht you werena interested," said the engineer, who
had now reduced his speed.

" I'm not much interested, but I'm duvellish keen," said
Para Handy. " Keep her goin' chust like that, Macphail ;
we'll soon be up wi' the *Shamrock* and the *Heather* ; they're
yonder off Loch Long."

A motor-boat regatta was going on at Dunoon ; the *Vital
Spark* seemed hardly to be moving as some of the com-
petitors flashed past her, breathing petrol fumes.

" You canna do anything like that," said Dougie to the
engineer, who snorted.

" No," said Macphail contemptuously, " I'm an engineer ;
I never was much o' a hand at the sewin'-machine. I couldna
lower mysel' to handle engines ye could put in your waistcoat pocket."

" Whether you could or no'," said Para Handy, " the
times iss changin', and the motor-launch iss coming for to
stop."

" That's whit she's aye daein'," retorted the engineer ;
" stoppin's her strong p'int ; gie me a good substantial
compound engine ; nane o' your hurdy-gurdies ! I wish the
wind would fresh a bit, for there's the *Shamrock*, and her
mainsail shakin'." He dived below, and the *Vital Spark*
in a little had her speed reduced to a crawl that kept her just
abreast of the drifting racers.

" Paddy's hurricane—up and doon the mast," said
Dougie in a tone of disappointment. " I would like,
mysel', to see Sir Thomas Lipton winnin', for it's there I get
my tea."

Para Handy extracted a gully-knife from the depths of
his trousers pockets, opened it, spat on the blade for luck,
and, walking forward, stuck it in the mast, where he left it.
" That's the way to get wind," said he ; " many a time I
tried it, and it never fails. Stop you, and you'll see a breeze

immediately. Them English skippers, Sycamore and Bevis, havena the heid to think o't."

" Whit's the use o' hangin' on here ? " said the engineer, with a wink at Dougie ; " it's time we were up the river ; I'll better get her under weigh again."

The Captain turned on him with a flashing eye. " You'll do nothing o' the kind, Macphail," said he ; " we'll stand by here and watch the feenish, if it's any time before the Gleska Fair."

Shamrock, having split tacks off Kilcreggan, laid away to the west, while *White Heather* stood in for the Holy Loch, seeking the evening breeze that is apt to blow from the setting sun. It was the crisis of the day, and the crew of the *Vital Spark* watched speechlessly for a while the yachts manœuvring. For an hour the cutter drifted on this starboard leg, and Sunny Jim, for reasons of his own, postponed the tea.

" It wants more knifes," said Para Handy ; " have you wan, Dougie ? " but Dougie had lost his pocket-knife a week ago, and the engineer had none either.

" If stickin' knifes in the mast would raise the wind," said Sunny Jim, " there would be gales by this time, for I stuck the tea-knife in an oor ago."

" Never kent it to fail afore ! " said Para Handy. . . . " By George ! it's comin'. Yonder's Bevis staying ! "

White Heather, catching the wind, reached for the closing lap of the race with a bone in her mouth, and Para Handy watched her, fascinated, twisting the buttons off his waistcoat in his intense excitement. With a turn or two of the wheel the mate put the *Vital Spark* about and headed for the mark ; Macphail deserted his engine and ran forward to the bow.

" The *Heather* hass it, Dougald," said the Captain thankfully ; " I'm vexed for you, considerin' the place you get your tea."

" Hold you on, Peter," said the mate ; " there's the *Shamrock* fetchin' ; a race is no' done till it's feenished."

His hopes were justified. *Shamrock*, only a few lengths behind, got the same light puff of wind in her sails, and rattled home a winner by half a minute.

"Macphail!" bawled the Captain, "I'll be much obleeged if you take your place again at your bits of engines, and get under weigh; it's any excuse wi' you for a diversion, and it's time we werena here."

FOG

In a silver-grey fog that was not unpleasant, the *Vital Spark* lay at Tarbert quay, and Dougie read a belated evening paper.

"Desperate fog on the Clyde!" he said to his shipmates; "we're the lucky chaps that's here and oot o't! It hasna lifted in Gleska for two days, and there's any amount o' boats amissin' between the Broomielaw and Bowlin'."

"Tck! tck! issn't that deplorable?" said the Captain. "Efter you wi' the paper, Dougald. It must be full o' accidents."

"The Campbeltown boat iss lost since Setturday, and they're lookin' for her wi' lanterns up and doon the river. I hope she hassna many passengers; the poor sowls 'll be stervin'."

"Duvvle the fear!" said Para Handy; "not on the Campbeltown boat ass long ass she has her usual cargo. I would sooner be lost wi' a cargo o' Campbeltown for a week than spend a month in wan o' them hydropathics."

"Two sailors went ashore at Bowlin' from the *Benmore*, and they havena been heard of since," proceeded the mate; "they couldna find their way back to the ship."

"And what happened then?" asked Para Handy.

"Nothing," replied the mate. "That's all; they couldna find their way back."

"Holy smoke!" reflected Para Handy, with genuine surprise; "they're surely ill off for news in the papers

nooadays ; or they must have a poor opeenion o' sailor-men.
They'll be thinkin' they should aalways be teetotalers."

The Captain got the paper to read for himself a little
later, and discovered that the missing *Benmore* men had
not lost themselves in the orthodox sailor way, but were
really victims of the fog, and his heart went out to them.
" I've seen the same thing happen to mysel'," he remarked.
" It wass the time that Hurricane Jeck and me wass on the
Julia. There wass a fog come on us wan time there so thick
you could almost cut it up and sell it for briquettes."

" Help ! " exclaimed Macphail.

" Away, you, Macphail, and study your novelles ; what
way's Lady Fitzgerald gettin' on in the chapter you're
at the noo ? It's a wonder to me you're no' greetin',"
retorted the Captain ; and this allusion to the sentimental
tears of the engineer sent him down, annoyed, among his
engines.

" It wass a fog that lasted near a week, and we got into
it on a Monday mornin' chust below the Cloch. We were
makin' home for Gleska. We fastened up to the quay at
Gourock, waitin' for a change, and the thing that vexed us
most wass that Hurricane Jeck and me wass both invited
for that very night to a smaal tea-party oot in Kelvinside."

" It's yoursel' wass stylish ! " said the mate. " It must
have been before you lost your money in the City Bank."

" It wassna style at aal, but a Cowal gyurl we knew that
wass cook to a chentleman in Kelvinside, and him away on
business in Liverpool," explained the Captain. " Hurricane
Jeck wass in love wi' the gyurl at the time, and her name
wass Bella. ' This fog 'll last for a day or two,' said Jeck
in the efternoon ; ' it's a peety to lose the ploy at Bella's
party.'

" ' What would you propose, yoursel' ? ' I asked him,
though I wass the skipper. I had aye a great opeenion o'
Hurricane Jeck's agility.

" ' What's to hinder us takin' the train to Gleska, and

leavin' the *Julia* here ? ' said Jeck, ass smert ass anything.
' There's nobody goin' to run away wi' her.'

"Jeck and me took the train for Gleska, and left the
enchineer—a chap Macnair—in full command o' the vessel
I never could trust a man o' the name o' Macnair from that
day on.

"It wass a splendid perty, and Jeck wass chust sublime.
I never partook in a finer perty—two or three hens, a pie
the size o' a binnacle, and wine !—the wine was chust
miraculous. Bella kept it comin' in in quantities. The coalman wass there, and the letter-carrier, and the man that came
for the grocer's orders, and there wassna a gas in the hoose
that wassna bleezin'. You could see that Hurricane Jeck
had his he'rt on makin' everybody happy. It wass him
that danced the hornpipe on the table, and mostly him that
carried the piano doon the stair to the dinin'-room. He
fastened a clothes-line aft on the legs o' her, laid doon a
couple o' planks, and slided her. 'Tail on to the rope, my
laads ! ' says he, ' and I'll go in front and steady her.' But
the clothes-rope broke, and the piano landed on his back.
He never had the least suspeecion, but cairried her doon
the rest o' the stair himsel', and put her in poseetion. And
efter a' oor bother there wass nobody could play. 'That's
the worst o' them fore-and-aft pianos ! ' said Jeck, ass vexed
ass anything ; ' they're that much complicated ! '

"We were chust in the middle o' the second supper, and
Bella wass bringin' in cigars, when her maister opened the
door wi' his chubb, and dandered in ! There wassna a train
for Liverpool on account o' the fog !

" ' What's this ? ' says he, and Bella nearly fainted.

" ' It's Miss Maclachlan's birthday '—meanin' Bella—
answered Jeck, ass nice ass possible. ' You're chust in the
nick o' time,' and he wass goin' to introduce the chentleman,
for Jeck wass a man that never forgot his mainners.

" ' What's that piano doin' there ? ' the chentleman asked,
quite furious.

" ' You may weel ask that,' said Jeck, ' for aal the use it iss, we would be better wi' a concertina,' and Bella had to laugh.

" ' I've a good mind to send for the polis,' said her maister.

" ' You needna bother,' said Bella ; ' he's comin' anyway, ass soon ass he's off his bate and shifted oot o' his uniform,' and that wass the only intimation and invitation Hurricane Jeck ever got that Bella wass goin' to mairry Macrae the polisman.

" We spent three days in the fog in Gleska, and aal oor money," proceeded Para Handy, " and then, ' It's time we were back on the hooker,' said Hurricane Jeck ; ' I can mind her name ; it's the *Julia*.'

" ' It's no' so much her name that bothers me,' says I ; ' it's her latitude and longitude : where in aal the world did we leave her ? '

" ' Them pink wines ! ' said Jeck. ' That's the rock we split on, Peter ! The fog would never have lasted aal this time if we had taken Brutish spirits.'

" It wass chust luck we found the half o' a railway ticket in Jeck's pocket, and it put us in mind that we left the boat at Gourock. We took the last train doon, and landed there wi' the fog ass bad ass ever ; ay, worse ! it wass that thick noo, it wassna briquettes you would make wi't, but marble nocks and mantelpieces.

" ' We left the *Julia* chust fornenst this shippin'-box,' said Jeck, on Gourock quay, and, sure enough, there wass the boat below, and a handy ladder. Him and me went doon the ladder to the deck, and whustled on Macnair. He never paid the least attention.

" ' He'll be in his bed,' said Jeck ; ' gie me a ha'ad o' a bit o' marlin'.'

" We went doon below and found him sleepin' in the dark ; Jeck took a bit o' the marlin', and tied him hands and feet, and the two o' us went to bed, ass tired ass anything, wi' oor boots on. You never, never, never saw such fog !

" Jeck wass the first to waken in the mornin', and he struck a match.

" ' Peter,' said he, quite solemn, when it went oot ; ' have we a stove wi' the name Eureka printed on the door ? '

" ' No, nor Myreeka,' says I ; ' there's no' a door at aal on oor stove, and fine ye ken it ! '

" He lay a while in the dark, sayin' nothing, and then he struck another match. ' Is Macnair red-heided, do you mind ? ' says he when the match went oot.

" ' Ass black ass the ace o' spades ! ' says I.

" ' That wass what wass runnin' in my own mind,' said Jeck ; ' but I thocht I maybe wass mistaken. WE'RE IN OOR BED IN THE WRONG BOAT ! '

" And we were ! We lowsed the chap and told him right enough it wass oor mistake, and gave him two or three o' Bella's best cigars, and then we went ashore to look for the *Julia*. You never saw such fog ! And it wass Friday mornin'.

" ' Where's the *Julia* ? ' we asked the harbour-maister. ' Her ! ' says he ; ' the enchineer got tired waitin' on ye, and got a couple o' quayheid chaps and went crawlin' up the river wi' the tide on We'nesday ! '

" So Hurricane Jeck and me lost more than oorsel's in the fog ; we lost oor jobs," concluded Para Handy. " Never put your trust in a man Macnair ! "

CHRISTMAS ON THE *VITAL SPARK*

THERE was something, plainly, weighing on Dougie's mind ; he let his tea get cold, and merely toyed with his kippered herring ; at intervals he sighed—an unsailor-like proceeding which considerably annoyed the engineer, Macphail.

" Whit's the maitter wi' ye ? " he querulously inquired. " Ye would think it was the Fast, to hear ye. Are ye ruein' your misspent life ? "

" Never you mind Macphail," advised the Captain ; " a chentleman should aalways hev respect for another chentleman in tribulation. What way's the mustress, Dougald ? " He held a large tablespoonful of marmalade suspended in his hand, while he put the question with genuine solicitude ; Dougie's wife was the very woman, he knew, to have something or other seriously wrong with her just when other folk were getting into a nice and jovial spirit for New Year.

" Oh, she's fine, thanky, Peter," said the mate ; " there's nothing spashial wrong wi' her except, noo and then, the rheumatism."

" She should aalways keep a raw potato in her pocket," said Para Handy ; " it's the only cure."

" She micht as weel keep a nutmeg-grater in her coalbunker," remarked the engineer. " Whit wye can a raw potato cure the rheumatism ? "

" It's the—it's the influence," explained Para Handy vaguely. " Look at them Vibrators ! But you'll believe in nothing, Macphail, unless you read aboot it in wan o' them novelles ; you're chust an unfidel ! "

Dougie sighed again, and the engineer, protesting that his meal had been spoiled for him by his shipmate's melancholy, hurriedly finished his fifth cup of tea and went on deck. There were no indications that it was Christmas Eve ; two men standing on the quay were strictly sober. Crarae is still a place where they thoroughly celebrate the Old New Year after a first rehearsal with the statutory one.

" If you're not feelin' very brusk you should go to your bed, Dougie," remarked the Captain sympathetically. " The time to stop trouble iss before it starts."

" There's nothing wrong wi' me," the mate assured him, sadly ; " we're weel off, livin' on the fat o' the land, and some folk stervin'."

" We are that ! " agreed Para Handy, helping himself to Dougie's second kipper. " Were you thinkin' of any wan parteecular ? "

" Did you know a quarryman here by the name o' Col Maclachlan ? " asked the mate, and Para Handy, having carefully reflected, confessed he didn't.

" Neither did I," said Dougie ; " but he died a year ago and left a weedow yonder, and the only thing that's for her iss the poorshouse at Lochgilpheid."

" Holy smoke ! " exclaimed the Captain ; " isn't that chust desperate ! If it wass a cargo of coals we had this trip, we might be givin' her a pickle, but she couldna make mich wi' a bag o' whinstones."

" They tell me she's goin' to start and walk to-morrow mornin' to Lochgilpheid, and she's an old done woman. She says she would be affronted for to go in the *Cygnet* or the *Minard*, for every one on board would ken she was goin' to the poorshouse."

" Oh, to the muschief ! " said Para Handy ; " Macphail wass right—a body might ass weel be at a funeral ass in your company, and it comin' on to the New Year ! " He fled on deck from this doleful atmosphere in the fo'c'sle, but came down again in a minute or two.

" I wass thinkin' to mysel'," he remarked with diffidence to the mate, " that if the poor old body would come wi' us, we could give her a lift to Ardrishaig ; what do you say ? "

" Whatever you say yoursel'," said the mate ; " but we would need to be aawfu' careful o' her feelin's, and she wouldna like to come doon the quay unless it wass in the dark."

" We'll start at six o'clock, then," said the Captain, " if you'll go ashore the now and make arrangements, and you needna bother aboot her feelin's ; we'll handle them like gless."

As an alternative to walking to the poorhouse, the sail to Lochgilphead by the *Vital Spark* was quite agreeable to the widow, who turned up at the quay in the morning quite alone, too proud even to take her neighbours into her confidence. Para Handy helped her on board and made her comfortable.

" You're goin' to get a splendid day ! " he assured her cheer-fully. " Dougie, iss it nearly time for oor cup o' tea ? "

" It'll be ready in a meenute," said Dougie, with delightful promptness, and went down to rouse Sunny Jim.

" We aalways have a cup o' tea at six o'clock on the *Fital Spark*," the Captain informed the widow, with a fluency that astonished even the engineer. " And an egg ; sometimes two. Jum 'll boil you an egg."

" I'm sure I'm an aawful bother to you ! " protested the poor old widow, feebly.

" Bother ! " said Para Handy ; " not the slightest ! The tea's there anyway. And the eggs. Efter that we'll have oor breakfast."

" I'll be a terrible expense to you," said the unhappy widow ; and Para Handy chuckled jovially.

" Expense ! Nonsense, Mrs Maclachlan ! Everything's paid for here by the owners ; we're allooed more tea and eggs and things than we can eat. I'll be thinkin' mysel' it's a sin the way we hev to throw them sometimes over the side " —at which astounding effort of the imagination Macphail retired among his engines and relieved his feelings by a noisy application of the coaling shovel.

" I have the money for my ticket," said the widow, fumbling nervously for her purse.

" Ticket ! " said Para Handy, with magnificent alarm. " If the Board o' Tred heard o' us chergin' money for a passage in the *Fital Spark*, we would never hear the end o't ; it would cost us oor certuficate."

The widow enjoyed her tea immensely, and Para Handy talked incessantly about everything and every place but Lochgilphead, while the *Vital Spark* chug-chugged on her fateful way down Loch Fyne to the poorhouse.

" Did you know my man ? " the woman suddenly asked, in an interval which even Para Handy's wonderful eloquence couldn't fill up.

" Iss it Col Maclachlan ? " he exclaimed. " Fine ! me'm ;

fine ! Col and me wass weel acquent ; it wass that that made me take the liberty to ask you. There wass never a finer man in Argyllshire than poor Col—a regular chentleman ! I mind o' him in the—in the quarry. So do you, Dougie, didn't you ? "

"I mind o' him caapital!" said Dougie, without a moment's hesitation. "The last time I saw him he lent me half-a-croon, and I never had the chance to pay him't back."

"I think mysel', if I mind right, it wass five shullin's," suggested Para Handy, putting his hand in his trousers pocket, with a wink to his mate, and Dougie quickly corrected himself ; it WAS five shillings, now that he thought of it. But having gone aside for a little and consulted the engineer and Sunny Jim, he came back and said it was really eight and sixpence.

"There wass other three-and-six I got the lend o' from him another time," he said ; "I could show you the very place it happened, and I wass nearly forgettin' aal aboot it."

"My ! ye're an awfu' leear ! " said the engineer in a whisper as they stood aside.

"Maybe I am," agreed the mate ; "but did you ever, ever, ever hear such a caapital one ass the Captain ? "

Sunny Jim had no sooner got the dishes cleaned from this informal meal than Para Handy went to him and commanded a speedy preparation of the breakfast.

"Right-oh ! " said Sunny Jim ; "I'll be able to tak' a job as a chef in yin o' thae Cunarders efter this. But I've naething else than tea and eggs."

"Weel, boil them ! " said the Captain. "Keep on boilin' them ! Things never look so black to a woman when she can get a cup o' tea, and an egg or two 'll no' go wrong wi' her. Efter that you'll maybe give us a tune on your melodian —something nice and cheery, mind ; none o' your laments : they're no' the thing at aal for a weedow woman goin' to the poorshouse."

It was a charming day; the sea was calm; the extraordinary high spirits of the crew of the *Vital Spark* appeared to be contagious, and the widow confessed she had never enjoyed a sail so much since the year she had gone with Col on a trip to Rothesay.

"It's five-and-thirty years ago, and I never wass there again," she added, just a little sadly.

"Faith, you should come wi' us to Ro'say," said the Captain genially, and then regretted it.

"I canna," said the poor old body; "I'll never see Ro'say again, for I'm goin' to Lochgilphead."

"And you couldna be goin' to a nicer place!" declared Para Handy. "Lochgilpheid's chust sublime! Dougie himsel' 'll tell you!"

"Salubrious!" said the mate. "And forbye, it's that healthy!"

"There wass nothing wrong wi' Crarae," said the widow pathetically, and Sunny Jim came to the rescue with another pot of tea.

"Many a time I'll be thinking to mysel' yonder that if I had a little money bye me, I would spend the rest o' my days in Lochgilpheid," said Para Handy. "You never saw a cheerier place——"

"Crarae wass very cheery, too—in the summer time—when Col wass livin'," said the widow.

"Oh, but there's an aawful lot to see aboot Lochgilpheid; that's the place for Life!" said Para Handy. "And such nice walks; there's—there's the road to Kilmartin, and Argyll Street, full o' splendid shops; and the steamers comin' to Ardrishaig, and every night the mail goes bye to Crarae and Inveraray"—here his knowledge of Lochgilphead's charms began to fail him.

"I didna think it would be so nice ass that," said the widow, less dispiritedly. "I forgot aboot the mail; I'll aye be seein' it passin' to Crarae,"

"Of course you will!" said Para Handy gaily; "that's

a thing I wouldna miss, mysel'. And any time you take the notion, you'll can take a drive in the mail to Crarae if the weather's suitable."

"I would like it fine!" said the widow; "but—but maybe they'll no' let me. You would hear—you would hear where I wass goin' in Lochgilpheid?"

"I never heard a word!" protested Para Handy. "That minds me—will you have another egg? Jum, boil another egg for Mrs Maclachlan!"

"You hev been very kind," said the widow gratefully, as the *Vital Spark* came into Ardrishaig pier; "you couldna hev been kinder."

"I'm sorry you have to waalk to Lochgilpheid," said the Captain.

"Oh, I'm no' that old but I can manage the waalk," she answered; "I'm only seventy."

"Seventy!" said Para Handy, with genuine surprise; "I didna think you would be anything like seventy."

"I'll be seventy next Thursday," said the widow, and Para Handy whistled.

"And what in the world are you goin' to Lochgilpheid for? —the last place on God's earth, next to London. Efter Thursday next you'll can get your five shillin's a week in Crarae."

"Five shillin's a week in Crarae!" said the widow mournfully; "I hope I'll be ass weel off ass that when I get to heaven!"

"Then never mind aboot heaven the noo," said Para Handy, clapping her on the back; "go back to Crarae wi' the *Minard*, and you'll get your pension regular every week —five shillin's."

"My pension!" said the widow, with surprise. "Fancy me wi' a pension; I never wass in the Airmy."

"Did nobody ever tell you that you wass entitled to a pension when they knew you were needin't?" asked the Captain, and the widow bridled.

"Nobody knew that I wass needin' anything," she exclaimed ; "I took good care o' that."

. . . .

Late that evening Mrs Maclachlan arrived at Crarae in the *Minard Castle* with a full knowledge for the first time of her glorious rights as an aged British citizen, and the balance of 8s. 6d. forced upon her by the mate, who had so opportunely remembered that he was due that sum to the lamented Col.

THE MAIDS OF BUTE

EVEN the captain of a steam lighter may feel the cheerful, exhilarating influence of spring, and Para Handy, sitting on an upturned pail, with his feet on a coil of rope, beiked himself in the sun and sang like a lintie—a rather croupy lintie. The song he sang was :

> " Blow ye winds aye-oh !
> For it's roving I will go,
> I'll stay no more on England's shore,
> So let the music play.
> I'm off by the morning train,
> Across the raging main,
> I have booked a trup wi' a Government shup,
> Ten thousand miles away."

" Who's that greetin' ? " asked the engineer malicioulsy, sticking his head out of the engine-room.

The Captain looked at him with contempt. " Nobody's greetin'," he said. " It's a thing you don't know anything at aal about ; it's music. Away and read your novelles. What way's Lady Fitzgerald gettin' on wi' her new man ? "

The engineer hastily withdrew.

" That's the way to settle him," said the Captain to Dougie and Sunny Jim. " Short and sweet ! I could sing him blin'. Do ye know the way it iss that steamboat enchineers

H

is aalways doon in the mooth like that? It's the want o'
nature. They never let themselves go. Poor duvvles, workin'
away among their bits o' enchines, they never get the wind
and the sun aboot them right the same ass us seamen. If I
wass always doon in a hole like that place o' Macphail's,
dabbin' my face wi' an oily rag aal day, I would maybe be ass
ugly ass himsel'. Man, I'm feelin' fine! There's nothing
like the spring o' the year, when you can get it like this.
It's chust sublime! I'm feelin' ass strong ass a lion. I
could pull the mast oot o' the boat and bate Brussels carpets
wi' it."

"We'll pay for this yet," said Sunny Jim. "Ye'll see
it'll rain or snow before night. What do ye say, Dougie?"

"Whatever ye think yoursel'," said Dougie.

"At this time o' the year," said the Captain, "I wish I
wass back in MacBrayne's boats. The *Fital Spark* iss a
splendid shup, the best in the tred, but there's no diversion.
I wass the first man that ever pented the Maids o' Bute."

"Ye don't tell me!" exclaimed Dougie incredulously.

"I wass that," said Para Handy, as modestly as possible.
"I'm not sayin' it for a bounce; the job might have come
anybody's way, but I wass the man that got it. I wass a
hand on the *Inveraray Castle* at the time. The Captain say
to me wan day we were passin' the Maids—only they werena
the Maids then; they hadna their clothes on—'Peter, what
do you think o' them two stones on the hull-side?'

"'They'll be there a long while before they're small enough
to pap at birds wi',' says I.

"'But do they no' put ye desperate in mind o' a couple o'
weemen?' said he.

"'Not them!' say I. 'I have been passin' here for
fifteen years, and I never heard them taalkin' yet. If they
were like weemen what would they be sittin' waitin' there
for so long, and no' a man on the whole o' this side o'
Bute?'

"'Ay, but it's the look o' them,' said the Captain. 'I

ye stand here and shut wan eye, they'll put ye aawfu' in mind o' the two MacFadyen gyurls up in Pennymore. I think we'll chust christen them the Maids o' Bute.'

" Well, we aalways caaled them the Maids o' Bute efter that, and pointed them oot to aal the passengers on the steamers. Some o' them said they were desperate like weemen, and others said they were chust like two big stones. The Captain o' the *Inveraray Castle* got quite wild at some passengers that said they werena a bit like weemen. ' That's the worst o' them English towerists,' he would say. ' They have no imachination. I could make myself believe them two stones wass a regiment o' sodgers if I put my mind to't. I'm sure the towerists might streetch a point the same ass other folk, and keep up the amusement.'

" Wan day the skipper came to me and says, ' Are ye on for a nice holiday, Peter ? ' It wass chust this time o' the year and weather like this, and I wass feelin' fine.

" ' No objections,' says I.

" ' Well,' he says, ' I wish you would go off at Tighnabruaich and take some pent wi' ye in a small boat over to the Maids, and give them a touch o' rud and white that'll make them more like weemen than ever.'

" ' I don't like,' said I.

" ' What way do ye no' like ? ' said the skipper. ' It's no even what you would caal work ; it's chust amusement ! '

" ' But will it no' look droll for a sailor to be pentin' clothes on a couple o' stones, aal his lone by himsel' in the north end o' Bute, and no' a sowl to see him ? Chust give it a think yersel', skipper ; would it no' look awfu' daft ? '

" ' I don't care if it looks daft enough for the Lochgilphead Asylum, ye'll have to do it,' said the skipper. ' I'll put ye off at Tighnabruaich this efternoon ; ye can go over and do the chob, and take a night's ludgin's in the toon, and we'll pick you up to-morrow when we're comin' doon. See you and make the Maids as smert as ye can, and by Chove, they'll give the towerists a start ! '

"Weel, I wass put off at Tighnabruaich, and the rud and white pent wi' me. I got ludgin's, took my tea and a herrin' to't, and rowed mysel' over in a boat to Bute. Some of the boys aboot the quay wass askin' what I wass efter, but it wassna likely I would tell them I wass goin' to pent clothes on the Maids o' Bute; they would be sure to caal me the manta-maker efter it. So I chust said I wass going over to mark oot the place for a new quay MacBrayne wass buildin'. There's nothing like discretioncy.

"It wass a day that wass chust sublime! The watter wass that calm you could see your face in it, the birds were singing like hey-my-nanny, and the Kyles wass lovely. Two meenutes efter I started pentin' the Maids I wass singin' to mysel' like anything. Now I must let you ken I never had no education at drawin', and it's wonderful how fine I pented them. When you got close to them they were no more like rale maids than I am; ye wouldna take them for maids even in the dark, but before I wass done with them, ye would ask them up to dance. The only thing that vexed me wass that I had only the rud and white; if I had magenta and blue and yellow, and the like o' that, I could have made them far more stylish. I gave them white faces and rud frocks and bonnets, and man, man, it wass a splendid day!

"I took the notion in my heid that maybe the skipper o' the *Inveraray* wass right, and that they were maids at wan time, that looked back the same as Lot's wife in the Scruptures and got turned into stone. When I wassna singin', I would be speakin' away to them, and I'll assure ye it wass the first time maids never gave me any back chat. Wan o' them I called Mery efter—efter a gyurl I knew, and the other I called 'Lizabeth, for she chust looked like it. And it wass a majestic day. 'There ye are, gyurls,' I says to them, 'and you never had clothes that fitted better. Stop you, and if I'm spared till next year, you'll have the magenta too.' The north end o' Bute iss a bleak, wild, lonely place, but when I wass done pentin' the Maids it looked like a lerge population.

They looked that nate and cheery among the heather ! Mery had a waist ye could get your arm roond, but 'Lizabeth wass a broad, broad gyrul. And I wassna a bad-lookin' chap mysel'."

Here Para Handy stopped and sighed.

" Go on wi' your baur," said Dougie.

" Old times ! old times ! " said the Captain. " By Chove ! I wass in trum that day ! I never saw finer weather, nor nicer gyurls. Och ! but it wass chust imachination ; when we pass the Maids o' Bute now, I know they're only stones, with rud and white pent on them. They're good enough for towerists."

HERRING—A GOSSIP

" OF aal the fish there iss in the sea," said Para Handy, " nothing bates the herrin' ; it's a providence they're plentiful and them so cheap ! "

" They're no' in Loch Fyne, wherever they are," said Dougie sadly ; " the only herrin' that they're gettin' there iss rud ones comin' up in barrels wi' the *Cygnet* or the *Minard Castle*. For five years back the trade wass desperate."

" I wouldna say but you're right," agreeably remarked the Captain. " The herrin' iss a great, great mystery. The more you will be catchin' of them the more there iss ; and when they're no' in't at aal they're no' there"—a great philosophic truth which the crew smoked over in silence for a few minutes.

" When I wass a hand on the gabberts," continued the Captain, " the herrin' fishin' of Loch Fyne wass in its prime. You ken yoursel' what I mean ; if you don't believe me, Jum, there's Dougie himsel' 'll tell you. Fortunes ! chust simply fortunes ! You couldna show your face in Tarbert then but a lot of the laads would gaither round at wance and make a ovial day of it. Wi' a barrel of nets in a skiff and a handy wife at the guttin', a man of the least agility could make

enough in a month to build a land o' hooses, and the rale
Loch Fyne was terrible namely over aal the world."

"I mind o't mysel'," said Sunny Jim; "they never sold
onything else but the rale Loch Fyne in Gleska."

"They did that whether or no'," explained Para Handy,
"for it wass the herrin's of Loch Fyne that had the
reputation."

"I've seen the Rooshians eatin' them raw in the Baltic,"
said Macphail, the engineer, and Dougie shuddered. "Eating
them raw!" said he; "the dirty duvvels!"

"The herrin' wass that thick in Loch Fyne in them days,"
recalled the Captain, "that you sometimes couldna get your
anchor to the ground, and the quality was chust sublime. It
wassna a tred at aal so much as an amusement; you went oot
at night when the weans wass in their beds, and you had a
couple o' cran on the road to Clyde in time for Gleska's breakfast. The quays wass covered wi' John O'Brian's boxes, and
man alive! but the wine and spirit tred wass busy. Loch
Fyne wass the place for Life in them days—high jeenks and
big hauls; you werena very smert if you werena into both o'
them. If you don't believe me, Dougie himsel' 'll tell you."

"You have it exact, Peter," guaranteed the mate, who
was thus appealed to; "I wass there mysel'."

"Of course I have it exact," said Para Handy; "I'll
assure you it's no' a thing I read in the papers. To-day
there's no' a herrin' in Loch Fyne or I'm mistaken."

"If there's wan he'll be kind o' lonely," said the mate.
"I wonder what in the muschief's wrong wi' them?"

"You might shot miles o' nets for a month and there's
no' a herrin' will come near them."

"Man! aren't they the tumid, frightened idiots!" said
Dougie, with disgust.

"If ye ask me, I think whit spoiled the herrin' fishing in
Loch Fyne was the way they gaed on writin' aboot it in the
papers," said Macphail. "It was enough to scunner ony
self-respectin' fish. Wan day a chap would write that it

was the trawlers that were daein' a' the damage ; next
day anither chap would say he was a liar, and that trawlin'
was a thing the herrin' thrived on. Then a chap would
write that there should be a close time so as to gie the herrin'
time to draw their breaths for anither breenge into the
nets ; and anither chap would write from Campbeltoon and
say a close time would be takin' the bread oot o' the mooths
o' his wife and weans. A scientific man said herrin' came
on cycles——"

"He's a liar, anyway," said the Captain, with conviction.
"They were in Loch Fyne afore the cycle was invented.
Are you sure, Macphail, it's no' the cod he means ? "

"He said the herrin' fishin' aye missed some years noo
and then in a' the herrin' places in Europe as weel's in
Loch Fyne, and the Gulf Stream had something to dae
wi't."

"That's the worst o' science," said the Captain piously ;
"it takes aal the credit away from the Creator. Don't you
pay attention to an unfidel like that ; when the herrin' wass
in Loch Fyne they stayed there aal the time, and only
maybe took a daunder oot noo and then the length o'
Ballantrae."

"If it's no' the Gulf Stream, then ye'll maybe tell us
whit it is ? " said the engineer, with some annoyance.

"I'll soon do that," said Para Handy ; "if you want to
ken, it's what I said—the herrin' iss a mystery, chust a
mystery ! "

"I'm awfu' gled ye told me," said the engineer ironically.
"I aye wondered. Whit's the parteecular mysteriousness
aboot it ? "

"It's a silly fish," replied the Captain ; "it's fine for
eatin,' but it hasna the sagacity. If it had the sagacity it
wouldna come lower than Otter Ferry, nor be gallivantin'
roond the Kyles o' Bute in daylight. It's them innovations
that's the death o' herrin'. If the herrin' stayed in Loch
Fyne attendin' to its business and givin' the drift-net

crews encouragement, it would have a happier life and die respected.

" Whenever the herrin' of Loch Fyne puts his nose below Kilfinan, his character is gone. First the Tarbert trawlers take him oot to company and turn his heid ; then there iss nothing for it for him but flying trips to the Kyles o' Bute, the Tail o' the Bank, and Gareloch. In Loch Fyne we never would touch the herrin' in the daytime, nor in winter ; they need a rest, forbye we're none the worse o' one oorsel's ; but the folk below Kilfinan have no regard for Chrustian principles, and they no sooner see an eye o' fish than they're roond aboot it with trawls, even if it's the middle o' the day or New-Year's mornin'. They never give the fish a chance ; they keep it on the run till its fins get hot. If it ventures ass far ass the Tail o' the Bank, it gets that dizzy wi' the sight o' the shippin' traffic that it loses the way and never comes back to Loch Fyne again. A silly fish ! If it only had sagacity ! Amn't I right, Dougie ? "

" Whatever you say yoursel', Captain ; there's wan thing sure, the herrin's scarce."

" The long and the short of it iss that they're a mystery," concluded Para Handy.

TO CAMPBELTOWN BY SEA

" MAN it's hot ; most desperate hot ! " said Para Handy, using his hand like a squeegee to remove the perspiration from his brow. " Life in weather like this iss a burden ; a body might ass weel be burnin' lime or at the bakin'. I wish I wass a fush."

The *Vital Spark* was lying at Skipness, the tar boiling between her seams in unusually ardent weather, and Macphail on deck, with a horror of his own engine-room.

" Bein' a fush wouldna be bad," said Dougie, " if it wass not for the constant watter. The only thing you can say for watter iss that it's wet and fine for sailin' boats on. If you were a fush, Captain, you would die of thirst."

> " Watter, watter everywhere,
>   And not a single drop of drink,"

quoted the engineer, who was literary.

The Captain looked at him with some annoyance. " It's bad enough, Macphail," said he, " withoot you harpin', harpin' on the thing. You have no consuderation ! I never mentioned drink. I wass thinkin' of us plowterin' doon in weather like this to Campbeltown, and wishin' I could swim."

" Can you no' swim ? " asked Sunny Jim with some surprise.

" I daresay I could, but I never tried," said Para Handy. " I had never the time, havin' aye to attend to my business."

" Swimmin's aal the rage chust now," remarked Dougie, who occasionally read a newspaper. " Look at the Thames in London—there's men and women swimmin' it in droves ; they'll do six or seven miles before their breakfast. And the Straits o' Dover's busy wi' splendid swimmers makin' their way to France."

" What are they wantin' to France for ? " asked Para Handy. " Did they do anything ? "

" I wouldna say," replied the mate ; " it's like enough the polis iss efter them, but the story they have themsel's iss that they're swimmin' for a wudger. The best this season iss a Gleska man caaled Wolffe ; he swam that close to France the other day he could hear the natives taalkin'."

" What for did he no' land ? " asked Sunny Jim.

" I canna tell," said Dougie, " but it's likely it would be wan o' the places where they charge a penny at the quay. Him bein' a Gleska man, he would see them d——d first, so he chust came back to Dover."

" I don't see the fun of it, mysel'," said Para Handy reflectively. " But of course, if it's a wudger——"

" That's what I'm throng tellin' you," said the mate.

H*

" It looks a terrible task, but it's simple enough for any man with the agility. First you put off your clo'es and leave them in the shippin'-box at Dover if you have the confidence. Then you oil yoursel' wi' oil, put on a pair o' goggles, and get your photygraph. When the crood's big enough you kiss the wife good-bye and start swimmin' like anything."

" Whit wife ? " asked the engineer, whose profound knowledge of life as depicted in penny novelettes had rendered him dubious of all adventures designed to end in France.

" Your own wife, of course," said Para Handy impatiently. " What other wife would a chap want to leave and go to France for ? Go on wi' your story, Dougie."

" Three steamers loaded wi' beef-tea, champagne, chocolate, and pipers follows you aal the way——"

" Beef-tea and chocolate ! " exclaimed the Captain, with astonishment. " What's the sense o' that ? Are you sure it's beef-tea, Dougie ? "

" I read it mysel' in the papers," the mate assured him. " You strike oot aalways wi' a firm, powerful, over-hand stroke, and whenever you're past the heid o' Dover quay you turn on your back, take your luncheon oot of a bottle and tell the folk on the steamers that you're feelin' fine."

" You might well be feelin' fine, wi' a luncheon oot o' a bottle," said Para Handy. " It's the beef-tea that bother me."

" Aal the time the pipers iss standin' on the paiddle-boxes o' the steamers playin' ' Hielan' Laddie ' and ' The Campbells iss Comin'.' "

" Aal the time ! " repeated Para Handy. " I don't believe wan word of it ! Not aboot pipers ; take my word for it, Dougie, they'll be doon below noo and then ; there's nothin, in this world thirstier than music."

" Do they no' get ony prizes for soomin' a' that distance ? " asked Sunny Jim.

" I'll warrant you there must be money in it some way," said the engineer. " Whatever side they land on, they'

ut roond the hat. There's naething the public 'll pay you
uicker or better for, than for daein' wi' your legs what
a engine 'll dae faur better."

" I could soom ony o' them blin'!" said Sunny Jim.
I was the natest wee soomer ever Geordie Geddes dragged
y the hair o' the heid frae the Clyde at Jenny's Burn.
air champion! Could we no' get up a soom frae here to
ampbeltown the morn, and mak' a trifle at the start and
enish?"

"Man! you couldna swim aal that distance," said the
aptain. "It would take you a week and a tug to tow you."

"I'm no daft," explained Sunny Jim; "the hale thing's
a the startin', for seemin'ly naebody ever feenishes soomin'
wer to France. A' I hae to dae is to ile mysel' and dive,
ad the *Vital Spark* can keep me company into Kilbrannan
ound."

"There's the photygraphs, and the beef-tea, and the
ipers," said the engineer; "unless ye hae them ye micht
s well jist walk to Campbeltown."

"Dougie can play his trump, and that'll dae instead o' the
ipers," said Sunny Jim. "It's a' in the start. See? I'll
imp in at the quay, and you'll collect the money from the
kipness folk, and pick me up whenever they're oot o' sicht.
ll dae the dive again afore we come into Campbeltown,
ad Dougie'll haud the watch and gie a guarantee I swam
ae hale length o' Kintyre in four oors and five-and-twenty
inutes. Then—bizz!—bang!—roon' the folk in Campbel-
own wi' the bonny wee hat again! See?"

"Man! your cluverness is chust sublime!" said Para
andy; "we'll have the demonstration in the mornin'."

The intelligence that the cook of the *Vital Spark* was to
vim to Campbeltown found Skipness curiously indifferent.
If he had been swimming FROM Campbeltown it might be
fferent," said the natives; so the attempts to collect a
ibscription in recognition of the gallant feat were poorly
ecognised and Sunny Jim, disgusted, quitted the water, and

resumed his clothes on the deck of the vessel less than
hundred yards from the shore. The *Vital Spark* next da
came into Campbeltown, and the intrepid swimmer, havin
quietly dropped over the side at not too great a distanc
swam in the direction of the quay, at which he arrived wi
no demonstration of excitement on the part of the populatio

"Swam aal the way from Skipness," Para Handy inform
the curious ; "we're raisin' a little money to encourage him
he's none of your Dover Frenchmen, but wan of Brutair
hardy sons. Whatever you think yoursel's in silver, chentl
men."

"Wass he in the watter aal the time ?" asked a nati
fisherman, copiously perspiring under a couple of guernse
and an enormous woollen comforter.

"He wass that !" Para Handy assured him. "If ye
don't believe me, Dougie himsel' 'll tell you."

"Then he wass the lucky chap !" said the native envious!
"It must have been fine and cool. What's he goin'
stand ?"

HOW TO BUY A BOAT

IT was shown in a former escapade of Para Handy's that .
wasn't averse from a little sea-trout poaching. He justifi
this sport in Gaelic, always quoting a proverb that a swit
from the forest, a bird from the hill, or a fish from the riv
were the natural right of every Highland gentleman. Sun
Jim approved the principle most heartily, and proposed
insert a clause including dogs, of which he confessed he ha
been a great admirer and collector in his Clutha days. Oste
sibly the Captain never fished for anything but flounders, a
his astonishment when he came on sea-trout or grilse in h
net after an hour's assiduous plashing with it at the mou
of a burn was charming to witness.

"Holy smoke !" he would exclaim, scratching his ea
"here's a wheen o' the white fellows, and us chust despera

r cod. It's likely they're the Duke's or Mr Younger's,
ıd they lost their way to Bullingsgate. Stop you! Dougie,
meenute and hand me up a fut-spar. . . . I'm sure and I
assna wantin' them, but there they are, and what can you
ake of it ? They might be saithe ; it's desperate dark the
ght ; what a peety we didna bring a lantern. Look and
e if you divna think they're saithe, Dougie."

" Whatever you say yoursel'," was the mate's unvarying
cision, and it could never be properly made out whether
e fish were saithe or salmon till the crew had eaten them.

There was one favourite fishing bank of the Captain's
conveniently close to the county police station. The
nstable was very apt to find a grilse on the inside handle
his coal-cellar door on mornings when the *Vital Spark*
ıs in the harbour, and he, also, was much surprised, but
ver mentioned it, except in a roundabout way, to Para
ındy.

" You must be makin' less noise oot in the bay at night,"
would say to him. " By Chove ! I could hear you mysel'
st night quite plain ; if you're not more caatious I'll have
display my activity and find a clue."

It was most unfortunate that the men of the *Vital Spark*
ould have come on a shoal of the " white fellows " one
rly morning when the river-watchers were in straits to
stify their job. The lighter's punt, with an excellent net
d its contents, had hurriedly to be abandoned, and before
eakfast the Captain had lodged a charge of larceny against
rties unknown at the police station. Some one had stolen
 punt, he said, cutting the painter of her during the calm
d virtuous sleep of self and mates. He identified the boat
 the possession of the river-bailiffs ; he was horrified to
rn of the nefarious purpose to which it had been applied,
t had to submit with curious equanimity to its confiscation.
cal sympathy was aroused—fostered unostentatiously by
e policeman ; a subscription sheet was passed round the
lage philanthropists—also on the discreet suggestion of

the policeman ; and the sum of two pounds ten and tenpen«
was collected—the tenpence being in ha'pence ingenious
abstracted by means of a table-knife from a tin bank in tʰ
possession of the policeman's only boy.

"You will go at wance to Tighnabruaich and buy yoursᵉ
another boat, Peter," said the policeman, when informaľ
handing over the money. "If you are circumspect aɩ
caautious you'll pick up a smert one chape that will serᵛ
for your requirements."

"I wouldna touch a penny," protested Para Handy, "
it wass not for my vessel's reputation ; she needs a punt
give her an appearance."

A few days later the *Vital Spark* came into Tighnabruaic
and the Captain, by apparent accident, fell into conver
with a hirer of rowing-boats.

"Man, you must be coinin' money," he said innocentlʸ
"you have a lot of boats."

"Coinin' money !" growled the boat-hirer ; "no' ʷ
weather like this. I micht be makin' mair at hirɩ
umbrellas."

"Dear me !" said the Captain sympathetically, "tha
a peety. A tidy lot o' boats, the most o' them ; it's a wonᵈ
you would keep so many, and tred so bad."

"You werena thinkin' maybe o' buyin', were ye ?" askᵉ
the boat-hirer suspiciously, with a look at the stern of tʰ
Vital Spark, where the absence of a punt was manifest.

"No," said the Captain blandly, "boats iss a luxury thᵉ
days ; they're lucky that doesna need them. Terriᵇ
weather ! And it's goin' to be a dirty summer ; there'ˢ
man yonder in America that prophesies we'll have rain even-
till Martinmas. Rowin' boats iss goin' chape at Millport.'

"If that's the look-out, they'll be goin' chape everywherᵉ
incautiously remarked the boat-hirer.

"Chust that," said Para Handy, and made as if to mᵒ
away. Then he stopped, and, with his hands in his pockᵉ
pointed with a contemptuous foot at a dinghy he had hᵉ

an eye on from the start of the conversation. "There's wan I aalways wondered at you keepin', Dan," said he ; "she's a prutty old stager, I'll be bound you."

"That ! " exclaimed the boat-hirer. "That's the tidiest boat on the shore ; she's a genuine Erchie Smith."

"Iss she, iss she ? " said the Captain. "I mind her the year o' the Jubilee ; it's wonderful the way they hold thegither. A bad crack in her bottom strake ; you wouldna be askin' much for her if a buyer wass here wi' ready money ? "

"Are ye wantin' a boat ? " asked the boat-hirer curtly, coming to the point.

"Not what you would caal exactly," said the Captain, "but if she's in the market I might maybe hear aboot a customer. What did you say wass the figure ? "

"Three pound ten, and a thief's bargain," said the boat-hirer promptly, and Para Handy dropped at his feet the pipe he was filling.

"Excuse me startin' ! " he remarked sarcastically, "you gave me a fright. It wass not about a schooner yat I was inquirin'."

"She's worth every penny o't, and a guid deal mair," said the boat-hirer, and Para Handy lit his pipe deliberately and changed the subject.

"There's a great run on them motors," he remarked, indicating one of the launches in the bay. "My friend that iss wantin' a boat iss——"

"I thocht ye said ye werena wantin' ony kind o' boat at a'," interjected the boat-hirer.

"Chust that ; but there wass a chentleman that spoke to me aboot a notion he had for a smaal boat ; he will likely take a motor wan ; they're aal the go. That swuft ! They're tellin' me they're doin' aal the hirin' tred in Ro'sa' and Dunoon ; there'll soon no' be a rowin'-boat left. If I wass you I would clear oot aal the trash and start a wheen o' motors."

"A motor wad be nae use for the *Vital Spark*," said the

boat-hirer, who had no doubt now he had met a buyer. " Hoo much are ye prepared to offer ? "

" What for ? " said Para Handy innocently, spitting on the desirable dinghy, and then apologetically wiping it with his hand.

" For this boat.   Say three pounds.   It's a bargain."

" Oh, for this wan !   I wouldna hurt your feelings, but if I wass wantin' a boat I wouldna take this wan in a gift.   Still and on, a boat iss a handy thing for them that needs it ; I'm not denyin' it.   I'll mention it to the other chentleman."

" Wha is he ? " asked the boat-hirer, and Para Handy screwed up his eyes, and was rapt in admiration of the scenery of the Kyles.

" What you don't know you don't ken," he replied mysteriously.

" Ye couldna get a better punt for the money if ye searched the Clyde," said the boat-hirer.

" I'm no' in any hurry ; I'll take a look aboot for something aboot two pound ten," said Para Handy.   " Ye canna get a first-class boat a penny cheaper.   I got the offer of a topper for the forty shillings, and I'm consuderin' it."   He had now thrown off all disguise, and come out in the open frankly as a buyer.

" Ye shouldna consider ower lang, then," said the boat-hirer ; " there's a lot o' men in the market the noo for handy boats o' this cless ; I have an offer mysel' o' two pounds fifteen for this very boat no later gone than yesterday, and I'm hangin' oot for the three pounds.   I believe I'll get it ; he's comin' back this afternoon."

" Chust that ! " said Para Handy, winking to himself. " I'm sure and I wish him weel wi' his bargain.   She looks as if she would be terrible cogly."

" Is Tighnabruaich quay cogly ? " asked the boat-hirer indignantly.   " Ye couldna put her over if ye tried."

" And they tell me she has a rowth," continued Para Handy, meaning thereby a bias under oars.

"They're liars, then," said the boat-hirer; "I'll sell ye her for two pound twelve to prove it."

The Captain buttoned up his jacket, and said it was time he was back to business.

"A fine boat," pleaded the boat-hirer. "Twa pairs o' oars, a pair o' galvanised rowlocks, a balin' dish, and a painter—dirt chape! take it or leave it."

"Would you no' be chenerous and throw in the plug?" said the Captain, with his finest irony.

"I'll dae better than that," said the boat-hirer. "I'll fling in a nice bit hand-line."

"For two pound ten, I think you said."

"Twa pound twelve," corrected the boat-hirer. "Come now, don't be stickin'."

"At two pounds twelve I'll have to consult my frien' the chentleman I mentioned," said the Captain; "and I'll no' be able to let you know for a week or two. At two pounds ten I would risk it, and it's chust the money I have on me."

"Done, then!" said the boat-hirer. "The boat's yours," and they went to the hotel to seal the bargain.

The boat-hirer was going home with his money when he heard the Captain stumping hurriedly after. "Stop a meenute, Dan," he said; "I forgot to ask if you haven't a bit of a net you might throw in, chust for the sake o' frien'ship?"

.   .   .   .   .

The boat-hirer confessed to his wife that he had made ten shillings profit on the sale of a boat he had bought for forty shillings and had three seasons out of.

Para Handy swopped the dinghy a fortnight later in Tarbert for a punt that suited the *Vital Spark* much better, and thirty shillings cash. With part of the thirty shillings he has bought another net. For flounders.

THE STOWAWAY

" DID you ever, ever, in your born days, see such umpidence ? " said the mate of the smartest boat in the coasting trade, looking up from his perusal of a scrap of newspaper in which the morning's kippers had been brought aboard by Sunny Jim.

" What iss't, Dougald ? " asked the Captain, sitting down on a keg to put on his carpet slippers, a sign that the day of toil on deck officially was over. " You'll hurt your eyes, there, studyin' in the dark. You're gettin' chust ass bad ass the enchineer for readin' ; we'll have to put in the electric light for you."

" Chermans ! " said Dougie. " The country's crooded wi' them. They're goin' aboot disguised ass towerists, drawin' plans o' forts and brudges."

" Now, issn't that most desperate ! " said Para Handy, poking up the fo'c'sle stove, by whose light his mate had been reading this disquieting intelligence. " That's the way that British tred iss ruined. First it wass Cherman clocks, and then it wass jumpin'-jecks, and noo it's picture post-cairds."

" Criftens ! " said Sunny Jim, who had come hurriedly down to put on a second waistcoat, for the night was cold : " Whit dae ye think they're makin' the drawin's for ? "

" Iss't no' for post-cairds ? " asked the Captain innocently, and the cook uproariously laughed.

" Post-cairds my auntie ! " he vulgarly exclaimed. " It's for the German Airmy. As soon's they can get their bits o' things thegither, they're comin' ower here to fight us afore the Boy Scouts gets ony bigger. They hae spies a' ower Britain makin' maps ; I'll lay ye there's no' a beer-shop in the country that they havena dotted doon."

" Holy smoke ! " said Para Handy.

He watched the very deliberate toilet of Sunny Jim with some impatience. " Who's supposed to be at the wheel at this parteecular meenute ? " he asked, with apparent unconcern.

"Me," said Sunny Jim. "There's naething in sicht, and I left it a meenute just to put on this waistcoat. Ye're gettin' awfu' pernicketty wi' your wheel ; it's no' the *Lusitania*."

" I'm no' findin' faault at aal, at aal, Jum, but I'm chust considerin'," said the Captain meekly. " Take your time. Don't hurry, Jum. Would you no' give your hands a wash and put on a collar ? It's always nice to have a collar on and be looking spruce if you're drooned in a collusion. Give a kind of a roar when you get up on deck if you see we're runnin' into anything."

" Collusion ! " said Sunny Jim contemptuously. " Wi' a' the speed this boat can dae, she couldna run into a pend close if it started rainin'," and he swung himself on deck.

" He hasna the least respect for the vessel," said the Captain sadly. " She might be a common gaabert for aal the pride that Jum hass in her."

The *Vital Spark* had left Loch Ranza an hour ago, and was puffing across the Sound of Bute for the Garroch Head on her way to Glasgow. A pitch-black night, not even a star to be seen, and Sunny Jim at the wheel had occasionally a feeling that the Cumbrae Light for which he steered was floating about in space, detached from everything like a fire-balloon that winked every thirty seconds at the sheer delight of being free. He whistled softly to himself, and still very cold, in spite of his second waistcoat, envied Macphail the engineer, whom he could see in the grateful warmth of the furnace-door reading a penny novelette. Except for the wheeze and hammer of the engine, the propeller's churning, and the wash of the calm sea at the snub nose of the vessel, the night was absolutely still.

The silence was broken suddenly by sounds of vituperation from the fo's'cle ; the angry voices of the Captain and the mate, and a moment later they were on deck pushing a figure aft in front of them. " Sling us up a lamp, Macphail, to see what iss't we have a haad o' here," said the Captain hurriedly, with a grasp on the stranger's coat-collar, and the engineer produced the light. It shone on a burly foreigner with coal-black hair, a bronze complexion, and a sack of onions to which he clung with desperate tenacity.

"Got him in Dougie's bunk, sound sleepin'," explained the Captain breathlessly, with the tone of an entomologist who has found a surprising moth. "I saw him dandering aboot Loch Ranza in the mornin'. A stowaway! He wants to steal a trip to Gleska."

"I'll bate ye he's gaun to the Scottish Exhibeetion," said Sunny Jim. "We'll be there in time, but his onions 'll gang wrang on him afore we get to Bowlin'. Whit dae they ca' ye for your Christian name, M'Callum?"

"Onions," replied the stranger. "Cheap onions. No Ingles."

"Oh, come aff it! come aff it! We're no' such neds as to think that ony man could hae a Christian name like Onions," said Sunny Jim. "Try again, and tell us it's Clarence."

"And what iss't your wantin' on my boat?" asked Para Handy sternly.

The foreigner looked from one to the other of them with large pathetic eyes from under a broad Basque bonnet. "Onions. Cheap onions," he repeated, extracting a bunch of them hastily from the bag. "Two bob. Onions."

"Gie the chap a chance," said Sunny Jim ironically. "Maybe he gie'd his ticket up to the purser comin' in."

"He hasna a word o' English in his heid," said Dougie. "There's something at the bottom o't; stop you, and you'll see! It's no' for his health he's traivellin' aboot Arran wi' a bag o' onions, and hidin' himsel' on board a Christian boat. I'll wudger that he's Cherman."

"It's no a German kep he's wearin' onyway," said Macphail, with the confidence of a man who has travelled extensively and observed.

"That's a disguise," said Dougie, no less confidently. "You

can see for yoursel' he hass even washed himsel'. Try him wi' a bit of the Cherman lingo, Macphail, and you'll see the start he'll get."

Macphail, whose boast had always been that he could converse with fluency in any language used in any port in either hemisphere, cleared his throat and hesitatingly said, " Parly voo Francis ? "

" Onions. Cheap onions," agreeably replied the stranger.

" Francis ! Francis ! Parly voo ? " repeated the engineer, testily and loudly, as if the man were deaf.

" Maybe his name's no Francis," suggested Sunny Jim. " Try him wi' Will Helm, or Alphonso ; there's lots o' them no' called Francis."

" He understands me fine, I can see by his eye," said the engineer, determined to preserve his reputation as a linguist. " But, man ! he's cunnin'."

" It's the wrong shup he hass come to if he thinks he iss cunnin' enough for us ! " said the Captain firmly. " It's the jyle in Greenock that we'll clap him in for breakin' on board of a well-known steam-boat and spoilin' Dougald's bunk wi' onions."

The stowaway sat nonchalantly down on a bucket, produced a knife and a hunk of bread, and proceeded to make a meal of it with onions. Immediately the crew was constituted into a court-martial, and treated the presence of their captive as if he were a deaf-mute or a harmless species of gorilla.

" What wass I tellin' you, Captain, at the very meenute I saw his feet stickin' oot o' my bunk ? " inquired the mate. " The country's overrun wi' Chermans. I wass readin' yonder that there's two hunder and fifty thousand o' them in Brutain."

" What a lot ! " said Para Handy. " I never set eyes on wan o' them to my knowledge. What are they like, the silly duvvles ? "

" They're chust like men that would be sellin' onions," said

Dougie. " Lerge, big, heavy fellows like oor frien' here ; and they never say nothing to nobody. You've seen hunders o' them though you maybe didna ken. They're Chermans that plays the bands on the river steamers."

" Are they ? are they ? " said Para Handy with surprise ; " I always thought yon chaps wass rivetters, or brass-feenishers, that chust made a chump on board the boat wi' their instruments when she wass passin' Yoker and the purser's back wass turned."

" Germans to a man ! " said Sunny Jim. " There's no' a Scotchman among them ; ye never saw yin o' them yet the worse o' drink."

" Ye needna tell me yon chaps playin' awa' on the steamers iss makin' maps," said Para Handy. " Their eyes iss aalways glued on their cornucopias."

" They're goin' aboot ports and forts and battleships drawin' plans," said the engineer. " Whit did the Royal Horse Artillery find the ither day at Portsmouth ? Yin o' them crawlin' up a gun to mak' a drawin' o't, and they had to drag him oot by the feet."

" Chust that ! " said Para Handy, regarding their captive with greater interest. " I can see mysel' noo ; he looks desperate like a Cherman. Do you think he wass makin' plans o' the *Vital Spark* ? "

" That's whit I was askin' him in German ! " said Macphail, " and ye saw yersel's the suspicious way he never answered."

" Jum," said the Captain, taking the wheel himself, " away like a smert laad and make up a cup o' tea for the chap ; it's maybe the last he'll ever get if we put him in the jyle in Greenock or in Gleska."

" Right-oh ! " said Sunny Jim, gladly relinquishing the wheel. " Will I set the table oot in the fore saloon ? Ye'll excuse us bein' short o' floral decorations, Francis ? Is there onything special ye would like in the way o' black breid or horse-flesh, and I'll order't frae the steward ? "

" Onions," said the stranger.

The foreigner spent the night imprisoned in the hold with the hatches down, and wakened with an excellent appetite for breakfast, while the vessel lay at a wharf on the upper river.

"There's money in't ; it's like a salvage," Dougie said to Para Handy, as they hurried ashore for a policeman.

"I canna see't," said the Captain dubiously. "What's the good o' a Cherman? If he wass a neegur bleck, you could sell him to the shows for swallowin' swords, but I doot that this chap hassna got the right agility."

"Stop, you!" said the mate with confidence. "The Government iss desperate keen to get a haad o' them, and here's Mackay the polisman."

"We have a kind o' a Cherman spy on board," he informed the constable, who seemed quite uninterested.

"The Sanitary Depairtment iss up in John Street," said the constable. "It's not on my bate." But he consented to come to the *Vital Spark* and see her stowaway.

"Toots, man! he's no a Cherman, and he's no' a spy," he informed them at a glance.

"And what iss he then?" asked the Captain.

"I don't ken what he iss, but he's duvellish like a man that would be sellin' onions," said Mackay, and on his advice the suspect was released.

It was somewhat later in the day that Dougie missed his silver watch, which had been hanging in the fo'c'sle.

CONFIDENCE

THE Captain of the *Vital Spark* and his mate were solemnly drinking beer in a Greenock public-house, clad in their best shore-going togs, for it was Saturday. Another customer came in—a bluff, high-coloured, English-spoken individual with an enormous watch-chain made of what appeared to be mainly golden nuggets in their natural state, and a ring with a diamond bulging out so far in it that he could hardly get his hand into his trousers pocket. He produced a wad of bank-notes, peeled one off, put it down on the counter with a slap, and demanded gin and ginger.

" A perfect chentleman ! " said Para Handy to his mate in a whisper ; " you can aalways tell them ! He'll likely have a business somewhere."

The opulent gentleman took his glass of gin and ginger to a table and sat down, lit a cigar, and proceeded to make notes in a pocket-book.

" That's the worst of wealth," said Dougie philosophically ; " you have to be aalways tottin' it up in case you forget you have it. Would you care for chust another, Peter ? I think I have a shullin' ."

Another customer came in—apparently a seaman, with a badge of a well-known shipping line on his cap.

" Hello, bully boys ! " he said heartily. " Gather around ; there's a letter from home ! What are we going to have ? In with your pannikins, lively now, and give it a name," and he ordered glasses round, excluding the auriferous gentleman who was taking notes behind.

" Looks like a bloomin' Duke ! " he remarked in an under-tone to Para Handy. " One of them ship-owners, likely ; cracker-hash and dandy-funk for Jack, and chicken and champagne wine for Mister Bloomin' Owner ! Ours is a dog's life, sonnies, but I don't care now, I'm home from Callao ! "

" Had you a good trup ? " asked Para Handy, with polite anxiety.

" Rotten ! " said the seaman tersely. " What's your line ? Longshore, eh ? " and he scrutinised the crew of the *Vital Spark*.

" Chust that ! " said Para Handy mildly. " Perusin' aboot the Clyde wi' coals and doin' the best we can."

" Then I hope the hooker's your own, my boy, for there's not much bloomin' money in it otherwise," said the seaman ;

and Para Handy, not for the first time, fell a victim to his vanity.

"Exactly" he said, with a pressure on the toe of Dougie's boot; "I'm captain and owner too; the smertest boat in the tred," and he jingled a little change he had in his pocket.

"My name's Tom Wilson," volunteered the seaman. "First mate of the *Wallaby*, with an extra master's papers, d——n your eyes! And I've got five-and-twenty bloomin' quids in my pocket this very moment; look at that!" He flourished a wad of notes that was almost as substantial as the one displayed a little before by the gentleman with the nugget watch-chain.

"It's a handy thing to have aboot ye," said Para Handy sagely, jingling his coppers eloquently. "But I aalways believe in gold mysel'; you're not so ready to lose it."

"I've noticed that mysel'," said Dougie solemnly.

Tom Wilson ordered another round, and produced a watch which he confidently assured them was the finest watch of its kind that money could buy. It had an alarm bell, and luminous paint on the hands and dial permitted you to see the time on the darkest night without a light.

"Well, well! issn't that cluvver!" exclaimed Para Handy. "They'll be makin' them next to boil a cup o' tea. It would cost a lot o' money? I'm no' askin', mind you; I wass chust remarkin'."

"Look here!" cried Tom Wilson impulsively; "I'll give the bloomin' clock to the very first man who can guess what I paid for it."

"Excuse me, gentlemen," said the man with the nugget watch-chain, putting away his note-book and pencil. "I'd like to see that watch," and they joined him at the table, where he generously ordered another round. He gravely examined the watch, and guessed that it cost about twenty pounds.

"Yes, but you must mention the exact figure," said its owner.

" Well, I guess two-and-twenty sovereigns," said the other, and Tom Wilson hastily proceeded to divest himself of the chain to which it had been originally attached. "It's yours!" he said; "you've guessed it, and you may as well have the bloomin' chain as well. That's the sort of sunny boy I am !" and he beamed upon the company with the warmth of one whose chief delight in life was to go round distributing costly watches.

" Wass I not chust goin' to say twenty-two pounds !" said Para Handy with some chagrin.

" I knew it wass aboot that," said Dougie; " chenuine gold ! "

The lucky winner of the watch laughed, put it into his pocket, and took out the wad of notes, from which he carefully counted out twenty-two pounds, which he thrust upon Tom Wilson.

" There you are !" he said; " I wouldn't take your watch for nothing, and it happens to be the very kind of watch I've been looking for."

" But you have only got my word for it, Mister, that it's worth that money," protested Mr Wilson.

The stranger smiled. " My name's Denovan," he remarked; " I'm up here from Woolwich on behalf of the Admiralty to arrange for housin' the torpedo workers in first-rate cottage homes with small back gardens. What does the Lords o' the Admiralty say to me ? The Lords o' the Admiralty says to me, ' Mr Denovan, you go and fix up them cottage homes, and treat the people of Greenock with confidence.' I'm a judge of men, I am, bein' what I am, and the principle I go on is to trust my fellow-men. If you say two-and-twenty pounds is the value of this watch, I say two-and-twenty it is, and there's an end of it ! "

Mr Wilson reluctantly put the notes in his pocket, with an expression of the highest admiration for Mr Denovan's principles, and Para Handy experienced the moral stimulation of being in an atmosphere of exceptional integrity and unlimited wealth. "Any wan could see you were the perfect chentleman," he confessed to Mr Denovan, ducking his head at him. "What way are they aal keepin' in Woolwich ? "

"I took you for a bloomin' ship-owner at first," said Mr Wilson. "I didn't think you had anything to do with the Admiralty."

"I'm its right-hand man," replied Mr Denovan modestly. "If you're thinkin' of a nice cottage home round here with front plot and small back garden, I can put you in, as a friend, for one at less than half what anybody else would pay."

"I haven't any use for a bloomin' house unless there was a licence to it," said Mr Wilson cheerfully.

Mr Denovan looked at him critically. "I like the look of you," he remarked impressively. "I'm a judge of men, and just to back my own opinion of you, I'll put you down right off for the first of the Admiralty houses. You needn't take it ; you could sell it at a profit of a hundred pounds to-morrow ; I don't ask you to give me a single penny till you have made your profit," and Mr Denovan, producing his pocket-book, made a careful note of the transaction lest he might forget it. " ' Treat the people of Greenock with confidence,' says the Lords of the Admiralty to me ; now, just to show my confidence in you, I'll hand you back your watch, and my own watch, and you can go away with them for twenty minutes."

"All right, then ; just for a bloomin' lark," agreed Tom Wilson, and with both watches and the colossal nugget-chain, he disappeared out of the public-house.

"That's a fine, smart, honest-lookin', manly fellow ! " remarked Mr Denovan admiringly.

"Do you think he'll come back wi' the watches ? " said Dougie dubiously.

"Of course he will," replied Mr Denovan. "Trust men, and they'll trust you. I'll lay you a dollar he would come back if he had twenty watches and all my money as well."

This opinion was justified. Mr Wilson returned in less than five minutes, and restored the watches to their owner.

"Well, I'm jeegered!" said Para Handy, and ordered another round out of admiration for such astounding honesty.

"Would you trust me?" Mr Denovan now asked Tom Wilson.

"I would," said the seaman heartily. "Look here; I've five-and-twenty bloomin' quid, and I'll let you go out and walk the length of the railway station with them."

"Done!" said Mr Denovan, and possessed of Wilson's roll of notes, went out of the public-house.

"Peter," said Dougie to the Captain, "do you no' think one of us should go efter him chust in case there's a train for Gleska at the railway station?"

But Tom Wilson assured them he had the utmost confidence in Mr Denovan, who was plainly a tip-top gentleman of unlimited financial resources, and his confidence was justified, for Mr Denovan not only returned with the money, but insisted on adding a couple of pounds to it as a recognition of Mr Wilson's sporting spirit.

"I suppose you Scotch chaps don't have any confidence?" said Mr Denovan to the Captain.

"Any amount!" said Para Handy.

"Well, just to prove it," said Mr Denovan, "would you be willin' to let our friend Wilson here, or me, go out with a five-pound note of yours?"

"I havena the five pounds here, but I have it in the boat," said the Captain. "If Dougie 'll wait here, I'll go down for it. Stop you, Dougie, with the chentlemen."

.   .   .   .

Some hours later Dougie turned up on the *Vital Spark* to find the Captain in his bunk, and sound asleep.

"I thocht you were comin' wi' a five-pound note?" he remarked on wakening him. "The chentlemen waited, and better waited, yonder on you, and they werena pleased at aal, at aal. They said you surely hadna confidence."

" Dougie," said the Captain, " I have the greatest confidence, but I have the five pounds, too.   And if you had any money in your pocket it's no' with Mr Denovan I would leave you."

THE GOAT

PARA HANDY, having listened with amazement to the story of the Stepney battle read by the engineer, remarked, " If it wassna in print, Macphail, I wouldna believe it ! They must be desperate powerful men, them Rooshian burgulars. Give us yon bit again aboot Sir Wunston Churchill."

" ' The Right Honourable gentleman, at the close of the engagement, went up a close and shook 127 bullets out of his Astrakan coat,' " repeated Macphail, who always added a few picturesque details of his own invention to any newspaper narrative.

" It was 125 you said last time," Para Handy pointed out suspiciously.

" My mistake ! " said Macphail frankly ;   " I thocht it was a five at first, but I see noo it's a seven.   A couple o' bullets more or less if it's anyway over the hundred doesna make much odds on an Astrakan coat."

" Man, he must be a tough young fellow, Wunston ! " said the Captain, genuinely admiring.   " Them bullets give you an awfu' bang.   But I think the London polisman iss greatly wantin' in agility ;   they would be none the worse o' a lesson from Wully Crawford, him that wass the polisman in Tarbert when I wass at the school.   Wully wouldna throw chuckies at the window to waken up the Rooshians ;   he wass far too caautious.   He would pause and consuder.   Wully wass never frightened for a bad man in a hoose :   ' It's when they're goin' lowse aboot the town they're dangerous,' he would say ;   ' they're chust ass safe in there ass in my lock-up, and they're no' so weel attended.'

" Wully wass the first polisman ever they had in Tarbert.

He wassna like the chob at aal, at aal, but they couldna get another man to take it. He wass a wee small man wi' a heid like a butter-firkin, full to the eyes wi' natural agility, and when he would put the snitchers on you, you would think it wass a shillin' he wass slippin' in your hand. If you were up to any muschief—poachin' a bit o' fish or makin' a demonstration—Wully would come up wi' his heid to the side and rubbing his hands thegither, and say a kindly word. I've seen great big massive fellows walkin' doon the street wi' Wully, thinkin' they were goin' to a Christmas pairty, and before they knew where they were they were lyin' on a plank in his lock-up. You never saw a man wi' nicer mainners ; he wass the perfect chentleman !

" ' Stop you there, lads, and I'll be back in a meenute wi' a cup o' tea,' he would say when he wass lockin' the door of the cell on them. ' Iss there anything you would like to't ? ' The silly idiots sometimes thocht they were in a temperance hotel by Wully's mainners, and they got a terrible start in the mornin' when they found they had to pay a fine. You mind o' Wully Crawford, Dougie ? "

" Fine ! " said Dougie. " He was the duvvle's own ! "

" ' Caaution and consuderation iss the chief planks in the armour of the Brutish constable,' Wully used to say, rubbin' his hands. ' There iss no need for anybody to be hurt.'

" It wass the time when Tarbert herrin'-trawlers wass at their best and money goin'. It wass then, my laads, there wass Life in Tarbert ! The whole o' Scotland Yaird and a regiment o' arteelery couldna have kept the Tarbert fishermen in order, but Wully Crawford held them in the hollow o' his hand——"

" It's a' very weel," said Macphail, " but they didna go aboot wi' automatic pistols."

" No, they didna have aromatic pistols," admitted Para Handy, " but they had aawfully aromatic fists. And you never saw smerter chaps wi' a foot-spar or a boat-hook. The wildest of the lot wass a lad M'Vicar, that belonged to Tarbert and wass called The Goat for his sagacity. He could punch his heid through a mill-stone and wear it round his neck the rest o' the day instead o' a collar. When The Goat wass extra lucky at the trawlin' the Tarbert merchants didna take the shutters off their shops and the steam-boat agents had to put a ton or two o' ballast in their shippin'-boxes. Not a bad chap at aal, The Goat—only wicked, wicked! The only wan that could stand up to him in Tarbert wass three Macdougall brothers wi' a skiff from Minard; him and them wass at variance.

" The Goat would be going through the toun wi' his gallowses ootside his guernsey and his bonnet on three hairs, spreading devastation, when the Free Church munister would send for Wully Crawford.

" ' You must do your duty, Wullium,' he would say, wi' his heid stickin' oot at a garret window and the front door barred. ' There's M'Vicar lowse again, and the whole o' Tarbert in commotion. Take care that ye divna hurt him.'

" ' There's nobody needs to be hurt at aal, wi' a little deeliberation,' Wully would say wi' his heid to the side, and it most dreadful like a butter-firkin. ' I'll chust paause and consuder, Mr Cameron, and M'Vicar, 'll be in the cell in twenty meenutes. Terrible stormy weather, Mr Cameron. What way's the mustress keepin' ? '

" Then Wully would put off his uniform coat and on wi' a wee pea-jecket, and go up to where The Goat wass roarin' like a bull in the streets of Tarbert, swingin' a top-boot full o' stones aboot his heid—clean daft wi' fair defiance.

" ' John,' Wully would say to him, rubbin' his hands and lookin' kindly at him, ' it's a wonder to me you would be carryin' on here, and them Macdougalls up on the quay swearin' they'll knock the heid off you.'

" The Goat would start for the quay, but Wully wass there before him, and would say to the Macdougalls, ' In to your boat, my laads, and on wi' the hatch; M'Vicar's vowing vengeance on you. Here he comes! ' He knew very well it wass the last thing they would do ; five minutes later and the three Macdougalls and The Goat would be in grips.

" ' Pick oot whatever bits belong to yoursel's, and I'll collect what's left of poor M'Vicar,' Wully would say to the Macdougalls when the fight wass done, and then he would hurl The Goat to the lock-up in a barrow.

" But that wass only wan of Wully's schemes ; his agility was sublime ! There wass wan time yonder when The Goat took a fancy for high jeenks, and carried a smaal-boat up from the shore at night and threw it into the banker's lobby. It wass a way they had in Tarbert at the time o' celebratin' Hallowe'en, for they were gettin' splendid fishin's, and were up to aal diversions.

" Wully went roond in the mornin' to M'Vicar's house, and ass sure ass daith he hadna the weight or body o' a string o' fish, but a heid on him like a firkin. If The Goat had kent what he came for, he would have heaved him through the window.

" ' You werena quarrellin' wi' Mackerracher last night and threw him ower the quay ? ' asked Wully, rubbin' his hands.

" ' I never set eyes on Mackerracher in the last fortnight ! ' said The Goat, puttin' doon a potato-beetle, as you might say disappointed.

" ' Tuts ! wassn't I sure of it ! ' said Wully, clappin' him on the back. ' Mackerracher's missin', and there's a man at the office yonder says he thocht he saw you wi' him. It's chust a case of alibi ; come awa' across to the office for a meenute ; he's waitin' there, and he'll see his mistake at wance.'

" The Goat went over quite joco to the polis-office, knowin' himsel' he wass innocent of any herm to poor Mackerracher, and wass fined in thirty shullin's for puttin' a boat in the banker's lobby. Oh, a cluver fellow, Wullium ! A heid like a butter-firkin !

" You would think The Goat would never be got to the

polis-office any more wi' such contrivances o' Wully Crawford. 'If that wee duvvle wants me again, he'll have to
come for me wi' the Princess Louisa's Own Argyll and
Sutherland Highlanders and a timber-junker,' he swore, and
Wully only laughed when he heard it. 'Us constables
would be havin' a sorry time wi' the like of John M'Vicar
if we hadna the Laaw o' the Land and oor wuts at the back
o' us,' he said, wi' his heid on the side, and his belt a couple
o' feet too big for him.

"Two or three weeks efter that, when the fishin' wass
splendid, and The Goat in finest trum, he wakened one
morning in his boat and found that some one had taken away
a couple o' barrels o' nets, a pair o' oars, and a good pump-
handle on him.

"'I'll have the Laaw on them, whoever it wass!' he says.
Tarbert will soon be a place where a dacent man canna leave
his boat withoot a watch-dog; where's Wully Crawford, the
polisman?'

"He went lookin' up and doon the toon for Wully, but
Wully wasna to be seen at aal, at aal, and some wan said he
wass over at the polis-office. The Goat went over to the
polis-office and chapped like a chentleman at the door withoot a meenute's prevarication.

"'Some wan stole on me through the night, a couple o'
barrel o' nets, a pair o' oars, and a good pump-handle, and
want you to do your duty!' says The Goat to the polis-
constable, and the head of him chust desperate like a butter-
firkin!

"'Did you lose them, John?' said Wully, rubbin' his
hands. 'Man! I think I have a clue to the depridaation;
have some of the very articles you're lookin' for in here,'
and he opened the cell door, and sure enough there was a
couple o' barrels o' nets in a corner. What did the silly idiot,
John M'Vicar, no' do, but go into the cell to look at them, and
the next meenute the door was locked on him!

"'A couple o' barrel o' nets and a pair o' oars or the like

I

o' that can be taken in charge withoot assistance from the
Princess Louisa's Own Argyll and Sutherland Highlanders,'
said bold Wully through the key-hole. ' Iss there anything
I could get for your breakfast to-morrow, John ? You'll
need to keep up your strength. You're to be tried for your
assault last Saturday on the Rechabite Lodge.'

" The Goat lay in the cell aal day and roared like a bull,
but it didna make any odds to Wully Crawford ; he went
aboot the toon wi' his heid more like a firkin than ever, and
a kindly smile. But when The Goat begood at night to kick
the door o' his cell for oors on end and shake the polis-office
to its foundations, Wully couldna get his naitural sleep. He
rose at last and went to the door o' the cell, and says, says he :
' John, ye didna leave oot your boots ; if you'll hand them
oot to me I'll gie them a brush for the mornin'.'

" M'Vicar put oot the boots like a lamb.

" ' There now,' said Wully, lockin' the door again, ' ye
can kick away till you're black in the face. Would you like
them oiled or bleckened ? ' And you never saw a man wi' a
heid more like a firkin o' Irish butter ! "

PARA HANDY'S VOTE

Para Handy had finished tea on Saturday night, and was
ruefully contemplating the urgent need for his weekly shave,
when Mary, his wife, was called to the outer door. She came
back to the kitchen to inform her husband that a gentleman
wished to see him.

" A chentleman ! " said Para Handy, with surprise
and even incredulity. " What in the world will he be
wantin' ? "

" He didna say," replied Mrs Macfarlane. " He said he
wanted to see you most particular, and wouldna keep you a
meenute. Whatever you do, don't go and buy another o'
thae Histories of the Scottish Clans."

" Could you not tell him I'm away on the boat, or that I'm busy ? " asked her husband, nervously putting on his jacket.

" I'm no' goin' to tell any lies aboot you," said Mrs Macfarlane. " It's nobody for money anyway, for we're no' in anybody's reverence a single penny."

" What the duvvle can the man be wantin' ? What kind o' look did you get at him ? Do you think he's angry ? "

" Not a bit of him ; he spoke quite civil to mysel', and he has a book wi' a 'lastic band on't, the same as if it was the meter he was comin' for."

" A book ! " said Para Handy, alarmed. " Go you out, Mary, like a cluver gyurl, and tell him that I slipped away to my bed when you werena lookin'. Tell him to come back on Monday."

" But you'll be away wi' the boat on Monday."

" Chust that ; but he'll be none the wiser. There's many a sailor caaled away in a hurry. Don't be a frightened coward, Mary. Man, but you're tumid, tumid ! The chentleman's no' goin' to eat you."

" He's no' goin' to eat you either," said Mrs Macfarlane. " He's standin' there at the door, and you'll just have to go and see him."

" I wish I wass back on the boat," said Para Handy in despair. " There's no' much fun in a hoose o' your own if you'll no' get a meenute's peace in't. What in the mischief iss he wantin' wi' his book and his 'lastic bands ? "

He went to the door and found an exceedingly suave young gentleman there, who said, " I'm delighted to find you at home, Captain Macfarlane ; my business won't take five minutes."

" If it's a History o' the Clans, we have it already," said Para Handy, with his shoulder against the door. " I ken the clans by he'rt."

" You have a vote in the College Division," said the visitor briskly, paying no attention to the suggestion that he was a book-canvasser. "I'm canvassing for your old friend, tried and true, Harry Watt."

"Chust that!" said Para Handy. "What way iss he keepin', Harry? I hope he's in good trum?"

"Never was better, or more confident, but he looks to you to do your best for him on this occasion."

"That's nice," said Para Handy. "It's a blessin' the health; and there's lots o' trouble goin' aboot. Watch your feet on the stair goin' down; there's a nesty dark bit at the bottom landin'."

"Mr Watt will be delighted to know that he can depend on you," said the canvasser, opening up his book and preparing to record one more adherent to the glorious principles of Reform. "He'll be sure to come round, and give you a call himself."

"Any time on Monday," said Para Handy. "I'll be prood to see him. What did you say again the chentleman's name wass?"

"Mr Harry Watt," said the canvasser, no way surprised to find that the voter was in ignorance on this point, an absolute indifference to the identity of its M.P.'s being not unusual in the College Division.

"Yes, yes, of course; I mind now, Harry Watt. A fine chentleman! Tip-top! He wass aalways for the workin' man. It's a fine open wunter we're havin' this wunter, if it wassna for the fogs."

"What do you think of the House of Lords now?" asked the canvasser, desirous to find exactly what his victim's colour was, and Para Handy shifted his weight on another leg and scratched his ear.

"It's still to the fore," he answered cautiously. "There's a lot of fine big chentlemen in it. Me bein' on the boat, I don't see much of them, except noo and then their pictures in the papers. Iss there any Bills goin' on the noo?"

" I think we're going to clip their wings this time," said the canvasser with emphasis ; and the Captain shifted hurriedly back to his former leg and scratched his other ear.

" Capital ! " he exclaimed, apparently with the utmost sympathy. " Ye canna clup them quick enough. They're playin' the very muschief over yonder in Ireland. There's wan thing, certain sure—I never could stand the Irish."

" Yes, yes ; but you'll admit a safe measure of Home Rule——" began the canvasser ; and the Captain found the other leg was the better one after all.

" I'll admit that ! " he agreed hurriedly. " Whatever you say yoursel'."

" See and be round at the poll early," said the canvasser. " It's on Thursday."

" I'm making aal arrangements," said the Captain cordially. " Never mind aboot a motor-car ; I can walk the distance. Give my best respects to Mr Harry ; tell him I'll stand firm. A Macfarlane never flinched ! He's no' in the shippin' line, Mr Harry, iss he ? No ? chust that ! I wass only askin' for curiosity. A brulliant chentleman ! He hass the wonderful agility, they tell me. Us workin' men must stand thegither and aye be bringin' in a bill."

" Of course the question before the electors is the Veto," said the canvasser.

" You never said a truer word ! " said the Captain heartily. " It's what I said mysel' years ago ; if my mate Dougie wass here he would tell you. Everything's goin' up in price, even the very blecknin'."

" See and not be carried away by any of their Referendum arguments," counselled the canvasser, slipping the elastic band on his book. " It's only a red herring dragged across the track."

" I never could stand red herring," said the Captain.

" And remember Thursday, early—the earlier the better ! " was the visitor's final word as he went downstairs.

" I'm chust goin' in this very meenute to make a note of

it in case I should forget," said Para Handy, ducking his head reassuringly at him.

"A smert young fellow!" he told his wife when he got back to the kitchen. "He took my name doon yonder chust as nate's you like!" and he explained the object of the caller's visit.

"It's the like o' me that should have the vote," said Mrs Macfarlane humorously. "I have a better heid for politics than you."

"Mery," said her husband warmly, "you're taalkin' like wan of them unfidel Suffragettes. If I see you goin' oot wi' a flag and standin' on a lorry, there'll be trouble in the College Diveesion!"

The Captain had hardly started to his shaving when Mrs Macfarlane found herself called to the door again, and returned with the annoying intelligence that another gentleman desired a moment's interview.

"Holy smoke!" said Para Handy. "Do they think this hoose iss the Argyle Arcade? It must be an aawful wet night outside when they're aal crowdin' here for shelter. Could you no' tell him to leave his name and address and say I would caal on him mysel' on Monday?"

On going to the door he found an even more insinuative canvasser than the first one—a gentleman who shook him by the hand several times during the interview, and even went the length of addressing him like an old friend as Peter.

"I'm lucky to find you at home," he said.

"You are that!" said the Captain curtly, with his shoulder against the door. "What iss't?"

"I'm canvassing for our friend——"

"It's no' ten meenutes since another wan wass here afore," broke in the Captain. "You should take stair aboot, the way they lift the tickets in the trains, and no' be comin' twice to the same door. I made aal arrangements for the Thursday wi' the other chap."

" Think it over again," said the canvasser, no way crestfallen, with an affectionate hand on the Captain's shoulder.
' Don't be misled by plausible stories. I have your name
down here since last election as a staunch upholder of the
Constitution. You must support Carr-Glyn."

" There's not a man in Gleska stauncher than mysel'," said
the Captain. " What did you say the chentleman's name
wass ? "

" Mr Carr-Glyn," said the canvasser. " One of the good
old sort ; one of ourselves, as you might say ; a nephew of
the Duke of Argyll's."

" The very man for the job ! I'll be there on Thursday ;
keep your mind easy on that. My mother wass a Campbell.
The Duke iss a splendid chentleman. Tremendous agility ! "

" The whole situation has changed in the last few days.
You see, the Referendum practically puts the final decision
upon every new constitutional change in the hands of the
individual elector, and the Lords are gone."

" Cot bless me ! you don't say so ? " said the Captain with
genuine surprise. " Where are they away to ? "

The canvasser rapidly sketched the decline and fall of the
hereditary principle in the Upper House.

" Holy smoke ! iss the Duke goin' to lose his job, then ? "
asked Para Handy with sincere alarm ; and the visitor
hastened to reassure him.

" If you like, I'll send round a motor-car on Thursday,"
said the canvasser, when he had satisfied himself that the
vote of Para Handy was likely to go to the side which had
his ear last.

" Don't put yoursel' to any bother aboot a car ; I would
sooner walk ; it's the least a body could do for Mr Glyn,"
said the Captain. " Tell him that I'll stand firm, and that
I'm terrible weel acquainted wi' his uncle."

" Thank you," said the canvasser. " Mr Carr-Glyn will be
highly pleased."

" You'll not answer the door the night again if a hundred

chentlemen comes to it," said Para Handy when he got back
to his wife.   " A man might ass weel be livin' in a restaurant."

" What day's the pollin' on ? " said Mary.

" On Thursday," said her husband.   " Thank Cot ! I'll
no' be within a hundred miles o't.   I'll be on the *Fital Spark*
in Tobermory."

HURRICANE JACK
OF THE *VITAL SPARK*

HURRICANE JACK

OF THE *VITAL SPARK*

I

HURRICANE JACK

"STOP you!" said Para Handy, looking at his watch, "and I will give you a trate; I will introduce you to the finest sailor ever sailed the seas. He's comin' aboard the vessel in a little to say good-bye to us before he joins a kind o' a boat that's bound for Valapariza. Am I right or am I wrong, Dougie?"

"That's what he said himsel', at any rate," said Dougie dubiously. "But ye canna put your trust in Jeck. He meant it right enough at the time, but that wass yesterday, and Jeck hass wan o' them memories for mindin' things that's no' to be depended on—ass short and foggy ass a winter day!"

"You'll see he'll come!" said Para Handy confidently. "Jeck's a man o' his word, a perfect chentleman! Forbye, I have the lend o' his topcoat."

"Who is the consummate and accomplished mariner?" I asked, delaying my departure from the *Vital Spark*.

"There's only wan in all the cope and canopy o' British shippin'," said the Captain. "'John Maclachlan' in the books, but 'Hurricane Jeck' in every port from here to Callao. You have heard me speak of him? An arm like a spar and the he'rt of a child!"

"I'll assure you there iss nothing wrong wi' his arm whatever," said the mate; "it's like a davit." But he offered no comment on the heart of the illustrious seaman.

"He'll be here in a chiffy," Para Handy assured me eagerly. "It's worth your while waitin' to meet him when you have the chance. You'll find him most agreeable ; no pride nor palavers about him ; chust like any common sailor. A full-rigged ship tattooed on his chest, and his hat wi' a list to starboard. A night wi' Jeck iss ass good ass a college education. You never saw such nerve ! "

"I'll wait a little," I said ; "life offers so few opportunities for seeing the really great."

Five minutes later, and a lanky weather-beaten person with a tightly-buttoned blue serge suit, a brown paper parcel in his hand, and a very low-crowned bowler hat at an angle of forty-five, dropped on to the deck of the *Vital Spark*.

"Peter," he said to the Captain anxiously, without preamble, "what did ye do wi' my portmanta ? "

"I never saw it, Jeck," said Para Handy. "Iss it runnin' in your mind ye lost it ? "

"Not exactly lost," said Hurricane Jack, "but it's been adrift in this old town since Friday, and I'm tackin' round my friends to see if any of them's wearin' a good Crimea shirt I had in it. No reflections upon anybody, mind—that was an A1 shirt," and he looked with some suspicion at the turned-up collar of my coat.

"Nobody here hass your shirt, Jeck, I'll assure you," protested the Captain. "What kind of a portmanta wass it ? "

"It was a small tin canister," said Hurricane Jack quite frankly, and, having said so, cheered up magically, unburdened his mind of his loss, and was quite affable when I was formally presented to his distinguished notice by the Captain. He had a hybrid accent, half-Scotch and half-American, and I flatter myself he seemed to take to me from the very first.

"Put it there ! " he exclaimed fervently, thrusting out a hand in which, on my response to the invitation, he almost crushed my fingers into pulp. "I'm nothin' but an old sailor-man, but if I can do anything for anybody at any time between now and my ship sailin', say the word, sunny boys ! "

I assured him there was nothing pressing that I wanted done at the moment.

"I told ye!" exclaimed the Captain triumphantly. "Always the perfect chentleman! He thinks of everything!" He beamed upon the visitor with a pride and gratification it was delightful to witness.

"We havena anything on the boat," remarked Dougie, with what, to stupid people, might seem irrelevance. Hurricane Jack, however, with marvellous intuition, knew exactly what was indicated, looked at me with some expectancy, and I had not the slightest difficulty in inducing them all to join me in a visit to the Ferry Inn.

The bright particular star of the British mercantile marine having given the toast, "A fair slant!" three minutes later, addressed himself to the disposal of the largest quantity of malt liquor I have ever seen consumed at one breath, put down the empty vessel with unnecessary ostentation, and informed all whom it might concern that it was the first to-day.

"The chentleman," said Para Handy, alluding to me, "would take it ass a special trate, Jeck, to hear some specimens of your agility."

I did my best to assume an aspect of the most eager curiosity.

"In the old clipper tred," Para Handy informed me in a stage whisper. "Wan of the very best! Namely in all the shuppin' offices! Took a barque they called the *Port Jackson* from Sydney to San Francisco in nine-and-thirty days. Look at the shouthers o' him!"

"If a bit of a song, now—an old come-all-ye, or a short-pull shanty like 'Missouri River,'—would be any good to the gentleman," said Hurricane Jack agreeably, "I'll do my best endeavours as soon as I've scoffed this off. Here's salue!"

Para Handy looked a little apprehensive. "What wass runnin' in my mind," said he, "wass no' so mich a song, though there's none can touch you at the singin', Jeck, but some of your diversions in foreign parts. Take your time, Jeck; whatever you like yoursel'!" He turned again to me with a glance that challenged my closest and most admiring attention for the performance about to take place, and whispered, "Stop you, and you'll hear Mr Maclachlan!"

The gifted tar was apparently reluctant to abandon the idea of a song, and rather at a loss which of the stirring incidents of his life to begin with.

"Vino," he remarked, and then, lest there should be any mistake about the word, he spelled it. "V-i-n-o, that's wine in the Dago lingo. Wherever there's land there's liquor, and down away in the Dago countries you take a wide sheer in, see, to a place like Montevidio. Montevidio's like here, see——" and he drew some lines on the counter with spilt ale; "and down about here's Bahia, and round the Horn, say just right here, there's Valaparisa. Well, as I say, you tack in to any o' them odd places, it might be for a cargo o' beef, and you're right up against the vino. That's Dago for wine, sunny boys! V-i-n-o."

"Didn't I tell ye!" exclaimed Para Handy ecstatically, looking at me. "Jeck hass been everywhere. Speaks aal their languages like a native. Yes, Jeck; go on, Jeck; you're doin' capital, Jeck!"

"Extremely interesting!" I said to the fascinating child of the sea. "Valparaiso now; it's pretty liable to earthquake, isn't it?"

"Take your time, Jeck; don't be in a hurry," said Para Handy anxiously, as if I had been a K.C. trying to trap a witness.

"Never saw the bloomin' place but it was pitchin' like a Cardiff tramp," said Hurricane Jack. "It's the vino. V-i-n-o. Silly thing, the Dago lingo; I know it fine, all the knots and splices of it, but it's the silliest lingo between Hell and Honolulu. Good enough, I guess, for them Johnny Dagoes. What this country wants is genuine British sailor-men, to sail genuine British ships, and where are they? A lot o' ruddy Dutchmen! None o' the old stuff that was in the Black Ball Line wi' me; it wasn't blood we had in our veins in them days, sunny boys, but Riga balsam and good Stockholm tar."

He suddenly put his hand into a pocket, dragged out a leather bag, and poured a considerable quantity of silver coinage on the counter.

"Set her up again, sunny boy!" he said to the barman; "and don't vast heavin' till this little pot o' money's earned."

"Always the perfect chentleman!" said Para Handy with emotion. "Money is nothing to Jeck; he will spend it like the wave of the sea." But he gathered it up and returned it, all but a shilling or two, to the leather bag, which was by force restored to its owner's pocket.

"What," I asked, "is the strangest port you have seen?"

Hurricane Jack reflected. "You wouldn't believe me, sunny boys," said he, "if I told you."

"Yes, yes, Jeck; the chentleman 'll believe anything," said Para Handy.

"The rummiest port I've struck," said Hurricane Jack, "is Glasgow. The hooker I was on came into the dock last week, the first time I've been home for three years, and I goes up the quay for a tot o' rum wi' a shipmate, Jerry Sloan, that comes out o' Sligo. It wasn't twelve o'clock——"

"At night?" asked Dougie.

"Certainly! Who wants rum in the middle o' the day? I'd been so long away, perusin' up and down the South America coasts and over to Australia, I'd clean forgot the Glasgow habits, and I tell you I got a start when I found the rum-shops battened down. There wasn't even a shebeen! They tell me shebeenin's against the law in Glasgow now. They'll soon be shuttin' up the churches!

"'This is the worst place ever I scoffed!' says Jerry, and he's a lad that's been a bit about the world. Next day Jerry and me takes a slant up-town to buy a knife, and blamed if there was a cutlery shop or an ironmonger's open in the whole village !

" ' The man that makes the knives in Sheffield's dead, and they're celebratin' his funeral, or this is the slowest town on the Western Hemisphere,' says Jerry.

" Next day we took another slant to buy boiled ham, and went into a shop that was full of ham, but the son-of-a gun who kept it said he daren't sell us anything but oranges ! So the both of us went back like billy-oh to the water-side and signed for Valaparisa. That's where the vino is, sunny boys, and don't you forget it ! V-i-n-o."

" Capital ! " said Para Handy, and, turning again to me, remarked : " It's wonderful the things you see in traivellin'. If you'll come over to the vessel now, we'll maybe get Jeck to give a stave o' ' Paddy came round.' "

But I tore myself away on the plea of urgent business.

II

THE MYSTERY SHIP

UP at the bar of the inn the crew of the *Vital Spark* mildly regaled themselves with munition ale which the Captain audibly surmised had been made on the premises after the last washing-day.

It seemed good enough, however, for a gang of young Glasgow Fair lads who were also in the bar, and made as much noise as if the liquor legislation of the past five years had been abandoned.

" They're only lettin' on," said Para Handy sadly. " Just play-actin' ! It's no' on ale o' this dimensions that they're keepin' up the frolic. A barrel o' that wouldna rouse a song in a Templar lodge."

He cut himself a plug of thick black twist, and chewed it to remove as speedily as possible the flavour of Macalister's still undemobilised beer.

" I say, old chap," said the cheekiest of the Glasgow youths, " what do ye chew tobacco for ? "

" Just to get oot the juice," said Para Handy. " Iss everybody weel aboot Barlinnie ? "

The trippers came surging boisterously up to his end of the counter ; there was about them an infectious jollity that slightly thawed even the saturnine Macphail.

" Is that your vessel at the quay ? " said one of the strangers after a while. " She looks a bit battered. Needin' paintin' an' that——"

Para Handy sighed.

" Ye may weel say it ! " he responded. " It would be droll if she wassna lookin' battered. Ye would read in the papers aboot the ' Mystery Ship ' ? "

" Often," said the Glasgow man.

" That's her," whispered Para Handy. " Q Boat 21— the chenuine article ! The cammyflage iss off her, and her cannons iss back at Beardmore's, but if ye had seen her a year ago ye would call her the gem o' the sea. Am I right or am I wrong, Dougie ? "

" Ye chust took the word oot o' my mooth," responded the mate with impressive alacrity. " The gem o' the ocean."

Macphail merely snorted.

" What was she for ? " asked one of the trippers, quite impressed.

" That's just the very words I asked the Admirality when they took her over," said Para Handy, " and they wouldna tell me. ' Ye'll fin' oot soon enough,' says they ; ' she's the very packet we're lookin' for to play a prank on Jerry. She looks like a boat that would have agility.'

" They painted her streakum-strokum like the batters o' a book I have at home called John Bunyan's ' Holy War,' so that ye couldna make her oot a hundred yerds off if ye shut your eyes ; they put a wireless instrument doon her funnel, and a couple o' nice wee guns at her stern, wi' a crate on the top o' them the same ass they were chickens,

and put on board her an old frien' o' my own by the name
o' Hurricane Jeck that's weel acquent wi' the ocean tred,
and another chap for a gunner. The hold was packed wi'
ammunition."

"Where did ye a' sleep?" asked one of the Glasgow
company.

"It wassna a place to sleep in that wass botherin' us,"
explained the Captain; "the trouble wass to find a place
to put doon the pail in when Dougie and me and Macphail
and Jeck was takin' oor baths in the morning."

"Oh, Jerusalem!" exclaimed Macphail to himself, with
his face in another mug of munition ale. "Baths!"

"'Had ye navy uniforms?" asked one of the intensely
interested strangers.

"The very latest!" Para Handy assured him. "I'll
assure you they did it handsome."

"'Q 21' on the guernsey in red, red letters," added Dougie.
"Tasty!"

"Every man a telescope and a heavily-mounted blue pea-
jacket," added Macphail, with an ironic humour that went
over the heads of the audience.

"But whit was the mystery bit?" inquired an impatient
listener. "Did ye sink onything?"

"Did we sink onything?" repeated Para Handy in an
impressive whisper, after looking round the bar, to assure
himself no person of German sympathies might be present.
"When I tell you, chentlemen, that Hurricane Jeck wass the
Admirality's man on board my boat, there iss no need to go
into the question aboot sinkin'."

"Perhaps the gentleman never heard o' Hurricane Jeck,"
suggested the engineer maliciously.

"Perhaps not by that name," said Para Handy briskly,
"but they would hear o' John Maclachlan, V.C., and that's
the same chentleman."

"I mind o' readin' the name o' a V.C. like that in the
papers," said an intelligent Glasgow man.

" There iss no more namely sailor in the Western Ocean tred," said Para Handy, " and no man livin' that did more to win the war than my old friend Jeck. Yon old fellow Tirpitz had a great respect for Jeck ; he gave orders to aal the German submarines to beware of Jeck in parteecular. But, mind ye—Jeck Maclachlan iss aalways the perfect chentleman ! He would sink your boat on ye the way ye would think it wass a favour."

" What sort o' lookin' chap is he ? " asked a Glasgow man.

" A great big copious kind o' fellow wi' fur in his ears and the he'rt of a child," said Para Handy with fervour. " He wass on the China clippers in his time ; there's not a quirk of navigation that Jeck iss not acquent wi', nor a British sailor that hass seen more life. Am I no' right, Dougie ? "

" Chust exactly what I would say myself," responded the mate. " Jeck's a clinker ! I never met a more soothin' man—very soothin' ! "

" Puts ye in mind o' Steedman's Powders," interpolated Macphail in a confidential whisper to Macalister, the publican. " Whit is it ye put in that beer ? It has a queer effect."

" Where did ye sail to ? " asked one of the strangers, eager to get on with what gave promise of being a most thrilling narrative.

Para Handy shook his head, and had another glass under pressure. " If I had a bit o' a map and two or three days wi' ye," he said, " I could show ye where we sailed. But it wouldna be fair to Jeck. Ye'll mind this was the Mystery Ship, and though I wass in command of her, Jeck wass for the Admirality. Would I dare put it any clearer, Dougie ? "

" Ye'll have to be caautious, Captain," said the mate anxiously. " Keep mind o' the regulations ! "

" Don't get into trouble, whitever you do ! " advised the engineer with a sardonic air.

Para Handy paid no heed to the engineer. He had sized up the Glasgow visitors as a most agreeable and vivacious party of fine young gentlemen whose acquaintance was well worth cultivating in the absence of more exhilarating elements in John Macalister's bar.

"Where are ye bidin'?" he asked them abruptly, and was informed that the bell-tent round the point, on the shore, was to be their residence for another week.

"Capital!" said Para Handy. "A tent's the very place for speakin' your mind; ye never ken who's aboot ye in a bar. Dougie and me'll go roond to the tent at supper-time and tell ye things aboot the Mystery Ship that'll make your blood run cold."

"Right-o!" said the Glasgow gentlemen with one accord.

"Mind ye!" warned the Captain, "strictly between oorsel's! If the Admirality thocht that we wass blabbin' the way we won the war, there would be trouble. We're no' a bit feared for oorsel's—Dougie and me—but we must consuder Jeck. It wass me that wass in command o' Q Boat 21, but it wass Jeck that had the agility. Just to let ye ken—we would be sailin' oot each trip wi' oor life in oor hands, and comin' back wi'——"

"Caautious, Captain! Caautious!" implored Dougie, with his eye on the clock.

"Half-past two; bar's closed, gentlemen!" announced Macalister, and his guests streamed out.

"Be round at the tent at six," said one of the Glasgow fellows.

"Ye can depend on it!" the Captain assured him. "And just to show ye the kind o' man he wass, I'll bring Hurricane Jeck's photygraf."

III

UNDER SEALED ORDERS

"THE first time the *Vital Spark* and us took up the line o' mystery shippin'," said Para Handy, settling down to his yarn, "she wasna camyflaged at aal, but in her naitural colour. I wass thinkin' to spruce her up a bit for the occasion wi' a yellow bead aboot her, and the least wee touch o' red aboot her funnel, but Hurricane Jeck, wi' the Admirality's orders, made us sail the way we were.

" ' This boat, my sunny boys,' says he, ' iss to look like any ordinar' packet that would be carryin' coals, or wud, or gravel,' and he wouldna let Dougie even wash his face for fear the enemy would have suspeecions she wass some vessel oot o' the usual. Indeed, I wass black affronted the way she took to sea—aal rust and tar, the deck reel-rall wi' buckets and boxes, a washin' o' clothes on the riggin', and everywhere Irish pennants. Am I right or am I wrong, Dougie ? "

" Ye have it exact, Captain," promptly agreed the mate ; " I have seen a bonnier boat on a valentine."

" ' The thing is to look naitural," says Jeck, and his notion aboot lookin' naitural wass to have us like a boat in a panto-mime, and a crew like a wheen o' showmen. He wouldna even let me put on my jecket ! And, oh, but Macphail wass the angry man ! Jeck's orders wass that we were to keep her at four or five knots, but make her funnel smoke like bleezes. Macphail had to burn up all his novelettes ; if he wass here himsel' he would tell ye."

" Where did ye start frae ? " asked one of the Glasgow men.

" I'll tell ye that withoot wan word o' devagation," said Para Handy. " We started from Bowling, under sealed orders that Jeck had at his finger-ends, and a lot o' impudent brats o' boys on the quay cryin', ' Three cheers for the *Aquitania* ! ' "

" Oor lives in oor hands ! " remarked Dougie solemnly. " We didna know but every minute would be oor next."

" There wass a lot o' talk at the time aboot submarines roond Arran, and we made oor course first for Loch Ranza," continued the Captain. " We never came on nothing—not a thing ! Jeck and me and Dougie put oot the punt at Loch Ranza, and went ashore to see the polisman. We took Jenkins wi' us—he wass the English chentleman in cherge of

the guns, and he would aye be scoorin' them wi' soft soap—
fair made pets o' them ! The polisman assured us Kilbrannan
Sound wass hotchin' wi' submarines the week before, and he
wass of opeenion they were shifted up Loch Fyne, for a whale
wass seen at Tarbert on the Friday.

"We carried on to Tarbert, and by good luck it wass
Tarbert Fair. Jeck threw open the boat for visitors, considerin' the occasion. They came on board in droves to
see a mystery ship, and Jeck put roond a hat in the aid of
Brutain's hardy sons. He gaithered seventeen shillin's, and
we stayed three days."

"Seventeen and ninepence ha'penny," said Dougie, apparently determined on absolute accuracy.

"I stand corrected, Dugald ; it wass seventeen and ninepence ha'penny," admitted the Captain, on reflection.

"It wass a chentleman's life under Jeck : ye never saw
a better hand for navigaation ! Duvvle the place did we
go into but there was sport—a displenishin' sale at Skipness
that lasted a couple o' days ; a marriage at Carradale wi'
fifteen hens on the table, and everybody hearty——"

"Kind, kind people in Carradale !" enthusiastically
testified the mate. "That homely ! Ye had just to stretch
your hand, and somebody would put something in it. It
wass wi' us bein' in the Navy."

"But did ye no' see ony submarines ?" impatiently inquired one of the Glasgow men.

The narrator refused to be hurried. "Jeck jaloosed,"
he proceeded, "that the Blackwaterfoot wass the kind of
a place where the Chermans might be lurkin' ; we went
ashore and scoured aal roond the inn, ootside and in, and up
as far as Shisken, lookin' at night for signals. We followed
a light for an oor, and tracked it to Shisken Inn ; it wass
only a man wi' a lantern.

"'My goodness ! aren't they cunnin' ?' said Jeck at
the end of the week, when there wassna ony sign o' the
Chermans. 'We'll have to go roond the Mull and see if

they're no' in Islay.' Ye'll mind o' him lookin' the book, Dougie ? "

" Fine ! " said the mate, without a moment's hesitation, but with a questioning look in his eye for Para Handy.

" It wass an almanac, and Jeck wass studyin' it like a book o' Gaelic songs.

" ' What are ye studyin', Jeck ? ' I asked him. ' Iss it the tides ye're lookin' ? '

" ' The tides iss aal right,' says Jeck ; ' I'm lookin' to see what day the wool market's on in Port Ellen.' Man ! ye couldna keep step to Jeck ; he wass chokeful o' naitural agility. We got into Port Ellen chust when the market started, and they couldna trate us better than they did. The English chentleman in charge o' oor guns said he had traivelled the world, and never seen the like o't. For a couple o' days his cannons got little scourin', I'll assure you !

" Jeck looked the map on Monday, and gave a start. ' Holy sailors ! ' says he, ' we forgot to caal on Campbeltown, and I have fifteen cousins there ! '

" We were chust goin' roond by Sanda, and it wass desperate dark, when a boat pops up and hails us. We couldna mak oot wan word they were sayin' !

" ' Now we're into the midst of it ! ' said Jeck, quite cool, puttin' oot the light and takin' off his slippers. ' Heave oot the punt and start the panic party ! ' "

" Whit was the panic party ? " asked one of the Glasgow men.

" Chust me and Dougie and Macphail. I assure you we were well put through oor drills at Bowling ! Whenever a U-boat hailed ye, ye understand, we were to get in the punt in a desperate confusion, and leave the English chentleman and Jeck on the vessel, below the crate where the guns wass.

" Macphail wass first in the punt, wi' his clock and a canister he kept his clothes in ; Dougie fell into the water, and wass nearly drooned, and I wass chust goin' to jump in when I minded and went back to get my papers——"

" ' John Bull ' and the ' Oban Times,' " explained the mate with unnecessary and misunderstanding minuteness.

" When we put off in the punt, the gallant Jeck, wi' his gunner below the crate, was usin' terrible language, bawlin' oot to the Chermans to egg them to come on. A stiff bit breeze wass blowin' from the south'ard. We waited to hear the battle and pick up Jeck and the English chentleman when it wass feenished——"

" Ye mind we were driftin', Captain," remarked the mate.

" As dark ass the inside o' a coo," pursued Para Handy, " and, as Dougie tells ye, we were driftin'. Believe it or no', but in oor hurry wi' the panic, we clean forgot the oars ! "

" Oor lives in oor hands ! " said Dougie lugubriously. " And me at the balin' dish. The chentlemen's gettin' tired listenin', Peter."

" Aal night we drifted in the punt, and it wass desperate dark, but a trawler towed us in to Campbeltown in the mornin'. There wass a demonstration when we landed, us bein' in the Navy, but it wass kind o' spoiled at first for me and Dougie, wonderin' aboot the vessel. And there she wass, lyin' at the quay ! "

" Criftens ! " said a Glasgow man, with an air of frank disappointment ; " I thocht she would be sunk by that time ! "

" Not under Hurricane Jeck ! " said Para Handy. " Ye'll mind o' Jeck's agility. He had sunk the other fellow, him and Jenkins, and that's the way he got the Victoria Cross. And it wassna fifteen cousins he had in Campbeltown, when the story went aboot ; the half o' aal the folk in Kintrye wass cousins to him."

" I have a bit here o' the Cherman boat," said Dougie, taking a fragment of a herring-box from below his guernsey. " Jeck picked it up for a sample. Any of you chentlemen that would like a souveneer——"

IV

A SEARCH FOR SALVAGE

" HURRICANE JECK got a great, great name wi' the Admirality for his cherenal agility, efter we sunk the Cherman submarine off Sanda," said Para Handy, " and they would be sendin' him letters every other day, but not an article in the way o' money, and Jeck got vexed. Ye never, never in your life saw a man in such a bad trum ; I declare the sparks would fly from him if ye rubbed his whiskers. He wass chust wicked ! Am I right or am I wrong, Dougie ? "

" Ye have it chust exact, Captain," chimed in the mate promptly. " His language wass deplorable for a Christian vessel."

" And, indeed, I wassna in tremendous good trum mysel' efter a fortnight or two o' danderin' roond the islands in the search o' Mr Tirpitz, wi' my boat pented in aal the colours o' a sixpenny kahouchy ball——"

" Chust makin' a bauchle o' the boat ! " said Dougie, with feeling.

" I had no money neither, and if it wass not that Jeck had a fine brass-braided deep-sea kep in the bottom o' his kist, we would be stervin'. Every noo and then he would go ashore wi' a Western Ocean chart rolled up under his oxter and the kep weel cocked, and come back wi' a dozen o' eggs, a pound or two o' poothered butter, and a hen. They're silly folk aboot them islands—chust ass Hielan' ass Mull ! —and when Jeck would cock his deep-sea kep at them, and wave the chart, and say he wass offeecial forger for the Navy, they would give him the very blankets !

" We went one day for water to a creek o' a place that was called Baghmohr, and spent the efternoon in pausin' and consuderin'. There iss a trig wee cotter hoose at Baghmohr, and a lot o' ducks aboot it ; Jeck went in to caal wi' his kep on, efter studying the ducks to see which wass the fattest, and all that wass at home wass a woman and a cat.

" Jeck is aye the chentleman ; he took off his kep and asked the woman in Gaelic where wass her husband.

" ' I don't ken where in the world he iss," said the wife, ' but he left this mornin' wi' an empty keg on his shouther, and him singin'.'

" ' Chust that ! ' said Jeck. ' It's a bonny place ye have here ; iss there chust the two o' ye ? '

" ' Bonny enough,' said the wife. ' There's only me and my man and the cat and the ducks, but it iss a terrible place for scandal ! '

" When Jeck came back withoot a duck I was dumfoondered. ' Surely ye hadna the right cock on your bonnet ? ' I says to him. ' I'm sure ye never saw finer ducks.'

" It wass then he told me aboot the keg. ' When a man goes away in them parts wi' an empty keg on his shouther, and him singin',' says Jeck, ' it's no' for holy water. We'll chust wait, Peter, till he comes back ! ' Oh, man ! Ye couldna be up to Jeck ! He iss chust a perfect duvvle for contrivance ! Am I right or am I wrong, Dougie ? "

" Oh, he's smert enough wi' his heid," frankly admitted the mate.

" We watched for the man comin' back wi' the keg till it was nearly dark," continued Para Handy, " and when he came, he hadna a keg at aal wi' him, but wass singin' that lood it put the fear o' daith on the very ducks.

" ' Whatever he went away for, it wassna in the keg he put it,' says Hurricane Jeck, ' but I'll bate ye anything he'll go back in the mornin', and Jenkins and me'll follow him up for fear that anything happens.'

" It wass hardly daylight when the man of Baghmohr wass out wi' a bowl at the well, and cold spring water didna please him, for before breakfast time he wass leapin' like a hare across the island.

" ' Put by your polishin' paste and put on your Sunday garments," said Jeck to Jenkins, ' and the two o' us 'll find oot where that fellow goes for the hair o' the dog that bit him.'

" Jenkins stopped scourin' his cannon, and they started off in chase o' the Baghmohr man, for Jenkins had the greatest respect for Jeck and his agility.

" Ye'll maybe no' believe me, but they tramped six miles till they came to a clachan where everybody wass singin' like a Sunday school choir, and it a Tuesday mornin' ! Every man in the place that had his wits aboot him wass doon on the shore aboot a cave wi' a great big puncheon o' rum in it. It had drifted ashore on the Sunday, but nobody put a hand on it till the Monday mornin'.

" They were singin' like hey-my-nanny when Jeck and Jenkins came in the midst o' them—Jeck wi' a terrible cock on his kep, and the North Sea chart as weel as the Western Ocean wan in his oxter, Jenkins wi' bell-mouthed troosers and a white string wi' a whustle on't.

" ' Birl your whustle ! ' commanded Jeck, and him throng buttonin' up his jecket.

" Jenkins birled his whustle the same's it wass for a British battle ; Jeck cocked his kep on three hairs, turned up wan side o' his moustache, and steps in front o' the biggest man in the company. What wass it he said, Dougald ? "

" Whatever ye say yoursel', Captain," replied the mate with deference.

" I canna mind the words exactly, but Jeck assured them it wass the jyle for them. ' You are fair pollutin' the island wi' the King's rum,' said Jeck, and him sniffin'. ' Ye ken ass weel ass I do that every article that drifts ashore belongs to the Admirality. Gie me a tinny, and I'll see what will require for to be done.'

" They passed him a tinny—Jeck filled it at the spigot-hole that they had made in the puncheon, took a good sup, and said, ' Chust what I wass jalousin'—Jamaica rum. Iss that not desperate, Jenkins? Chust you taste it, to make sure.'

" Jenkins tasted near a pint, shut his eyes wan efter the other, and said it wass rum, withoot a question.

" ' What ye'll do iss this,' says Jeck to the crofters, ' ye'll drive that spigot in again, put the puncheon on a cairt, and hurl it over to Baghmohr, where ye'll find oor gunboat lyin', and if ye're slippy aboot it I'll maybe let the thing blow by.'

" Jeck and Jenkins wass back at the boat by dinner-time, lookin' fine, and full o' capers, but the cairt wi' the puncheon in it didn't come till late in the efternoon. They said they had to travel seven miles to get a horse and cairt.

" We slung the goods aboard wi' the winch, and the men wass wantin' something for the salvage.

" ' I daurna do it,' said Jeck, ' it's against the regulations; forbye, ye didna bring your tinnies,' and in a few meenutes we had up the anchor, and were off to sea again.

" It would be near ten o'clock at night when Macphail the engineer took ill of a sudden, and nothin' would do him but a drop o' spurits. Jeck took a gimlet and bored a couple o' holes in the puncheon. He filled a cup for Macphail, and the silly fool had it swallowed before he found it wass nothing but a sample o' the Sound o' Sleat. Weren't they the black-guards! They had emptied the cask in their kegs and filled it up again wi' plain sea water! Oh, my! but Jeck wass angry!"

V

THE WONDERFUL CHEESE

" We were, wan time yonder, perusin' up and doon the Long Isle looking for mines," said Para Handy. " We looked high, and we looked low, on sea and land; many a droll thing we found drifting, but never came on nothing more infernal than oorsel's. Hurricane Jeck had a terrible skill for mines. At night he would take the punt, wi' a bit o' a net in her, and splash the mooths o' the burns for oors on end in search o' them. Not wan iota! The only thing he would get in the net would be a grilse or two, or a string o' troot ; Uist is fair infested wi' them.

" But wan night yonder he came back wi' a whupper o' a cheese ; he got it on the high-water mark.

" ' Capital ! ' I says to him ; ' that's something wise-like ! ' for I wass chust fair sick o' salmon—salmon—salmon, even-on.

" Jeck rolled the cheese on board ; sixty pounds wass in it if there wass an ounce ! I never saw a cheese that better pleased the eye. Wi' a cheese like yon and a poke o' meal, ye could trevel the world.

" But Jeck wass dubious. ' She looks aal right,' he says, ' but ye canna be up to them Cherman blackguards. We'll be better to trate that cheese wi' caaution. I didna put a hand on her mysel' till I walked three times roond her lookin' for horns, and when I lifted her it wass wi' my he'rt in my mooth and a word o' prayer.'

" ' Hoots, man, but ye're tumid, tumid ! ' I says to him. ' What harm's in a Cheddar-cheese ? Take her aft and put your knife in her.'

" He took oot his knife at that, and made to hand me't. ' Open her up yoursel', Peter,' says he, ' but first let me and the rest o' the crew get off a bit in the punt. I would be black affronted to be blown up wi' a Cherman cheese wi' a bomb inside o't.'

" I looked at the cheese, and, my goodness, it wass a whupper ! Ye could feed an airmy on't ! And I never wass as hungry in my life ! There iss something aboot a cheese on board a ship that grows on ye ! But I didna like the look o' Jeck, at aal, at aal, for he aye took care that the cheese wass on wan side o' the funnel, and he had a startled eye.

" ' I don't care a docken for cheese,' I says to him at last, ' but Dougie's fond o't. Gie the knife to Dougie.' By this time Dougie wass in the hold wi' a tarp'lain over his heid, but he heard me fine.

" Take it away and sink it,' he bawls ; ' cheese never agreed wi' me ; I promised my wife I would never taste it.'

" Jeck looked roond for Macphail, but he was off like a moose among his engines, and meh'in' like a sheep.

" The only man on the ship that wass quite cool and composed wass Jenkins, and he wass under the crate where his gun wass, and him sound sleepin'.

" ' Mind ye, I'm no' sayin' there is anything wrong wi' the cheese,' says Jeck. ' She may be a topper o' a cheese for aal I ken, but chust you put your ear doon close to her, Peter, and tell me if you don't hear something tickin'.'

" I made wan jump for the punt, and rowed away like fury !

" ' Heave that cursed cheese o' Satan over the side this instant, or there'll be the duvvle's own devastaation ! ' I roared to Hurricane Jeck. ' Ye were surely oot o' yer mind to meddle w'it.'

" I came back in twenty meenutes, and found Jeck and the gunner Jenkins had the cheese below a barrel.

" ' It's all right,' said Jeck ; ' it wass my mistake aboot the tickin' ; Jenkins couldna hear it. But aal the same, we'll better keep her at a distance till we come to some place where there's folk that is keener on cheese than we are.'

" For near a month—ay, more than a month—we pursued oor devagations roond the islands seekin' mines, and aye the cheese was in below the barrel. Nobody would touch it. Dougie had his Book oot every night, and indeed I wasna in the best o' trum myself, wi' my ear aye cocked for clockwork, and the boots never on my feet.

" Every other day Jeck would tilt the barrel up, and we could see that cursed cheese ass like a cheese ass anything

but lookin' duvelish glum. I couldna have worse night-
mares if I ate it. We gave it, between us, the name o'
Jerry.

"It wass the time o' the plewin' matches. The night
before a plewin' match we came into Portree, and a wheen
o' chentlemen were gatherin' prizes. Ye ken yoursel' the
kind o' prizes they have at a plewin' match—a smoked ham
for the best start-and-finish ; a trooser-length o' tweed
cloth from J. & A. Mackay, the merchants, for the best
oots-and-ins ; a gigot o' black-faced mutton for the best-
groomed horse ; a silver chain and pendulum for the largest
faimily plewman ; and a pair o' gallowses for the best-
dressed senior plewman at his own expense.

"The chentleman at the store had a fine collection o'
prizes when Jeck and me went in to look at them, and Jeck's
eye lighted up when he saw the gallowses. For months his
breeks wass hingin' on him wi' a lump o' string.

"'What ye're needin' to complete them prizes,' says he,
'iss a fine big sonsy Cheddar-cheese. I'll make a bargain
wi' ye. If ye'll let me into the plewin' competition, I'll gie
ye a prize o' the bonniest biggest keppuck between Barra
Heid and the Butt o' Lewis.'

"The man in charge o' the prizes looked hard at Jeck,
who had a gless in him, but not wan drop more than he could
cairry like a chentleman, and he says quite sharp, 'What's
wrong wi' the cheese ? '

"'There's nothing wrong wi' the cheese,' says Jeck ;
'she's a chenuine Thomas Lipton, but my mates and me iss
desperate keen on the agricultooral tred, and we'll gie the
cheese to promote the cheneral hilarity.'

"'Are ye sure ye can plew ? ' asks the other one, dubious.

"'I've been plewin' all my days,' says Jeck, quite smert ;
'chust look at the boots o' me ! '

"They agreed that Jeck would get into the competition,
and sent doon to the vessel to fetch the cheese, and all the
time they were away for't I wass in the nerves, for fear they

might jolt it. ' God help the harbour o' Portree this night,' says I to Jeck, ' if they start to sample Jerry ! '

"The plewin' match wass a great success. Jeck dressed himsel' in his Sunday clothes, and his Navy kep, and his hair was oiled magnificent. Ye never saw a more becomin' man between the stilts. He had got the lend o' a horse and plew from a cousin o' his on the ootskirts o' Portree.

"His plewin' wass lamentable, but he got the gallowses for bein' the best-dressed senior plewman at his own expense.

"A young man by the name o' Patrick Sinclair won the cheese, and Jeck and me helped him to hurl it in a barrow to his hoose. The whole time we were helpin' him home wi't my hert wass in my mooth for fear it would go off, and we laid it on the kitchen bed the same's it wass a baby !

"We got two good drams apiece from Sinclair's wife, and were no sooner oot o' the hoose than Jeck began to run for the ship ass fast as he could shift his legs, me efter him.

" ' It's time we were oot o' Portree,' says he, when we got on board ; ' there's likely to be trouble.'

" ' Do ye think that cheese 'll burst before we're started ? ' I asked him, busy lowsing the ropes.

" ' It's no the cheese I'm frightened for,' says Jeck, ' but it's Patrick Sinclair. I'm no' a bit vexed for him : a fine strong young man like that should be in the Navy when the land's at war, and no' idlin' his time away at plewin'. But when he opens up that cheese there'll be a desperate explosion.'

" ' What do ye think 'll be in it, Jeck ?   Will it be dunnymite ? '

" ' Duvvle the dunnymite ! ' says Jeck ; ' chust chucky stones ! Jenkins an' me scooped oot the inside o' the cheese between us in the last four weeks. We sliced the top off first, and used it for a lid. Three days ago, when you and the rest wass sleepin', we filled her up to the proper weight wi' stones and tacked the top on.' "

VI

THE PHANTOM HORSE AND CART

THE *Vital Spark*, with the labours of the day completed, dozed in her berth inside the harbour, enveloped in an atmosphere of peace and frying mackerel. From the stove-pipe rose the pale blue smoke of pine-wood : she had been loading timber. A couple of shirts were drying on a string ; the Captain felt them. " Duvvle a drop o' drouth iss in it, Dougie," he remarked to the mate impatiently ; " they'll no' be dry till Monday ! "

" My goodness ! " said the mate. " I wish I wass a shirt ! I'm that dry you could use me for a blot-sheet ! And there iss Jum again wi' his mackerel for the tea ; the fellow has no contrivance at the cookin'—mackerel even-on since we came roond Ardlamont ! Ye would think he was stockin' an aquarium. Fried mackerel iss the thirstiest fish that ever swam the sea ! "

" All right, chaps ! " Sunny Jim cried from the stove ; " to-morrow ye'll get boiled yins ! "

Dougie cast a pathetic look at the engineer.

" Issn't that the ruffian ? " said he. " Many a man that caals himself a cook would put his mind into the business noo and then and think o' something else than mackerel. It iss my opinion Jum goes doon to the slips wi' a pail at night and picks them up where the fishermen threw them over the quay in the mornin'. Man, I never, never, never wass so thirsty ! "

Macphail, the engineer, who was rather bored with mackerel himself, was in a nasty humour. " It's my opeenion," he remarked, " that that's no' a mackerel thirst at a', but the thirst ye started wi' last Saturday when ye got yer pay. There's naething 'll cure it for ye, Dougie ; it would tak' far mair money than ye earn, and it's worse noo that tratin's no permitted on the Clyde."

K

The mate was so indignant at the suggestion that trouble seemed impending, when Para Handy hurried to the restoration of a more peaceful humour with a defence of Dougie which, to subtler instincts, would have rather appeared an added insult.

"Never you mind him, Dougie!" said he; "Macphail iss aalways jibing. And he's aal wrong aalthegither; the worst man in the world can be turned from drink if his friends go aboot the thing wi' kindness. It's aal in the kindly word. That puts me in mind o' wan time yonder my old frien' Hurricane Jeck, made a Rechabite for life o' a man in Campeltown that up till then wass keepin' the distilleries goin' till his wife, poor body, wass near demented. It wass aal in the kindly word, and Jeck's agility.

"It wass long afore Jeck sailed on the clippers and made his reputation. Me and him and a bit o' a boy wass on the *Margaret Ann*, a gaabert that made money for a man in Tarbert. At that time, even, Jeck wass a perfect chentleman; his manners wass complete. To see him stavin' up the quay ye would think he wass off a steamboat, and 'twas him, I'll assure you, had the gallant eye! 'Peter,' he would say to me, and his bonnet cocked, 'I'm goin' for a perusal up the village, chust to show them the kind o' men we breed in Kinlochaline.' My chove! he had the step!

"There wass wan time yonder, we were puttin' oot coal in Campbeltown, and a cairter wi' the bye-name o' the Twister wass a perfect he'rtbreak to us wi' drink. He couped ower the side o' the cairt the best part o' the coals we slung to him, and came back from every rake wi' another gill in him. The cargo was nearly oot, and him no' over the side o' the quay yet wi' his horse and cairt, when his wife came doon an' yoked on us for leadin' her man astray.

"'Mrs MacCallum,' Jeck said to her, calm and gentle, 'there iss not a man on board this boat the day hass drunk ass much ass would wet the inside o' a flute; when wass the good-man sober last?'"

" ' The year they took the lifeboat over the Machrihanish ; he was at the cairtin' o't,' says she, and her near greetin'.

" ' It iss high time he wass comin' to a conclusion wi't ! ' said Hurricane Jeck. ' Away you home, and I'll send your husband back to ye a dufferent character. For the next three months have in a good supply of buttermilk ! '

" The woman went away. Her man came back to the boat ten meenutes efter, worse than ever. ' No more the night,' said Hurricane Jeck ; ' we'll put the rest oot in the mornin',' and the Twister made a course at wance wi' his horse and cairt for the nearest public-hoose.

" Jeck and me and the boy went efter him, and found the horse tied to a ring at the mooth o' a close. The Twister wass in the next door in the public-hoose, and so wass the rest o' Campbeltown, perhaps, for the street was like a Sunday mornin'.

" ' There's goin' to be a cairt amissin' here,' said Jeck, quite blithe wi' us, and made a proposeetion. We took the horse oot o' the trams and led it through the close to a washin'-green that wass at the back. We then took off the wheels o' the cairt and rolled them in beside the horse. Between us we lifted the body o' the cairt on its side and through the close wi't, too, like hey-ma-nanny, and back on the green we put on the wheels again and yoked the horse.

" ' There you are ! ' said Jeck. ' The first time ever a cairt wass here since they built the tenement ! Stop ye till ye hear what the Twister says when he finds it ! '

" Oh, man ! man ! I tell you it wass Jeck had the agility ! He wass chust sublime !

" It took nearly half an oor for the Twister to find where his cairt wass, and we gave him twenty meenits to himsel' before we went up to the close to see what he wass doin'.

" He had a bit o' string. First he would measure the width o' the close and then the cairt, and he was greetin' sore, sore !

" ' What iss't ? ' says Hurricane Jeck, quite kindly.

" ' Issn't this the fearful calamity that's happened ? ' said the cairter.   ' I canna get my cairt oot.'

" ' What cairt ? ' said Hurricane Jeck, quite cool—-oh, man, he was a genius !

" ' What cairt but this wan,' said the Twister.   ' The horse in some way that I canna fathom broucht it in, and noo I canna get it oot ! '

" ' Willyum,' said Jeck, and clapped his shouther, ' that's no' a horse and cairt at all ; it's just imaginaation !   Hoo on earth could a cairt get in here ?   Chust you go home like a decent lad, and stop the drinkin' or ye'll see far worse than cairts ! '

" We got him home.   ' Mind what I said aboot the butter-milk ! ' said Jeck to the Twister's wife ; ' he's fairly in the horrors ! '   And then we went back, took doon the cairt again and through the close, and to the yaird where it belonged, and stabled the horse as nate as ninepence.

" From that day on the Twister never tasted drink.   I can tell you he got the start !   It wass ten years efter that before he found oot it wass railly his cairt wass up the close, and no' a hallucinaation.   And by that time it wass hardly worth while to start drinkin' again."

VII

HURRICANE JACK'S LUCK-BIRD

PARA HANDY, with his arms plunged elbow-deep inside the waist-band of his trousers, and his back against a stanchion, conveniently for scratching, touched the animal misgivingly with the toe of his boot, and expressed an opinion that any kind of pet was unnecessary on the *Vital Spark* so long as they had Macphail.   " Forby," said he, " you would have to pay a licence for the beast, and the thing's no' worth it."

" Your aunty ! " retorted Sunny Jim, lifting the hedgehog

in his cap; "it's no' a dug. Ye divna need a licence for a hedgehog ony mair nor for a mangle. There's no' a better thing for killin' clocks; a' the foreign-goin' boats hae hedgehogs. Forbye, they're lucky."

But the Captain still looked with disapproval on the animal which Sunny Jim had picked up in a ditch along the shore that morning and brought aboard in a handkerchief.

"There wass never a beast on board this boat," said he, "but brought bad luck. I once had desperate trouble with a cockatoo; Dougie himsel' 'll tell you; and you mind yoursel' yon dog caaled Biler that you brought, that kept me ashore till the break o' day because it didna know me in my Sunday clothes? You never can tell the meenute you would get an aawful start from a hedgehog; you don't know when you might be sittin' doon on't suddenly. It might be worse than Col Macdougall's tortoise."

"What happened wi' it?" asked Sunny Jim.

"It wass the time o' the big Tarbert fishin's," said Para Handy, "and Hurricane Jeck wass home from sea and workin' a net wi' cousins that had a skiff caaled the *Welcome Back*. There never wass another boat that season had the luck o' the *Welcome Back*—she wass coinin' fortunes. She had only to dander over in the cool o' the evening to the Skate or Ealan Buie, and pick up an eye o' fish that would load her to the gunnle, and the others would be slashin' at it on the other side o' Otter and not a bloomin' tail.

"The other Tarbert boats wass desperate. They were sure there wass something in't, and one Sunday night they asked at Hurricane Jeck for an explanation. Jeck was a man that never took a mean advantage; he wass ass open ass the day.

" 'I'll not deceive you, sunny boys,' says he. 'If the *Welcome Back* iss gettin' fishin's, it's because she carries a luck-bird,' and he took a tortoise oot o' his top-coat pocket.

" 'She's no a bird at aal!' said one o' the MacCallums.

" 'Perhaps you'll tell me what she iss, then,' said Hurricane

Jeck, quite patient, and withoot a word o' divagaation. 'You
can see for yoursel' she's no' an animal.'

" ' I would say she was an insect,' says MacCallum, and
Jeck put the tortoise back in his top-coat pocket.

" ' If it waasna the Sabbath evenin',' says he, ' and me
wi' my reputation to consider, I would give you a lesson in
naitural history that would keep you studyin' in your bed
for a day or two.'

" There wass no doubt efter that in Tarbert that the
Welcome Back got her luck from Jeck's tortoise, and many
a crew in Tarbert tried to buy her. But Jeck was terribly
attached to her, and money wouldna tempt him. The beast
had wonderful agility—not nimble, if you understand, but
terrible sagacity. When Jeck would whustle to her she
would come and put her heid oot to be scratched, and she
knew his very step when he wass comin' doon the quay. My
own he'rt never warmed to them tortoises ; for aal the sport
that's in them you would be better wi' a partan, but Jeck aye
said she grew on you. There's beasts in nature I never could
see the use o'—lollipin' about wi' neither meat nor music in
them, chust like polismen ; and of aal the pets a man could
make a hobby of, I think a tortoise iss the most rideeculus.
You might ass weel be friendly wi' a floo'er-pot.

" Jeck caaled her Sarah efter an aunt he had in Stirling.
He wass never very sure aboot her sect, but he said he had a
feelin' in his mind that the name o' Sarah suited. When he
would be chirpin' to her and caalin' her Sarah, it made my
blood run cold ; he couldna be more respectful if she had a
sowl, and still-and-on he only bought her off a barrow in
Stockwell. I think mysel' it wass the great big he'rt o' him ;
Jeck must aye have something to be kindly to. Isn't that
so, Dougie ? "

" The very man," said Dougie. " If he wassna puttin' the
fear o' daith on his fellow-bein's, he wass lookin' aboot for
people to give money to."

" He wass ass chentle ass a child. He would be clappin'

Sarah on the back, and her wi' no more sense o' kindness than a blecknin' bottle. He could feed her from the hand. They said she would trot roond the deck behind him, cheepin' like an English curate, and when he went ashore he aalways had her in his pocket, feared the Tarbert men would steal her.

" Many a time I heard him comin' doon the quay at night, and him throng taalkin' away to Sarah in his pocket. If she had lived I don't believe he ever would have mairried. ' The best o' a tortoise,' he would say, ' iss that she never gives you any back chat.'

" There wass never a man more downed than Jeck when Sarah went and died on him. It wass the start o' the winter-time, and he said she took a chill. The *Welcome Back* wass at the long-line fishin', and from the day that Sarah slipped away the luck wass clean against them.

" Col Macdougall, a fisherman in Kilfinnan, wass a gentle-man that offered a bonny penny for the luck-bird when she wass in life, and her eye was hardly closed in daith when Jeck wass over at Macdougall's boat wi' her remains in a pocket-naipken.

" ' If ye're on,' says he, ' for Sarah noo, you can have her at a bargain,' says Jeck, and he clapped her doon on a thwart.

" ' She doesna seem to have much vivacity. What's wrong wi' her ? ' said Col, and he wass a man that played the bagpipes.

" ' Not one article iss the matter wi' the poor wee cratur, except that she's kind o' deid,' said Hurricane Jeck. He wass, in all respects, the perfect chentleman, and would never take advantage.

" ' Dear me,' said Col, ' isn't that a peety ! She wass worth her weight in gold when she wass livin'.'

" ' And she's worth her weight in silver noo she's deid,' said Jeck. He proved to Col that the luck-bird wass ass good ass ever, and went away wi' seven-and-sixpence in his pocket, leavin' Sarah's mortal elements behind him.

" ' I wouldna part wi' her,' said he, ' unless to a comfortable home.' There wass nothing wrong wi' Jeck ; he had the finest feelin's.

" Col put the late lamented in behind the stove o' his skiff, and started out for splendid fishin's. They werna in't. There didna seem to be a single cod or whitin' left in aal Loch Fyne. He would go doon to the den o' his skiff and turn poor Sarah over on her back, and give her the worst abuse because she didna come to his assistance, but Sarah was no more concerned than a smoothin'-iron.

" He used her for breakin' coal, and he used her for a toaster, and the winter slipped away. It wass a period namely still in Tarbert ass the Big New Year, money bein' rife, and Col wass oot wi' his bagpipes every evening till the month o' March. He wass over wi' his boat one night at Tarbert at a horo-yally, and came back on board, himsel', wi' his bagpipes aal reel-rall below his oxter, greatly put aboot because o' the barren fishin's.

" Doon to the den o' the boat he went, and struck a match, and turned up Sarah, who wass lyin' on her back.

" ' You're there,' said he, ' and the name to you of bein' lucky, but duvvle the tail iss Col Macdougall in your reverence. Paid good money for you, and there you are like a lump of stick, and the white fish laughin' at you ! '

" The next meenute and Sarah put oot her heid and started walkin' !

" He wass the valiant laad, wass Col, like aal the folk he came off, but at that he started squealin', for to see a deid tortoise wi' such agility, and took his feet from the skiff the same ass if the duvvle wass efter him. He fell and staved his arm on the quay, but still had the sense to throw his bagpipes into the middle o' Loch Tarbert.

" The parish munister, Macrae, wass gettin' ready for his bed wi' a drop o' toddy, when a ring came to the door, and a meenute efter Col Macdougall grabbed him by the elbow in the lobby.

" ' Oh, Mr Macrae,' said he, ' isn't this the visitaation ? Yonder's Sarah skippin' aboot the boat, and her a corpse since Martinmas. I'll assure you this'll be the bonny lessson for me ! '

" ' Whatna Sarah ? ' said the munister.

" ' Hurricane Jeck's tortoise,' said Col Macdougall, trumblin' aal over. ' Her ghost iss crawlin' through my boat, so I want to lead a better life, and I've drooned my bagpipes.'

" ' A tortoise,' said the munister, lookin' droll at Col Macdougall, who wass lamentably known to him for a musician. ' Are you sure it wass an actual tortoise ? '

" ' If you heard her bark ! ' said Col. ' She wass bitin' at the heels o' me, and her, as you might say, poor Jeck's relict since last Martinmas. I'll never touch the pipes again. Excuse me caalin', but I came to give a pound for the Foreign Missions.'

" ' What you want,' said the munister, ' iss to take the temperance pledge. You have been keepin' the New Year too long.'

" ' It's no' so bad as that,' said Col. ' I only saw but one o' them.'

" But Macrae took him into his study-room, and told him there wass nothing that would keep away tortoises but the temperance pledge. Col must keep teetotal for a twelve-month, and put his promise doon in black and white.

" ' And what aboot yoursel' ? ' said Col Macdougall, wi' his eye on the gless o' toddy.

" ' I'll sign it too if you want,' said the munister with much acceptance ; and Col agreed. The munister wrote out a line and said, ' I, Col Macdougall, promise to abstain from all intoxicatin' liquors for a twelvemonth,' and Col put his name to it.

" ' That's aal richt,' said the munister. ' Now for me,' and he signed at the bottom, ' George Macrae, M.A., witness.'

" ' That shows you,' said Para Handy, " that it's no'

K*

aalways lucky to have any kind of beast aboot the boat. Col staved his arm, and lost his pipes, and a pound for the Foreign Missions, and his liberty for a twelvemonth."

"He must have been an awful idiot that didna ken a tortoise sleeps a' winter," said Macphail, the engineer.

VIII

A ROWDY VISITOR

THE only man of the crew who dared to go ashore at Bunessan was Hurricane Jack. He had joined the *Vital Spark* again for a season, fed up with "going foreign." It was subsequent to the deplorable incident of the minister's hens, when Para Handy and his men had to fight their way to their vessel through an infuriated populace, and the *Vital Spark*, for the Ross of Mull, got the unpleasant reputation of being nothing better than a buccaneer.

It was nightfall when she came grunting into Loch Lathaich, and lay-to, while Jack went ashore in the punt on an urgent search for milk and butter.

The Captain gave him money to pay for these provisions. "Take a good big can wi' ye, and don't bring less than two or three prints o' butter," he instructed Jack. "Don't let on what boat ye're off, or they'll twist the neck off ye. And for God's sake, never let your eye light on a hen!"

"Anything at aal but hens!" implored Dougie. "They watch their hens like hawks. A body might lift a horse in Bunessan, and no' much said aboot it, but the loss o' a hen makes them fair demented."

"Right-o! sunny boys," said Hurricane Jack, and rowed off into the darkness.

He was gone for hours, and in the absence of the punt nobody could get ashore to look for him.

"I doot Jeck's in trouble," said Para Handy about midnight. "He has too flippant a style wi' him aaltogether !

After yon calamity we had wi' the Bunessan folk last Candlemas they're no' to be trifled wi'. We'll chust need to go roond to Tobermory and look for him in the polis-office. Wassn't I stupid to gie him the half-croon ? "

It was the early hours of the morning, and the crew were sound asleep on the *Vital Spark* when Jack came aboard again with a clatter to wake the dead, and apparently with some companion who required assistance.

" Bless my sowl ! " said the Captain, sitting up on the edge of his bunk. " Who on aal the earth hass he wi' him here ? He's far too flippant, Jeck, for a coastin' sailor ! "

" No consideration ! Not the least ! " said Macphail, the engineer, bitterly. " There's my sleep sp'iled for the night ! "

" Perhaps it's a chentleman he hass wi' him," said Dougie hopefully, listening to some terriffic banging up on deck. " It sounds like a chentleman from the hotel, that would have a gless or two in him. Jeck wouldna bring him unless he had something wi' him in his pocket. Light you the lamp, Peter."

The Captain was fumbling at the lamp when a shout of " Stand from under ! " came from Hurricane Jack on deck, and some frantic object, kicking wildly, landed between the bunks.

" Holy smoke ! " exclaimed Para Handy, and the next moment he was doubled up on the floor from a violent impact in the pit of the stomach.

For ten minutes pandemonium reigned in the sailor's narrow quarters, without its occupants being able to form any idea of the nature of this alarming visitation. The wooden sides of the bunks resounded with blows ; a galvanised pail and a box of potatoes were flung back and forward with the wildest racketing ; sea-boots were flying ; it looked as if the visitor meant to batter the *Vital Spark* to pieces.

Para Handy had gathered himself together and gone under

the blankets again. "I'm done for!" he proclaimed, gasping. "Whoever Jeck's friend iss, he iss no chentleman."

"It's an Englishman," said Dougie, sniffing, his nose the only part of him uncovered as he cowered in his bunk. "Ye can feel the smell o' him, he's in the horrors. Light you the lamp, Peter. Man! don't be tumid!"

There was an interval of silence, broken only by the Captain's groans and the visitor's noisy breathing. Macphail cautiously put out a leg, with the idea of rising to light the lamp himself, slipped on the potatoes with which the floor was strewn, and fell on the top of the Captain, who, putting up his hands to clear himself, seized an unmistakable frantic pair of horns!

"It's no' an Englishman at aal!" he yelled in terror; "it's the duvvle! He has on a wincey shirt, and I have him by the horns!"

Dougie's instant and vociferous praying was interrupted by the descent of Hurricane Jack with a lantern he had lit on deck, which revealed the mysterious and turbulent visitor as a shaggy yellow goat.

"What iss all the commotion?" angrily demanded the Captain, skipping briskly out of his bunk. "Ye're far too flippant, Jeck! Did ye get my butter and my milk?"

"I had the milk, right enough," said Hurricane Jack, "but I put the can down at my feet till I would talk wi' the fellow that had the goats, and this one emptied it before I noticed. It was milk I went for, and milk I was bound to bring, and the only way I could do it was to bring her ladyship here, the goat. Isn't she a topper?"

The goat, as if calmed by the presence of light on the subject, was lying down, peaceably chewing the top of a sea-boot with the utmost gusto.

"But did ye bring the butter?" pursued the Captain.

"There's no' an ounce of butter in Bunessan," said Hurricane Jack. "That's another reason for me bringin' ye the goat. If we're wantin' butter we must make it oorsel's.

A coo's oot o' the question on the *Vital Spark*, for we havena the accommodation, but a goat can pick up it's livin' anywhere, and it's far more hyginkic than a coo."

" I'm warnin' ye it's no' me that'll milk it ; I wou'dna lower mysel' ! " loudly declared Dougie. " I'll leave the vessel first ! "

" Where's my half-croon ? " inquired the Captain, having rescued half a boot from the still unsatiated visitor.

" It's cost me more than half-a-croon to get that valuable goat," said Hurricane Jack. " There's a swab o' an Irishman yonder on the roadside wi' a herd o' thirty goats he's takin' aboot the country, but I couldna go away wi' wan as long as he could coont them. It took me more than half-a-croon, but I left him yonder thinkin' he had a herd o' fifty."

" It's no' me that'll milk that brute ! " again protested Dougie. " I wadna be in the same boat wi't. Look at its eye ! Fierce ! Fair wicked ! Forbye, ye canna make butter wi' a goat's milk."

" Ye can ! " said the Captain ; " it's as easy ass anything. The best o' butter ! " He was looking now with more friendly eyes on the visitor, who was finishing off supper with a sock of the engineer's. The odd thing was that the engineer seemed in no way worried about his sock ; he was in a helpless paroxysm of laughter, lying in his bunk.

A violent altercation rose between the Captain, Jack, and Dougie—first, as to whether goat's milk would make butter, and second, as to which of the crew should be what the Captain called the " dairymaid." It came to wrestling. Pandemonium prevailed again, and the goat, apparently much refreshed by its meal, leapt into the fray with strict impartiality, butting at anything soft or hard that lay in the way of its lowered horns. Though seriously handicapped by the narrowness of the fo'c'sle limits, it had all the honours of the battle, and the three men ignominiously rushed on deck.

Macphail was still convulsed in his bunk, safe out of the conflict, and the goat turned joyfully to a change of diet in the form of raw potatoes.

Para Handy's head appeared in the companion.

" Macphail," he said coaxingly, " we forgot to bring her ladyship up wi' us. Slip you that piece o' marlin' roond her neck, and take her up on deck till we'll consuder who iss to be the master of this vessel."

" Come doon and get the beast yoursel'," retorted the engineer. " The dairy's no' in my depairtment."

" At least ye'll put up oor clothes," implored the Captain ; " Dougie and me'll get oor daith o' cold."

And now the mate's head appeared at the top of the companion. " Don't be stickin', Macphail," he pleaded piteously. " It's a cold east wind, and I want my garments. The Captain and me hass compromised the situation. I'm willing to do the milkin' and Jeck 'll churn."

" Good luck to the churnin' then ! " shouted the engineer. " The whole lot o' ye's a lot o' Hielan' stots. Your goat's a billy ! "

IX

THE FENIAN GOAT

A WHITE elephant would have been no more awkward a gift to the *Vital Spark* than the yellow goat which Hurricane Jack purloined from the Irish goat-herd in Bunessan. It had apparently been nurtured in the principles of Sinn Fein, and was utterly unamenable to restraint, law, order, or the chastening influence of a stiff rope's end. From dawn to dark it was up to mischief, and gave as much trouble as a cargo of rattlesnakes.

On account of its incorrigible bad character and its presumable origin, they called it Michael, and Hurricane Jack professed to have great expectations of the luck that would go with it as a mascot. But this consideration weighed less with the rest of the crew than the possibility of selling it at a pleasing price at some port of call remote from Mull.

"A capital goat!" said Para Handy. "Everything's complete! There's money in him! A fine big strappin' goat like that would be worth a pound."

"Ay, and more nor a pound!" calculated Dougie. "We would get far more than that even if we were selling his remains for venison."

"Naebody in their senses wants a billy-goat," said Macphail, the engineer, unfeelingly. "But perhaps ye could pass him off for a she if ye shaved him."

Michael really might have been shaved on the strength of the ironical suggestion; but already it was manifest that he was a goat to take no liberties with. He had broken away through the night from the stanchion to which they had tethered him, and roamed about the vessel, haughty and truculent, his eye for ever cocked for anything to butt at, and his appetite unappeasable.

The Captain had put his trousers over the stove to dry the night before; in the morning, all that was left of them was the blade of a pocket-knife, and Michael chewed his cud with an air of magnificent detachment.

Dougie was sent ashore on Oronsay for a bag of grass, and came back with withered bog hay, which Michael refused to put a tooth to, and strewed about the deck until it looked like the Moor of Rannoch in a droughty spring.

Two or three turnips that were in the bag seemed more to the passenger's fancy: they quickly disappeared, with the most stimulating effect on the consumer, who caught the Captain bending twice to tap his pipe on his boot, and on each occasion butted him clean across the hatches.

"I'll have his he'rt's blood!" roared Para Handy, dancing with rage. "It iss not a Fenian goat will be the master of my boat, and affront me behind my back! Get me a coal-slice or a shovel, Macphail, and I'll give him a bit o' Boyne Water!"

But Macphail, discretion itself, refused to involve himself in any way in a vulgar brawl, and retired among his engines.

For the rest of the day Michael was content to keep the ship's company interned abaft the funnel. Even Hurricane Jack, with a wonderful reputation for encounters with all sorts of wild forest animals in his voyages with the China clippers and the Black Ball Line, showed the utmost respect for Michael's lowered horns.

They threw lumps of coal at him till Macphail rebelled, finding himself in danger of being left with insufficient fuel to keep up a head of steam : the goat was no more affected than if it had been hailstones.

It was Dougie who had at last discovered that even an Irish goat has some human susceptibilities.

"There's no use o' batterin' away at that duvvle o' a beast," he said, "we should try kindness. I wonder would he take a lozenger ? " Since he had stopped smoking a month before, the mate incessantly devoured pan drops of a highly peppermint nature ; he never sailed from the Clyde without a half-stone of them.

Pan drops appeared to be a passion with Michael ; he devoured them readily from Dougie's hand, and became the most friendly goat in Britain, following the mate about the ship continually with his nose in the pocket where the sweets were.

In the Sound of Islay, Dougie's store of imperial pan drops went done, and Michael became more wicked than ever. He would tolerate no sound or movement of any kind on board his vessel. If timbers creaked—and creaking was a feature of the *Vital Spark*—he laid out with horns and hoofs at the nearest part of the bulwark ; if the man at the helm altered the course, the goat swept down on him at fifty knots.

The Captain positively wept ! "I don't believe that's a human goat at aal ! " he declared. "It's something supercanny. Iss it the will o' Providence that we're to be gybin' and yawin' aboot the Atlantic Ocean aal the rest o' oor days because a brute like that'll no' let us steer for harbour ? "

" We could trap him," suggested Hurricane Jack. " I've seen them trappin' the elephants in India."

" What way would ye trap him ? " inquired the Captain eagerly.

" We would need a pit, but the hold would do if we could get the hatches off—and then—and then we would need some cable, and a lot o' trees," explained Jack weakly.

" And whar the bleezes are ye gaun to get the trees ? " asked the engineer indignantly. " Are ye gaun to grow them ? I'll be clean oot o' coal to-morrow mornin', and ye daurna touch the sails."

" There iss nothing for it but abandon the ship and take to the punt," said Dougie lugubriously. " We're no far from Port Askaig."

" We'll do better than that ! " said the Captain, with an inspiration ; " ye'll row ashore yoursel' and bring back a poke o' sweeties. That'll maybe keep that cratur in trim till we reach Port Ellen."

Dougie succeeded in getting into the punt with difficulty, for Michael objected to having the only source of pan drops desert him. Half an hour later, a further supply of his favourite provender quite restored him to amiability, and they were able, at Port Ellen, to lead him ashore on a string.

" If we'll no' sell him we can wander him," was the Captain's idea. " Many a wan would be gled to have him."

" He would look fine in a great big park," remarked Hurricane Jack. " I've seen goats just like that one on the river Plate. They make wineskins o' them. Exactly the same in Bilbao."

" Watch you his eye. I don't like the look o't," said Macphail, as they went up the quay.

At that very moment Dougie's second supply of sweets was finished, and Michael, with the old Fenian ferocity aroused again, escaped from his halter, and proceeded to give animation to the scenery and populace of Port Ellen.

The first thing he altered was the structure of a shipping-box, whose vivid red colour apparently displeased him. A man who emerged from it was instantly butted back among its debris. The goat put its head through a large framed map of the Royal Route, and, thus embellished, swept up the town with the proud and lofty gait of a stag.

" I'm gaun to clear oot o' this for wan thing ! " cried Macphail, and bolted back to the vessel.

The others would have liked to follow him, but were irresistibly compelled to follow their property as he strewed terror and havoc in his track. Port Ellen shops hastily put up their shutters, unable to rescue barrels and boxes of goods displayed at their doors ; into the only one too late of closing its door the goat went bounding furiously, but calmed down instantly at the odour of peppermint.

Dougie went immediately after him.

" A pound of imperial pan drops ! " he gasped to the shopkeeper, who proceeded to weigh them out, all unsuspicious of the commotion in the street.

There was a woman customer at the counter.

" Do ye care for lozengers ? " Dougie asked her, calmly patting Michael.

" I whiles take them," she admitted.

" Then here's a present for ye," said Dougie, hurriedly thrusting the sweets in her hand. " Give wan or two to the goat ; he's desperate fond o' them."

" Come away oot o' this ! " he commanded his shipmates, as he hurriedly quitted the shop. " I have Michael planted on a wife, and he'll bide wi' her ass lang ass her poke holds oot."

" Whatna cairry on ! It iss chust lamentable ! " panted Para Handy, as they sped for their vessel.

The *Vital Spark* was leaving the quay when an infuriated carter ran up and bawled, " Stop you a meenute till I talk to ye ! "

" What are ye wantin' ? " asked the Captain.

" I'm wantin' a word wi' a bowly-legged man ye have there wi' whiskers on him, that tried to come roond my wife wi' a poke o' lozengers," roared the jealous carter.

" No offence at aal, at aal ! " cried Dougie, answering for himself. " I wassna flirtin' wi' her ; tell her to keep the sweeties for the goat. He's quite a good goat, and answers to the name of Michael."

" Take oot the chart and score oot Port Ellen," said the Captain a little later ; " that's another place we daurna enter in the Western Isles ! "

X

LAND GIRLS

ON the morning of Hallowe'en the *Vital Spark* puffed into the little creek where the cargo of timber was already waiting for her. The Land Girls who had felled, and snedded, and sawn the trees in the forest two miles off, and driven the logs down to the water's edge, completed their job by wading knee-deep in Loch Fyne, leading the horses that dragged the logs from the beach right out to the vessel's quarter, where the steam-winch picked them up and lowered them into the hold.

Amazing young women ! It was the first time Para Handy and his crew had seen their kind. Those girls, in their corduroy breeches, leggings, strong boots and smocks, with their bobbed hair, and Englified accent, made as much sensation as if they had been pantomime princesses.

They were not unconscious of the impression they created. They put, accordingly, a lot of sheer swank into their handling and hauling of the timber ; one or two boldly smoked cigarettes ; a little plump one, apparently known as Podger, who had come from a Midlothian Manse, actually stammered out a timid " d-d-damn ! " in the hearing of the crew, and blushed furiously as she did so.

"My goodness! chust look at them! Aren't they smert?" said Para Handy. "If they were in Gleska they would make money at the dancin'."

Dougie could not keep his gaze off them.

"I wish my wife could see them!" he remarked regretfully. "She never gets over the door to see anything. I'll wudger ye it would open her eyes. Chust fancy them wi' troosers!"

"That's the latest style, sunny boys," intimated Hurricane Jack, with all the assurance of a man of the world, up-to-date in all new movements. "First the vote and then the breeches. Ye can see them's no' common carteresses—born ladies!"

Jack's natural gallantry, even at the age of fifty-five, had made him oil his hair, put on his best pea-jacket, and borrow a pair of misfit boots which Dougie had bought a week or two before in Greenock, found far too small for him, and intended to take back to the vendor. They fitted Hurricane Jack like a glove.

"If my wife wass to go aboot in troosers wi' her hair cowed, I would bring her before the Session," said the Captain. "It's not naiture! There is not wan word aboot women wearin' breeches between the two boards o' the Bible."

"You look the Book o' Hezekiah!" said Hurricane Jack. "In the fifteenth chapter ye'll see there that a time would come, accordin' to the prophets, when women would arise in Babylon and put their husband's garments on, and the men go forth in frocks."

The Captain was plainly staggered. He had overlooked that bit. "Go you doon, Dougie," he said, "and look your Bible to see if Jeck iss right. I thocht I knew every word o' Hezekiah by he'rt."

Twenty minutes later the mate came back with the Bible and his specs on. "I canna put my hand on Hezekiah at all, at aal," he admitted. "What way do ye spell it?"

Hurricane Jack took the Bible from him and hurriedly

flicked through its pages ; then he turned to the dedication to " The Most High and Mighty Prince James by the Grace of God, King of Britain, France, Ireland, Defender of the Faith."

" Tach ! " he said ; " no wonder ye canna find it ! You might as well look a last year's almanac for the Battle o' Waterloo, as look in a Bible that's oot o' date completely for the Prophet Hezekiah."

" Anyway," said Dougie fervently, " ye'll never in aal your life see me in a frock. I never thocht much o' Hezekiah. He wass a waverer."

" I'll bate ye a pound to your pair o' boots ye'll wear a frock this winter," challenged Hurricane Jack.

" Done wi' ye ! " said Dougie. " Ye may as weel hand over the money."

By the time the vessel was loaded, her crew and the surprising ladies were on terms of the utmost cordiality. Only Macphail stood off—reserved and cynical. He knew about women, all they were up to, all they were capable of : for twenty years he had been studying them in novelettes. The profound impression created on his shipmates by these bob-haired, be-breeched huzzies merely amused him.

That was why he was not invited to the Hallowe'en party.

It was to take place that night at the forest huts, two miles off, where the girls lived and worked. The Captain and Hurricane Jack were to come in their Sunday clothes ; Dougie's despair was that his Sunday clothes were in Glasgow.

" That's all right ! " said the girls, languishing round him till his shyness made his very whiskers tickle him. " The wood manager is from home ; he's just your build of a man —with a suit in his wardrobe to fit you like a halo. We'll parcel it up and send it down to you in an hour."

" Nothing fancy, I hope ? " said Dougie nervously. " I canna stand knickerbockers. I never had them on my person."

" It's quite all right ! " Podger assured him. " Mr Taylor's taste is chaste. You can turn up the foot of the legs a little —that will be more convenient for the dancing.''

" But I'm no' goin' to dance ! '' protested Dougie in alarm. " The only dance I ken iss Paddy O'Rafferty.''

" Then we'll have it every now and then,'' said Podger, beaming on him. " But you needn't join in anything else. You can sit out on the doorstep and hold our hands.''

" My gracious ! '' said the mate to himself, " we're seein' life ! ''

In Mr Taylor's morning coat and a pair of shepherd-tartan trousers, Dougie was unmistakably the most conspicuous guest at the Land Girls' party. The garments were obviously made for an ampler person, but by the time the borrower had worked his way through several plates of mashed potatoes, which, he was assured, were full of threepenny-bits, but found loaded with nothing but buttons, and had consumed apples, nuts, cold ham, and tea till he perspired, there was not a single crease in the waistcoat.

" Mind, I'm no' goin' to dance wan step ! '' he confided to Hurricane Jack and the Captain. " It iss twenty years since I shook a foot at a pairty, and the only dance I ken iss Paddy O'Rafferty.''

" I doot it's oot o' date ; I'm no' goin' to dance mysel','' said Para Handy.

" Wi' a splendid pair o' shepherd-tartan troosers like that,'' said Hurricane Jack, " the thing for you to do, Dougie, is to drape yoursel' over the stern o' the piano and turn the music. Be up an' doin', man ! Cairry yoursel' like a sailor ! ''

To Dougie's horror Podger came up at this stage with a partner for him.

" Here's a lady who is dying to dance with you,'' she announced. " Her Sunday name is Miss Mathilde Vavasour MacKinlay, but you can call her 'Tilda. In the Greek that means ' very choice.' ''

" I can see that,'' said Dougie gallantly, " but if it's dancin' she wants, she'll better take the Captain. Wi' aal them buttons I swallowed, I'm no' in trum at aal, and the Captain's a fine strong dancer."

" Me ! " cried Para Handy, horrified. " I daurna dance a step for palpitation ! Jeck's the chentleman for 'Tulda ! He hass great experience in Australia, and the boots for't. There's no a man on the roarin' deep more flippant on his feet."

Hurricane Jack's performance for the rest of the evening justified this testimony ; he went through the country dances like a full-rigged ship among the lug-sail young lads who were in the party, and refrained from the waltzes and fox-trots only on the grounds of moral disapproval.

It was shortly after midnight when Podger, all in a tremble, pale with apparent alarm, though really from more application of powder than usual, came in to intimate that Mr Taylor had unexpectedly returned, and was to join the party as soon as he had had supper.

" And he'll want to wear these very clothes ! " she said to Dougie ; " what on earth are we to do ? "

" I'll go back to the boat and shift," said Dougie agreeably ; he had discovered a very obvious defect in the trousers. The pockets had been sewn up by Podger, and he had nowhere to put his hands.

" There's no time for that. He'll want them in fifteen minutes," said Podger. " We could loan you quite a good waterproof. He'd bring down the house if he found we had meddled with his wardrobe."

" 'Dalmighty ! What am I to do ? " bleated Dougie. " This iss a bonny habble ! And there iss not a pair of breeches in the company will fit me."

" Ye'll no' get mine, whatever ! " firmly declared Para Handy.

" Ye havena, by any chance, a kind o' kilt ? " inquired Hurricane Jack, who took contretemps of this sort with amazing calmness and resource.

"The very thing!" cried Podger. "There's 'Tilda's tartan skirt! It's good enough for a kilt. Go out to the hut at the back and we'll throw it in to you."

Twenty minutes later, attired, with the aid of Jack and the Captain, in a tartan skirt and a knitted jumper of a vivid yellow, Dougie was coaxed back to the ball-room.

A roar of uncontrollable laughter greeted his appearance. He stood for a moment, blinking and confused, in the middle of the room, in a nether garment much too short for a skirt and yet too long for a kilt, to which in other respects it bore no earthly resemblance.

"Dougie will now oblige wi' the Reel o' Hullichan for the sake of the cheneral hilarity," announced the Captain.

"I'll see you aal to the duvvle first!" cried the mate; "I didna come here for guisin'."

He bolted from the company, and an hour or two later, when Para Handy and Jack got back to their ship, they found him in bed still painfully conscious that he had been made to look ridiculous.

"Hoots, man!" said Hurricane Jack, "what for did ye run away? It wass chenerally admitted that ye were the belle o' the ball. Didn't I tell ye frocks wass goin' to be aal the go for men this winter, accordin' to the Prophet Hezekiah? I never, never, in aal my life got a better bargain in a pair o' boots!"

XI

LEAP YEAR ON THE *VITAL SPARK*

THE last cart of coals was no sooner out of the *Vital Spark* than the crew were up at the Ferry Inn with a bright new tin can Para Handy had bought three days before from a tinker in Ardrishaig. It would hold a gallon. To carry a gallon of ale from the Ferry Inn to the quay obviously did not require two sturdy sailormen and an engineer, but it was thought best that all of them should accompany the can to obviate any chance of accident.

" I have seen a can couped before noo," the Captain had remarked, with his eye on the engineer, who had offered to go alone ; " it takes a steady hand and a good conscience to cairry a gallon o' ale withoot spillin'."

" Wha are ye yappin' at noo ? " asked the engineer truculently.

" I am not yappin' at nobody," replied the Captain calmly. " I wass chust mindin' some droll things that happened in the way o' short measure wi' the last can that we had. Keep you calm, Macphail, and don't put on a bonnet that your heid doesna fit ! "

They went into the back room of the public-house, and, sitting down, carefully sampled a schooner each before presenting the wholesale order for a canful.

" What way did Jeck no' come ? " inquired Dougie. " I thocht he wass at oor back."

" Ye'll no' see Jeck for an oor or two," replied Para Handy. " He's away gallivantin'. I'm sure ye saw him washin' his face ? If you were to go over twenty minutes efter this to Mary Maclachlan's delf and sweety-shop, I'll wudger ye'll get Hurricane Jeck languishin' on the lady wi' his hench on the coonter, and smellin' like a valenteen wi' hair-oil. The last time we were here she made a great impression on Jeck wi' her conversation lozenges. He's no much o' a hand at flirtin' by word o' mooth, but he's desperate darin' when it comes to swappin' sweeties."

" I havena seen a conversation lozenger since the war," said Dougie. " They'll no' be printin' them."

" If they're no'," said Para Handy, " it's a blue look-oot the night for Jeck ! There wass never a gallanter man in oilskins, but he's tumid, tumid among women. It's my belief that Jeck would make a match of it wi' his namesake Mary Maclachlan if only he could summons up his nerve to ask her."

Macphail gave a sardonic laugh. "If bounce would dae, Jeck would be the champion lady-killer," he remarked unkindly. "The man's no' thinkin' o' merrage, in my belief; he has nerve enough to sample, every noo and then, the sweety boxes on the coonter."

There was genuine indignation in the Captain's reception of a remark so unflattering to the absent shipmate. He had to call in another schooner for himself and Dougie; Macphail this time he overlooked.

"Amn't I the forlorn poor skipper o' a boat to have an enchineer like you, Macphail, that's aalways makin' light o' other people!" he retorted. "Ye have chust been sailin' dubs aal your days, when Jeck wass makin' his name in the Black Ball Line and the China clippers. He wass sailin' roond the Horn before ye learned your tred in the gasfitter's shop in Paisley—that's where ye came from, and all ye ever learned aboot engines, or I'm mistaken!"

"I'm no' sayin' onything against the chap," said the engineer, "except that I don't think ony wise-like woman would ever mairry him. The man's fifty if he's a day!"

"He iss not a brat o' a boy, I admit," said the Captain, "but he's in the prime o' life and cheneral agility."

"It's time he wass married, anyway," chimed in Dougie. "It's a poor life, ludgin's. Are ye sure, Peter, he has a chenuine fancy for Miss Maclachlan?"

"She has him that tame he would eat oot o' her hand and jump through girrs," said the Captain. "Did he no' tell me himsel'? It's costin' him half his wages for hair-oil, pan drops, and 'Present-for-a-good-Boy' mugs every time he's in Lochfyne and goes to see her, but he canna, for his life, screw up his nerve to ask her."

"It's Leap Year; maybe she'll ask hersel'," suggested the engineer.

Para Handy's visage glowed at the suggestion. He banged the table.

"For a low-country man," he exclaimed, "ye have sometimes a wonderful sagacity, Macphail. If Mary Maclachlan would only put the word to Jeck and save him from confusion, it would be capital!"

"We could give her a bit o' a hint," proposed Dougie. "Break it to her gently that Jeck is bashful."

"I have a wonderful lot o' nerve mysel'," said the Captain, "but I'm no' wan o' them gladiators to risk my life in a delf shop. Perhaps Macphail would venture to put the position to Miss Maclachlan."

"Seein' it wass his idea——" said Dougie.

"I'll dae better than that," said the engineer; "if ye ring the bell for ink and a pen and paper, I'll write a nice wee letter for Jeck frae Miss Maclachlan that'll bring things to a heid and show if he's in earnest."

Macphail's forged Leap Year letter was a masterpiece of tact. It indicated that the ostensible writer was fully aware of the difficulty a sensitive gentleman might have in expressing his feelings to a young lady as sensitive as himself, and pointed out that as this was Leap Year, she was justified in making the first overtures. She remarked that Jack was no longer a youth, and was arriving at that period of life when he required some one to look after him. It was a position she felt thoroughly qualified to occupy. Though he might be of the impression that she was happy in her present position, it was far from being the case, and she was willing to change her condition on the slightest encouragement from him.

"Capital!" exclaimed the Captain when the note was finished. "Chust the way a girl like Miss Maclachlan would put it. If I wass not a married man and got a letter like that I would merry the girl, even if she was a bleck from South Australia."

"It should save a desperate lot o' hair-oil, that!" was Dougie's view. "I wonder where they'll get a hoose?"

A discreet boy, with instructions to say the letter was given him by a girl, was sent with it to the vessel, and the can and its convoy an hour or two later got on board.

Hurricane Jack was invisible. More remarkable was the fact that his dunnage bag and all his belongings were gone too. Inquiries on the quay brought out the information that he had left with the *Minard Castle* an hour ago, having got, as he explained to one informant, an unexpected letter which made his instant departure imperative.

" Holy sailors ! " exclaimed Para Handy, " isn't this the bonny caper ? Do ye think we scared him ? "

Para Handy and Macphail went down to the delf and sweety-shop to make inquiries, and found it in charge of Miss Maclachlan's sister.

" Did ye see any word o' Hurricane Jeck the night ? " he inquired.

" He was here two hours or more ago, and only stopped a minute," said the girl.

" Did he see your sister Mary ? " asked the Captain.

" Hoo could he see Mary ? " replied the girl. " She was married a week ago to Peter Campbell, and she's left the shop."

XII

BONNIE ANN

IT was Macphail the engineer who first discovered the fame of Bonnie Ann, and the little shop, half dairy, half green-grocery, where that gifted lady had far more young customers for her occult powers than for her excellent potted-head and home-made soda scones. The occult department of her thriving business was carried on behind the shop, in a room where she read tea-cups, disclosed the future vicissitudes of any love affair with the aid of a pack of cards, or—for a somewhat larger fee—took cataleptic fits, in the course of which she held communication with the dead.

Nor even then was Bonnie Ann's versatility exhausted ; she called this chamber of hers a " Beauty Parlour and Séance Saloon," and could guarantee the most ravishing complexions, busts of an agreeable contour, lustrous long hair, fascinating eyelashes, finger-nails to do credit to any lady, and an infallible cure for chilblains, corns, and cuticular blotches.

The notorious Madame Blavatsky was a bungling amateur in the magic arts compared with the shy, almost morbidly unostentatious Ann, who never advertised.

Macphail, having gone to Bonnie Ann for treatment of an ingrowing toe-nail, had been privileged to witness a trance performance, in which she conversed fluently with Mary Queen of Scots, and he returned to the *Vital Spark* immensely impressed.

" I'm tellin' ye, there's something in't ! " he declared to his shipmates. " She had Bloody Mary to the life, and I ken, for I've read history. Ye can get it a' in ' The Scottish Chiefs.' "

" Did she read the palm o' your hand ? " inquired Para Handy, his interest wakened.

" There's nane o' that hanky-panky about Bonnie Ann," replied the engineer. " Pure science ! She throws hersel' into a trance till ye only see the whites o' her eyes, and then ye hear the depairted jist the same's they were in the room. She's weel in wi' the Duke o' Wellington ; he tell't her three years ago we would win the war."

Dougie, the mate, was not surprised to hear of these wonderful manifestations. " The papers iss full o' them," he said. " It's aal the go wi' the titled gentry and Epuscopalian munisters. I heard mysel', wan night, a noise I couldna understand inside a kitchen dresser."

" I'm no' sayin' whether I believe in the spirits or no'," remarked Para Handy cautiously. " There iss spirits in the Scruptures, though they were different in the Holy Land, and no' up to capers—shiftin' sideboards, spillin' oil on the ceilin', rappin' in coal scuttles. But if Bonnie Ann hass the gift, we should give her a trial to see what she can make o' Hurricane Jeck."

Three weeks before, Hurricane Jack, alarmed at the apparent intentions of a lady who wished to take advantage of her Leap Year privilege and propose to him, had disappeared. He had left the *Vital Spark* without warning, and never been heard of since. Convinced—or almost convinced—that Jack had drowned himself—for they knew the lady—his three shipmates proceeded to Bonnie Ann's shop at night, and began negotiations diplomatically with an order for turnips and cabbages.

" Could we hae a word wi' ye at the back ? " inquired Macphail in a husky whisper over the counter. " I wass tellin' my mates aboot Bloody Mery."

Bonnie Ann, who apparently had got the adjective to her name from an ironic customer, looked at her watch, and intimated that it was shutting-up time.

" Forbye," she added, " if it's Mery Queen o' Scots ye're wantin', it's no' her nicht oot ; I couldna get her. A lot o' you sailor chaps thinks a beauty parlour and séance saloon is jist like a shebeen that ye can come intae ony oor o' the day or nicht and ring for the depairted the same's it was a schooner o' beer."

" It's no' Bloody Mery we're wantin'," explained Para Handy soothingly. " We'll no' put ye to the slightest bother. To let ye ken—a shipmate o' oors, Jeck Maclachlan, went missin' three weeks ago. He's no' in the polis-office, he's no' in his uncle's hoose in Polmadie, and he must be deid, fair play or foul. Could ye help us, Ann, to find oot something aboot Jeck ? "

He bent upon Bonnie Ann a gaze of compelling languishment.

" Awa' into the back," she said, " and I'll put up the shutters and jine ye in a meenute."

They were seated in the beauty parlour and séance saloon when she joined them.

She lit the gas and turned it down to a peep, after first having lowered the blind. Picking up, and gazing intently at, a crystal ball, the size of a satisfactory Seville orange, she muttered, " There's a man missin'. He has a tattoo mark on his airm—it's blue. He's been missin' three weeks ; his friends is anxious to hear aboot him."

" And that's the God's truth," exclaimed Dougie, awestruck by this swift, unerring comprehension of the situation. " He had a lend o' my pocket-naipkin."

" He's a sailor," continued Bonnie Ann. " The initials o' his name is J. M'L., and he's a Scotchman. He traivelled a lot on boats. He wasna a teetotaller, and whiles his language was coorse——"

" Holy Frost ! Jeck to the life ! " exclaimed Para Handy. " I doot he iss done for ; he never even came for his pay. Iss he on deck or under hatches, Annie ? "

" Did I no' tell ye ! " cried Macphail triumphantly. " Never mind the glessy, Annie ; throw us a trance, and get in touch wi' somebody that was in the sea tred when he was in the body. There's nae use botherin' Bonnie Mary o' Argyll to ask for Jeck : if he's in the Better Land, he'll be doon aboot the quay, or in a beershop whaur she wouldna care to venture."

" I could try the Duke o' Wellington," suggested Bonnie Ann. " Mind, I'm no' guaranteein' ony communication ; the duke, whiles, tak's a lot o' humourin'."

Para Handy looked dubious. " Is there no' a wee chape skipper chap could do the job ? His grace would be an expensive pairty. If Jeck iss there at aal, I'll wudger he's weel kent."

" In life he wass a toppin' singer, and he could play the trump," remarked Dougie helpfully.

Bonnie Ann put the crystal ball back on the chimney-piece, and pulled out a little table to the middle of the room.

" Ye'll hae to help yoursel's," she intimated, having placed chairs for them round the table. " Draw in."

" Don't put yoursel' to any bother, Annie," huskily implored the Captain, under a misapprehension. " We're chust efter a splendid tea."

"I wasna gaun to offer ye onything," said Bonnie Ann. "Ye needna be sae smert! A' put your baith hands flet on the table wi' me and concentrate your minds on—what did ye say the chap's name was—Maclachlan?"

"Better kent as Hurricane Jeck," explained Macphail, who entered into the ceremony with absolute enthusiasm. "If ye put some tumblers on the table he'll be wi' us in a jiffy."

This suggestion that the spirit of their departed shipmate was to join the company alarmed Para Handy, who hastily withdrew his hands.

"Bless my sowl!" he exclaimed, "are ye thinkin' to bring Jeck here in the spirit?"

"I thocht that was whit ye wanted," answered Bonnie Ann peevishly. "It's shairly no' to play catch-the-ten we're gaithered here!"

"And it's no' to see the ghost o' Jeck Maclachlan, I'll assure ye!" exclaimed Para Handy. "Take my advice, and don't you bother him, Annie. He wass a tricky lad in life, and dear knows what he would be up to in the spirit! Am I no' right, Dougie?"

"Ye're quite right, Captain," agreed the mate emphatically. "We're no' wantin' to see himsel' at aal, but chust to get the news o' him. Let him keep his distance! Could ye no' get him, Annie, to do something in the air wi' a tambourine?"

"As shair's daith I canna come the tambourine the nicht," pleaded Bonnie Ann; "I'm deid tired—bakin' a' the aifternoon. There's naething for't but to ask the Duke o' Wellington for your frien'."

"I don't believe the duke's a bit o' good; he'll go on haverin' aboot the battle o' Waterloo, and that's the wan battle Jeck wass never in," declared the Captain.

Macphail looked at the skipper with disgust. "Ye're makin' a fair cod o' the thing," he exclaimed. "Gie the woman a chance! Fling us a trance, Annie, and see whit the duke says."

Bonnie Ann sat back in her chair, shut her eyes, and in a minute or two was in wireless communication with the Iron Duke, who, in a falsetto baritone through her lips, conveyed the information that he had seen John Maclachlan in the last two days.

"What happened to Jeck?" inquired Para Handy, in an awestruck whisper.

The unfortunate seaman, it appeared, had fallen over the side of a ship in a storm, swam three days, and perished within sight of land.

"That's Jeck, sure enough!" exclaimed Dougie. "He was a capital sweemer!"

"Iss he happy, Annie?" whispered Para Handy. "Ask his Grace what sort o' trum he's in."

"The life and soul o' the place!" replied the Duke of Wellington. "As happy's the day's long. He sends his best respects to all concerned."

Having recovered from her trance, Bonnie Ann briskly collected a fee of five shillings which the crew of the *Vital Spark* made up with difficulty between them; saw her clients off the premises as quickly as possible, shut up her shop, and retired to the beauty parlour to make herself some supper.

The crew made for the quay in a state of considerable mental excitement, solemnised by the knowledge of their shipmate's fate, and were staggered to find Hurricane Jack himself on board the *Vital Spark*! He had arrived by the *Minard Castle*.

"'Dalmighty! where were ye, Jeck?" inquired Para Handy, who was first to recover himself.

"Oh, jist perusin' about the docks o' Gleska," said Jack airily. "I fell in wi' a lot o' fellows."

"Of aal the liars ever I heard," said the Captain viciously, "the worst iss the Duke o' Wellington!"

L

XIII

THE LEAP-YEAR BALL

SUNNY JIM, back again on one of his periodical short spells
of long-shore sailoring, went ashore on Friday morning with
a can for milk, and an old potato-sack for bread, and, such is
the morning charm of Appin, that he made no attempt to
get either of them filled until he reached the inn at Duror.
He wasn't a fellow who drank at any time excessively, but,
Glasgow-born, he felt always homesick in foreign parts unless
he could be, as Para Handy said, " convenient and adjaacent
to a licensed premise."   In a shop beside the inn he got his
bread, and he might have got the milk a mile or two nearer
Kintallen Quay, from which he had come, but a sailor never
goes to a farm for milk so long as he can get it at an inn.

" A quart," he said to the girl at the bar, and pushed the
can across the counter. As she measured out and filled his
can with ale, he sternly kept an averted eye on a bill on the
wall which spoke in the highest terms of Robertson's Sheep
Dips.

" What in the world do ye ca' this ? " he exclaimed,
regarding the can's contents with what to an unsophisticated
child would look like genuine surprise. " Michty ! what
thick cream ! If the Gleska coos gave milk like that, the
dairies would mak' their fortunes."

" Was it not beer you wanted ? " asked the girl, with
sleeves rolled up on a pair of arms worth all the rest of the
Venus de Medici, and a roguish eye.

" Nut at all ! " said he emphatically. " Milk. What ye
sometimes put in tea."

" Then it's the back of the house you should go to," said
the girl. " This is not the milk department," and she was
about to empty the can again, but not with unreasonable
celerity, lest the customer should maybe change his mind.

" Hold on ! " said Sunny Jim, with a grasp at it.   " Seein' it's there, I'll maybe can make use o't. See's a tumbler, Flora."

For twenty minutes he leaned upon the counter and fleeted the time delightfully as in the golden world. He said he was off a yacht, and, if not officially, in every other sense the skipper. True, it was not exactly what might be called the yachting season, but the owners of the yacht were whimsical. Incidentally, he referred to his melodeon, and at that the girl declared he was the very man she had been looking for.

" Oh, come aff it, come aff it ! " said Sunny Jim, with proper modesty, but yet with an approving glance at his reflection which was in the mirror behind her. " I'm nae-thing patent, but I'll admit there's no' a cheerier wee chap from here to Ballachulish."

" Ye would be an awful handy man at a ball," said the girl, " with your melodeon. We're having a leap-year dance to-night, and only a pair of pipers. What's a pair of pipers ? "

" Two," said Sunny Jim promptly.

" You're quite mistaken," replied the girl with equal promptness ; " it's only two till the first reel's by, and then it's a pair o' bauchles no' able to keep their feet. You come with your melodeon, and I'll be your partner."

He went back to the *Vital Spark* delighted, looked out his Sunday clothes and his melodeon, and chagrined his shipmates hugely by the narrative of his good fortune.

" What's a leap-year baal ? " asked Para Handy. " Iss there a night or two extra in it ? No Chrustian baal should last over the week-end."

" It's a baal where the women hae a' the say," explained Macphail, the engineer, whose knowledge was encyclopædic.

" Iss that it ? " said Para Handy. " It's chust like bein' at home ! It's me that's gled I'm not invited. Take you something wise-like wi' ye in your pocket, Jum ; I wouldna be in their reverence."

"I would like to see it," said Dougie. "Does the lady come in a kind of a cab for you?"

"It's only young chaps that's invited," explained Sunny Jim, with brutal candour.

The Captain looked at him reproachfully. "You shouldna say the like o' that to Dougie," he remonstrated. "Dougie's no' that terrible old."

"I was sayin' it to baith o' you," said Sunny Jim. "It's no' a mothers' meetin' this, it's dancin'."

"There's no man in the shippin' tred wi' more agility than mysel'," declared the indignant skipper. "I can stot through the middle o' a dance like a tuppeny kahoochy ball. Dougie himsel' 'll tell you!"

"Yes, I've often seen you stottin'," agreed the mate, with great solemnity. Para Handy looked at him with some suspicion, but he presented every appearance of a man with no intention to say anything offensive.

"You havena an extra collar and a bit o' a stud on you?" was the astonishing inquiry made by Dougie less than twenty minutes after Sunny Jim had departed for the Duror ball. "I wass thinkin' to mysel' we might take a turn along the road to look at the life and gaiety."

"Dougie, you're beyond redemption!" said Para Handy. "A married man and nine or ten o' a family, and there you're up to all diversions like a young one!"

"I wassna going by the door o' the ball," the mate exclaimed indignantly. "You aye take me up wrong."

"Oh, ye should baith gang," suggested the engineer, with malicious irony. "A couple o' fine young chaps! Gie the girls o' Appin a treat. Never let on you're mairried. They'll never suspect as lang's ye keep on your bonnets."

"I think mysel' we should go, Dougie, and we might be able to buy a penny novelle for Macphail to read on Sunday," said the Captain. "Anything fresh about Lady Audley, Macphail?"

Macphail ignored the innuendo. "Noo's your chance," he

proceeded. "Everything's done for ye by the fair sect : a lady M.C. to find ye pairtners ; the women themsel's comin' up to see if your programme's full, and askin' every noo and then if ye care for a gless o' clairet-cup on draught. I wouldna say but ye would be better to hae a fan and a Shetland shawl to put ower your heids when you're comin' hame ; everything's reversed at a leap-year ball."

He would simply have goaded the Captain into going if the Captain had not made up his mind as soon as Dougie himself that he was going in any case.

"Two-and-six apiece for the tickets," said the man at the door when Para Handy and his mate came drifting out of the bar and made a tentative attempt at slipping in unostentatiously.

"Not for a leap-year dance, Johnny," said the Captain mildly. "Everything is left to the ladies."

"Except the payin' ; that's ass usual," said the door-keeper, and the Captain and his mate regretfully paid for entrance. The room was crowded, and the masculine pre-dominated to the extent that it looked as if every lady had provided herself with half-a-dozen partners that she might be assured of sufficient dancing. One of the pipers had already lapsed into the state so picturesquely anticipated by the girl whom Sunny Jim called Flora ; the other leant on a window-sill, and looked with Celtic ferocity and disdain upon Sunny Jim, who was playing his melodeon for the Flowers of Edinburgh.

"You're playin' tip-top, Jum. I never heard you better," said the Captain to him at the first interval ; and the musician was so pleased that he introduced his shipmates to Flora.

"We're no' here for the baal at aal, at aal, but chust to put bye the time," the Captain explained to her. "I see you're no' slack for pairtners."

"Not at present," she replied ; "but just you wait till the supper's bye and you'll see a bonny difference."

She was right, too. The masculine did certainly not

predominate after midnight, being otherwise engaged. The fact that Flora was a wallflower seemed to distress Sunny Jim, who would gladly now relinquish his office of musician to the piper.

"That's a charmin' gyurl, and a desperate sober piper," said the Captain to his mate, who spent most of the time looking for what he called the "commytee," and had finally discovered, if not the thing itself, at all events what was as good. "Jum's doin' capital at the melodeon, and it would be a peety if the piper took his job."

They took out the piper, and by half an hour's intelligent administration of the committee's refreshments rendered him quite incapable of contributing any further music to the dancers.

"Now that's aal right," said the Captain cheerfully, returning to the hall. "A piper's aal right if ye take him the proper way, but I never saw one wi' a more durable heid than yon fellow. Man, Jum's doin' capital! Hasn't he got the touch! It's a peety he's such a strong musician, for, noo that the pipers hass lost their reeds, he's likely to be kept at it till the feenish."

"Lost their reeds!" said Dougie.

"Chust that!" replied the Captain calmly. "I took them oot o' their drones, and I have them in my pocket. It's every man for himsel' in Duror of Appin. You and me'll dance with Flora."

Nothing could exceed the obvious annoyance of Sunny Jim when he saw his shipmates dance with Flora to the music of his own providing. Again and again he glanced with impatient expectancy towards the door for the relieving piper.

"The piper 'll be back in a jiffy, Jum," said Para Handy to him, sweeping past with Flora in a polka or a schottische. "He's chust oot at the back takin' a drop of lemonade, and said he would be in immediately."

"You're doing magnificent," he said, coming round to the

musician again as Dougie took the floor with Flora for the Haymakers. " Ye put me awful in mind of yon chap, Paddy Roosky, him that's namely for the fiddle. Man, if ye chust had a velvet jecket ! Flora says she never danced to more becomin' music."

" That's a' richt," said the disgusted musician ; " but I'm gettin' fed up wi' playin' awa' here. I cam' here for dancin', and I wish the piper would look slippy."

" He'll be in in wan meenute," said Para Handy, with the utmost confidence, turning over the pipe reeds in his trousers pocket. " It's a reel next time, Jum ; you might have given us ' Monymusk ' and ' Alister wears a cock't bonnet ' ; I'm engaged for it to Flora."

Dance after dance went on, and, of course, there was no relieving piper. The melodeonist was sustained by the flattering comments of his shipmates on his playing and an occasional smile from Flora, who was that kind of girl who didn't care whom she danced with so long as she got dancing.

" Special request from Flora—would ye give us ' The Full-Rigged Ship ' the next one ? That's a topper," said the Captain to him. Or, " Compliments of Flora, and would you mind the Garaka Waltz and Circassian Circle for the next, Jum ? She says she likes my style o' dancin'."

" I wish to goodness I'd never learned to play a bloomin' note," said Sunny Jim.

But he played without cessation till the ball was ended, the fickle Flora dancing more often with his shipmates than with anybody else.

As they took the road to Kintallen Quay at six o'clock in the morning, Para Handy took some chanter reeds from his pocket and handed them to Sunny Jim.

" You should learn the pipes, Jum," he remarked. " They're no' so sore on you ass a melodeon. Man, but she wass a lovely dancer, Flora ! Chust sublime ! Am I no' right, Dougie ? "

"A fair gazelle! The steps o' her!" said the mate poetically.

"And we were pretty smert on oor feet oorsel's," said Para Handy. "It doesna do to have aal your agility in your fingers."

XIV

THE BOTTLE KING

THE *Vital Spark* at nightfall put into the little bay where her cargo of timber was assembled. On an ingenuous excuse of "takin' the air," Hurricane Jack, who had not been there before, went ashore at the earliest possible moment in the dark, and, trusting to an instinct usually unerring, searched for some place of cheer.

He came on the inn through a back yard, where were several vans and dogcarts, and a curious sort of chariot, highly ornamental to the feel, that puzzled him considerably, till he struck a match, and found it was a hearse.

The hearse, however, engaged his attention less intently than the enormous array of empty bottles which were piled up all round the yard. Crates were full of them, barrels were brimming over with them; they were in layers ten deep under the stable eaves, and tinkling with the water that fell through them from a broken rhone.

"Whatever they are in this place," said Jack to himself, "they're no' nerrow-minded. They must have a fine cheery winter of it! If they drank all that there must have been great tred wi' the hearse."

He opened that solemn vehicle, looked inside, and found it too was filled with the relics of conviviality, mostly wine-bottles.

"English gentlemen. Towerists. Shooters. The money them folk waste!"

He shook some of the bottles, to make certain they were

empty. "No fears o' them!" he reflected cynically. "It makes me sad. Puttin' bottles in a hearse—it's no' respectable; I wonder what the ministers would say!"

There was no access to the inn from the yard that he could find, so to save time he climbed a wall, and found himself on the other side of it, by that marvellous intuition of his, exactly at the door of the bar where all the winter business of the inn was done.

Nobody was inside but the innkeeper, who was washing tumblers in the light of a hanging paraffin-lamp, and was suspiciously flushed.

"A wet night," said Hurricane Jack, taking off his soaking cap and slapping it against the skirt of his oilskin coat to get rid of part of its moisture. "I'll take a small sensation."

The landlord looked surprised. "I thought you were from Balliemeanach," said he, "to order the hearse. Where in the world did ye come from?"

"From the boundin' deep," said Hurricane Jack. "My ship's outside there, as ye might say, on the doorstep."

The landlord looked immensely relieved.

"As sure as death," said he, "I thought ye were from Balliemeanach. Maclean the wudman had a couple o' glesses o' Cream de Mong here yesterday, and I havena slept a wink since, wonderin' would he get over it."

"Cream de Mong," said Hurricane Jack, with genuine interest; "if it's anything like that, I'll try it."

The landlord produced a bottle of green liqueur from below the counter. "Mind ye," he said, "it's at your own risk. I don't fancy the look o't mysel'. It was in the cellar when I came here three years ago, and I hadna the nerve to offer it to any one till Maclean was here in desperation yesterday, and me withoot a drop o' spirits in the hoose."

Hurricane Jack picked up the bottle, looked at it, and put it down again. "Starboard Light," he remarked. "I've seen it. They take it in cabins. I wouldn't use it to oil my hair. What I'm wantin's something to drink."

L*

A bottle of beer was promptly uncorked and put before him. " Ninepence," said the landlord.

" Holy sailors ! " exclaimed Hurricane Jack. " I could buy wine for that on the Rio Grande."

" There's a penny for the bottle," said the landlord. " Eightpence if ye bring back the bottle."

Jack, two seconds after, handed him back the empty bottle and eightpence.

" Ye're surely keen on empty bottles," he remarked.

" A penny apiece, and glad to get as many as I can ; they call me the Bottle King," said the landlord. " But someway, this while back, my mind's a' reel-rall."

Para Handy and Dougie were going to bed, and Macphail was there already, when Hurricane Jack got back to the ship and excitedly demanded a large spale basket.

" What on earth are ye goin' to do wi' a spale basket, Jeck ? " inquired the Captain. " Were ye fishin' ? "

" No, nor fishin' ! " retorted Jack ; " but there's a man up yonder at the inn that calls himsel' the Bottle King, and payin' a penny apiece for them. I think I can put a lot o' tred in his way." He had already found a basket.

Para Handy looked at him uneasily. " Iss it Peter Grant ? " he asked. " Ye'll no' get roond Peter wi' aal your agility. If it's buyin' bottles he is, ye'll no' put him off wi' jeely jars. Where in the name o' fortune are ye goin' to get the bottles ? There iss not wan bottle in this boat, unless it's under Macphail's pillow."

" Hoots, man ! " said Dougie, remonstrative ; " give Jeck a chance ! Jeck never yet put oot his hand farther than he could streetch his arm."

" Come on the pair o' ye, and see a pant ! " said Hurricane Jack. " We'll have to look slippy afore Grant shuts his shop."

" I hope it's nothing that 'll be found oot," said Para

Handy still uneasy. "Ye're a duvvle for quirks, Jeck, and I wouldna like the ship to get into trouble."

Ten minutes later they all trailed up to the inn with the empty basket.

The innkeeper was still washing tumblers when the Captain and Dougie, carrying a spale basket of empty bottles between them, came into his bar, and Hurricane Jack behind them.

"Three pints o' ale," said Jack, with the utmost confidence, "and here's two dozen bottles. We're glad to get rid o' them."

The Bottle King was frankly surprised at such a consignment from such a quarter.

"Wherever ye got them bottles, it wasna here," he said. "At least, as far as I can mind. My heid's a' reel-rall, but it doesna maitter. I'm willin' to tak' them," and, having emptied the basket, he produced the beer for his customers.

"Are ye sure they're no worth more than a penny the piece ? " inquired Para Handy. "We were gettin' tuppence for them in Port Askaig. Am I right, Dougie, or am I wrong ? "

"It wass tuppence in Port Askaig, and tuppence ha'penny in Port Ellen," replied the mate, with unhesitating assurance. "Bottles is scarce. They're no' makin' them. And ye never in your life saw bonnier bottles than them ; they're the chenuine gless."

"Pure plate gless," said Hurricane Jack. "Look at the labels—'Sherry Wine'—I'll wager there's a lot o' money in them."

"We have a shipload yonder o' them," said the Captain. "Could ye be doin' wi' a gross or two ? Chust for the turnover. We must aal put oor hand to the plew to help the government, Mr Grant."

The Bottle King for a moment suspended his washing of tumblers, with tremulous hands put on a pair of spectacles, and looked more closely at his purchase.

" God bless me ! " he exclaimed ; " them's my own wine bottles ! Where did ye get them ? "

" We got them in a hearse behind the hoose here," frankly admitted Hurricane Jack. " There's a thoosand deid men yonder, if there's wan."

" My Chove ! aren't you the ruffians ? " cried Peter Grant. " Sellin' me my own bottles ! I never could mind where I put them, and me lookin' for them high and low since the Old New Year. But tach ! it doesna maitter ; they caal me the Bottle King."

XV

" MUDGES "

" By Chove ! but they're bad the night ! " said Dougie, running a grimy paw across his forehead.

" Perfectly ferocious ! " said Para Handy, slapping his neck. " This fair beats Bowmore, and Bowmore iss namely for its mudges. I never saw the brutes more desperate ! You would actually think they were whustlin' on wan another, cryin', ' Here's a clean sailor, and he hasna a collar on ; gather about, boys ! ' "

" Oh, criftens ! " whimpered Sunny Jim, in agony, dabbing his face incessantly with what looked suspiciously like a dish-cloth ; " I've see'd midges afore this, but they never had spurs on their feet afore. Yah-h-h ! I wish I was back in Gleska ! They can say what they like aboot the Clyde, but anywhere above Bowlin' I'll guarantee ye'll no' be eaten alive. If they found a midge in Gleska, they would put it in the Kelvingrove Museum."

Macphail, his face well lubricated, came up from among the engines, and jeered. " Midges never bothered me," said he contemptuously. " If ye had been wi' me on the West Coast o' Africa, and felt the mosquitoes, it wouldna be aboot a wheen o' gnats ye would mak' a sang. It's a' a hallucination aboot midges ; I can only speak aboot them the way I find them, and they never did me ony harm. Perhaps it's no midges that's botherin' ye efter a'."

" Perhaps no'," said Para Handy, with great acidity. " Perhaps it's hummin' birds, but the effect iss chust the same. Ye'll read in the Scruptures yonder aboot the ant goin' for the sluggard, but the ant iss a perfect chentleman compared wi' the mudge. And from aal I ever heard o' the mosquito, it 'll no' stab ye behind your back withoot a word o' warnin'. Look at them on Dougie's face—quite black ! Ye would never think it wass the Sunday."

It was certainly pretty bad at the quay of Arrochar. With the evening air had come out, as is seemed, the midges of all the Highlands. They hung in clouds above the *Vital Spark*, and battened gluttonously on her distracted crew.

" When I was at the mooth o' the Congo river—" began the engineer ; but Para Handy throttled the reminiscence.

" The Congo's no' to be compared wi' the West o' Scotland when ye come to insects," said Para Handy. " There's places here that's chust deplorable whenever the weather's the least bit warm. Look at Tighnabruaich !—they're that bad there, they'll bite their way through corrugated iron roofs to get at ye ! Take Clynder, again, or any other place in the Gareloch, and ye'll see the old ones leadin' roond the young ones, learnin' them the proper grips. There iss a spachial kind of mudge in Dervaig, in the Isle of Mull, that hass aal the points o' a Poltalloch terrier, even to the black nose and the cocked lugs, and sits up and barks at you. I wass once gatherin' cockles in Colonsay——"

" I could be daein' wi' some cockles," said Sunny Jim. " I aye feel like a cockle when it comes near the Gleska Fair."

" The best cockles in the country iss in Colonsay," said the Captain. " But the people in Colonsay iss that slow they canna catch them. I wass wance gatherin' cockles there, and the mudges were that large and bold, I had to throw stones at them."

" It was a pity ye hadna a gun," remarked Macphail, with sarcasm.

" A gun would be no' much use wi' the mudges of Colonsay," replied the Captain ; " nothing would discourage yon fellows but a blast o' dynamite. What wass there on the island at the time but a chenuine English towerist, wi' a capital red kilt, and, man ! but he wass green ! He was that green, the coos of Colonsay would go mooin' along the road efter him, thinkin' he wass gress. He wass wan of them English chentlemen that 'll be drinkin' chinger-beer on aal occasions, even when they're dry, and him bein' English, he had seen next to nothing aal his days till he took the boat from West Loch Tarbert. The first night on the island he went oot in his kilt, and came back in half an oor to the inns wi' his legs fair peetiful ! There iss nothing that the mudges likes to see among them better than an English towerist with a kilt : the very tops wass eaten off his stockin's."

" That's a fair streetcher, Peter ! " exclaimed the incredulous engineer.

" It's ass true ass I'm tellin' you," said Para Handy. " Any one in Colonsay will tell you. He had wan of them names shed in the middle like Fitz-Gerald or Seton-Kerr ; that'll prove it to ye. When he came in to the inns wi' his legs chust fair beyond redemption, he didna even know the cause of it.

" ' It's the chinger-beer that's comin' oot on you,' says John Macdermott, that had the inns at the time. ' There iss not a thing you can drink that iss more deliteerious in Colonsay. Nobody takes it here.'

" ' And what in aal the world do they take ? ' said the English chentleman.

" ' The water o' the mountain well,' said John, ' and whiles a drop of wholesome Brutish spirits. There's some that doesna care for water.'

"But the English chentleman was eccentric, and nothing would do for him to drink but chinger, an' they took him doon to a shed where the fishermen were barkin' nets, and they got him to bark his legs wi' catechu. If it's green he wass before, he wass now ass brown's a trammel net. But it never made a bit o' odds to the mudges oot in Colonsay! I tell you they're no' slack!"

"They're no' slack here neithers!" wailed Sunny Jim, whose face was fairly wealed by the assailants. "Oh, michty! I think we would be faur better ashore."

"Not a bit!" said Dougie, furiously puffing a pipe of the strongest tobacco, in whose fumes the midges appeared to take the most exquisite pleasure. "There's no' a place ashore where ye could take shelter from them—it being Sunday," he significantly added.

"I'm gaun ashore anyway," said Macphail, removing all superfluous lubricant from his countenance with a piece of waste. "It wouldna be midges that would keep me lollin' aboot this auld hooker on a fine nicht. If ye had some experience o' mosquitoes! Them's the chaps for ye. It's mosquitoes that spreads the malaria fever."

They watched him go jauntily up the quay, accompanied by a cloud of insects which seemed to be of the impression that he was leading them to an even better feeding-ground than the *Vital Spark*. He had hardly gone a hundred yards when he turned and came hurriedly back, beating the air.

"Holy frost!" he exclaimed, jumping on deck, "I never felt midges like that in a' my days afore ; they're in billions o' billions!"

"Tut, tut!" said Para Handy. "Ye're surely getting awfu' tumid, Macphail. You that's so weel acquent wi' them mosquitoes! If I wass a trevelled man like you, I wouldna be bate wi' a wheen o' Hielan' mudges. They're no' in't anyway. Chust imagination! Chust a hallucination! Ye mind ye told us?"

"There's no hallucination aboot them chaps," said Macphail, smacking himself viciously.

"Nut at all!" said Sunny Jim. "Nut at all! If there's ony hallucination aboot them, they have it sherpened. G-r-r-r! It's cruel; that's whit it is; fair cruel!"

"I promised I would go and see Macrae the nicht," said the engineer. "But it's no' safe to gang up that quay. This is yin o' the times I wish I was a smoker; that tobacco o' yours, Dougie, would shairly fricht awa' the midges."

"Not wan bit of it!" said Dougie peevishly, rubbing the back of his neck, on which his tormentors were thickly clustered. "I'm beginning to think mysel' they're partial to tobacco; it maybe stimulates the appetite. My! aren't they the brutes! Look at them on Jim!"

With a howl of anguish Sunny Jim dashed down the fo'c'sle hatch, the back of his coat pulled over his ears.

"Is there naething 'at a' a chap could dae to his face to keep them aff?" asked the engineer, still solicitous about his promised visit to Macrae.

"Some people 'll be sayin' paraffine-oil iss a good thing," suggested the Captain. "But that's only for Ro'sa' mudges; I'm thinkin' the Arrochar mudges would maybe consuder paraffine a trate. And I've heard o' others tryin' whusky —I mean rubbed on ootside. I never had enough to experiment wi't mysel'. Forbye, there's none."

"I wadna care to gang up to Macrae's on a Sunday smellin' o' either paraffine-oil or whisky," said Macphail.

"Of course not!" said Para Handy. "What was I thinkin' of? Macrae's sister wouldna like it," and he winked broadly at Dougie. "Ye'll be takin' a bit of a daunder wi' her efter the church goes in. Give her my best respects, will ye? A fine, big, bouncin' gyurl! A splendid form!"

"You shut up!" said Macphail to his commander, blushing. "I think I'll gie my face anither syne wi' plenty o' saft soap for it, and mak' a breenge across to Macrae's afore the effect wears aff."

He dragged a pail over to the water-beaker, half-filled it with water, added a generous proportion of soft soap from a tin can, and proceeded to wash himself without taking off his coat.

" Ye needna mind to keep on your kep," said the Captain, grimacing to Dougie. "Mima 'll no' see ye. He's been callin' on Macrae a score o' times, Dougie, and the sister hasna found oot yet he's bald. Mercy on us ! Did ye ever in your life see such mudges ! "

" I'm past speakin' aboot them ! " said the mate, with hopeless resignation. " What iss he keepin' on his bonnet for ? "

" He's that bald that unless he keeps it on when he's washin' his face he doesna know where to stop," said Para Handy. " The want o' the hair's an aawful depredaation ! "

But even these drastic measures failed to render Macphail inviolate from the attack of the insects, whose prowess he had underestimated. For the second time he came running back from the head of the quay pursued by them, to be greeted afresh by the irony of his Captain.

" There's a solid wall o' them up there," he declared, rubbing his eyes.

" Isn't it annoyin' ? " said the Captain, with fallacious sympathy. " Mima will be weary waitin' on ye. If there wass a druggist's open, ye might get something in a bottle to rub on. Or if it wassna the Sabbath, ye might get a can o' syrup in the grocer's."

" Syrup ? " said the engineer inquiringly, and Para Handy slyly kicked Dougie on the shin.

" There's nothin' better for keepin' awa' the mudges," he explained. " Ye rub it on your face and leave it on. It's a peety we havena any syrup on the boat."

" Sunny Jim had a tin o' syrup last night at his tea," said the engineer hopefully.

"But it must be the chenuine golden syrup," said Para Handy. "No other kind 'll do."

Sunny Jim was routed out from under the blankets in his bunk to produce syrup, which proved to be of the requisite golden character, as Para Handy knew very well it was, and five minutes later Macphail, with a shining countenance, went up the quay a third time attended by midges in greater myriads than ever. This time he beat no retreat.

"Stop you!" said Para Handy. "When 'Mima' Macrae comes to the door, she'll think it's no' an enchineer she has to caal on her, but a fly cemetery."

XVI

AN OCEAN TRAGEDY

GEORGE IV, being a sovereign of imagination, was so much impressed by stories of Waterlooo that he began to say he had been there himself, and had taken part in it. He brought so much imagination to the narrative that he ended by believing it—an interesting example of the strange psychology of the liar. Quite as remarkable is the case of Para Handy, whose singular delusion of Sunday fortnight last is the subject of much hilarity now among seamen of the minor coasting-trade.

The first of the storm on Saturday night found the *Vital Spark* off Toward on her way up-channel, timber-laden, and without a single light, for Sunny Jim, who had been sent ashore for oil at Tarbert, had brought back a jar of beer instead by an error that might naturally occur with any honest seaman.

When the lights of other ships were showing dangerously close the mate stood at the bow and lit matches, which, of course, were blown out instantly.

"It's not what might be called a cheneral illumination," he remarked, "but it's an imitataation of the Gantock

Light, and it no' workin' proper, and you'll see them big fellows will give us plenty o' elbow-room."

Thanks to the matches and a bar of iron which Macphail had hung on the lever of the steam-whistle, so that it lamented ceaselessly through the tempest like a soul in pain, the *Vital Spark* escaped collision, and some time after midnight got into Cardwell Bay with nothing lost except the jar, a bucket, and the mate's sou'-wester.

" A dirty night ! It's us that iss weel out of it," said Para Handy gratefully, when he had got his anchor down.

The storm was at its worst when the Captain went ashore on Sunday to get the train for Glasgow on a visit to his wife, the farther progress of his vessel up the river for another day at least being obviously impossible. It was only then he realised that he had weathered one of the great gales that make history. At Gourock pierhead shellbacks of experi-ence swore they had never seen the like of it ; there were solemn bodings about the fate of vessels that had to face it. Para Handy, as a ship's commander who had struggled through it, found himself regarded as a hero, and was plied with the most flattering inquiries. On any other day the homage of the shellbacks might have aroused suspicion, but its disinterested nature could not be called in question, seeing all the public-houses were shut.

" Never saw anything like it in aal my born days," he said. " I wass the length wan time of puttin' off my sluppers and windin' up my watch for the Day of Chudgment. Wan moment the boat wass up in the air like a flyin'-machine, and the next she wass scrapin' the cockles off the bottom o' the deep. Mountains high—chust mountains high ! And no' wee mountains neither, but the very bens of Skye ! The seas was wearin' through us fore and aft like yon mysterious river rides that used to be at the Scenic Exhibeetion, and the noise o' the cups and saucers clatterin' doon below wass terrible, terrible ! If Dougie wass here he could tell you."

" A dog's life, boys ! " said the shellbacks. " He would

be ill-advised that would sell a farm and go to sea. Anything carried away, Captain ? "

A jar, a bucket, and a sou'-wester seemed too trivial a loss for such a great occasion. Para Handy hurriedly sketched a vision of bursting hatches, shattered bulwarks, a mate with a broken leg, and himself for hours lashed to the wheel.

It was annoying to find that these experiences were not regarded by the shellbacks as impressive. They seemed to think that nothing short of tragedy would do justice to a storm of such unusual magnitude.

Para Handy got into the train, and found himself in the company of some Paisley people, who seemed as proud of the superior nature of the storm as if they had themselves arranged it.

" Nothing like it in history, chentlemen," said Para Handy, after borrowing a match. " It's me that should ken, for I wass in it, ten mortal hours, battlin' wi' the tempest. A small boat carried away and a cargo o' feather bonnets on the deck we were carryin' for the Territorials. My boat was shaved clean doon to the water-line till she looked like wan o' them timber-ponds at the Port—not an article left standin'! A crank-shaft smashed on us, and the helm wass jammed. The enchineer—a man Macphail belongin' to Motherwell— had a couple of ribs stove in, and the mate got a pair o' broken legs ; at least there's wan o' them broken and the other's a nesty stave. I kept her on her coorse mysel' for five hours, and the watter up to my very muddle. Every sea was smashin' on me, but I never mudged. My George, no ! Macfarlane never mudged ! "

The Paisley passengers were intensely moved, and produced a consoling bottle.

" Best respects, chentlemen ! " said Para Handy. " It's me that would give a lot for the like o' that at three o'clock this mornin'. I'm sittin' here withoot a rag but what I have on me. A fine sea-kist, split new, wi' fancy grommets, all my clothes, my whole month's wages, and presents for the wife in't—it's lyin' yonder somewhere off Innellan. . . . It's a terrible thing the sea."

At Greenock two other passengers came into the compartment, brimful of admiration for a storm they seemed to think peculiarly British in its devastating character—a kind of vindication of the island's imperial pride.

" They've naething like it on the Continent," said one of them. " They're a' richt there wi' their volcanic eruptions and earthquakes and the like, but when it comes to the naitural elements——" He was incapable of expressing exactly what he thought of British dominance in respect of the natural elements.

" Here's a poor chap that was oot in his ship in the worst o't," said the Paisley passengers. Para Handy ducked his head in polite acknowledgment of the newcomers' flattering scrutiny, and was induced to repeat his story, to which he added some fresh sensational details.

He gave a vivid picture of the *Vital Spark* wallowing helplessly on the very edge of the Gantock rocks ; of the fallen mast beating against the vessel's side and driving holes in her ; of the funnel flying through the air, with cases of feather bonnets (" cost ten pounds apiece, chentlemen, to the War Office ") ; of Sunny Jim incessantly toiling at the pump ; the engineer unconscious and delirious ; himself, tenacious and unconquered, at the wheel, lashed to it with innumerable strands of the best Manilla cordage.

" I have seen storms in every part of the world," he said ; " I have even seen yon terrible monsoons that's namely oot about Australia, but never in my born life did I come through what I came through last night."

Another application of the consolatory bottle seemed to brighten his recollection of details.

" I had a lot o' sky-rockets," he explained. " We always have them on the best ships, and I fired them off wi' the wan hand, holdin' the wheel wi' the other. Signals o' distress, chentlemen. Some use cannons, but I aye believe in the sky-rockets : you can both hear and see them. It makes a dufference."

" I kent a chap that did that for a day and a nicht aff the Mull o' Kintyre, and it never brung oot a single lifeboat," said one of the Paisley men.

It was obvious to Para Handy that his tragedy of the sea was pitched on too low a key to stir some people ; he breathed deeply and shook a melancholy head.

" You'll never get lifeboats when you want them, chentlemen," he remarked. " They keep them aal laid up in Gleska for them Lifeboat Setturday processions. But it was too late for the lifeboat anyway for the *Vital Spark*. The smertest boat in the tred, too."

" Good Lord ! She didna sink ? " said the Paisley men, unprepared for such a denouement.

" Nothing above the water at three o'clock this mornin' but the winch," said the Captain. " We managed to make our way ashore on a couple o' herrin'-boxes. . . . Poor Macphail ! A great man for perusin' them novelles, but still-and-on a fellow of much agility. The very last words he said when he heaved his breath—and him, poor sowl, withoot a word o' Gaelic in his heid—wass, ' There's nobody can say but what you did your duty, Peter.' That wass me."

" Do ye mean to say he was drooned ? " asked the Paisley men with genuine emotion.

" Not drooned," said Para Handy ; " he simply passed away."

" Isn't that deplorable ! And whit came over the mate ? "

" His name wass Dougald," said the Captain sadly, " a native of Lochaline, and ass cheery a man as ever you met across a dram. Chust that very mornin' he said to me, ' The 5th of November, Peter ; this hass been a terrible New Year, and the next wan will be on us in a chiffy.' "

By the time the consolatory bottle was finished the loss of the *Vital Spark* had assumed the importance of the loss of the *Royal George*, and the Paisley men suggested that the obvious thing to do was to start a small subscription for the sole survivor.

For a moment the conscience-stricken Captain hesitated. He had scarcely thought his story quite so moving, but a moment of reflection found him quite incapable of recalling what was true and what imaginary of the tale he told them. With seven-and-sixpence in his pocket, wrung by the charm of pure imagination from his fellow-passengers, he arrived in Glasgow and went home.

He went in with a haggard countenance.

" What's the matter wi' ye, Peter ? " asked his wife.

" Desperate news for you, Mery. Desperate news ! The *Vital Spark* is sunk."

" As long's the crew o' her are right that doesna matter," said the plucky little woman.

" Every mortal man o' them drooned except mysel'," said Para Handy, and the tears streaming down his cheeks. " Nothing but her winch above the water. They died like Brutain's hardy sons."

" And what are you doing here ? " said his indignant wife. " As lang as the winch is standin' there ye should be on her. Call yoursel' a sailor and a Hielan'man ! "

For a moment he was staggered.

" Perhaps there's no' a word o' truth in it," he suggested. " Maybe the thing's exaggerated. Anything could happen in such a desperate storm."

" Whether it's exaggerated or no' ye'll go back the night and stick beside the boat. I'll make a cup o' tea and boil an egg for ye. A bonny-like thing for me to go up and tell Dougie's wife her husband's deid and my man snug at home at a tousy tea ! . . . Forbye, they'll maybe salve the boat, and she'll be needin' a captain."

With a train that left the Central some hours later Para Handy returned in great anxiety to Gourock, The tragedy of his imagination was now exceedingly real to him. He took a boat and rowed out to the *Vital Spark*, which he was astonished to see intact at anchor, not a feature of her changed.

Dougie was on deck to receive him.

" Holy smoke, Dougie, iss that yoursel' ? " the Captain asked incredulously. " What way are you keepin' ? "

" Fine," said Dougie. " What way's the mistress ? "

The Captain seized him by the arm and felt it carefully.

" Chust yoursel', Dougie, and nobody else. It's me that's prood to see you. I hope there's nothing wrong wi' your legs? "

" Not a drop," said Dougie.

" And what way's Macphail ? " inquired the Captain anxiously.

" He's in his bed wi' ' Lady Audley,' " said the mate.

" Still deleerious ? " said the Captain with apprehension.

" The duvvle was never anything else," said Dougie.

" Did we lose anything in the storm last night ? " asked Para Handy.

" A jar, and a bucket, and your own sou'-wester," answered Dougie.

" My Chove ! " said Para Handy, much relieved. " Things iss terribly exaggerated up in Gleska."

XVII

FREIGHTS OF FANCY

During several days on which the *Vital Spark* lay idle at Lochgoilhead, the crew spring-cleaned her. " My goodness ! ye wouldna think she would take such a desperate lot o' tar ! " said Para Handy, watching the final strokes of Dougie's brush on the vessel's quarter. There seemed, however, to be as much of the tar on the person and clothing of himself and his shipmates as on the boat.

" Ye're a bonny-lookin' lot ! " said Macphail, the engineer, who never took any part in the painting operations. " If ye just had a tambourine apiece, and could sing ' The Swanee River,' ye would do for Christy Minstrels."

But all the same, in spite of such tar as missed her when they slung it on, the *Vital Spark* looked beautiful and shiny, and the air for half a mile round had the odour of Archangel, where the Russians come from.

With his own good hand, and at his own expense, her proud commander had freshened up her yellow bead and given her funnel a coat of red as gorgeous as a Gourock sunset. He stood on one leg, in a favourite attitude of his when anything appealed to his emotions, and scratched his shin with the heel of his other boot.

" Man ! it's chust a trate to see her lookin' so smert !" he said with admiration. " The sauciest boat in the coastin' tred ! If ye shut wan eye and glance end-on, ye would think she wass the *Grenadier*. Chust you look at the lines of her—that sweet ! I'm tellin' you he wassna slack the man that made her."

Sunny Jim wiped his brow with the cuff of his jacket, and made a new smear on his countenance which left him with a striking resemblance to the White-Eyed Kaffir. His comparatively clean eye twinkled mischievously at Macphail.

" What I say is this," said he ; " there's no' much sense in bein' so fancy wi' a boat that's only gaun to cairry coals and timber inside the Cumbraes. Noo that we're block-aded, do ye no' think, Macphail, she should be cairryin' passengers ? "

" Holy smoke ! " ejaculated Dougie, with genuine surprise. " Ye might chust ass well say that the Admiralty should put some guns on her and send her to the Dardanelles."

Sunny Jim, with his back to the Captain, winked.

" There's maybe something in't," added Dougie hurriedly. " There's boats no better carryin' passengers aal winter, and I'll warrant ye there's money in't."

" It's the chance o' a lifetime ! " broke in the engineer, warming up to the play. " Half the regular steamers will be aff the Clyde for months takin' Gleska breid and the sodgers' washin's to the Bosphorus and thereabouts ; if you have ony say at a' wi' the owners, Peter, you advise them to let oot the *Vital Spark* for trips."

" Trups ! " said Para Handy, beaming. " Man, Jum, ye hit the very thing ! It wass always my ambeetion to get oot o' the common cairryin' tred and be a chentleman. I aalways said a boat like this wass thrown away on coal, and wud, and herrin' ; if she had chust a caibin and a place for sellin' tickets, I wouldna feel ashamed to sail her on the Royal Rowt."

Again his eye swept fondly over her bulging hull, with the tar still wet and glistening on it ; the bright new yellow stripe which made her so coquettish ; the crimson funnel.

" Of course, ye would need a band if ye went in for trips," suggested Macphail in a ruminating way. " Yin o' thae bands that can feenish a' thegither even if they're playin' different tunes, or drap the piccolo oot every noo and then to go roond and lift the pennies."

" Ach ! I wouldna bother wi' a band," said Para Handy. " A band's no use unless ye want to chase the passengers below to take refreshments, and we havena the accommodation. We maybe might get haud o' a kind o' fiddler. I mind when the tippiest boats on the Clyde had chust wan decent fiddler or a poor man wantin' the eyesight, wi' a concerteena. Tip-top ! "

He took a piece of twine from his trousers pocket and measured the standing room between the wheel and the engines ; Sunny Jim was in a transport of delight at a joke which went so smoothly.

" Two and a half," said Para Handy firmly, like a land surveyor. " I think there would be room for a no' too broad-built fiddler, if he didna bate the time wi' his feet. Stop you till we make a calculaation for the passenger accommodation. We'll need to make it cubic."

" There's only forty cubic feet allo'ed for every lodger in

the Garscube Road," said Sunny Jim. "That's the Act
o' Parliament. Ye can easy get the cubic space if ye coont
it longways up in the air, and there's naething to prevent it."

Para Handy stood on one leg again and scratched a shin,
with a look of the profoundest calculation.

"Ye couldna have cabin passengers," suggested Dougie,
snatching up an oil-can of Macphail's and pouring some of
its contents into his hands to clean the tar off.

"There's no' goin' to be no caibin in this boat," said
the Captain quickly. "Short runs and ready money!
Gourock and Dunoon, maybe, and perhaps a Setturday
to Ardentinny. I could get a dozen or two o' nice wee
herrin' firkins doon at Tarbert for passengers to sit on roond
the hatch."

"Do ye no' think it would look droll?" asked Dougie,
a little remorseful to have awakened such ecstatic
visions.

"What way would it be droll?" retorted his Captain
sharply. "I'm thinkin' ye havena much o' a heid for business, Dougie. If you would just consider—a shillin' a heid
to Hunter's Quay——"

"Ye would need a purser," suggested Sunny Jim.

"Allooin' I did!" replied the Captain. "Aal a purser
needs is a pocket-naipkin, a fancy tie, a flooer in his jaicket,
and a pleasant smile. There iss not a man on the Clyde
would make a better purser than yoursel' if ye showed the
right agility. I'm tellin' you there's money in't! The
people 'll chust come in and pay their tickets. Look at the
way they crood doon at the Gleska Fair! We could put
their wee tin boxes in the howld."

"Of course, we would have moonlight cruises," said
Macphail. "It's just found money—no extra cost for the
engineer and crew."

On the prospect of moonlight cruises the Captain pondered
for a moment. "No," he said. "I'm aal for daylight
sailin'; they slip in past ye in the dark withoot a ticket, or

give ye a Golden Text from the Sunday school that looks like the chenuine article, and then where are ye ? Forbye, it's no' that easy to watch a purser on the moonlight cruises ; he would make his fortune."

He looked at his bright new funnel ; imaginatively peopled the narrow deck with summer trippers ; smelled the pervading odour of paint and tar, and glowed all over at the thocht of his beloved vessel taking the quay at Dunoon on a Saturday afternoon with a crowd of the genteelest passengers seated on herring firkins, and a fiddle aft.

" I'll speak my mind aboot it to the owners whenever I get to Gleska ! " he declared emphatically. " It's no' a chance they should let slip. They might could put up a bit o' a deck-house where a body could get a cup o' tea and a penny thing at tuppence."

" And wha would serve the tea, like ? " asked Sunny Jim.

" There's nobody could do it cluverer than yoursel', Jum," said Para Handy. " You would wash your hands and put on a brattie, and every noo and then a chentleman would slup a penny in below his plate for a testimonial."

" That puts the feenish on it then ! " said Sunny Jim, with emphasis. " I jined this ship for a sailorman, and no' to hand roond cookies and lift the tickets."

" And the mate would need to wear a collar," said Dougie. " It's no a thing I fancy at aal, at aal."

" A bonny-like skipper ye would look withoot a bridge to stand on," wound up the engineer. " Besides, ye would need a Board o' Tred certificate."

The Captain's visage fell. His dream dispelled. " Perhaps ye're right," said he. " It would look a little droll. But, man, I aalways had the notion that the *Vital Spark* wass meant for something better than for cairryin' coals."

XVIII

SUMMER-TIME ON THE *VITAL SPARK*

PARA HANDY, on Saturday night, wound up the ship's Kew-tested 2s. 11½d. tin alarm chronometer with more than usual solemnity. It stopped as usual in the process, and he had to restore it to animation, after the customary fashion, by tapping it vigorously on the toe of his boot.

" If it wassna the law o' the land," he remarked, " I would see them at the muschief afore I would be tamperin' wi' the time o' day the way God made it. We'll have to come up the quay to oor beds next Setturday in broad daylight ; there's no consuderation for the sailor's reputaation."

" Science ! " said the mate, with bitterness. " Goodness knows what prank them fellows 'll be up to next ! There wass nothing wrong wi' the time the way it wass, except that it wass aalways slippin' past when ye werena thinkin'."

" There's the nock for ye, Jim," said Para Handy. " Ye'll stay up till two o'clock, and do the needful."

" What'll I stay up for ? " asked Sunny Jim indignantly.
" Ye can shift the handles noo ; it's a' the same."

" But it's no' aal the same ! If you would read the papers instead o' wastin' your time gallivanting, ye would see the Daylight Ack says two o'clock's the oor for shifting nocks. Ye daurna do it a meenute sooner."

Sunny Jim laughed. " Right-o, Captain ! " he agreed. " I'll sit up and dae the shiftin' for ye. You and Dougie better leave me your watches, too ; it'll be a' the yin operation."

" Can ye see the nock, Dougie ? What time iss't by the Daylight Ack ? " the Captain sleepily asked next morning without turning out of his bunk.

The mate unhooked the clock, and incredulously surveyed its face. " Stop you till I get my watch," he said, crawling out of his bunk. "Them German nocks iss not dependable; ye couldna boil an egg wi' them."

A rich resonant snore came from the bunk of Sunny Jim.

"Holy sailor!" exclaimed Dougie, having consulted his watch; "it's half-past ten o'clock! No wonder I wass hungry! That's your science for you!"

"Half-past ten o'clock!" said the Captain. "And chust you listen at the way that fellow iss snorin'! Up this meenute, Jum, and make the breakfast!"

It was with difficulty Sunny Jim was wakened, and then he proved of the most mutinous temper. "Ye can mak' your breakfast for yoursel's!" he protested. "If I'm to sit up till twa o'clock in the mornin' to shift the time, I'm no' gaun to rise till my sleep's made up."

Two seconds later he was snoring more resonantly than ever, in syncopated time with MacPahil, the engineer, who had volunteered to sit up till two o'clock with him, and who had a snore of an intermittent gurgling character like one of his own steam pipes.

Between them the Captain and the mate made breakfast. A blissful Sabbath calm was on loch and land when Para Handy put his head up through the hatch. The *Vital Spark* was bumping softly against her fenders at a deserted quay; the smoke of morning fires was rising in the village. The tide was ebbing, but not yet far from full.

"I didna think they could do't," said the Captain.

"Do what?" asked Dougie, finishing off the last of the marmalade.

"The tide," said Para Handy; "it's no' near where it wass at this time yesterday. It's shifted too."

"Chust what I told ye—science! The ruffians 'll do anything! Do you no' think, Peter, we'll get punished some day for all this schemin' and contrivance? Chust the work of unfidels! What way iss a man to ken noo whether it's Setturday night or Sunday morning? Many a wan 'll go wrong at twelve o'clock on the Setturday night and start whistling. Noo that they're starting takin' liberties wi' clocks and tides, ye'll see they'll cairry it further and play havoc wi' the almanacs. If they can rob us o' an oor they can steal a fortnight."

"Chust that!" agreed the Captain. "I could spare them a day or two at the Whitsunday term; that's the sort o' thing they should abolish." He sighed. "Indeed, it's a solemn thing, Dougie, to see the way they're flyin' aal round to new human devices; do ye no' think me and you should go to the church this morning?"

"Whatever you say yoursel'," said Dougie.

The bell was ringing as they went up the street, and had ceased when they reached the church. No other worshippers were visible.

"This place needs a great upliftin'," said Para Handy piously. "On a day like this, with the things of time upset and shifted, ye would think they would be croodin' in to hear Mr M'Queen. Have ye any losengers?"

"Not wan!" said Dougie, "but maybe he'll no' be long."

The beadle was shutting the door of the church as they approached to enter. "Where are ye goin'?" he asked, with a curious look at them.

"Where would we be goin' but to hear my good frien', John M'Queen," said the Captain fervently.

"Then ye'll better come back at half-past eleven," said the beadle dryly. "This is no' the place for you at all; it's the Sunday school."

"Holy sailors!" exclaimed the Captain; "what o'clock iss't?"

"Exactly half-past nine by the summer time," said the beadle, "but it's only half-past eight by naiture."

The Captain looked at Dougie. "Aren't we," said he, "the fools to be leavin' nocks and watches to fellows like Sunny Jim and Macphail! The tricky duvvles! There's no' an inch o' a chentleman between them. It's no' wan oor but three they put us forrit, and they're still snore-snoring yonder!"

XIX

EGGS UNCONTROLLED

SUNNY JIM, with his sleeves rolled up, a sweat-rag stuck in the waistband of his trousers, and his face much streaked with soot, clapped down a bowl of eggs before the Captain, rinsed his hands in a pail of water, dried them on his waist-coat, and sat down on the edge of his bunk to enjoy his breakfast.

A gloomy silence fell upon the crew when they saw the eggs. They were just plain ordinary eggs of oval shape, and no more soiled on the shells than usual, but their presence seemed momentous. Para Handy looked at them like one entranced; Dougie put a finger out and touched them gingerly; Macphail withdrew his incredulous gaze from them with a muttered exclamation, and starting furiously spreading bread with marmalade.

" Iss that eggs ? " said the Captain, like one who was uncertain whether they were eggs or curling-stones.

" Oh no ! Not at all ! " cried Macphail, with bitter irony ; " it's the best Devonshire bacon, fried kidneys, kippered herring, finnan haddies, omelets, pork sausages. Jim would never shove us off wi' eggs ! "

" They're duvelish like eggs ! " said Dougie lugubriously. " I never saw a better imitation. The look o' them fairly makes me grue."

" What way's the wind, Jum ? " said Para Handy mildly. " I don't feel the smell o' ham. Hurry you up, like a good laad, and bring us doon a wise-like breakfast."

" That's a' the breakfast that's gaun," said Sunny Jim. " There's no a bit o' ham in Tarbert."

" But, bless my he'rt ! there's many another thing than ham a body could enjoy ! " said Para Handy. " There's things like—fush, and—sausages, and—fush, that a man could eat wi' some diversion. You're awfu' nerrow, Jum !

ou havena no variety. Even-on it's eggs wi' you ; you avena had a thing but eggs since we left Bowling."

"Tak' them or leave them !" said the cook ; "the day 'll ome ye'll be gled to get them. I'm no' a Grand Hotel nor Italian Warehouse ; I can only gie ye what I can get, d there's dashed all left to eat in Tarbert since the Fair, less it's rhubarb."

The Captain chipped an egg with no enthusiasm. "Good- ss knows," said he, "what this country would come to ithoot the hens ! Everybody in the land is eatin' eggs— gs—eggs ! Half the year there's nothing in the morning r ye but an egg. What, in aal the world, iss in an egg ?"

"That's what I'm aye wonderin' when I start yin," said e engineer.

"There's nothing patent in an egg ; it's chust a thing ye ould expect from hens. If it wassna for the salt, ye might s weel be eatin' blot-sheet. Did ye ever see any dufference tween wan egg and another ?"

"Some o' them's bigger," suggested Dougie, scooping out s own, apparently without much interest in the contents.

"That's the thing that angers me aboot an egg !" con- nued the Captain. "It never makes ye gled to see it on e table ; ye know at wance the thing's a mere put-by cause your wife or Jum could not be bothered makin' mething tasty."

"We'll hae to get the hens to put their heids thegither, d invent a new kind o' fancy egg for sailors," said Sunny m, consuming his with ostentatious relish. "Ye can say hit ye like—there's naething bates a country egg ; and I n tell ye this, the lot o' ye, it's eggs ye're gaun to get for nner tae ; there's no a bit o' butcher meat in Tarbert !"

"Holy smoke !" exclaimed the Captain. "Eggs for nner ! Not a morsel more will I be eating ; you have oiled my breakfast on me !"

The *Vital Spark* had her coals discharged by noon, and the

M

Captain went ashore to a public-house for a change of diet
The very idea of eggs again for dinner was repugnant to him
and several schooners of beer intensified his inward feelings o
revolt against monotony of cuisine. There came into the bar
a man he thought he knew; he said, " Hallo, Macdougall!'
to him; " hoo's the fishin' ? " and they had a glass together

" What way's hersel'—the mustress keepin' ? " Para
Handy asked. " I hope she's splendid ? "

" She's no bad at aal," said the other, with a little
hesitation.

" Tell her I was askin' kindly for her health. I'm fine
mysel'. Yon's a nice bit hoose ye have, Johnny; it's
very creditable to aal concerned."

" It's no' that bad at aal ! " replied the other, thinking for
a moment. " What way do ye no' come up some night and
see us ? "

" Nobody would be better pleased ! " said Para Handy
" Iss your mother-in-law still wi' ye ? "

" Aye, she's yonder yet, but ach ! ye needna mind for her
come up some night, and have your supper. . . . Bring the
boys ! " Macdougall added with effusive hospitality. So far
he had not suggested another drink.

" If I go up, I'll better go mysel' ; there's four of us on
board," said Para Handy.

" Bring them all ! This very night at seven o'clock, and
I assure you, you'll have supper."

" Hoots ! That would be puttin' the wife to bother,'
said the Captain, with polite solicitude. " We would chust
be goin' to have a crack."

" Ye'll have a crack, and ye'll have your supper too ! '
said Macdougall firmly. " Mind and bring the boys ! Sharp
at seven, mind, and take your music."

The Captain hurried on board his vessel, watched his crew
disgustedly eat eggs, which he professed disdain for, and
when they had finished, told them of his invitation.

" Ye micht hae tell't us sooner ! " said Macphail, with genuine vexation. " There's a supper spoiled ! "

" A capital cook, Mrs Macdougall !—namely, in the place for cooking," callously said Para Handy. " I'm chust in trum mysel' for something else than eggs."

They dressed in their Sunday clothes, and went up at night to the house of John Macdougall.

" He's not at home, he's at the fishin' ! " said a lady whom the Captain shook warmly by the hand, and addressed as Katrin.

" I met him in the toon at twelve the day, and he asked us to be sure and come to supper," said the Captain, much surprised.

" What was he like ? " said she, with some amusement.

" A burly wise-like man, wi' a tartan kep ; I ken him fine ! "

She laughed ; she was a cheerful body. " That's no' my man at all, Captain," said she ; " but I'll tell ye who it was —his brother Peter ; they're as like as peas ! "

" Isn't this the bonny caper ! " said Dougie, with distress. They stood like sheep.

" It's no' the first time Peter played that trick," said the woman ; " he's a rascal ! If he had a house and a wife of his own, I would just advise ye to go up, and take him at his word, but seein' ye're here, ye'll just come in and have your supper."

They went in, with mingled hope and diffidence, and she boiled them eggs !

<h2 style="text-align:center">XX</h2>

<h2 style="text-align:center">COMMANDEERED</h2>

" STOP you ! We'll have a fine pant oot of Dougie ; he's ass timid ass a mountain hare," said Para Handy in the absence of his mate, who was ashore on one of the missions the crew of the *Vital Spark* entirely disapproved of—to buy some special and exclusive " kitchen " for his tea. He had an unpleasantly ostentatious way of eating ham or kippered herrings when the rest had nothing more piquant or interesting than jam.

As a consequence of some deliberation and rehearsal, when Dougie came back to the boat with his parcel he found an unusual bustle at an hour when, waiting for the tide to get her off at flood, the crew of the *Vital Spark* were apt to be yawning their heads off. The Captain was peeling his guernsey off, preparatory to washing himself—a proceeding in itself unusual enough to be surprising. Macphail, the engineer, was studying a map of the North Sea cut from some recent newspaper, and flourishing a one-legged compass. Sunny Jim was oiling the parts of a telescope he had won once in a raffle.

Such signs of unaccustomed activity could not but impress Dougie. " What's wrong wi' ye ? " he asked ; " ye're duvelish busy ! "

" We'll be busier yet before we're done ! " said the Captain, gravely and mysteriously, and turned his back to look over the shoulder of Macphail at the North Sea map. " Did ye find the place, Macphail ? " he asked anxiously.

" Ay ! " said the engineer. " It's just aboot whaur I said it was—a dangerous place, fair hotchin' full o' mines."

" Chust that ! " said Para Handy. " It's chust what I wass thinkin' to myself. Well, well ; we canna help it when the King and country caals. I'm only vexed aboot the boat." He stifled a sigh, bent over the enamelled basin, and hurriedly damped himself : it must be admitted the afternoon was cold.

" There's no' even the chance o' a medal on the job," said Sunny Jim. " That's what gives me the needle ! "

They behaved as if Dougie with his irritating groceries had no existence. He determined to show no curiosity.

" It might be sweepin' mines they mean," said Para

Handy in a little, drying his face. " Whatever it iss, it iss goin' to be a time of trial."

" It's me that's gled I can swim," said Sunny Jim. " The very first bang, and aff goes my galoshes ! It's no' sae bad for me, as if I had a wife and family."

Dougie pricked his ears.

" It's no' sweepin' mines," said the engineer emphatically. " If it was to sweep mines they wanted us they would put steel plates roond the bows and leave her light ; there wouldna be any sense in stuffin' her hold wi' cement and stones. Tak' you my word for it—she's gaun to jam the Kiel Canal. It's a risky job we're on, I'll warrant ye ! "

" I wouldna care so much if it wasna for my aunty," said Sunny Jim in a doleful accent, with a wink to the engineer. " I aye made up her rent. Perhaps it's to cairry troops we're needed."

" Not at aal ! " said Para Handy. " Where would ye put troops on the *Vital Spark*, and her hold filled up wi' causey and cement ? "

Dougie's curiosity could no further be restrained. " What in aal the earth are ye palaverin' at ? " he asked impatiently, and with some forebodings.

" I'm sorry to tell ye that, Dougald," said the Captain feelingly, " for it's a serious, serious business for us aal ; the boat is commandeered. I have a kind o' letter here from the Admirality"—he produced it with a flourish from his trousers pocket. " Chust a line in their usual way :—' Report at Renfrew ; get an extra dummy funnel and some wuden guns ; fill up wi' causey and cement, and take the North Sea for it. To Captain Peter C. Macfarlane.' "

" ' Peter C. Macfarlane,' " Dougie said surprised. " I never heard o' the ' C ' before ; where did ye get the title ? "

" They must have kent my mother was a Cameron," said Para Handy ; " and they're always for the stylish thing in the Admirality. Never you mind aboot the title, Dougald ;

have ye an extra shirt or two and a pair o' mittens ?   Ye'll
need them yonder."

" Where ? " asked the mate, alarmed.

" In the North Sea. Amnt' I tellin' ye we're commandeered ! "

" I'll see them to the muschief first ! " said Dougie warmly.
" If I'm to do the British Navy's work, it's no' in a cockle-
shell ! "   But his heart was in his boots.

For once his meal had no attractions for him, and the others,
for the first time, shared his private ham with surprising
appetite and relish, considering the tragic possibilities they
discussed.   So perfectly did they sustain their parts as
previously arranged among them that it never occurred to
him to doubt the story.

" Of course, ye'll break the news to your mustress the
best way that ye can," said the Captain, spreading jam on the
bread with a soup spoon ; " ye needna put the worst face
on the job ; chust say it's an East Coast cargo, and ye'll
send a postcaird home. I hope and trust ye kept up your
insurance ! "

" Of course, there's aye a chance they micht take us
prisoners," said Sunny Jim. " That wouldna be sae
bad."

" I ken a man that's no' goin'," said Dougie with profound conviction.

" There's nane o' us can get oot o't," said the engineer,
finishing the last of the ham in an absent-minded way. " I
think your letter makes that quite plain, Peter ? "

" It does that," said Para Handy, having scrutinised the
document again, and shoved it under his plate for further
reference if necessary. Dougie eyed it slyly, unobserved.

" The dashed thing is there's no' a uniform," said Sunny
Jim. " I wouldna mind sae much if we wore a blue pea-
jaicket wi' brass buttons, and the name o' the boat on oor
keps ; if I'm to be drooned for my country I would like to
be a wee bit tasty."

" There's a man I ken, and he's no' goin', whatever o't ! "
again said Dougie firmly.

The Captain had another inspiration. " Of course," said
he, " they're goin' to change the name o' the boat. There's
a cruiser caaled the *Vital Spark*, and if we were sunk it
would make confusion. The Chermans would be sayin' we
were the big one."

" There's one thing I can tell ye, and it's this—the man
that iss not goin' on this ploy iss me ! " said Dougie, and
slapped his knee.

" Toots, man ! ye shouldna be so tumid ! " said Para
Handy ; " Brutain's hardy sons ! "

The rule of the vessel was that a man who indulged in
extras to his tea had to wash the dishes, and Dougie was
left behind when the others went on deck. He lost no time
in reading the document the Captain had forgetfully left
below his plate, and a great illumination came to him when
he found it was nothing more than a second and final notice
demanding the Captain's poor-rates.

" My goodness ! wass there ever such a lot o' liars ? "
said their victim. " Spoiled my tea on me ! Stop you ! "

By and by he went up on deck, and found his shipmates
solemnly discussing the purpose of the dummy funnel and
the wooden guns.

" It's to draw their torpedo fire," the engineer suggested.
" When they're bangin' awa' at us the cruiser 'll slip bye."

" And then it's domino wi' us ! " said Sunny Jim lugubriously.

" There's wan thing I can say," said Para Handy unctuously,
" and it's this—that my affairs is aal in the best condeetion ;
quite complete. There's no' a penny that I'm owin'."

" Except your poor-rates," broke in Dougie, witheringly.
" There's your letter from the Admirality. It's in Berlin
the whole o' ye should be, and writin' Cherman telegrams."

XXI

SUNNY JIM REJECTED

WHEN tea was finished, Sunny Jim put on his Sunday clothes, turned up the foot of his trousers, oiled his boots, put his cap on carefully, with a saucy tilt to it, and then spent several minutes violently brushing what was left below it of his hair. Thus only could his curl be coaxed into that tasty wave above the forehead, and complete his fatal beauty for the girls.

" Capital ! " said Para Handy. " Never saw ye nicer, Jum ; chust a regular Napoleon ! Don't you shift another hair, or ye'll spoil yersel' ! "

" The only other thing I could recommend," said Macphail, " is to put some soap and water on a brush and gie a flourish aboot the ears."

Sunny Jim paid no attention. From the small tin box that held his dunnage he produced his mouth harmonium and a tin of Glasgow toffee, which he stowed in his jacket pockets.

" My goodness ! " said Dougie, the mate, " it's a desperate thing this love ; there's such expense in it ! There's a six-pence away on sweeties for another fellow's dochter ! "

" Of course, we'll have a bite o' something ready for ye, Jum, when ye come back," remarked the Captain with magnificent sarcasm. " Dougie 'll sit up. Will a bit of cold roast chucken do, or would ye like an omelet ? "

" Best respects to 'Liza," said the engineer rudely. " I think it's specs she's needin' if you're her fancy."

Sunny Jim calmly lighted a cigarette and buttoned up his jacket. " So long, chaps ! " he said. " It's a pity ye're a' that old ! Just a lot o' bloomin' fossils from the Fossil Grove, Whiteinch. Mak' yoursel's some gruel in a while, and awa' to your beds."

He was back to the *Vital Spark* in less than an hour in an obviously agitated state of mind.

" Bless me ! " said Para Handy, starting up ; " iss it that

time o' night ?   The way time has o' slippin' past when ye're a fossil !   Set you the table, Dougie, and put oot a chucken for his lordship.   Maybe ye would like a drop o' something, Jum ?   To start wi', like.   What way iss 'Liza keepin' in her health ?   My chove !   But yon's the beautious gyurl ! "

" Shut up ! " said Sunny Jim disgustedly.   " I'm done wi' her, onywey !   I wouldna trust a woman like yon the length that I could throw her ! "

" That's no far," said Macphail reflectively.   " Sixteen stone, if she's an ounce.   Tell me this—is she wearin' specs at last ? "

" It would need to be some sort o' specs she was wearin' to see onything in yon chap o' Mackay's she's awa' for a walk wi," said Sunny Jim with feeling.   " Naething at a' to recommend him but a kilt and a hack on his heel ! "

Dougie, who never lost his head even in the most exciting circumstances, asked the despondent lover abruptly if he had brought the tin of toffee back.   In a moment of aberration Sunny Jim produced it, and put it down on the top of a barrel, and it sped so quickly round them several times that when his turn came there were only two sticky bits left in the bottom.   He sucked them like one for whom toffee had no greater taste than gas-work cinders.   Such is the effect of unrequited love.

He was too profoundly grieved to be reticent.   " I had a tryst wi' her, right enough, chaps.   Eight o'clock, she said, at the factor's corner, and just at that very meenute she went sailin' past wi' Dan Mackay, that's hame frae the Territorials at Dunoon, lettin' on he's wounded, and a' the time, I'll bate ye, it's only a hack on his heel.

" ' It's eight o'clock, 'Liza,' says I, and gied her the wink.

" ' Fancy that ! ' says she, as nippy's onything.   ' But ye've loads o' time ; they're signin' on recruits in the armoury up till ten.   Did ye hear aboot the war ? ' says she afore I could get my breath.   ' It's fairly ragin' !   Corporal Mackay's gaun oot to the front as soon as his feet get better.'

M*

"And aff she went wi' Mackay, and left me standin' like a dummy! Yon's no gentleman! He hadna a word to say for himsel'. Naething to tak' the eye aboot him but a kilt and a hack on his heel!"

"Holy smoke!" said Para Handy sympathetically. "Isn't that the desperate pity? There's nothing noo in the heids o' the gyurls but sodgers. But ye canna blame the craturs! There's something smert aboot the kilt and the cockit bonnet."

"If I wassna one o' them old fossils from Whiteinch," remarked Dougie, with rancorous deliberation, "it wouldna be the like o' 'Liza Cameron, the tyler's dochter, could cast up to me a war wass ragin' and go off wi' another man—aye, even if he had a hack on every heel inside his boots."

Sunny Jim was distressed almost to the verge of tears. "I'm fair sick o' this!" said he. "I'm gaun to 'list! Every quay this boat comes in to somebody's shair to chip in something aboot my age and me no' bein' married, and whitna regiment I'm gaun to. The last trip we cam' up Loch Fyne I got as mony feathers as would stuff a bolster."

"I wass aye wonderin' what for so many feathers got into the porridge," said Dougie. "Did I no' say to the Captain yesterday, 'I'm fond o' porridge and I'm fond o' chicken, but I never cared to get them both mixed'?"

"Mind ye, it's no' that I'm feared to 'list," said Sunny Jim. "I never seen a German yet I couldna knock the napper aff, and it couldna be worse in the trenches than in the howld o' this old vessel shovellin' coal. But I'm feared they wouldna tak' me for a recruit——"

"If it's the bowly legs ye're thinkin' o'," said Macphail, "that's no ony obstacle; ye're just the very make o' a horse marine."

Para Handy measured the disconsolate lover with a calculating eye. "I doot," says he, "Jum hassna got the length for a horse marine unless they put him through a mangle first. The regiment for you, Jum, is the Bantams."

"I doot they wouldna pass me," said Sunny Jim. "But

to show that woman I'm game enough, although I'm no' bloodthirsty, I'll go up this very meenute and put in my name."

"You be fly and stand on your tiptoes!" Macphail cried after him as he climbed up on the quay from the vessel's rail.

He came back in half an hour a little more disconsolate than ever. "I tell't ye!" said he, "they wouldna sign me on," and stood with his back close to a glowing stove.

"No wonder," said the engineer. "Warpin' your legs still worse wi' standin' against the fire! Did I no' tell ye to get on the tips o' your taes?"

"You're a disgrace to the boat," said Para Handy, with genuine vexation. "I'm black affronted! If Dougald and me wass a trifle younger, it's no' wi' troosers on we would be puttin' past the time. Just bringin' a bad name on the boat —that's what ye are! What way would they no' take ye?"

"Just look at the legs o' him!" said the engineer, as if they made the question quite ridiculous.

"It would likely be his character," suggested Dougie sadly. "They're duvelish parteecular noo aboot the character; it's no like the old milishia."

"It's no' my legs at a'; there's naething wrang wi' my legs," said the disappointed candidate. "And they never asked aboot my character. But I kent fine a' alang they wouldna tak' me."

"What for?" asked Para Handy. "Ye have all your faculties aboot ye, and ye're in your prime."

"It was this e'e o' mine," explained Sunny Jim, and indicated his dexter optic, which had always a singularly stern expression even in his amorous hours.

"That wan?" exclaimed the Captain. "That's the best o' the pair, to my opeenion, it's aye that steady. What's wrong wi't?"

"It's gless," said Sunny Jim, blushing; "they found it oot at the first go-aff."

" Holy frost ! " said Para Handy. " Five years in this boat wi' us, and we never kent it. Did I no' think ye were chust plain skeely ! "

XXII

HOW JIM JOINED THE ARMY

" Jumpin' Jehosophat ! " said Para Handy. " Here's Macphail. I doot they havena lifted him."

Dougie's visage fell. He had been confident that the want of an engineer would keep them idle in Tarbert for at least a week. " Isn't that the trash ! " he said lugubriously. " Ye never could put dependence on him. Look you, has he any badge in his coat lapel ? He iss chust the man would let on a enchineer on the *Vital Spark* was a special tred. Ye canna be up to the quirks o' him."

" There is nothing on his coat lapel that I can see but a patch o' egg," said Para Handy, " and he had that when he started to go to Stirling. Ye'll see we'll no' get rid o' Macphail so easy ; they're gettin' gey parteecular in the airmy, and he never could keep the step."

" Oh, man ! if I had jist the ither eye ! " said Sunny Jim in a passionate outburst of yearning.

Macphail came down to the quay with the biscuit tin which fulfilled the function of a suit-case when he travelled. His gait was most dejected, and his general air of infestivity was accentuated by the fact that he wore his Sunday clothes and a hat that, having been picked up casually some years before at the close of a ball in Crarae, had never fitted.

" See's your canister in case ye break the bottle," suggested the Captain politely as his engineer stood on the edge of the quay and prepared to jump on board.

" We werena expectin' to see ye again withoot your kilt," said Dougie maliciously. Macphail's anatomical defects had been considered to render kilts so absurdly out of the question that his shipmates always insisted General Haig would instantly pick him for the Gordons.

Without a word the engineer sat down on his biscuit tin and burst into tears.

" Man, Macphail, I'm wonderin' at ye ! " exclaimed the Captain. " Your system's chust run doon wi' travellin' ; a little drop o' Brutish spurrits—have ye much left in the canister ? "

" Stand back and gie the chap breath ! " implored Sunny Jim. " I'll bate a pound they found there was something wrang wi' him internal. I wouldna bother, Mac, if it's checked in time ye'll maybe linger on for years."

" Tach ! " said Para Handy sympathetically. " I wouldna heed them doctors, Mac ; it's only guess-work wi' them. But to tell ye the truth I didna like yon chrechlin' cough ye had since ye went afore the Tribunal. The only hope I had wass ye were puttin' 't on. If I had chust a wee small drop of spurrits wi' some sugar in't—will ye no' sit on this bucket ? —a canister iss cold."

" Ye may be glad they wouldna take ye ! " said Dougie consolingly. " Even if it wass only for the sake o' yer wife and pickle children."

" That's the dashed thing ! " sobbed Macphail shamelessly ; " they're takin' me richt enough. I've passed the doctors at Stirling, and I have a ticket here to jine a regiment to-morrow at Fort Matilda."

" Oh, michty ! " exclaimed Sunny Jim with envy. " Whit regiment ? "

" I canna mind its name," said the engineer, drying his eyes with a piece of waste ; " but it starts wi' an F, and I'm to be a private. And me !—I don't ken the least wee thing aboot the way to be a private ! I was bred an engineer."

In proof of these lamentable tidings he produced an official document which declared he was physically fit in every respect, and a card with which to present himself to the office for recruits.

"Man alive! Did ye no cough at them?" asked Para Handy. "Yon chrechlin' cough wass chust a masterpiece."

"Cough!" exclaimed Macphail. "I coughed till ye would think it was the Cloch on a foggy night, but yon chaps never heeded. They put a tape aboot my chest, and chapped me between the shoulders, and listened could they hear my circulation. I was stripped stark naked——"

"My chove! issn't that chust desperate!" said the Captain, horrified.

"I don't care!" cried Macphail in an excess of indignation. "I'm no gaun to go, and that's a' aboot it!" He incautiously rose from his seat and stamped the deck.

"Wi' a little wee drop sugar in't, there's nothing better for a cough," said the Captain, hurriedly opening the biscuit tin. He looked disappointed. "Tach!" he said. "There's only an empty gill bottle and wan other garment. That iss not the way a chentleman would be travellin' from Stirling."

"See here!" said Sunny Jim with some eagerness. "Did they tak' your photograph?"

"No," said the melancholy engineer.

"Then gie me your tickets and I'll go to Fort Matilda in the name o' Dan Macphail. They'll never ken the difference. If it wasna this e'e o' mine was gless, I would hae listed a year ago. I've tried, and I've better tried to jine, but they'll no let ye jine wi' a glessy yin unless ye have lots o' influence."

"Ye canna hide that eye on them; it looks that flippant!" said the Captain incredulously.

Macphail hurriedly handed over his documents lest any debate should diminish the young man's ardour.

"They canna go back on the doctor's line!" said Sunny Jim. "It says here Dan Macphail is medically fit—that's me, and I'm faur better value for the British Airmy wi' my glessy than Macphail would be wi' a full set o' een and his Sunday specs and his he'rt no' in it. It's the chance o' my life!"

" I wash my hands of it ! " said Dougie, who had not yet recovered from his disappointment at the engineer's return. " It is against the Defence o' the Realm to pass gless eyes on the British Airmy, and ye'll get this boat in trouble."

" I jist have time to catch the boat for Greenock," said Sunny Jim. He put the documents in his pocket, buttoned his jacket, and climbed ashore.

XXIII

THE FUSILIER

THREE weeks after Sunny Jim stole into the Scottish Fusiliers under false pretences with the name and papers of Macphail, the engineer, and a glass eye he had previously made a dozen vain attempts to foist on recruiting officers as the natural article, he turned up in his uniform on the *Vital Spark*. He carried himself so erect that he had a rake aft like a steamer's funnel, his chest preceding him by about nine inches, and his glengarry bonnet cocked on three hairs. Every button glinted.

" Jumpin' Jehosophat ! " exclaimed the Captain. " It's on you they've made the dufference ! Wi' a step like that ye would make a toppin' piper. Ye're far more copious aboot the body than ye were."

" Broader in every direction ! " said Dougie, with genuine admiration. " By the time they're done wi' ye, ye'll be a fair Goliath."

Macphail looked sourly on his substitute, but even he could not restrain surprise. " I take the credit," said he, " for the makin' o' ye ; if it wasna for my testimonials ye wouldna be in the airmy yet."

Sunny Jim saluted his old shipmates with a rapid movement that threw his bonnet on to two hairs and an eyebrow, then cut away the right hand smartly.

" Cheer up, chaps ! " he said ; " the war's near by ;

I'm gaun oot wi' the very next draft to put the feenisher on it."

" Did they no' say nothin' aboot your eye ? " asked Para Handy, intently regarding that notorious organ.

" Oh, they just passed the remark that it was a fair bummer for the shootin'-ranges, seein' I wouldna need to shut it," said Sunny Jim. " But we had a kind o' a pant wi't the first day I was on parade. I was daein' the Swedish exercise, and sweatin' that much the glessy yin near slipped oot. I put up my hand to kep it, and the sergeant-major says, ' Whit's wrang wi' your eye, Macphail ? '

" ' There's something in it,' says I.

" ' Then fall to the rear three paces and tak' it oot,' says he, ' and no' mak' a bloomin' demonstration o' the squad ; the folk that's lookin' on'll think ye're greetin'.'

" I took it oot and slips it into my pocket, and when I steps into the ranks again the sergeant-major nearly fainted.

" ' Gless ! ' said he, when I explained it was a fancy yin. ' Man, it's no' a sodger you should be, but a war correspondent ; ye have half the full equipment for the job ! ' "

" And whit kind o' a situation hae ye ? " asked Macphail.

" Oh, I'm a cook," said Sunny Jim. " It's really a chef's job, for ye hae to be parteecular."

" Oh, my goodness ! " cried Macphail. " The Scottish Fusiliers is gaun to suffer."

" No fears ! " said Sunny Jim ; " cookin' in a camp is no' like cookin' in a coal-boat ; it's no' a pound o' boiled beef ham and a quarter loaf that's yonder ; the place is fair infested wi' the best o' butcher meat."

" Still and on it must be a hard life, James," suggested Para Handy. " Everything by word o' command, and no time for to pause and to consuder."

" It's a gentleman's life," declared the young recruit. " Naething hard aboot it, except that ye have to keep your teeth brushed. I don't think I could think o' goin' back to follow the sea when the war's past ; sodgerin' puts ye aff the notion o' a sedimentary life. I'm thinkin' o' gaun in for bein' a major; the best yins does it, and ye get a horse."

They gave the ambitious son of Mars a cup of tea, and two boiled eggs to it; he politely disposed of them, though it was evident such fare was rather homely for a chef. His new fastidiousness only came out when he asked for a saucer; he forgot that the only one on board was used for the engineer's black soap.

" The only thing that's wrang wi' the Fusiliers is that they spoil ye," he explained apologetically. " Every other day there's a duff."

" Whit like iss the other chentlemen in the business wi' ye? " inquired Dougie.

" The very best! " said Sunny Jim, with enthusiasm. " It's yonder ye meet wi' genteel society; regular gentlemen, tip-top toffs right enough. The chap that's lyin' next to me in the hut's in a capital business o' his ain aboot Dalry; I think it's linen drapery, for every sleeve he has is filled to the brim wi' hankies."

" Jehosophat! " said Para Handy. " Dougie will boil another egg for ye this meenute."

" I hope," said Macphail, " that ye'll no' mak' a Ned o' yoursel' in ony way in the airmy, seein' ye're there in the name o' Dan Macphail. The Macphails was aye respectable, and I wouldna care to have my reputation spiled."

Dougie laughed derisively. " The Macphails! " he exclaimed. " Everybody kens they came from Ireland—Fenians and Sinn Feiners."

" Your reputation," said Sunny Jim indignantly. " Ye're aye takin' oot your reputation and polishin' it up the same's it was a trombone or a cornet; no' much o' a reputation, and ye needna bother. To tell ye the truth, I found your reputation was the worst thing I could tak' wi' me to the Fusiliers. By George, they had your history in their books! "

" It's a lie! " shouted the engineer, reddening.

" It's as true as I'm tellin' ye! I wasna jined a week

when I went to my officer and tellt him straight I wasna
Macphail at a' ; and wasna gaun to stand the brunt o' bein'
Dan Macphail. For the recruitin' officer had Dan Macphail
doon in his books for a married man wi' five o' a family, and
they were gaun to tak' so much aff my pay every week for
your wife's allooance ! "

XXIV

PARA HANDY, M.D.

THE rain came down on Tarbert in a torrent. Dougie, while
the cards were being shuffled and dealt again, put his head
out by the scuttle, and looked up the deserted quay at the
blurred lights of the village.

" What in the wide world are ye doin' there ? " querulously
demanded Para Handy. " If ye keep that scuttle open any
longer we'll be swamped !   Come in and take your hand ; it's
no' ke-hoi we're playin'."

" It's a desperate night," said Dougie, shivering in an
atmosphere that, now the hatch was closed, was stuffier than
that of an oven. " Rain even-on ; ass black ass the Earl o'
Mansfield's waistcoat, and nothin' stirrin' in the place but
the smell o' frying herrin'."

" Herrin' ! " exclaimed the Captain, starting to his feet,
and slamming down his cards. " That puts me in mind I
wass to caal the night on Eddie Macvean, the carter. I
clean forgot !   I'm sorry to leave ye, laads, but ye'll get your
revenge to-morrow, maybe."

A minute later, and he was off the *Vital Spark*, with two
and ninepence in his pocket, the total amount of gambling
currency on the boat, not counting Dougie's lucky sixpence.

It was discovered by his shipmates, left behind, that the
cards he had abandoned were " rags " without exception.

.   .   .   .

Macvean was apparently alone in his house when the

Captain entered, sitting quite disconsolately by his fire, smoking.

" I wass up the toon for a message, Eddie," explained the visitor, " and I thocht I would gie ye a roar in the passin'. What way are ye keepin', this weather ? "

" I canna compleen," replied the carter in a doleful tone, as if he bitterly regretted his obviously robust condition of health. " Are ye fine yoursel' ? "

" What way iss the mustress ? " politely continued the Captain. " I hope she's keepin' muddlin' weel."

Eddie Macvean sighed profoundly. " That's the trouble in this hoose," he remarked ; " there's no come and go in her. She's that dour ! I got the finest offer o' a wee coal business in Lochgilphead, but she's that taken up wi' Tarbert for gaiety and the like, she'll no' hear tell o' flittin'."

" Chust that ! " commented Para Handy sympathetically. " Did ye no' try coaxin' her ? "

" It's no' the poker I would try wi' Liza Walker, you may be sure, Peter ! I have been throng coaxin' her aal this week wi' that much patience ye would think I wass coortin', but she'll no budge ! She says if I'm goin' to take her to Lochgilphead, it'll be in her coffin. Nothin' for her but gaiety ! It's them Young Women's Guilds that's leadin' them off their feet ! "

" Iss she oot at the Guild the night ? " inquired the Captain, with a well-simulated air of regret at the lady's absence.

" No," said the husband sadly, " she's away to her bed wi' a tirravee of a temper."

There was a loud banging on the wall which divided the room of Macvean's house from the kitchen ; he darted next door with significant alacrity, and was gone ten minutes.

" I canna make her oot at aal, at aal ! " he remarked on returning. " She's tellin' me where I'll get clean stockin's for mysel', and to send oot a pair o' sheets she has in the bottom of the kist for manglin'."

" Iss she angry ? " inquired Para Handy.

" That's the duvelish thing aboot her noo," replied the distracted husband. " She's quite composed, and caalin' me Edward. She says I wass a good man to her nearly aal the time we were together."

" God bless me ! " exclaimed Para Handy, staggered. " Ye should get the doctor. Never let the like o' that go too far ! It might be something inward ! "

There was another banging on the wall ; Macvean went out again, and came back more confounded than ever.

" I never saw Liza in my life like that before ! " he said. " She says she's quite resigned, and the only account against her iss a gallon of paraffin oil she got last Tuesday in the merchant's. I think she's kind o' dazed. She's wantin' a drink o' water."

" If I was you, Eddie, I would get the doctor," advised the Captain firmly. " Ye would be vexed if anything happened to her, and she died on ye in weather like this."

The carter returned from his wife's bedside with the empty cup and a look of greater anxiety.

" She says there's nothing wrong wi' her ; no pain nor nothing, except that when she dovers over she dreams she's in Lochgilphead poorhouse, and wakens wi' a start. Her voice is aal away to a whisper. When I spoke aboot the doctor she said I wassna to let him in the door ass long ass she had aal her faculties. I'm to gie ye her best respects, and tell ye her faith wass aye in the Protestant releegion. ' Tell Captain Macfarlane,' she says, ' to be a sober man, and be good to his family.' "

" It's the munister she's needin', Eddie, or a drop o' spirits," said the Captain gravely, though a little annoyed at the imputation. " Slip you oot and rouse the munister ; he'll be in his bed. Or, do ye think yoursel' ye would try the spirits first ? "

But another knocking summoned the carter, who returned to the kitchen, weeping.

" There's something desperate wrong wi' Liza ! " he blubbered ; " she wants me to go round to the baker's shop and order a seed-cake."

" What for ? " asked Para Handy, astonished.

" Goodness knows ! " said Macvean ; " the only seed-cake ever I saw wass at New Year or a funeral. I'm vexed I ever spoke about Lochgilphead ! Do ye think yoursel' there is any danger, Peter ? "

The Captain had no time to answer, for another knocking had called away his host, who returned in a little wringing his hands.

" There iss nothing for it but to go for the doctor," he said. " She's ramblin' ; she says I'm to try and keep the hoose together, and no' pairt wi' her mother's sofa."

" I'll go ben and see her," said Para Handy.

An oil-lamp on the chimney-piece lit up the room where Mrs Macvean was lying. The Captain was surprised to find her looking remarkably well, with the hue of health on her face, though a little embarrassed by his unexpected appearance. She whipped off her nightcap.

" What way are ye keepin', Mrs Macvean ? " he asked, in sympathetic tones.

The patient paid no heed to him, beyond putting up her hands to feel if her hair was tidy. In a feeble voice she remarked to her husband, " Edward, ye'll give my Sunday frock to Aunty Jennet, and my rings to Mary MacMillan ; she wass kind, kind to me ! "

" 'Dalmighty ! " said the Captain, scratching his ear. " Do ye no' think the least wee drop o' spirits would lift ye, Liza ? "

" Nothing 'll lift me noo but John Mackay, the joiner," sobbed the patient. " Tell him to keep my heid away from them M'Callums when he's carryin' me doon the stairs. . . . And oh, Edward ! " she continued, " I hope ye'll be happy in Lochgilphead, though it's a place I never cared for."

Her husband by now was prostrate with emotion, incapable of speech.

" Did ye order the seed-cake ? " she asked.

" It's aal right aboot the seed-cake," broke in Para Handy. " Mrs Cleghorn, the baker's widow, iss takin' it in hand. I wudger ye she'll make a topper ! She's terrible vexed to hear ye're poorly, and says ye're no' to bother. She's comin' in in the mornin' to make Eddie's breakfast."

Mrs Macvean at this sat up in bed with an amazing recovery of strength and speech, her visage purple with indignation.

" Comin' here ! " she cried. " She'll no' put a leg inside this door if I can help it ! I can see, noo, Edward, what ye're plottin'—to get me oot o' the road and mairry the bakehoose, but I'm no deid yet ! It's only you and your Lochgilphead——"

" It's aal right aboot Lochgilphead, Liza," said the Captain soothingly. " Edward's changed his mind ; he's goin' to cairry on in Tarbert."

" Cairry on ! " exclaimed the wife. " He'll no' cairry on wi' Susan Cleghorn anyway, and I'm goin' wi' him to Lochgilphead. If he had chust asked me the right way, I would be quite agreeable from the start. Away oot o' this, the pair o' ye, till I get on my garments ! "

XXV

A DOUBLE LIFE

" PHILANDERIN' ; what in the world's philanderin' ? " inquired Dougie, honestly eager for the definition of a word which Macphail the engineer had recently learned from a Blue Bell novelette, and was apt to drag into every conversation about the female sex.

" It's the same as flirtin', but fancier, if ye follow me," replied Macphail. " Many a chap starts flirtin' jist to pass the time and get the name o' being a regular teaser, and finds

himsel' married withoot knowin' hoo the devil it happened
to him. A philanderer's different. He has a' his wits aboot
him and doesna mak' a pet o' any woman in particular.
He'll have half a dozen o' them knittin' socks for him at
the same time in different localities, but the last thing he
would think o' wastin' money on would be a bride's-cake.
There's no philanderers in lodgin's; they're all supportin'
poor old mothers."

"The best philanderer I ever kent," said Para Handy,
"wass Hurricane Jeck. He wass a don at it when he wass
younger. He would cairry on wi' a whole Dorcas meetin'
if they didna crood roond him aal at wance. Ye never saw
a more nimble fellow, and there he iss—no' married yet, nor
showin' any signs o't."

"Hurricane Jeck's no' my notion o' a proper philanderer,"
commented the engineer with some acidity. "He hasna the
knowledge for't—a chap that never opens a book!"

"There's no books needed," retorted the Captain. "Jeck
had the gift by nature. I'm speakin' o' the time before
he went sailin' foreign, when he had his whuskers. We
were on the *Mary Jane* thegither, and faith I wasna slack
mysel', though I never had his agility. He wass ass smert
ass salt on a sore finger. There wassna a port inside o'
Paddy's Milestone where Jeck wass not ass welcome wi'
the girls ass Royal Cherlie! But I can tell ye it took some
management!

"I mind that wan time Jeck got into a nesty habble wi'
a couple o' girls in Gleska.

"He wass very chief at the time wi' a young weedow
wife in Oban that had a pickle money o' her own. If Jeck
wass not a rover he would have married her, for she wass
a fine big bouncin' woman quite suitable for a sailor, but
he couldna make up his mind between her and a girl called
Lucy Cameron he wass walkin' oot wi' any time the vessel
wass in Gleska.

"Wan time yonder when the *Mary Jane* wass in Oban

the weedow trysted Jeck to take her to the Mull and Iona Soiree, Concert, and Ball in the Waterloo Rooms in Gleska. Jeck wass always the perfect chentleman ; he would promise anything if it wassna that week.

" The night o' the Mull and Iona Gaitherin' came on, and Jeck clean forgot his engagement wi' Mrs Maclachlan. That very night he was booked for Hengler's Circus wi' Lucy Cameron. It wassna till the weedow came to his lodgin's in a cab, wi' a fine new pair o' white kid gloves for him and a floo'er for his button-hole, that the poor chap minded o' his promise.

" A lad less nimble in his wits would have thocht the poseetion hopeless, but Jeck wassna so easy daunted. Though he wass dressed aal ready for the Circus, he went to the Mull and Iona, clapped Mrs Maclachlan doon among a wheen o' freen's o' hers from Tobermory chust before the soiree started ; took a bloodin' nose, by his way of it, and wass oot in the street again in a jeffy, skelpin' it for Lucy Cameron's."

" Wasn't that the rogue ? " exclaimed Dougie admiringly.

" When the Mull and Iona wass singin' the chorus o' Farewell to Fuinary, or maybe aboot the time the orangers wass passin' roond in the Waterloo Rooms, Jeck wass sittin' across the street in Hengler's wi' Lucy Cameron, clappin' his hands at my namesake, Handy Andy the clown.

" Every noo and then he would take oot his watch when Lucy wassna lookin', and calculate hoo far the Mull and Iona folk would be in their programme, and in twenty minutes his nose began to blood again.

" ' Beg pardon ! ' says Jeck—for he was aalways the perfect chentleman—' but I'll have to go oot a meenute for a key to put doon my back.' And away he went like the wind across the street to the Waterloo Rooms.

" He was chust in time for the start o' the Grand March.

" ' Are ye better ? ' asked the weedow, quite anxious, never jalousin' Jeck wass a fair deceiver.

" ' Tip-top ! ' says Jeck, and into the Grand March wi' her like a trumpeter. It wass chenerally allooed there wassna a handsomer couple on the floor. He feenished Triumph wi' the weedow, saw her settled wi' another pairtner for Petronella, and then skipped like a goat across to Hengler's. Little did Lucy Cameron ken her lad wass at the dancin' !

" Every twenty minutes Jeck wass oot o' the circus on some excuse or other, and puttin' in a dance wi' the Oban weedow, then back again to Lucy. He wass so busy between the two o' them he couldna even get a drink, and at the Mull and Iona his condeetion was noticed. At the circus Lucy wass wonderin' too, for he aye came back wi' an oranger, or a poke o' sweeties from the baal, and a smell o' lavender, but as right as a Rechabite.

" For four mortal oors Jeck ran the ferry this way ; when the circus wass feenished he took Miss Cameron home, and then back to the Waterloo Rooms, where he made a night o't.

" He told me aal aboot it himsel' next day. ' If I hadna my health, Peter,' he said, ' I couldna do it. And the dash thing iss they're both fine girls ! I wass nearly poppin' the question to Lucy, and Mrs Maclachlan wass most attractive.'

" The thing would have passed aal right if it wassna that the ' Oban Times ' next week gave an account o' the Mull and Iona, wi' Jeck's name among the chentlemen that wass present, and Lucy saw it. She wass desperate angry !

" Jeck denied it ; said it wass aalthegether a mistake ; that somebody must have been tradin' on his reputation ; but Lucy's mother had a lodger in the polis force that made an investigation, and it wass all up wi' poor Jeck and the Cameron family.

" And it didna stop there neither, for the polisman informed the Oban weedow the way Jeck had been cairryin' on, and the next time Jeck made a caal on her in Oban to clinch things for a merrage, Mrs Maclachlan wouldna speak to him."

"That shows ye," said the engineer, "that he wasna a rale philanderer ; a philanderer's never found oot."

XXVI

THE WET MAN OF MUSCADALE

"TALKIN' aboot the health," said Para Handy, "the drollest man I ever saw that made a hobby o' his health wass a pairty in Muscadale caaled the Wet Man."

"What in the name o' goodness did they caal him that for ? " asked the mate.

"Chust because he wass never dry," replied the Captain. "He went aboot damp for forty years, and would be livin' yet if it wassna for the doctors. They took him to a cottage hospital in Campbeltoon, dried his clo'es on him, and packed him in a bed wi' hot-water bottles. He drank every drop that wass in the bottles before the mornin', and efter that they wouldna gie him any more, so he withered like the rose o' Sharon in the Scruptures. Died o' drooth, like a geranium in a floo'er-pot ! He wass over ninety years o' age, wi' aal his faculties aboot him till the end, and never used a towel."

"My goodness ! " exclaimed the mate.

"Many a time I'll be thinkin'," said Para Handy, "that the man in Muscadale wass born a bit before his time. If he wass spared another fifty years the world would see there iss a lot o' nonsense aboot science and the droggists' shops, and that long life iss aal a maitter o' moisture."

"If bein' wet would keep us healthy," interjected Macphail the engineer, "we would never dee at a' in the West Coast shippin' tred."

"There iss a lot o' rubbidge talked regairdin' damp," continued the Captain. "Colin MacClure in Muscadale proved it. He wass fifty years o' age when he took a desperate cold that he couldna get rid o' till he fell wan day in the watter in the Sound o' Jura, and when they fished him oot he hadna a vestige. A chrechlin' cough he had wass gone completely.

"From that day he wass a changed man, and pinned his faith in watter, ootside and in. He couldna pass a pump-well withoot a swig at it, and when any other fisherman would be takin' a Chrustian dram in moderation wi' his frien's, nothin' but a barrel and a balin'-dish would serve the Wet Man o' Muscadale."

"Issn't that chust duvelish!" exclaimed Dougie. "I would say there iss nothing worse for a man's inside than watter; look at the way it rots your boots!"

"He got heavy, heavy on the watter; aye nip-nippin' at it when he thocht that nobody wass lookin'. Many a time his wife—poor body!—had to go and look for him at the river-side and bring him home."

"I can take a little watter in moderation," said the mate; "a drop o't in your tea does herm to nobody, but it's ruinaation to be always tipplin' at it."

"It would be diabetes," suggested the engineer.

"There wassna a diabete in Colin's composeetion," said the Captain. "His constitution wass grand. He could eat tackets and sleep like a babe on a slab o' granite. A big bold healthy fisherman wi' a noble whusker on him!—wan o' the chenuine old MacClures that's in the 'History o' the Clans.' If there wass any germs o' any kind in the Wet Man o' Muscadale they would need to wear life-belts. The only time that Colin wass in danger for his health was in frosty weather; he would get ass hard then ass a curlin'-stone, and the least bit jar against the corner o' a hoose would knock a chip off him.

"'Be wet and ye'll be weel!' wass Colin's motto; he could prove it wi' the Bible. 'Noah,' he would say, 'made a fair hash o' the business in landin' on Ben Ararat; if it wassna for that, we would be sweemin' aboot the deep the day like fishes, in the best o' health and trum, and no need fo[r] your panel doctors.   Ye never heard o' a herrin' yet that ha[d] lumbago.'

"From the day that he wass picked oot o' the Sound o[f] Jura, he never let his clo'es dry on his back for fear o' trouble[,] and the very sight o' a dry shirt on a washin'-green woul[d] make him shiver.   He wass the wan man in Scotland y[e] would find lamentin' if it wassna rainin'.   Colin's notion o[f] comfort wass a good big hole in the roof o' the hoose, a dul[l] on the hearth, a thin alpaca jecket stickin' to his ribs, a[b]- plashin', and his sea-boots full o' watter."

"Did he no' get rheumatism?" inquired the mate[,] astounded.

"Not him!   He wass ass flippant on his feet ass an Iris[h] ragman, and never spent a penny on his health till the da[y] they buried him.   He cairried his notion to a redeeculou[s] degree, for he was staunch teetotal."

"If he was livin' the day he would get a' the watter h[e] needed in half a mutchkin," suggested the engineer cynically[.]

"That wouldna do for the Wet Man o' Muscadale," sai[d] the Captain.   "Ye see, he had to be wet ootside ass weel as[s] in.   Many a sore trauchle his wife had wettin' him wi' a[.] watterin'-can in the summer, the same's he wass a bed o[f] syboes.   She wass a poor wee cricket o' a low-country woman[,] and darena even dry the blankets efter washin' them for fear that Colin would get a cold.   On their golden weddin[']day she said to a neebour, ' Bonny on the golden weddin' ! My man's yonder sittin' on the ebb and steepin' like a lump o' dulse.'

"The Wet Man thrived so weel on the watter treatment that a lot o' the folk in the countryside aboot began to follow his example, and then nothin' would do for Colin but to start a new releegion.   At first he thocht, himsel', o' joinin' the Baptists, thinkin' that the Baptist churches had a pond in them the same ass the Greenheid Baths in Gleska, but when he heard that the Baptists only got a splash in a kind o' boyne and then came oot and dried themsel's, he wass fair disgusted.

" ' They're chust a lot o' back-sliders,' he says ; ' they havena the fundamentals o' releegion in them ! ' So he started a body o' his own they caaled the MacClurites. The other denominations gave them the by-name o' the Muscadale Dookers, and they suffered a lot o' persecution, them bein' so close on Campbeltoon. The MacClurites never used oilskins nor umberellas ; they're tellin' me the second cheneration o' them had web feet and feathers on them chust like jucks.

" The MacClurites quarrelled among themsel's aboot the doctrine ; some sayin' salt watter wasna the naitural element o' salvaation, and others that ye werena proper wet unless ye fell in the Sound o' Jura. It clean broke up the MacClurites, and they aal went back to the Wee Free Church ass dry ass anything, and died in the prime o' life at seventy or eighty.

" But Colin MacClure never flinched nor bowed the knee to Ramoth-Gilead. When the laird put rhones and a galvanised roof on his dwellin', he took his abode below high-water mark in a skiff turned upside doon that wass aalways flooded at every tide."

" He would be a' mildew," said the engineer.

" Fair blue-moulded ! " said the Captain. " For fifty years the clo'es wass never dry on him ; ye would think it wass gress wass growin' in his back, but he went aboot to the very last wi' wonderful agility. It is from scenes like them that Scotia's grandeur springs."

XXVII

INITIATION

THERE was absolutely nothing to do to pass the time till six o'clock, and Hurricane Jack, whose capacity for sleep under any circumstances and at any hour of the day or night was the envy of his shipmates, stretched himself out on the hatches with a fragment of tarpaulin over him. In about two seconds he was apparently dreaming of old days in the China clipper trade, and giving a most realistic imitation of a regular snorter of a gale off the Ramariz.

"There's some people iss born lucky," remarked the Captain pathetically. "Jeck could go to sleep inside a pair o' bagpipes and a man playin' on them. It's the innocent mind o' him."

"It's no' the innocent mind o' him, whatever it iss," retorted Dougie with some acidity. "It's chust fair laziness; he canna be bothered standin' up and keepin' his eyes open. Ye're chust spoilin' him. That's what I'm tellin' ye!"

Para Handy flushed with annoyance. "Ye think I'm slack," he remarked; "but I'm firm enough wi' Jeck when there's any occasion. I sent him pretty smert for the milk this mornin', and him wantin' me to go mysel'. I let him see who wass skipper on this boat. A body would think you wass brocht up on a man-o'-war; ye would like to see me aye bullyin' the fellow. There's no herm in Jeck Maclachlan, and there iss not a nimbler sailor under the cope and canopy, in any shape or form!"

Dougie made no reply. He sat on an upturned bucket sewing a patch on the salient part of a pair of trousers with a sail-maker's needle.

"There ye are!" resumed the Captain. "Darnin' away at your clothes and them beyond redemption! Ye're losin' aal taste o' yoursel'; what ye're needin's new garments altogether. Could ye no', for goodness sake, buy a web o' homespun somewhere in the islands and make a bargain wi' a tyler?"

"Tylers!" exclaimed Dougie. "I might as weel put mysel' in the hands o' Rob Roy Macgregor! They're askin' £6, 10s. the suit, and it's extra for the trooser linin'."

Para Handy was staggered. He had bought no clothes

himself since his marriage, and had failed to observe the extraordinary elevation in the cost of men's apparel.

"Holy Frost!" he cried. "That's a rent in itsel'! If that's the way o't, keep you on plyin' the needle, Dougie. It's terrible the price o' everything nooadays. I think, mysel', it's a sign o' something goin' to happen. It runs in my mind there wass something aboot that in the Book o' Revelations. I only paid £2, 10s. for a capital pilot suit the year I joined the Rechabites."

The mate suspended his sewing, and looked up suspiciously at the skipper.

"It's the first time ever I heard ye were in the Rechabites," he remarked significantly. "Hoo long were ye in them?"

"Nearly a week," replied Para Handy, "and I came oot o' them wi' flyin' colours at the start o' the Tarbert Fair. It wass aal a mistake, Dougie; the tyler at the time in Tarbert took advantage o' me. A fisherman by the name o' Colin Macleod from Minard and me wass very chief at that time, and he wass a Freemason. He would aye be givin' grips and makin' signs to ye. By his way o't a sailor that had the grip could trevel the world and find good company wherever he went, even if he didna ken the language.

"Colin wass high up in the Freemasons; when he had all his medals and brooches on he looked like a champion Hielan' dancer.

"He wass keen, keen for me to join the craft and be a reg'lar chentleman, and at last I thocht to mysel' it would be a great advantage.

"'Where will I join?' I asked him.

"'Ye'll join in Tarbert; there's no' a Lodge in the realm o' Scotland more complete,' says Colin. 'And the first thing ye'll do, ye'll go up and see my cousin the tyler; he'll gie ye a lot o' preluminary instruction.'

"The very next time I wass in Tarbert I went to the tyler right enough for the preluminaries.

" ' I wass thinkin' o' joinin' the Lodge,' I says to him, ' and Colin Macleod iss tellin' me ye're in a poseetion to gie me a lot o' tips to start wi'. What clothes will I need the night o' the meetin' ? '

" He was a big soft-lookin' lump o' a man, the tyler, wi' a smell o' singed cloth aboot him, and the front o' his jecket aal stuck over wi' pins ; and I'll assure ye he gave me the he'rty welcome.

" ' Ye couldna come to a better quarter ! ' he says to me, ' and it'll no' take me long to put ye through your facin's. There's a Lodge on Friday, and by that time ye'll be perfect. Of course, ye'll have the proper garments ? '

" ' What kind o' garments ? ' says I. ' I have nothing at aal but what I'm wearin' ; my Sabbath clothes iss all in Gleska.'

" ' Tut ! tut ! ' says he, quite vexed. ' Ye couldna get into a Lodge wi' clothes like that ; ye'll need a wise-like suit if ye're to join the brethren in Tarbert. But I can put ye right in half a jiffy.'

" He jumped the counter like a hare, made a grab at a pile o' cloth that wass behind me, hauled oot a web o' blue-pilot stuff, and slapped it on a chair.

" ' There's the very ticket for ye ! ' he says, triumphant. ' Wi' a suit o' that ye'll be the perfect chentleman ! '

" I wassna needin' clothes at aal, but before I could open my mouth to say Jeck Robe'son he had the tape on me. Noo there's something aboot a tyler's tape that aye puts me in a commotion, and I lose my wits.

" He had the measure o' my chest in the time ye wud gut a herrin', and wass roond at my back before I could turn mysel' to see what he wass up to. ' Forty-two ; twenty-three,' he bawls, and puts it in a ledger.

" He wass on to me again wi' his tape, like a flash o' lightnin' ; pulled the jecket nearly off my back and took the length o' my waistcoat, and oh ! my goodness, but he smelt o' Harris tweed, and it damp, singein' !

" ' Hold up your arm ! ' says he, and he took the sleeve-

length wi' a flourish, and aal the time he wass tellin' me
what a capital Lodge was the Tarbert one, and aboot the
staunchness o' the brethren.

" ' Ye'll find us a lot o' cheery chaps,' he says ; ' there's
often singin'. But ye'll have to come at first deid sober,
for they're duvelish particular.'

" By this time he wass doon aboot my legs, and the tape
wass whippin' aal aboot me like an Irish halyard. I wass
that vexed I had entered his shop withoot a dram, for if
I had a dram it wasna a tyler's tape that Peter Macfarlane
would flinch for.

" By the time he had aal my dimensions, fore and aft,
in his wee bit ledger, I wass in a perspiration, and I didna
care if he measured me for a lady's dolman.

" ' Do ye need to do this every time ? ' I asked him, put
aboot tremendous.

" ' Do what ? ' says the tyler.

" ' Go over me wi' a tape,' says I.

" ' Not at aal,' he says, quite he'rty, laughin'. ' It's only
for the first initiation that ye need consider your appearance.
Later on, no doot, ye'll need regalia, and I can put ye richt
here too.'

" ' It's only the first degree I'm wantin' to start wi',' I
says to him ; ' I want to see if my health 'll stand it.'

" ' Tach ! ' says the tyler ; ' ye'll get aal that's goin' at
the wan go-off. There's no shilly-shallyin' about oor Lodge
in Tarbert. Come up to the shop to-morrow, and I'll gie
the first fit on.'

" I went to him next day in the afternoon, and ye never
in aal your life saw such a performance ! The tape wass
nothin' to't ! He put on me bits o' jeckets and weskits
tacked thegither, withoot any sign o' sleeves or buttons on
them ; filled his mooth to the brim wi' pins, and started jag-
gin' them into me.

" Mind it's only the first degree ! ' I cries to him. ' Ye
maybe think I'm strong, but I'm no' that strong ! '

N

"Him bein' full o' pins, I couldna make oot wan word he wass mumblin', but I gaithered he wass tellin' me something aboot the grips and password. And then he fair lost his heid! He took a lump of chalk and began to make a regular cod o' my jecket and weskit.

"'Stop! Stop!' I cries to him. 'I wass aye kind o' dubious aboot Freemasons, and if I'm to wear a paraphar-nalia o' this kind, all made up o' patches pinned thegither, and chalked aal o'er like the start o' a game o' peever, I'm no' goin' to join!'

"The tyler gave a start. 'My goodness!' he says, 'it's no' the Freemason's ye were wantin' to join?'

"'That wass my intention,' I told him. 'And Colin said his cousin the tyler in Tarbert wass the very man to help me. That's the way I'm here.'

"'Isn't that chust deplorable!' says the tyler, scratchin' his heid. 'Ye're in the wrong shop aalthegither! The tyler o' the Masons' Lodge in Tarbert's another man aal the-gither, that stands at the door o' his Lodge to get the pass-word. I'm no' a Mason at aal; I'm the treasurer o' the Rechabites.'

"'The Rechabites!' says I, horror-struck. 'Aren't they teetotal?'

"'Strict!' he says. 'Ye canna get over that—to start wi'. And ye're chust ass good ass a full-blown Rechabite noo, for I've given ye aal I ken in the way o' secrets.'

"So that's the way I wass a Rechabite, Dougie. I wass staunch to the brethren for seven days, and then I fair pu' an end to't. I never went near their Lodge, but the suit o' clothes came doon to the vessel for me, wi' a wee boy for the money. It wass £2, 10s., and I have the weskit yet."

"£2, 10s. and aal that sport!" said Dougie ruefully. "Them wass the happy days!"

XXVIII

THE END OF THE WORLD

" WHEN men gets up in years—say aboot eighty or ninety —there should be something done wi' them," said Para Handy.

" What in the world would ye do wi' them ? " asked Dougie. " Ye darena wander them."

" Ye canna wander them nooadays ; the Government iss watchin' them like hawks, and, anyway, they'll never venture half a mile from the Post Office where they get their Old Age Pensions. I would put them aal oot on the island o' St Kilda, wi' a man in cherge. Any old man of ninety that wass dour and dismal I would ship him yonder wi' aal his parapharnalia. I'm no sayin' but here and there ye'll find an old chap worth his keep—chust as jolly and full o' mischief as if he wass a young man, but most o' them's a tribulation to their frien's, and always interferin.' Hurricane Jeck could tell ye."

The Captain's startling scheme for dealing with nonagenarians originated in a conversation on longevity among the people of Arran.

" Jeck," he continued, " had his life fair spoiled on him wi' an uncle he had in Govan. He wass ninety-two if he wass a day, but wasna pleased wi' that ; he would aye be braggin' that he wass a hundred. He lived by himsel' in a but-and-ben, and he made poor Hurricane's life a torment.

" Jeck at the time wass in his prime, and sailin' back and forrit, skipper o' a nice wee boat they caaled the *Jenet*. It wass years before he started goin' foreign. A more becomin' man on a quay ye never clapped an eye on—ass trig's a shippin'-box, and always wi' a nate wee roond broon hat.

" His uncle Wilyum wass a tyrant. In his time he wass a landscape gairdner——"

" What iss a landscape gairdner ? " asked Dougie.

"A landscape gairdner iss a man that scapes gairdens.
. . . But for twenty years old Wilyum lived on his money
and spent his time contrivin' what way he would make his
nephew Jeck a credit to the Second Comin' and the family
o' Maclachlan.

"He had every failin' that a man could have, Uncle Wilyum
—he wass lame wi' rheumatism, as deaf's a post, teetotal to
the worst degree, and never went to church but made a patent
kind o' releegion o' his own oot o' the 'Christian Herald' and
the 'Gospel Trumpet.' Chust an old pagan! Ye would be
sick listenin' to him on the prophet Jeremiah and the Second
Comin' and the opening o' Baxter's Seven Phials."

"Whatna man was Baxter?" inquired the mate.

"Chust Baxter!" replied Para Handy petulantly.
"The man that wass a prophet and wrote the 'Christian
Herald.'

"Nobody could be nicer to an uncle up in years than Jeck.
Many a firken o' herrin' and scores o' eggs he brocht from the
Hielan's for the old chap. He wass his only livin' relative
except a sister o' his that lived in Colonsay, and any money
that the old man left wass likely to be Jeck's.

"Money wass the last thing Jeck at the time had his mind
on ; he wass a born rover that asked for nothing better than
to dodge aboot the Western Hielan's in his own dacent boat,
or go percolatin' roond the Broomielaw wi' a cheery frien'
or two when his vessel wass in Clyde.

"There wass no more harm in Jeck than in a goldfish,
but the silly old body thocht he was a limb o' Satan, and never
missed a chance to board him wi' a bundle o' tracts. Jeck
had no sooner his foot on shore in Gleska than Uncle Wilyum,
wi' his sticks, would hirple up and follow him every place
he went to keep him oot o' temptation.

"He put the peter on't at last wan time he went efter Jeck
to the Oban and Lorn Soiree and Ball in the Waterloo Rooms,
and found him wi' a clove hitch round the waist o' a bouncin'
girl and them throng waltzin'.

" I can tell you Jeck got Jeremiah from his uncle Wilyum that night !

" ' The like o' you dancin' there wi' a wanton woman, and us on the verge ! ' says the old chap, groanin'.

" ' What verge ? ' says Jeck.

" ' Did ye no' hear ? ' says his uncle, lookin' fearful unsatisfactory.

" ' No,' says Jeck.

" ' That's what I wass thinkin',' says his uncle, whippin' oot a ' Christian Herald,' and showin' him a bit o' Baxter that said the end o' the world wass fixed for that day fortnight.

" ' Chust that ! ' says Jeck. ' I heard a kind o' rumour aboot it doon at Greenock ; but I'm no' botherin', for I'm goin' to take the boat for't when the time comes.'

" My goodness, but the old man wass staggered ! It had never entered his head to take to the sea for't when the end o' the world came, and he cocked his ears when he heard that Jeck wass goin' to get the better o' the Prophet Baxter wi' the *Jenet*.

" ' Will ye take me wi' ye ? ' he says to his nephew.

" ' Wi' aal the pleesure in the world,' says Jeck, who wass aye the perfect gentleman. ' Get you your bits o' sticks collected ; we'll put them in the hold for broken stowage, and ye'll come wi' me on Wednesday. We'll be roond the Mull before the trouble breaks oot.'

" Jeck wass only in fun, and you can imagine his consternation when a lorry came doon to his boat next day wi' aal Uncle Wilyum's plenishin', and the old man on the top o' a chest o' drawers wi' a bundle o' Baxter's prophecies !

" There's one thing aboot Jeck—he's never bate !

" He took the old man on board wi' all his dunnage, and started oot for Colonsay, where he wass takin' coals.

" It was the dreariest trip he ever made in aal his life ; for when the old man wassna takin' his meat or sleepin', he wass greetin' aboot the end o' aal things and swabbin'

his heid-lights even-on wi' a red bandana hanky, or groanin'
over the ' Christian Herald.'

" ' Tach ! I wouldna bother aboot the Prophet Baxter,'
says Jeck to him at last. ' Perhaps he wass workin' wi' a
last year's almanack, and fairly oot o't wi' his calculations.'

" But Uncle Wilyum said that wass blasphemy, and kept
on reelin' oot fathoms o' Jeremiah, till poor Jeck wass near
demented.

" ' What place iss this ? ' says Uncle Wilyum when they
came to Colonsay, and Jeck began dischairgin' coal.

" ' It's the end o' the world,' says Jeck, quite blithe.
' Away you ashore and see your sister Mary, and I'll send
up your furniture ass soon ass the coals iss done.'

" ' For aal the time we have thegether,' wailed his Uncle
Wilyum, ' is it worth my while ? '

" ' Worth your while ! ' cried Jeck. ' Of course it's worth
your while ! I'll bate ye Baxter never heard o' the Isle
o' Colonsay. It's forty years since ye saw your sister. Away
and spend your money on her like a chentleman.'

" Uncle Wilyum went ashore wi' his bundle o' the prophets,
and settled down wi' his sister, waitin' for the day o' tribulation. He lingered seven years, and shaved himsel' every
mornin', so as to be ready ; but Baxter failed him at the
last, and he died o' influenza, leavin' his pickle money to
his sister."

" That wass a pity for Jeck " said Dougie.

" Tach ! Jeck didna care a docken ! He wass enjoyin'
life."

XXIX

THE CAPTURED CANNON

As soon as it grew dark, when the quay was quite deserted
and the village seemed wholly asleep, the crew of the *Vital
Spark* set briskly about getting the gun ashore.

They passed two unrailed gang-planks between the vessel and the slip, took the tarpaulin off the mysterious mass of inert material at the bow and revealed a German 18-pounder, without its breech-block, exceedingly battered and rusty. Hurricane Jack fastened a stout rope to the gun itself, and going behind lifted up the trail of the carriage with an effort.

"Tail you on to the rope and pull like bleezes," he cried to Dougie ; "Macphail and Peter 'll shove roond the wheels o' her, and I'll hold up this cursed contrivance. . . . All thegither, boys ; heave ! "

Para Handy took up the task allotted to him, almost weeping. "Holy Frost ! " he wailed ; "isn't this the bonny habble we're in ? I wish we had never seen the blasted thing ; it's aal your fault, Jeck."

"There'll be trouble aboot this, you'll see ! " said Macphail, putting all his propulsive vigour into a wheel spoke. "I knew from the beginnin'. But ye wouldna listen to me ! "

"Shut up, and haul like Horse Artillery ! " growled Hurricane Jack. "Ye're no' in the Milishy."

By almost superhuman efforts they got the gun on to the slip, and up to the level of the wharf.

"What are we to do noo ? " panted the Captain. "We canna leave it here ; mind you, it's no' Crarae ; there's a polisman in the place."

"We'll hurl it doon the quay and oot on the ebb," said Hurricane Jack with confidence and alacrity. "Ye can put anything ye like under high-water-mark, there's no law against it. If we get it oot on the ebb noo it'll be covered wi' the tide afore the mornin'," and he picked up the trail again.

They trundled the piece noisily over the granite pier, perspiring at the task ; the weapon had never heard such lurid language in the process since it left the Hindenburg Line.

"If anybody catches us at this!" moaned Dougie apprehensively, blowing like a whale.

They were just on the verge of the sand when Macnaughton appeared in his official glazed tippet, but without his helmet. He had just been making his last round for the night.

"What in the name o' goodness are ye doin' here?" he inquired sternly. "Whose cairt have ye there?"

"It's no' a cairt," said Hurricane Jack, letting down the trail. "It's a quite good cannon the War Office sent for a War Memorial for the place. We're jist dischargin' it."

"Dischairgin' it!" exclaimed the constable, horrified, "ye'll waken the whole community!" He came closer, peered in the dark at the weapon, and had a sudden inspiration.

"I know your capers fine!" he exclaimed, throwing back his tippet to show his metal buttons. "We're no' that far behind in this place but we ken aboot that gun; it's the hue and cry o' the county."

"What did ye hear aboot it?" asked Hurricane Jack coolly taking a seat on the carriage.

"I have it aal here in my book," said the constable slapping his tail-pocket. "I might have ken't when I saw your boat come in this efternoon wi' a tarp'lin over the bows o' her, that you were up to some o' your dydoes. Ye got the gun from a hawker in Lochgilphead."

"Right enough!" acknowledged the Captain soothingly "But it wass his own gun; the burgh that got it from the War Office for a souvineer got sick o't, and gave him't for old metal."

"We took it for a speculation," added Hurricane Jack "Ye would think there's many a place in Loch Fyne would like a chenuine German cannon."

"We were goin' to make oor fortune wi't," said Macphail with bitter sarcasm. "Jeck assured us there was money in't."

"I ken aal aboot it," said the constable, with an air o

profound omniscience. " Ye've been cairryin' that lumber up and doon the loch for the last three weeks tryin' to palm it off on His Majesty's lieges. It's aal in my book ! Ye offered it for a pound in Cairndow ; the price wass down to ten shillin's at Strachur ; ye couldna sell't for a shillin' in Crarae, and ye left it on the quay there, but they made ye shift it."

" It's the God's truth—every word o't," confessed Hurricane Jack. " A German cannon's worse than a drunken reputation ; ye canna get rid o't."

The crew of the *Vital Spark* stood in the rain and dark round the degraded and rejected relic of Imperial power, and violently abused Jack.

" A bloomin' eediot ! I told him it would be left on oor hands ! " cried Macphail. " Whit could onybody dae wi' a cannon ? "

" There might be another war at any time," suggested Hurricane Jack defensively.

" I never wass ass black affronted in my life," bleated Para Handy. " The whole loch-side iss laughin' at us. The very turbine steamers blows their whistles when they pass and cry ' *Hood*, ahoy ! ' It's no' like a thing ye could break in bits and burn in Macphail's furnace ; it's solid iron in every pairt. Nobody hass a kind word for it ; we tried to get a minister to put it in his glebe, or fornent the door o' his manse, and he put his dog on us."

" Ye'll take it oot o' here anyway," said the constable firmly. " We have plenty o' trash o' oor own. It's a mercy I came on ye tryin' to leave it here and spoil the navigation ! "

" I never dreamt that a gun wass so ill to manœuvre," remarked the imperturbable Jack. " Do ye no' think, sergeant, there's anybody in the place would care for it for an orniment ? Anybody wi' a bit o' a gairden : they could cover it wi' fuchsias."

" No expense at aal ! " added Para Handy eagerly. " We would put it in poseetion. Many a wan would be gled to

N*

have it if it wass in London or in Gleska. It's a splendid cannon! Captured by the Australian Airmy. Cost the British Government £50 to take to Loch Fyne."

"I don't care if it cost £100," said the constable fiercely; "it's no' goin' to be palmed off on this community that suffered plenty wi' the war. Get it back on board your ship at wance, like dacent lads, and don't make any trouble."

"Dalmighty!" cried the Captain, wringing his hands, "are we goin' to have this Cherman abomination on oor decks the rest o' oor naitural lifes? . . . It's all your fault, Jeck, ye said there wass a fortune in it."

"My mistake!" admitted Hurricane Jack, most handsomely. "I wash my hands noo o' the whole concern."

"I would wash my hands too, if they werena aal blistered," said Dougie piteously. "What are we to do wi' the cursed thing? There iss no place we dare leave it."

"Could ye no' put it over the side o' the boat somewhere doon about Kilbrannan?" suggested the constable.

They stared at one another, utterly astounded.

"My Chove!" said Para Handy. "We never thocht o' that! Aren't you the born eediot, Jeck, that would have us cairtin' it up and doon the ocean for the last three weeks!"

"I didna want to see a good gun wasted," explained Hurricane Jack, rather lamely, and he picked up the trail again. "But maybe that's the best way oot o' the difficulty; get a ha'd o' the rope again, and pull, Dougie."

XXX

AN IDEAL JOB

As the *Vital Spark*, outrageously belching sparks and cinders from fuel eked out by wood purloined some days before from a cargo of pit-props, swept round the point of Row, Para Handy gazed with wonder and admiration at the Gareloch, full of idle ships.

" My word ! " he exclaimed, " isn't that the splendid sight ! Puts ye in mind o' a Royal Review ! "

" I don't see onything Royal aboot it," growled the misanthropic engineer, Macphail. " It's a sign o' the terrible times we're livin' in. If there was freights for them boats, they wouldna be there, but dashin' roond the Horn and makin' work for people."

" Of course ! Of course ! You must aye be contrairy," said the Captain peevishly. " Nothing on earth 'll please you ; ye're that parteecular. It's the way they chenerally make work for people that spoils ships for me. I like them best when they're at their moorin's. What more could ye want in the way o' a bonny spectacle than the sight o' aal them gallant vessels and them no' sailin' ? "

Macphail snorted as he ducked his head and withdrew among his engines. " There's enough bonny spectacles on board this boat to do me for my lifetime," he said in a parting shot before he disappeared.

Para Handy turned sadly to the mate. " Macphail must aye have the last word," he said. " The man's no' worth payin' heed to. Greasin' bits o' enchines every day o' your life makes ye awfu' coorse. I'm sure that's a fine sight, them ships, Dougie ? There must be nearly half a hundred there, and no' a lum reekin'."

" They're no bad," answered Dougie cautiously. " But some o' them's terrible in need o' a stroke o' paint. Will there be anybody stayin' on them ? "

" Ye may depend on that ! " the Captain assured him. " There iss a man or two in cherge o' every vessel, and maybe a wife and femily. The British Mercantile Marine iss no' leavin' ocean liners lyin' aboot Garelochheid wi' nobody watchin' them. A chentleman's life ! It would suit me fine, instead o' plowterin' up and doon Loch Fyne wi' coals and timber. Did I no' tell ye the way Hurricane Jeck spent a twelvemonth on a boat laid up in the Gareloch when tred was dull aboot twenty years ago ? "

" Ye did not ! " said Dougie.

" She wass a great big whupper o' a barquenteen caaled the *Jean and Mary*, wi' a caibin the size o' a Wee Free Church, and fitted up like a pleesure yacht.   She had even a pianna."

" God bless me ! " gasped the mate, half incredulous.

" Jeck had the influence in them days, and he got the job to look efter her in the Gareloch till the times got better. The times wass good enough the way they were for Jeck, wance he had his dunnage on board.   ' Never had a job to bate it ! ' he says ;   ' I wouldna swap wi' the polisman in the Kelvingrove Museum.' "

" I would think he would be lonely," said Dougie dubiously. " A great big boat wi' nobody but yersel' in it at night would be awfu' eerie."

The Captain laughed uproariously.   " Eerie ! " he repeated. " There iss nothin' eerie any place where Hurricane Jeck iss ; he had the time o' his life in the *Jean and Mary*.

" Wance they got their boat clapped doon in the Gareloch and Jeck in charge o' her, the chentlemen in Cardiff she belonged to forgot aal aboot her.   At least they never bothered Jeck except wi' a postal-order every now and then for wages.

" The wages wassna desperate big, and Jeck put his brains in steep to think oot some contrivance for makin' a wee bit extra money.

" It came near the Gleska Fair, and there wassna a but-and-ben in Garelochheid that wassna packed wi' ludgers like a herrin'-firkin.   When Jeck would be ashore for paraffine-oil or anything, he would aye be comin' on poor craturs wantin' ludgin's, so he filled the *Jean and Mary* wi' a fine selection.   For three or four weeks the barquenteen wass like an hotel, or wan o' them hydropathics.   Jeck swithered aboot puttin' up a sign to save him from goin' ashore to look for customers.

" Ye never saw a ship like it in aal your life !   It wass hung from end to end wi' washin's aal July, and Jeck gave ludgin's free to a man wi' a cornacopia that he played on the deck from mornin' till night."

" Wass it no' a terrible risk ? " asked Dougie.

" No risk o' any kind, at aal, at aal. The owners wass in Cardiff spendin' their money, and they never saw the Gareloch in their lifes but in the map. Jeck kent he wass doin' a noble work for the health o' the community—far better than the Fresh Air Fortnight !

" When the Fair wass feenished, and his ludgers went away, I'll assure ye they left a bonny penny wi' the landlord o' the *Jean and Mary*. He thocht the season wass done, but it wasna a week till he wass throng again wi' a lot o' genteel young divinity students that came from Edinburgh wi' a banjo.

" ' Gie me a bottle o' beer and a banjo playin', and it's wonderful the way the time slips by,' says Jeck. He learned them a lot o' sailor songs like ' Ranza, Boys ! ' and ' Rollin' doon to Rio,' and the folk in Garclochheid that couldna get their night's sleep came oot at last in a fury to the ship and asked him who she belonged to.

" ' Ye can look Lloyd's List,' says Jeck to them, quite the chentleman, ' and ye'll see the name o' the owners. But she's under charter wi' a man that's aal for high jinks and the cheneral hilarity—and his name iss John Maclachlan. If there iss any o' ye needin' ludgin's, say the word and I'll put past a fine wee caibin for ye, wi' a southern exposure.'

" They went away wi' their heids in the air. ' I ken what's wrong wi' them,' says Jeck. ' Oh, man ! if I chust had the spirit licence ! '

" That wass his only tribulation : he had ass good an hotel below his feet as any in the country, but he daurna open a bar.

" The summer slipped by like a night at a weddin' ; the cornacopia man went back to his work, but Jeck fell in wi' an old pianna-tuner that could play the pianna like a minister's wife, and aal the autumn Jeck gave smokin' concerts on the

Jean and Mary, where all the folk in charge o' the other vessels paid sixpence apiece and got a lot o' pleesure.

" ' If I had chust a brass band ! ' says Jeck, ' and a wise-like man I could trust for a purser, I would run moonlight trips. But it would be an awful bother liftin' the anchor ; perhaps I'm better the way I am ; there's no' the responsibility wi' a boat at moorin's.'

" But the time he showed the best agility wass when he had a weddin' on the ship. The mate o' another vessel was gettin' spliced in his good-mother's hoose in Clynder, where there wasna room for dancin'.

" Jeck hired the *Jean and Mary* to them ; the company came oot in boats from aal ends o' the Gareloch, wi' a couple o' pipers and that many roasted hens ye couldna get eggs in the shire for months efter it. They kept it up till the followin' efternoon, wi' the anchor lamp still burnin' and aal the buntin' in the vessel flyin'.

" A well-put-on young Englishman from Cardiff came alongside in a motor-lench in an awfu' fury, and bawled at Jeck what aal this carry-on meant. There wass sixty people on board if there wass a dozen.

" ' Some frien's o' my own,' says Jeck, quite nimble, and aye the chentleman. ' I have chust come into a lot o' money, and I'm givin' them a trate.'

" But that was the last o' Jeck's command in the *Jean and Mary* ; the poor duvvle had to go back and work at sailorin'."

ERCHIE

MY DROLL FRIEND

ERCHIE

I

INTRODUCTORY TO AN ODD CHARACTER

O N Sundays he is the beadle of our church; at other
times he Waits. In his ecclesiastical character there
is a solemn dignity about his deportment that compels most
of us to call him Mr Macpherson; in his secular hours, when
passing the fruit at a city banquet, or when at the close
of the repast he sweeps away the fragments of the dinner-
rolls, and whisperingly expresses in your left ear a fervent
hope that " ye've enjoyed your dinner," he is simply Erchie.

Once I forgot, deluded a moment into a Sunday train of
thought by his reverent way of laying down a bottle of
Pommery, and called him Mr MacPherson. He reproved me
with a glance of his eye.

" There's nae Mr MacPhersons here," said he afterwards;
" at whit ye might call the social board I'm jist Erchie, or
whiles Easy-gaun Erchie wi' them that kens me langest.
There's sae mony folks in this world don't like to hurt your
feelings that if I was kent as Mr MacPherson on this kind o'
job I wadna mak' enough to pay for starchin' my shirts."

I suppose Mr MacPherson has been snibbing-in preachers
in St Kentigern's Kirk pulpit and then going for twenty
minutes' sleep in the vestry since the Disruption; and the
more privileged citizens of Glasgow during two or three
generations of public dinners have experienced the kindly
ministrations of Erchie, whose proud motto is " A flet fit
but a warm hert." I think, however, I was the first to discover his long pent-up and precious strain of philosophy.

On Saturday nights, in his office as beadle of St Kentigern's he lights the furnaces that take the chill off the Sunday devotions. I found him stoking the kirk fires one Saturday, not very much like a beadle in appearance, and much less like a waiter. It was what, in England, they call the festive season.

" There's mair nor guid preachin' wanted to keep a kirk gaun," said he ; " if I was puttin' as muckle dross on my fires as the Doctor whiles puts in his sermons, efter a Setter-day at the gowf, ye wad see a bonny difference on the plate. But it's nae odds—a beadle gets sma' credit, though it's him that keeps the kirk tosh and warm, and jist at that nice easy-osy temperature whaur even a gey cauldrife member o' the congregation can tak' his nap and no' let his lozenge slip doon his throat for chitterin' wi' the cauld."

There was a remarkably small congregation at St Kenti-gern's on the following day, and when the worthy beadle had locked the door after dismissal and joined me on the pavement,

" Man," he said, " it was a puir turn-oot yon—hardly worth puttin' on fires for. It's aye the wye ; when I mak' the kirk a wee bit fancy, and jalouse there's shair to be twa pound ten in the plate, on comes a blash o' rain, and there's hardly whit wid pay for the starchin' o' the Doctor's bands.

" Christmas ! They ca't Christmas, but I could gie anither name for't. I looked it up in the penny almanac, and it said, 'Keen frost; probably snow,' and I declare-to if I hadna nearly to soom frae the hoose.

" The almanacs is no' whit they used to be ; the auld chaps that used to mak' them maun be deid.

" They used to could do't wi' the least wee bit touch, and tell ye in January whit kind o' day it wad be at Hallowe'en, besides lettin' ye ken the places whaur the Fair days and the 'ool-markets was, and when they were to tak' place—a' kind o' information that maist o' us that bocht the almanacs couldna sleep at nicht wantin'. I've seen me get up at three on a cauld winter's mornin' and strikin' a licht to turn up Orr's Penny Commercial and see whit day was the Fair at Dunse. I never was at Dunse in a' my days, and hae nae intention o' gaun, but it's a grand thing knowledge, and it's no' ill to cairry. It's like poetry—'The Star o' Rabbie Burns' and that kind o' thing—ye can aye be givin' it a ca' roond in your mind when ye hae naething better to dae.

" Oh, ay ! A puir turn-oot the day for Kentigern's ; that's the drawback o' a genteel congregation like oors—mair nor half o' them's sufferin' frae Christmas turkey and puttin' the blame on the weather.

" The bubbly-jock is the symbol o' Scotland's decline and fa' ; we maybe bate the English at Bannockburn, but noo they're haein' their revenge and underminin' oor constitution wi' the aid o' a bird that has neither a braw plumage nor a bonny sang, and costs mair nor the price o' three or four ducks. England gave us her bubbly-jock and took oor barley-bree.

" But it's a' richt ; Ne'erday's comin' ; it's begun this year gey early, for I saw Duffy gaun up his close last nicht wi' his nose peeled.

" ' Am I gaun hame, or am I comin' frae't, can ye tell me ? ' says he, and he was carryin' something roond-shaped in his pocket-naipkin.

" ' Whit's wrang wi' ye, puir cratur ? ' I says to him.

" ' I was struck wi' a sheet o' lichtnin',' says he, and by that I ken't he had been doon drinkin' at the Mull of Kintyre Vaults, and that the season o' peace on earth, guid-will to men was fairly started.

" ' MacPherson,' he says, wi' the tear at his e'e, ' I canna help it, but I'm a guid man.'

" ' Ye are that, Duffy,' I says, ' when ye're in your bed sleepin' ; at ither times ye're like the rest o' us, and that's gey middlin'. Whit hae ye in the naipkin ? '

" He gied a dazed look at it, and says, ' I'm no shair, but I think it's a curlin'-stane, and me maybe gaun to a bonspiel at Carsbreck.'

" He opened it oot, and found it was a wee, roond, red cheese.

" ' That's me, a' ower,' says he—' a Christmas for the wife,' and I declare there was as much drink jaupin' in him as wad hae done for a water-shute.

" Scotland's last stand in the way o' national customs is bein' made at the Mull o' Kintyre Vaults, whaur the flet half-mutchkin, wrapped up in magenta tissue paper so that it'll look tidy, is retreatin' doggedly, and fechtin' every fit o' the way, before the invadin' English Christmas caird. Ten years ago the like o' you and me couldna prove to a freen' that we liked him fine unless we took him at this time o' the year into five or six public-hooses, leaned him up against the coonter, and grat on his dickie. Whit dae we dae noo ? We send wee Jennie oot for a shilling box o' the year afore last's patterns in Christmas cairds, and show oor continued affection and esteem at the ha'penny postage rate.

" Instead o' takin' Duffy roon' the toon on Ne'erday, and hurtin' my heid wi' tryin' to be jolly, I send him a Christmas caird, wi' the picture o' a hayfield on the ootside and ' Wishin' you the Old, Old Wish, Dear,' on the inside, and stay in the hoose till the thing blaws bye.

" The shilling box o' Christmas cairds is the great peace-maker ; a gross or twa should hae been sent oot to Russia and Japan, and it wad hae stopped the war. Ye may hae thocht for a twelvemonth the MacTurks were a disgrace to the tenement, wi' their lassie learnin' the mandolin', and them haein' their gas cut off at the meter for no' payin' the last quarter ; but let them send a comic caird to your lassie —' Wee Wullie to Wee Jennie,' and they would get the len' o' your wife's best jeely-pan.

" No' but whit there's trouble wi' the Christmas caird. It's only when ye buy a shillin' box and sit doon wi' the wife

and weans to consider wha ye'll send them to that ye fin'
oot whit an awfu' lot o' freen's ye hae. A score o' shillin'
boxes wadna gae ower half the kizzens I hae, wi' my grand-
faither belangin' to the Hielan's, so Jinnet an' me jist let's
on to some o' them we're no' sendin' ony cairds oot this year
because it's no' the kin' o' society go ony langer. And ye
have aye to keep pairt o' the box till Ne'erday to send to
some o' the mair parteecular anes ye forgot a' thegither were
freen's o' yours till they sent ye a caird.

" Anither fau't I hae to the Christmas cairds is that the
writin' on them 's generally fair rideeculous.

" ' May Christmas Day be Blythe and Gay, and bring your
household Peace and Joy,' is on the only caird left ower to
send to Mrs Maclure; and when ye're shearin' aff the selvedges
o't to mak' it fit a wee envelope, ye canna but think that it's
a droll message for a hoose wi' five weans lyin' ill wi' the
whoopin'-cough, and the man cairryin' on the wye Maclure
does.

" ' Old friends, old favourites, Joy be with you at this
Season,' says the caird for the MacTurks, and ye canna but
mind that every third week there's a row wi' Mrs MacTurk
and your wife aboot the key o' the washin'-hoose and lettin'
the boiler rust that bad a' the salts o' sorrel in the Apothe-
caries 'll no tak' the stains aff your shirts.

" Whit's wanted is a kin' o' slidin' scale o' sentiment on
Christmas cairds, so that they'll taper doon frae a herty
greetin' ye can truthfully send to a dacent auld freen' and
the kind o' cool ' here's to ye ! ' suited for an acquaintance
that borrowed five shillin's frae ye at the Term, and hasna
much chance o' ever payin't back again.

" If it wasna for the Christmas cairds a lot o' us wad
maybe never jalouse there was onything parteecular merry
aboot the season. Every man that ye're owin' an accoont
to sends it to ye then, thinkin' your hert's warm and your
pouches rattlin'. On Christmas Day itsel' ye're aye expectin'
something ; ye canna richt tell whit it is, but there's ae thing

certain—that it never comes. Jinnet, my wife, made a breenge for the door every time the post knocked on Thursday, and a' she had for't at the end o' the day was an ashet fu' o' whit she ca's valenteens, a' written on so that they'll no even dae for next year.

"I used to wonder whit the banks shut for at Christmas, but I ken noo; they're feart that their customers, cairried awa' wi' their feelin' o' guid-will to men, wad be makin' a rush on them to draw money for presents, and maybe create a panic.

"Sae far as I can judge there's been nae panic at the banks this year.

"Every Ne'erday for the past fifty years I hae made up my mind I was gaun to be a guid man," he went on. "It jist wants a start, they tell me that's tried it, and I'm no' that auld. Naething bates a trial.

"I'm gaun to begin at twelve o'clock on Hogmanay, and mak' a wee note o't in my penny diary, and put a knot in my hankie to keep me in mind. Maist o' us would be as guid's there's ony need for if we had naething else to think o'. It's like a man that's hen-taed—he could walk fine if he hadna a train to catch, or the rent to rin wi' at the last meenute, or somethin' else to bother him. I'm gey faur wrang if I dinna dae the trick this year, though.

"Oh! ay. I'm gaun to be a guid man. No' that awfu' guid that auld freen's 'll rin up a close to hide when they see me comin', but jist dacent—jist guid enough to please mysel', like Duffy's singin'. I'm no' makin' a breenge at the thing and sprainin' my leg ower't. I'm startin' canny till I get into the wye o't. Efter this Erchie MacPherson's gaun to flype his ain socks and no' leave his claes reel-rall aboot the hoose at night for his wife Jinnet to lay oot richt in the mornin'. I've lost money by that up till noo, for there was aye bound to be an odd sixpence droppin' oot and me no' lookin'. I'm gaun to stop skliffin' wi' my feet; it's sair on the boots. I'm gaun to save preens by puttin' my collar stud in a bowl and a flet-iron on the top o't to keep it frae jinkin' under the chevalier and book-case when I'm sleepin'. I'm gaun to wear oot a' my auld waistcoats in the hoose. I'm——"

" My dear Erchie," I interrupted, " these seem very harm-less reforms."

" Are they ? " said he. " They'll dae to be gaun on wi' the noo, for I'm nae phenomena ; I'm jist Nature ; jist the Rale Oreeginal."

II

ERCHIE'S FLITTING

HE came down the street in the gloaming on Tuesday night with a bird-cage in one hand and a potato-masher in the other, and I knew at once, by these symptoms, that Erchie was flitting.

" On the long trail, the old trail, the trail that is always new, Erchie ? " said I, as he tried to push the handle of the masher as far up his coat sleeve as possible, and so divert attention from a utensil so ridiculously domestic and undignified.

" Oh, we're no' that bad ! " said he. " Six times in the four-and-forty year. We've been thirty years in the hoose we're leavin' the morn, and I'm fair oot o' the wye o' flittin'. I micht as weel start the dancin' again."

" Thirty years ! Your household gods plant a very firm foot, Erchie."

" Man, ay ! If it wisna for Jinnet and her new fandangles, I wad nae mair think o' flittin' than o' buyin' a balloon to mysel' ; but ye ken women ! They're aye gaun to be better aff onywhaur else than whaur they are. I ken different, but I havena time to mak' it plain to Jinnet."

On the following day I met Erchie taking the air in the neighbourhood of his new domicile, and smoking a very magnificent meerschaum pipe.

"I was presented wi' this pipe twenty years ago," said he, "by a man that went to California, and I lost it a week or twa efter that. It turned up at the flittin'. That's ane o' the advantages o' flittin's; ye find things ye havena seen for years."

"I hope the great trek came off all right, Erchie?"

"Oh, ay! no' that bad, considerin' we were sae much oot o' practice. It's no' sae serious when ye're only gaun roond the corner to the next street. I cairried a lot o' the mair particular wee things roond mysel' last nicht—the bird-cage and Gledstane's picture and the room vawzes and that sort o' thing—but at the hinder-end Jinnet made me tak' the maist o' them back again."

"Back again, Erchie?"

"Ay. She made oot that I had cairried ower sae muckle that the flittin' wad hae nae appearance on Duffy's cairt, and haein' her mind set on the twa rakes, and a' the fancy things lying at the close-mooth o' the new hoose till the plain stuff was taken in, I had just to cairry back a guid part o' whit I took ower last nicht. It's a rale divert the pride o' women! But I'm thinkin' she's vex't for't the day, because yin o' the things I took back was a mirror, and it was broke in Duffy's cairt. It's a gey unlucky thing to break a lookin'-gless."

"A mere superstition, Erchie."

"Dod! I'm no' sae shair o' that. I kent a lookin'-gless broke at a flittin' afore this, and the man took to drink a year efter't, and has been that wye since."

"How came you to remove at all?"

"It wad never hae happened if I hadna gane to a sale and seen a coal-scuttle. It's a dangerous thing to introduce a new coal-scuttle into the bosom o' your faimily. This was ane o' thae coal-scuttles wi' a pentin' o' the Falls o' Clyde and Tillitudlem Castle on the lid. I got it for three-and-tuppence; but it cost me a guid dale mair nor I bargained for. The wife was rale ta'en wi't, but efter a week or twa she made oot that it gar'd the auld room grate we had look shabby, and afore ye could say knife she had in a new grate wi' wally sides till't, and an ash-pan I couldna get spittin' on. Then the mantelpiece wanted a bed pawn on't to gie the grate a dacent look, and she pit on a plush yin. Ye wadna hinder her efter that to get plush-covered chairs instead o' the auld hair-cloth we got when we were mairried. Her mither's chist-o'-drawers didna gae very weel wi' the plush chairs, she found oot in a while efter that, and they were swapped wi' twa pound for a chevalier and book-case, though the only books I hae in the hoose is the Family Bible, Buchan's 'Domestic Medicine,' and the 'Tales o' the Borders.' It wad hae been a' richt if things had gane nae further, but when she went to a sale hersel' and bought a Brussels carpet a yaird ower lang for the room, she made oot there was naethin' for't but to flit to a hoose wi' a bigger room. And a' that happened because a pented coal-scuttle took ma e'e."

"It's an old story, Erchie ; ' c'est le premier pas que coûte,' as the French say."

"The French is the boys ! " says Erchie, who never gives himself away. "Weel, we're flittin' onywye, and a bonny trauchle it is. I'll no' be able to find my razor for a week or twa."

"It's a costly process, and three flittin's are worse than a fire, they say."

"It's worse nor that ; it's worse nor twa Irish lodgers.

" ' It'll cost jist next to naethin',' says Jinnet. ' Duffy 'll tak' ower the furniture in his lorry for freen'ship's sake, an' there's naethin' 'll need to be done to the new hoose.'

"But if ye ever flitted yersel', ye'll ken the funny wyes o' the waxcloth that's never cut the same wye in twa hooses ; and I'll need to be gey thrang at my tred for the next month or twa to pay for the odds and ends that Jinnet never thought o'.

"Duffy flitted us for naethin', but ye couldna but gie the

men a dram. A flittin' dram's by-ordinar; ye daurna be scrimp wi't, or they'll break your delf for spite, and ye canna be ower free wi't either, or they'll break everything else oot o' fair guid-natur. I tried to dae the thing judeecious, but I forgot to hide the bottle, and Duffy's heid man and his mate found it when I wasna there, and that's the wye the lookin'-gless was broken. Thae cairters divna ken their ain strength.

"It's a humblin' sicht your ain flittin' when ye see't on the tap o' a coal-lorry."

"Quite so, Erchie; chiffoniers are like a good many reputations—they look all right so long as you don't get seeing the back of them."

"And cairters hae nane o' the finer feelin's, I think. In spite o' a' that Jinnet could dae, they left the pots and pans a' efternoon on the pavement, and hurried the plush chairs up the stair at the first gae-aff. A thing like that's disheartenin' to ony weel-daein' woman.

"'Hoots!' says I to her, 'whit's the odds? There's naebody heedin' you nor your flittin'.'

"'Are they no'?' said Jinnet, keekin' up at the front o' the new land. 'A' the venetian blinds is doon, and I'll guarantee there's een behind them.'

"We werena half-an-oor in the new hoose when the woman on the same stairheid chappet at the door and tellt us it was oor week o' washin' oot the close. It wasna weel meant, but it did Jinnet a lot o' guid, for she was sitting in her braw new hoose greetin'."

"Greetin', Erchie? Why?"

"Ask that! Ye'll maybe ken better nor I dae."

"Well, you have earned your evening pipe at least, Erchie," said I.

He knocked out its ashes on his palm with a sigh. "I hiv that! Man, it's a gey dauntenin' thing a flittin', efter a'. I've a flet fit, but a warm hert, and efter thirty years o' the auld hoose I was sweart to leave 't. I brocht up a family in't,

and I wish Jinnet's carpet had been a fit or twa shorter, or
that I had never seen yon coal-scuttle wi' the Falls o' Clyde
and Tillitudlem Castle."

III

DEGENERATE DAYS

" THE tred's done," said Erchie.

" What ! beadling ? " I asked him.

" Oh ! there's naethin' wrang wi' beadlin'," said he ;
" there's nae ups and doons there except to put the books on
the pulpit desk, and they canna put ye aff the job if ye're no
jist a fair wreck. I'm a' richt for the beadlin' as lang's I
keep my health and hae Jinnet to button my collar, and it's
generally allo'ed—though maybe I shouldna say't mysel'—
that I'm the kind o' don at it roond aboot Gleska. I michtna
be, if I wasna gey carefu'. Efter waitin' at a Setterday nicht
spree, I aye tak' care to gie the bell an extra fancy ca' or
twa on the Sunday mornin' jist to save clash and mak' them
ken MacPherson's there himsel', and no' some puir pick-up
that never ca'd the handle o' a kirk bell in his life afore.

" There's no' a man gangs to oor kirk wi' better brushed
boots than mysel', as Jinnet 'll tell ye, and if I hae ae gift
mair nor anither it's discretioncy. A beadle that's a waiter
has to gae through life like the puir troot they caught in the
Clyde the other day—wi' his mooth shut, and he's worse aff
because he hasna ony gills—at least no' the kind ye pro-
nounce that way.

" Beadlin's an art, jist like pentin' photograph pictures, or
playin' the drum, and if it's no' in ye, naethin' 'll put it there.
I whiles see wee skinamalink craturs dottin' up the passages
in U.F. kirks carryin' the books as if they were M.C.'s at a
dancin'-schule ball gaun to tack up the programme in front
o' the band ; they lack thon rale releegious glide ; they
havena the feet for't.

" Waitin' is whit I mean ; it's fair done !

" When I began the tred forty-five year syne in the auld Saracen Heid Inn, a waiter was looked up to, and was well kent by the best folk in the toon, wha aye ca'd him by his first name when they wanted the pletform box o' cigaurs handed doon instead o' the Non Plus Ultras.

" Nooadays they stick a wally door-knob wi' a number on't in the lapelle o' his coat, and it's ' Hey, No. 9, you wi' the flet feet, dae ye ca' this ham ? '

" As if ye hadna been dacently christened and brocht up an honest faimily !

" In the auld days they didna drag a halflin callan' in frae Stra'ven, cut his nails wi' a hatchet, wash his face, put a dickie and a hired suit on him, and gie him the heave into a banquet-room, whaur he disna ken the difference between a finger-bowl and a box o' fuzuvian lichts.

" I was speakin' aboot that the ither nicht to Duffy, the coalman, and he says, ' Whit's the odds, MacPherson ? Wha the bleezes couldna sling roon' blue-mange at the richt time if he had the time-table, or the menu, or whitever ye ca't, to keep him richt ? '

" ' Wha couldna sell coal,' said I, ' if he had the jaw for't ? Man, Duffy,' says I, ' I never see ye openin' your mooth to roar coal up a close but I wonder whit wye there should be sae much talk in the Gleska Toon Cooncil aboot the want o' vacant spaces.'

" Duffy's failin' ; there's nae doot o't. He has a hump on him wi' carryin' bags o' chape coal and dross up thae new, genteel, tiled stairs, and he let's on it's jist a knot in his gallowses, but I ken better. I'm as straucht as a wand mysel'—faith, I micht weel be, for a' that I get to cairry hame frae ony o' the dinners nooadays. I've seen the day, when Blythswood Square and roond aboot it was a' the go, that it was coonted kind o' scrimp to let a waiter hame withoot a heel on him like yin o' thae Clyde steamers gaun oot o' Rothesay quay on a Fair Setturday.

" Noo they'll ripe your very hip pooches for fear ye may be takin' awa' a daud o' custard, or the toasted crumbs frae a dish o' pheasant.

" They needna' be sae awfu' feart, some o' them. I ken their dinners—cauld, clear, bane juice, wi' some strings o' vermicelli in't ; ling-fish hash ; a spoonfu' o' red-currant jeely, wi' a piece o' mutton the size o' a domino in't, if ye had time to find it, only ye're no' playin' kee-hoi ; a game croquette that's jist a flaff o' windy paste ; twa cheese straws ; four green grapes, and a wee lend o' a pair o' silver nut-crackers the wife o' the hoose got at her silver weddin'.

" Man! it's a rale divert! I see big, strong, healthy Bylies and members o' the Treds' Hoose and the Wine, Speerit, and Beer Tred risin' frae dinners like that, wi' their big, braw, gold watch-chains hingin' doon to their knees.

" As I tell Jinnet many a time, it's women that hae fair ruined dinner-parties in oor generation. They tak' the measure o' the appetites o' mankind by their ain, which hae been a'thegether spoiled wi' efternoon tea, and they think a man can mak' up wi' music in the drawin'-room for whit he didna get at the dinner-table.

" I'm a temperate man mysel', and hae to be, me bein' a beadle, but I whiles wish we had back the auld days I hae read aboot, when a laddie was kept under the table to lowse the grauvats o' the gentlemen that fell under't, in case they should choke themsel's. Scotland was Scotland then !

" If they choked noo, in some places I've been in, it wad be wi' thirst.

" The last whisk o' the petticoat's no roon' the stair-landin' when the man o' the hoose puts the half o' his cigarette bye for again, and says, ' The ladies will be wonderin' if we've forgotten them,' and troosh a' the puir deluded craturs afore him up the stair into the drawin'-room where his wife Eliza's maskin' tea, and a lady wi' tousy hair's kittlin' the piano till it's sair.

" ' Whit's your opinion about Tschaikovski ? ' I heard a wumman ask a Bylie at a dinner o' this sort the ither nicht.

" ' I never heard o' him,' said the Bylie, wi' a gant, ' but if he's in the proveesion tred, there'll be an awfu' run on his shop the morn's morn'.'

" Anither thing that has helped to spoil oor tred is the smokin' concerts. I tak' a draw o' the pipe mysel' whiles, but I never cared to mak' a meal o't. Noo and then when I'm no' very busy other ways I gie a hand at a smoker, and it mak's me that gled I got ower my growth afore the thing cam' into fashion ; but it's gey sair on an auld man to hear ' Queen o' the Earth ' five or six nichts in the week, and the man at the piano aye tryin' to guess the richt key, or to get done first, so that the company 'll no' rin awa' when he's no' lookin' withoot paying him his five shillin's.

" I've done the waitin' at a' kinds o' jobs in my time— Easy-gaun Erchie they ca' me sometimes in the tred—a flet fit but a warm hert ; I've even handed roond seed-cake and a wee drap o' spirits at a burial, wi' a bereaved and mournfu' mainner that greatly consoled the weedow ; but there's nae depths in the business so low as poo'in' corks for a smokin' concert. And the tips get smaller and smaller every ane I gang to. At first we used to get them in a schooner gless ; then it cam' doon to a wee tumbler ; and the last I was at I got the bawbees in an egg-cup."

IV

THE BURIAL OF BIG MACPHEE

ERCHIE looked pityingly at Big Macphee staggering down the street. " Puir sowl ! " said he, " whit's the maitter wi' ye noo ? "

Big Macphee looked up, and caught his questioner by the coat collar to steady himself. " Beer," said he ; " jist beer. Plain beer, if ye want to ken. It's no' ham and eggs,

I'll bate ye. Beer, beer, glorious beer ; I'm shair I've perished three gallons this very day. Three gallons hiv I in me, I'll wager."

" Ye wad be far better to cairry it hame in a pail," said Erchie. " Man, I'm rale vexed to see a fine, big, smert chap like you gaun hame like this, takin' the breadth o' the street."

" Hiv I no' a richt to tak' the breadth o' the street if I want it ? " said Big Macphee. " Am I no' a ratepayer ? I hiv a ludger's vote, and I'm gaun to vote against Joe Chamberlain and the dear loaf."

" Och ! ye needna fash aboot the loaf for a' the difference a tax on't 'll mak' to you," said Erchie. " If ye gang on the wye ye're daein' wi' the beer, it's the Death Duties yer freends 'll be bothered aboot afore lang."

And he led the erring one home.

Big Macphee was the man who for some months back had done the shouting for Duffy's lorry No. 2. He sustained the vibrant penetrating quality of a voice like the Cloch fog-horn on a regimen consisting of beer and the casual hard-boiled egg of the Mull of Kintyre Vaults. He had no relatives except a cousin " oot aboot Fintry," and when he justified Erchie's gloomy prediction about the Death Duties by dying of pneumonia a week afterwards, there was none to lament him, save in a mild, philosophical way, except Erchie's wife, Jinnet.

Jinnet, who could never sleep at night till she heard Macphee go up the stairs to his lodgings, thought the funeral would be scandalously cold and heartless lacking the cus- tomary " tousy tea " to finish up with, and as Duffy, that particular day, was not in a position to provide this solace for the mourners on their return from Sighthill Cemetery, she invited them to her house. There were Duffy and a man Macphee owed money to ; the cousin from " oot aboot Fintry " and his wife, who was, from the outset, jealous of the genteel way tea was served in Jinnet's parlour, and suspicious of a "stuckupness" that was only in her own imagination.

"It's been a nesty, wat, mochy, melancholy day for a burial," said Duffy at the second helping of Jinnet's cold boiled ham; "Macphee was jist as weel oot o't. He aye hated to hae to change his jaicket afore the last rake, him no' haein' ony richt wumman buddy aboot him to dry't."

"Och, the puir cratur!" said Jinnet. "It's like enough he had a disappointment ance upon a time. He was a cheery chap."

"He was a' that," said Duffy. "See's the haud o' the cream-poorie."

The cousin's wife felt Jinnet's home-baked seed-cake was a deliberate taunt at her own inefficiency in the baking line. She sniffed as she nibbled it with a studied appearance of inappreciation. "It wasna a very cheery burial he had, onyway," was her astounding comment, and at that Erchie winked to himself, realising the whole situation.

"Ye're richt there, Mistress Grant," said he. "Burials are no' whit they used to be. Perhaps—perhaps ye were expectin' a brass band?" and at that the cousin's wife saw this was a different man from her husband, and that there was a kind of back-chat they have in Glasgow quite unknown in Fintry.

"Oh! I wasna sayin' onything aboot brass bands," she retorted, very red-faced, and looking over to her husband for his support. He, however, was too replete with tea and cold boiled ham for any severe intellectual exercise, and was starting to fill his pipe. "I wasna saying onything aboot brass bands; we're no' used to thae kind o' operatics at burials whaur I come frae. But I think oor ain wye o' funerals is better than the Gleska wye."

Erchie (fearful for a moment that something might have been overlooked) glanced at the fragments of the feast, and at the spirit-bottle that had discreetly circulated somewhat earlier. "We're daein' the best we can," said he. "As

shair as death your kizzen—peace be wi' him!—'s jist as
nicely buried as if ye paid for it yersel' instead o' Duffy and
—and Jinnet ; if ye'll no' believe me ye can ask your man.
Nae doot Big Macphee deserved as fine a funeral as onybody,
wi' a wheen coaches, and a service at the kirk, wi' the organ
playin' and a' that, but that wasna the kind o' man your
kizzen was when he was livin'. He hated a' kinds o'
falderals."

"He was a cheery chap," said Jinnet again, nervously,
perceiving some electricity in the air.

"And he micht hae had a nicer burial," said the cousin's
wife, with firmness.

"Preserve us!" cried Erchie. "Whit wad ye like ?—
Flags maybe ? Or champagne wine at the liftin' ? Or
maybe wreaths o' floo'ers ? If it was cheeriness ye were
wantin' wi' puir Macphee, ye should hae come a month ago
and he micht hae ta'en ye himsel' to the Britannia Music-ha'."

"Haud yer tongue, Erchie," said Jinnet ; and the cousin's
wife, as fast as she could, took all the hair-pins out of her
head and put them in again. "They think we're that faur
back in Fintry," she said with fine irrelevance.

"Not at all," said Erchie, who saw his innocent wife was
getting all the cousin's wife's fierce glances. "Not at all,
mem. There's naething wrang wi' Fintry ; mony a yin I've
sent there. I'm rale chawed we didna hae a Fintry kind
o' funeral, to please ye. Whit's the patent thing aboot a
Fintry funeral ? "

"For wan thing," said the cousin's wife, "it's aye a rale
hearse we hae at Fintry and no' a box under a machine, like
thon. It was jist a disgrace. Little did his mither think
it wad come to thon. Ye wad think it was coals."

"And whit's the maitter wi' coals ? " cried Duffy, his
professional pride aroused. "Coals was his tred. Ye're
shairly awfu' toffs in Fintry aboot yer funerals."

The cousin's wife stabbed her head all over again with her
hair-pins, and paid no heed to him. Her husband evaded

her eyes with great determination. " No' that great toffs either," she retorted, " but we can aye afford a bit crape. There wasna a sowl that left this close behind the corp the day had crape in his hat except my ain man."

Then the man to whom Big Macphee owed money laughed.

" Crape's oot o' date, mistress," Erchie assured her. " It's no' the go noo at a' in Gleska ; ye micht as weel expect to see the auld saulies."

" Weel, it's the go enough in Fintry," said the cousin's wife. " And there was anither thing ; I didna expect to see onybody else but my man in weepers, him bein' the only freen' puir Macphee had but——"

" I havena seen weepers worn since the year o' the Tay Bridge," said Erchie, " and that was oot at the Mearns."

" Weel, we aye hae them at Fintry," insisted the cousin's wife.

" A cheery chap," said Jinnet again, at her wits'-end to put an end to this restrained wrangling, and the man Big Macphee owed money to laughed again.

" Whit's mair," went on the cousin's wife, " my man was the only wan there wi' a dacent shirt wi' tucks on the breist o't ; the rest o' ye had that sma' respect for the deid ye went wi' shirt-breists as flet as a sheet o' paper. It was showin' awfu' sma' respect for puir Macphee," and she broke down with her handkerchief at her eyes.

" Och ! to bleezes ! Jessie, ye're spilin' a' the fun," her husband remonstrated.

Erchie pushed back his chair and made an explanation. " Tucks is no' the go naither, mistress," said he, " and if ye kent whit the laundries were in Gleska ye wadna wonder at it. A laundry's a place whaur they'll no stand ony o' yer tucks, or ony nonsense o' that kind. Tucks wad spoil the teeth o' the curry-combs they use in the laundry for scoorin' the cuffs and collars ; they're no' gaun awa' to waste the vitriol they use for bleachin' on a wheen tucks. They couldna dae't at the money ; it's only threepence ha'penny a shirt, ye ken,

and oot o' that they hae to pay for the machines that tak's
the buttons aff, and the button-hole bursters—that's a tred
by itsel'. No, mem, tucked breists are oot o' date ; ye'll no'
see such a thing in Gleska ; I'm shair puir Macphee himself
hadna ane.   The man's as weel buried as if we had a' put on
the kilts, and had a piper in front playin' ' Lochaber no More.'
If ye'll no believe us, Duffy can show ye the receipted accoonts
for the undertaker and the lair ; can ye no', Duffy ? "

" Smert ! " said Duffy.

But the cousin's wife was not at all anxious to see accounts
of any kind, so she became more prostrate with annoyance
and grief than ever.

" Oot Fintry way," said Erchie, exasperated, " it's a' richt
to keep up tucked shirt-breists, and crape, and weepers, and
mort-cloths, and the like, for there canna be an awfu' lot o'
gaiety in the place, but we have aye plenty o' ither things to
amuse us in Gleska.   There's the Kelvingrove Museum, and
the Waxworks.   If ye're no' pleased wi' the wye Macphee
was buried, ye needna gie us the chance again wi' ony o' yer
freen's."

The cousin's wife addressed herself to her husband. " Whit
was yon ye were gaun to ask ? " she said to him.

He got very red, and shifted uneasily in his chair. " Me ! "
said he.   " I forget."

" No ye dinna ; ye mind fine."

" Och, it's a' richt.   Are we no' haein' a fine time ? " protested the husband.

" No, nor a' richt, Rubbert Grant."   She turned to the
others.   " Whit my man was gaun to ask, if he wasna such
a sumph, was whether oor kizzen hadna ony money put by
him."

" If ye kent him better, ye wadna need to ask," said Duffy.

" He was a cheery chap," said Jinnet.

" But was he no' in the Shepherds, or the Oddfellows, or the
Masons, or onything that wye ? "

" No, nor in the Good Templars nor the Rechabites," said

Erchie. " The only thing the puir sowl was ever in was the Mull o' Kintyre Vaults."

" Did I no' tell ye ? " said her husband.

. . . . . .

" Good-bye and thenky the noo," said the cousin's wife, as she went down the stair. " I've spent a rale nice day."

" It's the only thing ye did spend," said Erchie when she was out of hearing. " Funerals are managed gey chape in Fintry."

" Oh ye rascal, ye've the sherp tongue ! " said Jinnet.

" Ay, and there's some needs it ! A flet fit, too, but a warm hert," said Erchie.

V

THE PRODIGAL SON

JINNET, like a wise housewife, aye shops early on Saturday, but she always leaves some errand—some trifle overlooked, as it were—till the evening, for, true daughter of the city, she loves at times the evening throng of the streets. That of itself, perhaps, would not send her out with her door-key in her hand and a peering, eager look like that of one expecting something long of coming : the truth is she cherishes a hope that some Saturday to Erchie and her will come what comes often to her in her dreams, sometimes with terror and tears, sometimes with delight.

" I declare, Erchie, if I havena forgotten some sweeties for the kirk the morn," she says ; " put on yer kep and come awa' oot wi' me ; ye'll be nane the waur o' a breath o' fresh air."

Erchie puts down his " Weekly Mail," stifling a sigh and pocketing his spectacles. The night may be raw and wet, the streets full of mire, the kitchen more snug and clean and warm than any palace, but he never on such occasion says her nay. " You and your sweeties ! " he exclaims, lacing his boots ; " I'm shair ye never eat ony, in the kirk or onywhere else."

" And whit dae ye think I wad be buyin' them for if it wasna to keep me frae gantin' in the kirk when the sermon's dreich ? "

" Maybe for pappin' at the cats in the back coort," he retorts. " There's ae thing certain shair, I never see ye eatin' them."

" Indeed, and ye're richt," she confesses. " I havena the teeth for them nooadays."

" There's naething wrang wi' yer teeth, nor onything else aboot ye that I can see," her husband replies.

" Ye auld haver ! " Jinnet will then cry, smiling. " It's you that's lost yer sicht, I'm thinkin'. I'm a done auld buddy, that's whit I am, and that's tellin' ye. But haste ye and come awa' for the sweeties wi' me : whit'll thae wee Wilson weans in the close say the morn if Mrs MacPherson hasna ony sweeties for them ? "

They went along New City Road together, Erchie tall, lean, and a little round at the shoulders ; his wife a little wee body, not reaching his shoulder, dressed by-ordinar for her station and " ower young for her years," as a few jealous neighbours say.

An unceasing drizzle blurred the street lamps, the pavement was slippery with mud ; a night for the hearth-side and slippered feet on the fender ; yet the shops were thronged, and men and women crowded the thoroughfare or stood entranced before the windows.

" It's a wonnerfu' place, Gleska," said Erchie. " There's such diversion in't if ye're in the key for't. If ye hae yer health and yer wark, and the weans is weel, ye can be as happy as a lord, and far happier. It's the folk that live in the terraces where the nae stairs is, and sittin' in their paurlours readin' as hard's onything to keep up wi' the times, and naething to see oot the window but a plot o' grass that's no' richt green, that gets tired o' everything. The like o' us, that stay up closes and hae nae servants, and can come oot for a daunder efter turnin' the key in the door, hae the best o't. Lord! there's sae muckle to see—the cheeny-shops and the drapers, and the neighbours gaun for paraffin oil wi' a bottle, and Duffy wi' a new shepherd-tartan grauvit, and Lord Macdonald singin' awa' like a' that at the Normal School, and——"

" Oh, Erchie! dae ye mind when Willie was at the Normal ? " said Jinnet.

" Oh, my ! here it is already," thought Erchie. " If that laddie o' oors kent the hertbrek he was to his mither, I wonder wad he bide sae lang awa'."

" Yes, I mind, Jinnet ; I mind fine. Whit for need ye be askin' ? As I was sayin', it's aye in the common streets that things is happenin' that's worth lookin' at, if ye're game for fun. It's like travellin' on the railway ; if ye gang first-class, the way I did yince to Yoker by mistake, ye micht as weel be in a hearse for a' ye see or hear ; but gang third and ye'll aye find something to keep ye cheery if it's only fifteen chaps standin' on yer corns gaun to a fitba'-match, or a man in the corner o' the cairriage wi' a mooth-harmonium playin' a' the wye."

" Oh ! Erchie, look at the puir wean," said Jinnet, turning to glance after a woman with an infant in her arms. " Whit a shame bringin' oot weans on a nicht like this ! Its face is blae wi' the cauld."

" Och ! never mind the weans," said her husband ; " if ye were to mind a' the weans ye see in Gleska, ye wad hae a bonnie job o't."

" But jist think on the puir wee smout, Erchie. Oh, dear me ! there's anither yin no' three months auld, I'll wager. It's a black burnin' shame. It should be hame snug and soond in its wee bed. Does 't no' mind ye o' Willy when I took him first to his grannie's ? "

Her husband growled to himself, and hurried his step ; but that night there seemed to be a procession of women with infants in arms in New City Road, and Jinnet's heart was wrung at every crossing.

"I thocht it was pan-drops ye cam' oot for, or conversation-losengers," he protested at last; "and here ye're greetin' even-on aboot a wheen weans that's no' oor fault."

"Ye're a hard-herted monster, so ye are," said his wife indignantly.

"Of course I am," he confessed blythely. "I'll throw aff a' disguise and admit my rale name's Bluebeard, but don't tell the polis on me. Hard-herted monster—I wad need to be wi' a wife like you, that canna see a wean oot in the street at nicht withoot the drap at yer e'e. The weans is maybe no' that bad aff: the nicht air's no' waur nor the day air: maybe when they're oot here they'll no' mind they're hungry."

"Oh, Erchie! see that puir wee lame yin! God peety him!—I maun gie him a penny," whispered Jinnet, as a child in rags stopped before a jeweller's window to look in on a magic world of silver cruet-stands and diamond rings and gold watches.

"Ye'll dae naething o' the kind!" said Erchie. "It wad jist be wastin' yer money; I'll bate ye onything his mither drinks." He pushed his wife on her way past the boy, and, unobserved by her, slipped twopence in the latter's hand.

"I've seen the day ye werena sae mean, Erchie MacPherson," said his wife, vexatiously. "Ye aye brag o' yer flet fit and yer warm hert."

"It's jist a sayin'; I'm as mooly's onything," said Erchie, and winked to himself.

It was not the children of the city alone that engaged Jinnet's attention; they came to a street where now and then a young man would come from a public-house staggering; she always scanned the young fool's face with something of expectancy and fear.

"Jist aboot his age, Erchie," she whispered. "Oh, dear! I wonder if that puir callan' has a mither," and she stopped to look after the young man in his cups.

Erchie looked too, a little wistfully. " I'll wager ye he has," said he. " And like enough a guid yin, that's no' forgettin' him, though he may gang on the ran-dan, but in her bed at nicht no' sleepin', wonderin' whit's come o' him, and never mindin' onything that was bad in him, but jist a kind o' bein' easy-led, but mindin' hoo smert he was when he was but a laddie, and hoo he won the prize for com- poseetion in the school, and hoo prood he was when he brocht hame the first wage he got on a Setturday. If God Almichty has the same kind o' memory as a mither, Jinnet, there'll be a chance at the hinderend for the warst o' us."

They had gone at least a mile from home ; the night grew wetter and more bitter, the crowds more squalid, Jinnet's interest in errant belated youth more keen. And never a word of the sweets she had made-believe to come out particu- larly for. They had reached the harbour side ; the ships lay black and vacant along the wharfs, noisy seamen and women debauched passed in groups or turned into the public-houses. Far west into the drizzling night the river lamps stretched, showing the drumly water of the highway of the world. Jinnet stopped and looked and listened. " I think we're far enough, Erchie ; I think we'll jist gang hame," said she.

" Right ! " said Erchie, patiently ; and they turned, but not without one sad glance from his wife before they lost sight of the black ships, the noisy wharves, the rolling seamen on the pavement, the lamplights of the watery way that reaches to the world's end.

" Oh ! Erchie," she said piteously, " I wonder if he's still on the ships."

" Like enough," said her husband. " I'm shair he's no' in Gleska at onyrate without comin' to see us. I'll bate ye he's a mate or a captain or a purser or something, and that thrang somewhere abroad he hasna time the noo ; but we'll hear frae him by-and-bye. The wee deevil ! I'll gie him't when I see him, to be givin' us such a fricht."

"No' that wee, Erchie," said Jinnet. "He's bigger than yersel'."

"So he is, the rascal! am I no' aye thinkin' o' him jist aboot the age he was when he was at the Sunday school."

"Hoo lang is't since we heard o' him, Erchie?"

"Three or four years, or maybe five," said Erchie, quickly. "Man! the wye time slips bye! It doesna look like mair nor a twelvemonth."

"It looks to me like twenty year," said Jinnet, "and it's naething less than seeven, for it was the year o' Annie's weddin', and her wee Alick's six at Mertinmas. Seeven years! Oh, Erchie, where can he be? Whit can be wrang wi' him? No' to write a scrape o' a pen a' that time! Maybe I'll no' be spared to see him again."

"I'll bate ye whit ye like ye will," said her husband. "And if he doesna bring ye hame a lot o' nice things—shells and parrots, and bottles of scent, and Riga Balsam for hacked hands, and the rale Cheena cheeny, and ostrich feathers and a' that, I'll—I'll be awfu' wild at him. But the first thing I'll dae 'll be to stand behind the door and catch him when he comes in, and tak' the strap to him for the rideeculous wye he didna write to us."

"Seeven years," said Jinnet. "Oh, that weary sea, a puir trade to be followin' for ony mither's son. It was Australia he wrote frae last; whiles I'm feared the blecks catched him oot there and killed him in the Bush."

"No! nor the Bush! Jist let them try it wi' oor Willie! Dod! he would put the hems on them; he could wrastle a score o' blecks wi' his least wee bit touch."

"Erchie."

"Weel, Jinnet?"

"Ye'll no' be angry wi' me; but wha was it tellt ye they saw him twa years syne carryin' on near the quay, and that he was stayin' at the Sailors' Home?"

"It was Duffy," said Erchie, hurriedly. "I have a guid mind to—to kick him for sayin' onything o' the kind. I

o*

wad hae kicked him for't afore this if—if I wasna a beadle
in the kirk."

" I'm shair it wasna oor Willie at a'," said Jinnet.

" Oor Willie! Dae ye think the laddie's daft, to be in
Gleska and no' come to see his mither ? "

" I canna believe he wad dae't," said Jinnet, but always
looked intently in the face of every young man who passed
them.

.   .   .   .

" Weel, that's ower for anither Setturday," said Erchie to
himself, resuming his slippers and his spectacles.

" I declare, wife," said he, " ye've forgotten something."

" Whit is't ? " she asked.

" The sweeties ye went oot for," said Erchie, solemnly.

" Oh, dear me ! amn't I the silly yin ? Thinkin' on that
Willie o' oors puts everything oot o' my heid."

Erchie took a paper bag from his pocket and handed it to
her. " There ye are," said he. " I had them in my pooch
since dinner-time. I kent ye wad be needin' them."

" And ye never let on, but put on your boots and cam'
awa' oot wi' me."

" Of coorse I did ; I'm shairly no' that auld but I can be
gled on an excuse for a walk oot wi' my lass ? "

" Oh, Erchie ! Erchie ! " she cried, " when will ye be
wise ? I think I'll put on the kettle and mak' a cup o' tea
to ye."

VI

MRS DUFFY DESERTS HER MAN

" THEY'RE yatterin' awa' in the papers there like sweetie-
wives aboot Carlyle and his wife," said Erchie. " It's no'
the thing at a' makin' an exposure. I kent Carlyle fine ;
he had a wee baker's shop in Balmano Brae, and his wife
made potted heid. It was quite clean ; there was naething

wrang wi't. If they quarrelled it was naebody's business but their ain.

"It's a gey droll hoose whaur there's no' whiles a rippit. Though my fit's flet my hert's warm; but even me and Jinnet hae a cast-oot noo and then. I'm aye the mair angry if I ken I'm wrang, and I've seen me that bleezin' bad-tempered that I couldna light my pipe, and we wadna speak to ane anither for oors and oors.

"It'll come the nicht, and me wi' a job at waitin' to gang to, and my collar that hard to button I nearly break my thoombs.

"For a while Jinnet 'll say naethin', and then she'll cry, 'See's a haud o't, ye auld fuiter!'

"I'll be glowerin' awfu' solemn up at the corner o' the ceilin' when she's workin' at the button, lettin' on I'm fair ferocious yet, and she'll say, 'Whit are ye glowerin' at? Dae ye see ony spiders' webs?'

"'No, nor spiders' webs,' I says, as gruff as onything. 'I never saw a spider's web in this hoose.'

"At that she gets red in the face and tries no' to laugh.

"'There ye are laughin'! Ye're bate!' I says.

"'So are you laughin',' says she; 'and I saw ye first. Awa', ye're daft! Will I buy onything tasty for your supper?'

"Duffy's different. I'm no' blamin' him, for his wife's different too. When they quarrel it scandalises the close and gies the land a bad name. The wife washes even-on, and greets into her washin'-byne till she mak's the water cauld, and Duffy sits a' nicht wi' his feet on the kitchen-hobs singin' 'Boyne Water,' because her mither was a Bark, called M'Ginty, and cam' frae Connaught. The folk in the flet abin them hae to rap doon at them wi' a poker afore they'll get their nicht's sleep, and the broken delf that gangs oot to the ash-pit in the mornin' wad fill a crate.

"I'm no' sayin', mind ye, that Duffy doesna like her; it's jist his wye, for he hasna ony edication. He was awfu' vexed the time she broke her leg; it pit him aff his wark for three days, and he spent the time lamentin' aboot her doon in the Mull o' Kintyre Vaults.

" The biggest row they ever had that I can mind o' was aboot the time the weemen wore the dolmans. Duffy's wife took the notion o' a dolman, and told him that seein' there was a bawbee up in the bag o' coal that week, she thocht he could very weel afford it.

" ' There's a lot o' things we'll hae to get afore the dolman,' says he ; ' I'm needin' a new kep mysel', and I'm in a menoj for a bicycle.'

" ' I'm fair affronted wi' my claes,' says she ; ' I havena had onything new for a year or twa, and there's Carmichael's wife wi' her sealskin jaicket.'

" ' Let her ! ' says Duffy ; ' wi' a face like thon she's no' oot the need o't.'

" They started wi' that and kept it up till the neighbours near brocht doon the ceilin' on them.

" ' That's the worst o' leevin' in a close,' said Duffy, ' ye daurna show ye're the maister in yer ain hoose withoot a lot o' nyafs above ye spilin' a' the plaister.'

" Duffy's wife left him the very next day, and went hame to her mither's. She left oot clean sox for him and a bowl o' mulk on the dresser in case he micht be hungry afore he could mak' his ain tea.

" When Duffy cam' hame and found whit had happened, he was awfu' vexed for himsel' and begood to greet.

" I heard aboot the thing, and went in to see him, and found him drinkin' the mulk and eatin' shaves o' breid at twa bites to the shave the same as if it was for a wager.

" ' Isn't this an awfu' thing that's come on me, Mac-Pherson ? ' says he ; ' I'm nae better nor a weedower except for the mournin's.'

" ' It hasna pit ye aff yer meat onywye,' says I.

" ' Oh ! ' he says, ' ye may think I'm callous, but I hae been greetin' for twa oors afore I could tak' a bite, and I'm gaun to start again as soon as I'm done wi' this mulk.'

" ' Ye should gang oot,' I tells him, ' and buy the mistress a poke o' grapes and gang roond wi't to her mither's and tell her ye're an eediot and canna help it.'

" But wad he ?   No fears o' him !

" ' Oh ! I can dae fine withoot her,' he tells me quite cocky. ' I could keep a hoose wi' my least wee bit touch.'

" ' Ye puir deluded crature,' I tell't him, ' ye micht as well try to keep a hyena.   It looks gey like a collie-dug, but it'll no' sup saps, and a hoose looks an awfu' simple thing till ye try't ; I ken fine because Jinnet aften tellt me.'

" He begood to soop the floor wi' a whitenin'-brush, and put the stour under the bed.

" ' Go on,' says I, ' ye're daein' fine for a start. A' ye want's a week or twa at the nicht-schools, where they learn ye laundry-work and cookin', and when ye're at it ye should tak' lessons in scientific dressmakin'.   I'll look for ye comin' up the street next week wi' the charts under your oxter and your lad wi' ye.'

" For a hale week Duffy kept his ain hoose.

" He aye forgot to buy sticks for the fire at nicht, and had to mak' it in the mornin' wi' a dizzen or twa o' claes-pins. He didna mak' tea, for he couldna tak' tea withoot cream till't, and he couldna get cream because he didna ken the wye to wash a poorie, so he made his breakfast o' cocoa and his tea o' cocoa till he was gaun aboot wi' a broon taste in his mooth.

" On the Sunday he tried to mak' a dinner, and biled the plates wi' soap and soda to get the creesh aff them when he found it wadna come aff wi' cauld water and a washin'-clout.

" ' Hoo are ye gettin' on in yer ain bonny wee hoose noo ? ' I asks him ae dirty, wet, cauld day, takin' in a bowl o' broth to him frae Jinnet.

" ' Fine,' says he, quite brazen ; ' it's like haein' a yacht. I could be daein' first-rate if it was the summer-time.'

" He wore them long kahootchy boots up to your knees

on wet days at his wark, and he couldna get them aff him
withoot a hand frae his wife, so he had just to gang to his
bed wi' them on.   He ordered pipe-clay by the hunderwicht
and soap by the yard ; he blackleaded his boots, and didna
gang to the kirk because he couldna get on his ain collar.

" ' Duffy,' I says, ' ye'll mak' an awfu' nice auld wife if
ye leeve lang enough.   I'll hae to get Jinnet started to knit
ye a Shetland shawl.'

" Efter a week it begood to tell awfu' bad on Duffy's health.
He got that thin, and so wake in the voice he lost orders, for
a wheen o' his auldest customers didna ken him when he
cried, and gave a' their tred to MacTurk, the coalman, that
had a wife and twa sisters-in-law to coother him up wi'
beef-tea on wet days and a' his orders.

" Duffy's mind was affected too ; he gave the richt wicht,
and lost twa chances in ae day o' pittin' a ha'penny on the
bag wi' auld blin' weemen that couldna read his board.

" Then he ca'd on a doctor. The doctor tell't him he
couldna mak' it oot at a', but thocht it was appen—what
d'ye ca't ?—the same trouble as the King had, and that
Duffy had it in five or six different places. There was
naething for him but carefu' dietin' and a voyage to the
Cape.

" That very day Duffy, gaun hame frae his wark gey
shauchly, wi' a tin o' salmon in his pooch for his tea, saw his
wife comin' doon the street.   When she saw him she turned
and ran awa', and him efter her as hard's he could pelt.
She thocht he was that wild he was gaun to gie her a clourin' ;
and she was jist fair bate wi' the runnin' when he caught
up on her in a back coort.

" ' Tig ! ' says Duffy, touchin' her ; ' you're het ! '

" ' Oh, Jimmy ! ' she says, ' are ye in wi' me ? '

" ' Am I no' ? ' says Duffy, and they went hame thegither.

" ' There was a stranger in my tea this mornin',' says
Duffy : ' I kent fine somebody wad be comin'.'

" His wife tell't Jinnet a while efter that that she was a

great dale the better o' the rest she got the time she went
hame to her mither's ; it was jist the very thing she was
needin' ; and, forbye, she got the dolman."

VII

CARNEGIE'S WEE LASSIE

ERCHIE sought me out on Saturday with a copy of that day's
" News " containing a portrait of Carnegie's little daughter
Margaret.

" Man, isn't she the rale wee divert ? " said he, glowing.
" That like her faither, and sae weel-put-on ! She minds me
terrible o' oor wee Teenie when she was jist her age."

" She has been born into an enviable state, Erchie," I
said.

" Oh, I'm no' sae shair aboot that," said Erchie. " It's a
gey hard thing, whiles, bein' a millionaire's only wean. She
canna hae mony wee lassies like hersel' to play the peever
wi', or lift things oot o' the stanks o' Skibo Castle wi' a bit
o' clye and a string. I'm shair it must be a hard job for the
auld man, her paw, to provide diversions for the puir wee
smout. And she'll hae that mony things that she'll no' can
say whit she wants next. I ken fine the wye it'll be up
yonder at Skibo.

" It'll be, ' Paw, I'm wantin' something.'

" ' Whit is't, my dawtie, and ye'll get it to break ? ' Mr
Carnegie 'll say, and lift her on his knee, and let her play wi'
the works o' his twa thoosand pound repeater watch.

" ' I dinna ken,' says the wee lassie, ' but I want it awfu'
fast.'

" ' Whit wad ye be sayin' to an electric doll wi' a phono-
graph inside it to mak' it speak ? ' asks Mr Carnegie.

" ' I'm tired o' dolls,' says the wee yin, ' and, besides, I
wad raither dae the speakin' mysel'.'

" ' Ye're a rale wee woman there, Maggie,' says her paw.

" ' Weel, whit dae ye say to a wee totey motor-car a' for your ain sel', and jewelled in four-and-twenty holes ? ' says he efter that, takin' the hands o' his watch frae her in case she micht swallow them.

" ' Oh ! a motor-car,' says the wee lassie. ' No, I'm no carin' for ony mair motor-cars ; I canna get takin' them to my bed wi' me.'

" ' Ye're weel aff there,' says he. ' I've had the hale o' the Pittsburg works to my bed wi' me,' he says. ' They were in my heid a' the time when I couldna sleep, and they were on my chest a' the time when I was sleepin'.'

" ' Whit wye that, paw ? ' says the wee lassie.

" ' I was feart something wad gae wrang, and I wad lose a' the tred, and be puir again.'

" ' But I thocht ye wanted to die puir, paw ? ' says the wee lassie.

" ' Ay, but I never had ony notion o' leevin' puir,' says Mr Carnegie as smert's ye like, ' and that mak's a' the difference. If ye're no' for anither motor carriage, wad ye no' tak' a new watch ? '

" ' No, paw,' says the wee lassie, ' I'm no' for anither watch. The only thing a watch tells ye is when it's time to gang to bed, and then I'm no wantin' to gang onywye. Whit I wad like wad be ane o' thae watches that has haunds that dinna move when ye're haein' awfu' fine fun.'

" ' Oh, ay ! ' says her paw at that ; ' that's the kind we're a' wantin', but they're no' makin' them, and I'm no' shair that I wad hae muckle use for yin nooadays even if they were. If ye'll no hae a watch, will ye hae a yacht, or a brass band, or a fleein'-machine, or a piebald pony ? '

" ' I wad raither mak' mud-pies,' says the wee innocent.

" ' Mud-pies ! ' cries her faither in horror, lookin' roond to see that naebody heard her. ' Wheesh ! Maggie, it wadna look nice to see the like o' you makin' mud-pies. Ye havena the claes for't. Beside, I'm tellt they're no' the go nooadays at a'.'

" ' Weel,' says she at that, ' I think I'll hae a hairy-heided lion.'

" ' Hairy-heided lion. Right ! ' says Mr Carnegie. ' Ye'll get that, my wee lassie,' and cries doon the turret stair to the kitchen for his No. 9 secretary.

" The No. 9 secretary comes up in his shirt sleeves, chewin' blot-sheet and dichting the ink aff his elbows.

" ' Whit are ye thrang at the noo ? ' asks Mr Carnegie as nice as onything to him, though he's only a kind o' a workin' man.

" ' Sendin' aff the week's orders for new kirk organs,' says the No. 9 secretary, ' and it'll tak' us till Wednesday.'

" ' Where's a' the rest o' my secretaries ? ' asks Mr Carnegie.

" ' Half o' them's makin' oot cheques for new leebraries up and doon the country, and the ither half's oot in the back-coort burning letters frae weedows wi' nineteen weans, nane o' them daein' for themsel's, and frae men that were dacent and steady a' their days, but had awfu' bad luck.'

" ' If it gangs on like this we'll hae to put ye on the night-shift,' says Mr Carnegie. ' It's comin' to't when I hae to write ma ain letters. I'll be expected to write my ain books next. But I'll no' dae onything o' the kind. Jist you telegraph to India, or Africa, or Japan, or wherever the hairy-heided lions comes frae, and tell them to send wee Maggie ane o' the very best at 50 per cent. aff for cash.'

" Early ae mornin' some weeks efter that, when the steam-hooter for wakenin' the secretaries starts howlin' at five o'clock, Mr Carnegie comes doon stair and sees the hairy-heided lion in a crate bein' pit aff a lorry. He has it wheeled in to the wee lassie when she's at her breakfast.

" ' Let it oot,' she says ; ' I want to play wi't.'

" ' Ye wee fuiter ! ' he says, lauchin' like onything, ' ye canna get playin' wi't oot o' the cage, but ye'll can get feedin't wi' sultana-cake.'

" But that disna suit wee Maggie, and she jist tells him to send it awa' to the Bronx Zoo in New York.

" ' Bronx Zoo. Right ! ' says her paw, and cries on his No. 22 secretary to send it aff wi' the parcel post at yince.

" ' That minds me,' he says, ' there's a cryin' need for hairy-heided lions all over Europe and the United States. The moral and educative influence o' the common or bald-heided lion is of no account. Noo that maist o' the kirks has twa organs apiece, and there's a leebrary in every clachan in the country, I must think o' some ither wye o' gettin' rid o' this cursed wealth. It was rale 'cute o' you, Maggie, to think o't ; I'll pay half the price o' a hairy-heided lion for every toon in the country wi' a population o' over five hundred that can mak' up the ither half by public subscription.'

" And then the wee lassie says she canna tak' her parridge.

" ' Whit for no' ? ' he asks her, anxious-like. ' Are they no guid ? '

" ' Oh, they're maybe guid enough,' she says, ' but I wad raither hae toffie.'

" ' Toffie. Right ! ' says her paw, and orders up the chef to mak' toffie in a hurry.

" ' Whit's he gaun to mak' it wi' ? ' asks the wee yin.

" ' Oh, jist in the ordinar' wye—wi' butter and sugar,' says her paw.

" ' That's jist common toffie,' says the wee lassie ; ' I want some ither kind.'

" ' As shair's death, Maggie,' he says, ' there's only the ae wye o' makin' toffie.'

" ' Then whit's the use o' haein' a millionaire for a paw ? ' she asks.

" ' True for you,' he says, and thinks hard. ' I could mak' the chef put in champed rubies or a di'mond or twa grated doon.'

" ' Wad it mak' the toffie taste ony better ? ' asks the wee cratur'.

" ' No' a bit better,' he says. ' It wadna taste sae guid as the ordinary toffie, but it wad be nice and dear.'

" ' Then I'll jist hae to hae the plain, chape toffie,' says wee Maggie.

" ' That's jist whit I hae to hae mysel' wi' a great mony things,' says her paw. ' Being a millionaire's nice enough some wyes, but there's a wheen things money canna buy, and paupers wi' three or four thoosand paltry pounds a-year is able to get jist as guid toffie and ither things as I can. I canna even dress mysel' different frae ither folks, for it wad look rideeculous to see me gaun aboot wi' gold cloth waist-coats and a hat wi' strings o' pearls on it, so' a' I can dae is to get my nickerbocker suits made wi' an extra big check. I hae the pattern that big noo there's only a check-and-a-half to the suit ; but if it wasna for the honour o't I wad just as soon be wearin' Harris tweed.' "

" Upon my word, Erchie," I said, " you make me sorry for our philanthropic friend, and particularly for his little girl."

" Oh, there's no occasion ! " protested Erchie. " There's no condeetion in life that hasna its compensations, and even Mr Carnegie's wee lassie has them. I hae nae doot the best fun her and her paw gets is when they're playin' at bein' puir. The auld man 'll nae doot whiles hide his pocket-money in the press, and sit doon readin' his newspaper, wi' his feet on the chimney-piece, and she'll come in and ask for a bawbee.

" ' I declare to ye I havena a farden, Maggie,' he'll say ; ' but I'll gie ye a penny on Setturday when I get my pay.'

" ' I dinna believe ye,' she'll say.

" ' Then ye can ripe me,' says her paw, and the wee tot 'll feel in a' his pooches, and find half a sovereign in his waistcoat. They'll let on it's jist a bawbee (the wee thing never saw a rale bawbee in her life, I'll warrant), and he'll wonner whit wye he forgot aboot it, and tell her to keep it and buy jujubes wi't, and she'll be awa' like a whitteruck and come back in a while wi' her face a' sticky for a kiss, jist like rale.

" Fine I ken the wee smouts ; it was that wye wi' oor ain Teenie.

" Other whiles she'll hae a wee tin bank wi' a bee-skep on't, and she'll hae't fu' o' sovereigns her faither's veesitors slip't in her haund when they were gaun awa', and she'll put it on the mantelpiece and gang out. Then her paw 'll get up lauchin' like onything to himsel', and tak' doon the wee bank and rattle awa' at it, lettin' on he's robbin't for a schooner o' beer, and at that she'll come rinnin' in and catch him at it, and they'll hae great fun wi' that game. I have nae doot her faither and mither get mony a laugh at her playin' at wee washin's, too, and lettin' on she's fair trauchled aff the face o' the earth wi' a family o' nine dolls, an' three o' them doon wi' the hoopin'-cough. Oh ! they're no that bad aff for fine fun even in Skibo Castle."

VIII

A SON OF THE CITY

MY old friend came daundering down the street with what might have been a bag of cherries, if cherries were in season, and what I surmised were really the twopenny pies with which Jinnet and he sometimes made the Saturday evenings festive. When we met he displayed a blue hyacinth in a flower-pot.

" Saw't in a fruiterer's window," said he, " and took the notion. Ninepence ; dod ! I dinna ken hoo they mak' them for the money. I thocht it wad please the wife, and min' her o' Dunoon and the Lairgs and a' thae places that's doon the watter in the summer-time.

" Ye may say whit ye like, I'm shair they shut up a' thae coast toons when us bonny wee Gleska buddies is no' comin' doon wi' oor tin boxes, and cheerin' them up wi' a clog-wallop on the quay.

" It's a fine thing a flooer ; no' dear to buy at the start, and chaper to keep than a canary. It's Nature—the Rale Oreeginal. Ninepence ! And the smell o't ! Jist a fair phenomena ! "

" A sign of spring, Erchie," I said ; " thank heaven ! the primrose is in the wood, and the buds bursting on the hedge in the country, though you and I are not there to see it."

" I daursay," said he, " I'll hae to mak' a perusal doon the length o' Yoker on the skoosh car when the floods is ower. I'm that used to them noo, as shair's death I canna get my naitural sleep on dry nichts unless Jinnet gangs oot to the back and throws chuckies at the window, lettin' on it 's rain and hailstanes. When I hear the gravel on the window I cod mysel' it's the genuine auld Caledonian climate, say my wee ' Noo I lay me,' and gang to sleep as balmy as a nicht polisman.

" There's a great cry the noo aboot folks comin' frae the country and croodin' into the toons and livin' in slums and degenerating the bone and muscle o' Britain wi' eatin' kippered herrin' and ice-cream. Thoosands o' them's gaun aboot Gleska daein' their bit turns the best way they can, and no' kennin', puir craturs ! there's a Commission sittin' on them as hard's it can.

" ' Whit's wanted,' says the Inspectors o' Poor, ' is to hustle them aboot frae place to place till the soles o' their feet gets red-hot wi' the speed they're gaun at ; then gie them a bar o' carbolic soap and a keg o' Keatin's poother, and put them on the first train for Edinburgh.'

" ' Tear doon the rookeries,' says anither man, ' and pit up rooms and kitchens wi' wally jawboxes and tiled closes at a rent o' eighteenpence a-week when ye get it.'

" ' That's a' very fine,' says the economists, ' but if ye let guid wally jawbox hooses at ten shillin's a-year less than the auld-established and justly-popular slum hoose, will't no' tempt mair puir folk frae the country into Gleska and conjest the Gorbals worse than ever ? ' The puir economists thinks the folks oot aboot Skye and Kamerhashinjoo's waitin' for telegrams tellin' them the single apairtment hoose in Lyon Street, Garscube Road, 's doon ten shillin's a-year, afore they pack their carpet-bags and start on the *Clansman* for the

Broomielaw. But they're no'. They divna ken onything aboot the rent o' hooses in Gleska, and they're no' carin', for maybe they'll no' pay't onywye. They jist come awa' to Gleska when the wife tells them, and Hughie's auld enough for a polisman.

" Slums ! wha wants to abolish slums ? It's no' the like o' me nor Duffy. If there werena folk leevin' in slums I couldna buy chape shirts, and the celebrated Stand Fast Craigroyston serge breeks at 2s. 11¾d. the pair, bespoke, guaranteed, shrunk, and wan hip-pocket.

" When they're proposin' the toast o' the ' Army, Navy, and Reserve Forces,' they ought to add the Force that live in Slums. They're the men and women that's aye ready to sweat for their country—when their money's done. A man that wants the chapest kind o' chape labour kens he'll aye can get it in the slums ; if it wasna for that, my Stand Fast Craigroyston breeks wad maybe cost 7s. 6d., and some of the elders in the kirk I'm beadle for wad hae to smoke tuppenny cigars instead o' sixpenny yins.

" The slums 'll no' touch ye if ye don't gang near them.

" Whit a lot o' folk want to dae 's to run the skoosh cars away oot into the country whaur the clegs and the midges and the nae gas is, and coup them oot at Deid Slow on the Clyde, and leave them there wander't. Hoo wad they like it themsel's ? The idea is that Duffy, when he's done wi' his last rake o' coals, 'll mak' the breenge for Deid Slow, and tak' his tea and wash his face wi' watter that hard it stots aff his face like a kahootchy ba', and spend a joyous and invigoratin' evenin' sheuchin' leeks and prunin' cauliflooer-bushes in the front plot o' his cottage home.

" I think I see him ! He wad faur sooner pay twelve pounds rent in Grove Street, and hae the cheery lowe o' the Mull o' Kintyre Vaults forenent his paurlor window, than get his boots a' glaur wi' plantin' syboes roond his cottage home at £6, 10s.

" The country's a' richt for folks that havena their health

and dinna want to wear a collar to their wark, and Deid Slow
and places like that may be fine for gaun to if ye want to get
ower the dregs o' the measles, but they're nae places for ony
man that loves his fellow-men.

" And still there's mony a phenomena ! I ken a man that
says he wad stay in the country a' the year roond if he hadna
to bide in Gleska and keep his eye on ither men in the same
tred's himsel', to see they're no' risin' early in the mornin'
and gettin' the better o' him.

" It wadna suit Easy-gaun Erchie. Fine I ken whit the
country is ; did I no' leeve a hale winter aboot Dalry when I
was a halflin' ?

" It's maybe a' richt in summer, when you and me gangs
oot on an excursion, and cheers them up wi' our melodeon wi'
bell accompaniment ; but the puir sowls havena much
diversion at the time o' year the V-shaped depression's
cleckin' on Ben Nevis, and the weather prophets in the
evening papers is promisin' a welcome change o' weather
every Setturday. All ye can dae when your wark's done and
ye've ta'en your tea 's to put on a pair o' top-boots and a
waterproof, and gang oot in the dark. There's no' even a
close to coort in, and if ye want to walk along a country road
at nicht thinkin' hoo much money ye hae in the bank, ye
must be gey smert no' to fa' into a ditch. Stars ? Wha
wants to bother glowerin' at stars ? There's never ony
change in the programme wi' them in the country. If I want
stars I gang to the Britannia.

" Na, na, Gleska's the place, and it's nae wonder a' the
country-folks is croodin' into't as fast's they can get their
cottage homes sublet.

" This is the place for intellect and the big pennyworth of
skim-milk.

" I declare I'm that ta'en wi' Gleska I get up sometimes
afore the fire's lichted to look oot at the window and see if it's
still to the fore.

" Fifteen public-hooses within forty yairds o' the close-

mooth ; a guttapercha works at the tap o' the street, and twa
cab-stances at the foot. My mornin' 'oors are made merry
wi' the delightfu' strains o' factory hooters and the sound
o' the dust-cart man kickin' his horse like onything whaur
it 'll dae maist guid.

" I can get onywhere I want to gang on the skoosh cars
for a bawbee or a penny, but the only place I hae to gang to
generally is my wark, and I wad jist as soon walk it, for I'm
no' in ony hurry.

" When the rain's blashin' doon at nicht on the puir
miserable craturs workin' at their front plots in Deid Slow, or
trippin' ower hens that 'll no' lay ony eggs, I can be improvin'
my mind wi' Duffy at the Mull o' Kintyre Vaults, or daun-
derin' alang the Coocaddens wi' my hand tight on my watch-
pocket, lookin' at the shop windows and jinkin' the members
o' the Sons of Toil Social Club (Limited), as they tak' the
breadth o' the pavement.

" Gleska ! Some day when I'm in the key for't I'll mak'
a song aboot her. Here the triumphs o' civilisation meet ye
at the stair-fit, and three bawbee mornin' rolls can be had
efter six o'clock at nicht for a penny.

" There's libraries scattered a' ower the place ; I ken, for
I've seen them often, and the brass plate at the door tellin'
ye whit they are.

" Art's a' the go in Gleska, too ; there's something aboot
it every ither nicht in the papers, when Lord Somebody-or-
ither's no' divorcin' his wife, and takin' up the space ; and I
hear there's hunders o' pictures oot in yon place at Kelvingrove.

" Theatres, concerts, balls, swarees, lectures—ony mortal
thing ye like that'll keep ye oot o' your bed, ye'll get in
Gleska if ye have the money to pay for't."

" It's true, Erchie."

" Whit's true ? " said the old man, wrapping the paper
more carefully round his flower-pot. " Man, I'm only
coddin'. Toon or country, it doesna muckle maitter if, like

me, ye stay in yer ain hoose. I don't stay in Gleska ; not me ! it's only the place I mak' my money in ; I stay wi' Jinnet."

IX

ERCHIE ON THE KING'S CRUISE

I DELIBERATELY sought out Erchie one day in order to elicit his views upon the Royal progress through the Western Isles, and found him full of the subject, with the happiest disposition to eloquence thereon.

" Man ! I'm that gled I'm to the fore to see this prood day for Scotland," said he. " I'm daein' hardly onything but read the mornin' and evenin' papers, and if the Royal yacht comes up the length o' Yoker I'm gaun doon mysel' to wave a hanky. ' His Majesty in Arran. Great Reception,' says they. ' His Majesty in Glorious Health. Waves his hand to a Wee Lassie, and Nearly Shoots a Deer,' says they. ' His Majesty's Yacht Surrounded by the Natives. Escape round the Mull. Vexation of Campbeltown, and Vote of Censure by the Golfers of Machrihanish,' says they. Then the telegrams frae ' Oor Special Correspondent ' : ' OBAN, 1 P.M.—It is confidently expected that the Royal yacht will come into the bay this evenin' in time for tea. The esplanade is being washed with eau-de-Cologne, and a' the magistrates is up at Rankine's barber shop gettin' a dry shampoo.' ' OBAN, 1.30 P.M.—A wire frae Colonsay says the Royal yacht is about to set sail for Oban. Tremendous excitement prevails here, and the price o' hotel bedrooms is raised 200 per cent. It is decided to mobilise the local Boys' Brigade, and engage Johnny M'Coll to play the pipes afore the King when he's comin' ashore.' ' 6 P.M.—The Royal yacht has just passed Kerrara, and it is now certain that Oban will not be visited by the Royal party. All the flags have been taken down, and scathing comments on the extraordinary affair are anticipated from the local Press.'

" Maybe ye wadna think it, but his Majesty's gaun roond the West Coast for the sake o' his health.

" ' Ye'll hae to tak' a month o' the rest cure,' the doctors tellt him, ' a drap o' claret wine to dinner, and nae worry aboot business.'

" ' Can I afford it ? ' said his Majesty, that vexed-like, for he was puttin' aff his coat and rollin' up his sleeves to start work for the day.

" ' There's nae choice in the maitter,' said the doctors ; ' we order it.'

" ' But can I afford it ? ' again said his Majesty. ' Ye ken yoursel's, doctors, I have had a lot o' expense lately, wi' trouble in the hoose, and wi' the Coronation and aething and another. Could I no' be doin' the noo wi' Setturday-to-Monday trips doon the watter ? '

" But no ; the doctors said there was naethin' for him but rest. So his Majesty had to buy a new topcoat and a yachtin' bunnet, and start oot on the *Victoria and Albert.*

" It's a twa-funnelled boat, but I'm tellt that, bein' Government built, yin o' the funnels has a blaw-doon, and they daurna light the furnace below't if the win's no' in a certain airt.

" The yacht made first for the Isle o' Man, and wasna five meenutes in the place when the great novelist, Hall Corelli or Mary Caine, or whichever it is, was aboard o' her distributin' hand-bills advertisin' the latest novel, and the King took fright, and left the place as soon as he could.

" I'm tellin' ye it's a gey sair trauchle bein' a King. The puir sowl thought the Hielan's wad be a nice quate place where naebody wad bother him, and so he set sail then for Arran.

" ' What is that I see afore me ? ' said he, comin' up past Pladda.

" The captain put his spy-gless to his e'e, and got as white's a cloot.

" ' It's your Majesty's joyous and expectant subjects,'

says he. ' They've sixty-seven Gleska steamers oot yonder
waitin' on us, and every skipper has his hand on the string
o' the steam-hooter.'

" ' My God ! ' groaned the puir King, ' I thought I was
sent awa' here for the guid o' my health.'

" Before he could say knife, a' the Gleska steamers and
ten thoosan' wee rowin'-boats were scrapin' the pent aff
the sides o' the *Victoria and Albert*, and half a million Scottish
taxpayers were cheerin' their beloved Sovereign, Edward VII.,
every mortal yin o' them sayin', ' Yon's him yonder ! ' and
p'intin' at him.

" ' Will I hae to shoogle hands wi' a' that crood ? ' he
asked the captain o' the *Victoria and Albert*, and was told
it wad dae if he jist took aff his kep noo and then.

" And so, takin' aff his kep noo and then, wi' a' the Gleska
steamers and the ten thoosan' wee rowin'-boats hingin' on
to the side o' the yacht, and half a million devoted subjects
takin' turn aboot at keekin' in through the port-holes to
see what he had for dinner, his Majesty sailed into Brodick
Bay.

" ' The doctors were right,' says he ; ' efter a', there's
naething like a rest cure ; it's a mercy we're a' spared.'

" The following day his Majesty hunted the deer in Arran.
I see frae the papers that he was intelligently and actively
assisted in this by the well-known ghillies, Dugald M'Fadyen,
Donald Campbell, Sandy M'Neill, and Peter M'Phedran.

" They went up the hill and picked oot a nice quate he-
deer, and drove it doon in front o' where his Majesty sat
beside a stack o' loaded guns. His Majesty was graciously
pleased to tak' up yin o' the guns, and let bang at the deer.

" ' Weel done ! That wass gey near him,' said Dugald
M'Fadyen, strikin' the deer wi' his stick to mak' it stop eatin'
the gress.

" His Majesty fired a second time, and the deer couldna
stand it ony langer, but went aff wi' a breenge.

" ' Weel, it's a fine day to be oot on the hull onywye,'

says M'Phedran, resigned-like, and the things that the heid ghillie Campbell didna say was terrible.

"The papers a' said the deer was shot, and a bloody business too; but it wasna till lang efter the cauld-clye corpse o't was found on the hill.

"' Here it is ! ' said M'Fadyen.

"' I daursay it is,' said M'Neill.

"' It'll hae to be it onywye,' said the heid man, and they had it weighed.

"If it was sold in Gleska the day it would fetch ten shillin's a-pound.

"If there's ae thing I've noticed mair nor anither aboot Hielan' ghillies, it's that they'll no' hurt your feelin's if they can help it. I'm Hielan' mysel'; my name's MacPherson; a flet fit but a warm hert, and I ken.

"Meanwhile Campbeltoon washed its face, put a clove in its mooth, and tried to look as spruce as it could for a place that has mair distilleries than kirks. The Royal veesit was generally regairded as providential, because the supremacy o' Speyside whiskies over Campbeltoon whiskies o' recent years wad hae a chance o' being overcome if his Majesty could be prevailed on to gang through a' the distilleries and hae a sample frae each o' them.

"It was to be a gala day, and the bellman went roond the toon orderin' every loyal ceetizen to put oot a flag, cheer like onything when the King was gaun to the distilleries, and bide inside their hooses when he was comin' back frae them. But ye'll no' believ't—THE YACHT PASSED CAMPBELTOON !

"The Provost and Magistrates and the hale community was doon on the quay to cairry the Royal pairty shouther-high if necessary, and when they saw the *Victoria and Albert* they cheered sae lood they could be heard the length o' Larne.

"' Whit's that ? ' said his Majesty.

"' By the smell o't I wad say Campbeltoon,' said his

skipper, 'and that's mair o' your Majesty's subjects, awfu' interested in your recovery.'

" 'Oh man!' said the puir King, nearly greetin', 'we divna ken whit health is, ony o' us, till we lose it. Steam as far aff frae the shore as ye can, and it'll maybe no' be sae bad.'

"So the yacht ran bye Campbeltoon.

"The folk couldna believe't at first.

" 'They must hae made a mistake,' says they ; ' perhaps they didna notice the distillery lums,' and the polis sergeant birled his whustle by order of the Provost, to ca' the King's attention, but it was o' no avail. A rale divert !

"The yacht went on to Colonsay.

"That's the droll thing aboot this trip o' his Majesty's ; it's no' ony nice, cheery sort o' places he gangs to at a', but oot-o'-the-wye wee places wi' naethin' aboot them but hills and things—wee trashy places wi' nae nice braw new villas aboot them, and nae minstrels or banjo-singers on the esplanade singin' 'O! Lucky Jim!' and clautin' in the bawbees. I divna suppose they had half a dizzen flags in a' Colonsay, and ye wad fancy the King's een's no' that sair lookin' at flags but whit he wad be pleased to see mair o' them.

"Colonsay ! Man, it's fair peetifu' ! No' a Provost or a Bylie in't to hear a bit speech frae ; nae steamboat trips to gang roond the Royal yacht and keek in the portholes ; but everything as quate as a kirk on a Setturday mornin'.

"A' the rest o' Scotland wanted to wag flags at his Majesty Edward VII., and here he maun put up at Colonsay ! The thing was awfu' badly managed.

"If Campbeltoon was chawed at the yacht passin' withoot giein' a cry in, whit's to describe the vexation o' Oban ?

"Oban had its hert set on't. It never occurred to the mind o' Oban for wan meenute that the King could pass the 'Charin' Cross o' the Hielan's ' withoot spendin' a week there at the very least, and everything was arranged to mak' the Royal convalescent comfortable.

" The bay was fair jammed wi' yachts, and a' the steam-whustles were oiled. The hotels were packed to the roof wi' English tourists, some o' them sleepin' under the slates, wi' their feet in the cisterns, and gled to pay gey dear for the preevilege o' breathin' the same air as Edward VII.

" Early in the day somebody sent the alarmin' tidin's frae Colonsay that the *Victoria and Albert* micht pass Oban efter a', and to prevent this, herrin'-nets were stretched aff Kerrara to catch her if ony such dastardly move was made.

" But is was nae use ; Oban's in sackcloth and ashes.

" ' Where are we noo ? ' asked the Royal voyager, aff Kerrara. ' Is this Shingleton-on-the-Sea ? '

" ' No, your Majesty,' says the skipper of the Royal yacht, ' it's Oban, the place whaur the German waiters get their education.'

" ' Heavens ! ' cried his Majesty, shudderin' ; ' we're terrible close ; put a fire under the aft funnel at a' costs and get past as quick as we can.'

" It was pointed oot to his Majesty that the toon was evidently expectin' him, and so, to mak' things pleasant, he ordered the steam pinnace to land the week's washin' at the Charin' Cross o' the Hielan's—while the *Victoria and Albert* went on her way to Ballachulish."

x

HOW JINNET SAW THE KING

" I saw him and her on Thursday," said Erchie, " as nate's ye like, and it didna cost me mair nor havin' my hair cut. They gaed past oor kirk, and the session put up a stand, and chairges ten shillin's a sate.

" ' Not for Joe,' says I ; ' I'd sooner buy mysel' a new pair o' boots'; and I went to Duffy and says I, 'Duffy, are ye no' gaun to hae oot yer bonny wee lorry at the heid o' Gairbraid Street and ask the wife and Jinnet and me to stand on't?'

"'Right,' says Duffy, 'bring you Jinnet and I'll tak' my wife, and we'll hae a rale pant.'

"So there was the four o' us standin' five mortal 'oors on Duffy's coal-lorry. I was that gled when it was a' bye. But I'll wager there was naebody gledder nor the King himsel', puir sowl! Frae the time he cam' into Gleska at Queen Street Station till the time he left Maryhill, he lifted his hat three million seven hundred and sixty-eight thousand and sixty-three times.

"Talk aboot it bein' a fine job bein' a King! I can tell ye the money's gey hard earned. Afore he starts oot to see his beloved people, he has to practise for a week wi' the dumb-bells, and feed himsel' up on Force, Grape-nuts, Plasmon, Pianolio, and a' thae strengthenin' diets that Sunny Jim eats.

"I thocht first Jinnet maybe wadna gang, her bein' in the Co-operative Store and no' awfu' ta'en up wi' Royalty, but, dod! she jumped at the chance.

"'The Queen's a rale nice buddy,' she says; 'no' that I'm personally acquainted wi' her, but I hear them sayin'. And she used to mak' a' her ain claes afore she mairried the King.'

"So Jinnet and me were oot on Duffy's lorry, sittin' on auld copies o' 'Reynolds' News,' and hurrayin' awa' like a pair o' young yins.

"The first thing Jinnet saw was a woman wi' a wean and its face no' richt washed.

"'Fancy her bringin' oot her wean to see the King wi' a face like that,' says Jinnet, and gies the puir wee smout a sweetie.

"Frae that till it was time for us to gang hame Jinnet saw naething but weans, and her and Duffy's wife talked

aboot weans even on. Ye wad think it was a baby-show we
were at and no' a King's procession.

"Duffy sat wi' a Tontine face on him maist o' the time,
but every noo and then gaun up the street at the back o'
us to buy himsel' a bottle o' broon robin, for he couldna get
near a pub ; and I sat tryin' as hard's I could to think hoo
I wad like to be a King, and what kind o' waistcoats I wad
wear if I had the job. On every hand the flags were wavin',
and the folk were eatin' Abernaithy biscuits.

"At aboot twelve o'clock cannons begood to bang.

"'Oh my! I hope there's nae weans near thae cannons
or they micht get hurt,' says Jinnet.

"Little did she think that at that parteecular meenute
the King was comin' doon the tunnel frae Cowlairs, and
tellin' her Majesty no' to be frichted.

"When the King set foot in the Queen Street Station he
gied the wan look roond him, and says he, 'Is this Gleska,
can ony o' ye tell me ?'

"'It is that, wi' your Majesty's gracious permission,' says
the porter ; 'sees a haud o' yer bag.'

"'I mind fine o' bein' here yince afore,' says the King,
and gangs oot into George Square.

"'Whitna graveyaird's this ?' he asks, lookin' at the
statues.

"'It's no' a graveyaird ; it's a square, and that's the
Municeepal Buildin',' somebody tells him. His Majesty then
laid a foundation-stone as smert's ye like wi' his least wee
bit touch, and then went into the Municeepal Buildin's and
had a snack.

"He cam' oot feelin' fine. 'The Second City o' the
Empire !' he says. 'I can weel believ't. If it wasna for
my business bein' in London I wad hae a hoose here. Whit
am I to dae next ?'

"They took his Majesty doon Buchanan Street.

"'No bad !' says he.

"Then he cam' to Argyle Street, and gaed west, past

the Hielan'man's Cross at the heid o' Jamaica Street. He
sees a lot o' chaps there wi' the heather stickin' oot o' their
ears, and a tartan brogue that thick it nearly spiled the
procession.

"'The Hielan'man's Cross,' says he; 'man, ay! I've
heard o't. Kamerhashendoo. If I had thocht o't I wad hae
brocht my kilts and my pibroch and a' that.'

"A' the wey doon the Dumbarton Road the folk were fair
hingin' oot o' their windows, wavin' onything at a' they
could get a haud o', and the Royal carriage was bump-bump-
bumpin' like a' that ower the granite setts.

"'Whit's wrang wi' the streets o' Gleska?' says the King,
him bein' used to wud streets in London, whaur he works.

"'It's granite, if ye please,' says they.

"'Oh ay!' says the King; 'man, it mak's a fine noise.
Will we soon be there? I like this fine, but I wadna like to
keep onybody waitin'.'

"At Finnieston the folk cam' up frae the side streets and
fair grat wi' patriotic fervour. Forbye, a' the pubs were
shut for an 'oor or twa.

"'Whit I want to see's the poor,' says the King. 'I'm
tired lookin' at the folk that's weel aff; they're faur ower
common.'

"'Them's the poor,' he was tellt; 'it's the best we can
dae for your Majesty.'

"'But they're awfu' bien-lookin' and weel put on,' says he.

"'Oh ay!' they tells him, 'that's their Sunday claes.'

"And so the Royal procession passed on its way, the King
being supplied wi' a new hat every ten minutes, to mak' up
for the yins he spiled liftin' them to his frantic and patriotic
subjects.

"In ten to fifteen minutes he examined the pictures in
the Art Galleries—the Dutch, the English, the Italian, and
the Gleska schools o' painters; the stuffed birds, and the
sugaraully hats the polis used to hae when you and me was
jinkin' them.

P

" ' Och, it's fine,' says he ; ' there's naething wrang wi' the place. Are we no' near Maryhill noo ? '

" Ye see his Majesty had on a bate he could see the hale o' Gleska in five 'oors or less, an' be oot sooner nor ony ither king that ever set a fit in it. They wanted him to mak' a circular tour o't, and come back to the Municeepal Buildin's for his tea.

" ' Catch me,' says he. ' I'm gaun back to Dalkeith.'

" A' this time we were standin' on Duffy's lorry, flanked on the left by the Boys' Brigade, lookin' awfu' fierce, and the riflemen frae Dunoon on the richt. Every noo an' then a sodger went bye on a horse, or a lassie nearly fainted and had to be led alang the line by a polisman, and him no' awfu' carin' for the job. Duffy was gaun up the street to buy broon robin that aften he was gettin' sunburnt, and my wife Jinnet nearly hurt her een lookin' for weans.

" ' Look at thon wee wean, Erchie,' she wad aye be tellin' me, ' does't no' put ye in mind o' Rubbert's wee Hughie ? Oh, the cratur ! '

" ' Wumman,' I tellt her, ' this is no' a kinderspiel ye're at ; it's a Royal procession. I wonder to me ye wad be wastin' yer e'esicht lookin' at weans when there's sae mony braw sodgers.'

" ' Oh, Erchie ! ' says she, ' I'm bye wi' the sodgers ' ; and jist wi' that the procession cam' up the street. First the Lancers wi' their dickies stickin' ootside their waistcoats.

" ' Man, them's fine horses,' says Duffy, wi' a professional eye on the beasts. ' Chaps me that broon yin wi' the white feet.'

" Then cam' the King and Queen.

" ' Whaur's their croons ? ' asks Duffy's wife. ' I divna believe that's them at a'.'

" ' That's them, I'll bate ony money,' I says. ' Ye can tell by the hurry they're in.'

" ' Oh, the craturs ! ' says Jinnet, and then says she, ' Oh, Erchie ! look at the wean hanging ower that window. I'm feart it'll fa' ower.'

" Afore she could get her een aff the wean the King's cairrage was past, and the rest o' the Lancers cam' clatterin' after them.

" ' Noo for the brass bands ! ' says Duffy, lookin' doon the street. But there was nae brass bands. The show was bye.

" ' If I had kent that was to be a' that was in't, I wad never hae ta'en oot my lorry,' says Duffy, as angry as ony-thing, and made a breenge for anither bottle o' broon robin.

" ' Och, it was fine,' says Jinnet. ' I never saw sae mony weans in a' my days.'

" And the crood began to scale.

" His Majesty reached Maryhill Station exact to the minute, wi' his eye on his watch.

" ' Weel, that's bye onywye,' says he, and somebody cries for a speech.

" ' People o' Gleska,' he says, ' I have seen your toon. It's fine—there's naething wrang wi't,' and then the gaird blew his whustle, and the train went aff.

" The great event was ower, the rain begood to fa' again ; the Gilmorehill student hurried hame to blacken his face and put on his sister's frock. The coloured ping-pong balls strung ower Sauchieha' Street was lighted, the illuminated skoosh cars began to skoosh up and doon the street, the public-hooses did a fine tred.

" ' I'm gled it's a' bye,' says Jinnet, when we got hame to oor ain hoose.

" ' Indeed, and so am I,' says I. ' There wad be fine fun in this warld a' the time if we werena trying for't.' "

XI

ERCHIE RETURNS

FOR weeks I had not seen Erchie. He was not to be met on the accustomed streets, and St Kentigern's Kirk having been closed since July for alterations and repairs, it was useless to go there in search of its beadle. Once I met Duffy, and asked him what had become of the old man.

" Alloo you Erchie ! " was all the information he would vouchsafe ; " if he's keepin' oot o' sicht, he'll hae his ain reason for't. Mind, I'm no' sayin' onything against the cratur, though him and me's had mony a row. He's a' richt if ye tak' him the richt wye. But sly ! He's that sly, the auld yin, ye can whiles see him winkin' awa' to himsel' ower something he kens that naebody else kens, and that he's no gaun to tell to them. I havena seen the auld fuiter since the Fair week ; perhaps he's gotten genteel and bidin' doon at Rothesay till the summer steamboats stop. There's yin thing sure—it's no' a case o' wife-desertion, for Jinnet's wi' him. I can tell by the Venetian blinds and the handle o' their door. Sly ! Did ye say sly ? Man, it's no' the word for't. Erchie MacPherson's fair lost at the waitin' ; he should hae been a poet, or a statesman, or something in the fancy line like that."

It was with the joy of a man who has made up his mind he has lost a sovereign and finds it weeks after in the lining of his waistcoat, I unexpectedly met Erchie on Saturday.

" Upon my word, old friend," I said, " I thought you were dead."

" No, nor deid ! " retorted Erchie. " Catch me ! I'm nane o' the deein' kind. But I micht nearly as weel be deid, for I've been thae twa months in Edinburgh. Yon's the place for a man in a decline ; it's that slow he wad hae a chance o' livin' to a grand auld age. There's mair o' a bustle on the road to Sichthill Cemetery ony day in the week than there is in Princes Street on a Setturday nicht. I had a bit job there for the last ten weeks, and the only pleesure I had was gaun doon noo and then to the Waverley Station to see the bonny wee trains frae Gleska. They're a' richt for scenery and the like o' that in Edinburgh, but they're no' smert."

" But it's an old saying, Erchie, that all the wise men in

Glasgow come from the East—that's to say, they come from Edinburgh."

"Yes, and the wiser they are the quicker they come," said Erchie. "Man! and it's only an 'oor's journey, and to see the wye some o' them gae on bidin' ower yonder ye wad think they had the Atlantic Ocean to cross. There should be missionaries sent ower to Edinburgh explainin' things to the puir deluded craturs. Ony folk that wad put thon big humplock o' a hill they ca' the Castle in the middle o' the street, spilin' the view, and hing their washin's on hay-rakes stuck oot at their windows, hae muckle to learn."

"Still, I have no doubt Edinburgh's doing its best, Erchie," I said.

"Maybe, but they're no' smert; ye wad hae yer pouch picked half a dizzen times in Gleska in the time an Edinburgh polisman tak's to rub his een to waken himsel' when ye ask him the road to Leith.

"Did ye ever hear tell o' the Edinburgh man that ance ventured to Gleska and saw the hopper dredgers clawtin' up the glaur frae the Clyde at Broomielaw?

"'Whit are ye standin' here for? Come awa' and hae a gless o' milk,' said a freen' to him.

"'No, nor awa',' said he, glowerin' like onything; 'I've coonted 364 o' thae wee buckets comin' oot the watter, and I'll no move a step oot o' here till I see the last o' them!'

"The puir cratur never saw a rale river in his life afore. Och! but Edinburgh's no' that bad; ye can aye be sure o' gettin' yer nicht's sleep in't at ony 'oor o' the day, it's that quate. They're aye braggin' that it's cleaner than Gleska, as if there was onything smert aboot that.

"'There's naething dirtier nor a dirty Gleska man,' said yin o' them to me ae day.

"'There is,' says I.

"'Whit?' says he.

"'Twa clean Edinburgh yins,' says I.

"Och! but I'm only in fun. Edinburgh's a' richt; there's

naething wrang wi' the place ance ye're in it if ye hae a book
to read. I hate to hear the wye Duffy and some o' them
speak aboot Edinburgh, the same as if it was shut up a'thegither; hoo wad we like it oorsel's? I hae maybe a flet fit,
but I hae a warm hert, and I'll aye stick up for Edinburgh.
I had an uncle that near got the jyle there for running ower
yin o' their tramway caurs. They've no skoosh cars in
Edinburgh; they're thon ither kin' that's pu'ed wi' a rope,
and whiles the rope breaks; but it doesna maitter, naebody's
in ony hurry gaun to ony place in Edinburgh, and the
passengers jist sit where they are till it's mended."

" Well, anyhow, Erchie, we're glad to see you back," I said.

" Gled to see me back!" he cried. " I'll wager ye didna
ken I was awa', and the only folk that kent we werena in
Gleska for the past twa or three months was the dairy and
the wee shop we get oor vegetables frae.

"When I was in Edinburgh yonder, skliffin' alang the streets
as fast's I could, and nippin' mysel' every noo and then to
keep mysel' frae fa'in' asleep, I wad be thinkin' to mysel',
' Hoo are they gettin' on in Gleska wantin' Erchie Mac-
Pherson? Noo that they've lost me, they'll ken the worth o'
me.' I made shair that, at least, the skoosh cars wad hae to
stop runnin' when I was awa', and that the polis band wad
come doon to the station to meet me when I cam' hame.

" Dod! ye wad hardly believe it, but ever since I cam' back
I meet naebody but folk that never ken't I was awa'. It's a
gey hertless place Gleska that way. Noo, in Edinburgh it's
different. They're gey sweart to lose ye in Edinburgh ance
they get haud o' ye; that's the way they keep up the price
o' the railway ticket to Gleska.

" I was tellin' Duffy aboot Edinburgh, and he's gaun
through wi' a trip to see't on Monday. It'll be a puir holiday
for the cratur, but let him jist tak' it. He'll be better there
than wastin' his money in a toon. When Duffy goes onywhere on ony o' the Gleska holidays, it's generally to Airdrie,
or Coatbrig, or Clydebank he goes, and walks aboot the streets

till the polis put him on the last train hame for Gleska, and him singin' ' Dark Lochnagar ' wi' the tears in his een.

" He'll say to me next morning,' ' Man ! Erchie, thon's a thrivin' place, Coatbrig, but awfu' bad whisky.'

" There's a lot like him aboot a Gleska holiday. They'll be gettin' up to a late breakfast wi' no parridge till't on Monday mornin', and sayin', ' Man ! it's a grand day for Dunoon,' and then start druggin' themsel's wi' drams. Ye wad think they were gaun to get twa teeth ta'en oot instead o' gaun on a holiday.

" That's no' my notion o' a holiday, either in the Autumn or the Spring. I'm takin' Jinnet oot on Monday to Milliken Park to see her kizzen that keeps a gairden. We'll hae an awfu' wrastle in the mornin' catchin' the train, and it'll be that crooded we'll hae to stand a' the way. The wife's kizzen 'll be that gled to see us she'll mak' tea for us every half-'oor and send oot each time to the grocer's for mair o' thon biled ham ye aye get at burials. I'll get my feet a' sair walkin' up and doon the gairden coontin' the wife's kizzen's aipples that's no' richt ripe yet, and Jinnet and me 'll hae to cairry hame a big poke o' rhuburb or greens, or some ither stuff we're no wantin', and the train 'll be an 'oor late o' gettin' into Gleska.

" That's a holiday. The only time ye enjoy a holiday is when it's a' bye."

XII

DUFFY'S FIRST FAMILY

MORE than a year after the King's visit Erchie and I one day passed a piano-organ in the street playing " Dark Lochnagar." The air attracted him ; he hummed it very much out of tune for some minutes after.

" Do ye hear that ? " said he, " ' Dark Lochnagar ' ; I used ance to could nearly play't on the mooth harmonium. I learned it aff Duffy. Him and me was mairried aboot the same time. We lived in the same close up in the Coocaddens

—him on the top flet, and Jinnet and me in the flet below.
Oor wifes had turn aboot o' the same credle—and it was kept
gey throng, I'm tellin' ye. If it wasna Duffy up the stair at
nicht, efter his wark was done, rockin' awa' wi' a grudge to
the tune o' ' Dark Lochnagar,' it was me below at no' ' Auld
Lang Syne,' but yon ither yin ye ken fine. I daresay it was
rockin' the credle helped to mak' my feet flet, and it micht
hae happened in a far waur cause.

" It was Duffy's first wife ; she dee'd, I think, to get rid
o' him—the cratur ! Duffy's yin o' thae men wi' a great
big lump o' a hert that brocht the tear to his ain een when he
was singin' ' Bonny Annie Laurie ' doon in the Mull o' Kintyre
Vaults, but wad see his wife to bleezes afore he wad brush
his ain boots for Sunday, and her no' weel. She fair adored
him, too. She thocht Duffy was jist the ordinar' kind o'
man, and that I was a kind o' eccentric peely-wally sowl,
because I sometimes dried the dishes, and didna noo' an
then gie Jinnet a beltin'.

" ' His looks is the best o' him,' she wad tell Jinnet.

" ' Then' he's gey hard up ! ' I wad say to Jinnet when
she tellt me this.

" ' He's no very strong,'—that was aye her cry, when she
was fryin' anither pun' o' ham and a pair o' kippers for his
breakfast.

" Duffy's first wean was Wullie John. Ye wad think, to
hear Duffy brag aboot him, that it was a new patent kind o'
wean, and there wasna anither in Coocaddens, whaur, I'm
tellin' ye, weans is that rife ye hae to walk to yer work skliffin'
yer feet in case ye tramp on them.

" Duffy's notion was to rear a race o' kind o' gladiators,
and he rubbed him a' ower every nicht wi' olive-oil to mak'
him soople. Nane o' your fancy foods for weans for Wullie
John. It was rale auld Caledonia—parridge and soor dook,
that soor the puir wee smout went aboot grewin' wi' its
mooth a' slewed to the side, as if it was practising the wye
the women haud their hairpins.

" Mony a time I've seen oor Jinnet sneak him into oor hoose to gie him curds and cream ; he said he liked them fine, because they were sae slippy.

" ' Show your temper, Wullie John,' Duffy wad tell him when onybody was in the hoose ; and the wee cratur was trained at that to put on a fearfu' face and haud up his claws.

" ' See that ! ' Duffy wad say as prood as onything ; ' the game's there, I'm tellin' ye.'

" Then Duffy began to harden him. He wad haud him up by the lug to see if he was game, and if he grat that was coonted wan to Duffy, and Wullie John got nae jeely on his piece. He was washed every mornin', winter and summer, in cauld watter in the jaw-box, and rubbed wi' a tooel as coorse as a carrot-grater till the skin was peelin' aff his back.

" ' Ye need to bring oot the glow,' Duffy wad say to me.

" ' If it gangs on much further,' I tellt him, ' I'll bring oot the polis.'

" Wullie John was fair on the road for bein' an A1 gladiator, but he went and dee'd on Duffy, and I never saw a man mair chawed.

" Duffy's next was a laddie too—they ca'd him Alexander. Their was gaun to be nane o' their hardenin' dydoes wi' Alexander.

" It was aboot the time Duffy took to politics, and said the thing the Democratic pairty wanted was educated men wi' brains. He made up his mind that Alexander wad never cairry a coalpoke, but get the best o' learnin' if it cost a pound.

" He wasna very strong, was Alexander, and Duffy fed him maist o' the time on Gregory's mixture, cod-ile, and ony ither stuff he could buy by word o' mooth at the apothecary's withoot a doctor's line. Alexander was getting medicine poored into him that often he was feared to gant in case he wad jar his teeth on a table-spoon when his een was shut. He wore hot-water bottles to his feet in the deid o' summer, and if he had a sair heid in the mornin' afore he started for the

P*

school on the geography days he was put to his bed and fed on tapioca. Everything went wrong wi' puir wee Alexander. The hives went in wi' him, and the dregs o' the measles cam' oot. He took every trouble that was gaun aboot except gymnastics ; Duffy took him to Professor Coats, the bump-man, and had his heid examined ; the Professor said it was as fine a heid o' its kind as ever he saw, and Duffy put a bawbee on the bag o' coals richt aff, and began to put the money bye for Alexander's college fees.

" Alexander's a man noo, and daein' fine. He's in the gas office ; the only time he went to college was to read the meter there.

" Ye canna tell whit laddies 'll turn oot, and it's no' ony better wi' lassies. Duffy had a wheen o' lassies ; I forget hoo mony there was a'thegither, but when they were coortin' ye wad think ye were gaun doon the middle o' the Haymakers' country dance when ye cam' up the close at nicht.

" The auldest—she was Annie—was naething particular fancy ; she jist nursed the rest, and made their peenies, and washed for them, and trimmed her ain hats, and made Duffy's auld waistcoats into suits for the wee yins, and never got to the dancin', so naebody married her, and she's there yet.

" A' the chaps cam' efter her sisters.

" The sisters never let on aboot the coal-ree and Duffy's lorry, but said their paw was in the coal tred—a kind o' a coal-maister. It was a bonny sicht to see them merchin' oot to their cookery lessons in the efternoons, their hair as curly 's onything, and their beds no' made.

" The days they tried new dishes frae the cookery lessons at hame, Duffy took his meat in the Western Cookin' Depot, and cam' hame when it was dark. Yin o' them played the mandoline. The mandoline's a noble instrument ; it cheers the workman's hame ; a lassie gaun alang the street wi' a nice print dress, and a case wi' a mandoline, is jist the sort I wad fancy mysel' if I was a young yin and there wasna

Jinnet. A fruiterer married the mandoline. The nicht she was merrit, Duffy sang ' Dark Lochnagar,' and winked at me like a' that.

" ' Learn your dochters the mandoline, Erchie,' says he in my lug, ' and they'll gang aff your haunds like snaw aff a dyke. That's the advice I wad gie ye if ye had ony dochters left. I wad hae made it the piano, but we couldna get a piano up past the bend on the stair.'

" Efter the mandoline went, the boys begood to scramble for Duffy's dochters as if they were bowl-money. The close-mooth was never clear o' cabs, and the rice was always up to your ankles on the stair. Duffy sang ' Dark Lochnagar ' even-on, and aye kept winkin' at me.

" ' That's the mandoline awa',' says he, ' and the scientific dressmakin', and the shorthand, and the " Curfew must not Ring To-night," and the revival meetin's, and the no' very-weel yin that needs a nice quate hame ; they're a' gane, Erchie, and I'm no' gien jeely-dishes awa' wi' them either. I'm my lee-lane, me and Annie ; if ony o' thae chaps cam' efter Annie, I wad chase him doon the stair.'

" ' Man ! Duffy,' I says till him, ' ye're selfish enough workin' aff a' them ornamental dochters on the young men o' Gleska that did ye nae hairm, and keepin' the best o' the hale jingbang in the hoose a' the time in case they see her.'

" ' Let them tak' it ! ' says Duffy, ' I'm no' a bit vexed for them,' and he started to sing ' Dark Lochnagar ' as lood as ever, while Annie was puttin' on his boots.

" That was in Duffy's auld days. He married a second wife, and it was a fair tak'-in, for he thocht a wee green-grocer's shop she had was her ain, and a' the time it was her brither's.

" ' That's the mandoline for you, Duffy,' says I, when he tellt me.

" But that yin died on him too ; she died last Mertinmas ; Duffy's kind o' oot o' wifes the noo. And the warst o't is that his dochter Annie's gettin' married."

XIII

ERCHIE GOES TO A BAZAAR

THERE was a very self-conscious look on Erchie's face on Saturday when I met him with a hand-painted drain-pipe of the most generous proportions under his arm.

" It's aye the way," said he. " Did ye ever hae ony o' yer parteecular freen's meet ye when ye were takin' hame a brace o' grouse? No' a bit o' ye! But if it's a poke o' onything, or a parcel frae the country, whaur they havena ony broon paper, but jist ' The Weekly Mail,' and nae richt twine, ye'll no' can gang the length o' the street without comin' across everybody that gangs to yer kirk."

He put the drain-pipe down on the pavement—it was the evening—and sat on the end of it.

" So you are the latest victim to the art movement, Erchie? ' I said. " You will be putting away your haircloth chairs and introducing the sticky plush variety; I was suspicious of that new dado in your parlour the day we had the tousy tea after Big Macphee's burial."

" Catch me! " said Erchie. " Them and their art! I wadna be encouragin' the deevils. If ye want to ken the way I'm gaun hame wi' this wally umbrella-staun', I'll tell ye the rale truth. It's jist this, that Jinnet's doon yonder at the Freemasons' Bazaar wi' red-hot money in her pooch, and canna get awa' till it's done. She's bocht a tea-cosy besides this drain-pipe, and a toaster wi' puce ribbons on't for haudin' letters and papers, and she'll be in luck for yince if she disna win the raffle for the lady's bicycle that she had twa tickets for. Fancy me oot in Grove Street in the early mornin' learnin' Jinnet the bicycle, and her the granny o' seeven!

" Of course, Jinnet's no' needin' ony bicycle ony mair than she's needin' a bassinette, but she has a saft hert and canna say no unless she's awfu' angry, and a young chap, speakin'

awfu' Englified, wi' his hair a' vasaline, got roond her. She's
waitin' behin' there to see if she wins the raffle, and to pick
up ony bargains just a wee while afore the place shuts up—
the rale time for bazaar bargains if ye divna get yer leg
broken in the crush. I only went there mysel' to see if I
could get her to come hame as lang as she had enough
left to pay her fare on the skoosh car, but I micht as weel
speak to the wind. She was fair raised ower a bargain in
rabbits. It's an awfu' thing when yer wife tak's to bazaars ;
it's waur nor drink.

" It's a female complaint ; ye'll no' find mony men bothered
wi't unless they happen to be ministers. Ye'll no' see Duffy
sittin' late at nicht knittin' wee bootees for weans they'll
never in this warld fit, nor crochetin' doyleys, to aid the funds
o' the Celtic Fitba' Club. Ye micht watch a lang while afore
ye wad see me makin' tinsey 'ool ornaments wi' paste-heided
preens for hingin' up in the best room o' dacent folk that
never did me ony hairm.

" There wad be nae such thing as bazaars if there werena
ony weemen. In thoosands o' weel-daein' hames in this
Christian toon o' Gleska there's weemen at this very meenute
neglectin' their men's suppers to sit doon and think as hard's
they can whit they can mak' wi' a cut and a half o' three-ply
fingerin' worsted, that'll no' be ony use to ony body, but 'll
look worth eighteenpence in a bazaar. If ye miss your lum
hat, and canna find it to gang to a funeral, ye may be shair
it was cut in scollops a' roond the rim, and covered wi' velvet,
and that wee Jeenie pented floores on't in her ain time to
gie't the richt feenish for bein' an Art work-basket at yer
wife's stall in some bazaar.

" Maist weemen start it withoot meanin' ony hairm, maybe
wi' a table-centre, or a lamp-shade, or a pair o' bedroom
slippers. There's no' much wrang wi' that ; but it's a
beginnin', and the habit grows on them till they're scoorin'
the country lookin' for a chance to contribute whit they ca'
Work to kirk bazaars and ony ither kinds o' bazaars that's

handy. It mak's my hert sair sometimes to see weel-put-on-weemen wi' men o' their ain and dacent faimilies, comin' hame through back-streets staggerin' wi' parcels o' remnants for dressin' dolls or makin' cushions wi'. They'll hide it frae their men as long as they can, and then, when they're found oot, they'll brazen it oot and deny that it's ony great hairm.

" That's wan way the trouble shows itsel'.

" There's ither weemen—maistly younger and no' mairried —that's dyin' for a chance to be assistant stall-keepers, and wear white keps and aiprons, jist like tablemaids.

" That's the kind I'm feared for, and I'm nae chicken.

" When they see a man come into the bazaar and nae wife wi' him to tak' care o' him, they come swoopin' doon on him, gie him ony amount o' cleck, jist in fun, and ripe his pooches before he can button his jaicket.

" I'm no' sayin' they put their hands in his pooches, but jist as bad ; they look that nice, and sae fond o' his tie and the way he has o' wearin' his moustache, that he's kittley doon to the soles o' his feet, and wad buy a steam road-roller frae them if he had the money for't. But they're no' sellin' steam road-rollers, the craturs ! They're sellin' shillin' dolls at twa-and-six that can open and shut their een, and say ' Maw ' and ' Paw.' They're sellin' carpet slippers, or bonny wee bunches o' flooers, or raffle tickets for a rale heliotrope Persian cat. It's the flyest game I ken. When that puir sowl gets oot o' the place wi' naething in his pooches but his hands, and a dazed look in his een, the only thing he can mind is that she said her name was Maud, and that her hair was crimp, and that she didna put a preen in his coat-lapelle when she was puttin' the shillin' rose there, because she said a preen wad cut love. She said that to every customer she had for her flooers that day, wi' a quick look up in their face, and then droppin' her eyes confused like, and her face red, and a' the time, her, as like as no', engaged to a man in India.

" I wonder hoe it wad dae to hae a man's bazaar ? They ocht to have made the Freemasons' bazaar a man's yin, seein' the Freemasons 'll no tell the weemen their secrets nor let them into their lodges.

" A man's bazaar wad be a rale divert : naethin' to be sold in't but things for use, like meerschaum pipes, and kahootchy collars, and sox the richt size, and chairs, and tables, and concertinas—everything guaranteed to be made by men and them tryin'.

" The stalls wad be kept by a' the baronets that could be scraped thegither and could be trusted withoot cash registers, and the stall assistants wad be the pick o' the best-lookin' men in the toon—if ye could get them sober enough. If Jinnet wad let me, I wad be willin' to gie a hand mysel' ; for though I've a flet fit I've a warm hert, I'm tellin' ye.

" I think I see Duffy walkin' roond the St Andrew's Hall, and it got up to look like the Fall o' Babylon, tryin' to sell bunches o' flooers. Dae ye think he wad sell mony to the young chaps like whit Maud riped ? Nae fears ! He wad hae to tak' every customer oot and stand him a drink afore he wad get a flooer aff his hands.

" Can ye fancy Duffy gaun roond tryin' to sell tickets for a raffle o' a canary in a cage ?

" ' Here ye are, chaps and cairters ! the chance o' yer lives for a graund whustler, and no' ill to feed ! '

" Na, na ! a man o' the Duffy stamp wad be nae use for a bazaar, even wi' a dress suit on and his face washed. It wad need young stockbrokers, and chaps wi' the richt kind o' claes, wi' a crease doon the front o' their breeks—Grosvenor Restaurant chaps, wi' the smell o' cigars aff their topcoats, and either ca'd Fred or Vincent. Then ye micht see that the ither sex that hiv a' the best o't wi' bazaars, the wye they're managed noo, wad flock to the man's bazaar and buy like onything. And maybe no'."

Erchie rose off the drain-pipe, and prepared to resume his way home with that ingenious object that proves how the

lowliest things of life may be made dignified and beautiful—
if fashion says they are so.

"Well, good night, old friend," I said. "I hope Mrs
MacPherson will be lucky and get the bicycle."

"Dae ye, indeed?" said he. "Then ye're nae freen' o'
mine. We're faur mair in the need o' a mangle."

"Then you can exchange for one."

"I'm no' that shair. Did I ever tell ye I ance won a
powney in a raffle? It was at the bazaar oor kirk had in
Dr Jardine's time when they got the organ. I was helpin'
at the buffet, and I think they micht hae left me alane, me
no' bein' there for fun, but at my tred, but wha cam'
cravin' me to buy a ticket aff her but the doctor's guid-
sister.

"'There's three prizes,' says she; 'a powney wi' broon
harness, a marble nock, and a dizzen knifes and forks.'

"'I wad maybe risk it if it wisna for the powney,' I tellt
her; 'I havena kep' a coachman for years, and I'm oot o'
the way o' drivin' mysel'.'

"'Oh! ye needna be that feared, ye'll maybe no' get
the powney,' said she, and I went awa' like a fool and took
the ticket.

"The draw took place jist when the bazaar was shuttin'
on the Setturday nicht. And I won the powney wi' the
broon harness.

"I tore my ticket and threeped it was a mistake, but I
couldna get oot o't; they a' kent the powney was mine.

"It was stabled behind the bazaar, and had to be ta'en
awa' that nicht. I offered it to onybody that wanted it for
naething, but naebody wad tak' it aff my hands because
they a' said they had to tak' the car hame, and they wadna
be allooed to tak' a powney into a car wi' them. So they left
me wi' a bonny-like prize.

"I put its claes on the best way I could, fanklin' a' the
straps, and dragged it hame. We lived in the close at the
time, and I thocht maybe Jinnet wad let me keep it in the

lobby till the Monday mornin' till I could see whit I could dae. But she wadna hear tell o't. She said it wad scrape a' the waxcloth wi' its airn buits, and wad be a bonny-like thing to be nicherrin' a' Sunday, scandalisin' the neebours, forbye there bein' nae gress in the hoose to feed it on. I said I wad rise early in the mornin' and gaither dentylions for't oot at the Three-Tree Well, but she wadna let me nor the powney inside the door.

"It wasna an awfu' big broad powney, but a wee smout o' a thing they ca' a Shetland-shawl powney, and its harness didna fit it ony place at a'. It looked at the twa o' us, kind o' dazed like.

"'Ye're no' gaun to turn my hoose into a stable, and me jist cleaned it this very day,' said Jinnet.

"'And am I gaun to walk the streets a' nicht wi't?' I asked, near greetin'.

"'Put it oot in the ash-pit, and the scavengers 'll tak' it awa' in the mornin',' she said; and I did that, forgettin' that the mornin' was the Sunday.

"But it didna maitter; the powney wasna there in the mornin', and I took guid care no' to ask for't."

XIV

HOLIDAYS

"WELL, Erchie; not away on the Fair holidays?" I asked the old man one July day on meeting him as he came out of a little grocer's shop in the New City Road. The dignity of his profession is ever dear to Erchie; he kept his purchase behind his back, but I saw later it was kindling material for the morning fire.

"Not me!" said he. "There's nae Fair holidays for puir auld Erchie, no' even on the Sunday, or I might hae ta'en the skoosh car doon the wye o' Yoker, noo that a hurl on Sunday's no' that awfu' sair looked doon on, or the

' Mornin' Star ' 'bus to Paisley. But Jinnet went awa' on Setturday wi' her guid-sister to Dunoon, and I'm my lee-lane in the hoose till the morn's mornin', It's nae divert, I'm tellin' ye ; there's a lot o' things to mind forbye the windin' o' the nock on Setturday and watering the fuchsia. I can wait a municeepal banquet wi' ony man in my tred, but I'm no' great hand at cookin' for mysel'.

" Did I ever tell ye aboot the time the wife was awa' afore at a Fair, and I took a notion o' a seed-cake Duffy's first wife had to the tea she trated me to on the Sawbath ?

" ' It's as easy to mak' as boilin' an egg,' says Mrs Duffy, and gied me the receipt for't on condeetion that when I made it I was to bring her a sample. Something went wrang, and I brought her the sample next day in a bottle. It was a gey damp seedcake thon !

" I havena been awa' at a Fair mysel' since aboot the time Wullie was in the Foondry Boys, and used to gang to the Hielan's. I mind o't fine. Nooadays, in oor hoose, ye wad never jalouse it was the Fair at a' if it wasna for the nae parridge in the mornin's.

" Ye'll hae noticed, maybe, that though we're a' fearfu' fond o' oor parridge in Scotland, and some men mak' a brag o' takin' them every mornin' just as if they were a cauld bath, we're gey gled to skip them at a holiday and just be daein' wi' ham and eggs.

" But in thae days, as I was sayin', the Fair was something like the thing. There was Mumford's and Glenroy's shows, and if ye hadna the money to get in, ye could aye pap eggs at the musicianers playing on the ootside, and the thing was as broad as it was lang. Forbye ye didna get the name o' bein' keen on the theatricals if your faither was parteecular.

" I mind ance I hit a skeely-e'ed trombone, or maybe it was an awfuclyde, wi' an egg at Vinegar Hill. The glee pairty—as ye might ca' him if ye were funny—chased me as far doon as the Wee Doo Hill. I could rin in thae days ;

noo I've ower flet feet, though I've a warm hert too, I'm tellin' ye.

"If ye werena at the Shows in thae days ye went a trip wi' the steamer *Bonnie Doon*, and ye had an awfu' fine time o't on the Setturday if ye could jist mind aboot it on the Sunday mornin'. Duffy's gey coorse, bein' in the retail coal trade and cryin' for himsel'; I'm no' like that at a' mysel'; it widna dae, and me in the poseetion, but I mind aince o' Duffy tellin' me he could never fa' asleep at the Fair Time till his wife gave him the idea o' lyin' on his left side, and coontin' yin by yin a' the drams he had the night afore. He said it worked on him like chloryform.

"I hope ye'll no' mind me speakin' aboot drink; it's awfu' vulgar coonted noo, I hear, to let on ye ever heard that folk tak' it, but in thae days there was an awfu' lot o't partaken o' aboot Gleska. I'm tellt noo it's gaen clean oot o' fashion, and stane ginger's a' the go, and I see in the papers every Monday efter the Fair Setturday that 'there has been a gratifying decrease in the number o' cases at the Central Police Court compared wi' last year.' I'm that gled! I have been seein' that bit o' news in the papers for the last thirty years, and I hae nae doot that in a year or twa drunks and disorderlies 'll be sae scarce in Gleska at the Fair, the polis 'll hae to gang huntin' for them wi' bloodhounds.

"It's a fine thing the Press. It's aye keen to keep oor herts up. Ye'll notice, perhaps, that at every Gleska holiday the papers aye say the croods that left the stations were unprecedented. They were never kent to be ony ither wye.

"I daursay it's true enough. I went doon to the Broomie-law on Setturday to see Jinnet aff, and the croods on the Irish and Hielan' boats was that awfu', the men at the steerage end hadna room to pu' oot their pocket-hankies if they needed them. It's lucky they could dae withoot. When the butter-and-egg boats for Belfast and 'Derry left the quay, the pursers had a' to have on twa watches—at least they had the twa watch-chains, ane on each side, for fear the steamer wad capsize. I says to mysel', 'It's a peety a lot o' thae folk for Clachnacudden and County Doon dinna lose their return tickets and bide awa' when they're at it, for Gleska's a fine toon, but jist a wee bit ower crooked nooadays.'

" I hae nae great notion for doon the watter mysel' at the Fair. Jinnet jist goes and says she'll tell me whit it's like. Whit she likes it for is that ye're never lonely.

" And it's that homely doon aboot Rothesay and Dunoon, wi' the Gleska wifes hangin' ower the windows tryin' as hard as they can to see the scenery, between the whiles they're fryin' herrin' for Wull. And then there's wee Hughie awfu' ill wi' eatin' ower mony hairy grossets.

" But it's fine for the weans, too, to be gaun sclimbin' aboot the braes pu'in' the daisies and the dockens and the dentylions and—and—and a' thae kin' o' flooers ye'll can touch withoot onybody findin' fau't wi' ye. It's better for the puir wee smouts nor moshy in the back-coort, and puttin' bunnets doon the stanks. They'll mind it a' their days— the flooers and the dulse for naething, and the grossets and the Gregory's mixture. It's Nature ; it's the Rale Oreeginal.

" It does the wife a lot o' guid to gae doon the watter at the Fair. She's that thrang when she's at hame she hasna had time yet to try a new shooglin'-chair we got at the flittin' ; but ' it's a rest,' she'll say when she comes back, a' moth-eaten wi' the midges. And then she'll say, ' I'm that gled it's ower for the year.'

" That's the droll thing aboot the Fair and the New Year ; ye're aye in the notion that somethin' awfu' nice is gaun to happen, and naethin' happens at a', unless it's that ye get your hand awfu' sair hashed pu'in' the cork oot o' a bottle o' beer."

" You'll be glad, I'm sure, to have the goodwife back, Erchie ? " I said, with an eye on the fire-kindlers.

He betrayed some confusion at being discovered, and then laughed.

" Ye see I've been for sticks," said he. " That's a sample
o' my hoose-keepin'. I kent there was something parteecular
to get on the Setturday night, and thought it was pipeclye.
The grocer in there wad be thinkin' I was awa' on the ping-
pong if he didna ken I was a beadle. Will ye be puttin'
ony o' this bit crack in the papers ? "

" Well, I don't know, Erchie ; I hope you won't mind
if I do."

" Oh ! I'm no heedin' ; it's a' yin to Erchie, and does
nae hairm to my repitation, though I think sometimes your
spellin's a wee aff the plumb. Ye can say that I said keepin'
a hoose is like ridin' the bicycle ; ye think it's awfu' easy
till ye try't."

" That's a very old discovery, Erchie ; I fail to understand
why you should be anxious to have it published now."

Erchie winked. " I ken fine whit I'm aboot," said he.
" It'll please the leddies to ken that Erchie said it, and I
like fine to be popular. My private opeenion is that a man
could keep a hoose as weel as a woman ony day if he could
only bring his mind doon to't."

<h2 style="text-align:center">XV</h2>

<h1 style="text-align:center">THE STUDENT LODGER</h1>

It was with genuine astonishment Erchie one day had his
wife come to him with a proposal that she should keep a
lodger.

" A ludger ! " he cried. " It wad be mair like the thing
if ye keepit a servant lassie, for whiles I think ye're fair
wrocht aff yer feet."

" Oh, I'm no' sae faur done as a' that," said Jinnet.
" I'm shair I'm jist as smert on my feet as ever I was, and
I could be daein' wi' a ludger fine. It wad keep me frae
wearyin'."

" Wearyin' ! " said her husband. " It's comin' to't when

my ain wife tells me I'm no' company for her. Whit is't ye're wantin', and I'll see whit I can dae. If it's music ye're for, I'll buy a melodian and play't every nicht efter my tea. If it's improvin' conversation ye feel the want o', I'll ask Duffy up every ither nicht and we'll can argue on Fore Ordination and the chance o' the Celtic Fitba' Club to win the League Championship the time ye're darnin' stockin's. 'Wearyin'' says she! Perhaps ye wad like to jine a dancin' school; weel, I'll no' hinder ye, I'm shair, but I'll no' promise to walk to the hall wi' ye every nicht cairryin' yer slippers. Start a ludger! I'm shair we're no' that hard up!"

"No, we're no' that hard up," Jinnet confessed, "but for a' the use we mak' o' the room we micht hae somebody in it, and it wad jist be found money. I was jist thinkin' it wad be kind o' cheery to have a dacent young chap gaun oot and in. I'm no' for ony weemen ludgers; they're jist a fair bother, aye hingin' aboot the hoose and puttin' their nose into the kitchen, tellin' ye the richt wye to dae this and that, and burnin' coal and gas the time a man ludger wad be oot takin' the air."

"Takin' drink, mair likely," said Erchie, "and comin' hame singin' 'Sodgers o' the Queen,' and scandalisin' the hale stair."

"And I'm no' for a tredsman," Jinnet went on, with the air of one whose plans were all made.

"Of course no'," said her husband, "tredsmen's low. They're no' cless. It's a peety ye mairried yin. Perhaps ye're thinkin' o' takin' in a Chartered Accoontant, or maybe a polisman. Weel I'm jist tellin' ye I wadna hae a polisman in my paurlor; his helmet wadna gang richt wi' the furniture, and the blecknin' for his boots wad cost ye mair than whit he pyed for his room."

"No, nor a polisman!" said Jinnet. "I was thinkin' o' maybe a quate lad in a warehouse, or a nice factor's clerk, or something o' that sort. He wad be nae bother. It's just th ae makin' o' parridge in the mornin'. Ye're no' to thraw wi' me aboot this, Erchie ; my mind's made up I'm gaun to keep a ludger."

" If your mind's made up," he replied, " then there's nae use o' me argy-bargyin' wi' ye. I'm only your man. It bates me to ken whit ye're gaun to dae wi' the money, if it's no' to buy a motor-cairrage. Gie me your word ye're no' gaun in for ony sports o' that kind. I wad hate to see ony wife o' mine gaun skooshin' oot the Great Western Road on a machine like a tar-biler, wi' goggles on her een and a kahootchy trumpet skriechin' ' pip ! pip ! ' "

" Ye're jist an auld haver," said Jinnet, and turned to her sewing, her point gained.

. . . . . .

A fortnight after, as a result of a ticket with the legend " Apartments " in the parlour window, Jinnet was able to meet her husband's return to tea one night with the announcement that she had got a lodger. " A rale gentleman ! " she explained. " That weel put-on ! wi' twa Gledstone bags, yin o' them carpet, and an alerm clock for waukenin' him in the mornin'. He cam' this efternoon in a cab, and I think he'll be easy put up wi' and tak' jist whit we tak' oorsel's."

" I hope he's no' a theatrical," said Erchie. " Me bein' a beadle in a kirk it wadna be becomin' to hae a theatrical for a ludger. Forbye, they never rise oot o' their beds on the Sunday, but lie there drinkin' porter and readin' whit the papers say aboot their play-actin'."

" No, nor a theatrical ! " cried Jinnet. " I wadna mak' a show o' my hoose for ony o' them ! it's a rale nice wee fair-heided student."

Erchie threw up his hands in amazement. " Michty me ! " said he, " a student. Ye micht as weel hae taen in a brass baun' or the Cairter's Trip when ye were at it. Dae ye ken whit students is, Jinnet ? I ken them fine, though I was never at the college mysel', but yince I was engaged to hand roond beer at whit they ca'd a Gaudiamus. Ye have only to tak' the mildest wee laddie that has bad e'e-sicht and subject to sair heids frae the country and mak' a student o' him to rouse the warst passions o' his nature.   His mither, far awa' in Clachnacudden, thinks he's hurtin' his health wi' ower muckle study, but the only hairm he's daein' himsel' is to crack his voice cryin' oot impidence to his professors.   I'm vexed it's a student, and a fair-heided yin at that :   I've noticed that the fair-heided yins were aye the warst."

"Weel, he's there onywye, and we'll jist hae to mak' the best we can wi' him," said Jinnet.   "Forbye, I think he's a guid-leevin' lad, Erchie ;   he tellt me he was comin' oot for a minister."

"Comin' oot for a minister ! " said Erchie.   "Then that's the last straw !   I'm sorry for your chevalier and book-case ;   he'll be sclimbin' int't some nicht thinkin' it's the concealed bed."

The room door opened, a voice bawled in the lobby, " Mrs MacPherson, hey !   Mrs MacPherson," and the student, without waiting his landlady's appearance, walked coolly into the kitchen.

"Hulloo ! old chap, how's biz ? " he said to Erchie, and seated himself airily on the table, with a pipe in his mouth. He was a lad of twenty, with spectacles.

"I canna complain," said Erchie.   "I hope ye're makin' yersel' at hame."

"Allow me for that ! " said the student.

"That's nice," said Erchie, blandly.   "See and no' be ower blate, and if there's onything ye're wantin' that we havena got, we'll get it for ye.   Ye'll no' know whit ye need till ye see whit ye require.   It's a prood day for us to hae a diveenity student in oor room.   If we had expected it we wad hae had a harmonium."

"Never mind the harmonium," said the student.   "For music lean on me, George P. Tod.   I sing from morn till dewy eve.   When I get up in the morning, jocund day stands on the misty mountain top, and I give weight away to the

bloomin' lark. Shakespeare, Mr MacPherson. The Swan of
Avon. He wrote a fairly good play. What I wanted to know
was if by any chance Mrs Macpherson was a weepist ? "

" Sir ? " said Jinnet.

" Do you, by any chance, let the tear doon fa' ? "

" Not me ! " said Jinnet, " I'm a cheery wee woman."

" Good ! " said Tod. " Then you're lucky to secure a
sympathetic and desirable lodger. To be gay is my forte.
The last landlady I had was thrice a widow. She shed the
tears of unavailing regret into my lacteal nourishment with the
aid of a filler, I think, and the milk got thinner and thinner.
I was compelled at last to fold my tent like the justly celebrated Arabs of song and silently steal away. ' Why weep
ye by the tide, ladye ? ' I said to her. ' If it were by the
pint I should not care so much, but methinks your lachrymal
ducts are too much on the hair-trigger.' It was no use, she
could not help it, and—in short, here I am."

" I'm shair we'll dae whit we can for ye," said Jinnet. " I
never had a ludger before."

" So much the better," said George Tod. " I'm delighted
to be the object of experiment—the *corpus vile*, as we say
in the classics, Mr MacPherson—and you will learn a good
deal with me. I will now proceed to burn the essential
midnight oil. Ah, thought, thought ! You little know, Mr
MacPherson, the weary hours of study——"

" It's no' ile we hae in the room, it's gas," said Erchie.
" But if ye wad raither hae ile, say the word and we'll get it
for ye."

" Gas will do," said the student ; " it is equally conducive
to study, and more popular in all great congeries of thought."

" When dae ye rise in the mornin', Mr Tod ? " asked
Jinnet. " I wad like to ken when I should hae your breakfast ready."

" Rise ! " said Tod. " Oh, any time ! ' When the morn,
with russet mantle clad, walks o'er the dew on yon high
eastern hill.' "

" Is't Garnethill or Gilshochill ? " said Erchie, anxiously.
" I wad rise mysel', early in the mornin', and gang oot to
whichever o' them it is to see the first meenute the dew comes,
so that ye wadna lose ony time in gettin' up and started wi'
your wark."

The lodger for the first time looked at his landlord with a
suspicious eye. He had a faint fear that the old man might
be chaffing him, but the innocence of Erchie's face restored
his perkiness.

" I was only quoting the bard," he explained, as he left
the kitchen. " Strictly speaking, the morn with russet
mantle clad can go to the deuce for me, for I have an alarm
clock. Do not be startled if you hear it in the morning. It
goes off with incredible animation."

" Oh, Erchie, isn't he nice ? " said Jinnet, when the lodger
had withdrawn. " That smert, and aye talks that jovial, wi'
a lot o' words I canna mak' heid nor tail o'."

Erchie filled his pipe and thought a little, " Smert's the
word, Jinnet," said he. " That's whit students is for."

" I don't think he's very strong," said Jinnet. " If he
was in his mither's hoose she wad be giein' him hough soup
for his dinner. I think I'll jist mak' some for him to-morrow,
and put a hot-water bottle in his bed."

" That's richt," said Erchie ; " and if ye hae a haddie
or a kippered herrin', or onything else handy, it'll dae for
me."

" Ye're jist a haver ! " said Jinnet.

For a week George P. Tod was a model lodger. He came
in at early hours of the evening and went to bed timeously,
and was no great trouble to his landlady, whose cookery
exploits in his interest were a great improvement on anything he had ever experienced in lodgings before.

When he was in his room in the evenings Jinnet insisted on
the utmost quietness on the part of her husband. " Mr Tod's
at his hame lessons," she would say. " It'll no' dae to disturb

him. Oh, that heid wark ! that heid wark ! It must be an awfu' thing to hae to be thinkin' even-on."

" Heid wark ! " said her husband. " I ken the heid wark he's like enough at ; he's learnin' the words o' ' Mush Mush, tu-ral-i-ady ' to sing at the students' procession, or he's busy wi' a dictionary writin' hame to his paw to send him a post office order for twa pounds to jine the Y.M.C.A. But he's no' thinkin' o' jinin' the Y.M.C.A. ; he's mair likely to start takin' lessons at a boxin' cless."

But even Erchie was compelled to admit that the lad was no unsatisfactory lodger.

" I declare, Jinnet," he said, " I think he's yin o' the kind o' students ye read aboot but very seldom see. His faither 'll be a wee fairmer up aboot Clachnacudden, hainin' a' the money he can, and no' giein' his wife her richt meat, that he may see his son through the college and waggin' his heid in a pu'pit. Him and his faither's the stuff they mak' the six shillin' Scotch novells oot o'—the kind ye greet at frae the very start—for ye ken the puir lad, that was aye that smert in the school, and won a' the bursaries, is gaun to dee in the last chapter wi' a decline."

" Puir things," said Jinnet.

" Ye divna see ony signs o' decline aboot Mr Tod, do ye ? " asked Erchie, anxiously.

" I didna notice," replied Jinnet, " but he tak's his meat weel enough."

" The meat's the main thing ! But watch you if he hasna a hoast and thon hectic flush that aye breaks oot in chapter nine jist aboot the time he wins the gold medal."

" Och, ye're jist an auld haver, Erchie," said the wife. " Ye're no' to be frichtenin' me aboot the puir callant, jist the same age as oor ain Willie."

The time of the Rectorial Election approached, and Tod began to display some erratic habits. It was sometimes the small hours of the morning before he came home, and though he had a latch-key, Jinnet could never go to bed until her lodger was in for the night. Sometimes she went out to the close-mouth to look if he might be coming, and the first night that Erchie, coming home late from working at a civic banquet, found her there, Tod narrowly escaped being told to take his two bags and his alarm clock elsewhere.

"I was needin' a moothfu' o' fresh air onywye," was Jinnet's excuse for being out at such an hour. "But I'm feared that puir lad's workin' himsel' to death."

"Whaur dae ye think he's toilin' ? " asked her husband.

"At the nicht-school," said Jinnet. "I'm shair the college through the day's plenty for him."

"The nicht-school ! " cried Erchie. "Bonny on the nicht-school ! He's mair likely to be roond in Gibson Street batterin' in the doors o' the Conservative committee-rooms, for I ken by his specs and his plush weskit he's a Leeberal. Come awa' in to your bed and never mind him. Ye wad be daein' him a better turn maybe if ye chairged the gazogene to be ready for the mornin', when he'll be badly wantin't, if I'm no' faur mistaken."

Erchie was right—the gazogene would have been welcome next morning. As it was, the lodger was indifferent to breakfast, and expressed an ardent desire for Health Salts.

Erchie took them in to him, and found him groaning with a headache.

"The dew's awfu' late on the high eastern hills this mornin', Mr Tod," said Erchie. "Losh, ye're as gash as the Laird o' Garscadden ! I'm feart ye're studyin' far ower hard ; it's no' for the young and growin' to be hurtin' their heids wi' nicht-schools and day-schools ; ye should whiles tak' a bit rest to yersel'. And no' a bit o' yer breakfast touched ! Mrs MacPherson 'll no' be the pleased woman wi' ye this day, I can tell ye ! "

Tod looked up with a lack-lustre eye. "Thought, Mr MacPherson, thought ! " said he. "Hard, incessant, brain-corroding thought ! In the words of the Bard of Avon, ' He who increaseth knowledge increaseth sorrow.' "

"I aye thocht that was 'Ecclesiastes,' Mr Tod," said Erchie, meekly.

"In a way, yes," hastily admitted Tod. "It *was* 'Ecclesiastes,' as you say; but Shakespeare had pretty much the same idea. You will find it in—in—in his plays."

That afternoon began the more serious of Jinnet's experiences of divinity students. Nine young gentlemen with thick walking-sticks visited Tod's apartment *en masse*; the strains of "Mush Mush, tu-ral-i-ady," bellowed inharmoniously by ten voices, and accompanied by the beating of the walking-sticks on the floor, kept a crowd of children round the close-mouth for hours, and somewhat impeded the ordinary traffic of the street.

"There must be a spree on in auld MacPherson's," said the tenement. When Erchie came home he found Jinnet distracted. "Oh, whit a day I've had wi' them students!" she wailed.

"But look at the money ye're makin' aff your room," said her husband. "Wi' whit ye get frae Tod, ye'll soon hae enough for the motor cairrage and a yacht forbye."

"I'm feart to tell ye, Erchie," said Jinnet, "but I havena seen the colour o' his money yet."

"Study! study!" said Erchie. "Ye canna expect the puir lad to be thinkin' even-on aboot his lessons, and learnin' Latin and the rest o't, no' to mention 'Mush Mush,' and still keep mind o' your twa or three paltry bawbees."

"I mentioned it to him on Setturday and he was rale annoyed. He yoked on me and said I was jist as bad as the weedow he lodged wi' afore; that he was shair I was gaun to let the tear doon-fa'. He gied me warnin' that if I let the tear doon-fa' he wad leave."

"If I was you I wad start greetin' at yince," said Erchie. "And he'll leave onywye, this very Setturday."

That afternoon the students were having a torchlight procession, when, as usual, most of them marched in masquerade.

It was the day of the Rectorial Election, and the dust of far-flung pease-meal—favourite missile of the student—filled the air all over the classic slopes of Gilmorehill.   It had been one of Erchie's idle days ; he had been in the house all afternoon, and still was unbedded, though Jinnet for once had retired without waiting the home-coming of her lodger.

There came a riotous singing of students along the street, accompanied by the wheezy strains of a barrel-organ, and for twenty minutes uproar reigned at the entrance to the MacPherson's close.

Then Tod came up and opened the door with his latch-key. He had on part of Erchie's professional habiliments—the waiter's dress-coat and also Erchie's Sunday silk hat, both surreptitiously taken from a press in the lobby.   They were foul with pease-meal and the melted rosin from torches.   On his shoulders Tod had strapped a barrel-organ, and the noise of it, as it thumped against the door-posts on his entry, brought Erchie out to see what was the matter.

He took in the situation at a glance, though at first he did not recognise his own clothes.

" It's you, Mr Tod ! " said he.   " I was jist sittin' here thinkin' on ye slavin' awa' at your lessons yonder in the Deveenity Hall.   It maun be an awfu' strain on the intelleck. I'm gled I never went to the college mysel', but jist got my education, as it were, by word o' mooth."

Tod breathed heavily.   He looked very foolish with his borrowed and begrimed clothes, and the organ on his back, and he realised the fact himself.

" 'S all ri', Mr MacPherson," he said.   " Music hath charms.   Not a word !   I found this—this instuiment out-side, and just took it home.   Thought it might be useful. Music in the house makes cheerful happy homes—see adver-tisements—so I borrowed this from old friend, what's name —Angina Pectoris, Italian virtuoso, leaving him the monkey. Listen."

He unslung the organ and was starting to play it in the

lobby when Erchie caught him by the arm and restrained him.

"Canny, man, canny," said he. "Did I no' think it was a box wi' your bursary. I never kent richt whit a bursary was, but the lad o' pairts in the novells aye comes hame wi' a bursary, and hurts the spine o' his back carryin' his prizes frae the college. I jalouse that's the hectic flush on your face ; puir laddie, ye're no' lang for this warld."

Erchie stared more closely at his lodger, and for the first time recognised his own swallow-tail coat.

"My goodness!" said he, "my business coat, and my beadlin' hat. It was rale ill done o' ye, Mr Tod, to tak' them oot withoot my leave. It's the first time ever I was ashamed o' them. Jist a puir auld waiter's coat and hat. I wonder whit they wad say if they kent o't up in Clachna-cudden. The auld dominie that was sae prood o' ye wad be black affronted. My business coat! Tak' it aff and gang to your bed like a wise man. Leave the hurdy-gurdy on the stair-heid ; ye divna ken whit the other monkey micht hae left aboot it, and Jinnet's awfu' parteecular."

.   .   .   .   .

Next day Mr Tod got a week's notice to remove, and went reluctantly, for he knew good lodgings when he got them. He paid his bill when he went, too, "like a gentleman," as Jinnet put it. "He was a rale cheery wee chap," she said.

"I've seen faur worse," Erchie admitted. "Foolish a wee, but Nature, the Rale Oreeginal! I was gey throughither mysel' when I was his age. Ye never tellt me yet whit ye wanted wi' the ludging money."

"I was jist thinkin' I wad like to see ye wi' a gold watch the same as Carmichael's, next door," said Jinnet. "It's a thing a man at your time o' life, and in your poseetion, should hae, and I was ettlin' to gie ye't for your New Year."

"A gold watch!" cried her husband. "Whit nonsense!"

" It's no' nonsense at a'," said Jinnet. " It gies a man a kind o' bien, weel-daein' look, and I thocht I could mak' enough aff ludgers to buy ye yin."

" If it was for that ye wanted the ludger, and no' for a motor cairrage," said Erchie, " I'm gled Tod's awa'. You and your watch ! I wad be a bonny like la-di-da wi' a watch at the waitin' ; the folks wad be feared to tip me in case I wad be angry wi' them."

And so Erchie has not yet got a gold watch.

XVI

JINNET'S TEA-PARTY

ERCHIE'S goodwife came to him one day full of thrilling news from the dairy, where she had been for twopence worth of sticks.

" Oh, Erchie, dae ye ken the latest ? " said she. " The big fat yin in the dairy's gaun to mairry Duffy ! "

" Lord peety Duffy ! Somebody should tell the puir sowl she has her e'e on him. I'll bate ye he disna ken onything aboot it," said Erchie.

" Havers ! " said Jinnet. " It's him that's wantin' her, and I'm shair it's a guid thing, for his hoose is a' gaun to wreck and ruin since his last wife dee'd. Every time he comes hame to dry his claes on a wet day he's doon in the dairy for anither bawbee's worth o' mulk. The man's fair hoved up wi' drinkin' mulk he's no needin'. I hae catched him there that aften that he's kind o' affronted to see me. ' I'm here again, Mrs MacPherson,' says he to me yesterday when I went doon and found him leanin' ower the coonter wi' a tumbler in his haund. He was that ta'en he nearly dropped the gless."

" It wasna for the want o' practice—I'll wager ye that ! " said Erchie. " He could haud a schooner a hale nicht and him haulf sleepin'."

" ' I'm here again,' says he, onywye ; ' the doctor tellt me yon time I had the illness I was to keep up my strength. There's a lot o' nourishment in mulk.' And the big yin's face was as red as her short-goon.

" ' It's a blessin' the health, Mr Duffy,' says I ; ' we divna ken whit a mercy it is till we lose it,' and I never said anither word, but took my bit sticks and cam' awa'."

" And is that a' ye hae to gang on to be blamin' the chap ? " said Erchie. " Mony's a man 'll tak' a gless o' mulk and no' go ower faur wi't. But I think mysel' ye're maybe richt aboot the big yin, for I see Duffy's shaved aff his Paisley whiskers, and wears a tie on the Sundays."

Less than a week later the girl in the dairy gave in her notice, and Duffy put up the price of coals another ha'penny. He came up the stair with two bags for Jinnet, who was one of his customers.

" Whit wye are they up a bawbee the day ? " says she.

" It's because o' the Americans dumpin'," said Duffy. " They're takin' a' the tred frae us, and there's a kind o' tariff war."

" Bless me ! is there anither war ? " said Jinnet. " Weel, they're gettin' a fine day for't onywye. I hope it'll no put up the price o' the mulk."

Duffy looked at her and laughed uneasily. " I'm kind o' aff the mulk diet the noo," he said, seeing disguise was useless. " Ye're gey gleg, you weemen. I needna be tellin' ye me and big Leezie's sort o' chief this while back."

" Man ! dae ye tell me ? " said Jinnet, innocently. " A rale dacent lassie, and bakes a bonny scone. And she's to be the new mistress, is she ? We'll hae to be savin' up for the jeely-pan. I'm shair I aye tellt Erchie a wife was sair wanted in your hoose since Maggie dee'd."

" Jist at the very time I was thrangest," said Duffy, with regret. " I was awfu' chawed at her."

" Ye'll hae to bring yer lass up to see me and Erchie some nicht," said Jinnet. " It's a tryin' time the mairryin'."

Q

" There faur ower mony palavers aboot it," confided the coalman. " I wish it was ower and done wi', and I could get wearin' my grauvit at nicht again. Leezie's awfu' pernicketty aboot me haein' on a collar when we gang for a walk."

" Oh, ye rascal ! " said Jinnet, roguishly. " You men ! you men ! Ah, the coortin' time's the best time."

" Ach ! it's richt enough, I daursay ; but there's a lot o' nonsense aboot it. Ye get awfu' cauld feet standin' in the close. And it's aye in yer mind. I went to Leezie's close-mooth the ither nicht to whistle on her, and did I no' forget, and cry oot ' Coal ! ' thinkin' I was on business."

And thus it was that Jinnet's tea-party came about. The tender pair of pigeons were the guests of honour, and Jinnet's niece, and Macrae the night policeman, were likewise invited. Macrae was there because Jinnet thought her niece at thirty-five was old enough to marry. Jinnet did not know that he had drunk milk in Leezie's dairy before Duffy had gone there, and he himself had come quite unsuspicious of whom he should meet. In all innocence Jinnet had brought together the elements of tragedy.

There was something cold in the atmosphere of the party. Erchie noticed it. " Ye wad think it was a Quakers' meetin'," he said to himself, as all his wife's efforts to encourage an airy conversation dismally failed.

" See and mak' yer tea o't, Mr Macrae," she said to the night policeman. " And you, Sarah, I wish ye would tak' yin o' thae penny things, and pass the plate to Mr Duffy. Ye'll excuse there bein' nae scones, Mr Duffy ; there hasna been a nice scone baked in the dairy since Leezie left. There's wan thing ye'll can be shair o' haein' when ye're mairret till her, and that's guid bakin'."

Macrae snorted.

" What's the maitter wi' dough-feet, I wonder ? " thought Erchie, as innocent as his wife was of any complication. " That's the worst o' askin' the polis to yer pairties—they're no' cless ; and I'm shair, wi' a' Jinnet's contrivance, Sarah wadna be made up wi' him.''

" A wee tete mair tea, Mr Macrae ? Leezie, gie me Mr Macrae's cup if it's oot.''

Macrae snorted again. " I'll not pe puttin' her to the bother, Mrs MacPherson,'' said he, " Murdo Macrae can pe passin' his own teacups wisout botherin' anybody.''

" Dough-feet's in the dods,'' thought Erchie, to whom the whole situation was now, for the first time, revealed like a flash.

" I think, Jinnet,'' said he, " ye wad hae been nane the waur o' a pun' or twa o' conversation-losengers.''

They ate oranges after tea, but still a depression hung upon the company like a cloud, till Erchie asked Macrae if he would sing.

" Onything ye like,'' said he, " as lang's it's no' yin o' yer tartan chats that has a hunder verses, and that needs ye to tramp time wi' yer feet till't. I've a flet fit mysel', though my hert's warm, and I'm nae use at batin' time.''

Macrae looked at Leezie, who had all night studiously evaded his eye, cleared his throat, and started to sing a song with the chorus—

> " Fause Maggie Jurdan,
> She made my life a burden ;
> I don't want to live,
> And I'm gey sweart to dee.
> She's left me a' forlorn,
> And I wish I'd ne'er been born,
> Since fause Maggie Jurdan
> Went and jilted me.''

Leezie only heard one verse, and then began hysterically to cry.

" Look you here, Mac,'' broke in Erchie, " could ye no' mak' it the sword dance, or the Hoolichan, or something that wadna harrow oor feelin's this way ? ''

" Onything that'll gie us a rest,'' said Duffy, soothing his fiancée. " The nicht air's evidently no' very guid for the voice."

" Coals ! " cried the policeman, in a very good imitation of Duffy's business wail ; and at that Leezie had to be assisted into the kitchen by the other two women.

Duffy glared at his jealous and defeated rival, thought hard of something withering to hurl at him, and then said " Saps ! "

" What iss that you are saying ? " asked Macrae.

" Saps ! Big Saps ! That's jist what ye are," said Duffy. " If I wasna engaged I wad gie ye yin in the ear."

Jinnet's tea-party broke up as quickly as possible after that. When her guests had gone, and she found herself alone in the kitchen with Erchie and the tea dishes he carried in for her, she fell into a chair and wept.

" I'll never hae anither tea-pairty, and that's tellin' ye," she exclaimed between her sobs. " Fancy a' that cairry-on ower a big, fat, cat-witted cratur like thon ! Her and her lads ! "

" It's a' richt, Jinnet," said Erchie ; " you syne oot the dishes and I'll dry them if ye'll feenish yer greetin'. It's no' the last tea-pairty we'll hae if we hae oor health, but the next yin ye hae see and pick the company better."

XVII

THE NATIVES OF CLACHNACUDDEN

" You are looking somewhat tired, Erchie," I said to the old man on Saturday. " I suppose you were waiter at some dinner last night ? "

" Not me ! " said he promptly. " I wasna at my tred at a' last nicht ; I was wi' Jinnet at the Clachnacudden conversashion. My ! but we're gettin' grand. You should hae seen the twa o' us sittin' as hard as onything in a corner o' the hall watchin' the young yins dancin', and wishin' we were hame. Och, it's a fine thing a conversashion ; there's naething wrang wi't ; it's better nor standin' aboot the street corners, or haudin' up the coonter at the Mull o' Kintyre Vaults. But I'll tell ye whit, it's no' much o' a game for an auld couple weel ower sixty, though no' compleenin', and haein' their health, and able to read the smallest type withoot specs. I wadna hae been there at a', but Macrae, the nicht polisman that's efter Jinnet's niece, cam' cravin' me to buy tickets.

" ' I'm no' a Clachnacudden native,' says I till him. ' If it was a reunion o' the natives o' Gorbals and district, it micht be a' richt, for that's the place I belang to ; and if a' the auld natives cam' to a Gorbals swaree I micht get some o' the money some o' them's owin' me. But Clachnacudden ! —I never saw the place ; I aye thocht it was jist yin o' thae comic names they put on the labels o' the whisky bottles to mak' them look fancy.'

" Ye'll no' believe't, but Macrae, bein' Hielan' and no' haein' richt English, was that angry for me sayin' that aboot Clachnacudden, that he was nearly breakin' the engagement wi' Jinnet's niece, and I had to tak' the tickets at the hinder-end jist for peace' sake. Jinnet said it was a bonny-like thing spilin' Sarah's chances for the sake o' a shillin' or twa.

" So that's the wye I was wi' the Clachnacudden chats. Dae ye no' feel the smell o' peat-reek aff me ? If it wasna that my feet were flet I could gie ye the Hielan' Fling.

" But thae natives' reunions in Gleska's no' whit they used to be. They're gettin' far ower genteel. It'll soon be comin' to't that ye'll no can gang to ony o' them unless ye have a gold watch and chain, a dress suit, and £10 in the Savin's Bank. It used to be in the auld days when I went to natives' gatherin's for fun, and no' to please the nicht polis, that they were ca'd a swaree and ball, and the ticket was four-and-six for yoursel' and your pairtner. If ye didna get the worth o' your money there was something wrang wi' your stomach, or ye werena very smert. Mony a yin I've bin at, either in the wye o' tred, or because some o' Jinnet's Hielan' kizzens

cam' up to the hoose in their kilts to sell us tickets. There
was nae dress suits nor fal-lals aboot a reunion in thae days ;
ye jist put on your Sunday claes and some scent on your
hanky, wi' a dram in your pocket (if ye werena in the committee), turned up the feet o' your breeks, and walked doon
to the hall in the extra-wide welt shoes ye were gaun to dance
in. Your lass—or your wife, if it was your wife—sat up the
nicht before, washin' her white shawl and sewin' frillin' on
the neck o' her guid frock, and a' the expense ye had wi'
her if ye werena merried to her was that ye had to buy her a
pair o' white shammy leather gloves, size seeven.

" A' the auld folk frae Clachnacudden in Gleska were at
thae swarees, as weel as a' the young folk. Ye were packed in
your sates like red herrin' in a barrel, and on every hand ye
heard folk tearin' the tartan and misca'in' somebody at hame
in Clachnacudden. The natives wi' the dress suits that had
got on awfu' weel in Gleska at the speerit tred or keeping
banks, sat as dour as onything on the pletform lettin' on they
couldna speak the tartan. Ithers o' them—that had the richt
kind o' legs for't—wad hae on the kilts, wi' a white goat-skin
sporran the size o' a door-bass hung doon to their knees
fornent them, haudin' in their breaths in case the minister
wad smell drink aff them, and tryin' to feel like Rob Roy or
Roderick Dhu.

" In thae days they started oot wi' giein' ye tea and a poke
o' fancy breid—penny things like London buns and fruit-
cakes ; and between the speeches oranges were passed roond,
and wee roond hard sweeties, fine for pappin' at the folk in
front. Ye aye made a guid tea o't, the same as if ye never
saw tea in your life afore, and preferred it weel biled.

" When the tea was bye and the boys were blawin' as
much breath as they had left into the empty pokes, and
bangin' them aff like cannons, the chairman wad stand up
on the pletform and make a speech aboot Clachnacudden.
I used to ken that speech by hert ; it was the same yin for a'
the natives' reunions. He said that Clachnacudden was the

bonniest place ever onybody clapped eyes on. That the
Clachnacudden men were notorious a' ower the world for
their honesty and push, and aye got on like onything if they
were tryin', and didna tak' to the drink ; and that the Clachnacudden lassies were that braw, and nice, and smert, they
were lookit up to every place they went. When he said that
the natives o' Clachnacudden kent fine it was the God's truth
he was tellin' them, they got on their feet and waved their
hankies and cheered for ten meenutes.

"Havin' taken a drink o' watter frae the caraffe at his side
—efter makin' a mistake and tryin' to blaw the froth aff the
tumbler—the chairman then begood generally to say that
Gleska was a gey cauld, sooty, dirty, wicked place for onybody
to hae to live in that had been born in the bonny wee glens,
and the hulls, and hedges, and things aboot Clachnacudden,
but still

> 'Their herts were true, their herts were Hielan',
> And they in dreams beheld the Hebrides.'

At that ye wad see the hale o' the Clachnacudden folk puttin'
whit was left o' their pastry in their pouches and haudin'
their hankies wi' baith hands to their e'en to kep the tears
frae rinnin' on their guid waistcoats or their silk weddin'
goons. And the droll thing was that for a' they misca'd
Gleska, and grat aboot Clachnacudden, ye couldna get yin o'
them to gang back to Clachnacudden if ye pyed the train
ticket and guaranteed a pension o' a pound a week.

"Clachnacudden bein' Hielan', they aye started the music
efter the chairman's speech wi' a sang frae Harry Linn ca'd
' Jock Macraw, the Fattest Man in the Forty-Twa,' or some
ither sang that kind o' codded themsel's. Then the minister
made a comic speech wi' jokes in't, and tried to look as game
as onything ; and the folk frae Clachnacudden leaned forrit
on their sates and asked the wifes in front if they had mind
when his mither used to work in the tawtie field. ' Fancy
him a minister ! ' says they, ' and tryin' to be comic, wi' his

mither jist yin o' the MacTaggarts ! ' A' the time the puir minister was thinkin' he was daein' fine, and wonderin' if ' The Oban Times ' was takin' doon a' his speech.

" And then a lot o' nyafs in the back sates aye began to heave orange-peelin's at folk that was daein' them nae hairm.

" Efter the swaree was ower, the weemen went into the ladies' room to tak' aff their galoshes, and tak' the preens oot o' their trains, and the men went ower to the Duke o' Wellington Bar, rinnin' like onything, for it was nearly eleeven o'clock. The folk the hall belanged to started to tak' oot the sates for the dancin', and sweep the corks aff the floor ; and at eleeven prompt the Grand Merch started. Whiles they had Adams's or Iff's band, and whiles they jist had Fitzgerald, the fiddler that used to play on the Loch-goilhead boat. It didna maitter, for a' the Clachnacudden folk were fine strong dancers, and could dance to onything. Man ! I aye liked the Grand Merch. The man wi' the reddest kilts aye started it at the Clachnacudden, and when the Grand Merch got a' fankled, they jist started ' Triumph,' and did the best they could.

" That was in the grand auld days afore they got genteel. Nooadays, as I'm tellin' ye, it's a' conversashions, and they work aff their speeches on ye wi' no tea at a' and no pokes o' pastry, nor naething. Ye're no use unless ye hae the lend o' a dress suit, and your pairtner has to hae pipe-clyed shoon, a muslin frock no' richt hooked at the neck, her hair put up at Bamber's, and a cab to tak' her hame in. It's naething but the waltzin'. I'm prood to say I never waltzed in a' my born days, though they say I have the richt kind o' feet for't, me bein' so lang at the waitin'. And a' they auld classic dances, like La-va and the Guaracha Waltz and Circassian Circle's oot o' date ; I havena even seen Petronella for mony a day.

" And the music's a' spiled ; it's a' fancy music they hae noo, wi' nae tune ye can sing to't as ye gang up the back or doon the middle. Ye'll see them yonder wi' their piano, three fiddles, and a cornet. If I was gaun to hae a cornet I wad hae a cornet and no' a brass feenisher.

" Ye'll no' see ony o' the dacent auld Clachnacudden folk at their modern reunions ; the puir sowls has to bide at hame and gang to their beds early that they may get up in time to mak' a cup o' tea for their dochters that was at the conversashion. No ; Jinnet and me's no' keen on Clachnacudden or onything o' the kind nooadays ; we wad faur sooner stay at hame and read ' The Weekly Mail.' "

XVIII

MARY ANN

" I SEE frae ' The News,' " said Erchie, " that Mary Ann's no' gaun to see her kizzen on her nicht oot the noo, but has the kitchen table cleared for action wi' a penny bottle o' Perth ink and a quire o' paper to write letters to the editor, telling him and his readers that the country doesna ken her value.

" If ye're in the habit o' tryin' to keep a general, ye canna be shair but at this very meenute she's doon the stair, wi' her sleeves rowed up and her fingers a' Perth Blue Black, paintin' your wife's photograph as a slave-driver, and givin' your hoose a character that would mak' ye lose your nicht's sleep if ye kent it. Faith, it's comin' to it !

" The servant problem is the only ane that's railly o' ony interest to the country, as far as I can mak' oot frae hearin' things when I'm either beadlin', or waitin' at waddin'-breakfasts. Twa women canna put their heads thegither ower a cup o' tea withoot gaun ower a list o' a' the lassies they've had since last November ; and the notion ye get is that they change frae place to place that often they must hae motor cairrages.

" Mary Ann sails in with her kist and a fine character frae

Q*

her last place on Monday at 8 P.M., and aboot ten minutes efter that she's on the road again. She is the greatest traveller o' the age ; it is estimated by them that kens aboot thae things, that the average domestic, if she keeps her health and gets ony chance at a' gangs 15,000 miles every three years shifting her situation.

" It is the age of the lairge-built, agile, country girl ; no ither kind can stand the strain o' humpin' kists up and doon area stairs. An aluminium kist that when packed weighs only fifteen pounds has been invented specially for the ' strong and willing general, early riser, no washin', fond o' weans ' ; but in spite o' that, she canna get ower mair nor 250 to 263 different situations in the year.

" The Hielan's is the peculiar home o' the maist successful domestic servants, though a very gude strain o' them is said to come frae Ayrshire and roon' aboot Slamannan.

" They are catched young, carefully clipped, curry-combed and shod, and shipped to Gleska at the beginnin' o' the winter, wi' fine characters frae the U.F. minister. On the day they start their first situation they're generals, that say ' Whit is't ? ' quite angry, at the door to folk that come to their mistress's efternoon teas ; on the Wednesday they're wanting their wages up ; and on the Thursday they start in anither place as experienced hoose- and table-maids. At least, that's whit I gaither frae overhearin' the ladies : we have nae servant in oor hoose,—Jinnet does everything hersel'.

" When Mary Ann's no' packin' her kist, or haein' confabs wi' the butcher, or trimmin' a frock for the Clachnacudden natives' swarree and ball, she's lookin' the papers to see the rate o' servants' wages in Kimberley, near whaur the wars were. Some day she's gaun to Kimberley, or Australia, or ony ither foreign pairt, whaur intelligent cooks get the wages o' Cabinet Ministers, and can get mairrit jist as easy's onything.

" In the fine auld times servant lassies used to bide wi' ye

till they were that auld and frail ye had to have somebody
sittin' up wi' them at nicht.

"Yince they got a fit in yer hoose ye couldna get quat o'
them : they fastened their kists to the floor wi' big screw-
nails, and wad scarcely go oot the length o' the kirk for fear
ye wad shut up the hoose and rin awa' and leave them.
As for the wages they got, they were that sma', folks used
to toss up a bawbee to see whether they wad keep a servant
or a canary.

"But nooadays a man that's in the habit o' payin' ony
heed to the servant lassies that opens the door for him or
hands him his letters, thinks it's a magic-lantern show he's
at, wi' a new picture every twa seconds.

"He doesna see his wife except on the Sundays, for a'
the ither days o' the week she's cyclin' roond the registries
wi' five pounds o' change in silver, payin' fees.

"'Hoose-tablemaid, ma'am ? Certainly, ma'am ; we'll
see whit we can dae for ye between noo and the next Gleska
Exhibeetion,' says the registry, rakin' in the half-croons as
hard's she can.

"When there's a rumour gets aboot Dowanhill that a
servant lass, oot o' a situation, was seen the week afore last,
hundreds o' ladies mak' for the registries, and besiege them
in the hope o' catchin' her ; and of late, I'm tellt they're
engagin' trained detectives for trackin' plain cooks.

"Domestic service is the only profession in Europe the
day whaur the supply's less than the demand, and if I had
twa or three boys ready to gang oot and work for themselves, I wad sooner mak' them into scullery-maids than
apprentice them wi' an electrical engineer.

"In the last ten years wha ever heard o' a servant lassie
oot o' a situation ony langer than the time she took to rin
frae ae hoose to anither, if she had the richt number of hands
and een ?

"She disna need to gang onywhere lookin' for a place ;
the sleuth-hounds o' Dowanhill track her to her lair as soon

as she's landed at the Broomielaw or Buchanan Street Station, and mak' a grab at her afore she learns enough o' the language to ask her wye to a registry.

"A new servant in a hoose is like a Field-Marshal back frae the front,—she's trated wi' sae muckle deference. Ye daurna mak' a noise through the day for fear it'll spoil her sleep. Ye pit on the fire for her in the mornin', and brush her golfin' buits afore ye start for the office. Ye pay sixpence a day o' car fares for her to go and see her kizzens in case she's wearyin', puir thing! And if 'Rob Roy's' on at the theatre ye'll be as weel to let her know and gie her tickets for it, or she'll gie notice when she reads the creeticism in the paper and finds oot she missed it. Mair nor a dizzen societies have been started for giving medals and rewards to servant lassies that have been a lang lang while in the ae situation; they're worked on a graduated scale :—

"Hoosemaids, in one situation two months—Bronze medal of the Society and 30s.

"Generals, three months—Silver medal and fountain pen.

"Plain cook, six months—Gold medal, £5, and gramophone.

"Whit the country wants is the municeepilisation o' domestic service. The better hoosin' o' the poor's a thing that there's nae hurry for. Plain cooks and general servants that ken the difference between a cake o' black lead and a scrubbing-brush are a communal needcessity; they can nae mair be done without than gas, water, skoosh cars, or the telephone.

"The Corporations should import and train Mary Anns in bulk, gie them a nate uniform and thirty shillin's a week, and hire them oot 'oorly, daily, weekly, or monthly, as required, reserving for them a' the rights and privileges that belong to them, wi' limitation o' workin' 'oors, strick definition o' duties, stipulated nichts oot, and faceelities for followers. Look at the polis. Ye can depend on gettin' a polisman nine times oot o' ten if ye want him; a lassie to gang oot wi' the pramlater, or a hoose-tablemaid, should be jist as easy got by every ratepayer when wanted, and that's only to be secured by the Corporations takin' the domestic service into their ain haunds."

XIX

DUFFY'S WEDDING

I DID not see Erchie during the New-Year holidays, and so our greetings on Saturday night when I found him firing up the church furnace had quite a festive cheerfulness.

"Where have you been for the past week?" I asked him. "It looks bad for a beadle to be conspicuous by his absence at this season of the year."

"If ye had been whaur ye ocht to hae been, and that was in the kirk, last Sunday, ye wad hae found me at my place," said Erchie. "Here's a bit bride's-cake," he went on, taking a little packet from his pocket. "The rale stuff! Put that below your heid at nicht and ye'll dream aboot the yin that's gaun to mairry ye. It's a sure tip, for I've kent them that tried it, and escaped in time."

I took the wedding-cake. To dream of the one I want to marry is the desire of my days—though, indeed, I don't need any wedding-cake below my pillow for such a purpose. "And who's wedding does this—this deadly comestible—come from, Erchie?" I asked him.

"Wha's wad it be but Duffy's," said Erchie. "'At 5896 Braid Street, on the 31st, by the Rev. J. Macauslane, Elizabeth M'Niven Jardine to James K. Duffy, coal merchant.' Duffy's done for again; ye'll can see him noo hurryin' hame for his tea when his work's bye and feared ony o' the regular customers o' the Mull of Kintyre Vaults 'll stop him on the road and ask him in for something. His wife's takin' him roond wi' a collar on, and showin' him aff among a' her freen's and the ither weemen she wants to vex, and she's him learning to ca' her " Mrs D.' when they're in company. He wasna twa days at his work efter the thing happened when she made him stop cryin' his ain coals and leave yin o' his men to dae't, though there's no' twa o' them put thegither has the voice o' Duffy. I wadna wonder if his tred fell aff on accoont o't, and it's tellin' on his health. ' She says it's no' genteel for me to be cryin' my ain coals,' he says to me ; ' but I think it's jist pride on her part, jist pride. Whit hairm does it dae onybody for me to gie a wee bit roar noo and then if it's gaun to help business ? ' I heard him tryin' to sing ' Dark Lochnagar ' on Friday nicht in his ain hoose, and it wad vex ye to listen, for when he was trampin' time wi' his feet ye could hardly hear his voice, it was that much failed. ' Duffy,' I says till him, takin' him aside, ' never you mind the mistress, but go up a close noo and then and gie a roar to keep your voice in trim withoot lettin' on to her onything aboot it.'

" Yes, Duffy was mairried on Hogmanay Nicht, and we were a' there—Jinnet and me, and her niece Sarah, and Macrae the nicht polis, and a companion o' Macrae's frae Ardentinny, that had his pipes wi' him to play on, but never got them tuned. It was a grand ploy, and the man frae Ardentinny fell among his pipes comin' doon the stair in the mornin'. ' Ye had faur ower much drink,' I tellt him, takin' him oot frae amang the drones and ribbons and things. ' I'm shair ye've drunk a hale bottle.' ' Whit's a bottle o' whusky among wan ? ' says he. If it wasna for him it wad hae been a rale nice, genteel mairrage.

" Duffy had on a surtoo coat, and looked for a' the warld like Macmillan, the undertaker, on a chape job. He got the lend o' the surtoo frae yin o' the men aboot the Zoo, and he was aye tryin' to put his haunds in the ootside pooches of them no' there. ' Oh, Erchie,' he says to me, ' I wish I had on my jaicket again, this is no' canny. They'll a' be lookin' at my haunds.' ' No, nor yer feet,' I tellt him ; ' they'll be ower busy keepin' their e'e on whit they're gaun to get to eat.'

' If ye only kent it,' says he, ' my feet's a torment to me, for my buits is far ower sma'.' And I could see the puir sowl sweatin' wi' the agony.

" The bride looked fine. Jinnet nearly grat when she saw her comin' in, and said it minded her o' hersel' the day she was mairried. ' Ye're just haverin',' I tellt her, gey snappy. ' She couldna look as nice as you did that day if she was hung wi' jewels.' But I'll no' say Leezie wasna nice enough —a fine, big, sonsy, smert lass, wi' her face as glossy as onything.

" When the operation was by, and the minister had gane awa' hame, us pressin' him like onything to wait a while langer, and almost breakin' his airms wi' jammin' his top-coat on him fast in case he micht change his mind, we a' sat down to a high tea that wad dae credit to F. & F.'s. If there was wan hen yonder there was haulf a dizzen, for the bride had a hale lot o' country freen's, and this is the time o' the year the hens is no' layin'.

" There were thirty-five folk sat doon in Duffy's hoose that nicht, no' coontin' a wheen o' the neighbours that stood in the lobby and took their chance o' whit was passin' frae the kitchen. Duffy hadna richt started carvin' the No. 6 hen when a messenger cam' to the door to ask for the surtoo coat, because the man in the Zoo had his job changed for that nicht and found he needed the coat for his work ; so Duffy was quite gled to get rid of it, and put on his Sunday jaicket. ' Ask him if he wadna like a wee lend o' my new tight boots,' he says to the messenger frae the Zoo ; ' if he does, come back as fast's ye can for them, and I'll pay the cab.'

" Efter the high tea was by, the Ardentinny man never asked onybody's leave, but began to tune his pipes, stoppin' every twa or three meenutes to bounce aboot the player he was, and that his name was M'Kay—yin o' the auld clan M'Kays. Macrae, the nicht polis, was awfu' chawed that he brocht him there at a'. Ye couldna hear yersel' speakin' for the tunin' o' the pipes, and they werena nearly half ready for

playin' on when the bride's mither took the liberty o' stoppin'
him for a wee till we wad get a sang frae somebody.

" ' James 'll sing,' says the bride, lookin' as prood's ye like
at her new man. 'Will ye no' obleege the company wi'
" Dark Lochnagar " ? '

" ' I wad be only too willin',' he tellt her, ' if I had on my
ither boots and hadna ett thon last cookie.' But we got him
to sing ' Dark Lochnagar ' a' richt. In the middle o't the
man frae Ardentinny said if Duffy wad haud on a wee he wad
accompany him on the pipes, and he started to tune them
again, but Macrae stopped him by puttin' corks in his drones.

" Jinnet sang the ' Auld Hoose.' Man! I was prood o'
her. Yon's the smertest wumman in Gleska. The Rale
Oreeginal ! "

" Don't you yourself sing, Erchie ? "

" Not me ! I'm comic enough withoot that. A flet fit
and a warm hert, but timmer in the tune. Forbye, I was too
busy keepin' doon the man frae Ardentinny. He was determined to hae them pipes o' his tuned if it took him a' nicht.
I tried to get him to gang oot into the back-coort to screw
them up, but he aye said they were nearly ready noo, they
wadna tak' him ten meenutes, and he kept screechin' awa'
at them. It was fair reediculous.

" At last the bride's mither got him put into the kitchen,
and was clearin' the room for a dance. Duffy was very red
in the face, and refused to rise frae the table. ' Whit's the
use o' dancin' ? ' says he ; ' are we no' daein' fine the way
we are ? ' And then it was found oot he had slipped his
tight boots aff him under the table, and was sittin' there as
joco as ye like in his stockin' soles.

" The young yins were dancin' in the room to the playin'
o' a whustle, and the rest o' us were smokin' oot on the stair-
heid, when the man frae Ardentinny cam fleein' oot wi' his
bagpipes still gaspin'. He said it was an insult to him to
start dancin' to a penny whustle and him there ready to play
if he could only get his pipes tuned.

" ' Never you heed, Mac,' says I ; ' ye'll hae a chance at Macrae's waddin' if ye can get the pipes tuned afore then ; he's engaged to oor Sarah.'

" I was that gled when the cat-wutted cratur fell amang his pipes gaun doon the stair in the mornin' ; it served him richt."

" And where did Duffy and his bride spend their honeymoon, Erchie ? " I asked.

" They took the skoosh car oot to Paisley ; that was a' their honeymoon."

XX

ON CORPORAL PUNISHMENT

" On this question of corporal punishment in the schools, Erchie," I said to my old friend, " what are your views ? I've no doubt you're dead against any alteration on use and wont."

" Whiles," said Erchie ; " whiles ! I buy the paper ae day, and when I read the wye brutal and ignorant schoolmaisters abuse their poseetion, I feel that angry I could fling bricks at the windows o' a' the schools I pass on the wye to my wark; but the next day when I read whit perfect wee deevils a' the weans is nooadays, and hoo they'll a' turn oot a disgrace to their faithers and mithers if they divna get a beltin' twice a-day, I'm sair tempted to gae ower to my guid-dochter's in the Calton and tak' a razor-strop to wee Alick afore he gangs to his bed, jist in case he's bein' negleckit. That's the warst o' the newspapers ; they're aye giein' ye the differen' sets o't, and ye read sae much on the ae side and then the ither that ye're fair bate to mak' up your mind. My ain puir auld faither—peace be wi' him !—didna seem to be muckle fashed wi' the different sets o't in the newspapers ; he made up his mind awfu' fast, and gied ye his fit-rule ower the back o' the fingers afore ye could gie your wee brither a clip on the nose

for clypin' on ye. They may abolish corporal punishment
in the Gleska schools, but they'll no' pit an end to't in hooses
whaur the faither's a plumber and aye has a fit-rule stuck
doon the outside seam o' his breeks."

"Ah yes ! Erchie, but these paternal ebullitions of ill-
temper——"

"Ill-temper or no'," said Erchie, "it's a' in the scheme o'
nature, and an angry man's jist as much the weepon o' nature
as a thunderbolt is, or a lichted caundle lookin' for an escape
o' gas. If ye dinna get your licks in the school for bein' late
in the mornin', ye'll get fined an awfu' lot o' times for sleepin'
in when ye're auld enough to work in Dubs's ; so the thing's
as braid as it's wide, as the Hielan'man said."

"Then you seem to think a fit of anger is essential to
paternal punishment, Erchie ? That's surely contrary to all
sober conclusions."

"Sober conclusions hae naethin' to dae wi' skelpin' weans,
as I ken fine that brocht up ten o' a family and nearly a'
that's spared o' them daein' weel for themsel's. The auld
Doctor in oor kirk talks aboot love and chastisement, but in
my experience human nature wad be a' to bleezes lang afore
this if faithers and mithers didna whiles lose their tempers
and gie their weans whit they deserved. If you're the kind
o' man that could thresh a puir wee smout o' a laddie in
cauld bluid, I'm no', and I canna help it."

"And did you thrash your ten much, Erchie ? " I
asked, with a doubt as to that essential ill-temper in his
case.

"That has naethin' to dae wi't," said he, quickly. "My
private disinclination to hae the wee smouts greetin' disna
affect the point at a'. If oor yins needed it, I went oot for
a daunder and left the job to Jinnet. A woman's aye the
best hand at it, as I ken by my aunty Chirsty. When she
had the threshin' o' me, she aye gied me tuppence efter it was
done if I grat awfu' sair, and I took guid care I never went
wantin' money in thae days. I was only vexed she couldna

thresh me threepence-worth the time the shows were roond oor wye, and mony's the time I worked for't.

"When the papers mak' me wonder whether corporal punishment's guid for the young or no', I jist tak' a look at mysel' in Jinnet's new wardrobe looking-gless, and, except for the flet feet—me bein' a waiter—I don't see muckle wrang wi' Erchie MacPherson, and the Lord kens there was nae slackness o' corporal punishment in his days, though then it was simply ca'd a leatherin'. My mither threshed me because it wadna gae wrang onywye—if I wasna need'nt the noo I wad be need'nt some ither time; and my faither threshed me because there was a hard knot in the laces o' his boots, and he couldna lowse't. It didna dae me ony hairm, because I ken't they were fond enough o' me.

"In the school we were weel threshed in the winter-time to keep us warm, and in the summer-time a stirrin'-up wi' the tawse a' roond made up for the want o' ventilation. If I never learned much else in the school, I got a fair grup o' naitural history, and yin o' the tips I got was that a horse-hair laid across the loof o' the haund 'll split a cane or cut the fingers aff a tawse, when ye're struck by either the yin or the ither. I made twa or three cairt-horses bald-heided at the tail wi' my experimentin', but somethin' aye went wrang; the maister either let fly ower sudden, or it was the wrang kind o' horse—at onyrate, I never mind o' cuttin' the cane or the tawse.

"Whiles when I'm across at my guid-dochter's, I hear her wee laddie, Alick, greetin' ower his coonts, and fear't the maister 'll cane him because they're no' richt.

"'If a cistern wi' an inlet pipe twa-and-a-half inches in diameter lets in seventy-nine gallons eleeven quarts and seeven pints in twenty-fower and a half 'oors, and an ootlet pipe o' three-quarters o' an inch diameter discharges forty-eight gallons nineteen quarts and five pints in the six 'oors, whit o'clock will the cistern be empty if the ootlet pipe hiz a big leak in't?'

" That's the kind o' staggerer puir wee Alick gets thrashed
for if he canna answer't richt. I couldna dae a coont like
that mysel', as shair's death, if I was pyed for't, unless I had
the cistern aside me, and a len' o' the measures frae the Mull
o' Kintyre Vaults, and Jinnet wi' a lump o' chalk keepin'
tally. I'm no' shair that it's ony guid to thrash wee Alick
for no' can daein' a coont o' that kind, or for no' bein' able
to spell ' fuchsia,' or for no' mindin' the exact heights o' a'
the principal mountains in Asia and Sooth America.

" Noo wad ye like it yoursel' ? Ye canna put mathematics
into a callan's heid by thrashin' him ower the fingers, if he's
no' made wi' the richt lump in his heid for mathematics ; and
if Alick's schoolmaister gaes on thinkin' he can, I'll gae oot
some day to his school and maybe get the jyle for't."

" Come, come, Erchie," I protested ; " you are in quite
an inconsistent humour to-day ; surely Alick's thrashings
are all in the scheme of nature. If he is not punished now
for inability to do that interesting proposition in compound
proportion, he will be swindled out of part of his just payment
when paid for bricklaying by the piece when he has taken to
the trade, and the thing—once more as the Highlandman
said—is as broad as it's wide."

" Nane o' my guid-dochter's sons is gaun to tak' to treds,"
said Erchie, coldly ; " they're a' gaun to be bankers and
electreecians and clerks and genteel things o' that sort. If
I'm no' consistent aboot this, it's because o' whit I tellt ye,
that I've read ower mony o' thae letters and interviews in
the papers, and canna mak' up my mind. I ken fine a' the
beltin's I got in the school were for my guid, but—but—but
it's different wi' wee Alick."

" But we have all our wee Alicks, Erchie."

" Then we're a' weel aff," said Erchie, glowing, " fcr yon's
the comicalest wee trate ! The Rale Oreeginal."

" But the teachers don't understand him ? "

" That's the hale p'int," said Erchie, agreeably ; " the
teachers never dae. They're no' pyed for understandin' a'

the wee Alicks : a' that can be expected for the wages the schoolmaisters get in Gleska is that they'll haul the wee cratur by the scruff o' the neck through a' the standards. The schoolmaister and the mither ought to be mair prized and bigger pyed than ony ither class in the country, but they're no', and that's the reason their jobs are often sae badly filled up.

" If education was a' that folk think it is, there wad lang syne hae been nae need for cane nor strap. For mair nor a generation noo, every bairn has had to go to the school—a' the parents o' a' the weans in school the noo have had an education themsel's, so that baith at hame and in the school the young generation of the present day have sae mony advantages ower whit you and I had, they ought to be regular gems o' guid behaviour and intelligence.

" But I canna see that they're ony better than their grand-faithers were at the same age. Except my guid-dochter's boy Alick, I think they're a' worse.

" A' the difference seems to be that they're auld sooner than we were, smoke sooner, and swear sooner, and in a hunner wyes need mair leatherin' than we did. Education o' the heid's no' education o' the hert, and the only thing that comes frae crammin' a callant o' naiturally bad disposeetion with book-learnin' is that he's the better trained for swindlin' his fellow-men when he's auld enough to try his hand at it. I wad be awfu' prood o' every new school that's in Gleska if I didna ken that I had to pye a polis tax for't by-and-bye as weel as school tax."

" How glad we ought to be, Erchie, that we were born in a more virtuous age," I said, and Erchie screwed up his face.

" We werena," said he. " It's aye been the same since the start o' things. I've jist been sayin' to ye whit I mind o' hearin' my faither say to mysel'. There'll aye be jist enough rogues in the world to keep guid folk like you and me frae gettin' awfu' sick o' each ither."

XXI

THE FOLLIES OF FASHION

My old friend has a great repugnance to donning new clothes. His wife Jinnet told me once she had always to let him get into a new suit, as it were, on the instalment system : the first Sunday he reluctantly put on the trousers ; the second he ventured the trousers and waistcoat ; and on the third he courageously went forth in the garb complete, after looking out at the close-mouth first to see that Duffy or any other ribald and critical acquaintance was not looking.

I saw a tell-tale crease down the front of the old man's legs yesterday.

" New sartorial splendour, Erchie ? " I said, and pinched him for luck.

He got very red.

" You're awfu' gleg in the een," said he ; " am I no' daein' my best to let on they're an auld pair cleaned ? Blame the wife for't ! there's naethin' o' the la-di-da aboot easy-gaun Erchie. But weemen ! claes is their hale concern since the day that Adam's wife got the shape o' a sark frae the deevil, and made it wi' a remender o' fig-leafs.

" There's no much wrang wi' Jinnet, but she's far ower pernicketty aboot whit her and me puts on, and if she has naething else to brag aboot she'll brag I hae aye the best-brushed buits in oor kirk. She took an awfu' thraw yince at yin o' the elders, for she thocht he bate me wi' the polish o' his buits, and she could hardly sleep ower the heid o't till I tellt her they were patent.

" ' Och ! ' says she, ' is that a' ? Patent's no' in the game.'

" ' Onything's in the game,' says I to her, ' that's chaper nor heeling and soling.'

" It's bad enough," he went on, " to be hurtin' yer knees wi' new breeks, and haein' the folk lookin' at ye, but it's a mercy for you and me we're no weemen. You and me buys a hat, and as lang's the rim and the rest o't stick thegither, it's no' that faur oot the fashion we need to hide oorsel's. The only thing I see changes in is collars, and whether it's the lying-doon kind or the double-breisted chats, they hack yer neck like onything. There's changes in ties, but gie me plain black.

"Noo, Jinnet has to hae the shape o' her hat shifted every month as regular's a penny diary. If it's flet in June, it's cockin' up in July; and if the bash is on the left side in August, it has to be on the right side in September.

"Och! but there's no muckle wrang wi' Jinnet for a' that; she wanted to buy me a gold watch-chain last Fair.

"'A gold watch-chain's a nice, snod, bien-lookin' thing aboot a man,' says she, 'and it's gey usefu'.'

"'No, nor usefu',' says I; 'a watch-chain looks fine on a man, but it's his gallowses dae the serious wark.'"

"Still, Erchie," I said, "our sex can't escape criticism for its eccentricities of costume either. Just fancy our pockets, for instance!"

"Ye're right, there," Erchie agreed; "hae I no' fifteen pouches mysel' when I hae my top-coat on? If I put a tram-way ticket into yin o' them I wadna be able to fin' oot which o' them it was in for an 'oor or twa.

"Pockets is a rale divert. Ye canna dae withoot nine or ten in Gleska if ye try yer best. In the country it's different. Doon aboot Yoker, and Gargunnock, and Deid Slow and them places, a' a man needs in the wye o' pouches is twa trooser yins—yin for each haund when he's leanin' against a byre-door wonderin' whit job he'll start the morn.

"There's a lot o' fancy wee pouches that'll no' haud mair nor a pawn-ticket aboot a Gleska man's claes, but in the country they dae wi' less and dig them deep.

"Sae faur as I can see, the pouch is a new-fashioned thing a'thegither. Look at them auld chaps ye see in pictures wi' the galvanised or black-leaded airn suits on; if yin o' them wanted a pouch he wad need to cut it himsel' wi' a sardine-

opener, and then he wad peel a' his knuckles feelin' for his
hanky or the price o' a pint. I'm gled I wisna gaun aboot
when them galvanised airn suits was the go ; it must hae been
awfu' sair on the nails scratchin' yersel'. Yer claes were
made then in a biler-works. When ye went for the fit-on,
the cutter bashed in the slack bits at the back wi' a hammer
and made it easier for ye under the oxter wi' a cauld chisel.

" ' I want it higher at the neck,' says you.

" ' Right ! ' says he, quite game, and bangs in twa or three
extra rivets. And your wife, if ye had yin, had to gie your
suits a polish up every Friday when she was daein' the kitchen
grate.

" It was the same when the Hielan's was the wye ye read
aboot in books, and every Hielan'man wore the kilts.

" There was nae pocket in a pair of kilts.

" I daursay that was because the Hielan'man never had
onything worth while to put in a pocket if he had yin. He
hung his snuff-mull and his knife and fork ootside his claes,
and kept his skean-dhu in his stockin'.

" It's a proof that weemen's no' richt ceevilised yet that
they can be daein', like the men I'm speaking aboot, withoot
ony pooches. Jinnet tells me there's nae pooch in a woman's
frock nooadays, because it wad spoil her sate on the bicycle.
That's the wye ye see weemen gaun aboot wi' their purses in
their haunds, and their bawbees for the skoosh car inside their
glove, and their bonny wee watches that never gang because
they're never rowed up, hingin' just ony place they'll hook
on to ootside their claes.

" I was yince gaun doon to Whiteinch on a Clutha to see a
kizzen o' the wife's, and Jinnet was wi' me. Me bein' caury-
haunded, I got aff by mistake at Govan on the wrang side o'
the river, when Jinnet was crackin' awa' like a pengun wi'
some auld wife at the sherp end o' the boat, and she didna
see me.

" ' Oh ! Erchie ! ' she says when she cam' hame, ' the
time I've put in ! I thocht ye wis drooned.'

" ' And ye hurried hame for the Prudential book, I suppose ? ' says I.

" ' No,' says she, ' but I made up my mind to hae a pooch o' my ain efter this, if I merrit again, to haud my ain Clutha fares, and no' be lippenin' to onybody.' "

XXII

ERCHIE IN AN ART TEA-ROOM

" I saw you and Duffy looking wonderfully smart in Sauchie-hall Street on Saturday," I said to Erchie one morning.

" Man, were we no' ? " replied the old man, with an amused countenance. " I must tell ye the pant we had. Ye'll no' guess where I had Duffy. Him and me was in thon new tea-room wi' the comic windows. Yin o' his horses dee'd on him, and he was doon the toon liftin' the insurance for't. I met him comin' hame wi' his Sunday claes on, and the three pound ten he got for the horse. He was that prood he was walkin' sae far back on his heels that a waff o' win' wad hae couped him, and whustlin' ' Dark Lochnagar.'

" ' Come on in somewhere and hae something,' says he, quite joco.

" ' Not me,' says I—' I'm nane o' the kind ; a beadle's a public man, and he disna ken wha may be lookin' at him, but I'll tell ye whit I'll dae wi' ye—I'll tak' ye into a tea-room.' ' A' richt,' says Duffy ; ' I'm game for a pie or onything.'

" And I took him like a lamb to the new place.

" When we came fornent it, he glowered, and ' Michty ! ' says he, ' wha did this ? '

" ' Miss Cranston,' says I.

" ' Was she tryin' ? ' says Duffy.

" ' She took baith hands to't,' I tellt him. ' And a gey smert wumman, too, if ye ask me.'

" He stood five meenutes afore I could get him in, wi' his een glued on the fancy doors.

" ' Do ye hae to break yer wey in ? ' says he.

" ' No, nor in, I tells him ; look slippy in case some o' yer customers sees ye ! '

" ' Och ! I havena claes for a place o' the kind,' says he, and his face red.

" ' Man ! ' I says, ' ye've henned—that's whit's wrang wi' ye : come in jist for the pant ; naebody 'll touch ye, and ye'll can come oot if it's sore.'

" In we goes, Duffy wi' his kep aff. He gave the wan look roond him, and put his hand in his pooch to feel his money. ' Mind I have only the three flaffers and a half, Erchie,' says he.

" ' It'll cost ye nae mair than the Mull o' Kintyre Vaults,' I tellt him, and we began sclimmin' the stairs. Between every rail there was a piece o' gless like the bottom o' a soda-water bottle, hangin' on a wire ; Duffy touched every yin o' them for luck.

" ' Whit dae ye think o' that, noo ? ' I asked him.

" ' It's gey fancy,' says Duffy ; ' will we be lang ? '

" ' Ye puir ignorant cratur ! ' I says, losin' my patience a'thegither, ' ye havena a mind in the dietin' line above a sate on the trams o' a lorry wi' a can o' soup in your hand.'

" I may tell ye I was a wee bit put aboot mysel', though I'm a waiter by tred, and seen mony a dydo in my time. There was naething in the hale place was the way I was accustomed to ; the very snecks o' the doors were kind o' contrairy.

" ' This way for the threepeny cups and the guid bargains,' says I to Duffy, and I lands him into whit they ca' the Room de Looks. Maybe ye havena seen the Room de Looks ; it's the colour o' a goon Jinnet used to hae afore we mairried : there's whit Jinnet ca's insertion on the table-cloths, and wee beeds stitched a' ower the wa's the same as if somebody had done it themsel's. The chairs is no' like ony ither chairs ever I clapped eyes on, but ye could easy guess they were chairs ; and a' roond the place there's a lump o' lookin'-gless

wi' purple leeks pented on it every noo and then. The gasalier
in the middle was the thing that stunned me. It's hung a'
roond wi' hunners o' big gless bools, the size o' yer nief—but
ye don't get pappin' onything at them.

"Duffy could only speak in whispers. 'My jove!' says
he, ' ye'll no' get smokin' here, I'll bate.'

"'Smokin'!' says I; 'ye micht as weel talk o' gowfin'.'

"'I never in a' my life saw the like o't afore. This cows
a'!' says he, quite nervous and frichtened lookin'.

"'Och!' says I, 'it's no' your fau't; you didna dae't onywye. Sit doon.'

"There was a wheen lassies wi' white frocks and tippets on
for waitresses, and every yin o' them wi' a string o' big red
beads roond her neck.

"'Ye'll notice, Duffy,' says I, 'that though ye canna get
ony drink here, ye can tak' a fine bead onywye,' but he didna
see my joke.

"'Chaps me no'!' says he. 'Whit did ye say the name o'
this room was?'

"'The Room de Looks,' I tellt him.

"'It'll likely be the Room de Good Looks,' says he, lookin'
at the waitress that cam' for oor order. 'I'm for a pie and a
bottle o' Broon Robin.'

"'Ye'll get naething o' the kind. Ye'll jist tak' tea, and
stretch yer hand like a Christian for ony pastry ye want,'
said I, and Duffy did it like a lamb. Oh! I had the better
o' him; the puir sowl never saw onything fancy in his life
afore since the time Glenroy's was shut in the New City Road,
where the Zoo is. It was a rale divert. It was the first time
ever he had a knife and fork to eat cookies wi', and he thocht
his teaspoon was a' bashed oot o' its richt shape till I tellt
him that was whit made it Art.

"'Art,' says he, 'whit the mischief's Art?'

"'I can easy tell ye whit Art is,' says I, 'for it cost me
mony a penny. When I got mairried, Duffy, haircloth
chairs was a' the go; the sofas had twa ends to them, and

you had to hae six books wi' different coloured batters spread
oot on the paurlor table, wi' the tap o' yer weddin'-cake
under a gless globe in the middle. Wally dugs on the mantelpiece, worsted things on the chairbacks, a picture o' John
Knox ower the kist o' drawers, and ' Heaven Help Our Home '
under the kitchen clock—that was whit Jinnet and me
started wi'. There's mony a man in Gleska the day buyin'
hand-done pictures and wearin' tile hats to their work that
begun jist like that. When Art broke oot——'

" ' I never took it yet,' says Duffy.

" ' I ken that,' says I, ' but it's ragin' a' ower the place ;
ye'll be a lucky man if ye're no' smit wi't cairryin' coals up
thae new tenements they ca' mansions, for that's a hotbed
o' Art. But as I say, when Art broke oot, Jinnet took it bad,
though she didna ken the name o' the trouble, and the hair-
cloth chairs had to go, and leather yins got, and the sofa wi'
the twa ends had to be swapped for yin wi' an end cut aff and
no' richt back. The wally dugs, and the worsted things, and
the picture o' John Knox, were nae langer whit Jinnet ca'd
the fashion, and something else had to tak' their place. That
was Art : it's a lingerin' disease ; she has the dregs o't yet,
and whiles buys shillin' things that's nae use for onything
except for dustin'.'

" ' Oh ! is that it ? ' says Duffy ; ' I wish I had a pie.'

" ' Ye'll get a pie then,' I tellt him, ' but ye canna expect
it here ; a pie's no' becomin' enough for the Room de Looks.
Them's no' chairs for a coalman to sit on eatin' pies.'

" We went doon the stair then, and I edged him into the
solid meat department. There was a lassie sittin' at a desk
wi' a wheen o' different coloured bools afore her, and when
the waitresses cam' to her for an order for haricot mutton or
roast beef or onything like that frae the kitchen, she puts yin
o' the bools doon a pipe into the kitchen, and the stuff comes
up wi' naething said.

" ' Whit dae ye ca' that game ? ' asks Duffy, lookin' at
her pappin' doon the bools ; ' it's no' moshy, onywye.'

" ' No, nor moshy,' I says to him. ' That's Art. Ye can hae yer pie frae the kitchen withoot them yellin' doon a pipe for't and lettin' a' the ither customers ken whit ye want.'

" When the pie cam' up, it was jist the shape o' an ordinary pie, wi' nae beads nor onything Art aboot it, and Duffy cheered up at that, and said he enjoyed his tea."

" I hope the refining and elevating influence of Miss Cranston's beautiful rooms will have a permanent effect on Duffy's taste," I said.

" Perhaps it will," said Erchie ; " but we were nae sooner oot than he was wonderin' where the nearest place wad be for a gless o' beer."

XXIII

THE HIDDEN TREASURE

" I wish somebody would leave me some money," said Jinnet, " and the first thing I would dae wi't would be to buy ye a new topcoat. That yin's gettin' gey shabby, and that glazed I can almaist see my face in the back o't."

" Then ye're weel aff," said Erchie, " for there's seldom ye'll see a bonnier yin in a better lookin'-gless."

" Oh, ye auld haver ! " cried Jinnet, pushing him. " I wonder ye divna think shame to be talkin' like a laddie to his first lass ; and me jist a done auld body ! If I could jist get a shape I wad buy a remnant and mak' ye a topcoat mysel.' I could dae't quite easy."

" I ken fine that," said her husband, " but I'll bate ye would put the buttons on the wrang side, the wye ye did wi' yon waistcoat. It's a droll thing aboot weemen's claes that they aye hae their buttons on caurey-handed. It jist lets ye see their contrairiness."

" Oh ! it's a peety ye mairried me," said Jinnet ; " a contrairy wife must be an awfu' handfu'."

" Weel, so ye are contrairy," said Erchie firmly.

"It tak's twa to be contrairy, jist the same wye as it tak's twa to mak' a quarrel," said Jinnet, picking some fluff off his sleeve. "Whit wye am I contrairy I would like to ken?"

"If ye werena contrairy, ye would be thinkin' o' buyin' something for yersel' instead o' a topcoat for me, and ye're far mair needn't," said Erchie, and with that a knock came to the door.

"There's somebody," said Jinnet hastily; "put on the kettle."

.   .   .   .   .   .

"Come awa' in, Mr Duffy, and you, Mrs Duffy," said Jinnet; "we're rale gled to see ye, Erchie and me. I was jist puttin' on the kettle to mak' a drap tea."

Duffy and his wife came into the cosy light and warmth of the kitchen, and sat down. There was an elation in the coalman's eye that could not be concealed.

"My jove! I've news for ye the nicht," said he, taking out his pipe and lighting it.

"If it's that the bag o' coals is up anither bawbee," said Erchie, "there's nae hurry for't. It's no' awfu' new news that onywye."

"Ye needna be aye castin' up my tred to me," protested Duffy. "Whaur would ye be wantin' coals?"

"Mr MacPherson's quite richt," said Mrs Duffy; "everybody kens it's no' an awfu' genteel thing sellin' coals, they're that—that black. I'm aye at him, Mrs MacPherson, to gie up the ree and the lorries and start a eatin'-house. I could bake and cook for't fine. Noo that this money's comin' to us, we could dae't quite easy. Look at the profit aff mulk itsel'!"

"Dear me! hae ye come into a fortune?" cried Jinnet eagerly. "Isn't that droll? I was jist saying to Erchie that I wisht somebody would leave me something and I would buy him a new topcoat."

"That'll be a' richt," said Duffy. "If he'll gie me a haund

wi' this thing I called aboot the nicht, I'll stand him the finest topcoat in Gleska, if it costs a pound."

"If it's ca'in on lawyers and the like o' that ye want me to dae," said Erchie, "I'm nae use to ye. I've a fine wye wi' me for ministers and the like o' that, that's no' aye wantin' to get the better o' ye, but lawyers is different. I yince went to a lawyer that was a member in oor kirk to ask him if he didna think it was time for him to pay his sate-rents. He said he would think it ower, and a week efter that he sent me an account for six-and-eightpence for consultation. But I'm prood to hear ye've come in for something, Duffy, whether I get a topcoat or no'. I never kent ye had ony rich freen's at a'. Faith, ye're weel aff; look at me, I havena a rich freen' in the warld except—except Jinnet."

"Oh, I never kent she was that weel aff," cried Mrs Duffy.

"Is it her!" said Erchie. "She has that much money in the bank that the bank clerks touch their hats to her in the street if she has on her Sunday claes. But that wasna whit I was thinkin' o'; there's ither kinds o' riches besides the sort they keep in banks."

"Never mind him, he's an auld fuiter," said Jinnet, spreading a tablecloth on the table and preparing for the tea. "I'm shair I'm gled to hear o' your good luck. It doesna dae to build oorsel's up on money, for money's no everything, as the pickpocket said when he took the watch as weel; but we're a' quite ready to thole't. Ye'll be plannin' whit ye'll dae wi't, Mrs Duffy?"

"First and foremost we're gaun to get rid o' the ree, at onyrate," said Mrs Duffy emphatically. "Then we're gaun to get a piano."

"Can ye play?" asked Erchie.

"No," admitted Mrs Duffy, "but there's nae need tae play sae lang's ye can get a vinolia to play for ye. I think we'll flit at the term to yin o' yon hooses roond the corner, wi' the tiled closes, and maybe keep a wee servant lassie. I'm that nervous at havin' to rise for the mulk in the mornin'.

No' an awfu' big servant wi' keps and aiprons, ye understaund, but yin I could train into the thing. I'm no' for
nane o' your late dinners : I jist like to tak' something in
my hand for my supper."

"Och ay, ye'll can easy get a wee no' awfu' strong yin frae
the country, chape," said Erchie. "Ye must tak' care o'
yer ain health, Mrs Duffy, and if ye're nervous, risin' in the
mornin' to tak' in the mulk's no' for ye. But my ! ye'll no'
be for speakin' to the like o' us when ye come into your
fortune."

"It's no' exactly whit ye wad ca' a fortune," Duffy explained, as they drew in their chairs to the table. "But it's
a heap o' money to get a' at yince withoot daein' onything
for't."

"Will ye hae to gang into mournin's for the body that
left it ? " Jinnet asked Mrs Duffy. "I ken a puir weedow
wumman that would come to the hoose to sew for ye."

"Ye're aff it a'thegither," said Duffy. "It's naebody
that left it to us—it's a medallion. Whit I wanted to ask
ye, Erchie, is this—whit's a medallion ? "

"Jist a kind o' a medal," said Erchie.

"My jove ! " said Duffy, "the wife was richt efter a'. I
thocht it was something for playin' on, like a melodian.
Weel, it doesna maitter, ye've heard o' the hidden treasure
the newspapers 's puttin' here and there roond the country ?
I ken where yin o' them's hidden. At least I ken where
there's a medallion."

"Oh, hoo nice ! " said Jinnet. "It's awfu' smert o' ye, Mr
Duffy. I was jist readin' aboot them, and was jist hopin'
some puir body wad get them."

"No' that poor naither ! " said Mrs Duffy, with a little
warmth.

"Na, na, I wasna sayin'—— I didna mean ony hairm,"
said poor Jinnet. "Streetch yer hand, and tak' a bit cake.
That's a rale nice brooch ye hae gotten."

Erchie looked at Duffy dubiously. For a moment he

feared the coalman might be trying on some elaborate new kind of joke, but the complacency of his face put it out of the question.

" Then my advice to you, Duffy, if ye ken where the medallion is," said Erchie, " is to gang and howk it up at yince, or somebody 'll be there afore ye. I warrant it'll no' get time to tak' root if it's within a penny ride on the Gleska skoosh cars. There's thoosands o' people oot wi' lanterns at this very meenute scrapin' dirt in the hunt for that medallion. Hoo do ye ken whaur it is if ye havena seen it ? "

" It's there richt enough," said Mrs Duffy ; " it's in the paper, and we're gaun to gie up the ree ; my mind's made up on that. I hope ye'll come and see us sometime in our new hoose—house."

" It says in the paper," said Duffy, " that the medallion's up a street that has a public-hoose at each end o't, and a wee pawn in the middle, roond the corner o' anither street, where ye can see twa laundries at yince, and a sign ower yin o' them that puts ye in mind o' the battle o' Waterloo, then in a parteecular place twenty yairds to the richt o' a pend-close wi' a barrow in't."

Erchie laughed. " Wi' a barrow in't ? " said he. " They micht as weel hae said wi' a polisman in't ; barrows is like bobbies—if ye think ye'll get them where ye want them ye're up a close yersel'. And whit's the parteecular place, Duffy ? "

Duffy leaned forward and whispered mysteriously, " My coal-ree."

" But we're gaun to gie't up," explained his wife. " Oh, ay, we're gaun to give the ree up. Ye hae no idea whaur—where—I could get a smert wee lassie that would not eat awfu' much, Mrs MacPherson ? "

" I measured it a' aff," Duffy went on. " It's oor street richt enough ; the pubs is there——"

" ——I could bate ye they are," said Erchie. " If they werena there it wad be a miracle."

R

" ——and the laundries is there. ' Colin Campbell ' over yin o' them, him that bate Bonypart, ye ken, and twenty yairds frae the pend-close is richt under twenty ton o' coal I put in last week. It's no' M'Callum's wid-yaird ; it's my ree."

" My papa was the sole proprietor of a large wid-yaird," irrelevantly remarked Mrs Duffy, who was getting more and more Englified as the details of the prospective fortune came out.

" Was he, indeed," said Jinnet.   " That was nice ! "

" Noo, whit I wanted you to dae for me," Duffy went on, " was to come awa' doon wi' me the nicht and gie's a hand to shift thae coals.   I daurna ask ony o' my men to come, for they wad claim halfers."

Erchie toyed with a teaspoon and looked at the coalman, half in pity, half with amusement.   " Man, ye're a rale divert," said he at last.   " Do ye think the newspapers would be at the bother o' puttin' their medallion under twenty ton o' coal in your coal-ree, or onybody else's ?   Na, na, they can mak' their money easier nor that.   If ye tak' my advice, ye'll put a penny on the bag o' coal and gie short wecht, and ye'll mak' your fortune far shairer than lookin' under't for medallions."

" Then ye're no' game to gie's a hand ? " said Duffy, start-ing another cookie.   " See's the sugar."

" Not me ! " said Erchie promptly.   " I've a flet fit and a warm hert, but I'm no' a'thegither a born idiot to howk coal for medallions that's no' there."

.   .   .   .   .

Next day Duffy came up with two bags of coals which Jinnet had ordered.

" Did ye find the medallion ? " she asked him.

" I didna need to look for't," he replied.   " I heard efter I left here last nicht that a man found it in a back-coort in the Garscube Road.   Them sort of dydoes should be put doon by the polis."

" Oh, whit a peety ! " said Jinnet. " And hoo's the mistress the day ? "

" She's fine," said Duffy. " She's ca'in' me Jimmy again ; it was naething but Mr Duffy wi' her as lang's she thocht we were to get rid o' the ree."

XXIV

THE VALENTEEN

On the night of the last Trades House dinner I walked home with Erchie when his work was done. It was the 13th of February. There are little oil-and-colour shops in New City Road, where at that season the windows become literary and artistic, and display mock valentines. One of these windows caught my old friend's eye, and he stopped to look in.

" My ! " he said, " time flies ! It was only yesterday we had the last o' oor Ne'erday currant-bun, and here's the valenteens ! That minds me I maun buy——" He stopped and looked at me, a little embarrassed.

I could only look inquiry back at him.

" Ye'll think I'm droll," said he, " but it just cam' in my heid to buy a valenteen. To-morrow's Jinnet's birthday, and it would be a rale divert to send her ladyship yin and tak' a kind o' rise oot o' her. Come and gie's a hand to pick a nice yin."

I went into the oil-and-colour shop, but, alas ! for the ancient lover, he found there that the day of sentiment was done so far as the 14th of February was concerned.

" Hae ye ony nice valenteens ? " he asked a boy behind the counter.

" Is't a comic ye mean ? " asked the boy, apparently not much amazed at so strange an application from an elderly gentleman.

" A comic ! " said my friend in disdain. " Dae I look like the kind o' chap that sends mock valenteens ? If ye gie me

ony o' your chat I'll tell yer mither, ye wee—ye wee rascal!
Ye'll be asking me next if I want a mooth harmonium.   Dae
ye think I'm angry wi' the cook in some hoose roond in the
terraces because she's chief wi' the letter-carrier ?   I'll comic
ye ! "

"Weel, it's only comics we hae," said the youthful shopkeeper ; " the only ither kind we hae 's Christmas cairds, and
I think we're oot o' them."

He was a business-like boy—he flung a pile of the mock
valentines on the counter before us.

Erchie turned them over with contemptuous fingers. "It's
a gey droll age we live in," said he to me.   "We're far ower
funny, though ye wadna think it to see us.   I have a great
respect for valenteens, for if it wasna for a valenteen there
maybe wadna hae been ony Jinnet—at least in my hoose.
I wad gie a shillin' for a rale auld-fashioned valenteen that
gaed oot and in like a concertina, wi' lace roond aboot it,
and a smell o' scent aff it, and twa silver herts on't skewered
through the middle the same as it was for brandering.   Ye
havena seen mony o' that kind, laddie ?   Na, I daursay no' ;
they were oot afore your time, though I thocht ye micht hae
some in the back-shop.   They were the go when we werena
nearly sae smert as we are nooadays.   I'm gled I havena to
start the coortin' again."

He came on one of the garish sheets that was less vulgar
than the others, with the picture of a young lady under an
umbrella, and a verse of not unkindly doggerel.

"That'll hae to dae," said he, " although it's onything but
fancy."

"I hope," said I dubiously, " that Mrs MacPherson will
appreciate it."

"She's the very yin that will," he assured me, as he put
it in his pocket.   "She's like mysel' ; she canna play the
piano, but she has better gifts—she has the fear o' God and
a sense o' humour.   You come up the morn's nicht at eight,
afore the post comes, and ye'll see the ploy when she gets

her valenteen. I'll be slippin' oot and postin't in the fore-noon. Though a young lassie canna get her valenteens ower early in the mornin', a mairried wife's 'll dae very weel efter her wark's done for the day."

"It's yersel'?" said Mrs MacPherson when I went to her door. "Come awa' in. I kent there was a stranger comin' —though indeed I wadna be ca'in' you a stranger—for there was a stranger on the ribs o' the grate this mornin', and a knife fell aff the table when we were at oor tea."

"Ay, and who knocked it aff deeliberate?" interposed her husband, rising to welcome me. "Oh, she's the sly yin. She's that fond to see folk come aboot the hoose she whiles knocks a knife aff the table to see if it'll bring them."

"Oh, Erchie MacPherson!" cried his wife.

"I'm no' blamin' ye," he went on; "I ken I'm gey dreich company for onybody. I havena a heid for mindin' ony scandal aboot the folk we ken, and I canna understaund politics noo that Gledstone's no' to the fore, and I canna sing, or play a tune on onything."

"Listen to him!" cried Jinnet. "Isn't he the awfu' man? Did ye ever hear the like o' him for nonsense?"

The kettle was on the fire: I knew from experience that it had been put there when my knock came to the door, for so the good lady's hospitality always manifested itself, so that her kettle was off and on the fire a score of times a-day, ready to be brought to the boil if it was a visitor who knocked, and not a beggar or a pedlar of pipeclay.

"Tak' a watter biscuit," Jinnet pressed me as we sat at the table; "they're awfu' nice wi' saut butter."

"Hae ye nae syrup to put on them?" asked her husband with a sly glance.

"Nane o' yer nonsense," she exclaimed, and attempted a diversion in the conversation, but Erchie plainly had a joke to retail.

"I'll tell ye a baur aboot watter biscuits and syrup,"

said he. "When I was coortin' my first lass I wasna mair nor nineteen years o' age, and jist a thin peely-wally callant, mair like playin' moshy at the bools than rinnin' efter lassies. The lassie's faither and mither jist made fun o' us, and when I wad be gaun up to her hoose, lettin' on it was her brither I wanted to see, they used to affront me afore their dochter wi' speakin' aboot the Sunday School and the Band o' Hope I belanged to (because the lassie belanged to them tae), and askin' me if I was fond o' sugar to my parridge, and when I was thinkin' o' startin' the shavin'. I didna like it, but I jist had to put up wi't. But the worst blow ever I got frae them was yince when I gaed up wi' a new pair o' lavender breeks, and the lassie's mither, for the fun o' the thing, asked me if I wad hae a piece and jeely. I tellt her I wasna heedin', that I was jist efter haein' my tea ; but she went and spread syrup on a watter biscuit and handed it to me the same as if I was a wee lauddie wi' a grauvit on."

Jinnet laughed softly at the picture.

"Oh, ye may lauch," said her husband. "There was nae lauchin' in my heid, I'm tellin' ye. For there was the syrup comin' dreepin' through the holes in the watter biscuit, so that I had to haud the biscuit up every noo and then and lick in below't so as to keep the syrup frae gaun on my braw lavender breeks. A bonny object for a lass to look at, and it was jist to mak' me look reediculous her mither did it. She thocht I was faur ower young to be comin' efter her dochter."

"So ye were," said Jinnet. "I'm shair ye hadna muckle sense at the time, or it wadna be yon yin ye went coortin'."

"Maybe no' ; but I never rued it," said Erchie.

"She was as glaikit as yersel'," said Jinnet.

"She was the cleverest lass in the place," protested Erchie. "My ! the things she could sew, and crochet, and mak' doon, and bake ! "

"Her sister Phemie was faur cleverer than she was," said

Jinnet. " She couldna haud a candle to her sister Phemie
in tambourin' or in gingerbreid."

" And dancin' ! She could dance on a cobweb and no' put
a toe through't."

" Ye'll need a line wi' that yin, Erchie," said his wife, who
did not seem remarkably jealous of this first love.

" Ye should hear her singin'——"

" She wad hae been far better mendin' her wee brither's
stockin's, and no' leavin' her mither to dae't," said Jinnet.
" She was a gey licht-heided yin."

Erchie seemed merciless in his reminiscence,—I really felt
sorry for his wife.

" Ye may say whit ye like to run her doon, but ye canna
deny her looks."

" Her looks dinna concern me," said Jinnet abruptly.
" Ye're jist an auld haver ; think shame o' yersel' ! "

" Ye ken ye canna deny't," he went on. " It was alooed
all over the place she was the belle. I wasna the only yin
that was efter her wi' my lavender breeks. She kept the Band
o' Hope for nearly twa years frae burstin' up."

" I'll no' listen to anither word," protested Jinnet, now in
obvious vexation ; and mercifully there came a rapping at
the door.

She returned to the kitchen with an envelope and a little
parcel. Erchie winked at me, hugging to himself a great
delight.

" I wonder wha in the world can be writin' to me," said she,
looking at the addresses.

It'll likely be an accoont for di'mond tararas or dressmaking," said Erchie. " Oh you weemen ! Ye're a perfect
ruination. But if I was you I wad open them and see."

She opened the envelope first. It was Erchie's valentine,
and she knew it, for when she read the verse she shook her
head at him laughingly, and a little ashamed. " When will
ye be wise ? " said she.

Then she opened the little parcel : it contained a trivial

birthday gift from an anonymous friend in whose confidence only I, of all the three in the room, happened to be.   Vainly they speculated about his identity without suspecting me ; but I noticed that it was on her valentine Jinnet set most value.   She held it long in her hand, thinking, and was about to put it into a chest of drawers without letting me see it.

"Ye needna be hidin' it," said her husband then.   "He saw it already.   Faith ! he helped me to pick it."

"I'm fair affronted," she exclaimed, reddening at this exposure.   "You and your valenteens !"

"There's naething wrang wi' valenteens," said her husband. "If it wasna for a valenteen I wad never hae got ye.   I could never say to your face but that I liked ye ; but the valenteen had a word that's far mair brazen than ' like,' ye mind."

"Oh, Erchie !" I cried, "you must have been blate in these days.   The word was——"

He put up his hand in alarm and stopped me.   "Wheesht !" said he.   "It's a word that need never be mentioned here where we're a' three Scotch !"

"But what came over the first lass, Erchie ?" I asked determined to have the end of that romance.

He looked across at his wife and smiled.   "She's there hersel'," said he, " and ye better ask her."

"What !   Jinnet ?"   I   cried, amazed at my own obtuseness.

"Jinnet of course," said he.   "Wha else wad it be if it wasna Jinnet ?   She's the Rale Oreeginal."

XXV

AMONG THE PICTURES

"WHAUR are ye gaun the day ?" said Erchie to Duffy on Saturday afternoon when he came on the worthy coalman standing at his own close-mouth, looking up and down the street with the hesitation of a man who deliberates how he is to make the most of his Saturday half-holiday.

" I was just switherin'," said Duffy. " Since I got mairried and stopped gaun to the Mull o' Kintyre Vaults, there's no' much choice for a chap. I micht as weel be leevin' in the country for a' the life I see."

" Man, aye ! " said Erchie, " that's the warst o' Gleska ; there's nae life in't—naethin' daein'. Ye should try yer hand at takin' oot the wife for a walk, jist for the novelty o' the thing."

" Catch me ! " said Duffy. " She wad see ower mony things in the shop windows she was needin'. I was jist wonderin' whether I wad buy a ' Weekly Mail ' or gang to the fitba' match at Parkheid."

Erchie looked pityingly at him. " A fitba' match ! " said he. " Whit's the use o' gaun to a fitba' match when ye can see a' aboot it in the late edeetion ? Forbye, a fitba' match doesna improve the mind ; it's only sport. I'll tell ye whit I'll dae wi' ye if ye're game. I'll tak' ye to the Art Institute ; the minister gied me twa tickets. Awa' and put on your collar and I'll wait here on ye."

" Do ye need a collar for the gallery ? " asked Duffy, who thought the Art Institute was a music-hall. On this point Erchie set him right, and ten minutes later, with a collar whose rough edges rasped his neck and made him unhappy, he was on his way to Sauchiehall Street.

The band was playing a waltz tune as they entered the Institute.

" Mind, I'm no' on for ony dancin'," Duffy explained. " I canna be bothered dancin'."

" There's naebody gaun to ask ye to dance," said Erchie. " Do you think there couldna be a baun' playing' withoot dancin' ? It's jist here to cod a lot o' folk into the notion that they can be cheery enough in a place o' the kind in spite o' the pictures. And ye can get aifternoon tea here, too."

" I could be daein' wi' a gless o' beer," said Duffy.

R*

" No. They're no' that length yet," Erchie explained. " There's only the tea. The mair determined lovers o' the Fine Arts can dae the hale show in an aifternoon noo wi' the help o' a cup o' tea, so that they needna come back again. It's a great savin'. They used to hae to gang hame for their tea afore, and whiles they never got back. The Institute wasna popular in thae days ; it was that quate and secluded that if a chap had done onything wrang and the detectives were efter him he took a season ticket, and spent a' his days here. Noo, ye can see for yersel' the place is gaun like an inn. That's the effect o' the baun' and the aifternoon tea. If they added a baby incubator to the attractions the same's they hae in the East-End Exhibeetion, they would need the Fire Brigade wi' a hose to keep the croods oot. Ye hae nae idea o' the fascination Art has for the people o' Gleska if they're no' driven to't."

" My jove ! " exclaimed Duffy, at the sight of the first gallery. " Whit a lot o' pictures ! There'll be a pile o' money in a place o' this kind. Hiv they no water-shoot, or a shootin' jungle, or onything lively like that ? "

" Man, ye're awfu' common, whiles, Duffy," said Erchie. " I'm fear't I wasted my ticket on ye. This is no' an ordinary show for haein' fun at ; it's for enlargin' the mind, openin' the e'en to the beauties o' nature, and sellin' pictures."

" Are they a' for sale ? " asked Duffy, looking with great intentness at a foggy impression by Sidaner, the French artist.

" No' the hale o' them ; there's some on lend."

" I could hae lent them a topper," said Duffy,—" faur aheid o' onything here. It's a drawin' o' a horse I yince had in my first lorry ; it was pented for me by a penter that lodged above us, and had a great name for sign-boards. It cost me nearly a pound wan wye or anither, though I provided the pent mysel'."

" Ay, Art's a costly thing," said Erchie. " Ye'll seldom get a good picture under a pound. It's no' a'thegither the pent, it's the layin' o't on by hand."

" This yin's done by hand onywye," said Duffy, pointing to the foggy impression by Sidaner. " It's awfu' like as if somebody had done it themsel's in their spare time."

" You and me's no' judges o' that sort o' thing," said Erchie. " Maybe it's no' near so bad as it looks."

" Ye see," Erchie went on, " Art pentin's a tred by itsel'. There used to be hardly ony picture-penters in Gleska; it was a' shipbuildin' and calanderin', whitever that is, and chemical works that needed big lums. When a Gleska man did a guid stroke o' business on the Stock Exchange, or had money left him in thae days, and his wife wanted a present, he had his photygraph ta'en big size, ile-coloured by hand. It was gey like him, the photygraph, and so everybody kent it wasna the rale Art. Folk got rich that quick in Gleska, and had sae much money to spend, that the photygraphers couldna keep up wi' the demand, and then the hand-pentin' chaps began to open works in different pairts o' the city. Ye'll hardly gang into a hoose noo whaur ye'll no' see the guidman's picture in ile, and it micht be bilin' ile sometimes, judgin' from the agony on his face."

" My jove ! " said Duffy, " is it sore to get done that wye ? "

" Sore ! " replied Erchie ; " no, nor sore. At least, no' that awfu' sore. They wadna need to dae't unless they liked. When maistly a' the weel-aff Gleska folk had got their photygraphs done and then de'ed, the penters had to start the landscape brench o' the business. Them's landscapes a' roon' aboot "—and Erchie gave his arm a comprehensive sweep to suggest all the walls.

" They must be pretty smert chaps that does them," said Duffy. " I wish I had gone in for the pentin' mysel' ; it's cleaner nor the coals. Dae ye hae to serve your time ? "

" No, nor time ; ye can see for yersel' that it's jist a kind o' knack like poetry—or waitin'. And the plant doesna cost much ; a' ye need to start wi' 's paper, brushes, pent, and a saft hat."

" A saft hat ! "

" Ay ; a saft hat's the sure sign o' an artist. I ken hunners o' them ; Gleska's fair hotchin' wi' artists. If the Cairters' Trip wasna abolished, ye wad see the artists' tred union walkin' oot wi' the rest o' them."

The two friends went conscientiously round the rooms, Erchie expounding on the dimensions, frames, and literary merits of the pictures, Duffy a patient, humble student, sometimes bewildered at the less obvious transcripts of nature and life pointed out to him.

" Is there much mair o' this to see ? " he asked at last, after having gone through the fourth gallery. " I'm gettin' dizzy. Could we no' hae something at the tea bar if we gied them a tip ? They micht send oot for't. Or we micht get a pass-oot check."

" Mair to see ! " exclaimed Erchie. " Ye're awfu' easy made dizzy ! The like o' you wad faur raither be oot skreichin' yer heid aff at the fitba' match at Parkheid, instead o' improvin' the mind here. Ye canna get onything at the tea place but jist tea, I'm tellin' ye, and there's nae pass-oot checks. They ken better nor to gie ye pass-oot checks ; haulf o' your kind wad never come back again if yince ye escaped."

" My jove ! " said Duffy, suddenly, " here's a corker ! " and he indicated a rather peculiar drawing with a lady artist's name attached to it.

Erchie himself was staggered. " It's ca'd ' The Sleeper ' in the catalogue," said he. " It's a wumman, and her dozin'. The leddy that pented it wasna ower lavish wi' her pent. That's whit they ca' New Art, Duffy ; it jist shows ye whit weemen can dae if ye let them."

" And dae ye tell me there's weemen penters ? " asked Duffy in astonishment.

" Of course there's weemen penters."

" And hoo dae they get up and doon lethers ? " asked Duffy.

" I'm tellin' ye Art pentin's a brench by itsel'," said Erchie.

" The lady Art penters divna pent windows and rhones and hooses ; they bash brass, and hack wud, and draw pictures."

" And can they mak' a living at that ? "

" Whiles.   And whiles their paw helps."

" My jove ! " said Duffy, bewildered.

" We'll gang on to the next room noo," said Erchie.

" I wad raither come back some ither day," said Duffy. " I'm enjoyin' this fine, but I promised the wife I wad be hame early for my tea."   And together they hastily made an exit into Sauchiehall Street.

" I wonder wha won the semi-final at Parkheid," said Duffy. " We'll awa' doon the toon and see ; whit's the use o' hurryin' hame ? "

XXVI

THE PROBATIONARY GHOST

ONE day I observed Erchie going off the pavement rather than walk under a ladder.

" And are you superstitious too ? " I asked him, surprised at this unsuspected trait in a character so generally sensible.

" I don't care whither ye ca't supersteetion or no'," he replied, " but walkin' under lethers is a gey chancy thing ; and there's mony a chancy thing, and I'm neither that young nor that weel aff that I can afford to be takin' ony risks."

" Dear me ! " I said ; " I wouldn't be surprised to learn that you believed in ghosts."

" Do I no' ? " he answered.   " And guid reason for't ! Did I no' yince see yin ?   It was the time I had the rheumatic fever, when we were stayin' in Garnethill.   I was jist gettin' better, and sittin' up a wee while in the evenin' to air the bed, and Jinnet was oot for a message.   The nicht was wild and wet, and the win' was daudin' awa' at the window like onything, and I was feelin' gey eerie, and wearyin' for the

wife to come back. I was listenin' for her fit on the stair,
when the ootside door opens, and in a second there was a chap
at the kitchen door.

" ' Come in if your feet's clean,' says I, pretty snappy.
' Seein' ye've made sae free wi' the ae door ye needna mak'
ony ceremony wi' this ane.' I heard the hinges screechin,'
but naebody cam' in, and I looks roon' frae where I was
sittin' wi' a blanket roond me at the fire, and there was the
ghost keekin' in. He was a wee nyaf o' a thing, wi' a Paisley
whisker, a face no bigger than a Geneva watch, a nickerbocker suit on, Rab Roy tartan tops to his gowfin' stockings,
and pot-bellied to the bargain. I kent fine he was a ghost
at the first gae-aff.

" ' It's you,' says I. ' Come in and gies yer crack till
Jinnet comes. Losh, it's no' a nicht for stravaigin'.'

" He cam' glidin' in withoot makin' ony soond at a', and
sat doon on a chair.

" ' Ye're no' feared,' says he, trying to gnash his teeth, and
makin' a puir job o't, for they were maistly arteeficial.

" ' Feared ? ' says I. ' No me ! I never did onybody ony
hairm that wad mak' it worth ony ghost's while to meddle
wi' me. A flet fit but a warm hert.'

" ' We'll see aboot that,' says he, as cocky as onything. ' I
had a fine job findin' oot where ye were. Fancy me gaun
awa' doon to Millport on a nicht like this to haunt ye, and
findin' that ye had flitted up here last term.' And he begood
to gnash his teeth again.

" ' Millport ! ' says I. ' Man ! I was never near the place,
and I've lived in this hoose for seventeen year, and brocht up
a faimily in't.'

" I never seen a ghost mair vexed than he was when I tell't
him that. His jaw fell ; he was nearly greetin'.

" ' Whit's yer name ? ' he asked.

" ' Erchie MacPherson, and I'm no' ashamed o't. It's
no' in ony grocers' nor tylers' books that I ken o', and if I
ever murdered ony weans or onything o' that sort, it must hae

been when I was sleepin'. I doot, my man, ye're up the wrang close.'

"The ghost begood to swear. Oh my! such swearin'. I never listened to the bate o't. There was fancy words in't I never heard in a' my life, and I've kent a wheen o' cairters.

"'That's jist like them,' says he. 'They tellt me Millport; and efter I couldna find the man I was wantin' at Millport, I was tellt it was here, No. 16 Buccleuch Street. Fancy me bungin' awa' through the air on a nicht like this! My nicker-bockers is fair stickin' to my knees wi' wet.'

"'Peter,' says I (of course I didna ken his richt name, but I thocht I wad be nice wi' the chap seein' he had made such a mistake), 'Peter,' said I, 'ye're needin' yer specs on. This is no' No. 16, it's No. 18, and I think the man ye maun be lookin' for is Jeckson, that canvasses for the sewin'-machines. He came here last term frae aboot Millport. If he's done ony hairm to onybody in his past life—murdered a wife, and buried her under the hearth-stane, or ony daft-like thing o' that sort—I'm no' wantin' to hear onything aboot it, for he's a guid enough neebour, has twa bonny wee weans, comes hame regular to his tea, and gangs to the kirk wi' his wife. He's been teetotal ever since he came here. Gie the chap a chance!'

"'Jeckson!' said the ghost, and whips oot a wee book. 'That's the very man!' said he. 'Man! is't no' aggra-vatin'? Here's me skooshin' up and doon the coast wi' my thin flannels on lookin' for him, and him toastin' his taes at a fire in Buccleuch Street! Jist you wait. It shows ye the wye the books in oor place is kept. If the office was richt up-to-date, Jeckson wadna be flitted ten meenutes when his new address wad be marked doon. No wonder the Americans is batin' us! Weel, it's no' my faut if I'm up the wrang close, and I'm no' gaun to start the job the nicht. I'm far ower cauld.'

"There was an empty gless and a teaspoon on the dresser,

for Jinnet had been giein' me a drap toddy afore she gaed oot.
The ghost sat doon on a chair and looked at the gless.

" ' Could ye save a life ? ' said he.

" ' Whit wad be the use o' giein' it to you, Peter ? ' I asked
him ; ' ye havena ony inside, seein' ye're a ghost.'

" ' Have I no' ? ' says he.   ' Jist try me.'   So I pointed to
the press, and he took oot the decanter as smert's ye like
and helped himsel'.

" He turned oot a rale nice chap in spite o' his tred, and
he gave me a' the oots and ins o't.   ' I've nae luck,' he said.
' It's my first job at the hauntin', and I've made a kind o'
botch o't, though it's no' my faut.   I'm a probationer ; jist
on my trial, like yin o' thae U.F. ministers.   Maybe ye think
it's easy gettin' a haunter's job ; but I'm tellin' ye it's no'
that easy, and when ye get it, it's wark that tak's it oot o' ye.
There's mair gangs in for the job there than for the Ceevil
Service here, and the jobs go to compeetition.   Ye hae to pass
an examination, and ye hae nae chance o' gettin' yin if ye
divna mak' mair nor ninety per cent. o' points.   Mind ye,
there's mair than jist plain ghost-wark.   It used to be, in the
auld days, that a haunter wad be sent to dae onything—to
rattle chains, or gie ye the clammy hand, or be a blood-
curdler.   Nooadays there's half a dizzen different kinds o'
haunters.   I'm a blood-curdler mysel',' and he gied a skreich
that nearly broke a' the delf on the dresser.

" ' Nane o' that ! ' says I, no' very weel pleased.   ' Ye'll
hae the neebours doon on us.   Forbye, there's naething
patent aboot that sort o' skreich.   Duffy the coalman could
dae better himsel'.   That's no' the wye a dacent ghost
should cairry on in ony hoose whaur he's gettin' a dram.'

" ' Excuse me,' he says ; ' it's the dram that's ta'en my
heid.   Ye see, I'm no' used to't.   It's mony a day since I
had yin.'

" ' Are they that strict yonder ? ' I asked.

" ' Strict's no' the word for't !   If a blood-curdler on proba-
tion was kent to gang to his work wi' the smell o' drink aff

him, he wad lose his job ' : and he helped himsel' to anither dram.

" ' Weel, ye're no' blate onywye,' says I.

" ' Blate! Catch me,' says he. ' I wadna need to be blate at this tred, I'm tellin' ye. Jist you think o' the kind o' customers we hae to dale wi' ! They wad sooner see a tax-collector comin' into their hooses than yin o' us chaps. There's some hooses ye hae to gang to work in where it's easy. I ken a ghost that's been fifteen years on the same job, and gettin' fat on't. He has the name o' bein' the best white-sheet ghost in the Depairtmen', and he's stationed in an auld castle up aboot the Hielan's, a job he got because he had the Gaelic. He made it sae hot for the folk, walkin' aboot their bedrooms at a' 'oors o' the nicht, that naebody 'll stay in the place but himsel' and an auld deaf and dumb housekeeper. There's naething for him to dae, so he can lie in his bed a' nicht and no' bother himsel' aboot onything. It's a very different thing wi' anither chap I ken—a chain-clanker in England. He has to drag ten yairds o' heavy chain up and doon stairs every nicht ; and it's no easy job, I'm tellin' ye, wi' the folk the hoose belang to pappin' things and shootin' at whaur they think the soond comes frae. Oh ay ! there's a great run on the best jobs. My ain ambeetion is to be in the clammy-hand brench o' the business in some quate wee place at the coast. I hae my e'e on a likely thing at Rothesay. Of course the clammy hand's no' a very nice occupation for the winter, but this is a hoose that's shut up in the winter, and I wad only hae to work it in the fine summer nichts.'

" ' Hoo dae ye dae the clammy hand, Peter ? ' I asked him, and he just winked.

" ' If I was tellin' ye that,' says he, ' ye wad be as wise as mysel'. Never you mind, MacPherson ; ask me nae ques-tions and I'll tell ye nae lees. Weel, as I was sayin', I aye had a notion o' a quate job at the coast. I couldna stand Gleska ; there's such a rush aboot it, and sae mony stairs to sclim, and pianos aye playin' next door. And the accent's

awfu' ! Gie me a nice wee country hoose whaur somebody
hanged himsel', wi' roses on the wa', and dandelions in the
front plot. But there's plenty o' us lookin' efter jobs o' that
sort—far ower mony ; and it's generally them wi' influence
that gets them at the hinder-end.'

" ' That's whit everybody says aboot the situations here,
Peter,' says I. ' If they're nae use at their tred they talk
a lot aboot influence. I'm thinkin' ye wad soon get a job
at the coast if ye were fit for't.'

" He was the shortest-tempered ghost ever I seen. I had
nae sooner said that than he gied anither skreich, and disappeared in a blue lowe wi' an awfu' smell o' brimstone.

" ' Come oot o' that ! ' I says to him ; ' I can see the taps
o' yer gowfin' stockings ' ; and at that he gied a kind o'
shamed lauch and was sittin' in the chair again, helpin' himsel' to anither dram.

" ' I'll tell ye whit I'll dae wi' ye,' said he. ' I'll no' mind
aboot Jeckson at a', but I'll hing aboot your hoose for a week
or a fortnight, and they'll never ken at the office. I canna
think to gang into Jeckson's hoose if he's a teetotaler. Teetotalers is aye that—that—that teetotal. I wad never get
sittin' doon in Jeckson's to a jovial gless like this.'

" ' Ye're far ower jovial for me,' says I. ' See's that
decanter,' and I took it frae him. ' I'm awfu' prood to see
ye, but ye better be slidin' afore her ladyship the wife comes
in, or she'll put the hems on ye. She canna stand ghosts.'

" ' Michty ! ' said he, ' have ye a wife ? '

" ' The nicest wee wife in Gleska,' said I. ' And I wish to
goodness she was hame, for I'm awfu' tired.'

" ' Then I'm no' playin',' said the ghost. ' I'll awa' roon'
and gie Jeckson a cry afore he gangs to his bed.'

" He grabbed the decanter and emptied it into the tumbler,
gied ae gulp, and anither gnash to his teeth, and went awa'
withoot sae much as ' thenk ye.'

" Jinnet's step was on the stair. Fine I kent it ! Man,
that's the smertest wee wumman!

" ' There's nae livin' in this hoose wi' ghosts,' says I to her when she cam' in, and she had some grapes for me.

" ' Is there no', Erchie ? ' she said, lookin' at me, ' my ain puir auld man ! '

" ' Look at that decanter,' says I ; ' the rascal emptied it.'

" ' Hoots ! the decanter's a' richt,' says she, takin't frae the press ; and as shair's onything, there wasna a drap oot o't !

" And she put me to my bed there and then."

XXVII

JINNET'S CHRISTMAS SHOPPING

Jinnet had money in the Savings Bank. Erchie used to chuckle when some neighbour had gone out to whom she had casually mentioned the fact and say, " That's it, Jinnet, you be bragging o' your deposits like that, and they'll be thinking I mairried ye for your fortune." But the truth was that when their savings at first were lodged in Erchie's name, they had an unfortunate way of disappearing without Jinnet's knowledge, and it was to protect himself from himself that the husband finally opened the account in the name of his wife.

The first day she went to the bank with money it was with no little trepidation. " Maybe they'll no' tak' sae much as twenty-wan pounds," she suggested ; " it's a guid pickle money to hae the responsibility o'."

" Ay, and gled to get it ! " he replied. " That's whit they're there for. If it was twice twenty-wan they wad mak' room for't, even if they had to shift forrit the coonter. Ye hae nae idea o' the dacency o' thae banks ! "

" But whit if the bank was to burst ? " said Jinnet. " Lots o' folk losses their money wi' banks burstin', and hae to go on the Board a' the rest o' their days."

"Burst!" laughed Erchie. "Man! ye wad think it was a kitchen biler ye were talkin' aboot. It'll no' burst wi' a' we'll put into it, I'll warrant ye."

"Will ye hae to pay them much for takin' care o't?" she asked, still dubious of these immense financial operations.

Erchie laughed till the tears ran into his tea.

"Oh, my!" said he, "but ye're the caution! It's them that pays you. If ye leave the twenty-wan pound in for a twelvemonth, they'll gie ye something like twenty-wan pound ten shillin's when ye gang to lift it."

This troubled Jinnet worse than ever. "It's rale nice o' them," said she, "but I'm no' needin' their ten shillin's; we're no' that faur doon in the warld, and it's like enough they wad jist be takin' it aff some ither puir cratur."

But eventually the money was lodged in Jinnet's name. She used to take out her bank-book and examine it once a week, to make sure, as she said, "the money was still there," a proceeding at which Erchie would wink to himself, and with difficulty restrain his laughter.

On Saturday Jinnet expressed a wish that she had some of her money to make some purchases for Christmas and the New Year.

"Weel," said her husband, "whit's to hinder ye gaun to the bank and liftin' a pound or twa?"

Her face turned white at the very thought. "Me!" she cried. "I wadna ask for money at that bank if I was stervin'."

"But, bless my sowl! it's yer ain money; they canna keep ye frae gettin' it if ye want it," said her husband.

"I'm no carin'," Jinnet protested. "I divna like to ask for't, and them maybe busy. Perhaps the puir craturs havena got it to spare the noo."

"Weel, they can jist send oot for a wee lend o't frae some-body they ken," said Erchie. "It's your money, and if ye want ony o't oot they must gie ye't; that's whit banks is for."

" Will you no' gang for the twa pound ten for me, and I'll mak' something nice and tasty for your tea the nicht ? " said Jinnet coaxingly ; but Erchie had his own way of teaching Jinnet self-confidence, and refused. " They wadna gie't to me withoot a lot o' palaver," he explained ; " ye'll just hae to gang yersel'. Speak nice to them, and they'll no' touch ye. There hasna been a customer murdered in a Gleska bank for years and years." He explained the process she was to follow, and she set out with great misgivings.

" Weel, hoo did ye get on ? " Erchie asked her when she returned. " Ye got the money onywye—I can see by the wye yer nief's shut."

" Oh, Erchie ! " she cried hysterically, and dropped into a chair. " I wad never mak' a man o' business. My hert's in a palpitation—jist fair stottin'. I peety them that has the bother o' muckle money."

" My jove ! " said Erchie in alarm, " were they no' nice to ye ? If they werena nice and ceevil, I'll—I'll tak' oot every penny, and then they'll see whaur they are."

" Oh, they were as nice as they could be," Jinnet hurried to explain. " And I got the money a' richt. But oh ! I was that put-aboot. Thon slippy floor aye frichtens me, and the gentlemen inside the coonter in their wee cages like Duffy's goldy——"

" Goldies—ay, that's jist whit they are," said Erchie. " It's a fine bird a goldie if ye get a guid yin ; it can whustle better nor a canary."

" ——like Duffy's goldie, and that rale weel put-on. Each o' them had as muckle gold and silver aboot him as wad fill a bakie. I nearly fented when yin o' them spoke to me awfu' Englified, and askit whit he could dae for me the day. ' Oh,' says I, ' I see ye're throng ; I'll can come back anither time,' and I was makin' for the door when he cried me back, and said he wasna that throng but that he wad be gled to dae onything he could for me. I thocht he wad gie me the money

wi' a grudge when he found I wanted twa pound ten in silver,
but he coonted it oot like lichtnin', and bangs it fornent me.
A rale obleegin' lad he was, but no' lookin' awfu' strong ; I
think I'll knit him a pair o' warm socks or a muffler for his
New Year."

" Ye're a rale divert, Jinnet ! " said Erchie.

" I jist picked up the money withoot coontin' it and
turned to gang awa'. 'Hold on, Mistress MacPherson,'
he cries ; ' ye'll be as weel to coont yer siller afore ye
leave the bank in case I'm cheatin' ye,' and my face
got as red's the fire. 'I wadna hae the cheek to doot
ye efter seein' ye coontin't yersel',' I tellt him, and cam'
awa'. But I went up a close further along the street and
coonted it."

" I could bate a pound ye did," said Erchie.

And now, having got out her money, Jinnet had to go
shopping. Ordinary shopping had no terrors for her ; she
loved to drop into Lindsay, the grocer's, and discourse upon
the prices of simple things to eat, and feel important when he
offered to send his boy with the goods ; she was quite at home
in the little side-street shops where they sell trimming, and
bolts of tape, and remnants of print ; or the oil-and-colour
shops where she was known and could spend a pleasant ten
minutes' gossip over the purchase of a gallon of paraffin.
But Christmas shopping was no ordinary shopping, and was
entered on with almost as much apprehension as her expedition to the bank. It had to be done in big warehouses, where
the attendants were utter strangers to her, and had ways
frigid and unfamiliar.

" Put on your kep and come awa' doon the toon wi' me,"
she said to Erchie. " I hate gaun into some o' thae big shops
mysel'."

" Then whit wye dae ye no' jist gang into the wee yins ye
ken ? " he asked her. " If ye're feared they'll eat ye in the
big yins I wadna gang to them."

" Oh, that's a' very weel, but the wee yins havena the

turnover," she explained. " Ye get things far fresher at this time o' the year doon the toon."

" I'll gang wi' ye, for I ken that if I didna gang they wad tak' a fair lend o' ye," Erchie agreed at last ; " but mind, I'm no' gaun to stand lookin' in at baby-linen shop-windows or onything o' that sort. Me bein' a public man in a kind o' wye, it disna dae."

" I'll no' ask ye to dae onything o' the kind, ye pridefu' auld thing ye," she promised, and off they set.

She wanted a pair of gloves for a favourite grand-daughter, an umbrella for a sister of Erchie's, who was a widow and poor, and something as a wedding-present for Duffy's fiancée.

There was scarcely a drapery warehouse in Argyle Street whose window did not attract her. Erchie never looked into any of them, but patiently stood apart on the edge of the pavement or walked slowly ahead.

" Come here and see this at seevenpence three-fardens," she entreated him.

" It's fine, a rale bargain ; I wad tak' that," he replied, looking towards the window from afar off, and quite ignorant of what she alluded to, but determined not to be caught by any one, who knew him as waiter or beadle, looking into a shop-window full of the most delicate feminine mysteries of attire.

She went into the warehouse, while he walked on to the next shop—a cutler's—and looked intently in at the window of it, as if he were contemplating the purchase of a costly pocket-knife with five blades, a corkscrew, and an appliance popularly supposed to be for taking stones out of a horse's hoof. When he was joined by Jinnet, she had plainly begun to lose her nerve.

" I've got gloves," said she, " and a thing for Duffy's lass, but they're naither o' them whit I was wantin'."

" Of course they're no'," said Erchie. " Ye've got a grate consait o' yersel', if ye think a puir auld body like you can get exactly whit ye want in yin o' them warehooses wi' the big turnover ye aye talk aboot. Was it a peerie and a fiddle ye wanted that made ye tak' gloves ? "

" Oh ! dinna bother me, Erchie ; I canna help it ; the lassies that serve ye in there's that Englified and that smert that when they havena got whit I'm wantin' I jist aye tak' whit they can gie me."

" I've seen you in a big shop afore noo," said her husband, " and I ken fine the wye ye aye spile yersel' wi' them Englified smert yins. Ye gang forrit to the coonter as if ye were gaun to ask if they had ony windows to clean, or back-stairs to wash oot, and ye get red in the face and tak' yer money oot o' yer pocket to show ye have it, and ye lauch to the lassie as if ye kent her fine, and ye say, ' If you please ' to her ; or, ' Oh ! it's a bother to ye.' That mak's the lassie see at yince ye're no' cless ; she gets a' the mair Englified, lettin' on to hersel' she's the Duchess o' Montrose, and can put the like o' you in your place wi' the least wee bit touch. That's no' the wye to dae in a shop o' that kind. Ye should breenge up to the coonter, and cry ' Gloves ! ' as hard as Duffy cries ' Coals ! ' then sit doon withoot askin' on a chair, and wi' a gant noo and then watch them puttin' oot gloves by the hunderwicht in front o' ye, and them a' in the shakers in case ye'll no' think they're smert enough.

" Dinna be blate ; that's my advice to ye. Talk Englified yersel', and sniff wi' yer nose noo and then as if ye felt a nesty smell in the place, and run doon the goods like dirt. Never let your e'e rest on the folk that serve ye, unless they happen to hae a shabby tie on or a button aff some-where ; glower at that, and it'll mak' them uncomfortable, and——"

" Oh, that's a' richt, Erchie," said Jinnet ; " ye'll hae to come into the next shop I gang to, and show me the wye."

" No fears o' me," said Erchie promptly ; " I'm tellin' ye whit to dae, but I divna say I could dae't mysel'."

But when it came to the purchase of the umbrella he did go into the shop with her, and she got what she thought was a bargain, as well as the finest affability and courtesy from the gentleman who sold it.

"That's because I was wi' ye," said Erchie, when they came out.

" I daresay," she agreed ; " there's aye some use for a man."

XXVIII

A BET ON BURNS

DUFFY came round to Erchie's on Saturday night for the loan of a copy of Burns, which he knew the old man had on the shelves of what he called his chevalier and book-case. " I'm wantin' to learn a sang," said he, " for I'm gaun to the Haggis Club in the Mull o' Kintyre Vaults on Monday if I'm spared."

"Are ye, indeed!" said Erchie, drily. " Ye'll be takin' the new wife wi' ye ? "

" No fears o' me," said Duffy. " Wha ever heard o' a wife at a Burns meetin' ? "

" Oh ! I divna ken onything aboot it," said Erchie ; " I thocht maybe the weemen were gaun to thae things nooadays, though they didna go when I was young, and I thocht maybe you bein' sae lately mairried ye wanted to gie her a trate. It's a droll thing aboot Burns that though the weemen were sae ta'en up wi' him when he was leevin', they're no' awfu' keen on him noo that he's deid. There'll be thoosands o' men hurrayin' Burns on Monday nicht in a' pairts o' the warld, and eatin' haggis till they're no' weel, but I'll bate ye their wifes is no' there. No ; their wifes is at hame mendin' their men's sox, and chairgin' the gazogene for the morn's mornin', when it'll be sair wanted. And ye're gaun to a Haggis Club, are ye ? I didna ken ye were such a keen Burns hand."

" Me ! " cried Duffy—" I'm jist daft for Burns. Fifty or mair o' the members tak' their coals frae me. Burns ! Man, Erchie, I could gie ye Burns by the yaird—' Dark Lochnagar,' and ' The Flooers o' the Forest,' ' We're a' Noddin',' and ' Rollin' Hame to Bonnie Scotland '—

> ' Rollin' hame to Bonnie Scotland,
> Rollin' hame across the sea.' "

He sang the lines with gusto.

" Stop ! " said Erchie, in alarm, " stop ! There's nae deafenin' in thae ceilin's, and the folk abin 'll think I'm giein' Jinnet a leatherin'. Man ! I didna think ye kent sae mony o' Rabbie's sangs. It's a credit to ye. I'm shair ye divna need ony book to learn affa."

" To tell ye the rale sets o't, Erchie," said Duffy, " it's a bate. There's a chap yonder at the coal hill thrieps doon my throat Burns didna write ' Dark Lochnagar ' the wye I sing 't, and I want to show him 't in the book."

" Hoo much is the bate ? " asked Erchie.

" Hauf-a-croon," said Duffy.

" Then sell yin o' yer horses and pye the money," said Erchie, " for ye've lost the bate. Burns had nae grudge against his countrymen. They did him nae hairm. He didna write ' Dark Lochnagar ' the wye you sing it, for Burns never made his sangs wi' a saw ; in fact, he never wrote ' Dark Lochnagar ' at a' ; it was put oot by anither firm in the same tred, ca'd Byron."

" My jove ! " said Duffy, " I never kent that afore ! "

" There's lots o' things ye never kent," said Erchie. " Seein' ye're gaun to eat haggis on Monday nicht, ye micht tell us whit ye ken, no' aboot Burns's sangs, but aboot Burns himsel'."

" There was naething wrang wi' the chap," said Duffy, " if he just had stuck to his wark. When I'm sellin' coal I'm sellin' coal, and no' pentin' pictures. But there was Burns !—if he happened to come on a moose's nest in the field when he was plewin', or see a flooer in his road when he was oot workin' at the hye, he wad stop the plew, or lay doon his rake, and tak' the efternoon aff to mak' a sang aboot the moose or the daisy."

"A', and jist wi' his least wee bit touch," said Erchie, admiringly. "He was great, that's whit he was."

"Maybe he was, but it spiled the wark ; we wadna aloo that in the coal tred," said Duffy. "He didna ken what compeetition was. I've seen things in my ain tred a knacky chap could mak' a fine sang aboot if he was jist lettin' himsel' go."

"Then for mercy's sake aye keep a grip o' yersel'," said Erchie. "Mind ye hae a wife dependin' on ye ! "

"And then," said Duffy, "he was a bit o' the la-di-da. There's naething o' the la-di-da aboot me."

"There is not ! " admitted Erchie, frankly.

"But Burns, although he was a plewman to tred, went aboot wi' a di'mond ring spilin' folks' windows. If he saw a clean pane o' gless he never lost the chance o' writin' a bit verse on't wi' his di'mond ring. It was gey chawin' to the folk the windows belanged to, but Burns never cared sae lang's he let them see he had a rale di'mond ring that wad scratch gless."

"It was the fashion at the time, Duffy," said Erchie. "Nooadays when a poet has an idea for twa lines he keeps it under the bed till it sproots into a hale poem, and then he sends it to a magazine, and buys his wife, or somebody else's, a di'mond ring wi' whit he gets for't. Writin' on window-panes is no' the go ony langer. It's oot o' date."

"But I'm no' runnin' doon the chap," said Duffy. "Only I aye thocht it was him that wrote ' Dark Lochnagar.' Are ye shair it wasna ? "

Erchie nodded. "Nor ' Rollin' Hame to Bonnie Scotland ' either. He was far ower busy writin' sangs aboot the Marys, and the Jeans, and the Peggys at the time to write aboot ony o' yer ' Dark Lochnagars.' "

" So he was," admitted Duffy. " Yon's a rare yin aboot
Mary—' Kind, kind, and gentle is she—

> . . . kind is my Mary,
> The tender blossom on the tree
> Is half sae sweet as Mary.' "

" Calm yersel', Duffy," said Erchie, in dramatic alarm.
" I'm no deaf."

" That was written aboot ' Hielan' Mary,' " said Duffy.
" He met her at Dunoon the Fair Week, and I've seen her
monument."

" It's yonder as nate's ye like," said Erchie. " Faith ! it's
you that's weel up in Burns, Duffy."

" Oh ! I'm no' that faur back in my history," said Duffy,
quite pleased with himself. " But I could hae sworn it was
him that put thegither ' Rollin' Hame to Bonnie Scotland ' ;
it's his style. He micht be rollin', but he aye got hame. He
was a gey wild chap, Burns."

" I'm no' denyin't, Duffy," said Erchie. " But he hadna
ony o' the blessin's we have in oor time to keep him tame.
There was nae Free Leebrary to provide him wi' books to
keep him in the hoose at nicht, nae Good Templar Lodges to
help him in keepin' clear o' the horrors o' drink ; and Poosy
Nancy's public-hoose didna shut at ten o'clock, nor even
eleeven. If Burns had thae advantages, there's nae sayin'
whit he micht hae risen to ; perhaps he micht hae become
an M.P., and dee'd wi' money in the bank."

" Och ! there's worse than Burns," said Duffy. " I was
gey throughither mysel' when I was a young chap."

" Ah ! but ye couldna hae been that awfu' bad, for ye
never made ony poetry."

" I never tried," said Duffy ; " I was the youngest o' nine,
and I was put oot to wark early. So there wasna time for
me to try and be fancy in ony wye. But a gey wild chap,
Burns ! "

" Maybe no' that awfu' wild," said Erchie. " Ye're aye

harpin' on the wild. Burns was like a man takin' a daunder oot in a country road on a fine nicht : he kept his een sae much on the stars that sometimes he tripped in the sheuch. If it was the like o' you and me, Duffy, we wad be keepin' oor e'e a' the time on the road at oor feet to see if onybody hadna dropped onything, and there wad be nae fears o' us fa'in in the sheuch. Except for his habit o' makin' sangs when he micht be makin' money, Burns wasna very different frae the rest o' us. There was ae thing aboot him—he aye payed his way, and never forgot his freen's. He had a warm hert."

"Man, ye should be doon at the Mull o' Kintyre Vaults Haggis Club on Monday and propose the toast," said Duffy, admiringly.

"I'm better whaur I am," said Erchie ; "the best Burns Club a man can hae 's a weel-thumbed copy o' the poems on his chevalier and book-case, and a wife that can sing ' Ye Banks and Braes ' like oor Jinnet."

XXIX

THE PRODIGAL'S RETURN

A SAILOR-MAN with a thick black beard, and all his belongings apparently on his back,—for the dunnage-bag he carried was so poorly stuffed it could have held little more than a pair of sea-boots,—went into Erchie's close one afternoon, and slowly climbed the stair. He put the bag at his feet when he came to Erchie's door with " MacPherson " on the name-plate, scratched his head, hitched his waist-belt once or twice, and seemed in a mood to turn and flee rather than to ring or knock. At last he faintly tugged the bell-pull, and leaned against the door-post with the air of one who expected he might have some parley before getting admittance.

There was a step in the lobby, and Erchie himself in his shirt-sleeves came to the door,

" We're no' for onything the day," said he. " We have a sewin'-machine already, and we're a' in the Prudential Insurance, and the staircase windows were cleaned on Setturday, and——"

" Faither," said the sailor-man, " do ye no' ken me ? "

Erchie came closer and looked at the bearded face, and put his hand tremblingly upon the young man's shoulder.

" Willie ! " said he. " Willie ! " he repeated. " Man, ye're sair needin' shavin'." He shook his son, and " O, Willie," said he, " whit 'll yer mither say ? I suppose if I was the rale thing mysel', I should kill the fatted calf or start the greetin' ; but as shair's death we havena kept a calf in this hoose since ye left it yoursel', and I was never yin o' the greetin' kind. My goodness ! Willie ! "

He was so bewildered he forgot his visitor stood on the door-mat, until Willie lifted his dunnage-bag, and then he urged him into the kitchen.

" Where's—where's mother ? " said the sailor.

" She micht be deid and in her grave for you," said his father ; " but she's no'. She's doon at Lindsay the grocer's for a loaf. Oh, ye rogue ! ye rogue ! Whit 'll she say to ye ? Seeven years, come the fifth o' June ! Oh, ye're awfu' needin' shavin'. I hope—I hope the health's fine ? "

" Fine," said Willie, and sat in a chair uneasily, like a stranger.

" And whaur in a' the warld did ye come frae ? " said his father, putting the kettle on the fire. They had not even shaken hands.

" China and roond aboot there," said the son.

" China ! " said his father. " And hoo did ye leave them a' in China ? They're throng at the war there the noo, I see. I hope ye werena hurted."

" No, nor hurted," said Willie. " I hope ye're fine yersel' —and mother ? "

" Me ! said Erchie. " Jist a fair gladiator ! Divna ken my ain strength, and can eat onything, jist like a connoshoor. As for yer mother, she's wonderfu' ; a wee frail, but aye able to dae her turns. She'll be the gled wumman this—— Whit I mean to say is, ye should get a reg'lar leatherin' for your cairry-on. If I hadna my rheumatism in my shoother gey bad, I wad tak' a stick to ye. I'm pretty wild at ye, mind I'm tellin' ye. Whit dae ye think o' yersel', to gang awa' and no' write us for seeven years ? "

" No' an awfu' lot," said the son.

" That's hopeful," said his father. " I'm gled ye're no' puttin' the blame on us. And I'm gled ye havena ony brass buttons on your claes."

" Brass buttons ? " said Willie.

" Ay ! When your mother was wearyin' to hear frae ye, I used to be tellin' her that ye were likely a mate, or a purser, or something o' that sort, and that busy in foreign pairts liftin' the tickets in the fore saloon, where the dram's cheaper and maist o' the passengers go, that ye hadna time to write. Yince I took her doon to the docks and showed her a big ship gaun awa' to Australia, wi' the Captain on the tap flet, ca'in a handle and roarin' ' Let go that gangway ! ' and ' Nae smokin' abaft the funnel ! ' and she was as pleased as onything to see't. Ever since then she thinks o' her son Willie as a chap wi' brass buttons ca'in a handle the same as he was a tramway driver, and that busy he hadna time to write. I'm gled ye havena brass buttons," concluded Erchie, looking at his rather shabbily clothed scion. " It's mair to your credit that ye were jist a fool and no' a rascal."

" Man, ye're jist as great a caution as ever," said Willie, with the sincerest admiration.

" Duffy the coal-man tellt me he saw ye yince doon aboot the Broomielaw," said Erchie. " It was three years ago. I daursay ye were ower throng at the time to come up and see your mither and me. It's a guid wye up here frae the

Broomielaw ; it costs a penny on the skoosh car. Or maybe it was a wet day."

Willie's face got red. " It wasna only yince I was at the Broomielaw," he said. " I've been in Gleska four times since I left it."

" Were ye indeed ? " said his father. " Weel, weel, it was rale considerate o' ye no' to bother your auld mither and me. I'll wager ye werena needin' ony money."

" I was needin' money gey bad every time," said the son. " I aye had some when I landed, but it never got past the Broomielaw wi' me. And that's the wye I never cam near ye. I was ashamed, as shair's death. Every time I was in the Clyde I cam up here at nicht, or to the auld hoose afore ye flitted, and looked at the close or went roond to the back coort and looked at the kitchen window."

" It's a good thing I didna see ye there, or I wad maybe hae gien ye a clourin'."

" I wad hae liked it fine if ye had," said the young man. " A clourin' was the very thing I was needin', and I kent it mysel'. I was an awfu' fool, faither."

" That's jist whit ye were," Erchie admitted. " It's a lingerin' disease, and that's the warst o't. I hope ye'll maybe get ower't."

" If I didna think I had got ower't I wadna hae been here the nicht," said the son. " I'll warrant ye'll no' hae to complain o' me again."

Erchie took his hand. " Willie," said he, " gie me your thoomb on that. I ken the MacPhersons, if their mind's made up, and I think ye're auld enough noo to try your hand at sense. It'll no' hurt ye. Willie, Willie, it wasna mysel' I worried aboot thae seeven years, nor you either ; for I kent fine the prodigal wad come back, if it was only to see if his faither de'ed and left him onything. The prodigal son ! Awfu' needin' a shave ! Your mither 'll be the prood wumman this nicht."

Before Jinnet had come back from the grocer's Erchie put

his son into the parlour, so that the returned wanderer might not too abruptly confront his mother. She suspected nothing for a little, going about her ordinary offices in the kitchen till something fidgety in her husband's appearance directed her more close attention to him, and there was seen then an elation in his countenance that made her ask him what the matter was.

" Ye're awfu' joco," said she. " Are ye plannin' some baur for Duffy ? "

" Not me," said Erchie. " I'm jist wearyin' for my tea. And, by the wye, Jinnet," he added, " ye micht put doon anither cup for a frien' o' mine I'm expectin' frae abroad."

" Frae abroad ! " cried Jinnet, turning pale. " Ye havena heard onything o'—o'——"

" Have I no' ? " said Erchie. " There's a chap in the room at this meenute that wad be awfu' like Willie if he had a clean shave."

Ten minutes later Erchie joined his wife and Willie in the room. The dunnage-bag was being emptied before Jinnet by a son who was anxious to make the most of his gifts from foreign parts, though painfully conscious of their value.

" Oh, whit braw shells ! " cried his mither. " Jist the very thing I was needin' for the mantelpiece. The Carmichaels say wally dugs is no' the go noo at a'. It was rale thochtfu' o' ye to tak' them a' the wye frae abroad for me."

" And here a song folio and a pund o' sweet tobacco for you, faither," said Willie.

Erchie took them in his hand. " Man, that's the very thing," said he. " If ' Dark Lochnagar's ' in't, I'll be upside wi' Duffy."

" Whit's this ? " asked Jinnet, as the sailor brought forth for her a bottle containing some dark thick fluid.

" Riga balsam,—whit the sailors use for sair hands," said Willie.

s

"Oh, it's the very thing Erchie used to say ye wad bring back when ye cam," cried Jinnet in delight. "It'll be awfu' useful. I'm almost vext I havena onything sair aboot me the day."

"No' even a sair hert," said Erchie, and the son looked contritely at his mother.

JIMMY SWAN

THE JOY TRAVELLER

JIMMY SWAN

THE JOY TRAVELLER

STARS TO PUSH

MR SWAN, the work of the day accomplished, stood smoking at the Buck's Head door, and the sky was all a-glee with twinkling stars which are quite irrelevant to the story, and are merely mentioned here to indicate that it was evening. And yet, when I come to think of it, the stars deserve this mention, for their shining, so serene, and cool, and joyous, had some influence both on Jimmy and the story. They set him wondering on the mystery of things and on the purpose of his being and his life.

Behind him, in the hall of the hotel, the Boots, old Willie, piled his sample-cases ready for the boat at six o'clock next morning. The billiard-room seemed full of villagers; the sound of chaff and laughter and the clink of tumblers came from it occasionally. But Jimmy scarcely heard it—wrapt in contemplation of the stars.

From out the billiard-room, at last, there came a man who seemed to have decided, not a moment too soon—indeed, unfortunately, too late—that it was time for home. He fumbled for his top-coat, hanging with a dozen others on a stand, and he was forced to stretch himself a little over Jimmy's cases, piled up very high about the stand by Willie.

"A fine night, Mr Sloan," said Jimmy, who knew even recent incomers to Birrelton; and he helped him to put on his coat.

"There's naething wrang wi' the night," said Mr Sloan, "except for thae damn bags o' yours. . . . Perf'ly rideec'lous!

549

A body might as weel be on a steamer. . . . Shouldn' be allowed ! '' He was at that particular stage of fermentation where the scum of personal temperament comes bubbling to the top.

" Sorry they should be in your road," said Jimmy, affably. " They're often in my own. It's yin o' the chief drawbacks to bein' what the papers ca' an ambassador o' commerce."

"Ambass'or o' commerce ! '' hiccoughed Mr Sloan. " Nonsense ! Jus' a common bagman ! '' And two younger men who had joined him laughed at this brilliant sally.

" Right ye are ! '' said Jimmy. " Just a common bagman ! That's what I was thinkin', standin' here and takin' my bit smoke, and lookin' at the stars. Just a plain auld bagman sellin' silks and ribbons ! I wish my line was traivellin' for stars. My Jove ! if I had stars to push, I could get orders ! A line like that would gie me scope ; I'm sometimes sick o' wastin' words on Shantungs and on down-quilt patterns."

Mr Sloan was feeling nasty—distinctly nasty, having barked his shin on a sample case, and having an uneasy sense that he had forgotten something, and that he should have been home to his wife a good deal earlier. He wished to work himself into the proper spirit for a lively domestic altercation.

" What hae ye got in a' thae cases ? '' said he.

" Joy," said Jimmy, rappin' out his pipe upon his palm, and pursing up his mouth.

" Oh to bleezes ! '' said the man, " you're drunk.''

" Just touched a wee, perhaps, wi' drinkin' starlight," said Jimmy. " But still I'm tellin' ye, I'm a traiveller for joy, and there's my samples. If I was openin' up my bags to ye, it's likely ye would only see dry-goods. I saw them, last, mysel' as dry-goods when I packed them, but it just came on me here in lookin' at the stars I was mistaken ; there's naething in my bags but human joy."

The young men roared with laughter.

" 'Scuse me, Mr Swan," said Mr Sloan, a little more agreeably, " I've often seen ye gaun aboot, and thought ye were in the drapery line ; how was I to ken ye were traivellin' for beer ? "

" No," said Jimmy, solemnly, " not beer ! Wholesome human joy. Glowerin' at the stars there, I was tryin' to find some excuse for my paltry and insignificant existence, and then I minded I was an essential bit o' the mechanism for providin' dresses for the lassies o' Birrelton for next month's Territorial ball. Do ye think ye grasp me, Mr Sloan ? "

" But what aboot the joy ? " said Mr Sloan.

" That's joy," said Jimmy. " Youth, and a new frock ! I ran over a' my samples in my mind, and there's no' a one that's no' a swatch o' something meant for comfort, consolation, the pleasure o' the eye, or the pride o' life. What would life in Birrelton be withoot me, or the like o' me ? Man ! that's one o' my ties ye're wearin', Mr Sloan ! I wish ye would learn to put a better knot on't and gie the stuff a chance."

" Wha's tha' got to do wi' stars ? " asked Mr Sloan, vaguely. " You said ye were sellin' stars. Or was it beer ? I forget which."

" No," said Jimmy. " I'm not at present sellin' stars, though maybe that's in store for me if I could be a better man. I only mentioned stars because they set me wonderin' if an auld bagman was ony use at a' in that big scheme that put them twinklin' yonder. . . . Good night, gentlemen ! I'm aff to bed."

When they were gone, he watched the stars a little longer, finishing his pipe, and then went to the stand to take his coat upstairs with him. Instead of it he found the errant Sloan's.

" By George, I must get my coat," he said to Willie. " I have a pair o' gloves and a box o' chocolates for the wife in't."

.   .   .   .   .   .

Mr Sloan meandered home with that uneasy sense of something overlooked, forgotten, and only recollected what it was when his anxiously awaiting wife asked him if he had the mutton.

"Mutton!" he exclaimed with a sudden sinking of the heart. "What mutton?"

"Oh, John!" she said, "didn't you promise me to be sure and get a gigot for to-morrow? You know that it's the holiday, and all the shops 'll be shut. What am I to do for dinner?"

"As sure as death I clean forgot it, talkin' with a chap aboot the stars," said Mr Sloan, contritely, as she helped him to take off his coat.

She put a hand into its pockets and produced a pair of reindeer gloves and a box of chocolates. "What in all the world is this?" she asked him, and he stared, himself, confounded.

"I don't have ony mind o' buying them," said he; "but that's a' right: I likely meant them for a peace offerin'."

"You're just a dear!" she cried, delightedly; "although you did forget the mutton," and she put the gloves on, finding them a perfect size.

There was a ringing at the door.

.   .   .   .

"I'm very sorry to disturb you at this hour," said Mr Swan, "but there's been a slight mistake. I have a coat the very neighbour of your husband's, and we got them mixed between us at the hotel. This, I think, is his; I wouldn't trouble you, so late, but I have to leave by the early boat."

"Oh!" she said, despairingly, "I might have known!" and started pulling off the gloves. "Then these are yours, and the box of chocolates?" The tears were in her eyes.

"No," said Jimmy, firmly. "There was nothing in my pockets, Mrs Sloan: your husband must have bought them," and got his coat restored to him by a delighted wife.

"Who is he that?" she asked, when he was gone.

"Old Swan," said Mr Sloan, half sleeping.

"What is he?" she asked. "I liked the look of him."

"Travels for stars," said Mr Sloan, vaguely; "bags full of joy! Old Jimmy Swan! He's drunk!"

ON THE ROAD

JIMMY walked briskly up No. 3 Platform, glanced in at the door of the luggage-van and counted his cases, gave twopence to the boy who had carried round his rug and hand-bag, passed off the latest pantomime wheeze on the guard, whom he addressed as "Alick," and sank into his seat in the corner of the smoker just as the train, with a jolt, awoke to the necessity of doing something for its living. It was barely across the river when some one had produced a pack of cards, and Jimmy's rug was stretched between the knees of half a dozen men who played at Nap.

"Come UP to Brady's!" said Jimmy time and again, as he slammed an ace down in the centre of the rug and scooped in another shilling's-worth of coppers. On three occasions he went double Nap and got it.

"You've got all the luck the day, Mr Swan," said one of the players, an ambassador in the interest of Dray Gunn's biscuits, who looked anxiously out at every stoppage of the train.

"Wrong, my son," said Jimmy. "Cards are like commercial travelling—one-fourth luck, half pluck, and the balance don'tgiveadamness."

"Bluff, you mean," suggested Dray Gunn.

"Bluff's no use unless you have the stuff," said Jimmy, shuffling. "That's the Golden Text for to-day in cards or commercial travelling. . . . I don't care to mention it, Maguire, but what about that twopence? . . . Thanks."

"Where's this we're at?" asked the biscuit man at another station. "Stewarton. By Jinks! I should get

S*

out at Stewarton, but I'll take it on the way coming back. I'm not going to break up the company."

There was a young fellow in a corner seat who didn't play, but sat embattlemented round by a pile of magazines having snappy names, like " System," " Success," and the " World's Work." He read them with the fervour of a budding saw-bones studying for his First Professional. Sometimes he made notes on the back leaves of a traveller's order-book. Once he ate an apple, having pared it carefully first with an ivory paper-cutter, and Jimmy looked at him with paternal pity. It made him sad to see a fellow-creature recklessly spoil his appetite for dinner with such childish things as apples.

" Now that's a thing I never could do since I was a boy," said Jimmy—" eat apples in the middle of the day. It's a habit that grows on you till you become its slave. I don't say anything against the proper debauch of apples after business hours now and then—say at a Hallowe'en ; but get into the habit of nibbling, nibbling, nibbling away at apples at all hours of the day, and before you know where you are your relatives begin to say there really ought to be Some Place of Confinement for unfortunate people with such a weakness."

" It's much more natural to eat apples than half-raw beef-steaks," said the stranger.

" It's much more natural being dead than living," retorted Jimmy, cheerfully ; " for there's many more doing it, but hang it ! look at the fun there is in being quite alive ! I'm not blaming you, old man ; I have some bad habits myself, but they're all in the interest of the firm. When I retire from business I'm going to take a house beside a water-fall."

" Man is really not a carnivorous animal," said the apple-eater ; " he's frugiverous."

" I don't say that he's quite so bad as all that," said Jimmy, putting up the cards and handing them to their owner ; " but he's a serious problem any way you look at him."

The young fellow got out at the same station as Jimmy, who was three-and-sixpence up on the forenoon's gambling, and as cheerful as if he had won a horse and trap in a sixpenny raffle.

" On the road ? " asked Jimmy, mildly, as the porters trundled out cases for both of them from the van.

" Macdougall & Grant," said the other, handing him his card, and with the tone assumed by a visitor to Hamburg who says he is in the British Navy.

" A jolly good house ! " said Jimmy, genially, though it was a formidable rival of his own. " Good luck to you ! I'm Campbell & Macdonald ; name of Swan. So you're successor to old Kilpatrick ? Good old Kil. ! He and I began together on the road in the 'Seventies. Had it all our own way in these days. And a good man, too ! Kil. and I would come out of any town you like to name in Ayrshire, neck and neck, and we had the whole North journey in the hollow of our hands. But Kil. had to pay pretty sweet for it. . . . Kidneys, they tell me. Wonder how's his widow."

" That sort of way of making business is done," said the young man, replete with all the philosophy of " System " and " Success." " A man, to make his own way on the road now, has got to have some knowledge of psychology."

" Oh, blazes ! " said Jimmy, as they walked to the same hotel together. " What's that ? Don't tell me it's nuts, or lentil soup, or anything like that. Or do you mean bumps ? "

" It's the knowledge of human nature," said the young fellow, fervently. " You've got to study your customer. Don't waste his time. Come to the point. Tickle him with some novel lines. A customer is like a trout ; you mustn't throw the fly in with a splash. You must give him the idea that it's there by pure accident, and that if he doesn't hurry up and grab it some one else will have it before him. Once

he takes it, you must play him gently ; no jerk, no tug ; and
when you have his order in your basket, get out as quick as
possible before he has time to meditate and make it a couple
of dozen assorted instead of the level gross. The thing is
to watch your customer's eye."

Jimmy chuckled—one of those deep, rich, liquid chuckles
that add twenty per cent to his value for his salary. Across
the flush of his countenance went a hundred wrinkled lines—
the furrows of fun, irony, care, calculation, years, weather,
and a little droop at the corners of the mouth begot of that
sentiment known as tenderness which may be the greatest of
commercial assets. His deep eyes twinkled.

" Man, Watson," he remarked, falling into the vernacular
he has always made great play with in the villages : " Man,
Watson ! I fear you're far gone on aipples ! A chap canna
go about all day munchin' here and there all by himsel' at
aipples without doin' himsel' harm. If old Kil. heard ye, he
would turn in his grave. Ye'll no' get mony fish in your
basket that way, either in Galloway or Ayr. Do ye think
your customers are a' born idiots ? Take my advice, Mr
Watson ; I'm auld enough to be your faither : stop your
solitary aipple habit and burn a' your Yankee magazines.
There's only one way to catch and keep a customer—have
an honest liking for him as a human bein' just as clever in
his own way as yoursel', and see that your stuff's as good as
your warranty."

They dined together at the Buck's Head, where Jimmy
was *persona grata*. It couldn't very well be otherwise with
a guest who had been coming for twenty years ; who had a
new cure for the rheumatism of Willie the Boots (" mix the
two and take a half-a-teaspoonful every morning in a little
tepid water, Willie. None of your hunker-slidin', now : don't
put ony spirits into the water ") ; who was deeply interested
in the landlady's Orpington hens, and had heard in Glasgow
a week ago with joy of her being a grandmother ; who called
the landlord Bob, and had a rattling good cigar for him ;

and who asked the tablemaid when it was coming off with her and John Mackenzie. Jimmy, to the superficial vision, might seem an ordinary being surrounded by a rather shabby suit of Harris tweed, but as a matter of fact he bore, for twenty yards all round him, an aura, a personal atmosphere which took the chill from the coldest rooms, and someway gladdened every creature coming within its bounds.

He asked young Watson to join him in a drink; not that he wanted one himself, but just because it is a symbol of liberty, equality, and fraternity. And because he was Jimmy. But Watson wouldn't; he alone was impervious to the influence of auras.

" Good lad ! " said Jimmy heartily. " Then have a small lime-juice and soda. Nothing better for brightening up the —what-d'ye-call-it ?—psychologic eye."

A little later Jimmy went toddling round to Gardener's, the biggest draper in the place, in more respects than one, and found young Watson there before him, practising all he knew of the psychological on Mr Gardener, who maintained a great aloofness behind a desk from which it looked as if all the psychology in the world and a hundred steam-derricks could not for a moment budge him.

" Here I'm again, Bylie ! " Jimmy cried in at the door. " How's the wife ? But I observe you're engaged ; I'll see you later. See and be good to my friend Mr Watson—one of the best, and a good first journey means a lot for a young chap."

The aura appeared immediately to influence Bailie Gardener ; he ponderously raised himself from off his stool, and with a perfunctory glance at drawers and shelves discovered a few items in which his stock was short, though far from being so short as it might have been had Watson been the late Kilpatrick. The science of psychology otherwise had no more effect on him than a glass of buttermilk.

Half an hour later Jimmy came sailing in to Gardener's.

" They put some queer chaps on the road now, Mr Swan,"

said the Bailie. "I doot yon yin's no' the weight o' auld Kilpatrick."

"It's aipples," said Jimmy, roguishly. "Aipples, and low-browed underground smoking-rooms in Gleska, and black coffee in the forenoon, and Yankee magazines called 'Success.' I'm sorry for the chap ; a clever enough chap, mind ye, but spoiled wi' aipples. There's naething worse for wind. All the same, Bylie, we'll give the lad a chance ; he'll learn. There wasna a greater idiot than mysel' when I first set out for C. & M. . . . I have a clinkin' story for ye for your next night's lodge harmony."

Jimmy told the story as he walked behind the counter, pulled out drawers himself, and rapidly estimated how much of an order would bring the quantity of their contents to par. Bailie Gardener, sitting at the desk, complacently watched him turning over webs upon the shelving, running through the shirts, and totting up the blouses.

"Ye ken my stock better than mysel', I'm thinkin' sometimes, Mr Swan," said he, as Jimmy blandly booked what he reckoned should be the order.

"It's what ye call the psychologic eye," said Jimmy. "There's a whole lot o' books aboot it."

At high tea in the Buck's Head, Mr Watson seemed unhappy ; he had found the town a little unresponsive to the system of "Success" and the other snappy magazines, and in the aura of Jimmy he confessed it. Psychology itself could not have suggested a policy more likely to engage the sympathy of Jimmy Swan.

"I know, old man !" said he. "Dour ! I've been there myself. You'll find it'll be all right when they know you, if you treat them like men and not like bloomin' dominoes. Get it out of your head that you're out to sell and then to hook it ; you're out to make friends for yourself and the firm. You can't make friends by any process of philosophy, though you may get casual customers."

"And how can I make friends ?" asked Watson humbly.

" By being sure that you need them more than they need you," said Jimmy. " That's the start of it. Another way is to live, like me, to the age of five and fifty. And then your friends are apt to be far too many."

THE FATAL CLOCK

DAN SCOULAR, the third man in the Mantles, was to be married on Hogmanay, and the warehouse expressed its consolation in the customary way by means of a smoker and testimonial—James Swan, Esq., in the chair. For nearly twenty years there has been no presentation to an employee of C. & M. at which James Swan, Esq., has not firmly rapped on the table with the chairman's mallet, looked round the company with a pawky smile of the utmost self-possession, and said, " Gentleman all ! " preparatory to a speech which invested the occasion with almost national importance, and made the presentee determined that henceforth he should be worthy of the high encomiums passed upon his amiability, his genius, his industry, and general indispensability in the soft goods trade of Glasgow and the West of Scotland. Hundreds of brave and bright young gentlemen bound for matrimonial havens, or new drapery businesses of their own ; for Leeds, Bradford, London, Canada, or New South Wales, have gone out of Mancell's Restaurant with Gladstone bags, gold watches, writing desks, silver salvers, eight-day clocks, or gorgeously illuminated addresses, whose intrinsic values were merely trivial as compared with that superimposed on them by the eloquence of Jimmy Swan. They might lose the illuminated addresses or salvers before they got home, but the memory of his speech was always a fragrant possession.

For Dan Scoular's presentation, however, Mr Swan took up an unexpected attitude ; he would not consent to preside as usual, unless the testimonial took some other form than a marble timepiece, and Scoular's preference was

fondly set, as he told the committee, on this essential
domestic feature.

"Mr Swan's determined on something else," he was told.

"What does he think it should be?" asked Scoular.   "I'm
sure there's nothing wrong wi' a good-goin' clock."

"He doesn't care what it is, but he bars a timepiece, and
if we want him in the chair we'll have to meet his wishes."

"All right!" said Scoular; "make it a case o' cutlery.
It wouldn't be a testimonial at all unless we had him in
the chair."

So a case of cutlery it was, and Mr Swan agreeably pre-
sided. When the moment came for the presentation rites,
the cutlery case in tissue paper was suddenly produced in
due and ancient form, as if by sleight-of-hand, from under-
neath the table, and Mr Scoular assumed the appropriate
aspect of modest protestation and astonishment. As he said
in his reply, he had not for a moment expected his friends to
do anything so handsome.

Mr Swan sent the cutlery on a tour of the room that the
subscribers might have the pleasure of reading the inscription
on the case, and took the opportunity of expressing his gratification that the committee had selected this particular form
of gift.

"For a young man startin' a house of his own," he said,
"there are few things more appropriate than a case o' cutlery.
You have only got to lock it up and lose the key, and all
risk of early bankruptcy due to the good-wife's social am-
bitions is averted. If I thought for a moment that the
future Mrs Scoular was likely to use all that Sheffield steel
and electro-plate right off, I would advise Dan to swap it
at the earliest opportunity for a sewin'-machine. But what
she's sure to do, bein' a wise-like girl, as all of you know,
since she has been five years in the silk department, is to
place it carefully on the chiffonier, with a biscuit-barrel on
the top of it, till Dan becomes a partner. Meanwhile—
except perhaps at a christenin'—she'll use the cutlery that's

kept in the kitchen drawer. From scenes like these, gentle-men, auld Scotia's grandeur springs ! "

" What about the clock ? " cried some one in the back-ground, and Jimmy twinkled.

" I was just comin' to the clock," he retorted, dropping into the vernacular his warmer moods demanded. " Let me hasten to say, Mr Scoular, in case that remark has roused fond anticipations that are bound to be shattered, that there's naething mair for ye. There's no clock. And ye may thank me for there bein' no clock ; if some o' the com-mittee had their way o't, it's no' a dacent case o' cutlery ye would hae been gaun hame wi' on the Subway the nicht, but a ton or twa o' the monumental sculptor's art on a lorry.

" Gentlemen," he proceeded, " I've seen far ower mony o' the stately tenement homes o' Scotland brought to ruin under the weddin' gift o' a massive marble timepiece, some-times complicated wi' a couple o' objects reputed to be made o' bronze, and generously alluded to as ' ornaments.' It's a mean advantage to tak' o' ony young woman goin' to stay wi' a total stranger. For, remember, she has got to live wi' that timepiece a' day, and a' her days. Her man goes out to his work in the mornin' and comes back at night after a busy and cheerful day at the counter, and he never thinks o' her bein' shut up a' the time wi' an Italian monument that is for ever recallin' to her the shortness o' life and the solemnity o' the Necropolis. There's no escape from it for her, poor soul ! She canna lift it aff the mantelpiece and put it under a bed; it's as permanent in its place as a gasalier.

" The increasin' tyranny o' the marble timepiece has been obvious to some o' us for many years, but it is only within the last twa or three years I got a lesson in what it may lead to that has made me determined to discourage the marble clock as a presentation gift at ony function I may have the honour to be connected wi'.

" A customer o' mine in Mauchline went and got married three years ago. He was in the U.F. choir and in the

Rechabites—a thing that micht happen to onybody—and the choir and the Rechabites agreed on a conjoint testimonial. They gathered £12, 10s., and when they broke the news to him that he was in for a presentation, he said he would have a marble clock, and would like to get pickin' one for himsel' in Gleska.

"Up he came to Gleska, which is the peculiar home and haunt o' the marble clock in the most deleterious forms, and drags me awa' from the warehouse to help him at the buyin'. I did my best to put him aff the notion by tellin' him o' happy homes I had seen broken up through the habit o' having aye a tombstone in the parlour ; and I strongly urged a chiffonier and book-case, or sewin'-machine, or a bedroom suite o' furniture.   But no!   MacLeerie had set his he'rt on a polished black sarcophagus, and would have me, richt or wrang, to a shop where they sell them in broad day-licht without the police interferin'.   From scenes like these !

" I never thought there were sae mony ways o' bein' solemnly and distressingly ingenious in the cuttin' up o' black marble !   The miscreants that do that kind o' work appear to have attempted everything !   It was a pretty big shop, and it was full o' black monumental tombs that were made to look like Grecian temples, Roman altars, Rothesay villas, lighthouses, front elevations for Picture Palaces, tea-urns—ony mortal thing but clocks !   Yonder they were, tickin' awa' like onything, and we walked up and down between the plots o' them, quite low-spirited, the same as it was a cemetery.

" MacLeerie had but the one idea about a clock—that it should be big, and black, and heavy.   He picked the very biggest he could get for the money, and I tell you it was a whupper !   It was three feet long and two feet high if it was an inch ;   had the weight of a fire-proof safe, and was guaranteed a genuine reproduction o' the Madeleine Church in Paris.   MacLeerie said he liked, particularly, the Madeleine touch.

"I protested to the last. I implored him, if he must have a clock, to take a small inlaid mahogany one wi' a sonsy, honest face, and buy a bangle for the mistress with the balance o' the money, but he was on for the mausoleum, and he got it! From scenes like these!

"The first time I was back in Mauchline after his marriage, he took me up to his house, and showed me the Madeleine in poseetion. I couldna have believed that ony earthly mantelpiece would stand the strain, but he showed me how it was done wi' brackets o' angle-iron.

"'How in the world did ye get it up the stairs?' I asked, and he explained that it was hoisted through the window wi' a block-and-tackle.

"That clock was in supreme possession o' the parlour! It brooked no rivals! It dwarfed the piano, the what-not, the saddle-bag suite, and the ancestral portraits. It took your eye away from the carpet; I was twenty minutes in the room before I noticed the tantalus spirit-stand. A more commandin' article o' British furniture I never saw than George MacLeerie's clock!

"But it wasna goin'!

"It hadna gone since it was erected! You see the pendulum could only be started from the back, or by givin' the whole edifice a shake, and gettin' into the back or givin' it a shake was out o' the question; ye might as well try to shift or shake the Pyramids o' Egypt.

"I ate brides-cake and drank the health o' the couple in front o' that amazin' clock, and I declare it was like layin' the memorial-stone o' a new Post Office! From scenes like these!

"Well, gentlemen, what was the natural and inevitable outcome o' MacLeerie's vanity? For a while it looked as if the couple was gettin' on quite satisfactory. By and by I found MacLeerie a little dreich in settlin' his bills, and heard that his wife was launchin' oot in the social line wi' regular days-at-home, progressive whist, and a vacuum-cleaner. She was celebrated, ye understand, for having the biggest, heaviest, marble clock in Ayrshire, and she felt she had to live up to this distinction.

"She found, in a while, that her parlour furniture didna properly match the grand old Madeleine, and she had to get in a lot o' new things on the instalment system, includin' a pianolo and a fine new gramophone. The other ladies in the terrace would drop in on an efternoon and sit in front of the Madeleine listenin' to the music and thinkin' they were in Paris, and because the clock never went, they never knew the richt time, so that George's tea was seldom ready when he cam' hame. At last he didna come hame for his tea at a', but took onything that was handy at a public-house behind his shop ; he couldna bear the sight o' his mausoleum. When grocers' accounts and the like o' that came to the hoose, Mrs MacLeerie aye stuck them behind the Madeleine for safety ; and of course they never could be got oot again.

"The lang and the short o' it was that she, puir body, died one day in an effort to get below the clock and dust the mantelpiece, and her man, between her loss and his sequestration, was so put aboot that he only survived a few weeks after her.

"It was only then the marble clock was put to its appropriate purpose ; the works were taken out of it ; and it was re-erected on her final resting-place, where it mak's the brawest marble mausoleum in Mauchline. From scenes like these, gentlemen, auld Scotia's grandeur springs."

A SPREE

HAVING finished high tea at the George Hotel, Jimmy Swan, a little wearied after a cross-country journey of five-and-twenty miles in a badly-sprung waggonette, sought out his usual bedroom, and searched his bag for slippers.

They weren't there !

The ready-flyped extra socks were there ; the shirts with the studs in them ; the Cardigan waistcoat ; the chest-protector he had never used in all his life ; the little " house-wife " or bachelor's companion, with needles, thread, and buttons in it ; the sticking-plaster ; the bottle of fruit saline ; the pocket Bible and the Poems of Burns ; but not a hint of carpet slippers.

" I doubt Bella's gettin' a bit auld, like mysel'," he meditated. " It's the first time she forgot my slippers since we married. I'll hae to be awfu' angry wi' her when I get hame—if I can keep mind o't."

He went down to the Commercial Room and rang the bell for the Boots.

" Have ye a pair o' slippers, Willie ? " he inquired.

" There's no' such an article in the hoose, Mr Swan," said the Boots, " unless I got ye the lend o' the boss's."

" Oh, don't bother ! " said the traveller. " I'll can dae withoot."

" We used to hae a couple o' dozen pair for the use o' you commercial gentlemen," said Willie, " but nooadays naebody asks for them ; I suppose it's this new sanitary and high-jinkic education."

" The innkeepers made a great mistake when they stopped providin' slippers," said Mr Swan. " There was naething better for keepin' a customer in the hoose and no' stravaigin' roon the toon wastin' his money in other premises. If ever I start an inn, I'll hae a pair o' slippers, a rockin'-chair, and a copious free supply o' cake and speldrins for every customer. What's the result o' me no' hae'in' slippers ? I'm just goin' awa' ootbye for a walk to mysel', and there's no sayin' where I may forgaither wi' a frien' or twa. No man's hame for the nicht until he has aff his boots."

He lit his pipe, and walked through the little town at the hour when the cows, that had been milked for the evening, were released from their byres and driven back to their common pasture. The Free Church bell was ringing for the Thursday prayer-meeting. The shops were shuttered. An odour of burning oak from the bakehouse, commingled with the curious redolence from the hot oven-sole, impregnated the atmosphere until he got so far as the smithy, where a little earlier sheep's heads had apparently been singeing. From what had once been the U.P. chapel, and was now a hall for the Parish kirk, came the sound of choral voices.

Jimmy stood in front of the hall and listened. The combined Established and U.F. choirs were practising for the Ancient Shepherds' annual church parade, and at the moment singing Sullivan's " Carrow "—

<blockquote>
"My God, I thank Thee, who hast made
The earth so bright,
So full of splendour and of joy,
Beauty and light ;
So many glorious things are here,
Noble and right."
</blockquote>

Outside, on the pavement, he put in a restrained, but rich, resonant, and harmonious bass. A lifetime of encounter with bleak weather had not impaired his naturally mellifluent organ, and he counted no artistic joy so exquisite as the hearing of his own voice giving depth and body to the parts of a well-sung church tune. He knew all the words and harmonies of hundreds of hymns and Psalms ; they were ineradicable from his memory, which could never retain the words or air of a pantomine song for more than a week.

" That's Bob Fulton, my customer, puttin' them through their facin's for the Sabbath," reflected Mr Swan. " Good soprano, capital alto, bass no' sae bad, but tenor, as usual, no' worth a docken. Ye'll no' get a dacent tenor in Scotland out o' Gleska ; it must be something emolient and demulcent in Italian ice-cream."

A moment later, in a cessation of the singing, he put his head diffidently in at the hall door.

" Come awa' in, Mr Swan ! '' cheerfully invited the choir conductor. " We'll be nane the waur o' an extra bass.''

" Oh, ye are daein' splendid, Mr Fulton ! '' said Jimmy, joining the musicians, with many of whom he was well acquainted. " Good attack ; fine balance ; tempo tip-top ! Wi' an organ ye would just be as good as oor ain Cathedral.''

But to his vexation, the practice was at an end. And he had just administered a peppermint lozenge to himself before entering, to get the proper atmosphere, and tone up the larynx !

" Hang it a' ! '' he said, " the night's but young yet, and I was fair in the key for a spree o' Psalmondy.''

" The minister's for naething but the newer hymns on Sunday—except the Old Hundred to begin wi','' said Mr Fulton, and the commercial traveller made a grimace.

" New hymns ! '' said he. " New fiddlesticks ! He'll be takin' to Anthems next, and a solo soprano cocked up in the gallery cravin' the Wings o' a Dove wi' her mind on a new pair o' wings for her bonnet. There hasna been half a dozen new hymn tunes made in my time I would tolerate at my funeral ; there's only ' Peace, Perfect Peace ! ' ' St Margaret,' ' Lead, Kindly Light,' ' St Agnes,' ' Pax Dei,' and ' Carrow '—there's no' much more in their novelties to boast o'. I wouldna gie St George's, Edinburgh, for a' the rag-time stuff in Sankey.''

" Let us have a try at St George's,'' said the conductor ; " No. 141 in Carnie's Psalter—' Ye Gates Lift Up,' '' and the choir, to show Mr Swan the traveller what it was equal to, proceeded to sing with astonishing vigour and address. The summer shades in zephyrs and in hosiery ; new stripe and twill designs ; the Mona Lisa corset (specialty of C. & M.), the slump in Bulloch's order, and the rumour of sequestration for Macbain might never have been in the mind of Jimmy Swan ; he sang his bass like a soul transported high above the gross affairs of earth, and emulous of the cherubim. In the second part, where the voices of the males asked

Who of Glory, no other bass infused the phrase with so emotional a sense of wonder, inquiry, and reverence ; he might have been the warder Peter.

" Excellent ! " he exclaimed, when they were finished. " I liked particularly the lah-soh-fah-me o' the tenors ; it's the only bit we can aye depend on tenors gettin' a proper grip o', but a' your tenor, Mr Fulton, 's capital—what there is of it. If I might suggest another Psalm, it would be the Old 124th —' Now Israel may say and that truly.' "

And the Old 124th it was. The inspiring bass of the visitor was enjoyed as much by the choir as by himself, and when he took his upper B's with a clarity no less assured than the sonorousness of his lower G's, there was an ectasy in Jimmy's soul he would not barter for a fortune.

He got his choice of an hour of Psalmody—Selma and Kilmarnock, Coleshill and Torwood, and Dundee, " Oh, Send Thy Light Forth " and " By Babel's Streams " ; and Robin Brant, the joiner, leading bass, was put upon his metal. Himself a man in his prime, of six-feet-three, he was determined no grey-headed traveller from Glasgow, rather small in stature and slightly paunchy, should beat a voice that had been brought to its perfection by daily warblings, pitched in tone to the constant bizz of a circular saw. But Jimmy Swan was envious or emulous of no one, utterly delivered over to the art of harmony and the meaning of the lines. It would there and then have seemed but reasonable to him that the portion of the blest should be to sing eternal Psalms. The weariness of his journey was dispelled ; sharing a Psalm-book with another chorister, he rarely needed to glance upon its pages, he was doing what had been familiar and inspiring for him to do ever since the day the crackle left his adolescent voice, and he found he was a singer.

The rosy face was lit with animation ; the shrewd grey head just faintly moved in time to the wave of Fulton's pitchfork ; when at " Invocation " he said " my harp, my harp, my harp I will employ," there was an absolutely luscious " dying fall " in the opening notes for tenor and bass which gave the flexibility and colour of his voice magnificent exposition, and he knew it, for he glanced across at Fulton with the mute inquiry in his eye—" Did ye hear me that time ? "

" Ye're no' oot o' practice onyway, Mr Swan ! " said Fulton. " Where in a' the world do ye keep it up ? "

" Maistly on slow trains, when I ha'e a carriage to mysel'," said Jimmy. " Ye have no conception o' my compass on the N.B. Railway oot aboot Slamannan. But to tell the truth, I'm no' much use at solos ; I think I'm at my best when I swell the volume."

He went home to his inn with a pleasing sense of having spent a profitable evening. He had not only helped the harmony, but from a copious lore about psalm-tunes and their history he had entertained the choir to an instructive, though unpremeditated lecturette ; and pledged himself to Mr Fulton to give the same at greater length with the choir as illustrators at a public gathering when he next came round.

At the door of the George the innkeeper was standing speaking to Miss Bryce, the mantua-maker, one of Jimmy's customers.

" There you are, Mr Swan," he said, " I've been asking high and low for you ; I found you a pair of slippers."

" I've been employing my harp," said Mr Swan, serenely blissful, " and I've had a glorious night o't, Robert.

'So many glorious things are here,
Joyous and bright !'

Man ! it's a blessin' we're no' born dummies ! Good evening, Miss Bryce ; I'm just lookin' forward to seein' ye in the mornin'."

" I hear from Mrs Clark you're going to favour us some day with a lecture on Psalmody. I hope ye'll tell us some o' your funny stories!" said the mantua-maker, who had the greatest admiration for his gifts as a raconteur, and the traveller looked ruefully at his host.

"She's a worthy body, Robert, but she doesna understand the grandeur o' solemnity, and the joy o' sacred song —if ye happen to be bass," said Jimmy.

HIS "BÊTE NOIR"

ALWAYS, when Jimmy Swan is doing Birrelton, he puts off his visit to Joseph Jago's shop till the very last. The fact that there is a Joseph Jago mars, in some respects, the perfect bliss of his western journey, for of all his customers for a quarter of a century, Mr Jago is the only one to whose intelligence his peculiar humour has not penetrated. It is not because Mr Jago is old, for there are nonagenarians on the western journey who, for Jimmy Swan, are far more interesting than youngsters. Nor is it because Mr Jago is a dry old stick; Jimmy Swan makes a specialty of dry old sticks, and loves to hear them crackling when he puts, as it were, a match to them—the latest wheeze from the Merchants' Club, or a joke from "Punch," which does not circulate to any great extent in towns like Birrelton. To waste no unnecessary words on him, Mr Jago is old, and dull, and dismal, and deaf. Any one of these disabilities would seem a trifle to Jimmy Swan, but all of them combined in a single individual is more than even he can swallow.

Most distressing of all is Mr Jago's rooted conviction that C. & M.'s traveller is a wicked man of the world. He disapproves the knowing rake of Jimmy's business hat, his own idea of a tile being something much more solemn, straighter in its lines, and worn strictly perpendicular, only on Sundays and at funerals. Jimmy's patterned waistcoats, too, inspire distrust; for some unfathomable reason, fancy waistcoats are associated in Mr Jago's mind with horse-racing. And, finally, there is that unquenchable twinkle in Jimmy's eye. That twinkle, for Mr Jago, betokens many things—frivolity, foolish preoccupation with the things of time, theatres, public-houses, catch-the-ten, novelles, curling clubs, and Masons' meetings. When Jimmy Swan comes into Jago's shop, the owner always looks at him askance and troubled, feeling as he felt in 1876, when he was last away from Birrelton, and saw the frightful saturnalia of a Carters' Trip in Glasgow. It cannot be denied that Mr Swan is a first-rate traveller, and in that rôle indispensable to a country draper bound to keep abreast with the city's silly changes of fashions, but Mr Jago would have liked a man more grave ; he cannot rid himself of the belief that Jimmy laughs at him, and sometimes tries to pull his leg.

Jimmy, having swept up all the other soft-goods orders of the town, went into Joseph Jago's shop the other day with a stifled sigh, prepared for a depressing hour and the usual misunderstandings.

Old Jago gave him a flaccid hand as cold and unresponsive as a flounder, and groaned some unintelligible salutation with a hanging lip and a rheumy glance of disapproval on the tilted hat.

" I would have been round sooner, but I was having a bite at the inn," said Jimmy cheerfully.

" Better without it ! better without it ! " said old Jago, shaking his head. " It's a perfect ruination, morally and physically."

" Which do ye think the more deleterious ? " asked Jimmy smiling : " the tea or the ham and eggs ? "

" Oh, I thocht ye said drink," said Jago, taken aback.

" Not at all ! " said Jimmy. " Just a solemn, single-handed affair o' stoking boilers. That's no' cloves ye smell ; it's the camphor balls my wife persists in usin' to keep aff the moths. If you were a modern Gleska warehouse, Mr Jago, I wouldna need to go to the inn for tea ; I could have it in your room de luxe."

"My what ? " said Mr Jago, with a hand behind his ear.

"Room de luxe," said Jimmy patiently. "'De luxe' is French for a penny extra on the cup and a d'oyley naipken. All the big Gleska warehouses now, ye ken, have tea-rooms in them. The latest tip-top style o' decoration—Louis the Quatorze furniture and Adams friezes on the walls, Festoons. . . ."

"Balloons," said Mr Jago, with a crafty look of incredulity.

"Ay ! " said Jimmy, to save the time of explanation. "A band plays even-on behind a couple o' aspidestra palms, and ye can hear them quite plain daein' Maritana or the Count of Luxembourg quadrilles just the same as if it was in the West-End Park at the Exhibition."

"It's droll I never heard of it ! " said Mr Jago ironically.

"It's right, I'm tellin' ye," said Jimmy. "It's not only tea and buns they give ye ; if ye want a fish and chips or a luncheon *table d'hôte* at eighteenpence, it's there."

"I suppose ye'll have a place like that in C. & M.'s now ? " said Mr Jago, marvelling at the traveller's imagination.

"Not at all ! " said Jimmy. "We havena any o' these facilities in the wholesale houses, and we just step out and round the corner wi' a customer the way we did in '76 when ye were there."

"Ye're a terrible man, Mr Swan ! " said Mr Jago, shaking his head. "I think ye'll never be wise."

"I hope not," said Jimmy affably. "It doesna dae to be ower wise in this business."

Jimmy booked his orders as expeditiously as possible, but yearned to inform this obviously mistrustful mind of what it missed by vegetating in a shop in Birrelton. He got an unexpected opportunity. Old Jago turned again to the subject of Glasgow warehouse restaurants just to see how far the traveller's imagination would carry him.

"I suppose," said he, "they'll have the licence, Mr Swan ? Ye'll can get a dram ? "

"No fears o' ye ! " said Jimmy. "They havena got that

length yet. But there's no sayin'; they're aye gettin' on. Some o' them hae rooms where ye can get writin' and rest-rooms."

" What dae they charge for the best rooms ? " asked Mr Jago.

" There's no charge at all ; ye just go into them and sit down, and tak' your crochet wi' ye if ye like. There's naething more exhaustin' to the female frame than walkin' for hours up and down a warehouse looking for the hairpin department, or for some particular pattern o' taffeta not yet invented, worth a half a crown a yard but sold at eighteen-pence."

" Man, ye're a great wag, Mr Swan," said old Jago, with a cynical dry cough. " I wonder ye're no' frighted ! I suppose the customers 'll come sailin' in in their balloons ? "

" Balloons ? " said Jimmy, amazed to find Mr Jago attempting a joke.

" Yes, ye said there were balloons."

" I never mentioned such a thing, Mr Jago," said the traveller, and Mr Jago groaned in tribulation for this errant soul.

" Ye did, indeed ! " said he emphatically. " And may I ask if there's much advantage ta'en o' the fightin' rooms ? "

Mr Swan put off his hat and wiped his forehead. His customer was decidedly more distressing than usual.

" It's no' the National Sportin' Club I was talkin' about," he remarked, " nor the Suffrage Movement. I was speakin' o' Gleska warehouses, Mr Jago. There's nane o' them hae fightin' rooms that I ken o'. When I think o't, it's maybe an overlook."

" Do you know, Mr Swan, I canna believe a single word ye tell me ! " said the righteous draper, fixing a remonstrant gaze on the crimson dots on Jimmy's waistcoat. " Business is business, and it might occur to you that I'm no' so daft as to credit the shrewd drapery firms o' Gleska wi' fritterin' awa' their shop room, their time, tea, potato chips, and fancy luncheons, on customers comin' in aff the street for a bolt o' tape or a cut o' worsted. We're no' that far behind in Birrelton ; just last week there was a lassie frae a cocoa firm in England three days in the Store presenting cups of boilin' cocoa and Abernaithy biscuits to all and sundry. I'm perfectly certain it was for naething but the advertisement. But that's a very different thing from settin' up a restaurant and givin' awa' fish teas and fancy dinners and——"

" I didn't say you got the tea and the dinners for nothing," bawled Jimmy Swan.

" Ye needna speak so loud ; I'm no' so deaf as a' that," said Mr Jago. " And ye certainly declared there was no charge at all."

The traveller pocketed his order-book and packed his samples, incapable for a while of further disputation with this perverse and afflicted customer. But he was not done with him.

" It's a lang time since ye were in Gleska, Mr Jago," he remarked. " I'm no' surprised ye're dubious."

" I'm no' dubious at all ; I'm just astonished at ye, Mr Swan," said Jago.

Jimmy chuckled. " And yet," said he, " it's naething to what ye'll see in some o' the shops in London. There ye'll can play a game o' cairds or billiards while your wife's at the bargain counter fightin' for her life ; and the warehouse has a creche where the careful and devoted mother leaves her baby till she gets her pattern matched."

" Just that ! " said Mr Jago dryly. " Keep at it, Mr Swan, while you're warm. Do they haud your dog for ye ? "

" Upon my word they do ! " said Jimmy. " They'll keep your dog or stable your horse for ye, or garage your motor-car. They would do ony mortal thing to keep you on the spot ; I believe they would embalm ye if they thought your widow would come in at times to see ye."

" Oh, ye're an awfu' man ! " said Joseph Jago. " Do ye no' think, Mr Swan, ye've come to a time o' life when ye

should be settlin' doon to think soberly o' things ? It's no'
richt to be makin' a mock o' everything " ; and his voice
was full of a quaver of pious grief.

" Ach ! to the mischief ! " said the traveller in a discreet
undertone, as he tightened a strap on a sample case. " I
might as well try to talk to a skim-milk cheese ! "

FROM FORT-WILLIAM

WHEN Jimmy Swan is travelling in the North, sufficiently
remote from the Second City of the Empire to run any risk
of being taken immediately at his word, he proffers his
customers a Glasgow hospitality which would ruin C. & M.
if it were exercised at their expense. But C. & M. have
nothing to do with it ; the only person who has cause for
apprehension, if she knew the facts, is Mrs Swan. Her little
house in Ibrox couldn't hold a fiftieth part of the people
Jimmy invites to come and stay there. For the last week-
end on which there was an International Football Match at
Hampden, he had five-and-thirty customers urgently engaged
to come to Glasgow and sample the cosiest flat in Gower
Street. They were all to come from somewhere north of the
Caledonian Canal ; customers south of that got a genuine
Mazeppa cigar.

Nemesis waits on such commercial strategists. Jimmy
forgot, some weeks ago, that Fort-William is on the wrong
side of the Caledonian Canal, and instead of simply giving
Peter Macaskill a Mazeppa cigar, he invited him to come to
Glasgow soon and see the Kinemacolor pictures.

" I would like fine ! " said the draper eagerly, after hearing
all about them, and the Gower Street flat, and Bella's fairy
touch on pastry. " Would next week-end do ? "

" Capital ! " said Jimmy, beaming with delight, and
taking out his diary. " I see there's a fine train at ten
o'clock, and the fare's only 15s. 9d. return."

" Ay ; that's the fare for ordinar'," said Mr Macaskill ; " but there's a special week-end trip next Saturday at 9s. 6d. Depend on me bein' there."

" Good man ! " said Jimmy heartily. " If you don't come, I'll be awfully disappointed. Mind and bring a waterproof, and leave your presentation watch at hame."

A week later, at the breakfast table, he got a wire from his customer—" Arriving Queen Street 2.16." He scrutinised it through his spectacles with mock dismay.

" What's the matter, Jimmy ? " asked his wife anxiously. " Is Aunty Mary deid ? Or anything wrong wi' James ? "

" It's naething o' that sort at a'," he answered her. " It's the world that's gettin' ower wee. When I started on the road first, Fort-William was aboot the length o' Malta ; men were born, and grew up, and mairried, and were made deacons o' the kirk, and died in Fort-William withoot ever clappin' eyes on a railway train. Nooadays the great Scottish cigar belt is steadily pushin' north till a chap's hardly safe to hand oot onything but Mazeppas nearer hand than Ullapool and Lairg. The lang and the short o't is that Peter Macaskill's comin' this afternoon, and we'll have to put him up till Monday."

" Is he a good customer ? " asked Mrs Swan, no way perturbed.

" The best," said her husband.

" Then I'll have to ha'e a hen ! " said Mrs Swan emphatically, and Jimmy gently nipped her. In England, I believe, it takes the form of a caress.

Mr Macaskill came with a reassuring hand-bag little bigger than a gynæcologist's, and under Jimmy's guidance steadily worked his way through all the picture palaces within a radius of a mile from Sauchiehall Street. He had never seen the cinematograph before ; it fulfilled every demand of a truly artistic soul hitherto starved upon pictures in the " People's Journal " and monotonous scenic effects on Ben Nevis. The latest picture houses, where you could sit at a table earnestly drinking tea and eating penny sweet-cakes without the necessity for withdrawing your eyes for a single moment from the thrilling episodes of " The Bandit's Daughter," specially appealed to him ; he grudged every moment that they spent in the streets going from one show to another.

" He's like a new message-boy the first day in a sweetie shop," said Jimmy to his wife that night when their guest had gone to bed. " Another day o't would scunner him. I was never so tired mysel' o' cinemas in a' my days ; I've seen as mony 'o them, Bella, as'll dae me for a twelvemonth. I'll dream a' nicht o' horses gallopin' and tenements on fire. I almost wish the West Hielan' Railway wouldna pander to the rural districts wi' gi'en them week-end tickets at rideeculous rates ; the railway fares in Scotland's far too chape."

" Tuts ! he's a nice cheery chap, Mr Macaskill," said Mrs Swan. " I'm awfu' glad to see him," and Jimmy gently nipped her.

" So am I," said he. " The only thing to worry me would be that he might be a bother to yoursel'." And again he nipped her, this time on the ear.

On Sunday evening, still replete with hen, Mr Macaskill, whose salient characteristic was shrinking diffidence, became deeply and nervously engrossed in the contemplation of a penny time-table. Having cleared his throat noisily several times, he ventured the stammering remark that five in the morning was an early start.

" It depends on what ye're startin' for," said Mr Swan. " If ye're in a club, for instance, five o'clock in the mornin's no' a bit too early to go hame to supper."

" I was thinkin' o' the train to-morrow mornin' for Fort-William," said the guest, embarrassed. " It leaves Queen Street Station at ten minutes to six. I'm vexed to think o' puttin' ye up for such an hour, Mrs Swan."

" Hoots ! " said she, " there's surely a more wise-like train than that, Mr Macaskill ? "

T

" Unless ye think the polis have a clue to your identity,"
said Jimmy. " Is the afternoon train no' good enough ? "

" It would do me fine, but I'm an awful bother to ye,"
said Macaskill. " I'm takin' ye off your work."

" Not you ! " said Jimmy, with genuine warmth. " It's a
privilege. Stay till the 5.12 train in the afternoon, and see
some more o' the picture-houses ; there's dozens ye havena
seen yet. Ye'll can easy find them yoursel' if ye follow
the croods, and I'll meet ye at one o'clock for a bite o'
lunch."

So Macaskill spent the forenoon writing home to his wife
that he would be home to-morrow, and by four o'clock he
had covered several quite fresh picture-palaces and lunched
with Mr Swan. At five minutes past four he looked at his
watch, and stammered an allusion to the fact that there was
a place called Fort-William.

" There's no use o' ye goin' awa' there the day," said
Jimmy, politely. " The shop would be shut before ye got
hame, onyway ; wait till to-morrow and go back in style."

Mr Macaskill gulped an unuttered explanation that no
matter what day he went back he could not get from Glasgow
to Fort-William in time to find the shop open unless he
started at 5.50 in the morning, and that night Mrs Swan had
a splendid pie for supper.

" Ye're just a perfect wee wonder ! " said Jimmy, and he
nipped her.

On Tuesday, at breakfast, Mr Macaskill said, with something almost approaching firmness, that he must certainly
make tracks for home in the afternoon.

" Dear me ! " said Mrs Swan, " ye're surely awfu' tired o'
us goin' awa' already ! I'm sure to-morrow would be time
enough."

It shook him. He looked at the plump and rosy little
partner of James Swan the traveller ; marked the dimples
and the genial smile of her, and felt that nothing he could
do to please her must be left undone.

" Well," he said, " I maybe might could stay till to-morrow, but I must be there to open the shop on Wednesday mornin'.."

" Good man ! " said Jimmy Swan, effusively ; " I was just hopin' ye would change your mind. Man ! ye havena seen the half o' the picture-palaces ! "

Mr Macaskill wrote a letter home to say he was unfortunately detained till Wednesday, and with now unerring instinct for the real good stuff in Glasgow, found several picture-palaces on the south side of the river, where he spent the best part of the day, though by this time most of the films were become familiar.

He lost his way, and got back to Gower Street at night a little tired, but adamant in his determination to leave by the early morning train, if Mrs Swan would waken him at half-past four. That night there was for supper the finest brandered haddocks he had ever tasted.

" Look here, Bella ! " said Jimmy Swan, when the guest had gone to bed; "is this a domestic house or a sanatorium?"

" Don't be silly, Jimmy," said she. " I'm sure he's welcome ; and him a valuable customer o' yours."

" But, my goodness ! " said her husband, " if we keep him much langer awa' frae his shop he'll no' be a customer at all ! It'll no' be there ! Naething for me, after this, but the Mazeppa cigar, even, by heavens ! if it was in Thurso ! " But all the same he nipped her.

Of course, Mr Macaskill was not wakened in time for the early train ; it was impossible, with all that brandered haddock. Mr Macaskill manfully concealed his chagrin at breakfast-time. He stammered and stuttered, and agreed that, after all, the afternoon train would suit him better. There are only two trains in the day from Queen Street to Fort-William. He found he had overlooked some really creditable picture-palaces in the east end of the city, and renewed acquaintance with " The Bandit's Daughter."

That night, Mrs Swan had in a couple of friends who sang divinely, and some exquisite devilled kidneys. When their visitor talked of going on the morrow, she seemed to bridle up, and said she knew he was sorry he had come to Glasgow.

" Not at all ! " he eagerly declared. " I've had a tip-top time ! Ye've been awfu' good to me."

" Jimmy's oldest friend ! " she said (it wasn't, strictly speaking, true), " you'll vex me greatly if ye dinna bide till Friday."

" I should think so ! " said Jimmy.

So Mr Macaskill waited till Thursday, when Jimmy casually suggested Friday as a better day for setting out to Fort-William. Mrs Swan continued to have the most engaging suppers, and said that Friday was unlucky.

So Mr Macaskill did not leave till Saturday, having by that time discovered all the picture-palaces in the suburbs.

When Mr Macaskill got home to Fort-William after a week of absence, his wife was at the station in a condition of nervous prostration.

" What in all the world do ye mean by this carry on ? " she asked him, tearfully. " I was just makin' up my mind I was a widow woman. Just three clean collars and one pocket-naipken wi' ye, and ye stayed a whole week ! I'm black affronted ! "

" As sure as anything I couldna get away a minute sooner ! " said Macaskill, penitently. " Mr and Mrs Swan wouldna let me."

" Ye said ye would be back on Monday," said his wife. " And every day since then ye wrote me saying ye would be sure to be to-morrow."

" And every time I wrote I meant it," said Macaskill. " But ye don't understand the Swans, Margaret ; they're that hospitable ; every move I made to go, they raised some opposition. I believe they would keep me a' my days in Ibrox if I didna summon up my nerve at last, and pick up my bag and make a bolt for it."

" And what in the name o' Providence did ye find to do for a week in Gleska ? "

"Ye may well ask, Margaret!" said her contrite husband. "There's nothing yonder to be seen but picture-palaces. I went to them even on, day after day, and I can tell you I was sick o' them! I would sit in them for hours on end plottin' what way I could get away home from Gleska without hurtin' the feelin's o' Mr and Mrs Swan. Nothing could exceed their kindness, but they might have considered the possibility that I had my shop waitin' on me in Fort-William. I'm tellin' you, it's me that's the happy man to be home again, Margaret."

JIMMY'S SILVER WEDDING

"Do you know what Wednesday week is?" asked Mrs Swan, with a surprising attempt at archness for a woman who had brought up a fairly large family.

"Wednesday week's a lot o' things, Bella," said Jimmy, brushing his hair in a pensive humour induced by the reflection that it was not getting any thicker on the top. "It's the day I have to get up and work, for one thing. It's the day I'm nearly goin' to lose the train. It's the day C. & M.'s no' goin' to raise my salary. It's the day I'm no' goin' to get nearly as many orders as I think I deserve. It's the day I'm goin' to sell 1s. 4½d. Cotton Shantung at 1s., and muslin one-piece robes worth a guinea at 12s. 6d. It's the day I'm no' goin' to buy a motor-car or a steam yacht for ye. It's the day that's likely to be wet, for I'll be in Inverness. It's the day I'm goin' to wish to the Lord I had gone in for some other job than commercial travellin'. It's the day nobody's goin' to die and leave me anything. It's the day that's goin' to pass like any other day, and me a gey tired man at the end o't. Just the ordinary kind o' day, and when it's past it'll be bye!"

"Tuts!" said Mrs Swan, impatiently. "Do ye no' mind what happened five-and-twenty years ago come Wednesday week?"

Mr Swan put on his coat reflectively. "Five-and-twenty years ago? Let me see, now. Was that the day I was teetotal. Or was I hame at exactly the hour I said for my tea?"

"Never in your life," said Mrs Swan, with emphasis. "But the 13th o' July's an important date you might well keep mind o'. It's the day that we were married. It's our silver wedding."

Mr Swan gasped. "Silver weddin'!" he exclaimed. "Man, I'm astonished at ye, Bella! Ye're a' wrang wi' your calculations. It's no' a dozen years since we were married; I mind fine, for I was there!"

"And where did a' the weans come from, James Swan?" asked his wife.

"Oh, well! if you put it that way!" said Jimmy. "Well, say fifteen years."

"John's twenty-one, and if Annie had been spared she'd have been twenty-three on Saturday."

"Silver weddin'! my Jove, Bella, but that's a start! I aye thocht silver weddin's was for auld totterin' bodies wi' wan leg in the grave and the other on the road to the poorhouse. And look at us!" He surveyed himself in the looking-glass. "A fine, upstandin', fresh-complexioned, athletic young fellow, lacin' his ain boots every day he's awa' frae hame. And there's yoursel'—Bella Maclean or Swan; first in the Grand March, wearin' sky-blue dress with polka dots; the real and only belle of the ball; good for Wilton Drive! By jings, Bella, do ye mind the time I advertised ye? And there ye are yet, getting chubby a wee, but what an eye! and what a step runnin' up a stair! They're no' turnin' oot the same stuff nowadays at all. If only you could play the piano!"

Mr Swan did not go to Inverness on Wednesday week. Instead he took a silver wedding honeymoon holiday with his wife, and they went to Kirkfinn, chosen, first, because Mrs Swan had never been there; and, second, because there was never enough trade in the two or three drapers' shops of that sleepy village to tempt the commercial traveller to take his samples with him and combine sordid business with the poetic joys of a silver wedding celebration.

" Your cases 'll be in the van, Mr Swan ? " said Charlie, the Black Bull boots, at the station.

" Not this time, Cherlie," said Jimmy.   " Here's a bag ; that's all.   This is a special run ; I'm here with a sample wife—ah ! ye needna glower, ye rascal ; it's ma ain.   Ye'll no forget the extra pair o' boots in the mornin', and ye needna knock me up till nearly nine ; nae hurl to Kirk-michael for me to-morrow."

" And this is Kirkfinn," said Mrs Swan.   " It's no' that big, and still many a pair o' sox you lost in it."

" It's no' the size that coonts wi' toons on the northern circuit," said her husband, cheerfully ;   " it's the genial atmosphere, and there's whiles when Kirkfinn is awfu' hard on sox."

She was surprised that everybody seemed to know him as they went along the street.

" Of course they do ! " said he.   " What would hinder them?   I've been comin' here since the year o' the Tay Bridge storm, and they look on me as a kind o' institution like Ord-Pinder's Circus.   Ord-Pinder's clown and me's celebrities."

" It must be an awfu' dreich place in the winter," said Mrs Swan, though gratified by the public interest manifest in the lady accompanying a visitor who for more than a quarter of a century had seemed wedded only to a barrowload of sample-cases.

" Dreich ! " he exclaimed, derisively.   " Nae fears o't ! When things get slack they start a cookery-cless or a sale o' work for a new flag for the Rechabites.   There's nae dreich-ness about Kirkfinn, I'm tellin' ye ! "

" At any rate, it must be a healthy place ; everybody looks well up in years," said Mrs Swan.   " They'll no' take many troubles in a bracin' place like this."

"Troubles!" retorted Jimmy. "They take every trouble that's goin' except the tattie disease, and whiles I think they don't miss even that. But that's because they're in the Rechabite Tent, and get the benefit."

"If they're all in the Rechabites," said Mrs Swan, "it must be a very sober place."

"A Tent's no' a tenement hoose," said Jimmy; "it's easier to get oot and in to."

Though he protested business was the very last thing he would permit to intrude upon their honeymoon, their dinner at the Black Bull Inn was scarcely over when the habits of thirty years possessed him, and the first place he must take his wife was to one of his customers. They started out ostensibly to walk beside the river, but for half an hour they never got farther than Abraham Buntain's shop.

"Here I am again, Mr Buntain," said Jimmy, bursting in on the drapery counter. "You wouldna get the usual card notifyin' ye o' my comin', but it's all right. A special line in quiet grey summer-weight fancy tweeds, for immediate holiday wear," and he brought his wife forward with an arm about her waist.

"None of your nonsense, Jimmy," said Mrs Swan, blushing becomingly.

"If the wearer goes with the tweeds," said Abraham Buntain, gallantly, "you can put me down for an immediate delivery. Glad to see you in Kirkfinn, Mrs Swan. We all know Mr Swan in Kirkfinn, but it's the first time he has given us the chance to see who turns him out so creditably."

"Well, there she is," said Mr Swan in his professional manner. "Unique. Chaste pattern. None of your French models; British throughout. Durable. Unshrinkable— quite the contrary. A little dearer to begin with than flashier-looking stuff, but pays itself a thousandfold in the long run. The colours don't run."

"You're making them run pretty badly all the same," said Mrs Swan, with a smile, and blushing more than ever.

" I must say I like the style," said Mr Buntain, entering into the spirit of the thing.

" I should think you do ! " said Jimmy, buoyantly. " With any eyes in your head. It's a style that caught my fancy five-and-twenty years ago, and I've never tired of it. This season it's the tip-top of fashion—one of those Victorian revivals, you understand ; nothing like the old patterns ! Sometimes my eye's been caught—when I was younger, I mean—by a bit of Marquisite fancy voile or French foulard, but, bless your heart ! there's no wear in them, and no warmth. I don't conceal from you, Mr Buntain, that I consider mysel' pretty lucky."

Mr Buntain was prepared to make the silver wedding jaunt to Kirkfinn a satisfactory commercial proposition by giving a handsome order there and then for autumn lines, but Jimmy resolutely refused to book it now. " I'm not with C. & M. this week," he declared ; " I'm with Mrs Swan, and we're on our honeymoon—and oh, by the way, I want to buy her a costume-length of your homespun tweed." And he did it, too, at strictly local retail prices, refusing to avail himself of any trade discount.

" Before we go along the river, Bella," said Mr Swan, when they came out of Buntain's, " I want to run in and say how-d'ye-do to Miss Cleghorn. Here's her shop—a good old customer of mine."

" Good gracious ! " said Miss Cleghorn. " Your silver wedding ! I would never have thought it, Mr Swan, and I'm sure I wouldn't think it of you, Mrs Swan."

" She doesn't look a bit chafed, does she, Miss Cleghorn ? " asked Jimmy.

" She looks a good deal too good for you," replied the roguish shopkeeper.

" Don't spoil her by giving that away," said Jimmy. " It's the truth, but I've aye kept dark about it."

" Five-and-twenty years is a long time," pensively said Miss Cleghorn, who had lived that period at least in a state

T*

of virgin expectancy, and at times was apt to become impatient with the deliberation of the local matrimonial market.
" Did ye never tire of him ? "

" I tired of him the very first week I married him," laughed Mrs Swan, " and I think he tired of me in less."

" I did," said Jimmy, frankly. " And now I'm sure I wouldn't tire of her in fifty years. H'm ! Inscrutable are the ways o' nature ! I want to buy her one o' these Vienna sun-or-shower umbrellas we sent down to you last month, Miss Cleghorn."

" You're the happy pair ! " said Miss Cleghorn, when this second wedding gift had been presented. She, too, had an autumn order for C. & M. in readiness, but the traveller would have none of it this visit, saying he had not his order-book.

As they were leaving the shop she laughingly cried them back. " I wonder," said she, " if Mr Swan wouldn't book me an order for a husband ? "

" What kind ? " said Jimmy, whipping out the order-book whose possession he had just a moment before denied.

" Just one like yourself," replied Miss Cleghorn gaily, and still half meaning it. " I fancy I could not do better."

" Very good ! " said Jimmy, gravely, and he wrote down : " Husband ; middle-aged, but feeling fine ; not righteous overmuch, a fair to middling quality. Must sing bass, and be a good deal away from home."

" I'll get him for you ! " he declared as he pocketed the book.

A MATRIMONIAL ORDER

MISS CLEGHORN was a jocular body, or conscious that she had reached the desperate stage of spinsterdom, or was, more probably both, for a month having elapsed without James Swan implementing her order for a husband, she sent him a postcard with the expressive intimation, " Special order not yet invoiced." Jimmy took it home to his wife for her opinion as to whether his Kirkfinn correspondent was really in the market or only taking a rise out of him.

"I booked the order right enough," said he, "but I thought she was in fun."

"A maiden lady of Miss Cleghorn's age is never in fun about a thing like that, though she may think herself she is," said Mrs Swan. "Yon Kirkfinn's a very lonely place, nothing but the birds whistling, and even they get tired of it. You better hurry up and send the body what she wants before the season's over."

"It's no' in our line at all," said Jimmy; "she ought to apply to a Matrimonial Agency. They would send her down some samples or a likely fellow on appro."

"Ye were the sample yoursel', James," his wife retorted, "and she told ye she wanted something as near the pattern as possible."

"Bless your heart! I canna guarantee an absolute dupli-cate. There's no' mony o' my kind left, or we're aye picked up as soon as we're in the window. I have no idea where to look for the article she wants. All the bachelor chaps I ken are a bit shop-soiled and oot o' fashion."

"Ye were a bit shop-soiled yoursel', James Swan, when I got ye," said his wife. "But whit's a little Glasgow smoke? Ye were guaranteed to wash. Except that ye're a trifle frayed aboot the edges and wearin' thin on the top, ye're no discredit to your wife and family."

"She may be in fun," said Mr Swan, sitting down to tea, "but the honest truth is that Miss Cleghorn would be nane the waur o' a man. Yon shop o' hers would double its trade in a twelve-month if there was a man in it to give the genuine Gleska touch. Did ye ever see such windows? Tea-cosies and combinations, delaines and Turkey reds, sand-shoes and sun-bonnets; and every noo and then a bill to notify the public o' Kirkfinn that somebody's lost an umbrella. To the mischief wi' their lost umbrellas! It's no' her business

to be advertisin' for lost umbrellas ; let them come to her
and buy a new yin ! It's my opinion that when a case o'
goods from C. & M. comes to Miss Cleghorn she just coups
as much as she can o't into her windows, wi' her eyes shut,
and puts what's left in some cunning place below the counter
where she canna find it again.   The art o' shop-dressin', Bella,
is for men.   Miss Cleghorn, they tell me, is a tipper at
trimmin' hats, the thing she was brought up to, but she
has no more notion o' a well-trimmed shop than she has o'
operatic music."

" I saw that," said Mrs Swan.

" Then she wants nerve—— "

" Considering everything, I wouldn't say that was where
she was deficient," said Mrs Swan.

" I mean business nerve.   She's timid ; wi' the dozen
assorted type o' mind.   If I sent her a gross o' anything
—and she could easy sell it—she would take a fit.   So she
can never buy so cheap as Abraham Buntain can.   Her
selection is fair ridiculous ; if I didn't keep her right she
would still be tryin' to tempt Kirkfinn wi' tartan blouses
and silk mitts.   But where she fails most lamentably is in
credit to the wrong customers.   Any kind o' fairy story 'll
get roond Miss Cleghorn, and her ledger's mostly a' bad
debts.   ' Perhaps they havna got it, puir things ! ' she says.
Maybe no', but they've got her !   And still she makes no'
badly aff her business."

" Enough to keep a man ? " asked Mrs Swan.

" I'm tellin' ye the right sort o' man would double it.
What that shop wants is b-i-f-f—biff ! "

" What the shop seems to want, and what would suit Miss
Cleghorn otherwise, I think," said Mrs Swan, " is Will Allan
o' the Mantles."

Her husband stared at her with admiration.

" Ye're a most astonishin' woman, Bella ! " said he.   " I
never thought o' Allan, and he's the very man.   What made
ye think o' him ? "

" Oh, he comes from her quarter o' the country, and he's like hersel'—ye mind he had a disappointment in his youth."

" Had she ? " asked Mr Swan, amazed at his partner's knowledge.

" Of course she had ! " said Mrs Swan, emphatically. " Can ye think o' any other reason for a wyse-like woman like yon lookin' after a shop in Kirkfinn ? Forbye, she told me—when I met her on the Sunday."

That very night a letter from Mrs Swan was sent inviting Miss Cleghorn to spend some days with her in Glasgow.

Mr Swan took the earliest opportunity of having a little private conversation with Mr William Allan of the Mantle Department, and asked him casually to supper for the following Friday night. " I'll likely have one or two friends from the country," said he offhand. " There's one at least —a lady friend o' Bella's who hasna been in Gleska since the time the Haverley Minstrels were in Hengler's Circus."

" Lucky girl ! " said Mr Allan, cynically. " There's been nothing really doing in Glasgow since about that time. I mind of taking a lady friend to see the Haverleys." It seemed a pious and moving recollection.

" Was her name, by any chance, Dunlop ? " asked Mr Swan, with romantic interest.

" I don't know what it is now," said Mr Allan, pensively ; " but it was certainly not Dunlop at that time. Painful subject, Jimmy ; your wife knows all about it."

" She's gey close, the wife," said Mr Swan, craftily. " Any-way, this is a Miss Dunlop. Keeps a shop. No' far off fifty——"

" Prime o' life ! " muttered Will Allan of the Mantles, with sober conviction ; it was about his own age.

" ——Plump. Fair-complexioned. As cheery as another chap's weddin' ! It's a wonder to me, Will, that sort o' woman doesna marry, hersel'. Ye know Kirkfinn ? "

" Fine ! " said Mr Allan, emphatically. " I served my time there, but I haven't been near the place for twenty years. Painful subject, Jimmy ; your wife knows all about it."

" It's no great catch havin' a bit shop wi' a lot o' bad debts in Kirkfinn. It's the sort o' place where the most attractive kind of girl might sit on a sofa till it was a' sagged down waitin' for a lad to sit beside her, and die o' auld age before the springs recovered their elasticity. It's the sort of place where it's aye so long to the Cattle Show, or so long after it. When I'm in Kirkfinn, the Boots at the Inn has to pry open my door wi' an iron pinch to waken me— sound sleep's the one thing that Kirkfinn is famous for. That and hens ! Ye canna venture to walk through Kirkfinn without skliffin' your feet in case ye come on eggs."

" I aye liked poultry," confessed Mr William Allan. " And there's nothing wrong with Kirkfinn ; I sometimes wish I had never left it."

Miss Cleghorn promptly accepted the Glasgow invitation, with a quite unconvincing story of being seized for the first time in many years with a desire to see the autumn shows.

" Glad to say I've managed to fill that line for you," said Mr Swan, turning up his order-book. " ' Middle-aged, but feeling fine ; a fair to middling quality ; not righteous overmuch ; sings a kind of bass, and is a good deal away from home.' I can send it off to you at any time."

" None o' your nonsense, Jimmy ! " said his wife.

" I wouldn't insist on his being much away from home," said Miss Cleghorn, quite in the spirit of the thing. " You see it's pretty lonely in Kirkfinn. Is he on appro. ? "

" Not in these goods, Miss Cleghorn," said Mr Swan. " They get so easily chafed. And we don't keep a big stock. You see the whole demand nowadays is for thin fancy stuff that gratifies the eye for a season at the most, but has no wearin' quality, no body. But I'm no' askin' ye to buy a pig in a poke ; it's a Mr Johnson, and he's comin' here the night to supper."

Miss Cleghorn crimsoned. "Of course you understand I'm only joking, Mr Swan," she said, in nervous apprehension.

"So am I," said Mr Swan. "I'm the jokingest wee chap! Amn't I, Bella?"

When Mr and Mrs Swan retired to their bedroom that night, they sat down and laughed as heartily as consideration for the feelings of their guest next door would allow.

"My! didn't she get a start when she saw it was Will Allan?" said Mrs Swan.

"But did ye notice Will?" asked Jimmy, almost suffocated with suppressed amusement. "'I understood it was a Miss Dunlop,' says he, gaspin'. 'My mistake!' says I, 'the right name slipped my memory! Miss Cleghorn's up for autumn bargains; I had no idea that ye kent her.'"

"And they quarrelled twenty years ago!" said Mrs Swan, tremulous with the thought of the still romantic possibilities of life. "She told me all about it in Kirkfinn."

"Have ye any idea what about?" her husband asked.

"She told me," replied Mrs Swan in a paroxysm of restrained merriment. "You could never guess! It was because he would insist on partin' his hair in the middle! She considered it looked frivolous. And now—oh, Jimmy, I'm sore with laughing!—now he hasn't enough to part one way or another any more than yourself!"

"Tuts!" said Jimmy, rubbing his head. "A trifle like that! No wonder they made it up again so easily! I'm sort of vexed for C. & M.; they look like losin' a first-rate man in the Mantles."

A GREAT NIGHT

THERE are villages to which Jimmy Swan goes, burdened with all his sample-cases, as conscientiously as if he were visiting a metropolis, though it might appear that the profits on the orders he secures will hardly pay for the post-hiring. Among them is Birrelton, which is so unimportant that it isn't even given on the maps. When C. & M.'s ambassador of commerce puts his cases down in front of the only draper's shop in Birrelton, as he does twice a year, the whole vehicular traffic of the Main (and only) Street is diverted up the lane behind the smithy, and the populace realise that the long-familiar range of tweeds, prints, winceys, voils, and under-skirts in Dawson's window will be completely changed in a week or two in harmony with prevailing modes in Glasgow, London, Paris. Though their husbands don't suspect it, it is Jimmy Swan who dictates what the Birrelton women wear—at all events, the fabric and the pattern of it; Mr Dawson meekly leaves all the questions of æsthetics to the traveller, who postponed the era of crêpe de chine and ninon in Birrelton (it is said) for several years.

" About them foulards ? " Mr Dawson asks with diffidence, lest their suggestion might appear presumptuous.

" Foulards are no' use for Birrelton ; that's the stuff for you ! " says Jimmy ; and so it is.

Jimmy " takes in " Birrelton, not for any great profit in the place itself, but because it is on the road to several other important places. An hour of exposition and advice for Mr Dawson ; another hour to rest the horses and refresh himself, and Jimmy is on the road again, in the heavily-laden deep-sea wagonette himself and his cases call for.

Last week, however, a foundered horse broke down entirely under the stress of snowy weather, and the traveller found himself for the first time in his life compelled to stay a night in Birrelton. Its sleepiness lay heavy on his urban soul, and early in the afternoon he suggested to Mr Dawson that the village badly wanted cheering up in some way.

" It's aye a quiet time o' the year here," said Dawson apologetically. " And there's naething on till Friday week, when we hae a Parish Council meetin'."

" I'm no' goin' to wait for that," said Jimmy. " Could ye no' get up a concert in the aid o' something ? "

" A concert ! " exclaimed the draper. " There hasna been a concert here since Watty Sharp brought hame his gramophone."

" Has he got it yet ? " asked Jimmy. " We could hae a tip-top concert, wi' a gramophone for the nucleus."

As a result of active and immediate steps on the part of Mr Dawson and the traveller, the village bellman announced a Grand Concert in the Schoolroom at Eight o'clock that evening, James Swan, Esq., in the Chair. Collection in Silver in aid of Poor Coal Fund.

The school was crowded.

" Ladies and gentlemen," said the Chairman, standing up at a table furnished with a gramophone, a jug of water, and a tumbler, " the town of Birrelton has long been celebrated for its local talent in the music line. A bush is about the very worst place on earth you could keep a talent under ; the Bible says you should keep it on the house-tops. Look at Paderewski ! Look at Madame Melba ! But, passing on, I would ask your kind attention for a programme more than usually rich and varied in its items, a programme second to none, as I might say. Our object, I may say without the fear of contradiction, is a worthy one—to do a little for the Poor Coal Fund of Birrelton. The poor, as we know, we have always with us, and coals were never dearer. I will now ask Mr Duncan Tod to favour us with ' Scotland Yet ! ' "

The audience sat in petrified ecstasy while Mr Tod, the shoemaker, sang " Scotland Yet ! " in a high falsetto voice, impaired to a sad degree by difficulties of respiration and a nervousness which brought the perspiration to his brow, and compelled him constantly to dry the palms of his hands on a handkerchief whose more legitimate purpose was gently to wave in time with the refrain, in which the audience joined with the encouragement and example of Mr Swan. Mr Tod was apparently a sufferer from asthma ; at every bar there was a distinct interval in which, with pursed lips, he noisily recovered all his wind, which had apparently receded into the profoundest depths of his anatomy ; his efforts seemed to be attended with the utmost physical and mental agony.

" Thank heaven, that's bye ! " he audibly remarked when he was done, and resolutely refused to grant an encore, a desire for which is manifested by a Birrelton audience by whistling.

" We have a long programme," announced the Chairman, " and recalls must be strictly discouraged, but if time permits we may have a chance later on to hear Mr Tod, whose rendition of that fine old song shows us the stuff he is made of. Now we will be favoured by Mr George Steele of the Driepps —' Aft, aft hae I Pondered,' or ' Memories Dear.' "

Mr Steele, wearing an extraordinary suit of checks, which made him distinctly perceptible to the naked eye, dragged himself reluctantly to his feet at the very rear of the audience, came slowly forward, encouraged by exclamations of " Good old Geordie ! " by the younger members of the company ; cleared his throat loudly and carefully in a manner that almost amounted to ostentation ; fixed a baleful glance upon a high and distant corner of the room, and kept it immovably directed there while he sang—

" Aft, aft, as I ponder on the days o' my childhood,
    The days yince so happy—Oh come back again !
    When I pu'd the wild brambles that grew in the greenwood,
    And gied them awa' to my wee lovers then."

There were none of the studied and meretricious effects secured by so-called voice production in Mr Steele's performance ; his voice was the gift of nature, and suffused with such deep pathetic feeling that he wept himself to hear it. The tears, by the end of the second verse, were streaming down his cheeks ; in the middle of the third verse he broke down completely, overcome by his emotions, and abruptly sought his seat again with the remark, " As shair as daith, chaps, I canna come ' Memories Dear ' the nicht."

" Go on, Geordie ! " cried the audience, " ' The Auld Quarry Knowe.' "

In the circumstances the Chairman's veto on recalls was suspended while Mr Steele, bashfully coming forward again, attempted to repress emotions which did credit to his heart in singing the ditty mentioned.

But it was too much for him : he stopped at daffing wi' his Jessie on the Auld Quarry Knowe, and bolted ignominiously for the door.

" There's nothing like the old melodies," said the Chairman, ambiguously, " and I'm sure we all owe a deep debt of gratitude to Mr Steele. But, passing on, I have the pleasure to announce that the next item is of the comic gender—' Tobermory,' by Mr William Gilkison. I would respectfully ask for strict silence at the back while we are listening to our good friend Mr Gilkison."

Mr Gilkison, with a look of ineffable sadness on his face, came forward, assumed a large red-topped Tam o' Shanter, and stared fixedly at a young lady in front, who blushed violently as she rose and took her seat at the piano, which had not hitherto been called into use. There was no music.

" It goes something like this," whispered the vocalist, and he hummed a few bars in her ear.

" What key ? " she asked.

" Any key ye like," said he agreeably, " but I prefer the black yins."

After a few false starts, due to an absence of agreement between the singer and the accompanist, Mr Gilkison got fairly embarked on " Tobermory," and the youthful males of the audience signified their high appreciation of its quality by beating time on the floor with their feet and joining in the chorus.

Not even James Swan, Esq. could oppose successfully the

vociferous demand for an encore, and Mr Gilkison, with modest diffidence, not too well assumed, stood where he was at the side of the piano and plunged into " That's the reason why I wear the Kilt."

" I rise to a pint of order," said an excited little gentleman at the end of the first verse, and the audience cheered.

" What is your point of order, sir ? " asked Mr Swan, in the manner, self-possessed and firm, of the best Town Councils.

" Mr Gilkison's singin' a couple o' sangs I hae among the records for my grammyphone," said the interrupter. " Far better than he can dae them. By the man himsel'—Harry Lauder."

" I am sure," said the Chairman suavely, " that the audience will be only too delighted to have an opportunity of judging whether Mr Gilkison or Mr Harry Lauder is the best exponent, as I might venture to say, of the songs in question. It will be an added pleasure, Mr Sharp, to hear the songs twice, once by the ' vox humana,' and once by— by the gramophone."

But Mr Sharp, considerably incensed that his repertoire should have been forestalled, withdrew from the room in dudgeon, fortunately, as it seemed, forgetting to take his gramophone with him, and Mr Gilkison was permitted to finish his song without any further interruption.

" We now pass on with the programme," said the Chairman, " and as a change we will have the well-known song, ' Imitations,' by Mr Peter Gourlay."

The audience laughed.

" Not a song ! " whispered Mr Dawson, sitting beside the Chairman. " Imitations. Ventriloquial. Saws wud."

" I beg your pardon, ladies and gentlemen," said Mr Swan. " I find our friend Mr Gourlay's item is ventriloquial. Mr Gourlay will give imitations."

The artist came forward, singularly burdened with a draught-screen which he placed beside the table. Having secreted himself behind the screen, he produced sounds which were unmistakably suggestive of somebody sawing wood. From the same seclusion there followed what was understood to be an imitation of a joiner planing, and the audience cheered.

Mr Gourlay followed with an imitation, frankly in the open, without the aid of any draught-screen, of an infuriated wasp. He chased it over the table, up the wall, and round the back of his neck, and finally suggested its destruction by an abruptly terminated buzzing.

" I have heard all the best ventriloquial entertainers of the day," said Mr Swan, " but none of them had what I might boldly venture to call the realism of Mr Gourlay's great sawing and bumbee act. We will now pass on to the gramophone, the next item on our programme. Mr Sharp has unfortunately been called away by pressing engagements elsewhere, but perhaps there is some one present who understands the mechanism. It will form the second and concluding part of our evening's entertainment."

" Bob Crawford ! Bob Crawford ! " shouted the youths behind, and the young man alluded to, stuffing his cap in his trousers pocket, lurched diffidently forward, apparently with the reputation of being a skilled executant.

He selected a record, wound up the clockwork, looked anxiously about the table, and said, " Pins."

" Anything missing ? " asked the Chairman.

" Pins," said Mr Crawford. " Ye canna play a grammyphone without the pins, and I think that Sharp's awa' wi' them."

It proved to be the case ; the irate Sharp had successfully prevented any chance of Harry Lauder being placed in competition with Mr Gilkison, and, as nobody else would sing, the concert terminated with a speech, in which the Chairman said that the evening's entertainment had been of the most delightful character, far transcending the best that he had expected.

" Did ye hear what the collection in silver cam' to ? " he asked Mr Dawson, as they wandered up to the little inn.

" Eight-and-six," said Mr Dawson. " No' sae bad for Birrelton ! "

" Five shillin's for me, and the balance for the population," said Jimmy. " They have a better estimate o' whit a Birrelton concert's worth than me."

RANKINE'S ROOKERY

THE train for Fort-William stopped for a reputed five minutes at Crianlarich, and Jimmy Swan dropped off with another Knight of the Road for some refreshment. They entered a place in the station where the same was indicated, and found themselves before a counter covered with teacups and bell-shaped glasses, under which the management seemed to be experimenting in the intensive culture of the common Alpine or Edible Sandwich.

" They're thrivin' fine ! " said Jimmy, peering through the " cloches." " Put them out in a bed wi' a nice warm southern exposure as soon as the rain comes on, and they'll take a prize at the autumn show."

" Tea ? " said the lady behind the bar, already with a cup below the tap of a steaming urn.

" No tea," said Jimmy firmly ; " I had a cup on Sunday, and it doesn't do to make it into a habit. Say two bottles of lager beer, and—and a bunch of sandwiches."

" Licensed drinks in the refreshment room farther along the platform," said the lady, turning to another customer, and Jimmy and Mr Dawson went to the other refreshment room with great celerity, as there was no time to lose.

" Lovely weather," said Jimmy to the lady-attendant there. " Two lagers and a brace of sandwiches."

" We have no eatables here," said the lady, preparing to

pull the corks. " You'll get sandwiches at the other refreshment room farther along the platform."

" Great Scot ! " said Jimmy, " could you not combine both shops and have one regular Refreshment Room, the same as they have on the Continent ? It might be wicked, but it would be handy."

" This is not the Continent ; it is Crianlarich," said the lady tartly, and Jimmy smiled.

" I knew there must be something to account for it," said he. " Drink up, Dawson ; there's the whistle ! After all, there's nothing worse than the eating habit. That's one up in temperance reform for Crianlarich."

Back in the compartment, Mr Dawson, who has been gloomily reading a newspaper all the way from Queen Street, descanted upon this idiocy of the refreshment department at Crianlarich as one more proof that Great Britain, so-called, was precipitously going to the dogs. He represented a modest brand of East Coast whisky (patent still), which percolated through the country quite incognito as Genuine Old Matured, and which he said himself, in strict confidence to friends, was so young and robust it couldn't be put up in bottles without cracking them.

"No wonder there's all this labour unrest," he said; "every other day there's some new Act of Parliament that gets you on the neck. It's coming to 't when you can't get a bun or a biscuit at a station bar unless you take a cup o' tea to it," a manner of stating the case not strictly fair to Crainlarich.

" Keep it up ! " said a stranger, who had joined the train at Gairlochhead. " Blame Lloyd George ! "

Mr Dawson cordially accepted the invitation, and said things about Mr Lloyd George which it would greatly vex that statesman's wife to hear.

It then transpired that the stranger was a Comrade, who had his own views about the social and industrial chaos in the country, and a firm conviction that the most urgent reform demanded was the abolition of all landlords.

"Hear! hear!" said Jimmy Swan, and the Comrade beamed fraternally on him.

"Look at the land round here," the Comrade added with a sweep of the hand that comprehended the Moor of Rannoch, through which the train was now proceeding. "Nothing but deer! Nationalise it, and you'll see a healthy, prosperous, and contented population pouring back from the cities."

"I suppose you will," said Mr Swan agreeably. "When they start pouring they'll be well advised to bring waterproof top-boots with them and a good supply o' tinned meat, for the Moor o' Rannoch's not exactly the Carse o' Gowrie. I doubt they'll no' pour much at first unless they're dragged wi' ropes."

"I thocht you were a Land Nationalist," said the Comrade.

"So I am," said Jimmy. "I'm tired o' bein' a landlord."

"I didn't know you were a landed gentleman, Mr Swan," said Dawson in surprise. "All I have myself, in that line, is a couple o' flower-pots and a lair in Sighthill Cemetery."

"I'm one of the bloated miscreants," said Jimmy. "I've been one for nearly fifteen years, but lyin' low in case I would be suspected. You don't catch me goin' round wi' a nickerbocker suit and a couple o' retriever dugs. Forbye, it's no exactly land I'm laird o'; it's stone and lime; at least it was stone and lime when I saw 't the last time. If all the landlords were like me, the steamers bound for Canada would be crooded wi' them—third-class, and their beards shaved off for a disguise. . . . Do ye ken Dundee?" he asked the Comrade.

"I've been there," said the Comrade, with the air of one who could say more, but refrained from motives of politeness. "I was there last autumn."

"You're a lucky man," said Jimmy. "I had to cut Dundee out o' my circuit more than a dozen years ago, and hand it over to my fellow-traveller, Maclintock. And Dundee was a place where I aye did splendid business.

"Fifteen years ago," proceeded Jimmy, "I had no more

politics than a cow; at least if I had, my customers never discovered them."

"Sat on the fence?" suggested the Comrade nastily.

"Just that!" said Mr Swan. "There was so much glaur on both sides o' the fence I couldna' venture down withoot dirtyin' my boots. But I really didna give a rap for politics; I never could bring to them that personal animosity which political enthusiasm seems to demand. When it came to the elementals, I found that folk were much alike, whether Whig or Tory. But the Will o' an Uncle I had in Montrose, ca'd Geordie Rankine, that I hadna seen since I was a boy, put an end to this blissful frame of mind; he left me a land o' hooses in Dundee, and I found I was a red-hot Tory.

"The day I got the lawyer's letter and a copy o' the Will, I gave a dozen chaps in the warehouse a slap-up supper round in the Royal Restaurant, and I tell you the Landed Interests got their hair damped that nicht. There wasna a sealskin jaiket in the wareroom too good for Bella; and I bought mysel' a meerschaum pipe wi' a shammy-leather waistcoat on 't to keep it from bein' scratched. Next mornin' I was up wi' the very first train, that landed in Dundee before the milk, and I got a night-polisman to show me my estate. It was the best-known property in Dundee, as famous as the Tay Bridge, the Baxter Park, or the Bunnet Law, he said, and I saw what he meant when he took me to the most dilapidated tenement in one o' the most appallin' slums I ever set eyes on.

"'Do folk pay rent to get livin' in a place like that?' says I, dumbfoundered at the look o' my bonny property.

"'No fears o' them!' says he. 'It taks' the puir sowls a' their time to pay their fines on a Monday mornin' at the police-coort. The Corporation condemned the place to be demolished a couple o' years ago, and jist when they were gaun to dae 't themsel's at the landlord's cost he went awa' and died on them!'

"'And wha's the landlord noo?' I asked.

"'Some chap in Gleska,' says the polisman; 'I'll bet ye they'll nick him fast enough.'

"'Will they, faith?' says I to mysel', and I made tracks for the 7.49 a.m. for Gleska, wi' my collar turned up in case I might be identified afore I got to the station.

"When I got hame, the first thing my wife asked was if I had brought a picture postcard o' the property. I broke the news to her as gently as I could, and sent word to the lawyer in Dundee to sell the place for onything it would bring. He wrote me back that I might as well try to sell the Scourin'-burn for a mineral water works. My Uncle Geordie had given up all hope o' sellin' the place in the early 'Seventies. A man that lived in the tenement was factor for the property, and for his trouble was supposed to sit rent free, but he considered he ought to get something extra, him bein' factor, seein' nane o' the tenants ever could be got to pay a penny, and in that way were as well aff as himsel', withoot haein' his responsibility.

"I wrote to the lawyer, then, that I refused to accept the property; he could give it awa' for naething if he liked. He replied that the property was mine by the law o' Scotland, whether I wanted it or no', and that naebody would tak' it in a gift. He also sent a bill o' charges and another for rates and taxes.

"I paid them, and then he wrote that the tenement must be demolished by the Corporation's orders, at a cost which he put at £150. I never answered him, and he wrote once or twice a week till I had to flit, leavin' no address. I tell you I was gey annoyed at my Uncle Geordie.

"For five years I heard no more about my property except when I was in Dundee on business, and then it seemed to be growin' more notorious every month. Luckily it was Uncle Geordie's name that stuck to it, and 'Rankine's Rookery' was never, by any chance, associated wi' the traveller for C. & M. I used to go round and look at it; it was getting mair and mair disgraceful every time, and

every now and then the subject o' ' Rankine's Rookery '
would be up before the Council. It seemed there was some
legal difficulty about haulin' it down without due notification
to the owner, and the owner wasna to be found.

" ' Who is he ? ' the Labour gang would ask, indignantly,
and the Toon Clerk would reply that he was a man in Gleska,
but exactly whereaboots was undiscoverable.

" Then the Labour chaps would harangue aboot the
scoundrel battenin' on the rents o' the miserable wretches
livin' in his property, nae doot knockin' about in his motor-
caur and smokin' ninepenny cigars. Me ! I never battened
on as much as a penny bap aff the property, and the only
motor-caurs I travel in belang to the Gleska Corporation.

" The agitation aboot my tenement got so furious at last,
a dozen years ago, that I got frichtened, and since then I've
never gane near Dundee, in case I would be arrested. And
that's the way I'm for nationalisin' property, and daein'
awa' wi' landlords. Whether my property's standin' yet
or no' I never venture to inquire ; to indulge my curiosity
on that score might cost me far mair than I bargained for."

" That all bears out my argument," said the Comrade.
" The land must be for the people ! "

DIGNITY

" THE selling o' soap, butter, music, poetry, pictures, or
soft goods, is just as great an art as making them," said Mr
Swan, chipping the top off his second egg. " I was years
ago in a factory where they made Balmoral bunnets. They
had a big machine that just fair squirted oot Balmoral
bunnets ; the yarn went in at the one end by the ton, and
the bunnets poured out at the other, a' complete, even to the
toorie. I was spellbound lookin' at the thing, and the man
that had the factory says to me, ' That's a great machine,
Mr Swan. I see ye're lost in admiration.' ' That's just

what I am!' says I; 'but it's no' at the machine; I think
far more o' the men who can keep up wi 't at the sellin'.
Noo that keps are comin' in, it takes me a' my time to sell
a dozen bunnets in a year.'"

"That's quite true," said a man on the road for jams and
sweetmeats. "Every year commercial travelling grows
harder. I sometimes think the men that have to sell soor
draps and kali sookers after we're away 'll need to have a
college education."

Dunbar & Baxter's new young man, on his first journey,
stirred his coffee, and listened with great respect—indeed
with veneration—to these veterans of the road. What
roused this feeling in him was the thought that they should
have kept their jobs so long; his own beginning was so un-
propitious. Yesterday had been a rotten day, and he had
said to himself, "Another week like this, and it's back wi'
you to the counter, Willy!" It was not a pleasant feeling
for a chap who was doing his best. It was all the more
unpleasant because there were features of his new job that
greatly pleased him—the sense of freedom, space, and personal responsibility, so different from being in the shop;
the travelling by trains and steamers; the sight of new
places, the living in hotels—particularly the living in hotels.
To a young fellow who at home in Glasgow lodged in
Raeberry Street, and had no interest in any food he got
except the midday meal picked up at a restaurant, this
living in hotels was thoroughly and completely quite all
right. Deferential Boots and waiters; fish, ham-and-eggs,
and kidneys for one's breakfast (all together, mind you,
and no stinting!); a regular banquet called a lunch, and a
high tea quite as lavish as the breakfast! It would be a
deuce of a dunt to tumble back from these high altitudes
of luxury to the hopeless and prosaic levels of Raeberry
Street!

He nervously crumbled a breakfast roll and cleared his
throat, and meekly put a question.

" What would you say was the secret of success in our business, Mr Swan ? "

Jimmy flushed. He could have laughed, but remembered that he had one time been young on the road himself and full of strange illusions, and being a gentleman he made his best pretence at answering a question to which in the nature of things there is no answer.

" The secret of success, Mr Spens," said he, " is to be born lucky."

" But you need more than luck," said the jam man hurriedly. " You need brains, and pluck, and foresight, and habits of industry, and——"

"—And what's all that but bein' born lucky ? " broke in Jimmy. " There's many a one gets on dashed well without them, too ; but that's another kind o' luck."

" I'm not sure that I have either kind," said Spens, " but I'll guarantee I do my best to sell Dunbar & Baxter's flour, and I'm finding it a gey dreich business. I begin to think that I'm a failure."

Jimmy puckered up his face, so red and weathered, like a winter apple ; looked across the table at the lad with a twitching of his bushy eyebrows, and liked him for his unaffected innocence.

" Ye're all right, Mr Spens ! " said he with peculiar gentleness. " The worst ill-luck I ken is to be born self-satisfied, and that's been spared ye."

" The great thing," said the jam man, " is dignity. Aye stand on your dignity, and make the customer respect you."

This time Jimmy laughed without compunction. " Man, Simpson," said he, " I'm astonished at ye. If ye had to depend upon your dignity ye wouldna sell a sweetie. Do you ken the way Scotch travellers are the best in the world ? It's because they have nae dignity. A man wi' a sense o' dignity is like a man wi' a broken gallus ; he's aye feared something's goin' to slip. The thing is to have your galluses right, and then ye needna fash about your dignity. I'll tell

you and Mr Spens a story. I used one time to think dignity
was a great thing too ; that it was a thing ye wore like
a white waistcoat, and that the customer liked it. My
George ! I had as much dignity in these days as would do
for half a dozen o' statesmen or a couple o' point polismen.
When I started with C. & M. I scared away half my customers
by wearing my dignity like an ice-bag on my chest, and
talking London English. But I got a lesson, and the only
virtue ever I had in this life was that I never needed to get
the same lesson twice. For five years I was travelling every
season to Auchentee, a place whose only interest for me was
that it had three drapers' shops in 't. The drapers were all
MacLellans ; they were all related ; they were a' in the
same wee street. Auchentee's eight miles from the nearest
railway station. For five years I drove up to Auchentee
in a tip-top wagonette wi' my cases, and my hat cocked to
the side the same as I was the Duke o' Sutherland. I
lavished a' my art on the MacLellans : I choked the syvor
in front o' their shops wi' my cases ; I flourished sixpenny
cigars, and talked through the top o' my head like a man
from Sheffield.

" But there was naething doin' ! I never booked an order !
They were gettin' their stuff from Edinburgh ; they had aye
got their stuff from Edinburgh, and a' they kent aboot
Gleska was that it was on the maps. Three auld snuffy
deevils, I mind, they were—the MacLellans ; and when I
offered them bargains I would lose money on, they just
took another pinch o' snuff and said they couldna think
to change their house.

" One day I landed at the station, took my dinner at the
inn, and ordered the wagonette for Auchentee. It was
goin' to be my final visit ; if the MacLellans failed me this
time, they could go to bleezes. There was nae wagonette ;
it was awa' at a roup, and the only thing left on wheels was
a cairt. I said to mysel', ' There's no' much daein' wi'
dignity in Auchentee,' and I took the cairt. It was an awfu'

day o' wind and rain, and I had a fine silk hat, a cashmere mornin' coat, and a blue-sprigged waistcoat on. There I was, sittin' in the cairt wi' my cases piled behind me, far mair like an undertaker than a traveller for C. & M., and I tell you it was rainin'! When I landed in the main street o' Auchentee, I created a sensation. My hat was into pulp; I was drookit to the skin; a' the dignity I had could be spread oot on a threepenny bit, and ye would see the printin' through it.

"The whole toon gathered oot, and laughed; I was the bonny spectacle, cocked up there on MacGillvray's cairt, and naebody laughed looder nor the MacLellans. It was the first time they had ever seen I was a human bein', subject to the immutable laws o' nature. Now, folk that get a hearty laugh at ye aye feel kindly to ye after. One o' the MacLellans took me in and dried my clothes; another o' them gave me my tea; the third one put me up for the night, for the inn of Auchentee was full o' county gentlemen. And, what's mair, I got a slashin' big order from a' the three. The moral is that dignity's no' worth a dump in travellin'."

Ten minutes later Jimmy was smoking in the hall with Simpson.

"That's a great lesson!" said Simpson seriously.

"Ay, it's a great lesson right enough," said Jimmy, cleaning out his pipe. "It's a good enough lesson for a young man startin', just to put him on the right lines, but it wouldna be ony use to you. Ye see, I didna finish the story for Spens; I didna want to spoil it."

"What way spoil it?" asked Simpson.

"Well, you see, the three MacLellans a' worked in one another's hands; they a' went into bankruptcy three months efter that, and a' we got o' their accounts was ninepence in the pound!"

UNIVERSAL PROVIDER

THERE are small paraffin-oil-lamp towns in many parts of the country for which Mr Swan is Fairy Godfather, Perpetual Grand Plenipotentiary, and Deputy Providence. Half of his time in Glasgow is taken up with the execution of countless petty commissions for his rural customers and their friends, the selection and purchase of goods quite out of his own drapery line. I met him recently in a music-warehouse critically inspecting pianos on which he gave a masterly one-finger exposition of " We're a' noddin'." " For a customer of mine in Aviemore," he told me. " He wants a genuine £16 extra-grand, high-strung, Chubb-check-action walnut one with the right kind of candlesticks on it. I think this is about the article for Aviemore "—and he indicated one with gorgeous candlesticks and a singularly robust tone.

" Why don't they come and buy their own pianos ? " I asked innocently.

" They think they would be swindled," said Jimmy, " and I daresay they're right. Besides, they don't know a thing about pianos, and they know that I've bought hundreds of pianos in the past five-and-twenty years. I never bought one for a customer yet that failed to give satisfaction. It's all in the touch "—he touched a sprightly bar of " We're a' noddin' "—" and I could tell the right touch with my eyes shut."

" You must get some odd country commissions," I said, as we left the warehouse together when the transaction was completed. " I shouldn't care, myself, to buy pianos for other people."

" In my line," said Mr Swan, " I can't afford to be particular. I don't make a penny off the job directly, but it helps to keep a good customer on the books of C. & M. A piano's a simple matter ; I once had to buy a brass band for Larbert, and a dashed good brass band, too ; you never heard a

louder ! A customer of mine was chairman of the committee, and he said he couldn't trust another man in Glasgow
but myself to get the proper instruments. I got the dandiest
set you ever set eyes on, and seven-and-a-half off for cash,
that bought a tip-top banner, and they never expected the
money they had would run to a banner."

It is impossible to enumerate the variety and extent of
Mr Swan's private commissions for his country customers,
who haven't the time to come to Glasgow or sufficient confidence in their own judgment to buy either a piano or a
presentation silver albert and appendage for a young friend
going away to Canada. He has taken the blushing orders of
innumerable lads who felt the time had come for shaving,
but were coy about purchasing their first razor in a local
shop. There is no better judge of an engagement-ring in
Scotland ; and there is a piece of cardboard with a hole in
it in his waistcoat pocket almost every time he returns to
town from Perthshire. His knowledge of the cradle and
perambulator trade is copious, and more than once he has
executed telegraphic orders for a superior kind of oak coffin
unprocurable in Mull.

" I never made a mistake but once in my life," he says,
" and it cost me one of my very best Kirkcudbright customers.
She was a widow woman getting up in years, and she had
been reading somewhere or other that Society ladies kept
their fine complexions by putting on cosmetics. One day
after giving me a thumping good order for autumn goods,
she took me into the back of the shop and slipped five
shillings in my hand. ' I want you to send me that amount
of good cosmetic, Mr Swan,' she whispered. ' It's for—it's
for a friend.' ' Right you are, Mrs Lamont,' says I, and
made a note of it. The only place I ever saw cosmetic was
in a barber's shop, so I went to one in Gordon Street and
bought five shillings' worth, and sent it off to Mrs Lamont.
She would never look at me again ! You see it was what they
call Hong Grease cosmetic for sticking out the moustache,

U

and she distinctly had one. The best of it is that, so far as I can find out, there's not any other kind of cosmetic sold in the whole of Glasgow than the grease of the foresaid Hong."

The confidence of the agricultural districts in Mr Swan's good taste and commercial acumen is no greater than their faith in his ability to do any mortal thing for them that demands a knowledge of the world, and influence. When the drapers of the Western Journey want to start a son on a career in Glasgow, it is to Mr Swan they instinctively appeal for the requisite advice and aid. No boy is too hopelessly useless for Jimmy to find a job for in the city; the last decennial increase in our population is mainly made up of immigrants to whom he is credited with giving their urban start in life.

" Send him up to me," says Jimmy airily, " and I'll bet you I'll push him on to somebody."

The method of procedure in these cases is simplicity itself. " I take the young chap out to stay with me for a week," he told me ; " get his hair cut to begin with, and another kind of cap for him. Then I take him out and start him at one end of West George Street after breakfast and tell him to make his way to the other end, going up every stair *en route* and asking a job at every office till he gets one. He generally gets a job before the third day, just because he is a country-bred boy with a fine red face. Glasgow business men like to have an innocent country boy about the office ; it makes them think of what they might, themselves, have been. And the best way to start a boy in life in Glasgow is to let him understand that starting, like staying, all depends upon himself."

The fact that Mr Swan has often bazaar tickets and invitations to artists' exhibitions for disposal gratis to customers in from the country creates the impression that he can get a friend in anywhere, at any time, for nothing. He has rarely encouraged this flattering allusion at the cost of a pair of stall tickets for the pantomime, but no customer or customer's friend has ever failed to get a ticket for a football match, for Mr Swan has apparently the mysterious power of tapping inexhaustible supplies of free tickets for football matches.

"But the nerve of some folk is unbelievable," he told me. "Not long ago a customer from the North wrote asking me to get him a pass by the Caledonian Railway to London."

"Did you manage it ? " I asked.

"No," he answered, " I'm not exactly God. The best I could do for him was to give him an introduction to the guard and a list of places that he mustn't miss going to see in the Metropolis, so-called. I carefully explained to him that all the usual privileges in the way of free passes were suspended on account of the coal strike, so my reputation as The Universal Provider-to-the-North-for-nought is not in the least impaired."

Another customer of Mr Swan's found the air of Glasgow so exhilarating as compared with that of Dingwall that he spent an evening in a police cell, and had to send for C. & M.'s traveller to bail him out on the following morning. His peculiar dread was that the newspapers of the city would give a copious and sensational account of the unfortunate affair, which would be copied into the " Northern Star," and spoil the sober reputation of a lifetime. Mr Swan did not tell him that trivial indiscretions of this sort were never recorded in Glasgow newspapers.

"I'll fix it all right ! " he said. " You can depend on me. I have only got to pass the word along to the editors that you're a friend of mine, and the thing is done."

There is a draper now in Dingwall who is convinced that Mr James Swan has the British press in his pocket.

But the oddest commission Mr Swan ever got was to supply the parish of Birrelton with a minister. It would have staggered any other man, but Mr Swan set about its

execution with as much cheerfulness as if he had been asked
to send on a mouth harmonium.

Birrelton had spent some months of Sundays listening to
candidates for the vacant charge. Every one was better
than the other, and it was plainly impossible to get the congregation into a definite attitude of mind which would give
the pulpit to any particular one. After many squabbling
meetings the leading draper, who was ruling elder, said he
saw no hope of their ever agreeing upon a minister, and
proposed that Patronage should be re-established to the
extent of asking the traveller for C. & M. to pick a suitable
clergyman in Glasgow.

" So I got the job," said Mr Swan. " It took me a couple
of weeks. I knew exactly the kind of chap they would need
in Birrelton—not too fancy, you understand, for fear some
other kirk would grab at him before the Birrelton ladies'
presentation Geneva gown was right out of the tissue paper,
and still, on the other hand, not one so dull that he would
be likely to be left on their hands till he died at the age of
ninety. The minister they aye want in places like Birrelton
is a combination of the Apostle Paul, General Roberts, and
the cinematograph which never gives a word of offence to
anybody, and that kind of minister is not a glut on the
market. I did the best I could. I consulted all my acquaint-
ances, and every man Jack of them had a first-rate minister
he would recommend heartily for the vacancy. It was
always their own minister, and their eagerness to see him
doing well for himself by shifting somewhere else was most
significant.

" At last I found a young assistant something like the
thing I wanted, and put the Birrelton pulpit to him as a
business proposition. He jumped at it like a brave wee
man, and I wired to my customer—' Esteemed order will be
dispatched per passenger train on Monday.'

" He's a great success," said Mr Swan, tapping his pipe on
his boot-toe. " Everybody's delighted with him. I got a

letter from the session-clerk thanking me for putting such a fine minister their road, and asking me if I could recommend the best place to buy a silver tea and coffee service."

" You're a marvel, Mr Swan," I said.

" Not at əll ! " said Jimmy. " I'm only a business man. You can get any mortal thing you like in Glasgow if you have the business experience, and the ready money."

THE COMMERCIAL ROOM

His *confrère* Grant being temporarily off the Road on account of a prolonged attack of influenza, Jimmy Swan last week took up the Fifeshire journey for him, and put up one night at an hotel he had not visited for over a dozen years. In those dozen years some drastic changes had been made on the old Buck's Head. It had been re-created, mainly in the interest of golfers and the automobile traffic. Its geography was now unfamiliar to Jimmy, who, at one time, could have found his way through every corner of it in the dark. He had now the choice of sixteen wash-hand basins, all in a row ; a prominent announcement in the hall informed him that eleven bathrooms were at his august command ; a beauteous languid creature, with an amazing rick of yellow hair, put down his name and handed him a circular ticket with the number of his room.

" I hope," said he, " it's a southern exposure, and has a fire-escape and a telephone in it ? "

The fair being, with a wonderful pretence at talking into empty space, mentioned that the Buck's Head's bedrooms always gave satisfaction.

" Dinner, sir ? " said a German voice at his shoulder, and turning round, Jimmy sighed. At that exact moment he had remembered how old Willie Boyd, for twenty years the waiter and boots of the Buck's Head, as it used to be, was wont to welcome him.

"No; tea," he answered curtly. "And ham and eggs; with two boiled eggs to follow."

The Teutonic minion sped upon this mission; Jimmy washed his hands in five of the sixteen basins, in order to test the plumber work, and, still without having seen any signs of a proprietor, walked into the old Commercial Room. It had lost the printed designation on the door, and in some respects was fallen sadly from its old estate. He had it wholly to himself.

By-and-bye the waiter came in to intimate that tea was ready in the Coffee Room.

"Good!" said Jimmy. "But I want mine here. I suppose this is still the Commercial Room?"

"No, sir," said the waiter; "it is the Chauffeurs' Room; a Commercial Room we have not now got," and on that Jimmy said a bad word. He looked again about the room; there was the old familiar grate with a glowing fire in it; the sideboard and the chairs were as they used to be; there was no change in the steel engravings on the wall. A host of memories beset him.

"I don't care what it is," he said at last; "bring my tea in here. I suppose the Buck's Head has some sort of a landlord still; don't trouble to waken him, for I haven't got my motor-car wi' me this journey. I take it you haven't such a thing as a pair of commercial slippers? . . . No; of course not! It doesn't matter; I aye carry my own, and I used to put the house ones on just to please old Willie Boyd. Did ye ever hear of Willie Boyd, the Original Human Waiter?"

"Yes, sir," said the German. "He died."

Jimmy's face fell. If I were you, Fritz, I wouldn't put it so blunt as that," he said. "News like that should be broken gently; the man had a thousand friends, God bless him! . . . 'You must tak' another herrin', Mr Swan'; 'I wouldna risk the silverside the day, Mr Swan'; 'Still the rheumatics, gentlemen, but no' complainin''; 'A' to your

beds, now, like gude boys!' . . . Aye, aye! and Willie's
gone! No wonder I didna recognise the old Buck's Head!"

He took a solemn meal, and was ruminating wistfully at
the fire when the landlord plunged into the room with tardy
greetings. "Man, Mr Swan," said he, "the silly folk in
front there hadn't the least suspicion who ye were, and
never sent to the stable for me! I've been buyin' horse.
And what in a' creation are ye daein' here in the Chauffeurs'
Room?—I'm black affronted!"

"The room's fine, Mr Lorimer," said Jimmy Swan.
"Forbye, I clean forgot to bring my evenin' dress wi' me.
And it's still yoursel', John Lorimer! I'm glad to see ye;
I thought there was naething left o' the auld Buck's Head
but this grate and sideboard, and a wheen chairs. I hear
that Willie's gone."

"Three years ago," said the landlord, sitting down; "he
was gey frail at the hinder end."

"Was he? Dear auld Willie! Slept in himsel' at last;
I'll warrant ye it never happened once in twenty years wi'
a customer that Willie had to waken for the early mornin'
train! . . . Ye've made a wonderful change on the house
since I was here last, Mr Lorimer; but sittin' here my lone
at my tea, I was feelin' eerie."

"Tuts, man! ye should have gone to the Coffee Room,"
said the landlord. "It's perfectly ridiculous!"

"No," said Mr Swan; "I never could turn my back
on the auld Buck's Head Commercial Room; do ye know
it's the first I ever set foot in?"

"I mind!" said Mr Lorimer, chuckling; "you were a
little jimper at the waist then. You're gettin' fat, like
mysel', Mr Swan."

"That's not fat," said Jimmy, soberly; "it's philosophy.
. . . I mind on that occasion I asked a customer, old
David Graham, to come round to the Buck's Head at night
to see me, and it was wi' a gey red face I did it, I can tell
ye, for he micht hae been my father. He came in at night,

and in a little I asked him what he would ha'e. ' I drink naething but champagne,' says David Graham ; ' I'll ha'e a bottle.' My he'rt sunk into my heels ; the price o' a bottle o' champagne was mair than I would mak' o' profit on the journey ! But the deed was done ; I couldna back oot, and I rang the bell for Willie. ' A bottle o' good champagne and a bottle o' beer,' I said to him ; he never blinked an e'e, though I was but a boy, and oot he goes and comes in wi' twa bottles o' beer.

" ' I said champagne for one o' them,' says I, quite manly ; and David Graham—peace be wi' him ! a worthy man !— laughed in a quiet way, and says, ' Willie kens my auld trick wi' the young traiveller too weel to bring ony champagne in here. Na, na, laddie ; beer's better for us, and I doubt it'll be mony a day before ye'll be able to afford a bottle o' Pomeroy for a country customer ! '

" I'm sorry ye've given up the auld Commercial Room," proceeded Jimmy. " I look upon it in a kind o' way as consecrated. Auld times ! auld men ! "

" We had to move wi' the times, Mr Swan," said the landlord ; " I had to make a place for the chauffeurs somewhere, and our commercial trade is not what it used to be."

" I daresay no," said Jimmy. " Neither is commercial traivellin'. Do ye mind o' Cunningham and Stewart, Kerr, MacKay, J. P. Paterson, and MacLennan ? Where's the like o' them the day ? Kings o' the Road ! By George ! I've seen a polisman up in Brora touch his cap when a barrow passed wi' auld MacLennan's cases."

" Faith, aye ! This room has seen some cheery company ! " said Mr Lorimer.

" The first Sunday I took my dinner in't, I felt as if I was in the House o' Commons. Everything was done by ritual ; J. P. Paterson in the chair. I was formally introduced as if it was the twenty-ninth degree in Masonry ; Paterson made a canty speech, and wished me well on behalf o' the company, and they drank my health. And there was the usual bottle o' wine—I was jolly glad, I can tell ye ; it was port, for port was the only wine at the time that hadna the taste o' ink to me.   I've never seen a bottle o' port more ceremoniously disposed o' than the customary bottle on the Sunday in Commercial Rooms.   It was an education in the *haute politesse* !   At first it used actually to mak' me feel religious !   And always ' Mr President, sir ! ' and ' By your leave, gentlemen ! ' ''

" I havena sold a bottle o' port to a commercial in the past ten years, Mr Swan," said the landlord.   " They've lost the taste for wines, I'm thinkin'."

" Not them ! The only thing they've lost is the means o' payin' for them. There's no' mony pound-a-day men left on the Road, Mr Lorimer. And, onyway, port, I take it, is no' what it used to be.   Do ye know what I was thinkin' to mysel' sittin' here mopin' at the fire afore ye came in ? It was that naething nooadays was quite so good as it used to be.   The ham's gane aff, chops are no' so thick and sappy as they were before the Tay Bridge storm, and ye've a' lost the art o' branderin' them.   The cut off the joint is no' what it was, and finnen-haddies are completely aff, and there's no' the auld taste to potatoes. . . . And—and Willie Boyd's awa' frae the Buck's Head Inn ! And it hasna a Commercial Room ony longer ! ''

" The port's as good as ever it was," said Mr Lorimer with a twinkle.

" Take me in a bottle, then," said Jimmy Swan, " and join me in a sentimental glass to the auld Commercial Room, the memory o' honest Willie, an' the auld Knights o' the Road ! ''

THE CHANGED MAN

JAMES SWAN had a friend, a traveller in the line of Fancy Goods, who came originally—of all places in the world for a seller of photo-frames and jumping-jacks—from the Isle

U*

of Skye. His Christian name was Donald ; Jimmy always called him " Donald-of-the-Isles—the fusel-iles," and that, alas ! did no injustice to his salient weakness, which was a preference for mountain dew at its very freshest, before the warmth of the still was out of it. He took it in considerable quantities for years, with no apparent ill effect upon a constitution which seemed to be impervious to the erosive influence of moisture, like the Coolin hills or the Quiraing. The parlour what-nots of countless happy homes in the West of Scotland were laden with celluloid jewel-boxes, antimony silver ash-trays, fantastic cats with nodding heads, and Goss-ware, Presents from Dunoon, or Campbeltown, or whatever the case might be, which owed their prevalence in country shops almost wholly to the persuasive eloquence of Donald. He had a way of showing jumping-jacks and expounding the moral value of Teddy Bears that was positively irresistible anywhere ten miles out of Glasgow, his exposition of a doll that would say " Ma-ma," and horizontally shut its eyes was acknowledged to be unique. In Donald's hands it assumed the dignity of an epoch-making laboratory experiment by the late Lord Kelvin.

For Fancy Goods Jimmy Swan had the most extraordinary contempt. He looked (and not unreasonably) upon Fancy Goods as the proof that fancy itself, the cheapest and loveliest of all adornments, was, like porridge, almost obsolete in Scotland, and he never referred to Donald's stock of samples but as " dolls." " Anything fresh in the doll line, Donald ? " he would say ; " are shammy-leather legs goin' to hold their own this season ? " Or, " I see from the Board of Trade returns there's a slump in mouth-harmoniums ; I doubt you are losing ground, Donald."

But all the same they were the warmest of friends. It has recently been discovered by Professor Spiltzbaum of Heidelberg that the specific organism of alcoholism is a very minute motile coco-bacillus measuring from 1 to 2 micro-millimetres in length, with terminal spiral flagella.

In the body of its host, the unfortunate victim of the alcoholic disease, this anærobe has a curious tickling effect. It tickles the sense of confidence, laughter, toleration, and human kindness, and is the inveterate foe of those pink hæmatozoa which are now identified in bacteriological research as the cause of self-righteousness. Thus we have explained the remarkable fact that unfortunate victims of alcohol, like Donald, are often so much more jolly to meet than fine healthy fellows without a single coco-bacillus about them.

Donald was a good traveller, and could sell a gross of mechanical mice with broken springs in the time another traveller would be shutting up his umbrella and fumbling for his pencil. He was generous, tolerant, amusing, fearless, frank, and simple as a child when the coco-bacillus tickled with its spiral flagella ; he could be the most charming of companions, and most loyal of friends.

" I like Donald," Jimmy Swan would say. " I suppose it's because he's a bit o' an idiot like mysel', no' a'thegither given up to the main chance, nor always homeward bound. But I whiles wish he would settle doon and start the domestic and temperance virtues. I'm aye tellin' him that if he takes them up in the proper spirit they're almost as much fun as the other thing—forbye bein' money in your pocket."

Unfortunately the alcoholic bacillus in course of time by the assiduous application of its flagella in the tickling process wears them down to a stump, and deprived of its power to tickle to any great extent, it goes ramping round the whole intestinal system biting. An agonising thirst is created in the patient, only to be allayed by increased applications of mountain or other dew, with which, of course, are imbibed fresh colonies of the organism which take up the tickling, handicapped, however, by the increased difficulty of getting a dry spot to work on.

One day Donald came to his friend, Mr Swan, in a quiescent

moment of the bacilli, looking very blue, and borrowed £10 upon the touching presentation of a story about a Sheriff-Court summons.

The occasion was too obviously providential to be neglected, and Jimmy talked to him like a teetotal lecturer. "All I needed to be John B. Gough was a drunken past, my thumb-prints in the polis books, and a white dress muslin necktie," he said afterwards to his wife, describing the interview.

"Look here, Donald," he said; "not to put too fine a point on it, you're a d——d fool."

"It's the true word, Mr Swan!" admitted Donald, contritely.

"I'm the last man," said Jimmy, "to say a chap should begin in life by bein' a perfect model, for there's naething left for him to dae in the way o' self-improvement if he's perfect to begin wi', and the later part o' his life 'll be awfu' dreich. I started, mysel', wi' the full equipment o' a first-class idiot—worse than you, but for the last ten years I've got a wonderfu' lot o' pleesure and satisfaction tryin' to be better. I tell ye this—it's far more sport than keepin' a gairden!

"The way ye are," continued Jimmy, "you're just a wasted man! Ye have a' the qualities o' a good yin except the will to use them. Men no' half your weight, nor wi' half your wits aboot them, are laughin' at ye; I'll no' say that they're takin' the prizes you should have, for that's a point that would appeal to neither me nor you, but they're laughin' at ye—no, no! I'll no' say that o' human nature; rather will I say they're sorry for ye. That should sting a Skyeman!"

"There's something in it, Mr Swan," said Donald.

"Of course there is!" said Jimmy. "A man at your age canna learn much more, but he can get a lot of fun in unlearnin'. But for heaven's sake, Donald!—always in the proper spirit!—not too certain o' yoursel', nor too self-satisfied, nor too bitter on the weaker brethren."

Donald went away, impressed, and became a changed man.

Everybody noticed it, first of all his firm, which experienced a lamentable and unaccountable decline in the demand for autograph albums with real leatherette covers, mechanical steam-engines (with broken springs), celluloid dromedary inch-tapes, and golliwogs, on the West Coast journey. Donald was blatantly and offensively teetotal; once generous, he was now as hard as nails; once full of fun and kindliness, he was now as dull as crape; once fearless, he was become as timid as a mouse; once disingenuous as a child, he was become as crafty and suspicious as a shilling lawyer. The coco-bacilli, realising the situation, uttered an agonised shriek, and turned on their backs and died.

When he came to Jimmy Swan after a year to repay the borrowed money, Jimmy, who had not seen him much of late, looked at him with disappointed eyes.

" Do ye feel like a bottle o' cyder, Donald ? " he asked him.

" Thank goodness, I'm beyond that sort o' thing ! " said Donald. " Have ye a drop o' soda ? "

Jimmy gave it to him, sadly.

" Thank ye for the money, Donald," said he ; " it was good of ye to mind it. There's something aboot ye that puts me in mind o' the smell o' a wet leather school-bag. What way are ye gettin' on ? "

" Oh, not so bad," said Donald, solemnly. " I have the approval of my conscience, though the firm is not quite satisfied."

" Just that ! " said Jimmy, fingering the notes carelessly. " You're a muckle-improved man, but I'm feared I spoiled ye for a traiveller, and I ken I've lost ye for a friend. I told ye, man, to go about it in the proper spirit ! "

VITALISING THE GLOOMY GRANTS

JIMMY SWAN, with his hands in his jacket pockets, his hat at just the tiniest angle, his chest thrown out, and his waist reduced by a conscious effort of the abdominal muscles—which things all betoken a determination never to grow old, walked along Shore Street humming " Onward, Christian Soldiers." He was, if you take me, feeling good. The sun shone on the sea-front like a benediction ; enough and no more autumnal sting was in the air to give it bracing qualities ; he had done a good day's business yesterday at Inverness ; had slept like a babe, and breakfasted like a sailor ; was freshly shaved to that degree that his cheek was like a lady's ; he knew this journey's stuff was irresistible. It was going on in front of him—six weather-beaten cases in the wheel-barrow of Peter Melville, packed with sample lines to make the hair of any discerning draper fairly curl.

He felt as men feel who come with relief to long-beleaguered cities ; there ought to have been a band before him playing " Umpa-umpa-ump ! " and a few assorted banners. That was why he hummed, providing for himself a private and appropriate kind of military pomp. Other commercial travellers might sneak ingloriously into these northern towns and go cringing through the shops with self-depreciatory airs, inviting insults and rebuffs instead of orders—not so Mr Swan, ambassador of C. & M., Perpetual Grand Plenipotentiary and High Prince of the Soft Goods world, backed by a century's tradition, conscious of quality unassailable and prices strictly bed-rock, having due consideration for the quality.

In thirty years of the Road for C. & M. he had acquired a Psychic Touch with customers ; not only did his stuff talk for itself—why, C. & M.'s trade-mark on a web of Bolton sheeting was portentous as a statesman's speech !—but his manner magnetised, and he would insinuate a new line of

zephyr prints into the conversation like one who was quoting
a fine unhackneyed passage from Shakespeare. He did not
seem so much to seek to sell you goods as to give you the
inestimable privilege of taking part with the great firm of
C. & M. in a grand disinterested campaign to make the people
of Scotland wear the real right thing. No city superiority
or condescension, mind you! no bluff or airs! Jimmy
Swan had a shrewd appreciation of the psychological advantage of liking your man to start with; of being absolutely
disingenuous, and confident of the character of your own stuff.

No wonder he marched into R. & T. Grant's humming
"Onward, Christian Soldiers" in his mellifluous bass, while
Peter Melville out on the pavement took the straps from off
the cases.

He was no sooner at the counter and shaking hands with
Robert than he realised, intuitively, that the morning's sunshine and its bracing airs had no effect on the spirits of
that struggling drapery concern. The shop looked more
disheartened than it ever did before—more haphazard of
arrangement, more dingy, more out-of-date. Robert's eye
(the straight one) had the unmistakable lack-lustre of frustra-
tion and defeat. Thomas, the elder, totting up the greasy
ledger in a corner, stopped in the middle of a column and
came forward smiling automatically as to a customer, but
lapsing instantly into a mask of gloom, his voice subdued to
a funereal melancholy. The brothers were barely middle-
aged in years, but for long they had indulged a singular
illusion that solidity and success in commerce were only for
men who looked mature, and they had always carefully
cultivated an appearance of being twenty years older than
they really were. Gladstone collars, made-up padded neck-
ties, morning coats of the period of the Tay Bridge storm,
and—whiskers! And when I say whiskers, I mean actual
mid-Victorian side-wings, not mutton-chops, but fluffy cheek
appendages, the dire absurdity of which not even a doting
mother could condone.

" How's business ? " asked Mr Swan, with the cheerful air of one who is confident of learning that business was never better.

" Bad ! " said Robert Grant, laconically. " I don't think you need to open up your cases, Mr Swan, this trip."

The countenance of the traveller fell for a moment ; then he said airily, " Tuts ! it's only temporary. Everything's on the upward trend ; ye're maybe just a season later here in the North to feel it, but it's working up the Highland Line, and I make out that in less than a week the Boom will be the length o' Kingussie or Aviemore."

Robert Grant shook his head till his whiskers almost made a draught. " It's too late of comin' for us, Mr Swan," he said lugubriously. " Tom and me's tired o't. We're done ! What trade we ever had is goin' back. It was never a fat thing at the best, but now it's driftin' over to the Store across the street ; ye see they've started a drapery department."

" Let them start it ! " said Mr Swan, contemptuously. " I'm sure ye ken the slogan o' the Grants—' Stand fast, Craigellachie ! ' The new department at the Store should be a tonic to ye ; send ye brisker about your business than ever ye were before ; I never do so well myself as when I'm faced wi' solid opposition."

But the Grant brothers wagged their preposterous whiskers, and sunk their chins lower in their obsolete Gladstone collars, and assured their visitor that affairs were hopeless. Thank God they could still pay twenty shillings in the pound and have a little over, but there seemed to be nothing now for it but Canada. Everybody was going to Canada.

" What'll ye dae there ? " asked Mr Swan, bluntly.

They would look around them for a while, and no doubt hit on something, they remarked, and Robert's defective and erratic eye went flashing round the shop in a manner which suggested that at looking around in Canada he would be a perfect marvel.

James Swan walked to the door and looked at his open cases; threw out his chest and took a deep breath of the stimulating sea-born air, then turned back to the counter, and addressed the disconsolate brothers.

" Do ye ken what's the matter wi' this business and wi' you ? " he asked. " It's whiskers ! Nothing else but whiskers ! For the love of Peter shave yoursel's clean like me, or start a moustache, or a Captain Kettle beard wi' a peak to't, and be upsides wi' modern civilisation. Gie your cheeks a chance ; take aff these side-galleries and look like the year o' grace 1912, no' the start o' the Franco-Prussian war."

The brothers, too well acquainted with their visitor to resent this personality, smiled ruefully. " I see from the papers," said Robert, " that side whiskers are comin' into vogue again. Tom and me's just a little ahead o' the times ; we'll soon be in the height o' fashion."

" The height o' nonsense ! " cried Jimmy Swan. " There's no wise-like folk gaun back to whiskers ony mair than to the crinoline or the chignong. In either case the women wouldna stand it, and it's them that rule the fashions. Man, it's no' an age for whiskers ; ye need a face on ye as clean as the bow o' a cutter yacht to sail into the winds o' commerce nooadays, and there's the pair o' ye beatin' to the marks wi' spinnakers. There's naebody wears whiskers now but undertakers and men on the Stock Exchange that havena ony dochters to cod them into common sense. If any employee o' C. & M.'s came into the warehouse wi' a whisker on, the partners in the business would tak' fits, and the rest o' us would bray at him like cuddies. If the police o' Gleska saw a man your age wi' whiskers they would track him up a lane at night and hammer him wi' their batons. The way ye are, ye're an affront to me ; ye're no' a day aulder than mysel', and yet ye might be onybody's faithers. The first thing they would dae to ye in Canada would be to lay ye on a block and clip ye——"

He broke off with a chuckle which disarmed annoyance ; there were no customers of C. & M. for whom he had a greater respect—if only they would shave themselves ; and he knew they knew it.

" Ah, if it was only a question o' whiskers ! " said Thomas, sadly.

" It's ALL a question o' whiskers ! " vehemently retorted Jimmy Swan.   " There's naething criminal or immoral about whiskers, but in a drapery concern they're a Symbol.   Your fine half-Dundrearies are an indication o' your state o' mind.   The world is a' for youth—which I take to be onything under sixty, and there's the pair o' ye advertisin' that ye're nearly centenarians.   It's no' on your face only that there's whiskers ; they're in your philosophy and on your business.   Twa men your age, wi' health, and twenty shillin's in the pound, and an auld-established business, should be oot in the mornin's whistlin' like mavises and gambollin' round the shop like boys."

" I doubt we're not the gambollin' kind," said Robert humbly, for the first time in his life painfully conscious of his whiskers.   " But nobody can say we haven't paid strict attention to business." . . . " And walked in the fear of God," he added as an afterthought.

" That's it ! " said Jimmy Swan.   " More whiskers !   It would suit ye better to walk in His glory and sing the 27th Psalm.   It's no' in the fear and admonition o' the Lord ye're walkin', but in mortal terror o' the Store.   Bonny-like Grants ye are ?   Wi' a motto like ' Stand Fast ! ' that ought to stir ye up and stiffen ye like a trumpet !   Man, the very sound o't dirls like the tune Dunfermline ! "

" There's something in it ! " said Thomas tremulously. " Perhaps we were a little too timid about the Store, Robert ? "

" Ye couldna help it wi' thae whiskers ! " said Jimmy Swan.   " There's nothing worse for the nerve than fluff. Shave off your whiskers and I'll guarantee that between us

we'll make the Store look silly. I never saw the sense o'
Stores ; they don't get their stuff from C. & M."

" Could ye suggest anything, Mr Swan ? " asked Robert,
also infected by this fearless spirit. " Anything to, as it
were, buck us up in the business ? "

" Man, amn't I tellin' ye ?—Whiskers ! whiskers ! whiskers !
Get them aff ! Be as young as I am—twenty-six ; I only
begin to count from the day I married. It's a' nonsense
about bein' douce and demure, and auld-lookin'—at least,
in the drapery trade ; it may suit a'right wi' undertakers.
Take the whiskers aff your shop, and aff your stock, and aff
the dressin' o' your windows ! "

" There's maybe something in what you say," admitted
Robert, " but there seem to be such chances out in Canada ! "

" Of course there are ! " said Jimmy Swan. " Wherever
there's clean cheeks, there's chances, and every man in
Canada has a safety razor. But, bless your heart, man !
Canada's no' the only place ! If half the folk that went to
Canada had only stayed at home and shaved themsel's, and
took the side-wings aff their business, and the fluff frae their
way o' lookin' at things, there would be nae necessity to
emigrate. Are ye stupid enough to think this country's done
because the Store has added drapery ? It's a sign that it's
only startin', and that better men are wanted. Good luck
to them in Canada ! but let you and me stay here and shave
oursel's."

The brothers Grant looked at each other. " I think, after
all," said Thomas, " you might show us some of your winter
lines."

" Certainly," said Jimmy Swan with the utmost alacrity,
and humming " Onward, Christian Soldiers," went outside
to fetch his samples.

BLATE RACHEL

JIMMY SWAN, with a superb carnation in his coat-lapel, was leaning on the counter of the widow Thorpe, recounting all the splendours of a wedding he had been a guest at on the previous day, when he observed a tear was in the widow's eye. He promptly changed the subject, and went back to the claims of Union Shantung for good hard wear and smart appearance. " You never can tell," he thought, " when a widow woman's too far on in years to be sentimental ; the puir old body's envious." But he misunderstood.

" Everybody has luck but me," she said to him, indifferent, for the moment, to his Shantung samples ; " there's my lassie Rachel, and there's no' a man looks near her."

" Toots ! " said Jimmy blithely, " what's the matter wi' her ? Is she skelly-e'ed ? "

" There's naething wrang wi' her," replied the widow peevishly ; " she got a better chance, to start wi', in her looks than ever I got, but she's blate. Put her next a lad, and she's so shy she might be skelly in both e'es and he wouldna get a chance to see it."

" Blate ! " said Jimmy, with surprise. " That's a female disease I thought was oot o' fashion. Are ye sure it's no' her adenoids ? "

The widow positively wept as she disclosed the troubles she had had with Rachel. She had given her a first-rate educa-tion, up as far as Chemistry and Elocution ; she had lavished dress upon her to the point of gold watch-wristlets, petticoats of silk and patent American pumps ; she had taken her to hydros. " But there she is ! " bewailed the mother ; " goin' on eight-and-twenty, and I'll swear she never had a box o' chocolates I didna buy for her mysel' ! It's rale disheartenin', Mr Swan. I'd give a lot to see her settled down. But there ! —ye'll think I'm just a sly designin' woman."

The traveller smiled. " So far as I can see," he said, " the trouble is that ye're no' half sly enough nor much o' a dab at the designin', or otherwise, if Rachel's like the world, you should hae been a granny. I've never seen her."

"Come up the stair and ha'e a cup o' tea," said Mrs Thorpe; "I'm no' ashamed to let ye see her."

"I will!" said Jimmy with alacrity, and gave a little twitch to his superb carnation.

If Rachel Thorpe was blate she showed no signs of it to him. He told her three quite funny stories, led the conversation on to operas, and sitting down to the piano vamped his own accompaniment (three good chords and a twiddly one) to "Star of Eve," which, he explained, was a good deal finer when sung by a tenor who could really sing. Rachel, thus encouraged, gave a palpitating rendering of "The Rosary," the widow looking all the time at Jimmy in expectant anguish as if he were an *entrepreneur* who was testing a soprano.

"Capital!" he murmured at the end of every verse. "Expression! Feeling! Temperament! Particularly that rallantando bit! For such a heavy song, she's simply wonderful!" He finally presented her with the carnation.

"Now, can you tell what's the matter wi' her?" asked the mother when she got him back into the shop. "Time's aye slippin' past, and a' the diffies in the place are gettin' married, and Rachel's jist the way ye see her."

"A bonny, wise-like lass!" said he, with emphasis. "Perhaps it wasna fair to call her Rachel. Rachel, Ruth, Rebecca—ony o' them's a handicap in this dull material age, Mrs Thorpe; ye want a snappy, cheery sort o' name to give a girl a chance. 'Rachel's' solemn; it takes a lot o' pluck to put an arm about a Rachel. Ye should have ca'd her Jean. But she didna strike me as out o' the ordinar' shy; we got on together fine."

"Ah, yes," said Mrs Thorpe; "she got on a' right wi' you, for you're a married man, but if a lad comes to the house she hasna hardly got a word to say, and I've to do the talkin'."

"What do ye talk about to them?" asked Jimmy.

"Oh, anything at all," she answered, rather puzzled at the question. "Thank God, I never was at a loss for conversation! And Rachel, she sits fidgin'!"

"Yon's an interestin' photo album," said Jimmy, who had been personally conducted through it. "I suppose ye'll show them that?"

"Ye have to entertain them some way," said the widow sadly. "Especially if your daughter is a dummy."

"H'm!" said Jimmy, and rubbed his chin. "It's hardly fair to Rachel! There's half a dozen photos o' her yonder that amount to a complete exposure o' her past. 'Rachel as a baby'—nice, and wee, and fat; 'Rachel at the period o' the fringe,' 'Rachel when she won the ping-pong prize'—wi' a bolero jacketee, accordion pleats, and a motor kep. Ye shouldna rake up her past like that in front o' any chap ye're wantin' to encourage. It mak's her look like the History o' Scotland in monthly parts."

"I never thought o' that!" said Mrs Thorpe.

"Besides, the album, as a whole, is obsolete as a social and domestic cheerer-up. It's done! Ye might as well attempt to rouse enthusiasm wi' a game o' dominoes or a spellin'-bee. Any young man that you show through yon album is bound to get a fright when he sees three generations o' the Thorpes and a' their ramifications down to sixty-second cousins. It reduces Rachel to a mere incident. He's apt to say to himsel', 'Great Scot! she's no unique at all: there have been hundreds o' her!' And it's so unlucky there's so mony o' them deid! Brief life is here our portion, as the hymn says, but we needna rub it in to Rachel's friends that even the Thorpes get old and disappear; they want to think of her as in eternal youth, for ever gaily skippin' across the sands o' time in a hobble skirt and clocked silk stockin's."

"Ye're a droll man!" said Mrs Thorpe laughing.

"And then there's another thing," said Jimmy twinkling.

"I'll wager ye're far too anxious to be nice to any young man ye see in Rachel's company. That's no' the way to take the situation at all! My mother-in-law knew better than that when I was after Bella—that's the mistress. She forbade me to come near the house after her lassie, and used to look on me like dirt. She said the Swans were a' geese, and warned Bella to have naething to dae wi' me. Up till then Bella, wi' me, was just a lass for walkin' hame from the dancin' wi'; but when my pride was roused I up and married her! And the auld yin laughed!"

"That might do wi' others," said the widow, "but no wi' Rachel; she's so blate."

"Blate!" said Jimmy. "That'll be her salvation; there's far mair chance for a blate yin than the other kind. If she's really blate, and we had her down in Gleska she would be a novelty. Onything out o' the ordinar' takes in Gleska. Send her down for a week to Mrs Swan, to see the shops; there's nothing beats a change o' air for blateness."

"It's very kind of ye," said Mrs Thorpe. "She wouldna be the worse for't, maybe. But ye'll think I'm an awfu' designin' woman!"

"Good!" said Jimmy heartily. "Bella will be glad to see her. And as for the designin', Mrs Thorpe, God meant it."

RACHEL COMES TO TOWN

JAMES SWAN had mischievously described the girl from Banchory to his wife as "a spindly one wi' ruby hair, a voice like the start o' a gramophone, and clothes picked up in the dark at a jumble sale," and when the visitor jumped out of a taxi-cab, which also bore a substantial trunk, a leather hat-box, a neat morocco dressing-case, and a bag of golf-clubs, from the railway station, Mrs Swan immediately realised that she had been badly done.

" I can't believe a word you say to me, sometimes, Jimmy!"
she exclaimed with agitation, as the door bell rang.

There was nothing spindly about Rachel; her hair was a
glorious golden; her voice was sweet and mellow as a mavis'
song, and her dress alone was summed up in two seconds
by Mrs Swan as costing anything over £6, 10s.

" And where's the blateness of her ? " Jimmy was asked
at the earliest opportunity. " I thought from your description that you couldn't drag a word from her except in the
dummy alphabet."

Jimmy chuckled. " I only told ye what her mother said,"
he answered. " The case is desperate. She's goin' on eight
and twenty——"

" Just a child ! " said his wife from the point of view of
forty.

" Everybody in Banchory's gettin' married but hersel';
take her round the town before we go to Kirn, and give her
wrinkles."

" The only kind of wrinkles I have nowadays are the sort
a woman gets from being married," said Mrs Swan with a
look at herself in the overmantel mirror.

But really Rachel Thorpe required no wrinkles. Jimmy
was off the road for a week and busy at the warehouse;
for three nights in succession, when he came home at tea-
time, he found a vacant house and the fire out; a hitherto
conscientious wife was being dragged around the town at
the heels of the blate young thing from Banchory, and
wasn't even ashamed of herself.

" I never go anywhere, James," she said; " you never
take me over the door. I've seen more of Glasgow in the
past three days with Rachel than I've done in twenty years
with you."

The ladies together went to picture-palaces, tea-rooms,
parks; they paraded Buchanan Street and Sauchiehall
Street by the hour, fascinated by windows; they rode on
the outside of tramway cars as far as cars would take them;

one night they were not home till ten ; Rachel had insisted on a music-hall.

" Oh, it's all right ! " said Jimmy, meekly. " I'm vexed I never thought o' makin' ye a hot supper. I'll leave the door on the Chubb after this, and ye can jist slip in when ye like. There'll be something cold on the sideboard. But for goodness' sake don't start singin' and pullin' beer and make a row and wake me ; mind, I'm gettin' up in years."

" You should come out with us," seriously suggested the girl from Banchory. " What's the sense of sitting in here moping all alone when you might be enjoying yourself ? Mrs Swan and I are going to see ' 'Way Back in Darkeyland ' to-morrow night. I've just been telling her I hear it's fine."

" No," said he, ironically ; " I canna be bothered goin' anywhere unless I can get dancin' ; I'm vexed it's no' the social season ; you and Bella would like a ball."

On his wife had come the most extraordinary transformation. The fashion in which she put up her hair was preposterously antiquated, according to Rachel, who dressed it to look three times as thick as it was before, with glints of sunshine in its bronze that no one had hitherto suspected. Rachel also in an hour or two devised a hat for Mrs Swan, so chic and saucy that of itself it immediately knocked ten years off her age, and induced in the wearer a corresponding spirit of youthful gaiety. She took about a breadth from the width of her Sunday gown, reduced its length amazingly, bought the nattiest kind of shiny shoes, and displayed in the frankest manner a beautiful pair of shot-silk stockings. Her husband saw her one day jump on a car with Rachel, and they looked like a couple of soubrettes in " The Girl in the Film."

" Ye seem to have picked me up a' wrang, Bella," he said to his wife when they were alone that evening. " The idea was that Rachel Thorpe was to have her shyness polished off wi' a week in Gleska, and maybe learn a tip or twa on the way to get a sweetheart. There's no' that mony sweethearts disengaged in Gleska that ye can look for one a-piece. Besides, as lang as I hing on, it wouldna be respectable."

" Pooh ! " said Bella, radiantly ; " you want to see me going out a perfect fright. I never had a fling to myself since I was married, and now that Rachel's here I'm going to have it. Your idea of what is fit and proper in a married woman's fifty years behind the times. Rachel was quite astonished at the life I lead."

"And that's the girl her mither thinks is blate ! " said Mr Swan, derisively.

The Swans had taken three weeks of a house at Kirn ; they removed to the coast on Monday, and the girl from Banchory went with them. In two days she had taught Mrs Swan the game of golf, how to swing most effectively in a hammock, the two-step, " Hitchy-Koo " and divers other pleasing ditties, the right deportment for a walking-stick, and the way to clear the bows of a steamer by ten yards in a rowing-boat so as to get the rocking of the waves and a good view of the captain dancing with rage on the bridge.

Jimmy came down from town one afternoon, and saw them waiting for him on the pier. At first he had looked at them with amiable and even approving interest, for he did not, at a distance, recognise them. They had white serge skirts, white shoes and stockings, knitted sports-coats of a vivid mustard colour, knitted caps conform thereto in hue, and walking-sticks. They were distinctly making gallant play at coquetry with two young gentlemen he did not know, and to whom he was introduced with some embarrassment on the part of all concerned.

" There's just one thing ye have overlooked," he told his wife, who dropped behind with him while the blate girl from Banchory went up the pier between the two young gentlemen, putting down her feet with splendid artfulness so that nobody could help looking at them. Next to Mrs Swan's they were the neatest feet on the Cowal side of the coast that day.

" What do you mean ? What did I overlook ? " asked Mrs Swan, who seemed deliriously happy.

" The dug," said Jimmy, seriously. " Ye need a wee bit toy terrier under your oxter, and instead o' the walking-stick I would hae a tennis-racket. If I may ask, where did ye pick up thae twa misguided gentlemen ? "

" Oh, just on the quay," said Mrs Swan. " They're very nice. They came off a boat from Rothesay."

" Did they just wink at ye, or did you see them first and say, ' Ha, Berty ! ' ? "

" Nothing so common ! " said Mrs Swan, with dignity. " We pretended we didn't see them, but they would insist on speaking to Rachel."

" Just that ! " said Jimmy. " I'm goin' to write to Rachel's mother the night and tell her to get Rachel shifted back to Banchory as quick as possible, before my happy home is broken up."

His wife laughed. " Do you know who they are ? " she said. " They're just two Banchory friends of Rachel's, and the one with the fancy waistcoat wants to marry her. He came here specially to ask her, and she says she will."

" Could he no' ask her up in Banchory ? " asked Jimmy with surprise.

" No," said Mrs Swan ; " not without her mother over-hearing. She was always there, and kept cracking Rachel up so much that the poor lad never got a chance to shove a word in telling his intentions."

" That's exactly what I thought ! " said Mr Swan. " But what are you, at the age of over forty, comin' out so strong in the nutette line for ? "

" Just to cheer up and encourage Rachel ; just to make her think that married life's no' so dull as she would think if she saw me at my ordinary," said the amazing Mrs Swan.

A POOR PROGRAMME

" You're the last landlord on this side of the Clyde to keep slippers for your guests," said Mr Swan. " It's not that I'm needin' them myself, but I like to see them ; they're one of the few surviving relics of the age *de luxe* in the history of commercial travellin'."

" Do you know the way I manage to keep them, Mr Swan ? " said the landlord of the Queen's. " I got them big ! There's not a coffee-room pair of slippers here that's under easy number tens. It was a waiter, Alick Russell, put me up to 't. I lost about a gross of slippers every year through gentlemen finding them so good a fit they thought they were their own. ' Whit ye want,' says Alick, ' is big and roomy yins they canna walk upstairs to their bedrooms wi'.' I went away at once and bought three dozen pair of number tens. The only man they ever fitted was a cattleman from Perth. The rest just leave them."

Mr Swan put on his own slippers.

" You're surely not in for the night ? " said Mr Grant ; " there's a Territorial concert on."

Just for a moment Jimmy hesitated. " No," he said ; " I'm bye wi' country concerts ; they're too heatin' for my blood. If it was a swarry and a ball, or a Council meetin', I might risk it. That's the worst of bein' highly cultivated —I canna put up wi' ' Hitchy-Koo,' and they're bound to have ' Hitchy-Koo ' in Fochabers, especially wi' a Territorial concert. It's a hundred chances to one a Colour-Sergeant wi' a nearly-tenor voice 'll stand up and give ' The Phantom Army,' and as sure as daith I cannot stand ' The Phantom Army.' It was maybe good enough till the hundred thousandth time I heard it, but then it began to spoil my sleep. Forbye, ' The Phantom Army ' 's no' a song for Territorials ; it's far too personal."

" They have a lot of talent," said the landlord coaxingly.

"I know they'll have," said Mr Swan agreeably. "I notice in the country papers that they're always super-excellent. Did it ever occur to you, Mr Grant, that music's done in Scotland? I mean vocal music; of course there's aye the pianola. There are only two kinds o' singers now in Scotland—the real professional that needs an evening suit for't, and the young and healthy amateur who does 'Phil the Fluter's Ball' or 'No, John, No!' as if his life depended on it."

"The gramophone——" said Mr Grant.

"Of course! Quite right! The gramophone's the music master now; whenever 'Everbody's Doing It' comes out in a Glasgow Pantomime, they wire at once from Fochabers to send a dozen records. No time is lost! The latest rag-time tune is up at Thurso wi' the mornin' post, and everbody's whistlin't by tea-time.

"Half the folk in the country's sick-tired o' music, and the other half's tryin' to be Clara Butts and Harry Lauders—a thing that sounds quite easy when you hear it in a canister. Half the nice wee lassies that could sing like laverocks if they were content to sing the way that God intended them, fair sicken ye wi' tryin' to get cadenzas like the banker's Tetrazzini, ten-and-six the double-breasted disc. The other half realise they could never do anything within a mile of it, and they never try; they just put up their hair another way, and tell the chap they're fond of cookin'."

"But still it's a very decent programme," said the landlord producing it.

Mr Swan put on his glasses. "That's it! I knew it at once!" he said. "'The Prologue from Pagliacci, by Mr G. R. Williamson.' I don't ken Mr Williamson, but I'll bet ye he's a tall, thin, fair-haired chap in the Union Bank, and has a lisp. He'll be at least a light and easy baritone: he couldn't do 't unless. Then there's 'A Wee Deoch an' Doruis'—I ken that, too! He'll likely be a gas collector, a smart wee blackavised chap wi' a comic kind o' face and a

crackle up aboot the F. Comic singing is sappin' the manhood
o' the nation; it's worse than cigarettes. 'Angus Macdonald,' by Miss —— Oh! take it away and put it in the
larder! The only thing I see on the programme worth a
rap is 'God save the King'; that's about the only chance
that folk get now for singing.

"The place where people sing is Wales, and emulation o'
the gramophone hasna spoiled them," said Mr Swan, warming
to his subject. "Not being a solo vocalist myself, I always
thought harmonic music was the best, and that's the notion
o' the Welshmen. You see it gives a modest kind o' chap
like me a chance. Thirty years ago there was some sense o'
vocal music left in Scotland; there were choirs; now they
think a choir is jist a special place for sittin' in the kirk. So
long as there were choirs and glee parties there was some
hope for us, though we maybe werena just exactly Covent
Garden opera. We sang for singing's sake, and we didna
try to beat the gramophone.

"There's two things worth while in this world—gettin'
a Saturday to yoursel' and singin' bass in a choir that has a
decent tenor. I never was happier! And music—genuine
music—never got a better chance. So far as I'm aware
there was never anything positively rotten put in harmony;
quartet, glee, and catch were always decent. Three-fourths
of the agony of life to-day is due to that ridiculous preference for the solo. When the average amateur soloist comes
in leanin' heavily on himself wi' a couple o' music sheets—
one for the poor soul at the instrument and the other for
himself to hide his presentation watch-chain—I'm sorry for
him.

"I'm all for choirs and a good bass part for willing gentlemen! It's only wi' part-singing that ye'll stem the tide of
British musical decadence—what do you think of that for
rhetoric at this early hour o' evening, Mr Grant?"

"I like 'O, Who Will o'er the Downs?' and 'Kate
Dalrymple,'" said Mr Grant with modesty.

" Right you are ! " said Mr Swan emphatically. " You're tastes are sound ! They werena tripe—these songs—at any rate ! "

" All these remarks o' mine," continued Mr Swan, " are due to the fact that at a Glasgow public dinner the other night there was a choir. I havena heard a choir at a Glasgow public dinner for twenty years, and I'm thinkin' neither did the company. The usual idea o' a Glasgow dinner now is that a dozen men spoil a' the fun wi' makin' speeches. You'll never convince the poor deluded creatures that they have not something really new to say, and that folk don't want to hear them. Nobody ever does. It just fair spoils the coffee and cigars.

" At this dinner some daring innovator introduced a choir, the speakin' was cut down to the assurance that the Navy was right and trade was boomin', and the choir took up the rest o' the evening makin' us really happy. If dinners were a' like that one, they would be my hobby."

" Then you're not coming ? " said Mr Grant.

" Not me ! " said Jimmy, lighting his pipe ; " be sure and lock the door when ye come back. And tell the Pagliacci gentleman he hasna 't in him ! Tell him to start a decent choir."

BRODERICK'S SHOP

JAMES SWAN went into an Argyle Street shop on Saturday to buy a knife. It is one of the oldest ironmongery shops in town, but that was not the reason Jimmy went to it ; antiquity of itself makes no appeal to him ; he went to this particular shop because he knew the owner, who had for years been on the verge of losing money in it.

Elsewhere in Argyle Street it was the busiest hour of the day. All the world seemed out for buying. Drapery warehouses were crowded to the doors, the grocery shops, which also advertise, appeared too small for the folk who wanted into them ; the lust for giving money in exchange for something crowded the street itself with gutter merchants feverishly dispensing fruit, and flowers, and penny toys that last (with care) till Monday. Argyle Street blazed with light and roared with commerce ; electric moons, refulgent, made it bright as day ; a thousand windows gorgeously displayed their best ; the pavements streamed with life, and every other person had a parcel.

" Beautiful ! " said Jimmy to himself. " Tip-top ! Lovely ! And just to think that this was once a country lane ! "

He felt a genuine pride in Glasgow, and a personal pride that he was an essential part in its commercial activities. It was with almost a paternal eye he stopped to look at a window with a dummy figure wearing one of C. & M.'s " Incomparable " Long-Busk Corsets, there because himself had thrown no little poetry into its recommendation.

To step from the street into Broderick's ironmongery shop, however, was to leave the roar of battle and get into a mausoleum. A solemn hush prevailed there. A customer was standing at the counter, plunged in the patient contemplation of long rows of rather dusty shelves with nothing more attractive to the eye on them than screw-nail packages. In parts behind two shopmen blew or flicked the dust from other packages ; Broderick himself was on the ladder.

He came down at last, deliberately ; gave a friendly nod to Jimmy ; opened the parcel he had brought down with him, and found it was the wrong one. So he went up the ladder again, and in the course of time disposed of a key-ring to the customer for a penny. The customer gave sixpence for its payment. Mr Broderick picked the sixpence up and walked with dignity to some place far away in the back of his shop where he kept his cash-desk.

Jimmy took out his watch and held it in his hand.

The hum of the clamant, buying street came in, like some far murmur of a sea ; below the wan, old-fashioned gas-light over Broderick's door (" Established 1812 "), the multitude went skliffing past along the pavement, deigning not so much as a glance within. He hummed the funeral march from " Saul " to himself, and felt exceedingly sorry for Alick Broderick.

When Broderick had got the change for sixpence and dismissed his customer, he turned with a pathetic expansiveness to Jimmy.

" There's no' much profit aff a penny split ring, Jimmy," said he.

" I daresay no," said Jimmy, snapping up his hunter watch with a last glance at the dial. " Show me a shilling knife, and then shut up this shop o' yours, and come out and ha'e a dram."

" Indeed," said Broderick, " I might well shut it up for a' that's daein'. I never saw things worse " ; and he took out a case of knives with great solemnity.

" Alick," said Mr Swan, " do ye mind the day ye blooded my nose in old Maclean's Academy ? "

" Ay, fine ! " said Mr Broderick. " Ye stole my jawry-bool."

" Weel, I'm gaun to blood your nose the night," said Jimmy, smiling. " Ye better get oot your hanky. . . . Ye say that things were never worse. Where are your ears and e'en ? Take a daunder alang the street and hear things bumming. I could hardly get alang the pavement for folk fair daft to spend their money, and here are you sclimbin' ladders and wearin' oot your shoon to get change for a customer that wants a penny ring. It took ye exactly one minute and forty-five seconds to go away back there to your cash-desk."

" For a' that's daein'——" started Mr Broderick.

" For a' that's daein' — fiddlesticks ! " said Jimmy. " There's only six hundred minutes in a workin' day, and you have only the one pair o' legs on ye, and ye waste good minutes and good legs on the heid o' a penny ring. What ails

x

ye at a cash railway, man ?   Or if ye canna hae a railway,
can ye no' keep your cash beside your coonter ?   Naebody's
gaun to pinch it on ye !   When a customer sees ye makin' a
North Pole expedition awa' back there wi' his penny, he thinks
he has paid too much for the ring, and ye're away behind to
dance the hoolichan."

"There's naething to be done in business nooadays unless
ye advertise," said Mr Broderick sadly ;   "and I never was in
wi' advertisin'."

"Were ye no' ? " said Jimmy, sharply.   "What's your
window for but advertisin' ? "

"The cost's enormous," said Mr Broderick.

"Have ye ony money bye ye ? " asked Jimmy, boldly.

"Thank God I have a little," said Mr Broderick.

"It would need to be a lot," said Jimmy, "for it's you
that pays for other ironmongers' advertising, and nae thanks
for it."

"I don't understand ye, Jimmy," said his friend.   "How
do I pay for other folks' advertisin' ? "

"Who in heaven's name do ye think pays for't ? " said
Jimmy.

"The man that advertises."

"Not him !   He doesna pay a penny.   All he does is to
lend a little capital in advertising, that comes back a hundred-
fold.   The more he advertises, the bigger his profits at the
end of the year.   When did ye ever hear o' a big advertiser
failin' ?   The thing's unknown, and advertisin's only in its
infancy."

"Ay, but in the long-run it's the customer that pays for
advertisin'," said Mr Broderick.

"There, ye're wrang again ! " said Jimmy.   "What dae
ye charge for this shilling knife ? " and he picked up one that
met his fancy.

"Just a shillin'," said Mr Broderick.

"Well, I can go to any ironmonger's shop in Gleska that
advertises, and I'll get the same knife for a shillin'.   Things

are never ony dearer in a shop that advertises. So ye see it's neither the advertiser nor the customer that pays the newspapers."

" If it's no', wha is it, then ? " asked Mr Broderick, with genuine interest. He had never studied the point before.

"It's you, and the like o' you!" said Jimmy. " Every customer you lose through no' advertisin', and every shop that goes doon through no' advertisin', swells the volume o' business in the shops that advertise, and indirectly pays for other folks' advertising. I never see your name in the papers, but when I read a splash o' Grant & Richards, I say to mysel', ' There's some more o' Alick Broderick's money ! ' . . . Take you my tip, Alick, blaw the stour aff them shelves, and get a nice wee cash railway and a ladder that runs on wheels, and hing oot some dacent lights, and advertise, and ye'll no' complain o' naething daein'."

He paid for his knife and gave a genial chuckle. " Now take out your hanky, lad ! " he cried as he left the shop.

A hundred yards along the street he looked at a window of Grant & Richards, in whose shop a roaring trade was doing, and he saw a knife there priced at ninepence in every respect the counterpart of the one he had bought from Broderick.

" Stung ! " he said to himself, with a humorous grin. " Alick's got the best o' me again, and it's me that needs the hanky."

GENT.'S ATTIRE

THE utmost surprise was created last Friday in Campbell & Macdonald's warehouse when Mr Swan appeared in a familiar overcoat. In the memory of the oldest employee he had never previously been known to inaugurate the winter season in any other coat than one quite unmistakably fresh from the tailor's hands. Nothing less would have seemed becoming and appropriate to the oldest traveller for the

oldest soft goods firm in Glasgow. The tradition, long pre-
valent among the warehouse staff of C. & M., was that
Jimmy Swan owed much of his renown and success as a
traveller to the cut and fashion of his garments, always
meticulously fresh and trim, and worn with a certain distinction which was the envy and despair of the younger
travellers. They also tried to dress like gentlemen, but only
partially succeeded, and always stuck at the half-way stage,
where the best that can be said of a wearer of clothes is
that he is a knut. They knew it themselves, when Jimmy's
eyebrows would lift at the sight of their heliotrope wood-
fibre sox or what they had fondly thought a stunning effect
in waistcoats.

Yet here was Jimmy Swan in a last winter's greatcoat,
ready to start on the northern journey through towns and
villages to which, for years, he had been "the glass of fashion
and the mould of form"—the seasonal inspiration and
example of gent.'s styles as approved and passed in the
Metropolis!

A lapse! A decided and disquieting lapse! It was in-
conceivable that the best shops in, say, Aberdeen, would
give such orders as they used to do, to Jimmy Swan in a last
year's topcoat, however cunningly cleaned and pressed to
looked like new.

"Excuse the liberty, Jimmy," said Carmichael the mantle-
buyer, "but what's the matter wi' your tailor? Has your
credit stopped?"

Mr Swan, puffing a little, rose from the case he was bent
over, packing samples, and shrugged his shoulders.

"No," he answered. "If it's my coat you mean, it's just
economy. Quite a good coat!"

"Ah! well," conceded Carmichael, "we have all to exercise
some thrift or other these days."

"No' in the buyin' branch o' this establishment!" said
Mr Swan; "Mr Macdonald's notions o' economy are concentrated in the meantime on the expenses o' the man who

books the biggest orders for his firm, and—not to put too
fine a point on it—that's me ! ''

" Good heavens ! they're no' surely beginnin' to scrimp
YOU, Jimmy ? '' ejaculated Carmichael, genuinely shocked ;
it was understood in the shop that up to a pound a-day, Mr
Swan's bill for expenses passed the cashier unquestioned ;
that it was an historical right, like Magna Charta.

Mr Swan only smiled sadly. " Economy's a droll thing,
Alick," he remarked ; " it's like them Zeppelin bombs, ye
never ken where it'll licht, these days. Mr Macdonald has
all of a sudden found oot that my buyin' a topcoat or a suit
o' clothes noo and then from our country customers, involves
us, someway, in the Corrupt Practices Act. At least, it's
the best excuse he could think o' for knocking a bit aff my
expenses.''

Carmichael looked surprised. " What does it matter to
him where ye buy your clothes ? '' he asked. " But I never
dreamt ye bought any in the country.''

" Many and many a time ! '' said Jimmy. " But nobody
can cast up to me that I ever wore them ! ''

He shut down the lid of his case, and strapped it tightly.

" If ever you had been on the road sellin','' he said, when
that was done, " you would understand yoursel' what's
meant by my auld topcoat, and Macdonald's new economy.
Some o' you chaps get into the buyin' branch wi' little or
nae education to speak o' in human nature. A buyer's
cock-o'-the-walk ; he doesna even need to study to be
civil to the folk he deals wi' ; it's very different wi' the
bagman. I've seen me buy a Hielan' cape I wouldna be
dragged oot o' the Clyde by Geordie Geddes in, and wear it
a couple o' days in Dornoch just to please a draper and tailor
there I expected a thumpin' order frae.''

" Great Scot ! '' said Carmichael, horrified at the very
idea of Mr Swan in a Dornoch cape. " But do ye mean to
say they passed the price o' a cape in your expenses ? ''

" No quite ! '' said Jimmy. " I sold it at a loss o' a

pound when I got to Glasgow, and put the pound doon in my bill. This time last year old Macdonald himself would be the first to agree that it was a pound well spent on the Dornoch orders for fishermen's trousers I used to bring him. Do you know this, Carmichael? I one time went the length o' a suit o' kilts, complete even to the sporran! It was in Inverness, frae a customer that was awfu' namely for his kilts. But Mr Macdonald kicked at kilts; it cost me £2, 10s. to get rid o' them to a Hielandman that had a wee pub. doon on the Broomielaw.

"It is the firmly rooted conviction o' the drapery trade in the rural districts o' Scotland that it's fit to tackle gent.'s attire," continued Mr Swan. "They get the designs and plans for spring lounge suits frae last year's 'Tailor and Cutter' newspaper; heave a web o' tweed at their cutter the first fine day he's aff the spree, tell him the only change this season's in lapels, remind him that cotton lining's nae langer bein' put in breeks, then press a lump o' chalk and a fret-saw into his tremblin' hands, and order him to proceed.

"I've passed through the hands o' mair country cutters than any other man in Scotland. Ye never catch me wearin' onything but a genuine Glasgow suit, but for the sake o' business I've had to order suits in lots o' places no' the size o' Fochabers, where they put rabbit-pouches in your jacket whether ye poach or no', and would palm off a waistcoat wi' sleeves on ye if ye werena watchin'. There's at least a score o' country clothiers in Scotland that expect me to buy a suit or a topcoat frae them every year; the goods is sometimes waitin' ready for me when I land; if there's any difference in the length o' my sleeve since last year, they're ready to tak' in a hem.

"What do I dae wi' the clothes? I sometimes put them into my sample case and sell them in the next wee toon I come to as a model garment fresh from London, goin' at a dead-snip bargain. Some o' them I get rid o' in the packin'-shop at fifteen shillin's or a pound less than I paid for them;

many a time I'm left wi' a Harris tweed the wife can only use for cuttin' up to go under a runner carpet. But up till now the firm has played fair horney, and seen I didna lose on my diplomatic stimulation o' the tailor trade in the turnip districts."

" It's not fair ! " said Carmichael emphatically.

" It is not ! " agreed the traveller. " Macdonald's kickin' aboot 30s. I honestly spent in pushin' business in Clachna-cudden last October. I had aye to tak' a suit in Clachna-cudden ; Elshiner the draper seen to that. He had aye a range o' home-dyed, homespun tweeds for the local cattle show, and a cutter that took your measure a' wrang in Gaelic wi' a piece o' string. I've got suits frae Elshiner I could never sell onywhere at a third o' what they cost me ; they were that roary, and that defiant o' every law o' the male anatomy.

" Last October, when Elshiner's cutter was passin' the string all over my manly form, and stoppin' to tak' a snuff each time that Elshiner put doon the Gaelic figures in a pass-book, I says, ' Whit profit do ye expect to mak' aff this suit, Mr Elshiner ? ' "

" ' Thirty shillin's or thereabouts,' says he.

" ' Ah, well ! ' says I ; ' don't bother makin' it ; I'll pay the 30s. and we'll be a' square.'

" He took the thirty shillin's right enough, but his pride was touched, for he someway jaloused I didna appreciate his suits. And, if ye believe me, he has never given me an order since ! That's the way Macdonald's kickin'."

KEEPING UP WITH COCHRANE

IT is a stimulating thing to see a fellow-creature socially climbing, and up to a certain point Mr James Swan was quite delighted with the progress of his customer Watty Cochrane. He had in a sense been the making of Watty. It was he, nine years ago, who put Watty on to the excellent opening there was for an up-to-date drapery shop in Lairg. He selected his first stock for him ; got him a good credit from C. & M. ; put him up to the art of window-dressing ; and got him a wife with some sensible Glasgow notions of a mantua department.

"She's doin' fine," said Mr Cochrane, after eighteen months of married felicity. "She brought in last year £150 o' profit to the business, all out o' that bit room behind there, where I used to keep my lumber. She calls it an atelier, whatever that is ; so far as I'm concerned she might call it a fusilier, so long's she draws in business the way she does in homespun costumes."

"The main thing is she's up to guarantee," said Jimmy Swan. "I knew Kate Jardine was the sort to make a 'happy fireside clime,' and 'that's the true pathos and sublime o' human life,' as Burns says."

"There's nothing pathetic about £150," said Cochrane ; "it's nearly £3 a week. But when ye speak about a fireside climb, ye've hit the mark ; Kate and me's started climbin', and I lie awake at nichts sometimes wondering what I'll reach to if I keep my health. What would ye say to Provost Walter Cochrane, eh ? " And the draper rubbed his palms together.

The traveller looked at him with a critical eye. "'Well done!' I should say. 'Ye have fine shouthers for a chain, and the right sort o' chest for a door-knocker. But see and no' let your heid swell, Walter, or I'll be vexed I went and wasted Kate on ye!'"

After that, on every journey to the North he could see the climbing of Watty Cochrane. Mr Cochrane was made the Captain of the Golf Club, and immediately burst forth in knickerbocker suits. At the urgent solicitation of the citizens—at all events at the urgent solicitation of two of them, who were on his books—he went into the Town Council and became assured of undying local fame as the introducer of the ash-bin cleansing system. He talked more about ash-bins and destructors to Jimmy Swan on his visits than about the drapery business.

"How's the mistress?" Jimmy asked him sometimes; she was never to be seen.

"Up to the ears in the atelier," would Walter say with pride; "she's thrang on a weddin' job for Invershin."

"I hope," said Jimmy, "she's on the climb, too. There canna be much fun in sclimbin' if your wife's to stand at the foot a' the time and steady the ladder."

"I don't quite catch ye?" said Councillor Walter Cochrane, convener of the Sanitary Committee.

"What I mean," said Jimmy, "is that if you're goin' to climb awa' up to the giddy heights o' social and civic eminence ye seem to have your mind set on, and leave her up to the ears in the atelier, which is just the French for workshop, I'll consider I did an ill turn by Kate Jardine when I put her in your road. So far as I can see, this climbin's a' in the interest o' Walter Cochrane. If ye go on the way ye're doing, she'll soon no' be able to look at ye except through a bit o' smoked gless, the same's ye were an eclipse. I thought it was a wife I got for ye, and no' a heid mantle-maker."

"Do you know what she made last year in the dress-makin'?" asked Councillor Cochrane.

"I don't know, and I don't care," said Jimmy bluntly. "I could get ye scores o' dressmakers just as good from Gleska, but no' another wife like Kate Jardine, and I'm feared ye're tryin' to smother her in selvedges."

On Mr Swan's next journey to Lairg he was just in time to participate in a chippy little dinner given to a select stag company at the Inn to celebrate Councillor Cochrane's eleva-tion to the bench of Justices of the Peace. The dinner was the new J.P.'s. Councillor Cochrane was obviously becoming very fond of himself. He made three separate speeches in a newly-acquired throaty kind of voice, which he seemed to consider incumbent on a J.P. Several times he took occasion

X*

to allude to his last interview with the Lord-Lieutenant of the County.

" Who's he ? " Jimmy took an opportunity of asking.

" The Duke, of course," said Councillor Cochrane.

" Which o' them ? " asked Jimmy innocently. " I never can mind the names o' them unless I look up Orr's Penny Almanac."

" Sutherland," said the new J.P. " He's the Lord-Lieutenant o' the County, and makes all the J.P.'s. At least, the names are put before him, and he signs the Commissions."

" Plucky chap ! " said Jimmy. " Some men would bolt at the desperate responsibility. Listening to ye, there, Walter, I couldna help bein' sorry there's no' a uniform for J.P.'s the same as for Lord-Lieutenants. That heid o' yours 'll never get a chance until ye get a helmet."

The new J.P. considered the occasion incomplete without having his portrait done in oils, and he imported from Aberdeen a fearless young artist, who in five or six days achieved a masterpiece six feet high, wherein Councillor Cochrane was brilliantly revealed as the sort of man who is in the habit of sitting in a frock-coat suit, irrelevantly but firmly grasping a roll of vellum.

The consequence was that when Mr Swan returned to Lairg in autumn in the commercial interest of C. & M., he found his customer had flitted to a grand new villa. The fact was intimated casually over a counter piled with Jimmy's samples.

" Keep it up ! " said Jimmy with an air of resignation. " Lairg's gettin' ower small for ye. And how is she gettin' on, hersel', in the atelier ? "

" Thronger than ever ! " said Councillor Cochrane, triumphantly. " Workin' till all hours since the shootin' started."

" Puir Kate ! " said Jimmy. " She used to be the cheery yin when I kent her in Gleska. She used to hae her evenin's to hersel', and nae bother aboot a villa. What put the villa in your heid, Walter ? "

" It was," said Councillor Cochrane, " the portrait to begin wi'. You see, in the old house the portrait was so big in the wee parlour it fair drowned everything else. Besides, in my position——" and he closed abruptly with a gesture which plainly indicated that the position of a J.P. with the prospects of further civic dignities demanded a reasonable area of domestic space to move about in. " What I want ye to do for me, now," he proceeded, " is to send me up from the Clyde a flag-pole for the front o' the house."

" What do ye want wi' a flag-pole ? " said Jimmy with surprise. " Are ye goin' to start sclimbin' flag-poles next ? "

" No," said Councillor Cochrane : " but a bit of a pole goes well wi' a villa. I see a lot o' them in the villas down at Inverness. Many a time a body wants to hoist a flag. A flag-pole gives a kind o' finish."

The flag-pole was duly ordered by Mr Swan, who had dreams of a greatly inflated Cochrane painfully sprawling up and sitting on the truck with Kate Jardine sitting making costumes at the foot. For months he had no communication with his soaring customer, but at last he got a letter asking him to keep his eye about for a couple of iron cannons, second-hand. The letter came to Jimmy one morning as he sat at home at breakfast, and he groaned as he perused it.

" What's the matter, Jimmy ? " asked his wife.

" It's Watty Cochrane in Lairg," he told her. " He's goin' to shoot himsel', and he thinks himsel' that big it needs a couple o' cannons to do the job."

" Nonsense ! " said Mrs Swan.

" No, I'm wrang ! " said Jimmy, hastily, proceeding further with his reading of the letter. " They're for the front of the villa ; he wants them four feet lang and mounted, for he's noo a Bailie. I'll see him to the mischief first ! I've troked aboot for many a droll thing for my customers, but I draw the line at cannons. What'll he be wantin' next if they mak' him Provost ? "

Jimmy went up to Lairg on his next North journey with a plausible tale that there was a positive dearth of second-hand cannons in the West of Scotland, as they were all taken up by the Territorial artillery.

" It doesna matter," said Bailie Cochrane, looking slightly worried. " I thought they would make a kind of artistic finish to the villa, but I doubt I'll have to do without them. What I'm wantin' more's a forewoman. You would hear the news ? "

" No," said Jimmy.

" The wife's given up the atelier. . . . It's twins," said Bailie Cochrane.

THE HEN CRUSADE

" Do ye mind yon hen ye were good enough to send my wife for her stall at the Bazaar ? " asked Boyd the draper as Mr Swan was putting back his samples in their cases.

" Fine ! " said Jimmy. " I hope it was all right ? "

" It was right enough," said Mr Boyd, solemnly ; " but it caused a lot o' ill-will among the customers," and Jimmy, bent above his cases, indulged in a crafty wink to himself.

" There wasn't a body came to that Bazaar," went on the draper, " that didn't want to buy the hen. There was what I might call a regular furore about her. And because one hen couldna be sold to four hundred different folk, they took the pet and went away without buyin' anything. I canna understand it ; the folk in this place seem to be daft for poultry. . . . What are ye laughing at, Mr Swan ? "

" Was the Bazaar a success ? " asked Jimmy.

" Indeed and it was not ! They didna get half the money that they wanted, and I'm no' vexed ; it wasna wi' my will that my wife gave countenance to a Bazaar to buy an organ ; what we're needin's no' an organ, but a new minister ; we're all fair sick o' Cameron. . . . But what in a' the earth are ye grinnin' at, Mr Swan ? "

" I'll tell ye that," said Jimmy ; " I'm laughing at the continued triumph o' my Hen Crusade. You see, I'm utterly against Bazaars, Mr Boyd. They're the worst form o' Sweatin' that we have in this country. They're blackleg labour. They're bad for the shopkeeper's business, and they're bad for my firm, C. & M. If the craze for Bazaars went any further, I would soon be sellin' naething else but remnants, and folk would expect to get them gratis wi' a bonus ticket. Now, when a customer like yoursel' asks me for a trifle for his wife's stall, I darena well refuse ; but I took a survey of the situation some time since, and I saw how I could please my customer and at the same time put a spoke in the Bazaar. The common hen, Mr Boyd, humble, unostentatious, and industrious in life, becomes, when dead, the valued friend o' British commerce."

" Yours was the only fowl in that Bazaar," said Mr Boyd, " and it fair upset it ! "

" Exactly ! " said Jimmy, rubbing his hands with the greatest satisfaction. " Works like a charm, every time ! I'm strongly advising C. & M. to send a hen to every Bazaar that opens."

" Every person who came into that Bazaar made a dash at once for the produce stall and grabbed the hen, though it had a ticket ' Sold ' on it before the door was opened."

" The wife, I suppose ? " said Jimmy, innocently.

" Yes," said Mr Boyd, a little flushed. " It was a tidy hen ; well worth the half-crown you put on it."

" I always fix the price as low as that," said Jimmy, though that hen cost me exactly three-and-nine. If the price is low, the competition is the keener."

" At last my wife had to send the fowl home before it was torn to bits by exasperated customers ; but all the same everybody coming into that place till the latest hour at night was asking for the hen. And because we didn't have table-loads o' half-croon hens they took the huff and went away, as I say, without buyin' anything. The funny thing is they all kent there was a hen before they came near the place."

"They always do!" said Jimmy. "The rumour of something really useful in a Bazaar goes round a town like this like a fiery cross, and that's the phenomenon I take advantage of in my Hen Crusade. You see, it has got this length wi' Bazaars that they're filled wi' fancy-work no rational mortal soul could fancy. The first thing a woman does in the way o' contributin' to a stall is to cut up something useful and turn it into something ornamental, and the poor misguided body who buys it and brings it home is chaffed a lot about it by her husband. Then, in addition, there's, at all Bazaars, a great bulk o' stuff that's never meant for either use or ornament—it's just Bazaar stuff, made for sellin'. The buyer takes it home and puts it out o' sight till the next Bazaar comes on, and makes it her contribution. It goes from Bazaar to Bazaar till it drops in pieces, or till folk canna guess what it was first intended for.

"It's some years now since the hen came to me as an inspiration. There's something about a hen wi' its heid thrawed that strongly appeals to human nature. I thought to mysel' if I can introduce one fair good hen at a temptin' price to a Bazaar, the struggle for its possession will kill the interest in fancy-work that's far better bought from the retail shops that buy from C. & M. It's sure to be bought at the very start by the lady who has it in her stall, and that in itself's annoyin' to the other customers. But, further than that, it's well enough known to every woman who goes about Bazaars that the only thing she can bring home from them to please her man is something he can eat. He has no use for home-made toffee, and he wouldna thank her for the minister's wife's conception o' a seed-cake. A fowl, on the other hand, will never go wrong wi' him, and that's the way ye'll notice that the rumour o' a hen for sale at a Bazaar brings up a queue o' women to the doors an hour before they're open. Half o' them have explicit orders from their husbands to buy that hen, and the other half are planning to give him a nice surprise.

"When the crowd find that the hen's awa' wi't already at half-a-crown to the lady at the stall, it goes home indignant without a glance at the table-centres, and that's another Bazaar burst! I'm tellin' you, Mr Boyd, it's aye weel worth a draper's while to make his contribution to a kirk bazaar a sonsy hen marked down to a price that's temptin'. I've tried jucks, but jucks is no use; the public's dubious about jucks; ye can only rouse the spirit o' competition wi' a hen."

"You're an awfu' sly man, Mr Swan!" exclaimed the draper. "But I'm no vexed yon hen o' yours played havoc wi' the last Bazaar. I've quarrelled wi' the minister about that very organ, and now I havena any kirk to go to."

"It's surely no' for the want o' kirks," said Jimmy. "How many are there here for less than a thousand souls?"

"Five," said Mr Boyd sadly; "the Parish, the U.F., which I belong to, the Episcopalian that belongs to Mr Snodgrass of Blairmaddy, and two different kinds o' Frees, the Wee Frees and the——"

"Oh! never mind goin' into that," said Jimmy, "just say assorted. I never could tell the difference o' one Free Kirk from another, and I've studied the thing minutely, even to the way they cut their hair. A customer up in Ullapool tells me it's a' in the way ye carry your hat in your hand goin' up the aisle; if ye happen to carry it upside down you're seen to be a slider, and they fence the tables against ye at the next Communion, so ye have to join the other body."

"The worst of it with me," said Mr Boyd, "is that there's no' another body in the town I could take up wi' and respect myself. But I'm done wi' Cameron! He wants an organ and a lectern. It would suit him better if he stuck to the fundamentals."

" What exactly's that ? " asked Jimmy gravely, fastening a strap.

Mr Boyd was content to wave his hands in the manner which indicates that words are quite inadequate to express ideas. " It's a bonny-like thing," said he, " that I have to go to Glasgow for Communion Sunday ! I certainly will not go to the table under Cameron ! Could you recommend a sound U.F. in Glasgow, Mr Swan ? I'll take my wife and family."

" Cameron ? " said Jimmy, turning something over in his mind " The best kirk I can recommend's my ain, though ye'll have to thole the organ."

" I don't care ! " said Mr Boyd, as he took a note of it. " Anything at all to get awa' from Cameron ! "

Two weeks later all the family of Boyd came back from Glasgow looking rather downed. They had been to the Communion.

" What way did ye get on ? " a customer asked the draper on the day that followed their return.

" I didna get on at all ! " said Mr Boyd disgustedly. " A fair take-in ! It cost us £2, 10s. to go the week-end to Glasgow, and we a' went to the kirk that Swan the traveller recommended. There we were sittin' expectin' a rousin' sermon from the Rev. Walter Spiers, and sure o' havin' the fundamentals. When the bell stopped ringin', I heard a skliff o' feet from the vestry that struck me as familiar, and when I looked up to see who the beadle was snibbin' in the pulpit, who was this but Cameron ! "

LINOLEUM

MR JAMES SWAN has lived for fifteen years in Ibrox. For the first six months he thought it horrible, and ever since he has vexed himself to think how foolish he was not to have gone there sooner. That is life. Men are like pot plants. You shift a geranium into a new pot, and for weeks it wilts, disconsolate, till some fine sunny day it seems to realise that other geraniums seem happy enough in the same sort of pots, and that it isn't the pot that matters really. Whereupon the geranium (which is actually a pelargonium) strikes fresh roots into the soil, spreads out a broader leaf, throws out a couple of blossoms, and delights in making the best of it. It takes the first prize at the local flower show; content is the best fertiliser. Jimmy Swan, after fifteen years at Ibrox, thinks Ibrox is the centre of the solar system. Take him to Langside or Partickhill, and he feels chilly; at Dennistoun he feels himself a foreigner, and looks at passing tramcars for the Southside as an exile from Scotland, haunting the quays of Melbourne, looks at ships from the Clyde with the names of Denny or Fairfield on their brasses. Jimmy said to me the other day, "I canna think how people can live ony where else than Ibrox. It's the best place in the world." "How?" I asked. "Well," said he, "it's-it's-it's-it's Ibrox!" A little inconclusive, but I quite understood. Nine-tenths of us have our Ibrox; the people to be sympathised with are those who haven't.

But Jimmy got an awful start the other day! He came home from the North journey on a Saturday very tired, and exceedingly glad to see the familiar streets of Ibrox again. Nothing had changed; the same ham was in the grocery window, apparently only a slice the less, and he had exactly the high tea he expected, but his wife was different. She plainly nursed some secret discontent. Quite nice, and interested in his journey, and all that, but still——

It turned out to be the linoleum. The lobby linoleum. She put it to Jimmy if a lobby linoleum seven years old could honestly be regarded as quite decent.

"Tuts! there's naething wrang wi' the linoleum," said her husband. "As nice a linoleum as anybody need ask for; I never tripped on't yet."

" The pattern's worn off half of it," said his wife ; " Mrs Grant was in to-day, and I was black affronted. In her new house in Sibbald Terrace they have Persia rugs."

" Kirkcaldy's good enough for us," said Jimmy ; " just you wait for a year or twa and ye'll see the fine new linoleum I'll get ye."

It was then that the shock came. Mrs Swan, having brooded for a while on the remoteness of a new linoleum, intimated with a calm that was almost inhuman that she had been looking at some of the houses to let in Sibbald Terrace. Their present house was become impossible any longer. It had all the vices conceivable in any house built of human hands, and several others peculiar to itself, and evidently of their nature demoniac. It was cold, it was draughty, it was damp, it was dismal. Its chimneys did not draw properly ; its doors were in the wrong places ; its kitchen range was a heartbreak ; its presses were inadequate,—she took ten minutes to expose all its inherent defects as a dwelling, and left her astonished listener in the feeling that he had been living for fifteen years in an orange-box without knowing it.

" We'll have to flit ! " she said at last, determinedly.

" Sibbald Terrace is no' in Ibrox ! " said her husband, astonished at her apparent overlook of this vital consideration.

" All the better o' that ! " said the amazing woman. " I'm sick o' Ibrox ! You can say what you like, James Swan ; I'll no' stay another year in this hoose."

" Ye're fair fagged oot, Bella," said her husband, compassionately. " I doubt ye have been washin', efter all I told ye. Ye should stay in your bed the morn, and never mind the kirk. Sick o' Ibrox ? Ye shouldna say things like that even in fun ! "

It was at this stage, or a few days after it, I met Mr Swan. He was chuckling broadly to himself. " Did you ever flit," he asked me.

" Once," I said.

" That's enough for a lifetime," said he. " Men would never flit any mair than they would change their sox if it wasna for their wives. The advantage o' an auld hoose is that ye aye ken where your pipe is. My wife took a great fancy to flit the other day, and I said it was a' right; that I would look oot for a new house. At the end o' three days I said I had a fair clinker—vestibule wi' cathedral glass in the doors, oriel windows in the parlour, fifteen by eight lobby, venetian blinds, bathroom h. and c., wash-hand basin, electric light, tiled close, and only five stairs up.

" She says, ' Do ye think I'm daft ? Five stairs ! Is it in the Municipal Buildin's ? '

" ' No,' says I ; ' it's in Dalwhinnie Street.'

" ' Where in a' the earth is Dalwhinnie Street ? ' says she.

" ' It's a new street,' I said, ' near Ruchill. Ye take the car from aboot the foot o' Mitchell Street, come off at an apothecary's shop, and take the first turn to the right and ask a message-boy.'

" ' I'll not go to any such street, James Swan ! ' she says ; ' I would rather take a place ! ' and the dear lass was a' trimblin' wi' agitation."

" No wonder, Mr Swan," I said. " It sounded a very out-of-the-way locality. Where is Dalwhinnie Street ? "

" There's no such street," said Mr Swan : " at least if there is, I never heard o't. But ye see I wanted to put her aff the notion o' flittin'. And there was Bella, almost greetin' ! I let on I was fair set on Dalwhinnie Street because it was so handy for the Northern Merchants' Social Club. But Dalwhinnie Street, right or wrong, she would not hear tell o', and I said I would take another look round."

Mr Swan cocked his head a little and looked slyly at me. " Ye're a married man, yoursel'," said he. " Ye know what wives are. They're no' such intellectual giants as we are, thank God ! or else they would find us oot ; but once they've set their minds on a thing, Napoleon himself couldna shift them. Some days after that I cam' hame from Renfrewshire wi' a great scheme for takin' a house in the country. I said I had seen the very house for us—half-way between Houston and Bridge-of-Weir.

" ' Whereabouts is Houston ? ' says the mistress in frigid tones, as they say in the novels.

" ' It's half-way between the Caledonian and G. and S.-W. lines,' says I, ' and if ye're in a hurry ye take a 'bus if it's there.'

" ' What sort o' house is it ? ' she asked, turnin' the heel o' a stockin' as fast as lightning.

" ' Tip-top ! ' I says. ' Nine rooms and a kitchen ; fine flagged floor in the kitchen ; spring water frae the pump in the garden ; two-stall stable. Any amount o' room for hens ; ye can keep hunders o' hens. The grocer's van passes the door every Thursday.'

" She began to greet. ' That's right ! ' she says. ' Put me awa' in the wilds among hens, so that I'll die, and ye'll can marry a young yin. But mind you this, James Swan ; I'll no' shift a step oot o' Ibrox ! '

" ' Tuts, Bella ! ' I says, ' ye canna stay ony langer in this house ; it's a' wrang thegither.'

" ' There's naething wrang wi' the hoose,' says she, ' if I had jist some fresh linoleum.'

" ' Well, well,' says I ; ' ye'll get the linoleum '—and I was much relieved. ' I'll buy't to-morrow.' And I did. It cost me 4s. 6d. a yard.''

" Your wife is a very clever lady, Mr Swan," I said ; " she probably never thought of flitting, but badly wanted that linoleum."

" Of course ! " said Jimmy Swan. " I kent that a' alang ! But ye've got to compromise ! "

THE GRAUVAT KING

MOST people — even in the dry-goods trade — think the Muffler that made Mildrynie Famous, and that great woollen factory which gives employment to thousands of people in Mildrynie, and has in ten years made a fortune for the Drummonds, owed their conception wholly to Peter Drummond. A great mistake! Peter Drummond, of himself, never had any imagination, initiative, or enterprise ; till this day (between ourselves) he is a pretty poor fly, and his great national reputation as the Muffler King, his grand Deeside estate, his superb collection of Old Masters, his deputy-lieutenantship, and the marriage of his daughter Cissy to Lord " Tivitty " Beauchamp, are due under Providence to Mr James Swan, traveller for the Glasgow firm of Campbell & Macdonald. There is a marble timepiece of the most ponderous and depressing character in Mr Swan's parlour, with an inscription on it which marks an epoch in the history of industrial Scotland. It says—

To JAMES SWAN, ESQ.,

FROM

HIS FAITHFUL FRIEND,

PETER DRUMMOND.

3 *JUNE* 1903.

_____

" *Lest we forget.*"

The clock doesn't go ; it hasn't gone for years ; it is merely a domestic monument—of ingratitude.

Peter Drummond, in 1903, was a customer of Jimmy Swan's in Mildrynie. He and his brother Alick (now Alexander Lloyd Drummond, Esq. of Ballochmawn) had a tiny draper's shop in East Street, next door to a smiddy which seemed to do nothing else from one end of the year till the other but singe sheep's heads for the inhabitants of Mildrynie, who at that time numbered eight hundred souls and two policemen.

One day Jimmy Swan turned up at the door with his sample cases, and found the brothers much depressed. They were doing wretched business. Their shop was off the main street ; the propinquity of the smiddy and its perpetual odour of singed wool made the shopping public avoid it ; things were come to such a pass that the Drummonds were contemplating closing up and going off to Canada.

" There's naething to be done in this hole o' a place," said Peter, who spoke Scotch in these days.

" There's plenty to be done in ony place if you're the kind o' man to do it," said Jimmy. " Mildrynie's no' much size ; I've seen it missed a'thegither oot o' the maps ; but for a' that it's a wonderful place, for it's fair in the middle o' the world. If it's a hole, as ye say, it's a hole to be respected, for it's like a hole in the middle o' a grindstane."

" Nonsense ! " said Peter Drummond. " Aff the railway line, away up here in the North ; it's oot o' the world a'thegither."

" Fair in the middle ! " insisted Mr Swan. " Look you at a globe or a map o' the world, and ye'll see I'm richt. Every other place in the world's grouped roond aboot Mildrynie, just the same as if God had meant it to be great."

" Maybe that's so ! " conceded Mr Drummond on reflection ; " but my shop's no' in the middle o' Mildrynie, and so I whiles think I micht as weel ha'e my signboard up at the North Pole. That's the middle o' the world too."

" What do ye dae to attract customers ? " asked Jimmy, adjusting his carnation.

" Just what everybody else does that keeps a shop," said Peter Drummond.

" Error No. 1," said Jimmy. " The way to attract customers is to dae what naebody else is daein'. That's where the profit as well as the fun comes in. I would get sick-tired daein' the same as everybody else ; the only excuse ye have for bein' alive is that ye dae some things peculiarly in your own way."

" I carry a good stock, and I show everything at a reasonable price," said Peter Drummond.

" Error No. 2," said Jimmy, blandly. " Ye should start sellin' something at a quite unreasonable price."

" What dae ye mean ? " asked Mr Drummond.

" Sell it at what it costs ye. Here's a new line I have in woollen mufflers, as cosy as a fur-lined coat, and fastens wi' a snap. They'll cost ye half-a-croon each from C. & M., and that's even coontin' aff the discoont. The winter's comin' on ; you make a splash wi' the Mildrynie Muffler at half-a-croon, and ye'll get the folk to your shop, for naebody else sells them for less than three shillings. Once ye have the folk buying your mufflers at cost price, it'll be gey droll if ye canna sell them other things at a reasonable profit."

" There's something in't ! " said Peter Drummond.

On the next journey Mr Swan made to Mildrynie, he found that the half-crown muffler had moved the business slightly, but not enough to lift the spirits of the brothers Drummond. Their unpopular location and the smell of the smiddy were against a really popular and fashionable success.

" Do ye advertise ? " asked Jimmy.

" No," said Peter ; " naebody advertises here."

" My goodness ! that's the very chance for you then ! " exclaimed Mr Swan eagerly. " Chip in first before the others think o't. Advertise in the county paper—' The Real and Original Mildrynie Muffler ' ; ye'll sell them like Forfar Rock ! "

" But if naebody's wantin' mufflers ? " said Peter, sadly.

" Naebody was wantin' Beecham's pills a hundred years ago, and noo they canna dae withoot them. Look at the way that soap's come into fashion, even in the country districts—a' the result o' advertisin'."

"It's the smell o' the smiddy next door that spoils this street," said Mr Drummond.

"Error No. 4642 !" said Jimmy. "The smiddy 'll be a godsend if ye'll dae what I'm gaun to tell ye. Put you this advertisement in the local paper " —and he quickly drafted it out on a sheet of wrapping-paper—

THE MARVELLOUS MILDRYNIE MUFFLER,

ONLY HALF-A-CROWN.

DRUMMOND'S SHOP, 3 EAST STREET.

Follow your Nose and the Smell of Sheep's Head Singeing.

"I never saw an advertisement like that in a' my life," said Peter Drummond.

"Exactly !" said Jimmy. "That's the sort o' advertisement to advertise when ye're advertisin'."

On his next journey he found the Drummond business booming, and got an incredibly large order for Mildrynie mufflers at a price that left a reasonable profit for the retailer. But Peter was still a little depressed.

"There's money in't sure enough," said he ; "but they ca' me the Grauvat King, and I don't like it."

"Nonsense !" said Jimmy. "It's just as fine to be the Grauvat King as the Oil King, or the Diamond King, or the Cattle King ; it's a' the same to you so lang's ye get them on the neck. If you're the Grauvat King in Forfarshire, it's a' the easier for ye to be Muffler Monarch to the country at large. The Mildrynie Muffler's good enough to stand pushing just as far as Hielan' Whisky ; you get a pickle money thegither and advertise the Rale and Original Mildrynie Half-croon Muffler in a' the papers in the country, and ye'll mak' a fortune. Tell them the Mildrynie Muffler's made aff pure hygienic wool that's grown on high-pedigree Hielan' sheep that graze on the heathery slopes o' the Grampian Mountains, the land where the eagle soars and the cataract flashes ; that it's manufactured in the cottage homes o' the God-fearin',

clean, and industrious native peasantry, and is recognised
by the faculty as the one garment responsible for the sturdy
health and universal longevity o' the Scottish race, and
C. & M. 'll keep ye supplied wi' a' ye want; there's plenty o'
mills in bonny wee Gleska."

It was in recognition of this valuable tip that Peter
Drummond, a twelvemonth later, gave Mr Swan the timepiece—a poor solatium to Mr Swan for his loss of Drummonds' muffler trade when they opened the enormous works
of their own at Mildrynie.

JIMMY'S SINS FIND HIM OUT

MR JAMES SWAN picked up a bunch of violets, which he had
been refreshing in a tumbler while he wrote out his expenses
for the week, and placed it in his button-hole. From a
pocket he took a small case-comb, and, borrowing from
Pratt, the office " knut," the little mirror which Pratt kept
always in his desk to consult as often as the Ready Reckoner,
he went to the window and combed his hair.

" What side are sheds worn on this season ? " he asked
Pratt, whom it was the joke of the office to treat with mock
deference as arbiter of fashion, expert, and authority upon
every giddy new twirl of the world of elegance.

" To the left," said Pratt, without a moment's hesitation,
and with the utmost solemnity ; the parting of his own hair
was notoriously a matter of prayerful consideration. He was
a lank lad with a long neck ; it looked as if his Adam's
apple was a green one and was shining through—a verdant
phenomenon due to the fact that he had used the same
brass stud for three years.

" Can't be done on the left," said Mr Swan. " That's the
side I do my thinkin' on, and it's worn quite thin. I envy
ye your head o' hair, Pratt ; it'll last ye a lifetime, no'
like mine."

Pratt, with the mirror restored to him, put it back in his desk with a final glance at it to see that his necktie was as perfectly knotted as it was three minutes ago ; put on his hat and bolted from the office.

" They're a' in a great hurry to be off the day," said Mr Swan to himself. " I wonder what they're up to ? "

He was to find out in two minutes, to his own discomfiture.

At the foot of the stair which led to the upper warehouse he ran against Peter Grant of Aberdeen, who was in search of him.

" My Jove ! " said Grant, panting ; " I'm in luck ! I was sure ye would be awa' to't, and I ran doon the street like to break my legs."

" De-lighted to see ye, Mr Grant ! " said Jimmy with a radiant visage. " This is indeed a pleasant surprise ! But ye don't mean to tell me ye came from Aberdeen this mornin' ? "

" Left at a quarter to seven," said Grant. " I made up my mind last night to come and see it. And I says to mysel', ' If I can just catch Mr Swan before he goes to the field, the thing's velvet ! ' "

" De-lighted ! " said Jimmy, and shook his hand again. But the feeling of icy despair in his breast was enough to wilt his violets.

His sin had found him out ! There was only one inference to be drawn from Peter Grant's excited appearance ; he had carried out the threat of a dozen years to come and see a Glasgow football match, and expected the expert company and guidance of C. & M.'s commercial traveller.

And Jimmy Swan had, so far as Grant was concerned, a reputation for football knowledge and enthusiasm it was impossible to justify in Glasgow, however plausible they seemed in a shop in Aberdeen. Grant, who had never seen a football match in his life, was a fanatic in his devotion to a game which for twenty years he followed in the newspapers. Jimmy in his first journeys to Aberdeen had discovered this fancy of his customer, and played up to it craftily with the aid of the " Scottish Referee," which he bought on each journey North for no other purpose, since he himself had never seen a football match since the last cap of Harry M'Neill of the " Queen's," in 1881.

The appalling ignorance of Jimmy regarding modern football, and his blank indifference to the same, were never suspected by his customer, who from the traveller's breezy and familiar comments upon matches scrappily read about an hour before, credited him with knowing all there was to know about the national pastime.

When Jimmy was in doubt about the next move in a conversation with Grant, he always mentioned Quinn, and called him " good old Jimmy." He let it be understood that the Saturday afternoons when he couldn't get to Ibrox were unhappy—which was perfectly true, since he lived in Ibrox, though the Rangers' park was a place he never went near.

" I'll go and see a match some day ! " Grant always said ; he had said it for many years, and Jimmy always said, " Mind and let me know when ye're comin', and I'll show ye fitba'."

And now he was taken at his word !

What particular match could Grant have come for ? Jimmy had lost sight of football, even in the papers, for the past three months.

With an inward sigh for a dinner spoiled at home, he took his customer to a restaurant for lunch.

" I want to see M'Menemy," said Grant ; " it was that that brought me ; he's a clinker ! "

" And he never was in better form," said Jimmy. " Playin' like a book ! He says to me last Monday, ' We'll walk over them the same's we had a brass band in front of us, Mr Swan ! ' "

" Will they win, do ye think ? " Grant asked with great anxiety ; he was so keen, the lunch was thrown away on him.

"Win!" said Jimmy. "Hands down! The—the—the other chaps is shakin' in their shoes."

So far he moved in darkness. Who M'Menemy was, and what match he was playing in that day, he had not the faintest idea, and he played for safety. It was probably some important match. The state of the streets as they had walked along to the restaurant suggested a great influx of young men visitors; it might be something at Celtic Park.

He looked at Grant's square-topped hat and had an inspiration.

"If ye'll take my advice, Mr Grant," said he, "ye'll go and buy a kep. A hat like that's no use at a Gleska fitba' match; ye need a hooker. If ye wear a square-topped hat it jist provokes them. I'm gaun round to the warehouse to change my ain hat for a bunnet; I'll leave ye in a hat shop on the road and then I'll jine ye."

"What fitba' match is on the day?" Jimmy asked a porter in the warehouse.

"Good Goad!" said the porter with amazement at him; "it's the International against England."

"Where is it played?" asked Jimmy.

"Hampden, of course!"

"What way do ye get to't, and when does it start?"

"Red car to Mount Florida; game starts at three; I wish to goodness I could get to't," said the porter.

Jimmy looked his watch. It was half-past one.

He found Grant with a headgear appropriate to the occasion, and wasted twenty minutes in depositing his hat at Buchanan Street left-luggage office. Another twenty minutes passed at the station bar, where Jimmy now discoursed with confidence on Scotland's chances, having bought an evening paper.

"Will ye no' need to hurry oot to the park?" Grant asked with some anxiety. "There'll be an awfu' crood; twenty chaps wi' bunnets came on at Steenhive."

"Lot's of time!" said Jimmy with assurance. "We'll tak' a car. Come awa', and I'll show ye a picture palace."

It was fifteen minutes to three when they got to Hampden. A boiling mass of frantic people clamoured round the gates, which were shut against all further entrance, to the inner joy of Mr Swan, who lost his friend in the crowd and failed to find him.

"Where on earth were you till this time?" asked his wife when he got home to Ibrox two hours later.

"Out in the Queen's Park," said Jimmy truthfully. "Wi' luck I lost a man outside a fitba' match, and spent an hour in Camphill—no' a soul in't but mysel'—listenin' to the birds whistlin'."

A WAVE OF TEMPERANCE

ONE day last week an hotel in Falkirk had six commercial travellers from Glasgow in its commercial room at dinner, the president and *doyen* of them Jimmy Swan, who unfeelingly depressed the company by drinking ginger ale. It was not so much his choice of this unorthodox beverage that saddened them as his evident enjoyment of it; he lingered over it, and smacked his lips upon it, and cocked his eye to look through the bubbling glass as if it were Clicquot, 1904. The others suddenly realised that this ostentatious gusto carried some reproach on their preference for bitter beer—so they defiantly ordered in another pewter each.

"You should try sour milk, Mr Swan," said that hardened satirist, Joe M'Guire, the boot man; "it's said to be full o' the finest germs. If you drink sour dook you'll live to the age o' a hundred and fifty, and you'll well deserve it."

"Ginger," said the flour man, Wallace, "is all right in its own place. One time, I mind, I tried it—at the funeral o' an uncle o' mine who was a Rechabite; and I can tell you that so far as I was concerned that day he was sincerely mourned."

Jimmy Swan smiled blandly, and squinted again through his tumbler.

" Clean, wholesome, morally stimulatin', warmth-provokin', thirst-assuagin'—the nectar o' the gods ! " he said with the eloquence of an advertisement. " What's good enough for the King and Kitchener is good enough for me. You chaps should give it a trial ; it would save ye a lot o' money in aromatic lozengers."

Five minutes after the Crown Hotel commercial room was a debating club, with temperance and prohibition for its subjects. Mr Swan had by far the best of the argument, since none of the rest could agree upon what constituted the particular virtues or charm of alcohol, though they were unanimous in declaring their line of business made a judicious use of it absolutely indispensable.

" I've taken up that line mysel' in my unregenerate days —and that was up to a week ago," said Jimmy ; " but to tell the truth, I took a dram because I liked it ; my other reasons were a' palaver."

" But human geniality," said Peter Garvie (lubricating oils), who was reputed on the road to have as little geniality as a haddock—" it wants a glass o' something stronger than ginger ale to bring men together. You couldna show your friendliness to a man unless you bought him a glass o' something."

" Ye could buy him a pair o' gallowses," suggested Jimmy, and saying so, he finished the last of his ginger ale hurriedly, and put down the glass with a bang. He had an inspiration.

A little later six quite rational representatives of well-known wholesale Glasgow houses were, incredible though it may seem, in a solemn pact to suspend the ancient treating customs of their country for a week ; eschew all the alcoholic beverages, and maintain " the genial flow," as Jimmy called it, on a system more likely to benefit the sale of the goods they travelled in than standing rounds of beer or whisky-and-soda.

Two hours later M'Guire met Jimmy in the High Street, beaming with satisfaction at a well-filled book of orders ; his own success that day left no excuse for grumbling.

"It's a raw, cold day," said Jimmy, rubbing his hands. "Have ye any good in your mind ?"

"I don't mind if I do," said M'Guire, and absent-mindedly was making for the Blue Bell hostelry.

"Na ! na !" said Jimmy ; "mind the pledge ; there's naething'll cross my lips but a threepenny cheroot."

They went into a tobacconist's, and their cheroots were hardly lighted when Jimmy said, "Hurry up and we'll hae another."

"No fears !" said the boot man firmly, "I never smoked two cigars a day in my life except on Sunday, and I wouldna smoke this one noo if it hadna cost me threepence."

"Do ye feel the genial flow yet ?" asked Jimmy, as they walked along the street.

"Not a bit !" said M'Guire. "It's more like burned broon paper."

Jimmy chucked away his cigar and led him into a baker's shop.

"Two London buns, miss," said he. "The best. On draught" ; leaned one arm elegantly on the counter ; said, "Well, here's to us !" and ate his bun with a fair pretence at relish. M'Guire, who was renowned for being able to eat anything at any time, was finished before him.

"Hurry up, Jimmy !" he said. "We'll jist have another one, for the good o' the house."

"All right !" said Jimmy. "Make it a small one this time, miss. No ! I'll tell ye what—I'll split a parley this time, Joe ; I feel that bun in my heid already."

Wallace came round the corner just as they were leaving the baker's shop.

" Ye're just in time ! " said Jimmy. " An hour till the train goes and we're on the batter." He was munching the last of the parley he had shared with M'Guire, and Wallace dropped to the situation.

" What's it goin' to be ? " he asked with something less than the usual convivial abandon expected with the question.

" They're no' half fly wi' their drapery shops in Fa'kirk," said Jimmy, twinkling. " They should ha'e a back-door to them. Slip in to this yin," and he led them into the premises of one of his oldest customers.

" Back again, ye see, Mr Ross," he said to the draper. " It's somebody's birthday, and we're on the fair ran-dan. What are ye goin' to have, gentlemen ? "

" My shout ! " said Wallace. " Give it a name."

" I think I'll just have a small pocket-hankey this time," said M'Guire, and Jimmy Swan agreed that a pocket-hankey was the very thing he was thinking of having himself.

" We'll just have another ! " he said when they had got them. " Just one more hankey 'll no' do ye a bit o' harm. I'm feelin' fine ! A nasty raw cold day—ye need a hankey to cheer ye up."

M'Guire, who pretended to be looking all round the floor for a spittoon, declared he couldn't find room for another handkerchief, but could be doing with a 16 collar.

" Collars all round let it be," said Jimmy, " We'll just make a night of it. But mind ye, M'Guire, you're no' to start the singin' ! When it comes to collars, I'm aye prood to say I can either take them or leave them. I'm no' one o' these chaps that's nip-nip-nipping awa' at collars a' day —the ruination o' the constitution and the breakin'-up o' mony a happy home. Three White Horse collars, Mr Ross, and what'll ye take yoursel' ? "

Mr Ross was a pawky gentleman himself, and had heard of the commercials' compact from the traveller earlier in the day. He turned his back on them, having put forth the collars, and scrutinised the shelves behind him with profound shrewdness.

" At this time o' day I never touch a collar," he remarked. " It doesna agree wi' me before my tea. I think, if you'll allow me, seeing it's so cold a day, I'll just have a Cardigan waistcoat, Mr Swan," and he pulled down a box of those garments.

COUNTRY JOURNEYS

As the train pulled out of Buchanan Street Station, Slymon, the tea man, drew off a fur-lined glove and put his hand inquiringly upon the foot-warmer.

" Feel that, Mr Swan ! " he remarked, indignantly, and Jimmy did so.

" It's aff the bile, at any rate," he intimated cheerfully. " Or perhaps it's a new patent kind, like one of those Thermos flasks my wife got a present of at Christmas, guaranteed to keep the heat for four-and-twenty hours. She wrapped it up in flannel, put it in the bed, and was awfully disappointed. ' Is that your feet ? ' she asked me at two o'clock in the morning. ' It is not,' says I. ' Then the shop that sold John Grant that bottle swindled him ; it's an ice-cream freezer,' says the mistress."

" A railway foot-warmer filled with liquid gas is no use to me," proceeded the indignant Slymon, and for the next ten minutes he said things about The True Line which would have much distressed the directors of the Caledonian Railway had they been there to hear them.

Jimmy merely buttoned his coat a little tighter, tucked his rug more carefully round his legs, and looked compassionately upon his fellow-traveller.

" Man, Slymon," he remarked at last, " if you get so warm as that about the shortcomings of the Caley and every other system you'll work yourself into a perspiration that'll open all your pores, and get your death of cold when you go out

Y

at Larbert. It's your feet that's wrong to start with. Either your boots are tight or you're wearing the wrong kind of sox, or there's something up with your circulation. Thirty years ago the railways wouldn't even pretend to give us hot-water pans, and nobody in our line died of cold feet yet that I ever heard of."

"Travelling becomes more uncomfortable every year," said Slymon, irritably, and Jimmy snorted.

"Look here, Slymon!" he said, "you're making me feel old, and I don't like it. If you say travelling becomes more uncomfortable every year, I must be getting blind, or you must be thirty years younger than me, and I don't believe it. Here you are in a padded carriage—Third Class —fifty per cent. better than the First we used to use in the days before the Firm took on Macauslane for a managing director. There's an electric light you can read your paper by without losing the sight of an eye, a thing you always risked when even Firsts were lit by oil. Here's an air-tight window that doesn't rattle, and a ventilator that works; here's a bogey carriage running so smoothly that you could drink a cup o' tea—if you thought of it—without spilling a drop, and in the old days you couldn't take a tot from the bottom of a flask, but had to bite on the neck of it, and drink between the dunts."

"Oh, I daresay things have a bit improved in your time," said Slymon, cooling down; "but even now they might be better."

"We might be better ourselves," said Jimmy Swan. "It's a conviction of that kind that keeps me from kicking a lot of folk I meet.

"If you ask me," continued Jimmy, lighting his pipe, "there was far more fun on the road before cold feet came into fashion, and when the only kind of draught that did any harm was the kind you got in tumblers."

"Youth," suggested Mr Slymon, and Jimmy for a moment meditated.

" Ay, perhaps you're right," he said. " I sometimes envy the chaps that have it, and then again I'm vexed for them, knowing they'll never understand till it's bye what a jolly good thing it was. And whiles, again, I wonder if Youth in itself is ever half so fine as it's cracked up to be ; it's maybe only nice to an old man's eye because it's out of reach. The young that have it, anyway, make an awful hash wi't. I did, myself. . . . But all that has nothing to do with what we started out on—travelling.

" I've been on the road since the year the women wore the Dolly Vardens—d'ye mind the song ?—

'Come, dear, don't fear, let your ringlets curl,
     If you're out of fashion, you better leave the world,
     Your sweet and pretty face will wear a winning smile,
     If you buy a hat and feather in the Dolly Varden style.'

" Half my journeys then were made on gigs and wagonettes ; none of your hot-water bottles and hair-stuffed seats ! and I tell you, my feet never got time to get cold. If it wasn't gigs, and taking the reins myself for half the journey because the postboy had been out all night at a kirn or a coffining ; it was cargo boats that started at six o'clock in the morning, and the first bell would be ringing before the Boots chapped at my door.

" I see chaps noo gaun aboot on bicycles wi' a sample box o' biscuits strapped behind," continued Jimmy, lapsing into the vernacular as his feelings warmed. " They call themsel's Commercials, just like the rest o' us. I'm vexed for the chaps, do ye know ; I never can see ony hope for them bein' comfortably married. It's the same wi' tea."

" Tea's done ! " confessed Mr Slymon, lugubriously. " Between you and me. Everybody's selling it. I know iron-mongers handling Cooper's packages. There's wholesale people going among the farmers selling 20 lb. tins at what they call a wholesale rate, and never going near a grocer. I would sooner be on the road for specs or railway tunnels.

Y*

Blended tea !—that's the wheeze !   ' Fine silky liquor. . . .
Good body. . . . Rich Darjeeling flavour. . . . Soupçon of
Pekoe gives it character.' . . .''

" I know," said Jimmy, sympathetically.   " Worse than
horse-cowpin' !   The ordinary man kens nae mair aboot tea
than I ken aboot shortbreid.   And ye canna wonder at it ;
tea at the best's a skiddlin' thing ye tak' to wash doon
breid and butter.   The honestest thing ever I saw said aboot
tea was in a grocer's window in Inverness—' Our Unapproach-
able ; 2s. 6d.' ''

" Sooner be in specs, or railway tunnels," repeated Slymon,
sadly.

" I see you're no' very keen on a line wi' a lot o' heavy
cases, onyway," said Jimmy.   " Noo, I wadna care to be
without my cases.   It's the stuff that talks !   Stick it in
their e'e !   When I put oot my stuff in a wee bit shop in
Grantown it makes it look like a bargain day in Sauchiehall
Street, and the shopkeeper feels awfu' lonely and sees his
place infernal bare when I pack up the traps again.   So doon
he claps his bonny wee order ! . . .   The only thing that
would gie me cauld feet would be travellin' withoot my
cases.   There's a moral weight in them as weel as avoirdupois.
Man, on the quays and at the railway stations the porters
ken them.   ' That's C. & M.'s,' they say—' Auld Swan.'
And when they're oot in the straun in front of a country
shop, it's jist like a swatch o' Buchanan Street.

" I'll admit there's whiles when they're a nuisance, and
that puts me in mind o' a time in the North when I got cauld
feet richt enough.

" I had just got ower three weeks' rest at Christmas and
New Year, a time I always used for packin' and postin' kind
reminders to my customers.   There was nae Secret Commission Act then, and I tell ye I was a connoisseur at geese
and turkeys, and the genuine F. & F. currant bun.   I sent
them by the score.   I sent a hundred and twenty ' Chatter-
boxes ' every year to the children o' the drapery trade in

the West o' Scotland. All I needed to be Santa Claus was a reindeer. Macauslane put an end to that ; he found oot that the maist o' the weans that got the books belanged to customers a bit behind in the ledger.

" I got up to Golspie on a Hansel Monday, did my business there in an oor or twa, and then ordered a machine for Brora. I couldna even get a barrow ! Some minister was being inducted down at Dornoch, and every dacent trap in the place was aff to Dornoch wi' an elder.

" ' We could run ye up wi' a shandry-dan,' says the inn-keeper, ' but then it wouldna haud your cases.'

" ' I needna go to Brora wantin' cases,' says I. ' Shairly ye can dae something, Peter ? '

" ' There's naething in the yaird that would haud your cases except the hearse,' says Peter.

" ' Well, oot wi' the hearse ! ' says I, and less than twenty meenutes efter I was on the road to Dornoch, sittin' beside the driver on a hearse, and the latest lines in C. & M.'s Spring goods inside it. My Jove, but it was cauld !

" We drove richt up to the shop o' auld Mr Sutherland. Doon I draps frae the dickey o' the hearse, and in I goes wi' a face like a fiddler, and asks for a yaird o' crape.

" ' Dear me ! Mr Swan, wha are ye buryin' the day ? ' says Mr Sutherland.

" ' We're buryin' Annie,' says I.

" ' Whatna Annie ? ' says Mr Sutherland.

" ' Animosity,' says I—ony auld baur 'll pass in Brora—and he laughed like a young yin, though I must alloo he yoked on me later on for what he ca'd my sacrilege.

" It was the first and only time, sae far, I traivelled on a hearse, and I tell ye my feet were cauld ! "

RAISING THE WIND

Mr Swan had the counter of Cameron's shop piled high with the new season's samples of corsets, lingerie, hose, lace, ribbons, and dress material. He handled them, himself, as if they had been flowers—delicately, lovingly, caressingly, and called attention to their qualities in the ecstatic tones a dealer in pictorial art would use with a customer for Raphaels. Cameron, on the other hand—a rough, bluff, quite undraperish-looking man, who had been a baker until he came to Perth from Glasgow twenty years ago and married his cousin and her shop, had plainly no artistic pleasure in the stuff displayed by the commercial traveller ; he flung it about on the counter as if it had been dough. It made the traveller squirm to see him.

" Bright colours, rich effects," said Jimmy ; " that's the season's note. Look at this cerise and tango—it makes ye think o' a fine spring day and the birds whistling. It'll make up beautiful ! " He tossed it tenderly into billowy folds, which showed in it the most entrancing shadows, auriferous glints, and the flush of cherries. " This stuff in stripes (we call it 'peau-depeche,' from the man that thought o't first ; he was a Frenchman)—it's the finest tailorin' stuff I've ever handled, goin' to be a' the go when the King comes to the Clyde."

" Is he comin' ? " Cameron asked with sudden interest.

" In July," said Jimmy. " There's a rush on flags already oot at Coatbridge. It's goin' to be a drapery summer, I can tell ye ! Ye'll feel it even up in Perth."

And Cameron sighed.

" Na," said he ; " we'll no' feel't in Perth. We never feel onything here but cattle shows. We just kind o' driddle on frae yin year's end to the ither, and read about splendid things in the papers. I never see ye strappin' up your boxes, Mr Swan, but I wish ye would strap me up wi' them and take me back wi' ye to Gleska."

Cameron, in twenty years, since he had left St Mungo, had never returned to it even on the shortest visit. He spoke of it now with a sentimental air, and expressed a firm intention to go down and see the gaieties of July.

"I'll see a lot o' changes on Gleska," he said. "Twenty years! It looks like a lifetime! What would ye say yoursel', Mr Swan, was changed the most in Gleska in twenty years?"

Jimmy puckered up his brows and chewed a pencil, lost in thought.

"Well," said he, "there's the picture-palaces, where ye can get everything now except a dram and a bed for the night—they'll be new to ye. And then there's the Central Station; ye've never seen the Central since they altered it, have ye?"

"No," said Cameron sadly. "What's it like, noo?"

"Oh, it's beyond words!" said Jimmy, rolling ribbons up. "Ye could put the whole o' the folk in Perth between the bookstalls, and they would just look like a fitba' team. It's got the biggest, brawest, nameliest lavatory in Europe, doon a stair, where ye can get your hair cut, and a bath for sixpence. Lots o' men go down for baths and barberin', stayin' down for hours if they think their wives are lookin' for them."

Cameron laughed. "What do ye want wi' a bath in a station?" said he.

"I've kent o't bein' used for a bank," said Jimmy; "at least it served the purpose o' a bank in a way, for it got twa chaps I ken some money when they couldna get it otherwise."

"How that?" asked Cameron.

"It happened this way. Twa packers in our warehouse— Dan MacGhie and Willie Lovatt—got on the scatter a year ago at the Gleska Fair. They spent the half o' the day goin' round the town in search of the perfect schooner that was goin' to be the last, and they found their joint resources down to a single shilling. A shilling's a lot o' money in Gleska if it's tramway rides you're buying, but it doesna go far in the purchase o' liquid joy, and they were sore distressed. A' the banks were shut, but that didna matter ; they hadna ony money in the banks onyway. And the notion o' goin' hame at three o'clock was naturally horrible.

" Dan MacGhie's such a fool in the packin' business, ye would fancy the only way he could think o' keepin' his socks up would be to stand on his heid, but on this occasion he was pretty 'cute. ' I'll tell ye what, Willie,' said he. ' You'll hae a nice hot bath at the Central Station.'

" ' What dae I want wi' a bath ? ' says Willie. ' I had yin a while ago.'

" ' That's all right ! ' says Dan. ' You'll go down and have a nice wee bath to yoursel'. It'll cost ye sixpence, and ye'll take your time. Ye'll slip your coat and waistcoat oot to me. I'll go, like lightning, and put them in a fine wee pawn for a pound, and buy ye an alpaca jacket for three-and-six, and we'll have a' the odds. See ? Phizz ! '

" ' But ye'll be sure to come back ? ' says Willie. ' I have no notion o' goin' oot the New City Road in my galluses.'

" ' Right oh ! ' says Dan, and Willie went down wi' him and trysted a bath, and slips his coat and waistcoat oot to Dan.

" Dan takes the coat and waistcoat in an awfu' hurry down to Oswald Street, and into a nice wee pawn, and asks a pound on them. The man in the pawn ripes the pouches, and says he couldna gie more than seven-and-six.

" ' Seven-and-six ! ' says Dan. ' They belang to a landed gentleman ! '

" ' I don't care if they belanged to Lloyd George,' says the man in the pawn, ' seven-and-six is the value, and that's no' includin' the price o' the ticket.'

" Dan took the seven-and-odd-pence-ha'penny, after switherin' a wee, and went awa' doon the stair and along Argyle Street. He was disappionted. If he bought a lustre

jacket for Willie, there wasna goin' to be much left for fun.
A dishonest man would have just spent the money and gone
awa' hame withoot botherin' aboot Willie, but Dan MacGhie
wasna a chap o' that sort ; he had the true British spirit.

" He goes alang the street till he comes to a shop window
where there were clocks on the instalment system. If ye
paid the first instalment o' half-a-crown, ye got the nock wi'
ye, the notion bein' that ye paid the other seventeen-and-six
in monthly instalments. Dan goes in as bold as brass and
asks to see a nock. The man produced a fair clinker, fitted
up wi' an alarm that would waken ye even on a Sunday.
Dan tried the alarm, and made it birl, and said he thought
it would dae, although he would have preferred yin a little
quicker and louder in the action. He paid down half-a-crown
and signed his name and address for the rest o' the instalments, and awa' oot, like the mischief, to the Trongate.

" He went into a pawn in the Trongate and pledged the
nock. ' I want fifteen shillin's on that,' says he. ' It's a
Kew-tested, genuine, repeater nock, jewelled in every hole.'
The pawnbroker opened it wi' a knife the same's it was an
oyster, and looked inside it. ' I'll gie ten shillin's on't ! '
says he.

" ' My mither's nock ! ' says Dan, and him near greetin'.
' It cost five-pound-ten the year o' the *Daphne* disaster.'

" ' Half-a-quid ! ' says the pawnbroker ; ' take it or leave
it ! '

" Dan took the ten shillin's ; looked at the time on the
pawnshop clock, and ran like a lamplighter awa' back to
Oswald Street. He kent fine that Willie would be vexed
waitin' in the bath a' wet.

" He goes back to the first pawn and lifted Willie's coat
and waistcoat, payin' back the seven-and-six and interest.

" ' Ye havena been lang ! ' says the pawnbroker, surprised
to see him.

" ' No,' says Dan ; ' I forgot about a funeral I'm booked
for this afternoon, and I need my coat.'

"He got Willie's coat and waistcoat, and bunks awa' up to the Central Station and doon the stairs to the lavatory, and chaps at the door.

"'Is that you, Dan?' says Willie.

"'It is,' says Dan, and slips him in his clothes.

"'My goodness!' says Willie, 'and I was gettin' cauld! I was sure ye had forgotten all aboot me! What speed did ye come?'

"'Tip-top!' says Dan. 'I started wi' sixpence, and I've three shillin's. Come on oot and we'll have a pint!'

"That's Gleska!" said Jimmy Swan. "Oh, it's changed a lot since you were there last, Mr Cameron! And now, this shell-pink moire velours, just look at the style that's in it——"

"Ye're a terrible man," said Cameron.

ROSES, ROSES, ALL THE WAY!

From the 1st of May till well on in October no one for years has seen James Swan in business hours without a flower in his coat lapel. Any old kind of cigar is good enough for him, though his preference runs to black Burmese cheroots that look like bits of walking-stick; but when it comes to button-holes, he is a fastidious connoisseur. If the Karl Droschki rose is ever to have a perfume, you will find that Jimmy will anticipate the florists' shops by a week or two; he likes his button-holes large and redolent, and a scented Karl Droschki the size of a rhododendron is a joy he sometimes dreams of. In town he gets his daily flower by some arrangement with commercial friends in the neighbourhood of the Bazaar; on his business journeys he is rather unhappy anywhere out of the reach of fresh carnations, sweet peas, roses, or camellias; but even there he can make shift with a spray of lilac or of wallflower culled from vases in the coffee-rooms of the hotels.

" The button-hole is getting a bit out o' fashion," he told me recently ; " but I don't mind ; it will aye go very well in the coat of a middle-aged commercial gentleman with the right breadth in the chest for it. Give me a clean shave and a carnation, and I feel as cheery as a chap that earns his bread by singing. A flower in the coat goes a long way to conceal yon tired feeling in the morning ; it's a kind o' moral pick-me-up."

" I fancy," said I, " that it's also not without some beneficial effect on business " ; and Jimmy slyly chuckled.

" You may be sure o' that ! " said he. " Make your button-hole big enough, and the business man behind it's almost lost to sight ; there's wee shops yonder in the East End where they look on me and my carnations like a kind o' glimpse o' the country, where the mavie whistles and the milk comes from. They sniff as if it was the sea-breeze down at Millport—I tell you it puts a lot o' them in mind o' their mothers' gardens ! Give me that kind o' country sentiment, and I'll be busy wi' my wee bit book ! "

But Jimmy was not always a wearer of *boutonnières* and a connoisseur in cut flowers. Fifteen years ago, as he told me once, he would as soon have worn a wedding-ring or a Glengarry bonnet, and the only thing he knew about flowers was that certain ones were roses and the others weren't. His wife's pathetic struggles for bloom in a tiny front plot near the Paisley Road never, in these days, roused his slightest interest in horticulture. He is still inclined to regard flowers as a product best procured in shops, but his knowledge of them at the marketable age is now extensive. It began with an experience he had in Kirkcaldy.

For two years he had made the most valiant but unsuccessful efforts to get an order from a Kirkcaldy draper, who appeared to cherish the distressing delusion that he was well enough served by other wholesale firms than C. & M. Mr Dimister was the hardest nut Jimmy had ever tried to crack. At any hour of the day he was called on he was always too

desperately busy to look at anything, and never by any luck
was he to be got with a vacancy in his stock that Mr Swan
could replenish.

" Man, he was a dour yin ! " Jimmy said to me, narrating
the circumstances. " I don't object to a dour yin in reason,
for once ye nab a dour yin he's as dour to stop ye as he was
to start ye ; forbye it's aye a feather in your bonnet. But
Dimister was a perfect he'rt-break ; he had nae mair come-
and-go in him than Nelson's Monument—my jove ! the baurs
I wasted on that man ! I got the length o' jottin' the heids
o' my newest stories doon in a penny diary just to be sure o'
ticklin' him wi' something fresh, but devil the haet would
tickle Dimister ; he had nae mair sense o' humour than a
jyle door. There's folk like that.

" Ye have nae idea o' the patience I showed wi' the body !
I tried him on the majestic line, the same's I was sellin' peer-
ages, and I tried him on the meek—or at least as near on the
meek as I could manage wi' half a ton o' cases from C. & M.
in a couple o' barrows at the door. It was a' the same to
Dimister—he had nae mair interest in me than if I was selling
sheep-dip or railway sleepers. I tried him wi' kirk affairs,
put oot a feeler now and then on politics, and gave him a'
the grips in Masonry ; but it was nae use : he just hotched
on his stool, glowered ower his specs at me, and let me ken
there was naething doin'. For a' that was in the cratur's
business at the time, it wasna worth my while to bother wi'
him ; but my pride was up, and I swore I would have him,
even if I had to take a gun to't.

" One day I asked the landlord o' the hotel I was puttin'
up at where Dimister stayed, and went oot to look at the ootside o' his hoose. It was a nice enough bit villa, wi' a gairden
fu' o' floo'ers and a great big greenhoose. A letter-carrier
passin' told me Dimister was the champion rose-grower and
tomato hand in Fife.

" ' I have ye noo ! ' says I to mysel', and wired to my
friend in the Bazaar to send me oot three o' the finest roses in

Gleska by the first train, even if they cost a pound. They came in the aifternoon—fair champions !—I stuck them in my coat and went to call on Dimister.

"'Very sorry,' he says as usual; 'I'm not needin''—and then his eyes fell on my button-hole. It was the first time I ever saw a gleam o' human interest in the body's face. His eyes fair goggled.

"'That's a good rose,' he says, and came forward and looked at them closer. 'A Margaret Dickson; splendid form !'

"'No' a bad rose !' I says, aff-hand. 'It's aye worth the trouble growin' a good one when ye're at it,' and I passed them over to him wi' my compliments. Ye would hardly believe it, but he was mair pleased than many a man would be wi' a box o' cigars.

"'I didna know ye were a fancier,' says he. 'That's a first-rate hybrid perpetual.'

"'The craze o' my life !' says I, quite smart. 'What's better than a bit o' gairden and an intelligent interest in the works o' Nature ?'

"'Nature !' says he, wi' a girn. 'If Nature had her will o' roses, they would a' be back at the briar or killed wi' mildew and green-fly. But I needna tell you the fecht we hae wi' the randy—you that can sport a bloom like that !'

" The lang and the short o't was that I got a first-rate order there and then frae Dimister, and promised to go to his gairden next time I was roond and give him the benefit o' my experience wi' hybrid perpetuals. Me ! I didna ken a hybrid perpetual frae a horse-radish ! But I had my man ! And I have him yet ; there's no' a draper in the East o' Scotland that's mair glad to see me. When I had a day to mysel' in Gleska I went to my friend at the Bazaar, and learned as much aboot the rose trade in a couple o' hours as would keep me gaun in talk wi' Dimister for days. I bought a shillin' book on gairdenin', laid in a stock o' seedsmen's catalogues, and noo I ken far mair aboot the rose as a commercial plant than Dimister, though I never grew yin a' my days. What's the use ? What's shops for ? But every time I went to Dimister's, I aye had a button-hole that dazzled him. The droll thing is that havin' a button-hole grew into a habit ; I started it to get roon' auld Sandy Dimister, and noo I'd sooner go without my watch."

CITIZEN SOLDIER

MR JAMES SWAN sat at his Saturday dinner-table, and was about to draw his customary bottle of beer, when, on reflection, he put down the corkscrew and filled up his glass with water.

" Bilious, Jimmy ? " said his wife.

" No," he answered. " I'll wager there's no' a bilious man this day in the Citizen Corps. Two hours' route-merchin' on the Fenwick Road is the best anti-bilious pill I ken ; if it could be put up in boxes and sold in the apothecary shops, it would fetch a guinea a dozen. But ye couldna put Sergeant Watson in a box, and he's the main ingredient o' the route-merch pill. Watson's a fine, big, upstandin' chap, and it's a treat to see him handle his legs and arms the same's they were kahouchy, and double up a hill without a pech from him, but I wish he would mind at times our corps's no' made up o' gladiators or Græco-Roman wrestlers, that we're just plain business men, off and on about five-and-forty in the shade, wi' twenty years o' tramway travellin' and elevator lifts, and easy-chairs, bad air and beer in our constitution. It's no' to be expected we can pelt up braes on the Fenwick Road like a lot o' laddies."

" I hope you'll not hurt yoursel'," said Mrs Swan anxiousiy.

" Hurt mysel' ! I'm sore all over ! Sergeant Watson sees to that ! It's no' the Madame Pomeroy treatment for the skin he's givin' us, nor learnin' us the dummy alphabet ; he wouldna get a wink o' sleep this night if he thought we werena sore all over. ' The sorer ye feel,' says he, ' the sooner ye'll be fit.' I tell you he's a daisy ! I never knew I had calves to my legs nor muscles to my back before I joined this army. . . . My goodness, Bell, is that all the meat ye have the day ? That's no' a sodger's dinner."

" At any rate," said Mrs Swan, " I never saw you looking better or eating more."

" I don't know about my looks," said Mr Swan, " and that bit doesna matter, for I suppose the Germans are no great Adonises themselves, but I wish to Peter they had my legs ! " and he bent to rub them tenderly. " I've learned some-thing in the last month, Bell—that a body's body's no' just a thing for hangin' shirts and stockings on—the same's it was a pair o' winter-dykes. For twenty years I have been that intent on cultivatin' my intellect and the West Coast trade of C. & M., and dodgin' any kind o' physical effort that would spoil my touch wi' the country drapers, that I was turnin' into a daud o' creash, and slitherin' down this vale o' tears as if the seat o' my breeks were soaped. Do ye ken what Watson said to me one day, just the week I joined ? He saw me pechin', and had the decency to call a halt. ' Are ye all right ? ' says he ; and I told him I had the doctor's word for it that all my internal organs were in first-rate order, and as strong's as a lion's. ' Since that's the case,' says he, ' it's a pity we canna flype ye, for the ootside's been deplor-ably neglected.' "

" The idea ! " said Mrs Swan, bridling.

" Oh, the man was right enough ; a bonny job I could have made last month o' any German that came down the Drive wi' his bayonet fixed to look for beer ! I wouldna have the strength to hand him out a bottle. But let him try't now !—Oh, michty ! but I'm sore across the back ! "

" I hope you haven't racked yourself ? " his wife said, anxious again.

" The only thing I've racked's my braces. Just lie you

down on your hands and toes, face down, wi' your body stiff, and see how often ye can touch the floor wi' your chin."

" Indeed and I'll do nothing of the kind ! " said Mrs Swan. " I don't see what good that sort of thing's going to do if you have to fight the Germans. It's surely not on your hands and toes you're going to tackle them, James Swan ? "

Her husband laughed. " No," said he ; " and I'm no' expectin' to have to fight them even standing on the soles o' my feet, for the only Germans ye'll see in Scotland after this 'll come when their trouble's bye, wi' a pack, selling Christmas toys ; their whiskers 'll be dyed for a disguise, and they'll call themselves Maclachlans."

" And what on earth are you drilling for ? " said his wife. " I'm sure I wish you were on the road again. Since ever you were back in the shop six weeks ago, it's been nothing but darning socks for me, with your marching and parades."

Mr James Swan sighed, as he was helped to a man's size portion of the pie, which, to an appetite sharpened by his military duties, seemed quite inadequate.

" If ye want to know," said he, " I'm drilling mainly to make up the average for myself and for the country. The idea that the Black Watch and the Gordon Highlanders at a shilling or two a day per man were enough to keep us safe and let us carry on fine soft-goods businesses, allowing reasonable time for golf and football, was a slight mistake. It would have worked all right if the other chaps across the North Sea did the same, but you see they dinna. Instead of goin' in, like us, for a rare good time wi' athletic sports at half-a-crown for the grandstand seats, for tango dancin' and ke-hoi, the silly nyafs went, for a penny a day, into the army. So far as I can make out from the papers, they're all as tough as nails, and they cornered the toy trade too, and a lot o' other lines that's the inalienable right of the British business man. ' Our mistake, Maria ! ' said the Countess. All Britain is divided into two parts—the flabby-bellied and the fit ; I don't expect to have the luck to shoot a German, but at least I'm no' goin' to be a flabby."

" Then it's just for your health you're away parading ? " said Mrs Swan.

" No," said her husband. " For self-respect. Sergeant Watson's system's gey sore on the muscles for a week or two, but it's most morally elevatin'. Four weeks ago if I had attempted to lean on mysel' wi' any weight I would have crumpled up like a taper ; I'm sore all over just at present, but I feel that I could take a cow by the tail and swing it round my head. . . . What you want in this house, Bell, is more beef, and a more generous sense of what is meant by dinner. Are ye not aware, my dear, that a sodger gets a pound a day of beef without bone ? So far as I can judge, he needs it—every ounce ! "

"Man, ye're just a great big laddie!" said Mrs Swan, with a shake of her husband's shoulder.

He shook his head. " That's just the worst of it, Bell," said he ; " I'm no' ! The greatest luck in the world just now is to be a lad of twenty. When I was young there was hanged-all happened in the world to waken me in the morning sure that I was needed to do something : it was just, every day, a trivial wee world of business, and feeding, and playing, and sleeping ; no drums nor bugles in't, and nothing big enough to bother to roll my sleeves up for a blow at . . . James Swan, Commercial Traveller. . . . Sold stays ! . . . There was a destiny for ye ! And I go along the streets just now and I see a hundred thousand men in the prime o' life who haven't the slightest notion of their luck and the chance they're missing."

" What chance ? " asked Mrs Swan.

" To make a better, cleaner world of it ; to help to save a nation ; make themselves a name that, even if they perished, would be honoured by their people generations after. . . . Pass the water, Bell, please."

" Are you not going to take your beer ? " asked Mrs Swan.

"No," said Jimmy firmly.

"Why that?" she asked.

"Because I want to," he answered. "When we were doubling along the Fenwick Road I thought of that beer all the time. I could feel the very taste o't! But the oddest thing about Sergeant Watson's system is that it's learned me this—that the thing you're not particularly keen to do is the thing to do, and pays in the long-run best. So I'll just take water."

Printed in Great Britain by
WILLIAM BLACKWOOD & SONS LTD